# The Death of SHAKESPEARE

# S The Death of HAKESPEARE

*As It Was Accomplisht in 1616*
*& The Causes Thereof*

———◆◆◆◆———

## A Novel by Jon Benson

PART ONE

*Sherri — Thanks for the wonderful cover art*

*Jon Benson*
*by Douglas Clark Hathorn*

Copyright © 2016 Nedward, LLC

ISBN-10: 0-692-55930-2
ISBN-13: 978-0-692-55930-7

Library of Congress Control Number:  2015956043

Published by Nedward, LLC, Annapolis, Maryland

Cover Design by Gerard A. Valerio, with Sherri Ferritto

Maps drawn and hand-lettered by Joan B. Machinchick

The ₥ at the end of each chapter is the crown in the Earl of Oxford's signature.

*The Reader's Companion to The Death of Shakespeare*
contains endnotes that can be downloaded from
*www.doshakespeare.com.*

*To Elizabeth Regina, who took many secrets with her to the grave.*

*Degree being vizarded,*
*The unworthiest shows as fairly in the mask.*

        *Troilus and Cressida,* Act I, Scene 3


*Why write I still all one, ever the same,*
*And keep invention in a noted weed,*
*That every word doth almost tell my name,*
*Showing their birth and where they did proceed?*

        *Sonnet LXXVI*


*Far fly thy fame,*
*Most, most of me beloved, whose silent name*
*One letter bounds.*
*Thy unvalu'd worth*
*Shall mount fair place when Apes are turned forth.*

        *Scourge of Villainy,* John Marston (1598)

*To the Gentle Reader*

*This Booke, that thou here seest put,*
*It was for gentle Oxford cut;*
*Wherein the Author had a strife*
*With History to show Lord Oxford's life.*

*O, if only those who knew his wit*
*Had said the plays by him were writ,*
*There'd be no need to here reclaim*
*The name purloined by Shakespeare's fame.*

*Grave Spenser need not shift more nigh*
*Our Chaucer, nor Beaumont nearer Spenser lye;*
*Let them sleep, Westminster lords,*
*The world now knows the plays are Oxenford's.*
*Their every word sings he wrote the plays,*
*And in his Moniment Shakespeare slays.*

*Elizabeth knew of noble lords*
*Who wrote well but suppressed their words,*
*Or let them publish in another's name,*
*Thereby losing deservèd fame.*

*The author here his name must also feign,*
*Lest he, too, in academia, be slain.*
*Therefore, Gentle Reader, looke*
*Not on his name but on his Booke.—J.B.*

# Table of Contents

## Part One
### Prologue: Stratford-upon-Avon – April 23, 1616

## 1588

## 1589

# 1591

# 1592

iii

# Lineage Tables
*(at end of text after page 572)*

The Earls of Oxford

William Cecil, Baron Burghley

The Earls of Southampton

The Earls of Derby

Peregrine Bertie, Lord Willoughby de Eresby

The Earls of Pembroke

The Lords Hunsdon

The Sidney Family

# Glossary

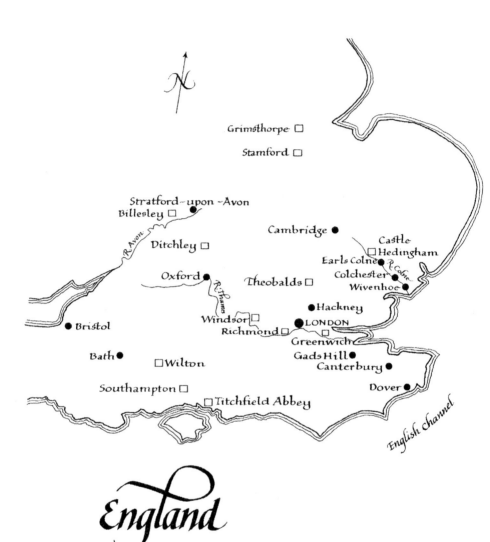

Grimsthorpe □

Stamford □

Stratford-upon-Avon
Billesley □ ●

Cambridge ●

Castle
□ Hedingham

Ditchley □

Earls Colne ●
Colchester ●
Wivenhoe ●

Oxford ●

Theobalds □

● Hackney

Windsor □
Richmond □ ● LONDON

Greenwich

● Bristol

Gads Hill ●
Canterbury ●

Bath ●

□ Wilton

Dover ●

Southampton □

□ Titchfield Abbey

R. Avon

R. Thames

R. Colne

English channel

England

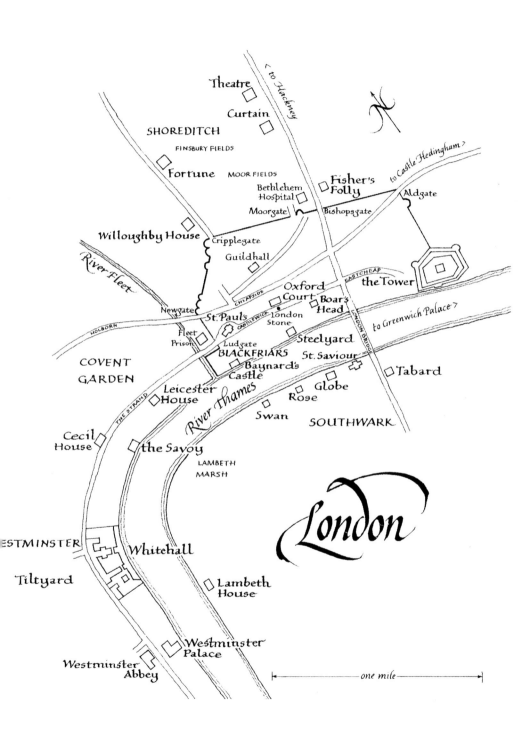

# The Death of
# SHAKESPEARE

Portrait of William Shakespeare from the cover of the *First Folio* (1623)

# 1616

## ~ Prologue ~
## Stratford-upon-Avon - April 23, 1616

The knock came earlier than expected. Anne Shackspear opened the door and looked out into the teeming rain. A man dressed in a brown cape and broad-brimmed felt hat filled the doorway. He pulled back the cape at his neck, exposing a white collar.

"Father," she said, swinging the door open. "We are so grateful you have come." The priest stepped inside. He took off his hat, uncovering a thick head of brown hair flecked with gray. His face was wide. Heavy jowls sagged either side of a thick-lipped mouth. He handed her his hat. "I am Anne Shackspear, she said nervously, as she took it. "Forgive me, Father, for I have sinned."

The priest offered his hand; Anne bent forward and kissed it. He peeled off the cloak and exposed the white collar again, which shone even brighter in the dark room. Anne was pleased to see that the priest was large. Priests should be well-fed, she thought. Let the Puritans show their bones like the cattle dying in the fields outside Stratford. She herself was a stump of a woman, made shorter by years of carrying milk pails on her father's farm. A large purse and heavy keys hung off her belt.

"William worried that a priest would be afraid to visit him here," she said, as she hung up the priest's cloak. "Where have you come from, Father?"

"Take me to him," the priest said, not answering her question.

Anne started for the stairs. "He has not gotten out of bed for days," she said over her shoulder, "for reasons my son-in-law, a doctor, cannot discover. Perhaps it's his grief over my second daughter's marriage, so recently besmutched." The priest followed close behind, almost pushing her up the stairs. She stopped prattling. At the top, she pointed to a dark bedroom.

"Leave us," the priest said. Anne went back downstairs as the priest entered the room and closed the door behind him. Shackspear lay in a wide bed with turned posts but no canopy. A silk tapestry that depicted scenes from *The Book of Martyrs* hung on the wall over his head, a recent acquisition from how clean and bright it was in contrast to the rest of the dingy room. A small portrait of Shackspear hung on the wall on the other side of the bed.

Shackspear looked up and saw the priest. "Father!" he exclaimed. "Thank you for coming! I despaired I would leave this life before I was confessed."

The priest walked over to the bed. His eyes swept the room. "Have you sinned, my son?"

"Yes, Father! My conscience hath a thousand tongues, one for every sin I have committed! They crowd the bar," he cried, waving a bony finger over the priest's head, as if a gallery of wraiths behind the priest were hooting 'Guilty! Guilty!'

The priest looked mildly surprised. "What kind of sins, my son?"

"*I stole a man's name, Father.*"

"Is that a crime?" The priest smiled indulgently. "I thought you were going to confess to something worse, like murder."

Shackspear shook his head. "What I did was far worse. Killing a man only shortens his life. *Stealing his name means no one will remember him after he is gone! It's as if he had been erased! As if he had never been born!*"

He reached over and picked up a document from the nightstand. He handed it to the priest. His hand was shaking. "I have written a confession based on the one Father Campion gave my father." The priest made the sign of the cross. Shackspear saw this and was pleased.

The priest took the confession and started to look through it. "And whose name have you stolen?"

"The Earl of Oxford's, Father. The Queen made me do it. She said the Earl would write plays and my name would go on them, and if I ever told anyone …" He made a slashing movement across his throat. "But she is dead now, as so many others are …" He lost his train of thought, his eyes drifting away.

"Have you told this to others?"

"Only to my wife and daughters."

"And what do they say?"

"They laugh at me. They say I'm an old man. They know nothing of the theater. They can't even read. Confess me, Father."

"Where *are* the plays?"

"Oxford kept them."

"And the drafts he wrote?"

"He kept everything, even the foul papers. But they would've done you no good if you had them. He wrote the way water bugs skitter across a pond, or lightning runs across the sky. No one could read what he wrote; except Robin, of course, or Lyly when Lyly was his secretary. Oxford wrote all the time. And, when he wasn't writing, he was dictating. *And putting my name on it!*'

Shackspear stopped as if he suddenly remembered something. "'Twas only right, of course," he said, a firmness appearing in his voice for the first time. "After all, who made the plays work so the public would pay good money to see them? *I did.* Who was it added parts he'd never thought of, or rewrote speeches that would have drowned a fish? *I did.* Without me, the Earl would have been just another recluse scribbling away in some moldering castle. *I gave his ideas to the world!*"

"You did," the priest agreed.

Shackspear thought the priest didn't believe him. He bristled. "I did, I tell ye. Oxford resisted at first, of course, he being a lord and me a commoner, but he finally began to understand what I could bring to our 'partnership.' I brought him back to Earth, I did, and I became famous."

"At least in London."

"Aye, in London, but not in Puritan-diseased Stratford!" This turn in the conversation appeared to confuse him, and for a moment he didn't say anything, seemingly lost. Then he looked up at the priest. "When the Queen died, Oxford wanted to go back on our 'contract.' He wanted me to tell the world that he had written *Hamlet* and *The Merchant* and all the rest. But how could I give up being the immortal playwright I had become and return to being just a nameless actor again? 'Our Roscius!' Jonson would call out when I walked into the Mermaid. I was famous! I would never die as long as there was a theater somewhere and people could read."

"So you said no."

Shackspear nodded. "I told Oxford he was dying, not me, and I would continue to enjoy the fame Fortune had given me, thank you very much. And so he died, a never writer to an ever reader. And I'm the only one left who knows the truth."

"Yes," the priest said quietly.

Shackspear's river of words dried up. He lay still, staring off in space. Then he turned to the priest. "I wasn't facing God then—Oxford was! But now it's my turn, Father, and God won't ask me what I did—*he will know!*"

The priest made no comment. He looked around the room. "Do you have any books? I don't see any."

Shackspear laughed. "No. I can read, mark you, and write. I had a good education down the street in the Guild Hall but I never liked reading and writing. Acting took me to London. I thought I was good, but no one else did. But there was lots of money to be made by putting on shows and I decided that, if I couldn't be a player, I could be a manager. None of the players knew how to run a business. It was easy to step in and fill the void. I became their manager. They're all rich now because of me."

"Well, you certainly suffer from the sin of pride," the priest remarked. "And you lack humility, my son. You are the same man who hid grain while his neighbors starved, aren't you?" Shackspear sat up. "And didn't you work with 'Pimping Billy,' who arranged for women to lie on their backs while men on top paid silver to you and Francis Langley?" Shackspear's jaw dropped. The priest went on, his voice rising. "Do you think brief religion can make up for foul deeds committed over a lifetime? A short 'Hail Mary' availeth you not, I'm afraid."

Shackspear was terrified. "Do not abandon me, Father. For the love of Mary and Jesus, do not let me go to my Maker clothed in sin." He reached over and grabbed the Confession from the nightstand. He pressed it into the priest's hands. "Give this to Sir Francis Bacon. He is an honest man. He will see to it that justice is done. Swear it," Shackspear begged, pulling on the priest's sleeve.

"I swear," the priest said without emotion.

"Then confess me, Father, for I have sinned."

The priest took the Bible off the nightstand and put it on the bed. He placed Shackspear's hand on the Bible and began to chant in Latin when Shackspear pulled his hand away and sat upright.

"Wait! You're not a priest! You're Nicholas Skerret!"

"Skerres," the larger man growled. "*Nicholas Skerres*! You never got anything right, did you, Willum!" He grabbed a pillow and slammed it down over Shackspear's face like a mason smashing a tile into wet mortar. He climbed onto the bed and leaned all his weight into the pillow.

"You made me stand with a spear in *Julius Caesar*," he said through clenched teeth, "but your only role was croaking 'swear, swear' from beneath the stage in *Hamlet*!" Shackspear's cries were muffled, his legs vainly kicking to throw off the man on top of him. "When I asked for better parts, you said I couldn't act. 'Just business,' you told me. Well, what thinks you now of how I played my part? *You knew me not!*"

Shackspear was still struggling, but his life was ebbing away.

"For you, the world became a stage where you played 'author,' but now you exit to a grander stage where the role of ghost surely awaits you. It's just business, eh?"

Shackspear finally stopped moving. Skerres climbed off the bed. He laid a finger along Shackspear's neck. "He's dead!" Skerres said to himself after a moment. "The last living person who knew the truth is no more." He slipped the pillow back under Shackspear's head, fluffing it up and straightening the bedclothes.

He turned his attention to the nightstand. He opened the drawer and with his thick fingers pawed through the jars of ointment and medicines inside, finally pulling out a gold ring. "A seal ring," he said, holding it up. He could read the initials "WS" in reverse. "He won't be needing *this* anymore." He dropped the ring into a pocket inside his belt.

He pulled a poem out of a second drawer. He picked up a candle and read it aloud:

*Good friend for Jesus sake forbeare.*
*To dig the dust encloased heare:*
*Blesse be the man that spares these stones,*
*And curst be he that moves my bones.*

Skerres sniffed. "If this was cheese," he said, looking at Shackspear, "you'd have been dead before I got here. You want this on your gravestone? You deserve it." He put the poem back in the drawer.

He picked up the pages of a will and scanned them quickly. He noticed that Shackspear had left nothing for his playhouse friends in London. Picking up a quill, Skerres dipped it into the pot of ink sitting on the nightstand and added: "*and to my Fellowes, John Hemynges, Richard Burbage, and Henry Cundell, XXVI viij Apeece, to buy them ringes*" between the lines on the third page The signature lines were blank. Shackspear had put off signing the will. "Too late now," Skerres muttered to himself. "Maybe Anne Shackspear will sign it."

He walked around the bed to look more closely at the portrait on the far wall. Something was odd. Shackspear's eyes looked like they were both right eyes. Or were they left eyes? Skerres glanced back at Shackspear's face. He couldn't tell. The bulbous head was right, but the tunic was too small, and the shoulder-wings were oversized. Was the right arm the left in reverse? And the ruff: it made Shackspear's head seem to float in the air. "Martin's done better than this," Skerres muttered to himself. Then he saw the bold line that started under Shackspear's chin and ran up the side of his head. A broad grin spread across Skerres's face.

"A mask!" he said aloud. Laughter began to rumble through his belly. His tiny brown eyes disappeared into the folds of his face. "Martin did a portrait of him as a mask and the fool hung it in his own bedroom!" His laughter grew until it filled the room. He finally forced himself to stop. He put a serious look on his face, straightened the clerical collar he was wearing, and went downstairs.

"He is resting peacefully," he said to Anne Shackspear at the bottom of the stairs. "Are there any books or papers in the house? I want to make sure there's nothing here that might embarrass the Church."

"No books, Father. We have to hide our faith in our hearts."

"I'll look around." He strode off into the house, but was back shortly.

"I leave," he announced.

"Bless you, Father." Anne helped him on with his cloak. "I'm sure William well-liked your visit."

"He did."

Anne opened the back door. Skerres jammed his hat down over his head and stepped out into the rain. He went down the garden path, past the barn, oblivious of Venus, Shackspear's barren mare, watching him as he went by. He walked past Holy Trinity Church to a wooden bridge that swayed back and forth in the surging waters of the Avon. He crossed the bridge and continued on a mile to a carriage waiting under a grove of sycamores. Two horses, coach fellows, stood in the rain. The driver sat up high, huddled under an enormous cape. Skerres opened the door to the carriage and got in. Two men waited inside. A few minutes later a side window opened and the seal ring Skerres had taken from Shackspear's nightstand was thrown out onto the ground. This was followed by a thump that came from inside the carriage. The driver flipped the cape off his head and snapped his whip. The horses came to life and the carriage careened up onto the road, crushing the ring into the mud as it disappeared into the night toward London.

# 1588

## Fisher's Folly - September 27, 1588

I t was a cold, crisp day, a day that tells the trees it's time to start tucking in for winter; a day that stills the songbirds and sends them south. "And a good day to see the Queen," Oxford thought to himself as he came out onto the second-floor gallery that ran around the inner courtyard in the center of Fisher's Folly.

"Nigel!" he called out. The night air had strung a necklace of diamonds along the railing in front of him. He touched one and it instantly disappeared.

"My lord," a voice answered from nearby. A tall man dressed in a dark green jacket appeared. The lapels of his jacket were black, as was his hair, which had been slicked over his head and knotted at the back.

"Must I do everything?" Oxford asked. "You know I see the Queen today. Where is my dresser?"

"I regret to say, my lord, that he is no longer in your service."

"And why is that?"

"Because he has not been paid, my lord."

"Not been paid?"

"Yes. I have your clothes ready, your lordship," Nigel said, gesturing to the room behind him. Oxford was about to follow him when he saw two men fencing in the courtyard below. He leaned over the railing and watched them for a moment.

"No, no, no," he called out. "Anthony, your back foot is wrong. It should be pointing away from your opponent." He rotated his right foot so that it was pointed down the walkway. Whether the men below could see his foot was unclear.

"A faint "my lord" floated up from the courtyard below.

"And where is the rest of the play you've been working on?"

"Two sheets in folio, my lord. The rest, up here," the man called Anthony said, tapping the right side of his head with his index finger.

"Then I suggest you 'distill' your play onto paper before you continue with John Lyly here, lest he spit you on his sword, leaving your work in naught but airy thought." His words marched away from him in tiny clouds in the cold morning air as he spoke. "Like my breath here, so quickly gone."

Nigel leaned out of the room. "My lord, neither the Sun nor the Queen waits for anyone, even the Earl of Oxford."

"True," Oxford said. He began to turn away when he saw a hostler walking two horses across the courtyard toward the gate that opened onto Bishopsgate Street. "Ho!" he shouted. "Let go those horses!" The man looked up but did not stop. The two fencers stepped aside to let him pass. "Nigel! Why are my horses being taken away?"

Nigel came back out and looked over the railing. "Because they have not been paid for, my lord."

"Even so," Oxford said, "they are *my* horses and they cannot be repossessed *without benefit of law*! Fetch my solicitor! Tell him to file a writ!"

"I have already spoken with Malfis, my lord. He said that the owner can take them back. We haven't finish paying for them."

"Why was I not told this?"

"You were, my lord."

Oxford lowered his voice. "Is there nothing left?"

"Very little. Few who live here pay for their room and board. They all claim they are providing you a service. John Lyly, for example says you need him as secretary when the 'Muse' seizes you."

"True," Oxford said. "And I see the Queen today," he continued, his face brightening, "and she will order me to write plays to ornament her court now that the Spanish have run for home." He leaned on the railing:

> *The lively larke stretcht forth her wing,*
> *The messenger of morninge bright*

A sparrow landed on the railing to his right and bounced toward him.

"Shoo!" he said. The bird hopped back and gave him a baleful look. "I sing only to larks this morning."

"My lord," Nigel said, a pained look on his face.

Oxford followed. "And which doublet have you chosen for me today?"

"A new one," Nigel said, a touch of enthusiasm appearing in his voice for the first time. He held up a doublet of gray silk woven with a tiny thread the shade of green one sees only on the surface of a small pond in August. The front of the doublet was speckled with small tufts that appeared to be pearls but which, upon closer examination, were a complicated weaving of satin thread the color of polished pewter.

The fabric of the upper part of the doublet continued out beyond the shoulders, which were ruffed and flared to suggest the sleeves that were not there. The front of the doublet was ornamented with a cascade of gold and black pearls, real this time, arranged in three diagonal lines across the front.

Oxford was pleased. "Good. Good," he said, feeling the silk.

Nigel held up a long-sleeved silk shirt and starched ruff to frame the garment in white. Oxford put on the shirt.

"And the cape," Nigel said. It was made of black velvet. A border of faux pearls, backgrounded by specks of gold, edged the cape. A boar's head the size of a small plum had been embroidered over the heart.

Oxford swung the cape over his left shoulder and turned to look at himself in the glass. His left hand pulled the cape across his chest, flashing a gold thumb ring emblazoned with another boar's head. "Well done," he said.

Nigel's chin rose slightly. "I know the gimlet-eyed ladies at court will count the threads that close the button holes and frown if they see anything other than what is expected of the Seventeenth Earl of Oxford."

"But where did you get the silver to pay for this, seeing that my horses are being repossessed and my dresser has gone home for lack of money?"

Nigel slid the cape off Oxford's shoulder. "I thought you would be disappointed to learn you had nothing new to wear before the Queen today because I had spent what is left on horses and dressers."

This was said without innuendo or criticism of any kind. Nigel considered himself fortunate to be in service of the man surveying himself in front of the mirror. The earls of Oxford stretched back 500 years. Nigel's father had served Oxford's father. Money was tight but there were benefits, of course, such as special privileges from other noble families, from merchants, and, most importantly, from the law courts when leniency was needed. Consequently, those in service stayed when money was in limited supply, the dressing-boy being an exception to the rule.

Oxford, for his part, had no idea how he was financed. That was Nigel's job. He paid as little attention to money as he did to the disappearance of the chamber pot each morning. He adjusted the sleeve of his shirt and looked at Nigel in the mirror. His faithful steward seemed a bit weary. Maybe it was the hubbub from the writers and painters moving in and out all the time, and the parties that went on into the night.

"You seem a bit off, Nigel, what with having to manage me and keep me moving forward, like the way a summer voyage can take the sweetness off a barrel of Malmsey."

"I know nothing of Malmsey, my lord," Nigel said. "I am not privileged to sample such delights."

"You've never taken a sip when word has come down to send more up to the table?"

Nigel shook his head. His master was in a bantering mood, which always made Nigel feel awkward. He preferred to serve in silence. He had no time for frivolity. Work filled his day. As chief steward, he had to deal with the Folly, as well as Castle Hedingham in Essex, Oxford Court in London, and the Earl's other properties. Rising before dawn, he would open a leather book and list the tasks for that day, checking them off as he completed them. He also had no sense of humor, a grave failing in anyone in service to the Earl of Oxford. Consequently, he mistook Oxford's comment about the Malmsey as criticism.

"I have never tasted of the Malmsey," he said, straightening a sleeve.

Oxford laughed. "Of course not." He put his hand on Nigel's shoulder. "You have always been my honest servant, Nigel, but I am not used to honesty. The court is full of lies. If someone lies, I am usually able to recognize it but there are times …"

Nigel thought Oxford was still talking about him. "My lord," he protested, moving squarely in front of Oxford, "I assure you that I have never tasted of the Malmsey."

Oxford realized that Nigel had no idea what he was talking about. "Of course not," he said, taking the ruff from Nigel's hand and slipping it around his neck. "Thank God for that."

Nigel, relieved, busied himself with the rest of Oxford's attire. He handed Oxford the sheath containing his sword, a rapier of damask'd steel. Oxford buckled a narrow belt inside his cape and thrust the sheath down his leg. The matching dagger was slipped inside the belt on the other side. Nigel handed him a felt hat, also black, its short cylindrical top separated from the narrow brim by a border of faux pearls and speckled gold that mimicked the border on the cape. A pair of black gloves completed Oxford's outfit.

The Earl of Oxford turned to face himself in the mirror. He placed one foot out, tilting his head to one side. Thinning sandy-colored hair swept over his head. Eyebrows arched over hazel eyes, giving an air of permanent questioning or slight surprise to his face. He laid a finger alongside the trim mustache that fledged his upper lip. "How can she refuse me?" he asked the image in the glass. "Such *sprezzatura*," he said to Nigel, drifting off. His steward had no idea what *sprezzatura* meant. He let his master drift for a moment and then tugged on his sleeve. "Yes," Oxford said to himself. He ducked into a nearby room, coming out with a sheaf of rolled-up papers tied with a ribbon. "Scenes to dazzle her majesty," he announced, waving the roll of papers around like it was a consul's baton and he was Caesar returning from Gaul. Nigel smiled, having seen dozens of rolled-up plays littering the rooms in the Folly.

"But I have no horse," Oxford said, disappointed. "I must go on foot, then."

"Your whiffler waits in the street."

Oxford headed for the stairs.

Nigel watched him go. He had once again overcome his master's lack of purpose and direction to send him out the door a worthy descendent of his ancestors. He took out a small leather book and squinted at the list of tasks he had written down that morning before the house awoke. He scanned the page and realized he had failed to note that his master was to see the Queen. This failure took away some of the satisfaction he felt. He quickly added 'dress his lrdshp for the Qn' as an interlineation and drew a line through it. Snapping the book shut, his feeling of quiet competence returned.

⸺⸻◆✦✦◆⸻⸺

Oxford went out through the entrance into Bishopsgate Street where he found his whiffler waiting for him.

"Good morrow, Tobias."

Tobias nodded. He was a large African man, ebony in color. He was dressed in a tawny over shirt emblazoned with a blue boar on the right shoulder. A dark purple hat with a rolled-up brim was on his head; thick leather boots protected his feet. His two immense fists hung either side of him like resting hammers. In one he held a gilded pomander given to Oxford's grandfather by a French count. A trail of smoke floated away from the smoldering mixture of cinnamon, cloves, musk, and other aromatics Nigel had stuffed into it.

"Holla! Make way for the Earl of Oxford," Tobias cried, as he moved out into the street. He pushed people away with one hand while he swung the pomander in dangerous arcs over their heads.

The street stank of urine, manure, rotten cabbage, and mutton fat. Oxford raised a perfumed glove to his face to ward of the odors that assaulted him. Bethlehem Hospital, or Bedlam as it was known to the citizens of London, was directly across the street. Bedlam was where the city dumped its insane.

Bishopsgate, the main entrance through the Roman wall for travelers coming from the north, was only a few yards from the Folly. The gate was straddled by a three-story tower. A narrow window in the center of the second floor looked out on the street like the eye of a cyclops. Thick oak doors bound with black iron, normally closed at night, were open this bright September morning as a press of people pushed into each other trying to get through the gate. The people stank of sweat and unwashed clothes, of rotting teeth, and of the rancid cheese and sour milk they had eaten before setting out that morning.

"Holla! Make way for the Earl of Oxford," Tobias continued to call out.

The street widened inside the gate. Oxford stepped around Tobias and started to breathe again. Narrow alleys led off into dark corners.

He turned right at one of them. Swan Alley ended at a narrow door. Tobias took up station just outside while Oxford opened it and stepped inside, a silver bell announcing his arrival. He closed the door and was immediately hit by the fragrances that filled the shop. Chaos, most people snorted when they had gotten their breath. Oxford, on the other hand, loved the perfumes and aromatic scents that greeted him. He tried to separate and identify each one, something he had done many times in the back of the store. The owner of the shop suddenly appeared from behind a curtain.

"Signore Baldini!" Oxford exclaimed, moving off through the barrels and boxes that filled the room.

"My lord," Signore Baldini answered with decidedly less enthusiasm. He attempted a slight bow. He had thin hair and a thinner mustache. He wore a brown tunic and loose breeches. His beard was short, his hair unkempt. He held a long-necked pitcher in his left hand.

"*Maestro* Baldini," Oxford said with added emphasis. "I see the Queen this morning, and I *must* have something with which to amaze her. Have you completed your work on the recipe we were working on last spring, the one with musk oil and a hint of bergamot?"

Signore Baldini looked pained. "My lord," he said, "I value your friendship, your kind help when I came here all the way from Venice, your references to your many friends at court," he said, now animated, waving his hands, but Oxford interrupted him.

"And?"

"But no one pays me," he burst out.

Oxford was dismayed.

"How can you say that?" he asked. "Haven't I paid for the gloves you've given me, the perfumes, the cedar boxes?"

Baldini made another face.

"Haven't I?" Oxford asked, beginning to sense that his knightly honor was under attack.

"Si, si," Baldini agreed, the word coming out of him the way a splinter is pulled out of a flesh wound, slowly and painfully. "But not always right away."

"Oh, but eventually, I'm sure," Oxford said quickly. "So what have you for me? What can I take to the Queen and once again dazzle her with your magic?"

Baldini sighed. He took out a small leather pouch and held it out for Oxford to sniff. "Now this, my lord," he said, making sure that Oxford could not grab the pouch, "is something the Queen has never smelled." He opened the pouch. "The essence of a desert bush from Morocco that blooms once a year, and then only under moonlight."

He slipped a small vial out of the pouch and held it up for Oxford to see. It was a celestial blue slightly darker than the color of a robin's egg. "Taken off a Spanish captain drowned in Ireland this past month. A well-made cork kept out the ocean out and saved the essence he was carrying. The scavengers sold the vial to a merchant in Dublin."

"And the cost to me?" Oxford asked.

"Two pounds, six."

"Done." Oxford reached over and grasped the vial. Baldini resisted for a moment, perhaps in imitation of the Spanish captain, but finally let go. Oxford took the leather pouch and headed for the door. "Two pounds, six," he said, confirming what he owed Baldini.

13

Baldini sighed as he watched the vial and Lord Oxford disappear. He heard Oxford head down the alley, the heavy footsteps of Tobias following him. "No piu soldi," he said mournfully, returning to the back of the store, muttering to himself.

---

Coming out into Bishopsgate Street, Oxford headed downhill toward the river. As he and Tobias got closer, the fishmongers began to fill the street. The smell of seaweed, dried fish, fresh fish, oysters, mussels, and clams mixed with the stench of yesterday's catch. Oxford's glove came back up as Tobias led the way, pushing through the fishmongers crying out the names of the fish they were selling: "*Sweet salmon, barbell, trout, chevin, perch, smelt here.*" A woman closer to the river was waving her arms: "*Bream, roach, dace, and gudgeon,*" she cried.

Oxford and Tobias arrived at the river stairs next to Fishmongers Hall where people were boarding tilt boats, sculls, and other boats to carry them across the Thames. An old wherry idled upstream, kept in position by a broad-shouldered man leaning on his oars. He saw Oxford and spun the boat around and backed it into the stairs.

"Three hours," Oxford said to Tobias. He stepped into the boat. "Good day, John. I am to the Queen." The boatman put his back into the oars, propelling the boat out into the river.

Oxford looked at London Bridge to his left. The day was bright and windy. Flags flew off the houses on the bridge. "A new play," Oxford said to the boatman, waving the roll of papers.

"Would that ye could take her one of my poems."

"Do you have one?"

"Aye," he said. Without missing a stroke, he handed Oxford a piece of paper folded into a tiny square.

"I'll see what I can do," Oxford said, slipping the paper into a pocket.

The tide was going out and the piers that supported the bridge funneled the river into narrow sluices that foamed and roared. Oxford sat down as the wherry disappeared into the darkness under the bridge to be spit out the other side into an anchorage crowded with ships. With the tide pushing them downriver, they were soon alongside Greenwich Palace.

## ~ 2 ~
## Greenwich Palace

The Queen had spent the past year away from the seacoast while the Spanish threatened to invade England. The high wrought-iron fence that kept people from wandering onto the grounds of the palace would have done little to stop armed troops if the Spanish had decided to sail up the Thames and attacked London. With the defeat of the Armada, Elizabeth had returned to Greenwich, her favorite palace, and the place where she had been borne. One of the first things she did was to send word for Oxford to appear before her.

The palace was three stories high and crowded up to the water's edge to take in the view and fresh air from the river. Bright sunlight silvered the water as Oxford's boat approached. It ran up the polished railings either side of the granite steps and exploded in waves of shimmering light across the building's windows.

"She beckons," he said to himself, as he stepped onto the bottom step. A page waited at the top.

"My lord," the page said. He doffed his cap and bowed, showing thick dark hair as shiny as the wing of a cormorant just up from chasing a fish. The boy was young but handsomely dressed—somebody's favorite at court, Oxford thought. He took note of the boy's black worsted doublet and green side gown. A pair of black pumps, crosscut for corns, were newly polished with soot and grease and shone like the top of his head. Oxford took the boy to be about twelve and wondered why he had not been met by an officer.

"I am honored to escort you today," the page announced, standing up as he put his hat back on his head.

"As well you should," Oxford replied, sweeping past him toward the east end of the palace where the royal apartments were located.

"I regret to inform your lordship," Oxford heard the page say from behind him, "that her majesty expects you in the Summer Room." Oxford, with a slight frown, turned to follow the boy to a door opposite the landing stairs. The page opened the door and stepped aside to let Oxford stride past him into the gallery.

Oxford had not been back in the palace since he and the Queen had spent many weeks there as lovers years earlier. The sight of the old building brought back memories of dreams dashed when Elizabeth decided he could not be her consort.

"I am a great admirer of your plays, my lord," the page said, interrupting Oxford's train of thought as they crossed the gallery, their hard-nailed shoes clattering on the slate floor.

"Are you," Oxford said. "But they are performed when servants are not usually in attendance."

"A servant can be invisible, my lord, like paintings on a wall or rugs on the floor. No one notices me when I slip into a corner. Invisible to the others, I inhale the nectar of your words."

"'*The nectar of my words*,'" Oxford repeated. He was amused. "And which of my plays have you seen?" He half-expected the boy to name something by Marlowe or Greene.

The page opened a door as they entered another hallway. A number of people were coming and going. They nodded to Oxford as they passed. "The best by far was *The True Tragedy of Richard the Third*. Pure magic. I was back in Richard's time, peering into his throne room."

Oxford was surprised. "Any others?"

"I didn't like *The History of Errors*," the page said, then caught himself. He looked up to see how Oxford reacted, but Oxford was apparently not offended. Reassured, the page went on. "A twin who loses his brother? The plot seemed too thin to carry so many words, like a pail with too much water in it."

Oxford glanced at the boy. "Interesting. Go on."

"*Hamlet, the Prince of Denmark*. The Queen didn't like that one."

"True." Oxford remembered the Queen telling him there were too many tragical speeches. "What about you?"

"I didn't like it neither. I liked *The Spanish Tragedy*, though. More action. Fewer speeches."

"You think I wrote *The Spanish Tragedy*?"

"Well," the page chattered on, opening another door, "Mr. Kyd's been living at Fisher's Folly for years. What else has he done? Everyone knows you helped John Lyly hatch his *Euphues*." They continued down the hall. "But I liked *Edmund Ironside* and *Thomas of Woodstock* best of all. That's what you should keep writing about—the kings of England!"

Oxford could not resist smiling at the boy's eager face. "I'll consider it."

They were now walking across another large room. "Begging your pardon, my lord, but may I ask if there is room at the Folly for one more writer who's been bitten by the muse."

"And who might that be?"

"Me," the page said.

"And who is me?"

"Robin, my lord, but they call me 'Scribbler.'"

"And what do you scribble, Robin?"

"Stories, my lord."

"And poetry?"

"No, my lord."

"Some would say that a man is nothing without poetry."

"That may be so," the page said, opening the door to the next room, "but I am not yet a man. And I have no ink in my pot for poetry." He looked up at Oxford, his eyes bright. Oxford said nothing as the two of them walked deeper into the palace. The boy thought he was losing Oxford's interest. "And I can play the lute."

"Ah, you scribble on frets as well as on paper."

"Most commendably, my lord." The boy snatched the cap off his head and went to one knee, presenting the top of his shiny head once again. "I will serve you truly if you put me in your trust: I will say little; fear judgment; fight when I cannot choose otherwise, and eat no fish."

Oxford nodded. "The last, of course, the most important." He waved him up. "So how is it that you are a page here at court, Robin?"

"I am an orphan, my lord. The Earl of Leicester took me in because he liked my music. He decided I would make a worthy gift to give to the Queen. He thought she would like my music."

"And does she?"

"She does, my lord, but I want to be a writer."

"But you can't leave the Queen's service without her permission."

"She will let me go, my lord. The Earl passed away a fortnight ago and was apparently much loved by the Queen."

"More in death than in life," Oxford commented, unable to stop himself from sniping at the now-dead earl. "He never really took my place in her heart, he said to himself. "That was impossible. She only said so out of politics. But, then again, who ever knew what Elizabeth was really thinking." He pushed away thoughts of Leicester and the Queen.

"My playing now incites her to tears," Robin went on. "She says it reminds her of him."

"I see," Oxford said as they strode into another hallway. He looked down at the boy. "Come not tomorrow, then, young Robin, but the day after. Three o'clock in the afternoon. You know where?"

"Oh, yes, my lord. Just outside Bishopsgate."

"Aye."

"Where all the writers are," the boy said excitedly.

"Not yet. We've haven't had the pleasure of your company."

"Oh, my lord," the page said, his face crimson with embarrassment. "I cannot thank you enough."

"Oh, but you will," Oxford said. "You will play at supper. I miss good music at even time."

"My lord, I shall not disappoint."

A servant appeared in front of them who gestured for Oxford to follow him. He gave Robin a sharp glance that sent the boy out of sight. The servant opened a door to a small room. "Please wait in here, my lord. Her majesty will send for you."

Oxford stepped into the room. The servant closed the door and disappeared. Oxford sat down on a bench along one of the walls. Silence settled over him. He leaned back and breathed in the air, the scent of the old palace bringing back memories of the time he had spent with Elizabeth, and later, his inner voice reminded him, with Anne Vavasor, Elizabeth's lady-in-waiting, who had delivered herself of a child in a bedchamber next to the Queen's. The memory made him smile. *Oh, did all hell break loose that night.* Oxford ran but was caught as he was about to board a ship and bundled back to London to join Anne and her new baby in the Tower.

The Queen had been furious. A lady-in-waiting was supposed to be a virgin, like her sovereign. Many dallied but kept their affairs quiet. Getting pregnant and delivering a baby in the next room was unthinkable, but what made Anne's pregnancy even worse was that it had been kept secret from Elizabeth. She hated secrets. After all, if a pregnant lady-in-waiting could be hidden under her very nose, *what else was going on without her knowledge?* Her anger doubled when Oxford was identified as the father. Even though their affair had ended years earlier, she reacted as though she and Oxford were married and he had cheated on her! He always thought her rage was more about him than the wounded decorum of her court.

"A woman scorned," Oxford said to himself, "even if she would deny any such feelings if asked!" He didn't understand women, starting with his mother, who had abandoned him to Burghley when his father suddenly died. Oxford was twelve at the time. Then there was little Nan, Burghley's daughter, whom Burghley had made him marry. She was another mystery, like a fish that keeps wiggling away from you. And Anne Vavasor! His vixen mistress! Nothing mysterious about her, he thought, as he remembered her narrow face, her aquiline nose, her dark searching eyes, and the tumultuous times they had spent together jousting with words and making love between silken sheets.

Anne had retired to the country after her release from the Tower, taking the baby with her. Oxford had not seen her since, but the fireworks Anne had brought to their relationship were not something he wanted now. He needed more quiet now, he realized, to write the plays that thronged his head, like the quiet he had enjoyed when he lived for a year on the palace grounds in a tiny cottage tucked away under a grove of lofty pine trees. He chuckled to himself as he remembered the parties he had hosted in that little cottage when he would stand up and tell outrageous stories to his guests, all witless themselves, come to revel in his wit, which flowed like wine.

The door opened, startling him. Sir Thomas Heneage stepped into the room. Sir Thomas was a big, ruddy-faced man of Oxford's age whose large head made him lean forward over his spindly legs as if the weight of his upper torso was about to topple him over forward. Sir Thomas was, among other things, a minor poet whose poetry looked and sounded like him—plodding and top-heavy. His wealth came not from his verse but from the property he acquired by marrying a wealthy widow. He made another fortune by investing in the voyages of Sir Francis Drake, while Oxford put himself in debt by financing the voyages of Martin Frobisher. Drake plundered the Spanish Main and returned with ships full of gold; Frobisher returned with a unicorn horn, a few natives, and rocks that turned out to be worthless.

As if that wasn't enough, the Queen had elevated Heneage to the rank of Vice Chamberlain and Treasurer of the Chamber, offices that gave him power over domestic and foreign affairs. This day, for some reason, he was dressed in a bright yellow doublet and purple hose, reinforcing the view of the rest of the court that if one of them could come up with a new way of looking elegant, Heneage would show up in an outfit that would redefine the word "inelegant."

"Ah, Oxford," Sir Thomas said. "How nice to see you."

"How dost thou, Sir Thomas."

"Well, thank you." Sir Thomas put a beefy hand on Oxford's shoulder. "The Queen is in a good mood, I must say, to the relief of all of us. She's been much taken of late with the loss of Leicester, the old dog. You know he may have poisoned himself when his wife, unknowingly, gave him the very draught he had brought home to poison her?"

"Really," Oxford said, having already heard the story. It was not difficult to believe. Leicester's first wife, Amy Robstart, had been "found" years ago at the bottom of a staircase. Leicester thought this freed him to wed Elizabeth and become king in all but name. Elizabeth had flirted with the idea for a while but the rumor that Amy had been pushed down the stairs would not go away and Elizabeth eventually made it clear that Leicester would not be marrying England's "Virgin Queen." The irony of Leicester being hung on his own petard was a pleasant idea to Oxford, but he suddenly realized the switched cup of poison might be something he could use in a play he was working on. He drifted away, thinking of various possibilities.

Sir Thomas thought Oxford had gone silent because he did not want to enjoy a quiet chortle over Leicester's fall. Sir Thomas adopted a more businesslike attitude. "In any event," he went on, taking his hand off Oxford's shoulder, "don't incite the old boot today. We've worked for days to make her smile. If you get into a row with her, she'll take it out on us once you're gone." Oxford's face showed surprise at this suggestion. "Don't give me that look. The two of you are so alike. We dread your visits. Fortunately, you haven't seen her for some time now."

Oxford gave Sir Thomas a thin smile. "I'll do my best."

"Good," said Sir Thomas, too self-absorbed to notice Oxford's sarcasm.

"With your permission," Oxford said.

"By all means."

Oxford opened the door and stepped into a small room that everyone called the Summer Room. The far wall was glass that looked out on the park behind the palace. The other three walls were covered with hangings imported from Belgium. The floor was freshly covered with rushes. A leather chair stood against the wall opposite the windows. The back was straight and rose six feet from the floor. The arms were dark wood and unpadded. The wooden legs were straight and unornamented. A visitor might think it was a small throne, particularly when Elizabeth sat on it, but the chair's Spartan simplicity suggested that other chambers were reserved for show while business was conducted in this room.

Elizabeth sat erect in the chair. She was wearing a silk robe over a black dress with a top made of white taffeta. Black taffeta backgrounded the robe and the dress. A simple chain suspended a silver cross above her breasts where the square-cut white top showed the fair skin for which she was famous. Her hair was piled on top of her head and held in place by an ivory comb that stood straight up at the back of her head.

Elizabeth was of middle height, slender, and straight. Her nose rose in the middle. Her forehead was large and fair. Her eyes were gray as glass.

Oxford had not seen her in some time. She was now fifty-five. Despite the layers of makeup, he could see that her attempts to prove she was immune to the ravages of time were failing. Her aging face and thinning hair surprised him. The rich red hair he had held in his hands years earlier was now the color and texture of burnished straw.

A large arras covered the wall across from Oxford. It showed the death of Acteon, the hunter who had stumbled upon the goddess Diana bathing in a forest pool. Diana had changed Acteon into a stag for his effrontery and his dogs had run him down. The weaver had skillfully caught the fright on Acteon's face as the dogs seize him by the throat. Don't cross Diana, Oxford thought to himself as he looked at the wall hanging. What better sign to hang on the wall of a room in which Her Majesty dispenses justice? Or accepts gifts, such as the play he held under his arm. He gave it a satisfying squeeze.

Three ladies-in-waiting stood against the wall in the corner nearest the windows. Their low chatter stopped as Oxford stepped into the room and knelt on the rushes.

"Ah," the Queen said. "My Lord of Oxford."

"Elizabeth . . ." he said, pausing just long enough to let everyone think he was greeting her by her Christian name. Such familiarity would have been unacceptable from any subject, even from a lord as senior as Oxford, but before the Queen and her attendants could draw in their breath, Oxford followed 'Elizabeth' with 'Regina,' making it clear that he was addressing her in Latin.

The ladies-in-waiting relaxed, but the Queen did not. She knew he was punning on the word 'vagina,' for he had called her 'Vagina Regina' more than once when they had been lovers. She was not pleased.

The ladies-in-waiting, of course, had no idea that Oxford might be referring to a very private part of the Queen's anatomy, but they could tell they had missed something because they could see that the Queen was angry. They averted their eyes, expecting an outburst, but the Queen did nothing. She sat there, as still as an Egyptian statue, her hands gripping and ungripping the arms of her chair while she glared at Oxford, who kept his head down, awaiting her response. She wanted to strike him, but realized that his outrageous statement was like a burst of fresh air from a window suddenly thrown open. Few knew of the promises they had exchanged years earlier and how duty had pried them apart to set her on a course that would deny her a husband and send him back to his wife.

She looked down at his bowed head and marveled at how two words, one her name, the other her official title, separated by a pause and a pun, could bring back memories of a time when she could not get enough of him. Two simple words that sent a message only she would get. How more economical could a wordsmith be, she wondered? He would, of course, deny anything was intended beyond his simple greeting if she were so witless as to ask. At the same time, "regina," once it had delivered its hidden pun, immediately restored decorum to the room.

Elizabeth smiled slightly, a smile seen by the ladies in waiting. Oxford also saw it but, while the Queen's mouth might flicker with a smile, her eyes told him he was to go no further.

"Welcome, cousin," Elizabeth said, gesturing with her long-fingered hands for Oxford to rise. "Do your words always carry double meanings, my lord?"

He stood up. "Always, Your Majesty."

"As they do now," she said, the faint smile still on her face, which, in the interest of resuming a more regal bearing, she was trying to erase.

"Your Majesty sees all," Oxford deadpanned.

"If I did, I would have no need of Walsingham's spies."

"Or Lord Burghley's."

"Yes."

"May I?" Oxford stepped forward with his gift. He opened the pouch and handed it to her. The Queen took out the porcelain vial and held it up. She loved gifts. "The essence of a desert bush from Morocco," Oxford told her, "that blooms only once a year, and then only in moonlight." The Queen inhaled the scent from the bottle.

Oxford continued. "Pried from the hand of a Spanish captain found in the surf off Sligo Bay. A scent never before experienced outside of Africa."

"We like it," the Queen said. "'Tis a fitting gift for one as you to give your Queen." She handed the vial and the leather bag to one of the ladies who had soundlessly appeared at her side.

"I am humbled," Oxford said, bowing. "I have come hither with great expectations to hear what Your Majesty wishes to command of me."

"Still seeking Harwich?"

"I expect Your Majesty has something more important for me than overseeing a small port at the mouth of the River Orwell."

"I do, but not a position of command, as you have pressed me for all these years."

He couldn't stop himself from scowling. "I expect no favor in that regard, since you have never favored my requests for command."

"And for good reason." Her voice rose slightly. "You see connections we don't see, and this allows you to write plays and poetry that we marvel at, but generals must deal with reality and make decisions. Seeing a thousand possibilities can cripple someone who has too much imagination."

"So you seek out men who have little or no imagination, like Hatton," Oxford said, his voice dripping with sarcasm, "a sheep without teeth."

"Yes. Better the 'mutton' who cannot bite than the 'boar' whose teeth can raze," she said, alluding to a letter Hatton had written her arguing that she should prefer him over Oxford for these very reasons.

"But it is my duty to add to the luster of my forefathers," Oxford went on, trying to remain calm. "You have denied me that opportunity. You have denied me my heritage."

"I have denied you nothing. I sent you north to second Lord Sussex and you threw yourself at the Scots in such a reckless manner that you had to be rescued. England can ill afford to throw away another poet. I will not have another Sidney."

"Sidney! A little poet made great by an early death."

Elizabeth frowned. "Sir Philip lies not long in the ground, my lord."

"Yes, and none too soon. English poetry is the better without him."

"Jealousy ill becomes you, my lord."

"'Tis not jealousy, Your Majesty. Sidney's ideas would have crippled poetry. Accent and rhythm would have died away. Every poet alive should be grateful he is gone. God obviously called him home."

"A curious statement, coming from a man who has been linked to the devil in more ways than one. When were *you* last inside a church?"

"Last week," Oxford said. "St. Paul's."

"No doubt to wander through the bookstalls. Did you stay for the sermon?" She spied the papers under his arm. "And what else did you bring with you?"

"A new play, Your Majesty, with scenes never seen anywhere, even in Africa."

"No." She said, waving a hand as if to dispel an odor that had suddenly filled the room. "We will have no more plays."

"No more plays? Plays are my life."

"Being the Seventeenth Earl of Oxford is your life, my lord. The playhouse is for bawds. Let Lyly and Greene write plays; you must write poetry."

"Poetry cannot compare to plays."

"Poetry exceeds playwriting on every level. Look at *Astrophel and Stella*, Sidney's great poem."

"Sidney again! How many people have sat in rapt attention while they listened to *Astrophel and Stella*?"

> *Not at first sight, nor with a dribbled shot*
> *Love gave the wound, which while I breathe will bleed.*

Oxford snorted. The Queen made no effort to stop him. She and the ladies in the room waited. They all knew he could repeat anything he had heard once, no matter how long it was. Oxford, unaware that he had been ceded the floor, raced on:

> *But known worth did in time of mine proceed,*
> *Till by degrees it had full conquest got;*
> *I saw and liked, I liked but loved not.*

"This is drivel!" he exclaimed, throwing up his hands. "Love's 'dribbled shot? 'At length to love's decree I, forced, agreed? 'Tis the forced gait of a shuffling nag! He was a facile poet, Your Majesty, imitative at best, and sentimental and silly at worst. He could hiss like a serpent—*Sweet swelling lips well maist thou swell*—gobble like a turkey—*Moddels such be wood globes*—and quack like a duck—*But God wot, wot not what they mean.*"

He stood before her, hands on his hips. He could tell the Queen was trying not to laugh.

"How much better this," he said, turning and striking a menacing pose: "Evil Richard sending Earl Rivers to his death:

*Wilt thou be ringleader to wrong, must you guide the realm?*
*Nay, overboard all such mates I hurl, whilst I do guide the helm.*
*I'll weed you out by one and one, I'll burn you up like chaff;*
*I'll rend your stock up by the roots.*

"Richard snarls and paces across the stage, a moving, breathing embodiment of everyone's fear—an evil king! A thousand pairs of eyes, nay three thousand, watch him plot and scheme, the illusion being more real than reality."

"Illusion?" Elizabeth cried out. "Thou knowest nothing of illusion. You write a poor play and get hissed off the stage. I govern poorly and people rush in to end my reign and send me after my father."

"True," Oxford agreed, loving the return to the way they had argued during their courtship, "but your words, severing me from my work, kill me as much as if you had cut off my head!"

The Queen was not moved. Lips pursed, she looked away. Nevertheless, Oxford thought she was wavering a little.

"I am filled with characters who rage for admission to the world. Generals order me to let them strut the stage; Machiavels push at me to work their wiles on gulls and fools; murderers clamor for attention so that they can poison good people and cry out when they are undone. I am bloated with a sickness that can only be cured by being bled through my pen, my blood, freighted with pirates and peasants, coursing down my arm to come out as stark scratchings that turn white pages into living, breathing art." His outburst had drained him. "I am touched with fire," he said in a subdued voice.

"Then you needs douse it, my lord. Your Queen commands it."

Oxford looked at her, anger supplanting the disappointment visible on his face. "For my Queen?" he asked. "Or for someone else?" He walked over to the arras. He stopped and assumed a dramatic pose. "The people say that Lord Burghley doth age and his hearing fades. Thus, we must raise our voices so that he misses nothing!"

Unsheathing his rapier in one swift movement, he hooked the edge of the arras and flipped it aside, exposing an older man standing sideways in a doorway hidden by the hanging.

"Behold!" Oxford exclaimed. "My former father-in-law, a god these many years, listening to us like Zeus watching the Greeks squabble before Troy."

Burghley, his dignity ruffled, walked into the room. He was wearing a dark green coat, open down the front to expose the gold chain and symbol of his office as Lord Treasurer. He was white-headed and bearded, but no one would mistake him for a king or general as he strode across the room to take up his position beside Elizabeth. Born the son of a minor bureaucrat, he had been knighted by Elizabeth for his devotion during the years her brother and sister ruled England and while she herself waited to find out whether she would succeed her sister Mary or be executed as the bastard daughter of Anne Boleyn. In 1571 she made him Baron Burghley so that his daughter could marry Oxford and his grandchildren could inherit Oxford's titles. Otherwise, the marriage would have been morganatic. Thus, in an odd twist, Burghley owed his rise to the peerage to Oxford. Of course, Pondus, as he was called behind his back because of his long speeches, had planned all this long before he had taken custody of twelve-year old Edward de Vere in 1562 when the Sixteenth Earl of Oxford had suddenly and mysteriously died.

"So now we know why the Queen doth command her most loyal subject to stop writing plays. Pondus must not let the playhouse taint his granddaughters before they are married off."

"The essence of civilized behavior," Burghley began, his nose in the air, "is the ability to enact gracefully and convincingly upon a public stage the role that fortune has selected for you. For Her Majesty, it is to be Queen of England. For me, it is to be Lord Treasurer. For you, it is to be …"

"Oh, shut it!" Oxford said.

Burghley stopped in mid-sentence, shocked.

The Queen intervened.

"Let me read you something, Edward," she said, using his given name for the first time. She took out a small book and opened it to the title page. "*Il Cortegiano*," she said, "by a learned Italian gentleman named Baldassare Castiglione. A certain lord we know paid handsomely to have this work translated into Latin." She peered at him knowingly. "I believe it was your cousin, Arthur Golding, who translated it."

"My uncle," Oxford corrected her, "and it was Ovid's *Metamorphosis* he translated, not Castiglione."

"Yes," the Queen went on smoothly, ignoring the double correction, "your mother's brother. Who was your tutor when you were young."

"As you are Tudoring me now," Oxford could not help himself from punning.

Burghley took this to mean that Oxford thought the Queen was 'tutoring' him, a pleasant thought to Burghley. The Queen knew Oxford had taken her family name and turned it into a verb. A smutty one at that, she realized. She forced herself to ignore it.

"A most gracious knight, Castiglione," she said, "and the finest defender of our courtly traditions."

"Yes, yes," Oxford said impatiently.

"You even wrote the preface, which Gabriel Harvey, of all people, said was a 'courtly epistle more polished than the writings of Castiglione himself.'"

Oxford knew what was coming. He felt like the patient watching a chirurgeon preparing his instruments to lance a boil.

"The preface most impressed me." She turned to a page near the front of the volume. Oxford had not seen the small book come into her hands.

The Queen looked over the top of the book at him. "You admit, do you not, that Signore Castiglione propounded the very rules of proper behavior?"

Oxford nodded.

"And do you still find what *you* wrote in the preface to be apt? It's in choice Latin, but let me see if I can translate it fairly." She held the book out in front of her:

*And great as all these qualities are, our translator has wisely added one single surpassing title of distinction to recommend his work. For indeed what more effective action could he have taken to make his work fruitful of good results than to dedicate his Courtier to our most illustrious and noble Queen, in whom all courtly qualities are personified, together with those diviner and truly celestial virtues?*

She closed the book. "I read this to Sir Philip Sidney after you and he quarreled at the tennis court. I told Sir Philip then, as I am telling you now, that there are degrees between earls and gentlemen, and that it is incumbent upon each to respect their superiors. Furthermore, princes must of necessity maintain the degrees descending between the people's licentiousness and the anointed sovereignty of the crown, and that the consequence of a gentleman's neglect of nobility, in the former case being Sidney's disrespect of you, and in this case your refusal to accept my suggestion that you leave playwriting to others, will result in the peasantry insulting us both."

"Yes, yes," Oxford said, impatiently. "The end of society as we know it because those who walk behind will kick the heels of those who walk in front."

The Queen looked at him archly but could not tell if he was being sarcastic or was angry.

"The heavens themselves," she continued, "observe degree, priority and place, proportion, season, form, office and custom, in all line of order," but Oxford interrupted her before she could go further.

"Your Majesty," Oxford pleaded, coming toward her, "that all may be true, but do not take playwriting away from me."

"My lord, my court has need of poets, not playwrights."

"Quite so," Burghley murmured.

"Pondus, I am neither ward to you nor son-in-law. I am that I am, and I will serve myself first."

"Before you serve your Queen?" Elizabeth asked.

"Madame, when your grandfather Henry Tudor took the crown from Richard, my forefathers lay fourteen-deep in the soil of England!"

Everyone in the room gasped.

"How dare you," Elizabeth said, her eyes flashing. "I am your sovereign Queen, no matter how many of your ancestors preceded mine. You durst not speak thus to me."

"Or take liberties with the royal person," Oxford went on blithely, "as I was wont to do in times past."

"Stop!" Elizabeth shouted. She stood up. Her robe fell off her shoulders. It hit the floor before a lady-in-waiting could catch it. "Follow me," she said, striding past him toward the glass doors at the rear of the room. She flung them open and headed up the hill behind the palace in long angry strides. Oxford followed. When she arrived at the top, she pointed to a spot on the bench that circled the giant beech at the top. "Sit!" she commanded, treating him like a dog. He felt like one. He sat down. Once again, he had gone too far. She placed herself in front of him, her head held back in anger, her hands on her hips.

"I may not be able to make the sun come up in the west, but, by God, I can make any man a traitor. There are always Catholic plots that need another conspirator. Wouldn't Lord Howard or Charles

Arundel be happy to tell a court about your Catholic leanings to pay you back for the months they spent in the Tower after you said they were conspiring to unseat me?"

"But I spoke the truth about them."

"Yes, but, if the investigation were reopened, would they not swear you told them that Joseph was a wittol, that Jesus was only a man, and that Mary was a whore!?"

"Not true," Oxford protested weakly.

"True, my lord, and you know it. But even if not, such fine points will matter little once they are given an opportunity to testify against you."

Oxford looked up. He had angered her, yes, but so much that she would send him to the Tower again? She had become the commanding presence he had fallen in love with years earlier. Her age had disappeared. Her anger had transformed her into the fiery spirit with whom he had fallen in love. She, however, was not playing the part of an old lover. She was furious at his insolence. Never far from thinking she was being laughed at by her subjects, she could not tolerate any sign of disrespect. Oxford's words, coming from a senior lord in open court, made the affront worse.

"Don't ever do that again," she said in a low voice.

He bowed his head.

She paced up and down in front of him, clenching and unclenching her fists, as if the sight of his face would cause her to strike him. Finally, she stopped pacing. A soft breeze fluttered a few leaves past them. Oxford thought they looked like silent servants trying to sweep something away. She sat down next to him.

"There are no keyholes up here to listen to what we say. You can lean on this tree or the flowers that fringe this retreat and they will not blab or know of what we speak. Not so elsewhere, where we must always keep an ear open, listening in the darkest part of night to footsteps in the hallway outside. Are they the measured pace of a guard walking by with even step, indifferent to the sound he makes, or are they the footsteps of someone trying to move swiftly to harm our person?"

She looked toward the river. A mile away a flower girl was walking down the road to the river to sell her flowers to passengers coming ashore. Elizabeth pointed toward her.

"You see that girl? She dreams of being me. At times, I wish I could be her, but I cannot: I must be Queen of England. I cannot gambol in flowered fields or loll in lover's arms. All that has been denied me."

"Not so," Oxford said softly. "We exchanged rings and promises about eternal love. It was attested to by the holy close of lips and sealed by the archbishop at Croydon."

"A moment's lapse."

"Three or four weeks," Oxford lamented.

"We cannot change the roles that have been given us."

"You thought so once."

"I did, but in the coolness after so much heat I realized I would not be Queen if you were my consort."

"I would have been a star in your court."

"*I* would have been a star: *you* would have been the sun. We all know what happens when the sun comes out: the stars disappear."

The two of them sat there, staring out over the top of the palace at the river. A ship was moving downriver, the tops of its masts and uppers visible over the palace roof. Neither spoke. She touched his shoulder, surprising him.

"A touch," she said, "of something I can never have again."

She withdrew her hand. She rose from the bench.

"My marriage bed is England, and no sight of well-formed flesh shall sway me from what is good for England. I must be Queen, and you must be my senior lord."

Oxford began to speak softly:

> *Being your slave, what should I do but tend*
> *Upon the hours and times of your desire?*
> *I have no precious time at all to spend,*
> *Nor services to do, till you require.*

Elizabeth waved a hand, telling him to stop. She knew the sonnet, one of many he had written to her. It threatened to take her back to times when she lay in his lap and let his poetry envelope her like the warm wind that was gently stroking her now.

> *Nor dare I chide the world-without-end hour*
> *Whilst I, my sovereign, watch the clock for you,*
> *Nor think the bitterness of absence sour*
> *When you have bid your servant once adieu ...*

"Enough!" she said with just enough irritation to silence him. She turned away, looking down the hill toward the palace.

30

Oxford leaned toward her. "If you won't revisit those days with me, let me at least write plays, Bess. My loss, first of you, and now of playwriting, is a double loss I cannot bear. 'Tis the swirling height of mounting eagles when I write *'enter the young Prince, with Ned and Tom,'* book-ended by the tired pen of a spent lover when I close the tale with 'Finis.'" He waved the roll of papers he still held in his hand. "No simple poem this. No brief arrow shot into the sky, but textured stories no one has read or heard. I can no more resist their birth than the sun can stay its course at sunrise."

She said nothing. He thought she was softening.

"I saw the power of the stage at Cambridge when the students put on a play in front of you that was so anti-papist you stormed off, calling for the torches: 'Give me light: away!' you cried. 'Twas the moment I knew that poetry had been eclipsed. To write words that move one person while they read a poem is a wonderful thing; to write words that cause a sovereign to call for light and flee nothing more fearsome than actors on a stage is much, much more."

He leaped up.

"What I will write will far exceed what Titian painted when I was in Venice, because a painting is dead as soon as the painter puts down his brush. It's like the stag's head over the fireplace at Hedingham, which is no longer alive. The same is true of poetry, dead as soon as the pen is lifted from the page, or sculpture, frozen the moment the sculptor puts down his chisel."

He swirled around.

"What I will write will live! I will take the audience to Venice to watch pickpockets lifting purses from the gulls who walk the Grand Canal, or bring them into a throne room to watch the murder of a king. The audience will call for light, as you did, though the darkness be nothing more than the gossamer threads I have woven in my mind."

He looked intently at her.

"Do not take away my pen. Let me leave a name behind me. Do not let Burghley silence me."

His hope that Elizabeth had softened was wrong.

"I do not do this for Burghley," she said, a sharp edge back in her voice. "I do this because I will not allow the foremost noble in my realm to become a penny-a-page playwright, no matter how good his plays may be. And if they be more than good, the effect on my kingdom will be worse, since you, who should be first in upholding the noble character of my realm, will become known for your plays, and my reign will dissolve into nothing but contests over words and money. Nigh unto forty winters have creased thy brow, Edward; far more mine. Death shall soon make us all kin—you, me, and the flower girl who now goes happily to the wharf below. I will not let you tarnish the nobility of my court by writing plays and stain your name at the same time."

*"What name!"* Oxford exploded, the anger he had been pushing down bursting out of him. He jumped up. "Had I writ, my name would have lived on in the mouths of men. 'Twas what Achilles feared: that he would do no deed worthy of being spoken of after he was gone. I will leave nothing behind me. My name will be buried where my body lies."

"Write poetry," Elizabeth said, resisting the urge to put her hand on his shoulder again. "Honor my court with poetry, poetry only you can write."

He tore the papers in his hands into shreds and threw them away. They fluttered down the hill like birds scattered by the wind, hunting for a home they would never find. He refused to look at her. "I write none more," he said. He turned and set off down the hill.

It was an hour before she followed him. Burghley was waiting inside the door. "He would have made a terrible playwright," he sniffed. "I saw *Hamlet*. Too many tragical speeches."

"He would have been a *great* playwright," Elizabeth countered. "I have staunched someone that England has never seen, and may never see again."

"He must be an earl," Burghley intoned, "as you must be a virgin and bear no children."

She looked at him, making no effort to mask her disdain. "Thank you, my lord." And with that she brushed past him into the palace.

## ~ 3 ~
## The Boar's Head

Oxford saw no one on his way back through the palace, not even a Yeoman of the Guard. He waited for a boat to take him across the Thames to a world without honor or hope. "The sun will not show his head this day," he said, looking up at a sky that had turned gray and foreboding. "'*Framed in the front of forlorn hope, past all recovery, I stayless stand,*'" he began to recite, when a voice interrupted him.

"Your Grace?"

John the boatman was holding onto an iron ring below him. Oxford climbed down into the boat.

"Did ye give her my poem?" John asked.

Oxford felt for the poem but couldn't find it. He had lost it in the Palace. "Aye, John. But don't expect anything. Her mind is full of matters."

The sound of his voice cut him like a knife. It was a fitting end to a day of denigration and defeat: "Forced to lie to an honest man, and an artist at that!" he thought ruefully. How far he had come from the boy who believed that his family's motto—*Vero nihil verius*—*Nothing truer than truth*— would be the pole star to guide him through life.

"Then I rest content. Someone will surely read it."

"Aye," Oxford said. He looked away. The Thames, muddy and brown, roiled past them. He thought it looked like an oily beast, leering up at him as it surged by the boat.

They were quickly under the bridge and into the boats crowding the landing like cattle pushing their way into a feed bin. Oxford stepped ashore. *And now?* His legs had gone numb. *Back to the Folly?* No. The papers that littered the rooms in the Folly would look like broken glass in an abandoned house, each page mocking his dream of being a playwright.

A woman carrying a tray of fish knocked into him as she went by. "Mind yer back, yer lordship!" she called out. The blow pushed him forward, away from the river. He headed uphill, his mind a blank. He turned left at Eastcheap. Moments later he found himself in front of the snarling head that hung crookedly from a black iron frame and told the world that the Boar's Head Tavern was inside. The front of the building leaned out over the street. Repaving and debris had raised the pavement over the years so that the entrance was below the street. Oxford stepped down and pushed open the heavy wooden door.

The roar of voices, along with the aromas of trussed chickens, bacon fat, turtles in their shells, ducks, herons, and pheasants, welcomed him. Enormous posts held up the ceiling. They were covered with graffiti and papers announcing someone's latest literary effort. Knuckle bones paved the floor. Smoke from burning tobacco, a new vice introduced by Raleigh, filled the air. Booths lined the walls. Trestle tables in the middle were filled with men playing games and arguing.

Oxford worked his way through the smoke to the rear of the tavern and threw himself into a booth. He dumped his rapier and cape into a corner. A large man was sleeping on the other side of the table, a knee projecting upward like an uprooted tree. An immense belly rose and fell like an ocean being heaved by storms far away.

"Jack," Oxford hissed. The snoring continued. Oxford leaned over and twisted one of the man's fingers. The man snorted, but did not raise his head. "Jack," Oxford repeated. "Wake up, ye fat slug!"

The man finally raised his head. He opened one eye. The eye smiled, if one eye could smile, but the face slept on. The effort drained him. The eye slid shut like a window being closed against a summer thunderstorm. The man called Jack slumped back under the table.

"Jack!" Oxford repeated, louder this time. He poked the man hard in the stomach, finally waking him. Jack sat upright, looking dazed. He was wide at the shoulders. An oversized head was crowned by a tangled lion's mane. His face wore the brown sheen of a ripe medlar. His shirt, expensive when new, was soiled and torn. An enormous buckle, tilted from the strain of holding in such a large belly, held the ends of a leather belt. Soiled and tattered gaskins fell to his knees. A finely woven straw hat lay crushed on the seat next to him.

"My lord," Jack said in a deep basso profundo. A barmaid was going by. He reached out for her and, without looking, reeled her in. "Peaches, my lass. Ale for his lordship and me."

The girl was plump and big-bosomed, with strawberry hair and the complexion of, indeed, a fresh peach. "Sir John Falstaff," she announced contemptuously, "risen from the dead to eat and drink more. And all without paying."

"Peaches!" Jack protested. "I always pay. You know that!"

"Not in my lifetime. A large ale, my lord?"

Oxford nodded.

"Always large," Falstaff said, reaching out for her again.

She twisted away. "For someone so large," she said, "I would not be jesting about size, Sir John. Forget not the mouse that was et by the cat because he could not fit back in his hole."

"A mouse? I be a *lion* in this jungle."

Oxford lowered his head. Peaches and Falstaff saw his reaction and stopped their bantering. Peaches headed back to the kitchen.

Oxford looked at the fat man across the table from him. Has he always been this fat? he wondered. They had first met at Cecil House when Oxford was only fourteen. The boy earl had found Falstaff irresistible. Burghley was aghast when he found out that they had become companions. Dire consequences were predicted, he announced, but here they were, years later, sitting opposite each other.

Oxford had a grim look on his face, which Falstaff instantly recognized had nothing to do with his attempt at being witty. "So what's more important than sleep?" he asked, trying to sound churlish, which he could not.

"The Queen says no more plays."

"She's closing the playhouses?"

"No. She's ordered me to stop writing plays."

"Oh," Falstaff began to stroke the end of one of his mustaches. There were two of them, one each side of his face. They grew larger as they spread out across his cheeks. "Not to worry, Edward. Let her make her pronunciamentos. You shall go on as before and she will forget, as she has done in the past."

"Not this time, my friend. This time she means it."

Falstaff demurred. "She won't be able to keep your plays off the stage. She loves them. And you."

Peaches returned with beer for both of them.

"*Did* love me."

"*Still* loves you," Falstaff insisted, "and your plays."

"She doesn't need me anymore. She has Marlowe and Kyd, and Greene and Lyly."

Falstaff snorted. "Those university boys have not the wit to write plays for her. She will tire of them. She will relent. *Je vouz assure.*"

"And what makes you so sure of that?" Oxford asked, wanting to believe him.

Falstaff placed a thick index finger alongside his nose. "I know because my nose tells me."

"Your nose?"

"My nose. *La Nez.*

"Le Nez," Oxford corrected him.

"Of course. *Le nez.* A mere slip of the tongue, a loose connection twixt my teeming brain and my addled tongue. How could my nose be anything but masculine?" He turned to show it in profile. "Don't the French consider it the marker of a man? François the First had *un grand nez.* They say the first part of him to arrive was determined by the beauty of the lady he was approaching." Oxford was in no mood for jokes. "In my case," Falstaff went on, "*my nose knows.*" A look of contentment came over him. "Oh, I am a poet after all."

"Three words do not make a poet."

"Why not? Marlowe made you cry with scarce more." Falstaff placed his hand over his heart. "'*Come live with me and be my love,*'" he proclaimed. Oxford started to argue but a man in a nearby booth jumped up.

"Learned gentlemen and friends," he cried, placing his hand over his heart. Falstaff immediately snatched his away from his chest. "Let me fill your ears with poetry that I hope will titillate your fine senses."

The tavern quieted. Such outbursts were common. The speaker climbed onto a bench, his hand still pressed against his chest. His eyes were small, his mustache wispy, his accent provincial. His hair was brown and greasy and plastered to his head. His clothes were the weeds sold to newcomers in Three Needle Street to make them think London would accept them as gentlemen:

> *A parliemente member, a justice of the peace,*
> *At home a poor scare-crowe, at London an ass,*
> *If lowsie is Lucy, as some folk miscall it,*
> *Then Lucy is lousie whatever befall it.*

The patrons started laughing. Sir Thomas Lucy was well-known, if not well-liked. The speaker continued:

> *He thinks himself great, yet an ass in his state,*
> *We allow by his ears but with asses to mate.*
> *If Lucy is lowsie as some folke miscall it,*
> *Sing Lowsie Lucy whatever befall it!*

Cheers rang out, but Oxford had heard enough. He walked over to the man, who was bowing to whistles and applause.

"They applaud your insolence and not your art," Oxford told him.

The man recognized Oxford. "My lord! I trust I do not offend."

"Only the gods of poetry. What work is this from?"

"A snippet of a larger work, my lord, *The Poacher of Arden Forest*."

"The Queen deserves it."

"Thank you, my lord."

"No thanks are due." Oxford turned to the patrons in the tavern. "Who needs a university education when talent like this comes so naturally?" Oxford turned back to him. "You are gifted, young sir."

"Sweet words, coming from one whose plays rank in Heaven."

"Oh, they do rank, sir. They fester worse than weeds. What do you call yourself?"

"William Shackspear, my lord."

"Shack-Spear?"

The man did not hear the wonder in Oxford's question. He was still reveling in the euphoria of being praised by the Poet Earl. "I am from Stratford-upon-Avon, my lord. I may only be the son of a glover, but I have high aspirations. I just missed the fleet when it sailed."

"How unfortunate. You could have served with us on the *Bonaventure*."

"Indeed," Shackspear went on hurriedly. He assumed a dramatic pose. "Now I shall be Aeschylus and commemorate our great victory. And my name shall live on forever, as long as men live and breathe!"

"Really. And how came you to this lofty profession?"

"Your plays, my lord! I heard *Hamnet* in Stratford! I was swept away on a river of words! I even named my son after your play," he said, thinking this detail would cement their relationship.

"Hamnet?" Oxford asked incredulously. "The play is called *Hamlet*, my dear man, not *Hamnet!*"

"It is?" Shackspear's face fell. He suddenly looked cross-eyed. "I saw it at the Guild Hall. It was difficult to hear. I thought the name was Hamnet. Nothing was printed, of course," he babbled on, frightened that his good fortune was now washing away because he had misheard one letter in a name. "Oh, well, Hamnet or Hamlet. What difference does a letter make?" he asked, his voice now carrying a tone of false light-heartedness. "You still have your play, and I still have my son." He looked as if this conclusion fixed all.

Oxford's face was frozen in disbelief. "Yes," he finally forced himself to say. "And I'm sure he's a fine lad. But Aeschylus actually *fought* at Marathon. You missed the fleet, so you cannot be Aeschylus. Homer is a better choice. He was not at Troy. Call yourself Homer, young man. You shall be England's Bard."

"Oh, thank you, my lord," Shackspear gushed. "Thank you."

Oxford turned and headed for the door. Falstaff followed.

"Hamnet!" Oxford muttered to himself as they crossed the room.

"Son of a glover," Falstaff said, repeating Shackspear's phrase.

"Do you think he's related to you?" Oxford asked.

"To me?"

"Shack-Spear. Fall-Staff. Spear. Staff. The two names are not that far apart."

Falstaff's face darkened. "That pizzle-pup is no relation to me. Thou hast a way of offending with words, my lord, words that 'spear' people, if I may say so. Cast them not at me."

They were at the door, which suddenly opened to reveal a young man in the livery of a page.

"My lord," the young man said, bowing to Oxford. "My Lady Mary, Countess of Pembroke, requests your presence tomorrow at 11 o'clock. She is staying at Cecil House."

"I shall be there."

"My lord," Peaches said from behind them. She had Oxford's sword and cloak in her arms.

"Thank you, Peaches. Nigel would have left my service if I had returned without these. You are too kind to keep looking after me."

"And me," Falstaff added, a twinkle in his eye.

"Ye fat chuff," Peaches said. She pushed him toward the door. "Off with ye!"

"I'm making progress, I am," Falstaff said to Oxford's backside as they climbed the steps to the street. "Last time she called me a stinking sack of Sheffield …"

## ~ 4 ~
## Cecil House – The Next Day

Cecil House was a three-story turreted manse on the north side of the Strand, midway between London and Westminster. The house had been constructed in the form of an H, with the bottom of the H facing the Strand. The ends of the wings had been connected by two extensions that formed three courtyards. The southernmost courtyard opened onto the Strand through an archway that was adorned with statuary to suggest the approaches to the great colleges at Cambridge and Oxford.

Liveried servants who stood guard either side of the open archway spied Oxford coming down the Strand. He had come alone. One of the servants thumped the ground with a large staff and began to announce his arrival: "Edward de Vere, Seventeenth Earl of Oxford, Lord Great Chamberlain of England," but Oxford had no interest in going through the main gateway and running into Burghley or his son, Robert. Instead, he went by the servant and headed for an opening in the wall farther along the Strand that was used by tradesmen and suppliers. He took a set of stairs just inside the service entrance to the third floor, where Lady Mary waited for him.

As he began climbing the stairs, he remembered the first time he had come to Cecil House. He was twelve years old. His father had died a few days before, making him a royal ward. The Queen appointed Lord Burghley Oxford's guardian, and Burghley had wasted no time in ordering Oxford to Cecil House. Oxford took Burghley's order as a command to take his rightful place at court. He had supped a few years earlier with the Queen at Castle Hedingham and imagined she would be seeking out his advice. He made the journey down to London on a magnificent stallion at the head of eighty gentlemen on horseback and one hundred yeomen who followed on foot.

Oxford vividly recalled Burghley welcoming him as he rode up to Cecil House and then immediately dismissing the men who had accompanied him. "Greetings, fine gentlemen," Oxford recalled Burghley saying. "Our thanks to you for escorting Lord Oxford safely to his new home. He has no need of retainers here. Be gone, therefore, and safe passage back to Hedingham."

Oxford had protested. "My lord," he remembered saying: "take not these gentlemen from me so that I am without means to show

how worthy I am." "Boy," Burghley said, as he watched the men turning their horses to leave, "you have neither the resources nor the time to traipse around London trying to impress people. Your worth has not yet been determined."

Oxford was humiliated. He not only recalled how Burghley had transformed him from a noble lord into a "boy," but how heavy Burghley's arm felt across his shoulders as his new "father" steered him into Cecil House. Worse, his mother promptly abandoned him. In a letter to Burghley not long after Oxford had arrived at Cecil House, his mother wrote that "circumstances did not permit her resuming her motherly duties." He never saw her again. She remarried soon thereafter and died five years later.

Cecil House brought back more than memories of being alone, however, or learning to survive the rigorous education all the wards were given by Burghley and his wife, Mildred. Oxford also remembered how Burghley had forced him to marry his own daughter, Nan, a vapid girl Oxford had come to dislike as the two of them grew up in Cecil House. Refusal was out of the question, of course: Burghley was his guardian and controlled who Oxford would marry.

Oxford's reluctance to marry Nan was not just because he didn't like her; he didn't want to be married at all, and the marriage had not been a happy one. The dashing young poet had all the qualities expected of an English nobleman: he could ride, hunt, fence, and dance. In 1571, he won the tournament at Westminster Palace in front of the Queen. She was smitten with him and took him into her bed. Nan was banned from court, lest her "scolding eye" take away the fun the Queen was having with Oxford.

He had refused to bed Nan at first, thinking he could get an annulment if the Queen decided to marry him, but the Queen's ardor soon faded. She moved on to other lovers and Oxford resigned himself to accepting Nan as his wife. Over the years, Nan gave him two sons and three daughters. The sons died at birth or shortly thereafter; the daughters survived. When Nan died in June, just a few months before, Oxford was at sea on the *Bonaventure* fighting the Spanish. Before Oxford could return, Burghley had buried her and taken his granddaughters into his care.

"There's a good chance they're here," Oxford suddenly realized as he climbed the stairs to the third floor. He knew nothing about raising children, much less daughters, and had not seen them for how many months? He couldn't recall. Would he have acted differently if Nan had left a son behind? Was he reenacting what his mother did to him?

The thought made him uncomfortable. He didn't want to think about his daughters. They were another failure, like playwriting.

He faltered for a moment. He didn't like being in Cecil House, but his promise to see Lady Mary forced him to stay the course. He knew she would be waiting for him in a suite of rooms overlooking the rear yard that extended north into Covent Garden.

At last Oxford arrived at the third floor. A servant outside her suite opened the door to let him in. Oxford walked in and found Lady Mary comfortably ensconced in a large chair in front of a window. She was a small woman with bright, black eyes. Her dark hair was held at the back of her head in a bun. A simple shawl wrapped around her shoulders and flowed into her lap, a study in elegant simplicity. Only a few years older than Oxford, Lady Mary had always been more of a great-aunt to him than a contemporary. She was an accomplished poet and translator of French and Latin texts. The deification of her brother, Sir Philip Sidney, the previous year, had only added to her reputation as the foremost woman of letters in England.

"Edward," she said warmly, holding out her hand.

"My dear Lady Mary," Oxford said as he kissed her hand. Without further preamble, he announced: "The Queen says no to plays."

"Urged on, you think, by my illustrious host." Her wry tone told him that the Queen's order was no secret to her.

"Aye. He wants no stain on his family name while he sells off his granddaughters to the highest bidders."

Lady Mary disagreed. "Elizabeth, not Burghley, is the one who has taken away your pen, Edward. She sees greatness ahead for England. She intends to surround herself with witty courtiers to impress the dignitaries who will come from Europe now that England has ascended to a new place in the world. There will be balls and concerts, and even plays, but they will not be written by you."

Oxford slumped in his chair. "Can you not help me?"

Lady Mary shook her head. "She visited me at Wilton last month. She told me she was going to command you to stop writing plays. I gently reminded her that she had been richly rewarded by your plays, but she would have none of it. 'Playwriting and nobility do not go hand in hand,' she insisted."

"I shall to Italy," Oxford said. "I can be a free man there and write whatever I want."

Lady Mary frowned. "If you do, you will prove a bigger fool than many think you are now. You have no money to run to Italy, Edward. And you are too old to shift to a new country. "

Oxford sighed. Lady Mary put a hand on his arm.

"You carry a noble name, Edward. Part of the burden of being an earl is that you cannot be a common playwright. I am a woman, whose worth is diminished by my sex. Stale custom presses us both down, but I have not stopped writing. Neither can you. The plays must come out, whether there is an audience to hear them or not."

"No, I am done."

Lady Mary's eyebrows rose slightly. "You are *not* done. There are many chapters yet to be written in the play that is your life."

Oxford didn't want to hear her. They sat in silence for a few moments.

"I saw your daughters this morning," Lady Mary said. "Three more reasons you cannot go to Italy." Oxford looked away. "Wilton is at your disposal. Come stay with me. Help me with translating Philipe de Mornay's *A Discourse on Life and Death*. We can even translate more Psalms."

"Very kind of you," Oxford said. "To leave the city is good advice, but I shall go to Bilton, where I can bury myself in long walks in the Forest of Arden."

"Another good choice. And you will find tongues in trees there, and books in running brooks. You will see men and women behind every bush to fill you plays when you return to your library and find a fresh fire waiting there to warm you, like this fire that warms us here."

"I shall leave tomorrow."

"I'm afraid not. The Queen plans a celebration at St. Paul's. She wants you to lead the procession. It will start at Westminster."

Oxford was aghast. "And when will that be?"

"She did not say. It could be next week; it could be months from now."

Oxford groaned. He walked over to a window and realized he was looking down into the privy garden where he had stabbed an undercook he had found spying on him from behind a hedge. Oxford had been only seventeen. He had run over to the hedge and stabbed blindly into it. The sword went into the cook's leg. The poor man died in less than twenty minutes. Oxford shuddered and turned away. "Too many memories here," he said to himself. "I have to be gone."

"There is one more thing," Lady Mary said from behind him. "Lord Burghley wants an audience with you when your visit with me is over. He says he has a gift for you, and a request."

Oxford turned around, his anger boiling out of him. "A gift? The man never gives; he only takes. I shall leave without speaking to him."

"And make me an ingrate for allowing you to go on your way without seeing him?" She was obviously becoming irritated with Oxford's theatrics. "Or worse, leaving the impression that I told you to leave without seeing him?" She shook her head. "No, I will not allow you to give him an opportunity to take something away from me years hence." She reached for a bell cord and pulled it. "You will find him in the library. Find out what he wants. He will keep you waiting, of course, to show you his station in power to make up for what he lacks in nobility. Put up with it." A servant appeared at the door. "Tell Lord Burghley that Lord Oxford will see him in the library." The servant bowed and left.

"Remember, Wilton is always there for you," she repeated. "See your children before you leave, and send me a note about what the old goat wants."

Oxford stood up. "I am remiss in not asking after your boys, William and Philip. Are they well?"

She nodded, pleased to be asked about them. "They grow bigger every day. They bring nothing but noise and mud into the house." She tried to look disgusted but Oxford could see she was proud of them. "Someone took Philip, only five, to see *Tamburlaine*! Did you take him? No one will say who did it."

Oxford laughed. "Not guilty, this time."

"All he talks about is the theater! He's built a stage in his room and spends the day stabbing kings and rescuing dolls he's made from mops and sticks. You didn't do that when you were young, did you?"

"No, my lady." He was lying, of course, and she knew it.

She waved him out. "Don't forget to write."

On the stairs he met Henry Wriothesley, the Third Earl of Southampton. Henry, sixteen now, had become a ward when his father had suddenly died, like Oxford's. Henry was tall and thin, with fine features. His auburn hair, streaked with touches of red, hung in long tresses. A wisp of a mustache smudged his upper lip. He was wearing an ornate shirt covered with stitched designs in gold thread of gods and goddesses frolicking over a black background. Azure blue leggings tightly wrapped his thin legs. His feet were shod in black boots made more for dancing than for the outdoors. He stopped and draped his long fingers over the balustrade, his eyes flashing insolence only those with ancient titles can produce without effort.

"My Lord of Oxford," he said, bowing slightly.

"Henry," Oxford said. "How goest thou?"

"Well, my lord."

"I am to Lord Burghley."

"Oh," Southampton replied. He put his hand to his breast. "Would that I were done with my Lord Burghley. How did you survive in this house? My spirit is crushed with dancing at seven, French at nine, Latin at ten, and prayers, always more prayers."

"And advice."

"Oh, yes. 'Neither a borrower nor a lender be,' and so on. What need I of these strictures? I will be a landed gentleman when I come of age, and I shall be able to content myself without all these rules."

"He is lord of the realm, Henry, more so than the Queen, and thus you must kiss the ring that is closest to the throne if you wish to survive in this world."

Southampton nodded. "Five more years," he sighed.

"Which will fly by, my lord. He awaits me in the library. Adieu."

"Adieu, my lord."

⸺⸺⸺✦✦✦⸺⸺⸺

Oxford found the library empty. Closing the door behind him, he inhaled the musty scent of old leather and parchment he had learned to love while living in the house. He had once thought that simply breathing the air in the library would add new facts and arguments to his store of knowledge. The rooms set aside at Cambridge and Oxford did not equal the collection Burghley had assembled at Cecil House.

Bookcases in the center of the room rose twenty feet into the air, mimicking Stonehenge in their appearance and mystery. The far wall was all glass, mullioned into narrow panes crowned at their tops with scarlet griffins and bright blue saints. The other walls were covered with books. The ceiling was a Dutch painter's idea, in garish blues and blinding white, of Moses receiving the Ten Commandments from God, hidden behind a summer cloud. Oxford began to pull a book from a case when a door in the wall behind him opened and Lord Burghley stepped into the library.

"Good morning, Edward," Burghley said warmly. He walked into the room with his head held back, an affectation he had acquired when young to make himself appear taller than he was. His pointed beard was neatly trimmed.

"My Lord," Oxford said, bowing slightly. He saw that Burghley was wearing felt slippers that were scuffed and worn. Oxford wondered if this was a sign of cordial familiarity or contempt.

"How good to see you."

"You saw me yesterday, my lord."

"So I did," Burghley said, a slight wheeze now detectable in his voice, "but that was at court. Much more relaxed here, don't you think?" He walked past Oxford and fingered the books Oxford had been looking at. "Ah, you wanted to see if I had replaced the copy of Ovid's *Metamorphoses* you took with you when you left my house so many years ago." He had a bemused look on his face.

Oxford bristled. "I much liked the book, my lord, and that you would scarce miss it since you liked neither Ovid nor Arthur's translation. You said noble minds have no need of poetry or plays. Or of Ovid and his *Metamorphoses*."

"Indeed, indeed," the older man said, walking over to a straight-backed wooden chair and gingerly lowering himself into it. "I don't approve of the Spanish either, but I read their dispatches. Besides, we know that your uncle, while he was your tutor, translated Ovid in this very room with you hanging over his shoulder. His translation contains lurid details not found in the original. Arthur wrote nothing thereafter except dull, plodding church epistles. Methinks you did more than watch him as he penned his translation."

Oxford was not surprised that Burghley was fishing for information as stale as whether his ward had helped Arthur Golding translate the *Metamorphoses*. Oxford's silence told Burghley he would not oblige him. Without showing any reaction, the older man turned to his right and took a leather-bound book off a small table.

"This," Burghley said, holding the book out to Oxford, "is newly arrived from Paris. *Essais*, by Michel de Montaigne. You may have heard of him. Extraordinary book. I am sure you will find it interesting."

Oxford put the book under his arm without looking at it. "Yes, I've read Montaigne," he said to himself, "but I'm not going to let you know it." He waited for Burghley to go on.

"We may disagree on many subjects, Edward, but not on the value of this library. It is yours, if you wish, to use whenever you see fit."

"And the price of admission is ..."

"Nothing," Burghley replied. He looked amused at Oxford's suspicion, but then became more serious. "However, there is one thing you might help me with."

A look of annoyance flashed across Oxford's face. Burghley saw it. He got up and walked over to the bookcase behind Oxford and began straightening a row of books. Oxford had seen him do the same thing every morning with his servants.

"In my many positions of responsibility," Burghley went on, "I am always being asked for favors. I don't resent it. I like finding solutions to problems. It gives me great satisfaction. But sometimes, I need help."

Oxford's irritation was growing by the minute. He knew Burghley was moving books and stretching out the conversation to annoy him. He felt like a fish on the end of a line, and Burghley was jigging it back and forth before setting the hook.

"Yes, to the point," Burghley said, sensing Oxford's impatience. "Videlicet, I will be brief." He turned to Oxford. "There is a certain knight who has been a staunch friend of mine for many years. His health is declining. His wife recently died, leaving him with the care of their only child, a daughter now fifteen. Unfortunately, the father's financial situation has also declined through debts incurred by investing in voyages to the new world."

They both knew that Oxford had lost thousands of pounds on similar voyages while Burghley's investments had been successful. Oxford tried to look as though this dig had missed him, but Burghley knew it hadn't. He went on.

"My friend wants his daughter to marry a respectable man but cannot provide a dowry sufficient to attract someone worthy of her. I have offered to help him find a suitable husband. I have also spoken with Archbishop Whitgift about arranging an appointment to an appropriate vicarage so that the daughter's new husband can support her."

"And?"

"I understand that there is a young man living at Fisher's Folly whose name is Colin Sanderson. He was sent to Cambridge to obtain a divinity degree but was diverted from his appointed profession by the playhouse. I wonder if you might speak to Mr. Sanderson to see if he would be interested in the idea herein expressed."

"That is all?"

"Just so," Burghley replied. "With, I would hope, encouragement that the young man consider the proposal earnestly."

Oxford had no reason to help Sanderson, or *not* to help him. The young man had accomplished little while living at the Folly. He was a dullard who should be shown the door, but Oxford was reluctant to help Burghley when he couldn't see what Burghley really wanted, for Burghley always wanted more than what seemed apparent at first. Oxford decided to dig a little further, if only to irritate his former father-in-law.

"Methinks the young lady is enamored of someone else. 'Tis likely true, since young ladies of that age are constantly in love. And her father likes not the man she angles for, so he wants to force her into a marriage that will be more acceptable to himself, if not to her."

Burghley's face told Oxford that he had struck something close to the heart of the matter, despite the older man's denial. The old fox may not have been thinking of the girl or her feelings, but Oxford sensed something else was afoot.

"Don't make this more than it is, Edward. The marriage I propose will benefit them both." Burghley was ruing the fact that Oxford always made everything more difficult than it had to be.

"I think you force them to marry so they will do well at court."

"This couple will not go anywhere near court," Burghley said, letting a small amount of authority reenter the conversation.

"Then why meddle in this? What difference does it make whom she marries? I would think you would be more understanding. After all, didn't your father threaten to disinherit you when he found out you had married Mary Cheke?"

This was too much for Burghley. Personal matters, such as his first marriage and his father's violent reaction to it, were out of bounds. Mary had given him his first child, Thomas, and then obligingly died before his father's lawyers had finished drawing up the papers that would have made Burghley a pauper. With Mary dead, Burghley was able to keep his inheritance and remarry, but it was not a pleasant memory. He would not let himself recognize any similarity between the proposal he was putting forward to Oxford and his own marriage to Mary Cheke, but suddenly he realized Oxford may know more than he was letting on. "Does he know I had to marry Mary because she was pregnant?" he asked himself. His dislike of his former son-in-law ratcheted up another notch, but he told himself he must not let Oxford win. He smiled, not caring that Oxford could tell it was a false smile.

"Imagination may be well and good in the playhouse, Edward, but it is of little use when dealing with the real world. Don't make more of this than it is. I am passing on a simple request to find a husband for the daughter of an old friend. I recognize that you do not think well of me, but I hope that you will put aside your personal pique for once and give Sanderson an opportunity to advance himself."

"What say you of the girl?" Oxford asked, still not convinced.

"I know nothing of the girl except that she is of age and her father loves her. But what of that? Whitgift will set Sanderson up for life. He is not a landed gentleman who can ignore the need for money." This was another dig; Oxford had no interest in money, except to spend it. Burghley pressed on. "And the Folly will not be there forever. If you close its doors, where will Sanderson go? By encouraging him to consider my offer, you do your friend a service and make us both look good in the eyes of the father. What say you?"

Oxford hated to give in to Burghley but he could not stand in the way of Sanderson's good fortune. "I will speak to him, my lord."

"Excellent." Burghley said. "The library is yours," he added, implying a quid pro quo had been struck, an arranged marriage for Sanderson in exchange for access to the library. This was obviously not true but the old fox wanted to make Oxford pay for being so difficult. Smiling, now that he'd gotten his way, Burghley turned to another topic.

"Your daughters miss you," he said, enjoying the opportunity to make Oxford squirm even more. "Surely you would like to see them while you are here?" The syrup was back in his voice.

Oxford had been thinking of nothing but heading for the front door but could find no way to refuse, gracefully or not. He suddenly heard Lady Mary's voice encouraging him to see his daughters."

"Certainly."

Burghley rose. "I believe they are in the morning room." He led the way out of the library and down the hall where his granddaughters waited. The three girls sat lined up on straight-backed chairs. A nurse stood at attention close at hand, projecting a distinct absence of friendliness.

"Ladies," Burghley announced. "Your father would like a word with you." He stepped back into the hall, leaving Oxford alone with his daughters. Lisbeth, the oldest, now fourteen and looking every bit a woman, sat in the chair farthest to Oxford's left, her head turned away from him. Bridget, five, sat next to Lisbeth. Her face and body posture mimicked her older sister's. Oxford had not remembered her dark hair. Susan, three, sat in the chair farthest to the right, her feet not long enough to reach the floor. She leaned forward and fixed her eyes on Oxford. "Papa!" she said brightly. She got down and began to come to him. The nurse intercepted her and put her back on her chair.

The nurse stepped back. "My lord, I present your daughters, Lisbeth, Bridget, and Susan."

"Ladies," Oxford began. He took a step closer to them. He cleared his throat. "It is with distinct pleasure that your father finds you looking so well," he began. The two oldest kept their faces turned away but Susan continued to smile at him. He smiled back at her. "I, uh, regret that I was at sea when your mother passed away," he began, at which point Lisbeth began to make a low guttural sound. Oxford looked at her. "I had no idea she was ill," he continued, trying to ignore Lisbeth, but she turned to look at him, her eyes filled with anger.

"She wasn't ill," she blurted out in a tone of voice she would use to correct a slow learner at school. "She killed herself!"

Oxford recoiled in shock at this.

"Grandpapa said we must never say that," Bridget said.

"I don't care. It's the truth. She drowned herself!"

"Drowned herself?" Oxford asked. "Where?"

"You know where," Lisbeth said, looking away from him. "And you know why. She couldn't take the humiliation of being married to you anymore, so she threw herself into the lake at Hatfield!"

Oxford was stunned. "I have heard nothing about your mother drowning. As I said, she died while I was at sea, fighting the Spanish. When I returned to port, a messenger told me your mother had died at Hatfield because she couldn't breathe. Your grandfather buried her before I returned. No one has said anything about a drowning."

"'Twas no illness," Lisbeth insisted, "though 'tis true she could not breathe. She could not breathe because she drowned!"

"No, she didn't," Bridget said forcefully. "She didn't kill herself. She wouldn't do that. It was an accident. Every one said it was an accident. You're the only one who says she threw herself into the lake."

Oxford looked at the nurse, whose hands were folded across her skirt. Her face told him that she believed Lisbeth, not Bridget, and was enjoying Oxford's discomfort.

"Lisbeth," Oxford said. "Bridget is right. I have just left your grandfather. He would have told me if your mother had killed herself."

Lisbeth remained unmoved. Bridget's face showed that she liked Oxford's support, but she tried to hide it. Susan was watching with big eyes, understanding very little of what was going on.

Oxford pressed on. "Your mother could not have been buried in sacred ground if she had done away with herself. The church would not have allowed it."

Bridget's head went up and down. "See?" she said to her sister.

Lisbeth turned and addressed Susan but her words were directed at her father. "The fact that she lies in Westminster Abbey means nothing. If mother had thrown herself into the lake, grandpapa would not have liked that to become known, would he?" She turned to Oxford. "Don't you agree, my lord?"

Oxford had no answer to this. The possibility that Nan had taken her own life was an outrageous idea, but Oxford found himself unable to dismiss Lisbeth's claim outright because he knew that, if Nan had killed herself, Burghley would have done everything he could to keep it a secret. Maybe Burghley couldn't trick God, but he was fully capable of tricking the Church of England. Heaven could wait.

But what if Nan had taken her life because of the way I treated her? Oxford suddenly asked himself. This realization threatened to overwhelm him. Lisbeth's angry face added to his disorientation as he saw more and more of himself in her as she spoke. She had the same sadness in her eyes, the same protruding nether lip. He had the dizzying feeling he was bantering with himself. The child he had never known had suddenly appeared in front of him, accusing him of heinous crimes in words and gestures that aped the way he spoke. And she knew he had made it public knowledge that she was not his child! No wonder she hates me! he thought.

"Lisbeth," he began, but the nurse interrupted him.

"My lord," she said, a thin smile on her face. "It is not convenient that my ladies remain with your lordship. Let me bring them back at a time when they can more easily listen to your plaints."

Nursemaids did not tell a lord what to do. Oxford waved a hand at her. "Thank you, ma'am, but I will speak with my daughters now."

The nurse's eyebrows rose. She turned and gestured to the girls. Lisbeth stood up and headed toward the door. Bridget followed. Susan kept looking at Oxford. The nurse gestured for her to follow and Susan slid off the chair. The nurse took her hand and began to tow her toward the door. Susan kept her eyes on her father until she was out of sight and the door had been closed behind them.

"'Sblood!" Oxford bellowed. "Mary, Mother of God! He offers me his library, not fifteen minutes ago, all smiles and teeth, breakfast between them, and then leads me in here knowing that my daughters would accuse me of murdering their mother!"

Oxford stormed toward the door but it opened before he got there. Burghley stood in the doorway.

"What hath discomfited you, my lord? I heard loud oaths not fit to be uttered in my house."

"*Damn you and your house!*" Oxford shouted. "My daughters accuse me of causing Nan to throw herself into the waters behind Hatfield House!"

"Lisbeth, no doubt."

"Aye, but she speaks for the rest."

"Being the oldest, she would. Being your daughter, she sees hidden motives in many places, and drama everywhere. She voiced this fear shortly after Nan died. She said it came to her in a dream. Hazel was there to comfort her."

"Then why did Hazel not disabuse her of this horrid slander when Lisbeth did utter it just now in my presence?"

"Because Hazel has orders not to speak on the subject, our thought being that the less said the sooner this fantasy will wither away."

"And you say that Nan did not do away with herself?"

"Edward," Burghley went on mildly. "Do you think the Archbishop would have allowed me to bury her in Westminster if she had taken her own life?"

"He would if you had not told him how she died."

Burghley's face assumed a pained expression.

"Nan was my only daughter, my lord, long before she became your wife. She was the mother of my grandchildren. If she had taken her life, I would have blamed myself for failing to turn her away from despair, and my grief would have become focused on you, my dear sir, if I had thought that your treatment of her had driven her to it."

"And you say otherwise?"

Burghley's shoulders slumped. He suddenly looked the grieving father. "She developed a cough. Her lungs filled with water. Neither potion nor herb could clear her chest. 'Tis true she drowned, but she drowned in her own bed, not in the lake behind the house. Lisbeth took the story of her mother's passing and added the lake as the cause. Dr. Foreman says that Lisbeth cannot accept that a simple cough carried off her mother. Thus, she invents a more dramatic death."

Burghley was convincing, but Oxford also knew his former father-in-law was capable of planting seeds in the minds of his grandchildren to make them believe Oxford *had* killed their mother, and then denying he ever thought of such a thing. What greater revenge, Oxford wondered, could the old man have than turning his three granddaughters against their father? Burghley had looted Oxford's estates and forced him to marry Nan. He had made sure the Queen denied him a command, and, when Oxford sought permission to write plays, Burghley made her say no again.

"Edward," Burghley said quietly.

Did Burghley drown Nan? Oxford asked himself. He shuddered. Madness lies that way. I begin to sound like Lisbeth. Dazed, he walked past Burghley out the door.

# ~ 5 ~
# St. Paul's Cathedral

Sunday, November 24, 1588, dawned bright and blustery. A hundred knights, their servants by their sides, assembled at Westminster to ride with the Queen to the gates of London where she would receive greetings from the Lord Mayor to celebrate England's victory over the Spanish Armada. Aldermen in scarlet gowns trailed the knights, who were followed by the rich and powerful, the ambassadors from various countries, and other lords on horseback. Oxford bore the sword of state in front of Elizabeth, who was carried high on a litter so that she appeared to be floating on air. A silken canopy shielded her from the sun. It was so encrusted with jewels and gold that the two noblemen who bore it had to be replaced every quarter-mile. For the final leg, as the Queen entered the church, Oxford and the Marquess of Winchester bore the canopy.

The church had been cleared of bookstalls and food shops to make room for the people who came to hear the Archbishop rail against the Pope and claim that God favored the English. The Queen sat to the Archbishop's right. Oxford and the other lords sat in the pews in the middle of the church.

A few minutes after the service began, while latecomers were still sliding into their seats, Robert Cecil, head bent low, disappeared unseen into the north vestry and went out a narrow door into the churchyard. He padded away up Aldersgate to St. Martin's le Grand, a small church of Puritans who would have none of the ceremony and pomp now taking place in St. Paul's. To these simpler churchgoers, the celebration at the larger church was the work of the Devil who had recreated the Catholic Church and all its sinful excesses in the Church of England.

Robert was twenty-six years old, short in stature, and hunchbacked. His deformity had kept him from a normal childhood. "It is an unwholesome thing," a servant of the Earl of Essex had been overheard to say, "to meet a man in the morning which hath a wry neck, a crooked back or a splay foot." No one doubted the servant was referring to Robert. It was not a gentle age when it came to those born with infirmities. The taunts and jokes forced Robert to the edges of society where he brooded and watched, the outsider looking in. Without friends, he became adept at manipulating other men blessed

53

with fairer features. His father recognized this early on and began to groom his second son to enter government service.

Burghley loved all his children, including Robert, but he had a selfish reason to nurture the skills of the son others called 'Toad' and worse. Burghley dreamed of building a dynasty of Cecil advisors after he was gone. Robert was an apt pupil. Burghley loved talking to his son's upturned face, and saw much of himself in Robert.

Others, however, had a different view. They were put off by Robert's appearance and his silence, which they took as disapproval. Some called him *Robertus Diabolus*, and wrote doggerel linking him to Lucifer and Machiavelli. Gabriel Harvey, thinking that Robert had blocked a request he had made, declared that Robert was "a friend from the teeth outward but no man's friend from the heart inward."

Robert, this day of national celebration, was alone as he labored awkwardly uphill toward St. Martin's. The cane he leaned on was no affectation; he needed it as he crossed the cobblestones and stone curbs that lay in his path. Breathing heavily from the effort, he finally arrived at the rear of the church. He opened a side door into a small chapel. Inside, a young girl dressed in a wedding dress waited for him.

"Robert," she cried, rushing to him. She wrapped her arms around him. The two held each other, swaying back and forth.

"I can't go through with this, Robert. I don't love Colin. I don't want to spend my life in Melton Mowbray."

Cecil gently held her away from him so that he could look at her one more time. She was his height, with brown hair and a plain face that was now streaked with tears. She had just turned sixteen.

"I should never have come to work at your house," she lamented.

"No, Frances, it is I who am at fault." Tears formed in his eyes as he gently stroked a hair away from her face. "You gain by this marriage. You will soon forget me. I, however, have lost love forever."

"Your father could have done more," the girl said bitterly. "He could have made our marriage happen. He did not, and I marry someone else."

"Not so," Cecil said sadly. "'Tis true he refused me permission at first. I told him I loved you and begged him not to deny me your love, particularly since Fortune had so ill-served otherwise. He finally relented. He went to your father but your father insisted that he was bound to the bargain he had made with the earl. You must marry Colin Sanderson, one of the earl's retainers. My father spoke with the earl, who merely laughed, and said it was a good match."

54

"Why would he do that?" the girl asked through her tears.

"The earl hates my father."

"Why is that?"

"Father made him marry my sister. I asked Father to go to the Queen, which he did, but she would not intervene, Oxford being one of her favorites."

"Did you think to approach the earl yourself?"

Robert shook his head. "We lived together when I was young. He was much older than I. The earl treated me kindly at first. He would take me riding on his back up and down the hallway until Father stopped him. The earl turned sullen later on and ignored me."

"The beast!"

A servant stuck her head in the room. "The family waits, Miss."

Cecil gave the girl one more kiss and pushed her toward the door. Dragging the train of her dress behind her, she walked out of his life.

Cecil opened the door to the street and stepped out into the swirling wind. "Beast," he muttered to himself. He straightened the ruffles on his white shirt and retraced his steps to St. Paul's. The service was over. He went around to the entrance. Oxford and Burghley came out side by side. Robert glared at Oxford as they passed. Oxford caught the intensity in Robert's face.

"Your son doth cast a most malicious look on me, my lord."

Burghley was smiling broadly. "Perchance it is because the woman he loves has just married Colin Sanderson at St. Martin le Grand."

"Colin Sanderson? You said Colin Sanderson was to marry the daughter of an old friend of yours. You made no mention of Robert."

"Did I not?"

"No, you did not."

"I must have misspoken. Colin Sanderson has now married the scullery maid Robert fell in love with. I could not let Robert marry a scullery maid, could I? Bad for the family, and a decision he would later regret once his passion for her had burned itself out."

"But you did not tell him this to his face, did you," Oxford said, his voice rising. "Oh, no. 'The hand that does the deed should not be seen.'" Burghley knew this was a reference to the letters that sent Mary Queen of Scots to the block. Some claimed he had forged them.

They were almost to the far side of the square. "Really, Edward," Burghley went on. "How could I let him think that I had prevented him from marrying his love? I would have lost him forever. So I told him the girl's father had made an arrangement with you that she would marry Colin Sanderson."

"Me?" Oxford asked.

"Yes. As it involved one of your retainers, your permission was required."

"Sanderson is *not* one of my retainers."

"Robert does not know that, of course. He thinks this is all your doing, done to him out of your meanness to me."

"I never did Robert wrong," Oxford protested.

"No," Burghley said, a harder tone appearing in his voice, "but you abused my daughter unmercifully. You accused her of infidelity while you consorted with every woman in England, from the upstairs maids to the Queen. Nan, a patient Griselda if there ever was one, waited for you to show her the respect and husbandly duty you owed her, but you never did. You treated your hunting dogs better." He glared at Oxford. "Now that she is gone, I intend to avenge her by giving you the punishment you so richly deserve. But I grow old, and may not be able to carry out all the promises I made to Nan as I knelt beside her tomb. Robert will be my agent after I am gone. Making him your enemy was brilliant, if I may say so."

"My lord!"

Burghley was enjoying Oxford's dismay. "Robert would have eloped with the girl if I had opposed him, but he is trained in the law and understood that a promise to marry could not be broken without the consent of all. He thinks I spoke with the girl's father but, of course, I never did. And I had no need to speak with you, although I told Robert I had. He believes you have denied him his love. He will succeed me, God willing, and continue my work in denying you whatever you want." He rearranged the coat over his shoulders. "This is my gift to Nan," he said, more to himself than to Oxford. He started to shamble off, smiling.

"He'll never believe it," Oxford called after him.

Burghley stopped. "Face it, Edward, you have lost. Be a good boy, now, and come to supper at my house. The Queen will see something by John Lyly, but I imagine you already know that."

## ~ 6 ~
## Oxford Court - The Same Day

Oxford walked away from the cathedral in a daze. Without thinking, he headed for his family's long-time London residence, a three-story granite on Candlewick Street manse next to St. Swithin's. He had never spent a night in it: He preferred the Folly when he was in town and Castle Hedingham forty miles northeast of London when he wanted to be quiet. But now, he thought to himself, he needed a place to go to ground, somewhere nearby. Oxford Court was only a short walk away from Paul's. He was soon there. He looked up at the ancient vines, as thick as a blacksmith's forearm, that laced the upper stories and kept the front from falling into the street and crushing the passersby maneuvering around London Stone, a jagged piece of white marble that had been the center of London since Rome ruled it as Londinium.

An iron-banded oak door marked the entrance. A bronze boar's head, blackened with age, snarled from the middle of the door. The bronze ring it once held had been stolen long ago, a thief knowing that the porter inside was deaf. Oxford had no key.

A garden enclosed by a high wall separated the house from St. Swithin's to the right. There was a narrow door into the garden. Oxford worked the latch and managed to open it. He stepped into the garden and shut the door behind him. A stone bench faced a fountain full of leaves and broken sticks. Oxford sat down on the bench and looked up at the decaying house that loomed over him. Oncoming night began to chill the air.

Cursed by Lord Burghley, he said to himself. Like Niobe, he felt he was slowly turning into stone like the bench he sat on. The garden began to transform itself into a theater. The fading sunlight became a falling curtain, "signaling the end of my life," Oxford said to himself. He had started out so well, he remembered, striking London Stone as he had ridden by on his way to Cecil House. Looking back, he realized his arrival had been the apogee of his life. Everything had been stripped from him in the following years. It was time to end his life; time to emulate a noble Roman and spell *finis* to his failed hopes. He cast about for a tool he could use to end his life, a pointed trowel, perhaps, or a pruning knife left by the gardener: *A knife, a key to Ope the door to death,* he muttered to himself, and began to laugh, a sardonic, bitter laugh that filled the silent courtyard. "Even at the door to death I cannot stop myself from voicing my trivial thoughts in faltering verse." He looked up at the Moon now sliding over the rooftops. "I shall sit here," he announced to the empty courtyard, 'till the Moon falls on me and the walls topple and crush me."

---

Nigel found Oxford hours later, still as a statue, staring into the darkness. "My lord," he said, bustling into the garden from the house. "When you didn't return from court, I thought you might be at the Boar's Head. I looked for you there but found you not. I looked into the Steelyard …"

"And found me not there as well," Oxford said.

"Yes." Nigel came to attention and waited for instructions. The pleated ruff he had fussed over that morning lay over Oxford's shoulders like the petals of a wilted flower. All of Mistress Vanderplasse's tricks were of no use against a damp evening. He did not dare ask the fate of the elegant Spanish hat he had placed on his master's head before Oxford had left for St. Paul's.

"Tell Malfis to sell Fisher's Folly. He may take his fees out of the proceeds. That will cause him to move at greater speed than he is accustomed to."

"Certainly. And the writers and painters …"

"Will have to find other patrons. As you have so often reminded me, Nigel, I am a relic who has outlived his usefulness *and* his money. I am defeated. I shall retire to the countryside."

"And where shall we be removing ourselves?"

Oxford looked up. "*We?*"

Nigel's eyebrows flickered. "I serve you, my lord; I served your father before you, and my father served your father before that."

"Little that I deserve it," Oxford muttered.

The thought of agreeing with this comment never crossed Nigel's mind. "And when do we depart?" he asked.

"Before the Christmas festivities begin. I will not stay here to be entertainment for the court." He stood up. "I will now to bed."

"Aye, my lord." Nigel stepped aside as Oxford walked around the fountain and into the house. As he disappeared, Nigel heard Oxford reciting a poem: *What plague is greater than the grief of mind?*

## ~ 7 ~
## Lyly, Falstaff, and Robin

The front door to Oxford Court opened onto a great hall that ran back to a wide set of stairs at the rear of the house. A day room was to the right; a library to the left. Malfis was leaving through the front door just as John Lyly came bustling into the house. Lyly was a small man with furtive, darting eyes, a round pate ringed by thinning hair, and pipe-stem arms that were now wrapped around a roll of papers.

"My lord," he called out to Oxford standing at the top of the stairs as he skittered crab-like across the immense pieces of slate that paved the hall. "Is the Folly really to close? What furious constellations borne in the night sky have made your lordship think to do so? What villain by birth, by nature, by soil, by descent, by education, by practice, by study, by experience, has convinced your lordship to close the very hall that has been the birth-mother of every mother-wit these past years?"

"Enough!" Oxford cried. "Would that I had never unleashed *Eupheus* and all his words!" He sighed. "The Queen has commanded me to stop writing plays. There is no money. The Folly must close."

"But what shall *I* do, my lord?"

"Seek your fortune with the Earl of Rutland. He has dreams of forming Rutland's Men. If so, he will need plays."

"But I have no new plays, my lord. My muse has forsaken me."

"Your muse has forced you off his lordship's tit in the hope that you would give birth to something original."

"But nothing new has been conceived," Lyly whined.

"Change the title to one of your plays. Rutland won't read it. And, when it's performed, the audience won't notice they've heard it before."

Lyly's eyes lit up. "Thank you, my lord!" he cried, bowing quickly. He scurried back across the hall and out the front door, which had barely closed when Falstaff and Robin burst in. Falstaff was huffing and puffing as he retraced the path John Lyly had taken across the hall. Robin clung to him like a fish attending a whale, hovering first on one side and then the other, his eyes as big as Dutch pancakes as he took in the trophy heads Oxford's forbears had hung on the walls high above them. Falstaff and Robin, one immense, the other a pint pot by comparison, stopped at the bottom of the stairs. "My lord," Falstaff began, gripping the railing as he recovered his breath. "Mallard-Head, here, tells me you're closing the Folly."

"Mallard-Head?" Robin exclaimed, coming out from behind Falstaff.

Falstaff looked down at the page. "You told me you dip your head in mallard-grease, didn't you?"

"Never!" Robin cried out. He looked up at Oxford. "My lord, nothing but capon grease touches the top of my head, I warrant it."

"I'm sure."

"I did not enter your service to be called 'Mallard-Head,'" Robin went on doggedly.

"Robin you shall be," Oxford declared, coming down the stairs and casting a baleful eye at Falstaff.

"My lord," Robin immediately said, bending his knee.

"My lord," Falstaff said in a different tone. "There'll be plays this afternoon as part of the celebration begun yesterday at St. Paul's!"

"No, no more plays."

"'Tis what you need most of all. To the theater we go for to see a new play. That'll wake ye up! "

"I do not want to see any more plays, thank you, Jack."

"Aye, you do," Falstaff insisted. Robin began inching away, uncomfortable at the way Falstaff was talking to his lordship. "Don't let the Queen deprive you of enjoyment. Did I let myself get down when I lost my arm at Zutphen?"

Robin took another step away.

"You didn't lose your arm at Zutphen," Oxford said. He was in no mood to clown with Falstaff, but he saw Robin's reaction out of the corner of his eye.

"I grew it back!" Falstaff announced, waving his arm around. Robin gasped. Oxford frowned harder, but Robin's astonished upturned face had morphed Falstaff's ridiculous statement into a piece of theater. Falstaff stood at the bottom of the stairs, his head cocked, his arm sticking straight out, as if to say, "How do you like that, eh? Isn't that what you want to see? A little drama?" The corner of Oxford's mouth fluttered.

"Ah, Robin, there's life in the old boy yet! *The Poacher of Arden Forest* is the play. The playing of it will be at the Rose."

"I know it not."

"A new play by William Shackspear." Oxford didn't recognize the name. "Ham<u>n</u>et," Falstaff said.

"Oh, God. No, not Hamnet."

"'Tis just the physick ye need."

"No, no—," but Falstaff would have none of it. "Tut, tut. A fresh shirt and a pair of boots is all ye need." He tipped his head back. "Nigel!" he bellowed in a voice more suited to a carnival barker than a guest in a nobleman's house. Nigel appeared at the railing. "A shirt and a pair of boots for his lordship, if you please." Nigel disappeared. "However, we cannot delay, my lord, because lovely Peaches awaits me at the Boar's Head." Falstaff started back across the hall, Robin in tow. "We shall go ahead, my lord, and be your whifflers for the day."

Robin hurried to keep up. "Why is it 'Peaches' and not 'Peach'? There is only one of her."

"Ah, but there are two of these," Falstaff said, making the shape of a pair of breasts with his hands.

"Well, you may be seeing 'Peaches' today," Robin went on, "but I'll wager she'll not be showing you her 'peaches.'"

"Tut, boy. You underestimate me. I've studied the word for breast in every language: *la poitrine* in French; *pecho* in Spanish; *mammella* in Italian. In fact, the Sea of Marmora is named after a breast."

"*Like bloody hell*," Oxford called out. He had stopped at the top of the steps to listen to Falstaff's blather. "The word 'Marmora' comes from the Greek for 'marble,' not from 'mammary.' There is only one 'r' in 'mammary,'" he said, his voice rising, "*as there is no 'n' in 'Hamlet*!'"

"True," Falstaff said. He stopped to consider what Oxford had said. "Then I must needs be 'mammarized.'"

"God," Oxford muttered.

"I think," Robin said, as if he hadn't heard what Falstaff had said, "that 'breast' is too formal a word for those things that women have and try to conceal from men."

"It's better than 'tits,'" Falstaff suggested.

"Yes. 'Tits' is a useless, Anglo-Saxon word."

"Watch it, little page. I don't come from that Norman-Frenchy stock. I be solid Sheffield Saxon." He winked at Oxford.

Robin kept on. "Anglo-Saxon words are words from a farmyard language. And 'tits' is one of the worst!" Falstaff looked at the boy. Oxford came down a few steps. "They are all one syllable; stabs of sound; base thoughts. 'Fits,' which describes a man who is crazy; 'hits,' a word that describes the action of striking someone; 'pits,' where everything bad or rotten is thrown; 'quits,' for people who give up; and 'sits,' for where you put your smelliest part, *which leads us to 'shit!'*"

"Bravo!" Oxford said. "We have a poet here. If the word 'tits' could have passed John Lyly's lips the way it flies out of Robin's mouth, the little man would never have written, "hills and mountains crowned with castles whose locks can be picked with a tongue!""

"Oooo," Robin said, disgusted at the image Lyly's words created.

"So you are a wordsmith, Robin."

"I am, yer lordship."

"Well, if 'tits' is a word not worth speaking, what is *your* choice?"

"'Boob,'" Robin immediately said. "The 'b' looks like two breasts, and begins and ends either side of two Os, which also look like two breasts. That's what I call double reinforcement."

"Good, good," Falstaff agreed, assuming the voice of a scientist announcing the discovery of a new Moon, "but I prefer 'bosom,'" he announced. "It begins with a B, like 'boob,' but the two Os either side of the S remind one of snakes, and 'bosom' ends with another B, this time lying on its side disguised as an M."

"Sir John has an excellent fantasy," Oxford said in a dismissive tone of voice, "but, as Augustus said of Haterius, *sufflaminandus erat — it is sometimes necessary that he should be stopped!*"

"Too late," Falstaff said, as he headed for the door. He was obviously pleased with himself. "We're going to be late for the Boar's Head. Which reminds me of *my* favorite Latin phrase: *Deus magnum; vita bona; alimentarium mirabilis—life is good, God is great, and food is wonderful!*" He pushed open the door, Robin behind him.

"Which is the *only* Latin he knows," Oxford called after them. "Watch out, Robin. If the Queen marries a Spaniard, Sir John will turn Catholic in a twinkling!"

"Aye," Falstaff said, as he disappeared, a now startled Robin close behind him. "If they change the gates to Heaven, lad, I'll knock on the door they give me. One must be nimble and quick, ye know."

## ~ 8 ~
### *The Poacher of Arden Forest*

Oxford caught up with Falstaff and Robin at Fisherman's Wharf. He found Sir John a disappointed man: Peaches had not been waiting for him with his midday meal of conger eel and fennel.

The boat landed at Falcon Stairs, a short distance from the Rose, a new theater built the previous year by Philip Henslowe to compete with the Theater and the Curtain a mile north of London. The two older theaters had been operated as one to choke off competition. Henslowe had responded by building the Rose across the river in Southwark which, as soon as it opened, began to attract theatergoers who found it easier to take a wherry across the Thames than to trudge a mile up a muddy road to the Theater or the Curtain in Shoreditch.

The good weather had brought out a sizable crowd that streamed past Henslowe as he stood on a raised platform to greet them. He rubbed his hands together as he watched the playgoers drop their pennies into a metal box held by a burly man who clutched the box to his chest.

As Oxford approached, Henslowe waved a welcome. "Your lordship!" he called out. The muddy area in front of the platform had been churned into a pudding by the playgoers who had already arrived. Henslowe tiptoed at the edge of the platform but would not risk dirtying his latest pair of good-luck shoes, which were narrow-heeled and made of bright violet leather.

Oxford, having avoided the worst of the mud, stepped up onto the wooden floor and returned Henslowe's greeting. Falstaff followed with a nod in Henslowe's direction, but Henslowe had already turned to the next group of people behind them. Robin skittered around them to drop three pennies into the strong box and went off to find cushions for them. He followed his master and Sir John into the theater where they climbed the stairs to one of the tiers that overlooked the pit.

"You noticed the new shoes," Oxford said to Falstaff as they went up the stairs.

"Aye, and a pretty color they are, aren't they?" Falstaff chuckled. "But he'll not get mud on them, he won't. Not on opening day."

"It would ruin his good-luck charm, wouldn't it?" Oxford smiled. Then his face darkened. "Hamnet!" he said angrily.

"From what we heard at the Boar's Head," Falstaff said, as they found their seats, "it won't last long in front of this crowd."

The pit filled quickly. A player came out and placed his right foot at an angle he obviously thought was dramatic. He inclined his head toward the highest tier and announced the play.

"*The Poacher of Arden Forest*," he sang out in a high falsetto voice, "by a writer that shall be known to all who know lit-triture and good plays."

Falstaff chuckled. "Mark that the author has not given us his name. If the play fails, he can keep himself hidden. If it succeeds, he can write another, and say it's by the author of the *Poacher*."

"Is he clever enough to have come up with that himself?" Oxford asked. His face showed that he didn't think so. Falstaff had to agree. "Probably not."

---

The play failed. Shackspear had penned a tragedy about a poor man trying to feed his family by poaching deer on a nearby estate. The poacher is captured and executed, but the excessive posing by the players and the long monologues drowned out whatever plot there was. Laughter greeted the poacher when he fired an arrow aimed at an open window but which struck the wall two feet from a woman's head. The groundlings took the woman for the intended target and the play for a comedy. They began to throw fruits and vegetables in the first act. In the second, people began to leave, streaming past a stricken Henslowe who was wringing his hands and wishing them well.

As the third act began, Falstaff stood up.

"My apologies, my lord," he said, "but what I thought would be medicine for you is sickness to me."

Oxford waved him away. "A play in its death throes is something so horrible that I cannot bring myself to leave. I will stay."

Robin pointed his face at the stage, but it was obvious he had seen enough. "Go on," Oxford said. Robin quickly ran after Falstaff.

At the end, Oxford was the only person left in the theater. Shackspear came out onto the stage. Oxford began to clap slowly. Shackspear looked up and recognized him. "My lord," he said. Oxford got up and headed down the stairs. Shackspear intercepted him.

"I am undone," Shackspear said, taking up a position that blocked Oxford's path. "Undone in only a few short hours. After so much work. Mr. Henslowe will never take another script from me."

"And with good reason," Oxford said, but he saw the anguish in Shackspear's face and was reminded of his own dreams and how Elizabeth had crushed them. Is Shackspear any different, he wondered? But how can we have anything in common? Shackspear is a provincial gull who believe he can, without noble breeding or education, write tragedies. He should be in Stratford tending sheep. Still, the loss on Shackspear's face was real.

"'Twas better done than they appreciated," Oxford said.

"You think?"

"Yes." Oxford turned to go.

Shackspear plucked his sleeve. "With a little polishing, do you think it might be saved? After all, I heard *Hamlet* was not well received the first time it graced the boards, and look how tall it stands today!"

Any sympathy for Shackspear disappeared. Citing *Hamlet* as an example of a bad play made good by a "little polishing" was too much. "*Polish away*," Oxford said, turning away again.

Shackspear clutched Oxford's sleeve. "But my lord, I just need some advice, a little wisdom from a more experienced . . ."

Oxford pulled his arm away. "That's as may be, but don't look to me for it."

"But I have another play."

"Another?"

"*Procne's Revenge*," Shackspear said, a slight touch of hope in his voice. "Rape. Incest. Imprisonment. A tongue cut out in front of the pit, the beheading of a child who is fed to his father in a meat pie!"

Oxford's mouth fell open.

"Perhaps my lordship does not know the story?"

"Of course I know it: Book Six; Ovid's *Metamorphoses*."

"Well, then," Shackspear went on blithely, "it's the perfect follow-up to *The Spanish Tragedy*. All I hear from Henslowe is, 'Give me another *Spanish Tragedy* and your career is made!'"

This stopped Oxford, who had started to leave again. Shackspear was right. *The Spanish Tragedy* had taken London by storm. Whoever wrote the next *Spanish Tragedy* would own the London stage.

"I come with good education," Shackspear said, sensing Oxford's train of thought. "I attended the Stratford Grammar School."

"Where, no doubt, you learned Greek."

"Yes. Of course."

"Μία γλώσσα δεν είναι ποτέ αρκετή,"

"Can we speak English?" Shackspear pleaded.

"I was Sophocles, you know." Oxford said mysteriously.

"You have helped so many, my lord," Shackspear said. "I can be one more who could spread your fame. My stories, your great knowledge of the world ..." Oxford said nothing. Shackspear thought Oxford was interested. "I have learned how to put a story together," he went on, but I'm not good at the writing of it. All I need are a few classical allusions to flesh out *Procne's Revenge* and I'm on my way."

Oxford looked at Shackspear in amazement: a few classical illusions was all he needed? He almost laughed out loud. But then he had a different thought: "What if I took his play and made it worse?" A smile began to spread across his face. Shackspear saw it. Oxford had decided to help him. In fact, Oxford was imagining how much fun it would be to see how absurd he could make Shackspear's play. Yes, that would be the challenge: to make Shackspear's play so awful that the Queen would realize how much she had lost by barring him from writing plays! The quicker this was accomplished, the quicker she would ask him to write plays again and send Shackspear back to Stratford where he belonged.

"On one condition," Oxford said, freezing Shackspear into rapt attention. "Anything I do to help you must remain secret?"

"Absolutely," Shackspear said, his face beaming. "*Absolutely secret!*" He dropped his voice into a conspiratorial hush. "Absolutely secret."

"If anyone learns I have helped you, I will deny it ever happened and sue you for slander."

"My lips are sealed," Shackspear said, suppressing a wide grin that kept trying to break out across his face. He looked like a kid who had just been told summer recess had come a week early.

"Moreover," Oxford went on, "if you violate this agreement, your punishment will not be meted out by the courts but by me, and it will be sudden, severe, and rendered at the moment you least expect!"

This took away some of Shackspear's euphoria, but he quickly agreed.

"Then give me your arms," Oxford said. He seized Shackspear's wrists, locking his hands around them. "How shall you swear, William Shackspear?"

Shackspear saw a wild look in Oxford's eyes. What need had the earl of an oath, he wondered? No one in the theater believed in God. He licked his lips. "I swear by Heaven to keep our arrangement secret!"

"Swear not by Heaven, for Heaven commits no sin."

A new Moon had just slid over the thatched roof of the Rose. Shackspear saw it over Oxford's shoulder. "Then I swear by the Moon," he said, throwing his head back in a dramatic pose.

"Nay," Oxford said, "The Moon monthly changes."

Shackspear gulped. He wracked his brain. "I swear by my son," he blurted out, "whom I revere and adore."

This brought Oxford up short. He remembered the Queen giving birth to a son during the time they were lovers, but the baby had not lived. "He was but one hour mine," Oxford remembered. A decade later, Nan gave him a son who lived longer, but only by a few weeks. Oxford could still see the boy's tiny coffin being lowered into the ground, Nan weeping beside him. If such short lives were dear to him, how much dearer must Shackspear's son, now three, be to him?

"Upon your son, then," Oxford said. He released Shackspear's arms, who stepped away, rubbing his wrists.

"I will not let your lordship down," Shackspear began, but Oxford interrupted him.

"Don't grovel. You have the manuscript?"

"Yes, my lord."

"How complete is it?" Oxford asked.

"Oh, it needs work here and there." The slightly cross-eyed look Oxford had seen in the Boar's Head reappeared. Shackspear was lying.

"Are there any words on paper?" Oxford asked.

"Oh, yes, my lord. Upwards of forty pages at least."

"Be at Oxford Court tomorrow at ten. If anyone asks, you have come for payment on bills assigned to you by my creditors." Oxford turned away, leaving a very happy William Shackspear behind him.

## ~ 9 ~
### *Procne's Revenge*

Nigel escorted Shackspear into the library. Oxford came in a few minutes later. "You have it?"

"Indeed, my lord." Shackspear pulled out a set of loose papers and handed them to Oxford, who spread them out on a large table.

"I recognize this fist, and it is not yours. Robert Greene wrote these pages. How came you by them?"

Shackspear shrugged. "He had a row with Burbage and threw them in Burbage's face. I was there. I saw it happen."

"But how did *you* get them?"

"Both of them walked out. When they didn't come back. I picked up the pages. Abandoned property, they were, right, my lord?" Shackspear was warming to his tale. "Like a shilling someone drops in the street."

Oxford started to have second thoughts about helping Shackspear but remembered how eager he was to write another play, "Even a play designed to fail," he muttered to himself. He started to read the pages Shackspear had given him.

"Terrible," he said after a few minutes. "Greene is a fool to think Burbage would take this. No wonder it ended up on the floor."

Shackspear was aghast. "But revenge, my lord, and horror are what sells a play these days. Tereus rapes his wife's sister. Then he cuts out her tongue 'close to the trembling root' to keep her silent and locks her in a shed. But the sister gets a message out and Tereus's wife slays their son and bakes him in a meat pie! When the husband asks for his little boy, the wife serves him his son in the pie! Now, what could be better than that?"

"Yes, yes. And they all become birds, the mutilated sister a sparrow that has no song, the rapist a kingfisher, and so forth. Were they going to fly off the stage at the end?"

"No, no," Shackspear said, missing the sarcasm in Oxford's voice. "The play ends with the husband howling as he runs out the back of the stage chasing his wife and her sister!"

Oxford did not agree. "*The Spanish Tragedy* has Heronimo killing the man who killed his son. That's good old-fashioned revenge, but a play about a wife trying to avenge the rape and mutilation of her sister is a play written for women. *Procne's Revenge* will not do."

Shackspear's face fell. "But?" he asked hopefully.

"But?" Oxford asked, more to himself than Shackspear. He started walking around the library. Shackspear stifled himself.

"But what if the play was about more than the rape of a girl? What if she is raped by someone who doesn't do it out of lust but as an act of revenge? That would take *The Spanish Tragedy* a step further. "

"It certainly would," Shackspear said enthusiastically.

Oxford ignored him. "There must be something that makes the rapist want to violate the girl. No, make it two rapists. Brothers."

"Spurred on by their evil mother," Shackspear volunteered.

"Yes," Oxford said, irritated at the interruption but having to admit that adding the mother was a good idea. "Their mother."

Shackspear forced himself to remain silent. Oxford had accepted a suggestion. Good, good, he said to himself.

Oxford was now at the far end of the library. "The father of the girl who is raped will be called Titus. The mother will command the brothers to rape the girl because Titus has executed one of her sons."

"But wouldn't Titus kill *all* her sons?"

"In real life, yes, but this is a play."

Shackspear saw a flicker of excitement on Oxford's face. How cleverly his lordship had adopted and made his own the horrific scene Shackspear had proposed!

"Titus will be a Roman general," Oxford went on. "*The Spanish Tragedy* takes place in Spain, so we must take the story back to Rome."

Shackspear nodded again.

"And Titus will have fifty sons, like Priam at Troy!"

"Fifty?" Shackspear exclaimed.

"To bring in the Trojan War."

"But Henslowe will never pay for fifty players to appear onstage."

Oxford shrugged. "Then Titus will have twenty-five sons, to bring in an allusion to the Trojan War." He glanced at Shackspear, whose face showed that twenty-five was still too many. "Twenty of whom will be dead when the play begins," he added.

"Wonderful!" Shackspear said, clapping his hands.

Oxford was looking at the drapes that covered the window at the end of the room. "I cannot see the reason for the first death, but it will come. The rape scene calls to me now."

"Yes," Shackspear said. "Nothing like a good rape scene."

"Not because of the rape but because the young woman has her tongue cut out."

"Oh," Shackspear muttered. "Well, that's good too."

"In the story you borrowed, she cannot speak, but she quickly realizes she can use her hands to weave a message. That will not do. Leaving the mother's sons alive to revenge their brother's death is necessary to the plot and will not be noticed, but leaving the girl with hands weakens the story. The rapists will lop them off."

"Lop, my lord? I know not this word."

"'Lop' is the sound the axe makes when it separates the head from the shoulders." Oxford chopped the back of his neck with his hand.

Shackspear shivered. "Would it not be better to use 'cut off', my lord, a phrase people know?"

"If you had grown up in London you would know 'lop'," Oxford said. "'Cut off' is a description of the action; 'lop' is the sound itself. And if you ever tell anyone that I am helping you, it will be the last sound you ever hear!"

Shackspear shuddered.

"And if you *do* speak of our secret, make sure someone brings lots of angels to the executioner so that he brings his sharp axe to cut your head off."

Shackspear's eyes got bigger. "Is that why it took two strokes to cut off Mary's head?"

Oxford nodded. "Mary sent the money but the messenger took it to Lord Burghley, who decided he had a better use for it."

Shackspear gulped.

Oxford walked over to the window. He stopped in front of the drapes, which were made of red silk. He looked at them closely. Shackspear thought Oxford was looking *through* them. "Yes," Oxford said in a low voice. "By God, I know what it is like to be without tongue *and* hands!" A look of rage suddenly flashed across his face. Shackspear took a step backward but the earl calmed down as he fingered the edge of the drape in front of him. He suddenly ripped a length off one edge and tore it into three pieces. "*John Lyly!*" he called out, stuffing one of the ribbons into his mouth. "*John Lyly!*"

Shackspear thought Oxford had gone mad. Nigel appeared in the doorway. "I believe, your lordship," Nigel said calmly, "that Mr. Lyly is, at the moment, on horseback to the Earl of Rutland where, upon your suggestion, he seeks employment as one of the Earl's servants."

"Oh." Oxford said. He pulled the ribbon out of his mouth. "Well, if he be gone, who shall capture my words?"

"I will, your lordship," Robin said, putting his head into the room.

Oxford waved him into the room. "Come hither, young Robin. Lend me your hand and I will give you my words."

Nigel took an ink pot and a quill out of a cupboard and handed them to Robin who sat down at the table. Robin jammed the quill into the ink pot and looked up. Oxford began to dictate.

"Dragged away by, Demetrius and Chiron, the young woman, Lavinia, protests the attack, but her cries only spur on the two brutes. Their mother is watching. Lavinia sees the mother and begs to die rather than be deflowered by her sons. The mother laughs:

Mother:     *Remember, sons, I pour'd forth tears in vain,*
                    *To save your father from the sacrifice;*
                    *But her fierce father would not relent;*
                    *Therefore, away with her, and use her as you will,*
                    *The worse to her, the better loved of me.*

Lavinia:     *O gentle queen,*
                    *With thine own hands kill me in this place!*

Mother:     *So should I rob my sweet sons of their fee?*
                    *No, let them satisfy their lust on thee.*

Oxford saw that Robin had stopped writing. Mouth open, the boy was looking at Oxford with big eyes. Shackspear stood next to him, gaping as well. "Think you be at the theater?" Oxford demanded. Robin quickly bent over the table. "Lose not a word!"

Oxford took off around the table, waving the ribbons. "I am Lavinia. The two sons pursue me. They run me down." Oxford stumbled to one knee. "They cut off one of my hands, and then the other." He staggered to his feet, pulling his hands into his shirt sleeves, the red ribbons fluttering from the ends of his arms. "Reaching down my throat, they clutch my tongue with taloned fingers and rip it out as well!" Oxford stuffed the third ribbon into his mouth and then slowly pulled it out, letting it hang down his chest. "Once this is done, Demetrius and Chiron will speak thus to Lavinia:

| Demetrius: | *So, now go tell, if thy tongue can speak,* |
| | *Who 'twas that cut thy tongue and ravish'd thee.* |
| Chiron: | *Write down thy mind, bewray thy meaning so,* |
| | *If thy stumps will let thee play the scribe.* |
| Demetrius: | *See, how with signs and tokens she can scrowl.* |
| Chiron: | *Go home, call for sweet water, wash thy hands.* |
| Demetrius: | *She hath no tongue to call, nor hands to wash;* |
| | *And so let's leave her to her silent walks.* |
| Chiron: | *If t'twere my case, I should go hang myself.* |
| Demetrius: | *If thou hadst hands to help thee knit the cord.* |

"After which, all three of them will go off laughing."

Robin kept his head down, the words burning the ink he stroked across the page in front of him.

"But," Oxford asked, "how can Lavinia tell her tale of woe without hands?"

"She can hold a stick in her stumps and draw pictures in the sand," Shackspear volunteered.

Oxford turned to look at him. "Bravo," he said quietly. "And so she shall."

Shackspear was thrilled. A second suggestion accepted! He and Oxford were surely partners now!

In fact, however, Oxford was trying to keep himself from laughing at the sight of Lavinia holding a stick in her stumps and trying to write something!

Nigel appeared in the doorway.

"A Queen's Messenger, my lord."

"I am not at home." He swept the papers on the table into a pile and handed them to a slack-jawed Shackspear. Shackspear took the papers and watched Oxford, Nigel, and Robin disappear into the hall. "I am not a fine-antlered deer in one of her royal parks," he could hear Oxford angrily saying. "If she does not want plays by me to light the Christmas revels, she gets not me as well. Now, where is Malfis?"

Shackspear followed Oxford into the hall. Despite being dismissed, he was walking on air. "The bits with the ribbons! Brilliant! Dismissed? Yes, but not told to leave," he assured himself. He decided to wait. He took up a position outside the library, the script in his hands.

"Malfis is in the day room, your lordship," Nigel said.

Oxford found Malfis examining a painting on the wall. "You bring me news of Bilton?" Oxford asked.

"Good morning, my lord," Malfis said, bowing slightly. He was an older man, thin and lean, with the black, piercing eyes of a lawyer who had heard every excuse and lie uttered by man and was finding it difficult, at this late stage of his life, to believe anything. He always looked out of sorts, as if he were trying to digest a bit of beef. "My lord, you leased Bilton in 1574 to Lord Darcy and sold the fee to John Shuckburgh in 1580."

"Why was I not told about this?"

"You were, my lord. However, you were newly married at the time and in love with the Queen, if I remember rightly." He looked at the painting again to show that he said this without hint of disapproval.

"But I loved the time I spent at Bilton. I lingered there during the Queen's progress in 1572. A pleasant manor, I remember, with many rooms, and a long view down to the Avon River."

"Indeed, my lord, but Bilton is not available. However, Billesley Hall may be."

"Ah, I was thinking of Billesley, not Bilton. Is it still owned by Sir Thomas, my grandmother Trussell's grandson? If so, he would surely grant me leave to stay there."

"Unfortunately, he is not the owner anymore. Sir Thomas has this past summer been convicted of robbery on the public highway in Kent and sentenced to death."

"Robbery? Sentenced to death? How can that be?"

"He is but a young lad, my lord, full of vinegar, and the robbery seems to have been committed on a drunken lark."

"Good God."

"There is hope the Queen will pardon him. Young men oft engage in such conduct, particularly when spirits run high and wine runs free. I can recall another young lord waylaying two servants years ago in the same county. On Gads Hill, if memory serves me right. The servants were in the pay of the young man's former guardian and wanted to press criminal charges, particularly when the more senior of them had been fired upon, breaking the girth of his saddle and dropping him to the highway. If they had, the young lord involved in that caper might have been convicted and sentenced to death, as Sir Thomas has been."

Oxford listened to this in dismay. Malfis was describing the very incident in which Oxford and his friends had fired upon two of Lord Burghley's servants as they passed Gads Hill. Oxford was twenty-three at the time. He had only wanted to scare them for spying on him. He remembered laughing as the servants rode off at high speed, and giving it no more thought.

"However," Malfis continued, seeing the shock on Oxford's face, "Sir Thomas's misfortune may be to your lordship's benefit."

"How so? I would not wish such a misfortune on any man, much less a kinsman."

"Of course not, but, because of Sir Thomas's conviction, title to Billesley Hall has passed to the Crown. I have spoken with Lord Burghley's secretary about leasing it to you. With the proceeds from the sale of Fisher's Folly, you have sufficient funds to do so."

"And Lord Burghley will consent because it will get me away from the Queen and cost him nothing."

"He has already consented. You can leave tomorrow. A skeleton staff has been left behind while the Queen decides what to do with it."

Oxford looked at Malfis with new appreciation. "Thank you."

"My duty, your lordship" Malfis bowed.

"I have not treated you with the courtesy you deserve."

"It is a lawyer's lot to deal with unpleasant matters that others would prefer to ignore."

"But tell me, Malfis, why am I not loved like my father, Earl John, whom everyone refers to as the Good Earl?"

"Yes, he was a good man, indeed. He was of your height but of greater girth. He had large hands, like a blacksmith's, which were always open and friendly. When he was at Castle Hedingham, he would visit the pubs nearby. The people were not used to a man of such ancient nobility willing to sit down and try to drink them under the table, but they liked him for it. He was impulsive and without guile, which was one of the reasons women found him so attractive, even though he was not. You have, of course, met Lady Katherine, your half-sister by your father's first wife?" Oxford's face showed that he had. "Lady Katherine is much like her mother," Malfis said.

"I *have* met Katherine," Oxford said, "and, she is a shrew. If she be anything like her mother, I can understand my father's wanderings."

"And wander he did, particularly after he was widowed. Her death freed him, of course, but he had no heir. His friends urged him to marry and beget a son. Those who thought they had his best interest at heart pushed him to marry a woman named Dorothy Fosser. Your father apparently agreed, and the marriage was arranged, but your father didn't wait. On the night of July 7, 1548, he used a ladder to spirit Dorothy out of a second-story bedroom. He put her over his shoulder and carried her off to enjoy privileges that he was supposed to enjoy only *after* the wedding ceremony."

Malfis was tight-lipped when it came to passing on confidential information about his clients but Oxford was Earl John's son and entitled to know such important details about his father. Oxford detected a faint hint of appreciation for Earl John's recklessness, qualities a lawyer had to suppress in order to succeed in the practice of law. Oxford, too, also found himself with new appreciation for his father. "But he didn't marry her."

"No, the day before the wedding, your father rode to Belchamp St. Paul and married your mother, Margery Golding. The marriage was unusual for a number of reasons. Most importantly, it was done without royal consent, a *sine qua non* for a senior lord in those days."

"As it is today," Oxford added, awed by his father's reckless conduct.

"Furthermore, the marriage took place at the Golding residence, not in a church."

"And what said Dorothy Fosser?"

"She and her family were furious, of course. They claimed that your father had married Dorothy secretly at the height of their passion."

This shocked Oxford. If his father had married Dorothy Fosser, his father's marriage to Oxford's mother would be null and void, and Oxford would be illegitimate. "Was this true?"

Malfis smiled. "Of course not. Your father's marriage to your mother was an excellent one. You were born, and your mother gave your father a bonus in your sister Mary."

Oxford's face darkened. "Not that she would linger over my father's grave once he was gone. She remarried so quickly that the funeral meats could have furnished the marriage table."

"Being a woman, she was no doubt at a loss for companionship."

"I was not invited to the wedding." Oxford said, more to himself than to Malfis. "My mother had consigned me to Burghley, like I was so much furniture she didn't need any longer. When she died seven years later, I refused to attend her funeral. Burghley thought I did this out of spite, but, in truth, I knew I could not carry her coffin and hold in my grief. The sight of her lifeless body would have been too bright a sign that she would never ask me to walk in the garden again with her. If tears had cracked my face, I would have been humiliated forever."

This confession made Malfis uncomfortable. He didn't like clients who thought a frank discussion of legal matters opened the door to more personal matters. He had paid the price for listening to a powerful person unburden himself more than once, and knew he was sailing in dangerous waters. "But, what good fortune it was that your father married a Golding," he said brightly, "a distinguished family filled with statesmen and eminent scholars like your uncle, Arthur."

"Yes," Oxford said. A crooked smile lit up his face. "Imagine if my mother had been Dorothy Fosser: *I would have been the son of a servant!*"

"Indeed," Malfis said. "Just one day can make all the difference, as can one word instead of another."

Oxford pushed away what it might have been like to be common. "I will retreat to the country," he announced, "where I can find myself again. How goes the sale of the Folly?"

"Nearly done." Malfis reached into the small valise he was holding and held up a piece of parchment. "The transfer should take place before the end of the year. With this indenture, I have bonded your account so that the funds for you to move to Billesley are now available. Nigel has emptied Fisher's Folly of everything worth removing. However, a daughter of the buyer, Anne Cornwallis, has found a sheaf of poems left behind that are apparently in your hand. She asked if she can keep them."

"She can," Oxford said. "I am done with poetry."

"You don't want to review them?"

"No."

"One of them appears to have been written by Anne Vavasor," Malfis said, watching Oxford to see if this changed anything.

"I am done with Anne Vavasor as well," Oxford added.

"Very well." He put the parchment back into his valise. "One more thing, my lord. As I left Fisher's Folly I was accosted by a beggar who called himself Tom O'Bedlam. He gave me a message for you."

"Which was?"

"The beadles took him before he could finish but he said you should not sell your house. He said, 'Tell nuncle not to sell his house; even a snail needs a house to put his horns in.'"

"Anything else?"

"He said they were carrying him off because he sees God everywhere, 'In you, in the Earth, in the sky, but they'— he meant the beadles—'only see God in church on Sunday.'" Oxford considered this. "Why does he call you 'nuncle'?" Malfis asked.

"Because I am not his uncle."

"Oh."

Oxford took his hand. "You have served me well, Malfis. Thank you."

Shackspear, who had become impatient waiting, put his head into the room. "Sorry to bother you, my lord, but if we could keep working on, you know," he said, gesturing with his thumb toward the library.

"I am to Billesley," Oxford said, walking around Shackspear and into the hall. Malfis retrieved his cane from where he had hung it on the back of a chair. He glided across the hall, his cane tapping on the slate floor in time with the great clock that stood along the wall.

Shackspear watched the lawyer disappear in one direction, Oxford, in the other.

"What about the play?" he asked.

"I shall work on it at Billesley."

"Shouldn't I come with you to help?"

"No!" Oxford said. He was angry, but then stopped himself. He had just apologized to Malfis for treating him poorly over the years and here he was treating Shackspear the same way. Shackspear deserved none of the courtesy Malfis had earned but something in Oxford told him he could do better. "Stratford is but five or six miles from Billesley," he said. "Why don't you visit your family there? After all, they must miss you, mustn't they?" He heard himself slipping back into sarcasm. He was suddenly tired of Shackspear. "If you go down, send a message around before you come over to Billesley."

"Yes, my lord," Shackspear said.

# ~ 10 ~
## Billesley Hall – Christmas Eve, 1588

The Avon River finally came into view. Stratford lay on the other side. Billesley Hall was now a scant six miles away.

The tired horses clattered over Clopton Bridge and into Stratford. The change in pavement made the horses think a barn was in the offing. They slowed but Oxford and Robin urged them on. The horses, sensing that the end of the journey was near, picked up the pace.

The fading light turned the Avon into a dark band that meandered back and forth in the dusk, paralleling the road south from Stratford. Thickets and fields rose gently from the river on the left and continued uphill before disappearing into a thick forest on the right. In warmer weather, sheep and cattle would have looked up to see who was coming along the road, but the countryside was empty of life this dark December day.

A skein of geese came down the slope from the right arguing with each other about where to spend the night. They flew low in a ragged formation, barely clearing Oxford's head as they passed over him. Three broke left, too tired to go on, but the main group continued on toward the river bottom and ignored them. The three stragglers, complaining loudly, rejoined their companions as the flock disappeared in the darkness. They looked lost and homeless, an apt welcome for a man who was without a home or a sense of purpose.

The horses soon turned uphill away from the river. They struggled past a derelict chapel and entered the walled enclosure that faced away from the river. Billesley Hall had been built of lias limestone in the 14th century. Extensions of the main house flanked the courtyard. The main door was thick oak banded with black iron and framed by stone posts made of gray ashlar that curved inward at the top like the peak of a bishop's miter. The door opened and Nigel stepped out to greet them. Tobias followed. They had brought Frangellica but she remained hidden, as was her custom, in the kitchen.

"Good even, my lord," Nigel said. Tobias took the reins to Oxford's horse. "And to you, Robin."

"Nigel," Oxford said, as he swung down from the horse. "A long day, made longer by a gray sky."

"Come in, my lord."

"Where are the servants?"

"The promised 'skeleton' staff has decamped."

Inside, Oxford was greeted by the damp smell of an abandoned house. The mustiness reminded him of all the other houses he had lived in, each house telling him as he entered that no one had lived there long enough to leave memories of love and laughter. He followed the candles into the dining room where he found a bowl of veal and green scallions, the steam from the broth rising into the cold air of the room. Thin slices of hard, day-old manchet bread surrounded the bowl. Oxford pulled out a chair at the end of the table and sat down. He stuck a spoon into the bowl. In the absence of any servants, Nigel stood next to the doorway to act as butler. Tobias and Robin went into the kitchen to eat. Robin had offered to play the lute but Oxford had waved him away.

He filled his mouth with Frangellica's creation and leaned back to savor it. The cook herself made no appearance. She rarely came out of the kitchen. She always said that her food spoke better for her than the little English she had learned. She had first cooked for Oxford in Venice when he had lived in a house that overlooked the Isle of Murano. Her younger brother, Orazio, had served as Oxford's page while Oxford was in Italy and came back with Oxford to England. Orazio stayed a year. Upon his return, he convinced his sister to go to England and cook for the *Inglese* she had served in Venice. Oxford was living in the Savoy apartments at the time. When he moved to Fisher's Folly, she went with him, as she did when he moved to Oxford Court, and to wherever the Queen ordered Oxford to attend during her progresses around England. The move to Billesley was a new stage in Oxford's life, however, one that Frangellica recognized as signaling something ominous, but she did not complain that her master had decided to remove himself to a cobweb-filled country estate that sat in the middle of nowhere far from London. When word came from Nigel that they were leaving London, Frangellica quickly gathered up the vegetables and dried herbs she had and loaded them into the cart that would take them to Oxford's new domicile.

As Oxford ate, the silence began to press in on him. He was used to the noise of a bustling city but here the only sound accompanying his supper was his spoon striking the lip of the earthenware bowl in front of him. No wind blew outside. No clock tick-tocked in the hall outside like a well-fed house guest snoring after dinner. As he listened, Oxford realized he could hear Nigel breathing in and out as his faithful steward, ramrod-straight, stood next to the doorway behind him. He then realized he could even hear his *own* breathing.

He was soon startled by a cat that suddenly appeared at the other end of the table, having leaped silently onto it from some dark corner of the room. His body was deep black; his face, paws, and bib were white. Enormous eyes, far bigger than appropriate for such a small face, looked down the length of the table. The cat sat down, wrapping his tail across the tops of its forepaws.

"What's his name?" Oxford asked Nigel.

"No one knows, my lord. He was here when we arrived. Frangellica calls him *Nulla Nome*."

"'*A cat with no name*,'" Oxford said. "How fitting." He leaned back to let Nigel spoon more stew into his bowl. "But he looks not gaunt."

"Frangellica reports there are no mice in the kitchen."

The cat had apparently heard enough. He turned and leaped back into the darkness.

Oxford pushed back his chair, making a harsh, grating noise as the wooden legs slid across the stone floor. "I am tired," he said, standing up. "Show me my room."

Nigel took a taper from the hall outside and headed up the stairs. Oxford followed him. At the top, Nigel showed Oxford into a room with a fireplace that was already warming the room. A carved fascia of vines and grapes decorated the mantel and mimicked the frieze that ran along the top of the carved oak panels in the hall below. A huge canopied bed faced the fireplace. Oxford's writing desk was already positioned under the windows along the far wall that looked downhill toward the Avon.

"Thank you, Nigel," Oxford said, walking over to the fireplace.

"May I suggest a glass of Frangellica's liqueur, your lordship? She says it will ease the burden of your journey."

"That is kind of her, but no. Please thank her for me."

"I will, my lord." Nigel hesitated in the doorway.

"Yes?" Oxford asked.

"Would your lordship allow me to escort Frangellica to Stratford this evening? Being Christmas Eve, she would like to take part in the services at Holy Trinity Church."

"Wouldn't Frangellica be found dead than inside an Anglican church?"

"Indeed, my lord, but she is far from home and this is Christmas Eve. She thinks it is far better for the Lord to see her in an Anglican church than in no church at all."

Oxford smiled. "And so she shall. You have my permission."

"Thank you, my lord."

"Will Tobias and Robin accompany you? These roads are dark, and brigands may be about."

"On Christmas Eve?" Nigel obviously didn't think this was a concern.

"Will Tobias and Robin go with you?"

"Tobias is a heathen, my lord, and is worshipping an arrangement of sticks in his room. Robin is scribbling in his. He declined to come with us. He said you would think less of him if he did."

"Why would he think that?"

"He said he heard that you doubted Christ's divinity, that you said Joseph was a wittol, and that the blessed virgin was, well …"

"Yes, yes," Oxford said. He sighed. His words, spoken without the raised eyebrow and sardonic tone in which they had been delivered, implied he had no religion at all and that he laughed at those who did. Oxford was beginning to realize how much longer words lived on in the memories of men after the breath that uttered them had died away, and how, in contrast, all the words he had hoped to write would never be heard. "How ironic," he thought. "My reputation will determined by flippant remarks spoken among friends over dinner instead of the poetry and plays I imagined would make me immortal. Reading only those remarks, future historians will twist his words and paint a picture of me that will be inaccurate, if not slanderous.

"I was *in poculis* at the time, Nigel, but Robin has apparently taken my supper-time sarcasm as fact. Please tell him he has my permission to go and I will not think less of him if he does."

"Thank you, my lord." Oxford's consent pleased Nigel greatly. Yet he remained standing in the doorway.

"Yes?" Oxford asked once more.

"We would, of course, welcome your presence as well."

Oxford smiled. "That is most gracious of you, Nigel, but I will spend the night here. Your joy in celebrating the birth of Jesus does not need the shadow my presence might cast over the occasion."

"Very well, my lord." Nigel bowed and left the room.

Oxford listened to Nigel descend the stairs. He knew he couldn't go with his little household. "No, I, who am of little faith, cannot enter the kingdom of heaven this night, or hope for a better life in the hereafter."

He turned to the fireplace, its warmth and light reaching out to him.

"Faith is the leap I cannot make, and thus my hell is here on Earth. If I told Nigel I shared his beliefs, my words would deceive him. And if there *is* a god, He would surely see through my lies. Ergo, I remain here, alone, where I belong."

He noticed a small door in an alcove in the corner of the room. He walked over and opened it. The door gave access to a small porch that looked south toward the Avon in the distance. A circular fishpond, full of debris, was dimly visible down the hill. Beyond the pond were the remains of a moat filled with ice. A stone pigeon-house could be seen alongside the lane that went down to the road to Stratford.

Oxford looked out into the cold night and sighed, his breath coming out in clouds that looked tired and gray, so unlike the bright clouds he had seen floating away from him as he prepared to see the Queen in September with the hope that he would be writing plays for her. How much had changed in such a short time. He was suddenly bone weary. He went back into the house, closing the door behind him. He walked over to the bed, dropping his clothes onto a chair and then putting on a nightdress Nigel had left for him. He reached down and pulled out the bedpan from beneath the bed. He lifted the nightdress and emptied his bladder. A slight movement caught his eye. The cat with no name walked around the other side of the bed and looked at the bedpan Oxford was filling.

"Ah," Oxford said, as he finished. "*Nulla Nome.*" He pushed the bedpan under the bed. "It won't do for you to have no name," he said, pulling the covers back. "Everything must have a name. What shall yours be, eh?" The cat sat down, staring at him from the floor. "I cannot call you *Christian*, not being Christian myself, nor *Christmas*, since neither you nor I are participating in tonight's events. Besides, you look decidedly more ancient than Jesus, with those deep eyes sucking my soul into yours. Eh? What I shall call you?"

The cat remained motionless, as if *he* were waiting for an answer to a question he had asked Oxford.

"Ah, I see" Oxford said. "*Nulla voce* as well. For your silence, I shall call you Socrates. He never answered questions either. You are Socrates, then, reborn as a cat in the year 1588. What say you to that?"

The cat leaped onto the extra quilt that covered the end of the bed.

"An answer." Oxford said, climbing into the bed. Being built for a lord, the bed it was wide enough to sleep four, and thus was more than ample for one man and one cat. Socrates began walking around in a circle at the bottom of the bed, kneading the quilt with his paws to test it for softness. He eventually settled down, wrapping himself into a tight ball with his head down, his eyes still staring at Oxford.

"I know not cats," Oxford said to Socrates, whose eyes were beginning to look sleepy. "You may stay the night since the house is empty and it is Christmas. Beyond that, I make no promise."

Oxford turned over and was soon asleep. He didn't hear Nigel slip into the room and slide the bedpan out from under the bed nor see his faithful servant helping Frangellica negotiate the frozen path down the hill in the darkness to the road where they turned left and disappeared toward Stratford.

# 1589

## ~ 11 ~
## Shackspear Pays an Unwelcome Visit

O xford was sitting at his writing desk looking down the slope toward the Avon when Tobias appeared in the doorway.

"Frangellica, she say you spend too much time inside. We walk."

Oxford smiled. "I do not walk: I ride. A lord in my country rides."

"You have no horses."

"No horses? We came here on horses. What happened to them?"

"Nigel borrowed them; Robin took them back."

"To London?"

"Aye, my lord."

"Has he returned? I have not seen him."

Tobias grimaced. Talking always gave him a headache. "He is back, my lord. You not see him because you are inside too much."

Frangellica appeared behind Tobias, her arms folded across her chest. She tried to get around Tobias but he blocked her. She glared at Oxford. Tobias nodded toward her. "She says you walk."

"Sì, sì la mia nonna" Oxford said, extending his hands outward to ask for understanding if not forgiveness. "Ma per me, non è possible uscire," but Frangellica interrupted him.

"No, è possibile. È necessario!"

Oxford sighed. "Then I shall walk."

Frangellica nodded and disappeared.

He put on a coat, hat, and boots and followed Tobias out into the bright sunlight, the snow crunching under his feet. Tobias led the way down to the road where they turned right. They had walked less than a mile when a horseman galloped up. It was Shackspear!

"My lord," Shackspear said, jumping off the horse and dropping to one knee in the snow.

"What are you doing here?"

"I know you said I should stay away, my lord," Shackspear continued, "but Henslowe presses me for a play."

"What's that to me?"

"You promised to help me with *Procne's Revenge.*"

"Yes, but I didn't say when."

Shackspear groaned. Oxford waved him up. Shackspear staggered to his feet, brushing the snow off his knee.

"My good lord," Shackspear went on, but Oxford interrupted him.

"You shouldn't have promised. The fault lies with you."

"Yes, yes," Shackspear agreed quickly.

"Don't grovel. If you want me to work on it, you must go away. As for you, Stratford lies only a few miles behind me. No doubt, you are passing by on your way to visit your family."

Shackspear groaned. He looked like a tavern patron who had been given a bill he couldn't pay. He remounted his horse and turned it in the direction from which he had come.

Oxford was surprised by this. "Stratford lies there," he said, gesturing over his shoulder. "Why do you post in the opposite direction? Don't you want to find out what your wife is up to when she thinks you are far away in London?"

"No, my lord."

"No? You are married to an Anne, are you not?" Shackspear nodded. "As was I. Is she faithful, your Anne?"

"I care not."

"You care not?"

"No. I didn't want to marry her in the first place. She was twenty-six; I was eighteen. Some tomfoolery in a field got her with child."

"Well, one part of you worked like a man," Oxford said, glancing at Tobias, whose face, as usual, showed nothing.

"The woman I wanted to marry lived in Temple Grafton. But when Anne found out she was pregnant, well," he looked away, "that was the end of that dream."

This brought Oxford up short. He knew something of dreams that had turned out badly, particularly dreams about women. Hadn't Burghley forced him to marry Nan? He did not like thinking about the similarities between Shackspear's marriage and his own.

Shakespeare wasn't finished. "The townspeople smiled at the wedding because they knew I was trapped, like them. Then I saw your play." He was careful not to mention its name. "Then I knew. I would go to London, become a playwright, and fill my pockets with money."

This shocked Oxford as much as hearing Shackspear did not care whether his wife was cheating on him in Stratford. The theater was apparently nothing more to the Stratford man than a way to make money, like the tannery was to Shackspear's father—gloves in his father's case, tickets to plays in Shackspear's. But why he did he care, Oxford asked himself? The man was no more than advertised. Still, Oxford couldn't stop himself from asking after Shackspear's son. "Don't you want to see your son?"

Shackspear admitted that he did. "But if I see his face, my lord, I will be trapped again. In staying to love him, I will be another failed father, like my father before me, and his before him. When I make my fortune, my lord, my son and Stratford will welcome me."

"Well, then, you must return to London as soon as possible."

"But there is no fortune for me there, my lord, unless …," but Oxford put up his hand.

"No. I must have complete silence. Go!"

Shackspear sighed. "Very well, my lord." He turned his horse toward London and rode off.

Tobias stepped up next to Oxford. "A man cannot see the horns on his own head until he sees them in his wife's face, my lord."

Oxford looked at Tobias with new interest. "That's very good. How came you by this knowledge?"

"Women are the same everywhere, my lord."

Oxford realized his faithful whiffler was another man he did not know. "You have had experience with them?" he said.

"I caught my wife with another man. I killed them both with one spear thrust." He grinned. Oxford realized he was looking at what must have been the last thing Tobias' wife ever saw. He shivered.

"And how have you fared since?"

"Well, my lord."

"But you have decided not to live with them."

"I will *never* live with them." His face darkened. "I will play with them but not stay till morning. White or black, they all same. They will pen you in. They will put shoe your feet and bridle your mouth. And then," he said, his voice lowering, "they will cheat you."

"Let us continue our walk," Oxford said, setting off in the same direction Shackspear had gone. He motioned for Tobias to walk alongside him. "Have you been hereabouts?"

"Yes, my lord. The ladies in the nearby villages like me."

"How much?" Oxford asked.

The grin reappeared on Tobias' face. "I am asked to return."

"I see."

A crow screeched from the wood to their right.

"We have no bird like that in Africa," Tobias said, frowning. "So much noise, so little beauty."

"Well," Oxford announced, moving off down the road, "you must take me into the forest some day and teach me how to hear all these things." He picked up the pace. Tobias, more sensitive to moods than words, was pleased. His master was back.

When they returned to the house, they found a horse tied to the hitching post, breathing heavily in the cold air. A messenger waited inside.

"My lord," the man said, bowing as Oxford and Tobias came up. "The Queen has summoned Parliament for February the ninth."

"Less than two weeks," Oxford said. "I shall be in attendance." He motioned for Nigel to take care of the man. "Where is Robin?"

Robin came running down the stairs. "My lord," he said.

"We are to London in less than a fortnight. You and Nigel will leave tomorrow to open Oxford Court. Tobias and I will follow."

"We have no horses," Nigel said.

"So I heard."

"May I send Robin to hire what we need in Stratford?"

"Yes. Send him now." Oxford headed for the stairs.

Robin called after him. "Shouldn't we work on *Procne's Revenge* before you leave? We will no doubt meet Mr. Shackspear in London."

"We already have. This day in fact. But, right now, I need to capture a sonnet I have in my head." He turned to the stairs. "*So shall I live, supposing thou art true, / like a deceived husband,*" Oxford said to himself as he bounded up the stairs.

## ~ 12 ~
## Westminster Palace

Oxford was stepped off the boat onto the steps of the old palace wharf. He went past the Chapel of St. Stephen to the palace entrance reserved for the lords and clergy. The immense doors were immediately opened to let him in. He walked down a long hallway to a room where he found Lord Burghley donning ceremonial robes. Burghley had a black skullcap on his head and clutched the state purse, a large bag made of heavy fabric fringed with enameled coats of arms and silk tassels. A servant was placing a jewel-encrusted mantle over his shoulders. Baron Hunsdon, Lord Chamberlain, was putting on a white ermine robe. Other nobles were putting on the robes they were entitled to wear as ministers and judges at the opening of Parliament.

"My lords," Oxford said as he slipped his arms through the openings in a red velvet robe a servant held out for him. A murmur acknowledged his presence. A second servant appeared with the Sword of State, an ancient two-handed battle sword Oxford carried in formal ceremonies. Oxford took the sword and held it upright, pointing the tip at the ceiling. The blade was etched with detailed engravings that danced in the light from the flickering torches that lined the room.

Burghley walked sideways across the few steps that separated him from Oxford. "My Lady Mildred lies abed," he said in a voice too low for the others to hear, "and little hope remains for her." Burghley's eyes were red; his face was haggard. For a moment, Oxford felt sorry for him. Lady Mildred may have been a shrew but Burghley loved her deeply. "Her last day is close upon her. You did me the favor of being at sea when Nan died. Do me likewise when Mildred passes. "

"I protest, my lord. I never did Lady Mildred harm."

"You abused our daughter," Burghley hissed. "Worse, you have had the audacity to outlive Nan, and it now appears that you will outlive Mildred as well. Those of us who believe there is justice in Heaven have great difficulty accepting the loss of Nan and Mildred while He allows *you* to go on living and breathing."

Oxford stood in front of Burghley, the tip of the Sword of State wavering between them. "The old man is not himself," thought Oxford. "His wife's approaching death is unraveling him."

"Get out of my way," Burghley said, pushing the tip of the sword to one side. He walked away. Oxford followed him into the room where the Queen would greet Parliament. Paintings covered the walls and ceiling depicting stories from the Old Testament in a profusion of glorious color. The royal throne dominated the end of the room. Oxford took his place to its left, Burghley on the other side.

The other lords and ministers took their places in front of the throne. The Queen entered, carrying emblems of her position as ruler of England. Once she was seated, the members of the House of Commons filed in from St. Stephen's and took their places behind the bar. The archbishop blessed the assembled gathering. Elizabeth welcomed them. Sir Christopher Hatton, Lord Chancellor, rose from his seat and announced the purposes of the session, after which everyone adjourned to the Great Hall for a banquet and a play. Business would be conducted the following day.

The Great Hall had been built by William II in 1099. Immense hammer-beams held up a peaked roof. It was home to the Queen's Bench, the Court of Chancery, and the Court of Common Pleas, often all at the same time, with sufficient room left over for wig stalls, booksellers, and food stands. Ramshackle buildings slumped against the ancient walls outside and sheltered taverns and alehouses that provided food and lodging to those attending court from outside London.

The courts and all its attendant structures had been swept out of the Hall to ready it for the opening of Parliament and the great feast that would follow. Rich tapestries had been taken out of long-term storage and hung under the direction of Sir Edmund Tilney, Master of the Revels. A raised platform had been built at the bottom of the stairs that descended into the great room at the south end. A long table had been set up on the platform for the Queen and her ministers. Long trestle tables and benches filled the rest of the Hall.

Elizabeth walked down the stairs to the platform and took her seat at the table. The lords and ministers filled the chairs to her left and right, with Burghley next to her on one side, Hatton on the other. Oxford took a chair at the far end.

An army of servants brought in platters of cold, hot, fried, and steamed oysters, roast game, and joints of mutton. More servers filled tankards with ale. A group of musicians began to play. A cake, decorated with glazed carrots and parsnips, capped the meal. The Queen ate a bite, rose, and left. The servants immediately began clearing the platform for the play that would follow.

Oxford wandered outside and found Robin waiting at the door. A shriek of laughter was heard from the other side of the square. Falstaff was relieving himself over the embankment, his piss arching high through the air. Three women surrounded him, laughing and shrieking. He strutted over to Oxford and Robin.

"They all want to know if Jack's staff is still large and running well," he said as he came up to them. "I was paddling in their packets."

"And they in your codpiece," Oxford said.

"Well, if jewels there be, 'tis only fitting they be played with," Falstaff said, with a wink at Robin.

"Aren't you a little old for paddling and playing?" Robin asked.

Falstaff frowned. "How old do you think I be, young sir?" He was suddenly looming over Robin like a tree about to fall.

"I have no idea," Robin said, trying to make himself small.

"Of course ye don't, and no one ever will."

One of the three women called out to him across the square.

"Where's my tiller?" Falstaff called back loudly, as he fished in the folds of flesh and cloth that covered his lower extremities, leering at the women on the other side of the square. They shrieked and giggled.

"Tiller?" Robin asked. "For such a large boat, shouldn't you have a wheel?"

Falstaff glowered. "I'm not talking boats here, boy. I'm talking what ye use on a farm to till the rich, dark earth." He smiled at the women and made a rocking motion with his hips. "Though the earth I till is long-legged, fresh, and moist."

Robin made a face. "You're going to be arrested for waving that thing around."

"A felony, for sure," Falstaff said.

"Spare me," Robin said, putting up a hand.

Falstaff began to move off toward the women.

"You'll miss the play," Oxford announced, turning to head back to the Hall.

"I'll be quick."

"Not at your age."

Falstaff groaned. He took off his oversized straw hat and waved it at the women. He turned to trundle after Oxford. "What I do for art," he muttered, sliding his pants around so that they lined up with his legs, now moving toward the open door funneling people into the Hall.

Their progress was interrupted by a man who suddenly appeared in front of them. He was tall and dressed in Puritan black. Unlike many of the other people who had filled the Hall and spilled outside, he wore no ruff. His eyes were heavy-lidded, almost as if he were asleep.

"My lord," the man said, bowing to Oxford.

"Mr. Spenser," Oxford replied.

Edmund Spenser stood up. "I have taken the liberty of inscribing a dedication in my new work that includes praise of my Lord of Oxford," he said, smiling. He bowed again.

Oxford returned the bow. "One can always accept another dedication, particularly if it says kind things about me. But if you come for money, there is none to be had."

"Oh, such base needs are not the goal of artists such as you and I. Sir Walter Raleigh has brought me to speak with the Queen. I hope for a pension so I can finish *The Fairie Queene*. I have, as she earlier commanded me, removed myself to the estate she gave me in Ireland where I have been working to produce art that will sing her praises."

"Ah, more words of praise."

"Yes," Spenser said, a contented smile sliding across his face. "Words I hope will please her, as well as you."

"But she has kept you waiting."

"Indeed, my lord."

"You will get used to it. But have you come to see the play?"

Spenser wrinkled his nose. "No, my lord. I was here with Sir Walter for the feast, but I am now off to St. Margaret's for the afternoon service."

"Without Sir Walter, it appears."

"Yes. He prefers the play."

"A better choice."

Spenser was confused.

"For Sir Walter, if not for Mr. Spenser," Oxford said.

Spenser realized Oxford had been playing him. "But the play is not one of yours," he could not keep himself from saying.

"It is not."

"'Tis said that you have fled the court and sit in an idle cell far from London."

"My Ireland," Oxford replied. Everyone but Spenser knew the Queen's decision to gift him an estate in Ireland was tantamount to banishment and intended to get him out of England.

Spenser missed Oxford's sarcasm. "So the gentle spirit from whose pen large streams of honey and sweet nectar flow has been stilled?"

"He knows I write no more," Oxford said to himself, "and he likes it." Oxford had the feeling he was watching his own funeral. "Am I?" He was suddenly angry.

"Of course not," he said with conviction. "I shall undoubtedly have something soon that will give you a new target to strike at in your struggle to save England from immoral art and bad poetry."

"Indeed," Spenser said, irritated for having wasted his time in stopping to talk to Oxford. "My lord," he muttered.

Oxford watched him walk away.

"If he thinks," Falstaff said, "that a poem long in length but short on the painting of women's parts can save a man from debauchery, he is a bigger fool than I thought he was."

"Edmund Spenser is a chicken scratching in barnyard dirt. But the Queen likes his poetry. Therefore, she deserves it. Let us see how the *Comicall History of Alphonsus, King of Arragon*, fares this afternoon, the latest work from that red-bearded, two-fisted drinker, Robert Greene."

A lady dressed in a long gown suddenly glided out of the crowd and came over to Oxford. She was fine-boned with a narrow face, an aquiline nose, and ivory complexion. Her beauty, however, came not from her features but from her dark eyes that flashed as she came up to Oxford.

"My lord," the woman said. Her hand came up to lightly touch his arm, stopping him.

Falstaff and Robin kept walking. Robin had never seen the woman before but Falstaff knew she was Anne Vavasor, a former lady-in-waiting to the Queen who had become infamous when she delivered a baby in a closet adjacent to the royal bedroom some eight years earlier. Oxford was identified as the father of the child. Oxford had not seen her since the Queen had thrown them into the Tower.

"Anne," Oxford said. Her perfume enveloped him, painfully reminding him of how long it had been since he had been with a woman, much less a woman of the beauty Anne Vavasor possessed.

"It is good to see you," she purred, giving Oxford's arm a gentle squeeze, as if her hand wanted to explore him further. Her eyes flitted from his mouth to his eyes and back, like a butterfly touching flowers in a garden, drinking in and recharging her memories of him.

"It has been a busy time."

"Yes, and I heard you were everywhere last year," she said, in the lilting voice Oxford remembered so well, "outfitting your ship and chasing the Spanish across the seas."

"Only one Englishman of many." He looked over at Falstaff and Robin patiently waiting for him. He wanted to move but couldn't: part of him screaming to get away from her; another part wanting more of her perfume, her voice, and her smiling eyes.

"My regrets about Nan. I heard you were at sea when she died."

"She was buried before I got back."

"At the urging of good Lord Burghley, I am sure," Anne continued in a honeyed voice, her hand still on his arm. "And so you are finally free to make your own choices about how you spend your time, or who you live with."

Oxford stiffened. Anne continued to caress his arm. Her voice sank an octave. "We had so much, you and I. The heat, the passion, the joy you found in my bed. Don't you remember?"

"Yes, and the fireworks. Always the fireworks."

"But we are older now, aren't we? And wiser? We have much to build on."

"I am not so sure." He looked away. He remembered her wit, and the stroke and counterstroke of the words they flung at each other as they played and fought, but he knew that Anne's beauty and the memory of the times they had shared together was not enough to renew their relationship. "I heard you were married," he said, thinking this might bank her fires.

"To a sea captain who is always at sea," she purred, "who may not find me at home when he returns." She squeezed his arm again. "You *do* remember the poetry you bathed me in, don't you?" She leaned into him. "The poetry *you* wrote?" Her perfume swept over him again, stopping whatever thought had been was running toward his tongue.

*I saw a fair younge ladye come her secret teares to wail,*
*Clad all in colour of a vow and covered with a vail.*
*From sighes and shedding amber teares into sweet songe she broke,*
*And thus the echo answered her to every woorde she spoke*
*O heavens (quoth she) who was the first that bred in me this fevere?*

Oxford pulled away. "Those words do not come to me now."

She laughed. "'Twas you who bred the fever. You are the only one who can quench it!" She leaned into him, looking into his eyes.

"You forget the disputes, the pain."

"I remember them well, the sonnet you sent me when it was over:

*My Mistress' eyes are nothing like the sun,*
*Coral is farre more red then her lips,*
*If snow be white, why then her breasts are black,*
*If hairs be wires, black wires grow from her head!*

My hair *was red*, and you made it into wires, and said it was black!"

"Your hair *was black*," Oxford protested. "You only dyed it red."

"To ape the Queen, to win you from her."

This remark stopped them both. How quickly they had returned to sparring with each other, sending verbal volleys across a net between them which, at one time, would have thrilled Oxford.

Anne moved closer. "We both know that I can joust with you on any tiltyard, be it made of words or silken sheets. I can be a partner who can ruffle your hair and make you laugh. I am no poet but I can be the apprentice who takes your gold and buffs it brighter, sending it back to you with love and wit!"

"Never," Oxford said with more force than he expected. "That a woman conceived me, I thank her. But that I should marry again, never. I will live a bachelor, thank you very much, and thereby do no woman wrong by mistrusting her."

This surprised Anne. "You mistrusted me?"

"A man's mother is always known; his father …"

Anne's face hardened. "You think our son is not yours?"

Oxford looked away. Anne moved to look him full in the face.

"I say, *our son?* I gave you the use of my heart, a double heart for your one. Edward is the son you and I made. He only needs his father to hoist him on his shoulder and tell him the world is his oyster."

"Then find the man who fathered him," Oxford said quietly.

95

Anne was dismayed. "How can you say that?" She caught herself. She looked away. "I should have known. You've not reached out to him, or me." Oxford saw the hurt in her eyes. "A woman damned on suspicion alone cannot prove her faithfulness no matter what she does."

Oxford knew she was right. His suspicion that Nan had cuckolded him permeated every corner of their marriage.

"That's why there is trust," Anne said, speaking now more as a friend than a lover. "Trust is believing that someone is faithful to you. We do it by giving someone the power to hurt us."

She stepped away, smoothing the front of her dress.

"I pity our son, who is fatherless. He is yours, as God knows. If you looked, you would see yourself in his face. As for me, I feel nothing but sadness for you. One cannot love without trust. Without it, you are sentencing yourself to a life without love."

"Whatever truth there is in your words, I am not the man for you. I am sorry."

"So am I. Fare thee well, Edward. I would have been your wife had I the power to make thee love me again, and I would have been a good one too. I will continue strange."

Oxford watched her walk away. Falstaff and Robin drifted over.

"Whatever I write, my lord, it will not be about women," Robin said.

"Ah, but you do not know them yet."

"And never will, seeing that they give off an invisible scent that drives men mad."

"You think you will be immune?"

"I shall keep my distance, my lord, and suffer not their advances."

"Oh, this will be a wonder to see. What do you think, Sir John?"

"Long odds, my lord."

"I don't think he can do it. I don't know anybody who has."

"There's yer answer."

## ~ 13 ~
## Billesley Hall

*T*he *Comicall History of Alphonsus, King of Aragon* was exactly what Oxford thought it would be—a rambling string of battles between armies, a head that belched fire, and goddesses in billowy white robes. The only surprise was that Shackspear was Calliope. He caught Oxford as everyone was leaving the Great Hall. "My lord," he said, plucking Oxford's sleeve. "Mr. Henslowe begs me for my *Procne*. You see how they treat me," he reached up to tug at his wig. "I have no power as an actor. If I have my *Procne*, I shall be a made man *and someone else will be Calliope!*"

Oxford was in no mood to talk to Shackspear. He stalked off. He and Robin returned to Oxford Court and left immediately for Billesley.

---

On the way back to Warwickshire, Oxford realized that Spenser's snide remarks had irritated him. "Have I put my pen away?" He did not like watching Spenser chuckle over this. It was as if Oxford had gone to his own funeral and seen how soon he would be forgotten. "I have too long put off Shackspear *and the Spensers of the world,*" he told Robin as they descended into the Avon valley. "*Alphonsus* needs competition. Through Shackspear, I will give the Queen such poor fare that she will have to bring me back."

Robin was thrilled. He did not know what Oxford was talking about, but if his master had decided to return to the world of playwriting, *God bless them everyone.* Oxford went on to explain how he was going to take Shackpear's idea and fill it with mutilated characters and dead bodies. "Ovid," Robin reminded his master. "I've read every story."

They arrived at Billesley cold and tired. "Supper in the library," he said to Nigel as he swept past him, tossing his coat and hat on a chair. "Robin!" he called out. Robin was coming in the door behind him. The young man was more tired than Oxford was. "My lord," he said, breathing heavily.

"Pen and ink!" Robin followed Oxford into the library where he picked up an inlaid ebony tray that held quills, ink, and a special knife, small and bone-handled, used to shape quills into pens. Paper was at hand. Robin drew one leaf into position, dipped a quill into the ink pot, and waited.

Oxford stopped at the window, looking out into the evening dusk. "What lines come to mind when you think of *The Spanish Tragedy*?" he asked.

Robin was too tired to play word games but the answer came to him immediately. "'*First take my tongue and afterwards my heart,*'" he said.

"And the stage directions that follow?"

"'*He bites out his tongue.*'" Robin's eyes got bigger. "I saw Burbage play Hieronimo once and he spit his tongue clear across the stage!"

"Which, I warrant, was the high point of the play?"

Robin nodded. He was awake now. "The soldiers had seized Hieronimo to find out who helped him stab the king's son, but before they could torture him, Hieronimo bites off his tongue and spits it out!" Robin had obviously relived the moment more than once. "Before *The Spanish Tragedy*, everyone died offstage. Master Kyd put death upfront, where the audience got their money's worth."

"So what say you about a play in which the bodies keep falling like heavy rain, not just at the end, but throughout the play?"

Robin nodded again. Like everyone else in 1589, he loved gore, but the joy of recalling Hieronimo spit his tongue across the stage began to fade as he noticed an eerie light in Oxford's eyes. The muse had seized his master again. The first time was when Oxford announced he had to "pull" a sonnet out of his bosom. Oxford had closeted himself in his room that time and not asked Robin to assist him. The second time was when Oxford stuffed ribbons into his mouth and paraded back and forth as a mutilated woman at Oxford Court. Shackspear and Nigel had been there at the time, and so Robin did not feel as uneasy as he did now.

"The play I will write will be about a mother's loss of her son, not a father's loss, for how much more than the father doth the mother mourn the loss of a baby. The mother doth mourn from nature; the father from laws written by men. A mother knows who her child is; the father can never be as certain."

"Nor can the child," Robin added brightly.

This brought Oxford to a halt. Robin was an orphan and obviously thinking of himself. "But does what Robin say apply to me as well?" Oxford asked himself. "Was Earl John really my father? I don't look like Earl John. Earl John was much bigger." He pushed the thought away.

"Shackspear suggests a play where a woman is raped and mutilated, but that will not be enough." Robin waited. He felt like he was in the calm before a storm. His master still had that eerie look. "I am going to write a play about a spiral of deaths, tit for tat, leading up to a bloodbath at the end that leaves only a few alive to tell the audience who has died and who has lived!"

Robin gulped. "Master Kyd would be, well, ah, *out-Kyded.*"

Oxford smiled. He liked the idea of twisting Kyd's name into a verb, but resisted the temptation. "This is business," he said to himself.

"Hieronimo is driven mad by the injuries he suffers at the hands of others. But his suffering will pale when compared to what I will visit on Titus."

"So what will Lavinia do once she loses her hands and tongue?" Robin asked. This scene obviously interested him.

"She will parade back and forth across the stage while the play goes on, presenting her bleeding stumps and mouth to the audience over and over again."

"Which will silently scream horror more loudly than words!"

Oxford smiled. "You begin to understand the theater, my little Robin. Now, you must set down how Titus loses his hand." Robin blinked. Oxford waved a hand to ward of any questions. "Tamora will capture two of Titus' sons. Aaron the Moor, a Barabas, will come to Titus and tell him Tamora will give him back his sons if someone in Titus's family gives up a hand. Titus immediately volunteers one of his hands. He finds a knife and says the following to Aaron:

> *Come hither, Aaron; I'll deceive them both:*
> *Lend me thy hand, and I will give thee mine.*

The stage direction that follows will be: *Aaron chops off Titus' hand.*"

Disbelief spread across Robin's face. "Lend me thy hand, and I will give thee mine?" Would anyone say thus? Particularly when it sounds like "Come live with me and be my love?"

"Shh," Oxford said. "Sometimes a line carries more meaning than was intended."

"But what of Marlowe?"

"I know him not, but think he will laugh when he hears this."

"So, Aaron leaves with Titus's hand."

"Yes."

"Does Titus get his sons back?"

"No. A messenger returns with the hand Titus gave Aaron and the *heads* of his two sons. The messenger puts them on a table next to the ever-bleeding, ever-present Lavinia. Titus goes mad. He tells his brother and Lavinia to carry the two heads and his lopped-off hand:

> *Come, brother, take a head;*
> *And in this hand the other I will bear.*
> *Lavinia, thou shalt be employ'd:*
> *Bear thou my hand, sweet wench, between thy teeth.*

"Oh, was there ever a play like this?" Robin asked himself as he took this down. He looked up. "But the brother only carries one head. He could carry both heads. Titus could carry his hand with his other hand. Why make Lavinia 'bear it between her teeth?"

"How see you this as they troop across the stage?"

"Most ghastly."

"Yes. Dramatic vision can sometimes overcome logic. And let the pedants expectorate ink on why Lavinia carried anything!"

Robin shivered as he wrote this down. "I protest. Such a plot will be hooted down by the audience."

"Of course, it will."

Robin was lost. He looked up at Oxford.

"If the Queen does not want my plays on her stage, I will give her what she deserves: absurd plots, mad characters, bad poetry, and more deaths than a coroner sees at the height of the plague!"

Robin looked at him, eyes wide.

"*This be Shackspear's play,*" Oxford thundered, "*not mine.*" The eerie glow reappeared in his eyes. "I shall have fun taking Greene and Kyd and Marlowe and smearing their entrails across the stage!"

"Marlowe? Entrails?"

"First digested by me, like a piece of boiled beef, and then spit out, like Hieronomo's tongue, across the stage! To your pen!"

The two of them worked far into the night. Robin tried to keep up but became more and more tired as Oxford showed no signs of stopping. Oxford finally turned around and found the boy with his head on the pages in front of him, an ink blot on the side of his cheek. "And so to sleep, young scribbler."

## ~ 14 ~
## The Return to Oxford Court

Tobias got Oxford to accompany him on a walk into the Stratford countryside. They meandered through the woods and fields around Billesley Hall but said little to each other. Tobias thought Oxford's silence meant that his master was listening to nature but Oxford was realizing that he was missing London more and more, the noise of the Boar's Head, the wit combats, and yes, even the court.

"I shall return to London," he announced upon his return to the Hall. He left the next day. Robin went with him. Nigel and Frangellica followed later. Oxford instructed them to bring everything with them.

When he arrived at Oxford Court, he closeted himself in his room to finish *Titus Andronicus*. It was two days before Nigel and Frangellica came clattering up, the trunks and baggage piled into a two-wheeled cart they had borrowed from Billesley Hall. Nigel found his master in the library, bent over a sea of papers strewn across the top of the table. Oxford acknowledged Nigel with a grunt, but kept writing. Nigel returned an hour later with a bowl of soup.

"My lord," he announced as he came into the room. He held a large tureen in front of him. He slid it onto the corner of the table and lifted the lid.

The aroma from the soup washed over Oxford. He looked up. "Turtle soup!" he said. "Where found you this?"

"Frangellica sent a boy ahead to buy a bowl from Sally, the soup vendor on Lombard Street." He ladled some into a bowl.

Oxford picked up a spoon. "I thought Frangellica would never let you serve a soup someone else made."

"Indeed, my lord, but she knew you loved Sally's turtle soup and thought you would appreciate a warm, welcome home."

"This is the perfect antidote to all the execrable food I ate in Warwickshire. Thank her for me."

Nigel was pleased.

"I once offered a bowl to Tobias," Oxford said, "but he said he only eats animals that live on land and eat grass, not something pried out of an upside-down bowl that spends its life underwater."

Oxford did not offer Nigel some soup, or think to ask whether Nigel had ever tasted turtle soup. What Nigel liked or disliked was not something to be shared with his master, which, Oxford realized, was how it should be.

"Sally is Richard Topcliffe's sister," Oxford said, leaning back to let Nigel spoon more soup into his bowl.

"He who pries confessions out of innocent men?" Nigel was surprised at this. "But Topcliffe would never let his sister sell soup on the street, would he?"

Oxford shook his head. "Sally's tough enough to tell him to go hang himself."

Nigel decided this was more than he needed to know. "Will you be having your meals in the library, my lord?"

"Yes. I need to finish this. I need fireworks, surprises. I shall tie a message to an arrow and fire it at the heavens asking for help." He laughed. "Arrows fired at the heavens." He slid down the table, searching through the papers on the table, when he saw Socrates looking at him from the end of the table.

"You brought the cat?"

Nigel couldn't tell whether his master was glad the cat had reappeared or was irritated by its presence. "If I must say, my lord, he brought himself."

"How so?"

"He watched us leave Billesley from the front hall window and is now sitting on the library table. How this was accomplished, I know not."

"Is this Frangellica's doing?"

"She likes not the cat, my lord."

Socrates, with a disdainful look, walked over to one of the many pages scattered on the table and sat down in the middle of one.

"The bugger has cheek," Oxford said.

"Shall I remove him, my lord?"

"No."

"Very well, my lord." Nigel left the cat and his master eyeing each other.

# ~ 15 ~
## Oxford's "Hand" in *Titus Andronicus*

Oxford was bent over the table. Socrates sat erect at the other end, watching. Oxford would write down the page in front of him, turn the page sideways and write up the side, then across the top and down the other margin. If the reverse side was blank, he would turn over the page and use that as well, and when he had filled it up both sides, he would begin writing on a new page, muttering to himself all the while in a tone so low that it sounded like the drone of carpenter bees boring through the table.

Robin sat sleepily near the door, waiting. A fly came in through an open window, bred by the warmth of the early spring day. It landed on the table next to Robin, who promptly smashed it, startling Oxford and Socrates.

"What did thou strike at, young Robin?"

"That which I have killed, my lord; a fly."

"Out on thee!" Oxford exclaimed, putting his pen down. His eyes were red from lack of sleep. His fingers were black with ink. "Thou art a murderer!"

"'Twas a fly, my lord."

"Had he not a father and a mother?"

"He was an ill-favor'd black fly, my lord, as black as Aaron the Moor."

Oxford looked dazed. He glanced around the library.

"My lord," Robin said, getting up to come over to Oxford. "You look not well."

"Yes. My mind teems with Titus." He tried to focus. "Thou hast done me a charitable deed, Robin." He turned back to the table. "We must have flies in this play." He picked up his pen and began to write again. "Arrows over the rooftops, masks, and two boys baked in a pot pie."

Robin sat down next to the door again. The sound of the carpenter bees returned. As Oxford finished covering a page with his wild, Italic script, he would fling it to his right and grab a new sheet.

Socrates would watch Oxford scribbling furiously on the new page while he waited for the ink to dry on the page Oxford had flung aside, which event would occur shortly before Oxford was done with the page he was working on. Socrates would then move over and sit on it as Oxford attacked the next page, the two of them engaged in an unconscious slow-motion pas de deux Robin had long ago ceased to notice.

As night fell, Robin lit candles and began to clean up the room. "Good night, my lord," he said, moving to the door. Oxford grunted, letting Robin know the page was free to go.

———————◆◆◆◆◆——————

Robin came down to the library the next morning and found Oxford wrapped in a frayed blanket, asleep in a chair before the fireplace. The fire had burned out. Socrates was nowhere to be seen.

"My lord," Robin said, shaking Oxford gently. Sunlight was pouring into the room. "Shackspear craves a word with you."

Oxford sat up. He looked rumpled and confused. "Who?"

"Shackspear. He has come for the script."

"Let him in."

Shackspear appeared in the doorway. He bowed. "My lord," he said. He saw the papers strewn across the table.

Oxford waved him in. Socrates leaped from the table to the open window and disappeared.

Shackspear went directly to the table and, gathering the pages against his chest, sank into one of the chairs, and began reading them. Grunting to himself, exclaiming every once in a while, he raced through the pages, stacking them to his left as he finished them.

For an hour Oxford sat and watched while Robin stood in the doorway and took in the scene. Shackspear surprised them; he could read, although not quickly. No one said anything. When Shackspear finally scanned the last page, he added it to the pile with a flourish.

"Hands everywhere," he cried, looking up, an expression of delight on his face. He grabbed a sheet. "Here's Lavinia, blessing Titus in the first scene: '*O bless me here with thy victorious <u>hand</u>.*' The very hand Titus will chop off!" He grabbed another page. "Here's Tamora, urging her sons on to vengeance: '*Your mother's <u>hand</u> shall right your mother's wrong.*' And Marcius and Quintius at the pit with Saturninus's body: '*Help me with thy fainting <u>hand</u>;*' '*reach me thy <u>hand</u>;*' and, '*thy <u>hand</u> once* *more.'* This chorus of 'hands' reaches fever pitch when Titus confronts Lavinia, bleeding from her mouth and arms:

> *Speak, Lavinia, what accursed <u>hand</u>*
> *Hath made thee <u>handless</u> in thy father's sight?*
> *Give me a sword, I'll chop off my <u>hand</u> too;*
> *For they have fought for Rome, and all in vain;*
> *'Tis well, Lavinia, that thou hast no <u>hands</u>;*
> *For <u>hands</u>, to do Rome service, are but vain.*

"The word 'hand' is on every page. In the scene where Titus cuts off his hand and gives it to Aaron the Moor it's almost *every other word*," Shackspear exclaimed, shaking his head in wonder. "And when he has only one hand, he says, '*O, here I lift this one <u>hand</u> up to heaven.*'" He looked at Oxford. "What makest you of this?"

"You like it?" Oxford asked, not answering Shackspear's question.

"*I love it!*" Shackspear said. "Especially, the last scene where you have Titus ask the emperor if he agrees that a woman who has been shamed should be killed. When the emperor says yes, Titus stabs Lavinia, *his own daughter!* He then tells the emperor that the sons of his new queen *are in the pie in front of him!* Titus stabs the queen but is killed by the emperor, who immediately dies on the sword of Lucius, Titus's sole surviving son!" Shackspear looked at Oxford, eyes wide. "Wonderful!" He scooped up the pages. "May I?"

Oxford nodded.

Shackspear headed for the door. "They're going to love this!" he exclaimed as he disappeared into the hallway.

Oxford looked over at Robin. "He's learning fast," Oxford said quietly. "But his day of reckoning is fast upon him. I have filled the play with words the way a cart is oe'rloaded with night soil on its way to the midden. I want Shackspear laughed off the stage when the audience hears the actors go on and on about 'hands.' Marcus implores Titus not to encourage Lavinia 'to lay such violent <u>hands</u> upon her tender life,' to which Titus replies:

> *What violent <u>hands</u> can she lay on her life?*
> *Ah, wherefore dost thou urge the name of <u>hands</u>;*
> *O, <u>handle</u> not the theme, to talk of <u>hands</u>,*
> *Lest we remember still that we have none.*
> *Fie, fie, how franticly I square my talk,*
> *As if we should forget we had no <u>hands</u>,*
> *If Marcus did not name the word of <u>hands</u>!*

"So what do you say, my lord, when you speak of hands?"

Oxford looked at his hands, turning them over. "They are not mine anymore," he said quietly. "They are Shackspear's. The name on the play will be *William Shackspear.*" He looked at Robin. "I am Lavinia, Robin, sans hands, sans tongue, sans voice."

"'Twas Elizabeth who cut them off."

"I must get some sleep," Oxford said. He got up and started for the door.

## ~ 16 ~
## *Titus Andronicus* at the Rose

The conclusion of *Titus* was greeted with thundering applause. The packed audience whistled and threw shoes. Young men seized their neighbors' arms and mimed cutting them off; others pulled cloths from their mouths and staggered back and forth as they acted out the pain of having their tongues ripped out.

Falstaff was leaning against the rear wall, a look of bemusement on his face. Robin was staring in shock, as was Oxford. "Circe's charm hath turned them all to swine," he muttered.

Shackspear walked onto the stage and the din increased. Gentles," he called out, opening his arms in a Jesus-like gesture.

"Son of a glover!" Falstaff muttered.

"It seems I have misjudged what the audience wants," Oxford said. He looked to his left at the boxes filled with people hanging over the railings, waving at Shackspear far below. "Even the upper balconies love *Titus*." He shook his head.

Falstaff heaved himself up. "To the Boar's Head," he announced.

The three of them descended the stairs. Below, in the vestibule, Shackspear and Henslowe were wishing everyone good afternoon. John Greene appeared. He was almost the equal of Falstaff in height and girth, with flowing red hair and a pointed beard. He pointed his beard at Shackspear. He looked like the bow of a Greek trireme about to ram an enemy ship. He jammed himself to one side of the patrons leaving the theater and leaned in toward Shackspear.

"I thought I heard *Procne's Revenge* in there," he growled.

"How could that be, Master Greene?" Shackspear said, his face glowing. He had just heard the voice of God: an audience that loved him. Even Robert Greene looming over him couldn't dampen his enthusiasm. "The play is new," Shackspear said. "You had a play about a woman who loses her tongue, but it wasn't good enough to make it to the stage. Isn't that right, Mr. Henslowe?" Henslowe's face moved in multiple directions but he said nothing. He had on new shoes, lavender in color, and his attention was focused on keeping them out from under the many feet crowded into the small vestibule. Greene gritted his teeth. He pushed past Henslowe and went out the door.

Christopher Marlowe appeared, elegantly dressed in a morning jacket he never wore while he was at Cambridge. "My congratulations," he said, in a voice that was as velvety as the jacket he was wearing, as he came up to Shackspear. "Most interesting, particularly the claim by Aaron the Moor that he stood corpses up and carved initials on their chests:

> *Oft have I digg'd up dead men from their graves,*
> *And set them upright at their dear friends' doors,*
> *Even when their sorrows almost were forgot;*
> *And on their skins, as on the bark of trees,*
> *Have with my knife carved in Roman letters,*
> *'Let not your sorrow die, though I am dead.'*

"Is this not Barabas in *The Jew of Malta*: *'And every moon made some or other mad / And now and then one hang himself for grief / Pinning upon his breast a long great scroll?'* It doesn't scan right, but, still, you show a delicacy in subject matter, if not in poetry, that belies your provincial roots." He studied Shackspear. "Yes, 'tis many an ugly plant that puts forth lovely flowers. Welcome to the lists, Master Shackspear." He moved on.

Shackspear was beaming. Oxford pushed past him, heading for the door. Shackspear turned to follow him, but Henslowe grabbed him. "Master Shackspear, the patrons demand a new play."

Shackspear eyes were fixed on Oxford, who was moving away from him. Just then identical twin girls, no older than fifteen or sixteen, elbowed their way past Oxford on their way out of the theater.

"Twins," Oxford said, watching the two girls go out the door.

"Twins," Shackspear immediately repeated to Henslowe.

Falstaff thought Oxford had taken a fancy to the two girls. "My lord, they may be too young for someone of your greatness, although," and here his voice began to trail off, "two *is* always better than one."

Robin frowned. Oxford laughed. "If I write again, it may be about twins, Sir John, but it won't be about a tumble with children."

"Oh," Falstaff said, but then immediately thought he may have objected too soon.

Robin could see the thought run across the big man's face. "For the love of bread and beer," he muttered, turning away.

Henslowe was still holding onto Shackspear. "A comedy? A tragedy?"

"A comedy," Oxford called back, loud enough for Shackspear to hear.

"A comedy," Shackspear repeated. He pulled away from Henslowe. "My lord," Shackspear said, catching up to Oxford. "Will ye help me again?"

"Hah!" Oxford said, not breaking stride.

"My lord, you said a comedy. About twins."

"I spoke without thinking."

"My lord, I cannot do it without your help."

Oxford stopped an angry look on his face. "It is time you knew that I filled *Titus* with ridiculous scenes and words, expecting the audience to laugh and send you back to Stratford."

Shackspear looked like he had been slapped. "My lord does injustice to himself in doing injustice to me." Oxford was surprised by this. The newest London playwright was not through. "I know you can laugh at me in five different languages. I know little Latin and no Greek, but I know the theater business, and you don't. I don't care if Christopher Marlowe thinks my lines don't scan. I don't want praise from Cambridge dons. I want money because money buys respectability. You were born with both; I was born with neither. I will build my fortune by presenting plays that people will pay money to see. And, if you help me, they will pay and pay and pay. I want the biggest house in Stratford. I want my father to have arms. I want people to call me 'Master Shackspear,' like Marlowe just did out of ignorance." Oxford was taken aback. Shackspear was showing him no deference. Worse, he was talking about the theater as if it were nothing more than a business. Shackspear pressed on. "You have the ideas; I know how to make them work on the stage."

Oxford was trying to recover from being lectured by an upstart from the provinces, but to be told he did not know how to stage a play was too much. "I am forbidden by the Queen from writing plays," he announced dismissively. "I consider that prohibition includes writing plays *for others*." He started moving toward the river again.

Shackspear went with him. "But that didn't stop you from helping me with *Titus*," he said, the anger in his voice dropping a bit. "You didn't think it would succeed, but it did. People will demand to see it. Over and over again. That is success. What more could you ask for?"

Oxford slowed his pace.

"If you care not if I reap the praise, why give up the writing of it?"

Falstaff cleared his throat. "Avast, my lord."

Oxford came to a halt. He looked from one to the other.

Shackspear ignored Sir John. "The characters that fill your mind will never be birthed if you give up now. Help me and you can sit in the rafters of the Rose and feed on the ambrosia an audience feeds you when you take them to foreign countries, or present them with murders committed in palaces they know only by name."

Oxford was surprised that Shackspear knew the word ambrosia. And the roar of the audience *is* food for the gods, he thought.

Shackspear pressed on. "If you write no more, the Queen will have won. But if she sees new plays that remind her of what she has lost, she may put your pen back in your hands."

Oxford studied Shackspear. Where had he learned such crafty speech? How had he teased out the very thoughts that had driven Oxford to help Shackspear with *Titus* in the first place?

"If she gives me back my pen, you will no longer be the bard from Stratford-upon-Avon."

Shackspear agreed. "If you stop writing, I am no more, but you are you no more as well. If you give me plays, I will live on, as will your hope of being allowed to take the bows that will be given to me. We are partners in this venture, your lordship." He cocked his head. "If ye say aye."

Oxford glanced at Falstaff and Robin. Their frowns told him Shackspear's proposal was a bad idea. Oxford turned to Shackspear.

"Not just one set of twins, then," he said, surprising them all. "Two sets."

Shackspear's face broke into a wide smile. "Two?"

Oxford was surprised himself. The words tumbled out of him, as if he had reached up and opened a drawer that was overstuffed with ideas. "One set of twins will be noblemen, the other, their servants. Henslowe has two actors who look like twins. They shall be the noblemen. Burbage has a similar pair who can play the servants. A shipwreck has separated one nobleman and his servant from the others. One pair has been living in Ephesus. The other pair will arrive looking for their counterparts but not reveal who they are."

"And so confusion results," Shackspear said, excitedly.

"*A Comedy of Errors*," Oxford announced.

"Wonderful!" Shackspear said, clapping his hands.

## ~ 17 ~
## Gray's Inn - *The Comedy of Errors*

Oxford and Robin were climbing Chancery Lane, which was not much of a hill for them but a mountain to Falstaff. "Wherefore is the play to be performed at Gray's Inn and not at the Rose?" he asked, resting for a moment with one hand on his knee. "The Rose is but a boat ride from the Boar's Head, not a trek uphill like this!"

"Henslowe liked not the script."

"Ne did Shackspear," Robin added.

"Why so?"

"Too many words," Oxford said.

Robin disagreed. "He couldn't follow the confusion once the characters started mistaking each other. And no one dies in it."

Oxford shrugged. "He wanted a play, so I gave him one, but not one he could understand ..."

"Or make money off. That's why we're going to the Inn. The students will love it!"

"You think so?"

"It's unusual."

They walked into South Square, a long, tree-lined promenade bordered by brick offices, each guarded by a gate and a porter. Ahead of them lay the Hall, where the students ate their meals. The Hall dated from the 1300s. Burleigh and Sir Thomas Walsingham had attended the Inn. The Queen had recently donated a wooden screen to the Inn, carved from the transom of a captured Spanish galleon.

The three men made their way around to the entrance to the Hall. They walked in and looked up at the afternoon sunlight pouring through the stained-glass windows. The tables and chairs that usually filled the Hall had been replaced with makeshift chairs and stools. Workers were finishing the assembly of a set of risers along the two sides of the Hall. A large group of students arrived from the Inner Temple nearby, followed by an ambassador from a far-away country who had been told that a lively performance was to be expected.

Shackspear moved through the crowd and came up to Oxford. "My lord," he said, "The Inn has agreed to pay £10 for the performance."

"You shall be well-paid, then," Oxford said.

"Not so, my lord! A play Henslowe accepts will net far more. I need a play the fools in the pit want to see."

"Well," Oxford said, gesturing to the gentlemen and ladies behind him waving their fine handkerchiefs at each other like peacocks in a jungle clearing, "you have enough fools here tonight to determine if the play succeeds or no."

"Oh, them," Shackspear said, his voice rising as the babble around him increased. "They'll tell each other they liked it because they'll be too embarrassed to admit they didn't understand it. But the sad thing is that they're not paying a groatsworth to hear it. I need plays that people will pay money to see. I know you have 'em. Give me another one, but make it bleed. More action—fewer words!"

"Fewer words," Oxford repeated. "And how can I pass up a good word to make a play shorter or simpler?"

Shackspear threw up his hands. "Let me see the next one so I can suggest what might make it better."

Oxford bristled. "You? Make it better?"

Shackspear realized he had gone too far. "Begging your pardon," he said, acting the groveling provincial Oxford had first seen in the Boar's Head. "I helped you with *Titus,* and that play made people forget they saw *Tamburlaine* or *The Spanish Tragedy.* Now we have *The Comedy of Errors* and there's no blood, no revenge, and, and," and here his voice trailed off, "we have a mother who pops out of a door who didn't know one of her sons had been living in the same town for 18 years!"

"She was an abbess," Oxford said, calmly dismissing Shackspear's criticism. "Abbesses don't walk the seawall every night."

A trumpet sounded.

"I have to go," Shackspear said, turning to push through the crowd.

The audience stopped talking. A duke came out on the stage, accompanied by a gaoler dragging a man in chains. The audience quickly learned that the man was the father of twin sons, one of whom had gone missing with his wife. The father had come to Ephesus to search for his missing wife and son, not knowing that, because he was from Syracuse, the laws of Ephesus required his death. The duke made

112

it clear that the man should expect no clemency. To everyone's surprise, the father tells the duke to end his life:

> *Proceed, noble duke, to procure my fall,*
> *And by the doom of death end woes end all.*
> *Yet this my comfort: when your words are done,*
> *My woes end likewise with the evening sun.*

There was murmuring in the audience. "Priggin' flummery!!" someone announced behind Oxford, who smiled and looked at Robin. "Anyone can come up with a story," he said. "The difficulty is deciding where to begin. Look here. The father has been searching for 20 years, yet the play begins on the day he arrives in Ephesus, not when the loss occurs. The law says he must die, and he shows the audience he is so burdened by grief that he welcomes his death, thereby supplying all the history one needs to understand where he has been and what has happened to him."

"And thus the audience is hooked," Robin said.

The laughter began when the son from Syracuse mistook his brother's servant for his own. He had given his servant gold and, believing that he was talking to the same man, demanded to know where it was. The servant had no idea, not being the servant who had been given the gold. The confusion from the mixed identities grew, and the laughter continued as the characters on stage kept having conversations with people they thought were someone else. The confusion increased as the play unfolded, but it was not the finale that made the play famous as the "Night of Errors." It was a scene where a servant tries to explain that he is being pursued by a kitchen-wench:

> Servant: *Marry, sir, she's the kitchen-wench, and all grease;*
> *and I know not what use to put her to but to make a*
> *lamp of her and run from her by her own light.*
>
> Master: *What complexion is she of?*
>
> Servant: *Swart, like my shoe, but her face nothing like so*
> *clean kept: for why she sweats.*
>
> Master: *That's a fault that water will mend.*
>
> Servant: *No, sir, 'tis in grain; Noah's flood could not do it.*
>
> Master: *What's her name?*
>
> Servant: *Nell, sir; but her name and three quarters will not*
> *measure her from hip to hip.*
>
> Master: *Then she bears some breadth?*

Servant: *No longer from head to foot than from hip to hip: she is spherical, like a globe; I could find out countries in her.*

Master: *In what part of her body stands Ireland?*

Servant: *Marry, in her buttocks: I found it out by the bogs.*

Master: *Where Scotland?*

Servant: *I found it by the barrenness.*

As the servant described how a large woman could be made up of countries, the students began jumping up and down on the scaffolding. They knew this was a parody of Lord Burghley's insistence that young people should be tested on their knowledge of England before they were allowed to go abroad. "Where is the thighbone of England?" he would ask. If he did not like the answer, he would tell the applicant to stay home and discover his own country first.

Master: *Where England?*

Servant: *I looked for the chalky cliffs, but I could find no whiteness in them.*

Master: *Where Spain?*

Servant: *Faith, I saw not; but I felt it hot in her breath.*

Master: *Where America, the Indies?*

Servant: *O, sir! upon her nose, all o'er embellished with rubies, carbuncles, sapphires, declining their rich aspect to the hot breath of Spain, who sent whole armadoes of caracks to be ballast at her nose.*

Master: *Where stood Belgia, the Netherlands?*

Servant: *O, sir! I did not look so low!*

At which point the stands came down with a crash.

The play halted momentarily while the wreckage was cleared and the injured were helped out. Some of those who viewed themselves as coming from a better station in life decided Shackspear was the one who had stooped too low and went out the door, muttering and shaking their heads. The rest stayed for the last act and gave Shackspear a rousing round of applause.

Oxford did not stay to see Shackspear bask in his new-found fame. Shackspear must not have stayed either, for he was heard knocking on the door to Oxford Court early the next morning.

## ~ 18 ~
## A Summons from the Queen

Shackspear wanted to come in the door but Tobias was blocking him.

"The Queen has sent for me!" Shackspear cried, struggling to get past the African. "I am told Lord Oxford is to accompany me! Tobias, you do your master no service by barring me from seeing him!"

Shackspear's pleas had no effect on the much larger man, who took Shackspear by the neck and was about to throw him out when a queen's messenger stepped around him into the hall.

"A message for the Earl of Oxford," he announced loudly, as if Tobias were standing at the other end of the hall.

"I will fetch him," said Tobias, but Oxford appeared at the top of the stairs.

"Yes?"

"My lord, the Queen requests your presence at Greenwich at two this afternoon."

"Regarding what?"

"Her Majesty did not share that with me."

Oxford waved a hand, which, in the etiquette of the court, constituted both a dismissal and Oxford's agreement to appear at the palace. The messenger left. Shackspear used the opportunity to push past Tobias.

"My lord, I, too, have been summoned. The messenger told me it was about *The Comedy of Errors* last night. Her Majesty is not pleased with the confusion and injuries." He stopped at the bottom of the stairs. Oxford said nothing. "She thinks I wrote the play."

"Of course she does."

"But I didn't!" Shackspear cried out. "*You* did!" He stood there, fear washing back and forth across his face like the tides at Gravesend. "You don't expect me to lie to the Queen, do you?"

"We have an agreement, bonded with the blood of your son."

"My lord," Shackspear said, wringing his hands. "No contract can withstand the Queen."

"Then how will you explain your name on the playbills?" Oxford started coming down the stairs. "How will you explain the praise heaped on you last night? I, for one, would never lie to the Queen. I will tell her a wondrous new talent has come to London from Stratford-upon-Avon. This new light has written two excellent plays."

Shackspear was aghast. "My lord, please don't tell the Queen I wrote the plays!" He moved to one side to let Oxford step off the bottom stair. "I must tell her that *you* wrote the plays."

"And *I* must tell her that *you* wrote the plays."

"Then, she will wonder which of us is telling the truth!"

"I expect so." Oxford headed toward the back of the house.

"If you say you didn't write the plays and I say you did, she will believe you, me being nothing and you being a most senior lord!"

"'Tis very probable," Oxford said. He pushed open a door and disappeared.

"What shall I do?" Shackspear wailed.

A rumpled Falstaff slid around the corner to the library. He hobbled stiffly down the hall to Shackspear. He put a beefy arm on his shoulder. "Good morrow, Master Shackspear. You must to the Queen," he said in a voice so low that anyone listening would have thought they were conspirators discussing the commission of a foul deed.

"Yes," Shackspear said. "But, she thinks I wrote the plays!"

"But that's what you wanted, wasn't it?" Falstaff asked. Shackspear nodded glumly. Falstaff gave Shackspear a squeeze. "Watch out for what you wish for, eh?" Shackspear nodded again. "But," Falstaff went on exuberantly, "*carpe diem*. This is your chance to convince the Queen that you *did* write the plays. What an opportunity for you to show her how great an actor you are! Your audience will be the Queen! Not just a narrow box jammed with groundlings who have nothing better to do than throw fruit and crack nuts. If you play your part well, you will be famous!"

"*Or dead!*" Shackspear cried out. He threw off Falstaff's arm and started for the door, then stopped. "No. I'll wait for the earl. We'll go together. He will not abandon me."

"Not good," Falstaff said, shaking his head. "The earl is always late. You don't want to be late for the Queen, do you?"

Shackspear let out a "Yipe!" and started running toward the door. Falstaff threw his head back and laughed as the would-be-playwright disappeared into Candlewick Street.

—————◆◆✕◆●————

Oxford went to the palace alone. He found Shackspear cowering in an outer room. He went by him without acknowledgement and stepped into a room where he could wait out of sight. The Queen would know where he was.

It was an hour before a page came to get him, a not humiliating length of time, Oxford thought, considering how long she had kept him waiting on other occasions. The page did not take him to the summer room, however, but to a Privy Council chamber Elizabeth used for smaller meetings. She was seated on a dark, high-backed chair raised off the floor on a wooden platform. She was wearing a black, high-necked dress with a minimum of lace. Her eyes were lidded. Burghley stood to her right, the emblems of his office hanging down his chest. His hand was on a white staff that rested on the floor next to him and extended up beyond the top of his head. Various other officials stood around the room. There were no ladies-in-waiting.

Oxford bowed to Elizabeth and moved to his right. Another door opened and Shackspear was thrust into the room. He nearly fell over himself bowing to the Queen as a servant pushed him across the room Burghley stepped forward.

"The playhouses are for bawds. They corrode the common good, promote the work of the devil, and spread disease. Last night the 'disease' came to Gray's Inn. The 'pestilence' was brought into an institution in the heart of London that girds the very civilization that we enjoy here in England. The effect on the young men last night will be difficult to erase, but we shall triumph over evil, as we always do."

Queen Elizabeth interrupted. "I liked not the rioting. The performance of this play was against everything I stand for."

"Hear, hear," Burghley murmured in agreement.

Elizabeth looked at Oxford. "I order you to stop writing and suddenly there is a new playwright in town whose plays sound very much like yours. It takes very little effort to realize that you are the author of these new plays, not him," she said, waving a painted fingernail at Shackspear, who nearly fainted when he heard that the Queen did not think he had written the *Comedy of Errors*. "Did you really think you could get this mountebank from Warwickshire to play-act as author and no one would notice?"

Shackspear blinked. He wasn't sure he liked being called a mountebank, even by the Queen. He wasn't even sure what a mountebank was. Oxford, for his part, was enjoying Shackspear's confusion. He leaned toward him and whispered loud enough for Elizabeth to hear him: "She knows it was me because she has many eyes and ears, and very long arms."

"And thank God I do," Elizabeth nearly shouted. "Otherwise you and other rabble in my kingdom would be doing things I would not know of."

"Like impersonating foreign dignitaries so expertly that she knew not it was me!" Oxford explained to Shackspear, as he continued to act like the two of them were sharing a good story the others in the room could not hear. Shackspear, for his part, was horrified that Oxford was using him to gibe at the Queen.

Elizabeth banged her fist on the arm of her chair.

"Why dost thou constantly gall me?"

Oxford bowed. Such movements were a silent language that newcomers took years to understand. They were a ballet that could communicate many levels of meaning in a single gesture. Oxford's bow was sincere. The Queen realized he was done with being flippant.

"A thousand pardons," he said, lowering his voice to sound both respectful and deferential. "I went too far. Thinking I was about to be executed, speaking figuratively if not in fact, I thought it mattered little what I said to the executioner."

"You think it does?" Elizabeth asked archly.

"You had no need to order me here today if your only purpose was to rage at me for penning two trivial theater pieces. You could have banned me from the court and had your servants drop me at the Fleet Prison."

"A not unpleasant idea."

Burghley uttered a sound like the lowest register in a pipe organ. Shackspear was flopping around in front of them like a fish in the bottom of a boat. Part of him wanted to run; the other part kept telling him to stay where he was. The Queen looked down at him.

"Oh, get out," she said. Shackspear bolted for the door. Elizabeth turned back to Oxford. She reached down and pulled up a slim book. "*The Arte of English Poesie*," she said, opening it. Oxford sighed. He knew what was coming. "I am most upset over the riotous behavior at Gray's Inn last night. While I attempt to govern my subjects, books declare I have failed."

She turned to a page near the beginning of the book. "Here is a book by a publisher who claims he does not know the author but which 'was intended to please our Sovereign Lady the Queen, and for her recreation and service chiefly devised.' This unknown author writes that there are 'many notable gentlemen in the Court that have written commendably, and suppressed it again, or else suffered it to be published without their own names. There are sprung up a crew of Courtly makers, Noblemen and Gentlemen of Her Majesty's servants, who have written excellently well as it would appear if their doings could be found out and made public with the rest, *of which number is first that noble gentleman Edward Earl of Oxford!.*'"

She closed the book. "I tell you no more plays and you get that Warwickshire hack to be your visor. You write a play that likens a woman's parts to countries, the performance of which literally brings down the house! To add insult to injury, Richard Field comes out and identifies you as the best writer in my court!"

"Field is from Stratford, Your Majesty," Oxford went on casually. "He may even be a relative of Shackspear's."

Elizabeth's eyebrows rose. "So, is this part of your plot against me?" Her voice took on a darker, more threatening tone.

Oxford became serious. "I had no knowledge that Mr. Field would print a book heaping praise on me, Your Majesty, and would have asked him to forgo the honor had I known."

"But he had obviously seen *The Comedy of Errors*. Why did you go against our wishes and command?" She tilted her head back the way a scorpion does before it strikes.

"I wanted to be admired, Your Majesty, even if I was unknown. I wanted to see if my efforts outshined those of other writers penning plays for the stage."

Burghley harrumphed. "To live by writing plays is a disgrace. It is not commerce, like the monopolies in wine or tin. It is art. Art is degraded if it be rewarded by lucre."

"No 'lucre' has touched my hands, my lord. And I received no 'praise' either, because I am not identified as the author."

"Regardless," Burghley went on, "Her Majesty did not intend that you could circumvent her order by simply changing the name of the author on the title page."

"Why not?" Elizabeth asked, surprising them both. She got up and walked into the middle of the room. "With the Armada defeated, those who want to harm our person will redouble their efforts to find someone in England to end my reign. The Spanish would have succeeded this year if God had not sent a storm to scatter their ships."

"With all due deference, Your Majesty," Oxford said, "the Spanish were turned back by stout English seamen, like those who crewed the *Bonaventure*."

"It was the storm," she said, making it clear that she would hear no more about brave English seamen. "Next time there will be no storm. We must come up with ways to stop the Spanish at our beaches and, at the same time, reduce the number of those who would harm us. My people receive information from two sources: the playhouse and the pulpit. A third source has now appeared: pamphlets written by someone who calls himself Martin Marprelate."

Oxford volunteered his opinion immediately. "Rank heresy, Your Majesty. I have read one."

"Many would disagree with you, my lord. So far, his slanders against our person have gone unrebutted. My churchmen are of no help; they believe it is beneath their dignity to debate him."

Oxford stepped forward. "Your Majesty," he said, bowing.

She studied him for a moment. "We have need of a response, but it must come from persons who will not be seen as speaking directly for us."

"They will be loyal subjects," Oxford said, "incensed by the libels printed by this scurrilous priest."

"Loyal, yes," the Queen said, "but anonymous."

"I know anonymous."

"I will entrust you with the carrying out of this policy."

"I am deeply honored."

Burghley was suddenly apprehensive. He stepped forward. "Do not lay the serpent before the fire, Your Majesty, lest you awaken it from its sleep."

Oxford's eyes flashed. Elizabeth set off walking, silencing them both with a gesture of her hand.

"That leaves the playhouse. We are not pleased with the present fare. *Tamburlaine* glorifies a shepherd who rises from nothing to rule the world. Rulers should come from noble families. Robert Greene tries to emulate Marlowe by recycling goddesses. Kyd gives us Hieronimo, who would have become king had he not killed everyone within arm's reach. But what is worse is that none of these plays show our glorious history. Holinshed in his *Chronicles of England, Scotland, and*

*Ireland*, has provided all the stories a playwright needs, yet no one has come forward to pick up the challenge."

Oxford went down on one knee. "I know one who can."

The Queen looked down at him, a smile flickering across her face. "Always so modest," was all she said.

"Your Majesty," Burghley began again, but Elizabeth let him know that she would brook no interruption.

"Rest easy, my Lord Burghley. Your family's reputation shall remain intact." She walked back to her chair and sat down. "Come here," she said to Oxford. "Listen carefully. You will arrange to have pamphlets written that will have my people laughing at Martin Marprelate."

"'Twill be done, Your Majesty."

"In return, I will allow you to write plays for the stage, *provided* no one knows you are the author. Your visor, now trembling in the hall outside, will be the author, not you."

Oxford, surprised, agreed.

"Furthermore, you will write history plays. I want to see Talbot fresh-bleeding on the stage. I want to hear my people shouting 'huzzah' when Henry V conquers the French at Agincourt. Do you understand?"

"I do."

"I expect these efforts will require a certain amount of money, which I know you do not have. You will need to pay the authors of the pamphlets and finance the plays that will tell our history on the stage. Since the money your father left you is gone, some assistance must be provided."

"Your Majesty," Burghley protested, but she waved him silent again.

"If you are agreeable to these terms, I will provide you with a stipend of £1,000 annually, payable in quarterly installments."

"Your Majesty!" Burghley gasped. "Such largess has never been awarded to any peer of the realm."

"If my Lord of Oxford's resources are limited," she went on without looking at Burghley, "it may be due to the management of his estates while he was in your care as a royal ward. Some have noted that, while my Lord of Oxford's worth declined, yours increased."

Burghley's face went red. "I have never misused my Lord of Oxford's funds," he began, but Elizabeth interrupted him again.

"Soothe yourself, my lord," she said. "Some of the revenue I now give to Lord Oxford will be used for the maintenance of your three grandchildren, who you now support alone."

This caught Burghley off guard. The thought that some of the money would benefit him dampened his opposition. On his part, Oxford heard a command that he use part of the annuity for his daughters. Oxford and the Queen both knew that Burghley's love of wealth might exceed his love for his children in some circumstances. The Queen continued.

"I will backdate the annuity to the first of the year to increase the funds you start with." She waved a hand and a servant brought her a document. She examined it, then returned it to the servant. "Read this to Lord Oxford," she commanded. The servant held the document at arm's length and began to read it:

> *Elizabeth, etc., to the Treasurer and Chamberlains of our Exchequer, Greeting. We command you of Our treasure being and remaining from time to time within the receipt of Our Exchequer, to deliver and pay, or cause to be delivered and paid, unto Our right trusty and well beloved Cousin the Earl of Oxford or to his assigns sufficiently authorized by him, the sum of One Thousand Pounds good and lawful money of England. The same to be yearly delivered and paid unto Our said Cousin at four terms of the year by even portions: and so to be continued unto him during Our pleasure, or until such time as he shall be by Us otherwise provided for to be in some manner relieved; at which time Our pleasure is that this payment of One Thousand Pounds yearly to Our said Cousin in manner above specified shall cease. And for the same or any part thereof, Our further will and commandment is that neither the said Earl nor his assigns nor his executors nor any of them shall by way of account, imprest, or any other way whatsoever be charged towards Us, our heirs or successors. And these Our letters shall be sufficient warrant and discharge in that behalf. Given under our Privy Seal at Our Manor of Greenwich, the six and twentieth day of June in the thirty-first year of Our reign.*

Burghley's shoulders slumped.

Elizabeth motioned for the servant to give the document to Oxford. "You realize, Edward, that by entering into this bargain, you are giving your soul to Shackspear."

"If I am allowed to write, Your Majesty, my soul shall be in my words, so give me my soul now, and be damned with what happens afterwards!" He seized the quill from the servant and scrawled his signature across the bottom of the document.

The servant took the document back to the Queen, whose eyebrows rose.

"Seven checks?" she said. "A crown?"

"With a line through it."

"Which means?"

"I am *not* king."

"No, you are not."

She looked like she was about to explode. Oxford hurried on. "Your Majesty may recall that Sir Philip Sidney carried a shield in the 1581 tournament with the word ~~SPERAVI~~ on it. He did this to show that any hope he had of inheriting the Earl of Leicester's estate had been dashed by the birth of a son to the earl's wife."

"So you borrowed the idea from Sir Philip?"

"No, he borrowed it from me. And I got the idea from you."

"From me?" Her eyes widened.

"When you and I were closer, you promised to marry me. You said you would make me King of England. If you had, I would have been Edward VII. However, you decided otherwise. Since then, I have signed my name with seven checks below my name and a crown with a line through it to show the world that I am *not* king of England, which has been the most significant event, or *non*-event, of my life."

Elizabeth gasped. Her most senior earl had crafted a signature that bordered on treason. Her head spun. He would *never* have been more than consort, no matter how many titles she gave him, and he knew it, yet here he was blithely claiming he would have been king! She could not imagine another peer thinking of such an outrageous idea, much less using it on an official document she would see, and the very one that awarded him an annual pension of £1,000! She felt dizzy. "Why do I always get two when I see only one," she said, more to herself than to him.

"Your Majesty?"

"One moment you are the man who out-performed everyone else at tilts and tournaments, who spoke sweet discourse, and flowered into a man worthy of his noble birth; the next moment you are a jackdaw sitting on a fence cawing at the world as it goes by."

Oxford tried to look offended but couldn't. A feeling of elation was sweeping over him: "She is going to let me write plays!" It was like apple brandy rising through him on a cold winter day, or the thrill of seeing the geese come into view.

Elizabeth was wondering whether she had made a mistake in asking him to help her. He reminded her of the red stallion she used to ride at Hatfield when she was a girl. Given his head, the stallion would fly over the countryside, but he was unpredictable and threw her more than once. She was advised to ride another horse and she never got on the red stallion again. Oxford had given her the same type of excitement but he was just as unpredictable. She was about to cancel the entire arrangement when she reminded herself she needed a reply to Martin Marprelate as well as plays about English kings. She handed the warrant back to the servant, her lidded eyes telling Oxford what she thought of his signature.

"Shackspear is to know nothing of this. If he finds out, the annuity I hereby give you, *despite your seditious signature*, will be canceled."

Oxford nodded.

She turned to a servant at the door. "Bring Shackspear back in."

A thoroughly frightened Shackspear was led into the room. "Come here," she said. Shackspear, clutching his hat to his chest, shuffled over to a spot a half-dozen feet in front of Elizabeth. She looked him up and down. "I am told you wish to be an actor."

Shackspear, surprised, nodded yes.

"I am going to ask you to play the greatest role anyone could ever play. I am giving Lord Oxford permission to write plays for the theater on the condition that you are listed as the author." Shackspear's jaw dropped. "No one else can know about this, *ever*," she continued, leaning in toward him. "Do you understand?"

Shackspear looked at Oxford and back at the Queen, who was watching him intently. "Yes, Your Majesty."

"Can you keep this secret?"

Shackspear nodded. "To my grave," he said, crossing himself, his hat flapping back and forth across his chest like he was beating a rug.

"In your role as author, you will supervise the performances of the plays. Lord Oxford will provide money to help with costs of production. As author, you will be asked questions. Don't answer them. Smile and let your inquisitors answer their own questions, for their answers will always be better than yours. What say you?"

"I agree, Your Majesty."

"And if you are found out, there will be no more plays with your name on them." Shackspear nodded. "It is a figure in rhetoric that drink, being poured out of a cup into a glass, by filling the one doth empty the other. Lord Oxford shall be the cup; you shall be the glass. For everyone agrees that ipse is he: you are not ipse; he is."

Shackspear blinked. He had no idea what she was talking about.

Elizabeth gestured to Burghley. "Escort Master Shackspear out." Burghley took this as a suggestion to leave. He was ready to go.

"With Your Majesty's permission," he said, a touch of disapproval in his voice.

Burghley and Shackspear left the room. Elizabeth turned to Oxford.

"More humor," she said, "and fewer tragical speeches."

"But how does Your Majesty know about my plays, seeing as your attendance at the theater has not been noted."

"Timothie Bright used to take notes for me in the shorthand he invented," Elizabeth said. "He got the gist of what he saw but it always took two or three transcripts to come up with a whole play, and even then there were errors. Walsingham found a Flemish student who had perfect recall but he died of the plague. Henry V," she said. "Your first subject."

"Our greatest king," Oxford said, bowing low, "before we had our greatest Queen."

"Since I am England's first and *only* queen, your words bring gifts that are instantly withdrawn. 'Tis ever thus with you."

"Ever."

"Stop it! I know not how many languages you speak when we think you speak but one." She waved him out.

"As I thought Your Majesty spoke when we spoke as one." He was giddy.

Elizabeth looked at him sharply.

Oxford bowed. "With your permission," he said. She held up a hand to stop him.

"Nothing about me."

Oxford nodded.

"*Nothing*," she repeated. "And I mean it."

Oxford nodded again.

"Nothing." He had a mischievous grin on his face.

"Oh, get out!" Elizabeth said, suppressing a smile. She told herself she must be queen despite his attempts to take her back to earlier times when the word 'nothing' referred to a very private part of her body.

Oxford ran into Burghley coming back in to the room. The older man was in a foul mood. He thought Oxford had been meeting with the Queen behind his back. He was convinced that Elizabeth was incapable of coming up on her own with the idea of letting Oxford write plays.

"You have been having intercourse with the Queen," he fumed.

"Yes. Many times."

"I thought so," Burghley said, missing the meaning of Oxford's remark.

"By God, Burghley, I shall skewer you on my pen before I'm done and leave you wriggling on the page for people to laugh at down the centuries!"

"And who will care," Burghley said. "When they put you in the ground—and God bless that day—your name will go with you. You will be forgotten."

"Oh, no I won't."

Oxford opened the door and glanced back to see if Elizabeth was watching. She was. The faint smile on her face told him he was a rogue, and she loved him for it.

## ~ 19~
## The Boar's Head

Oxford leaped off the wherry onto Fisherman's Wharf. He was ecstatic: the Queen said he could write plays. But who could he share his good fortune with? People swirled around him, gentry climbing in and out of boats, fishermen landing their catches, but he might as well have been alone in the middle of an empty field for all they meant to him.

"I'll to the Boar's Head," Oxford said to himself, fending off a fishmonger whose large basket of sole was about to take his head off.

The Boar's Head was almost empty. Peaches brought him a tankard of ale. She smiled as she turned to leave and he smiled back, but he couldn't celebrate his good fortune with her. She did not like plays. "I seen one," she'd told him once, her pretty nose wrinkling: "I didn't like it."

Should he go to Oxford Court, he wondered? Nigel would be happy for him but have no sense of what it meant other than the money. Lady Mary, the Countess of Pembroke, would also be pleased, and for better reasons, but she was far away on her estate at Wilton. Anne Vavasor would have rewarded him handsomely, but the price he would have to pay for seeking her praise was too much.

He took a sip of beer. Had he pushed everyone away? Nan? Anne Vavasor? The Queen? His children? Everyone? Was there no one left?

He suddenly felt very old. He was almost 40. How had this happened so fast? What had he done with all those years? Penned a few silly plays? Sold his estates and spent all his money? Cut people with words? How could the most senior lord in England, more learned and witty than anyone in Elizabeth's court, find himself completely alone? Everyone he had ever met began filing by his mind's eye, smiling or frowning, winking or throwing kisses, glaring or shouting. He was an island in the middle of a sea of people, like he was at a play, looking in but not a part of what was going on. He truly had no one. Burghley had his Mildred, Earl John, his Dorothy. Even John Lyly had his Gretchen, though he paid a dear price for her.

"But the Queen is also alone," Oxford suddenly thought. This gave him comfort. He imagined Elizabeth standing in one of her rooms thinking about him as she looked across the Thames toward

London, their two souls communing across the water, each equally alone. They finally had something in common.

He sighed. He drained the tankard in front of him and stood up. Time to go, but where? He headed for the door, which flew open as he got there, nearly knocking him over. Falstaff filled the doorway, dripping wet from the rain that had started to fall.

"My lord!" Falstaff exclaimed, pushing into the inn and showering Oxford with water like a spaniel just returned from the river with a bird. "How went the audience with the Queen?"

"Well," Oxford began, but Falstaff put his arm over Oxford's shoulders and steered him back into the tavern. He pushed Oxford onto a bench and sat down opposite him. "Tell me *all* about it," he said.

Oxford's tankard was still where he had left it. Before he could reach for it, Peaches appeared and refilled it. She put a full one down in front of Falstaff. He tried to grab her but she wriggled away from him. He laughed and hoisted the tankard, draining it in one long, noisy gulp.

"Ah," he said, wiping his mustache when he was done. "But now I have my lord here, just back from the Queen. And looking very strange, I must say. She could not bar you from writing plays any more 'cause she's already done that. So what'd she take away this time?" He reached under the table and tried to grab Oxford's private parts.

"My wife took those years ago."

"Tut, tut," Falstaff said, wagging his head. "No philosophee. Too early in the day for that kind of noise. So?"

Oxford was trying not to grin. His attempts made him look silly, which puzzled Falstaff even more. Big John cocked his head and glowered at Oxford, as if to say, *I'm not going to ask again. What happened?*

"She says I can write plays," Oxford finally said, a broad grin breaking out across his face. "As long as Shackspear gets the praise," he quickly added.

Falstaff was now thoroughly confused. "Is that good?"

"Good *and* bad. I get to write but he gets the praise."

"Tut the pronunciamentos of old men!" Falstaff exclaimed. "This is a bountiful barricado! You've slipt into Troy, my boy. The city is yours."

"Troy?" Oxford asked. He was the one now confused.

"The world of playwriting!" Falstaff announced. He leaned forward. "You are Agamemnon. The Queen is your goddess, who has opened the door to the city of plays. You will slip into the city by hiding inside the Trojan Horse, or, shall I say, the '*Horse known as Shackspear*.'" He put his head back and laughed at the image. "The plays will come spewing out! And someday soon you will be hailed as the true author of the plays!" Here he imitated a trumpet, blaring so loudly that Oxford had to put his hands over his ears. Falstaff stopped.

Oxford looked up at him, frowning. "'Spewing'? A 'Horse known as Shackspear'?"

"An Ass known as Shackspear, then?"

"Ridiculous," Oxford snorted, but whether it was the elation at being allowed to write plays or the silliness of Falstaff's image, a grin began to spread across his face.

"*Aha!*" Falstaff cried. "Even the Earl of Oxford appreciates my 'literary' efforts!"

Oxford shook his head, but the silly grin was frozen on his face.

"Peaches, my lass!" Falstaff called out. "More beer. And food! We need food!" Peaches came up, ready to take his order. "Fetch the fattest humble bee from Lord Burghley's garden and snip off its honey bags," he began, but she groaned and started for the kitchen. "Okay, okay," Falstaff said, clutching her skirt to keep her from escaping. "Some of your roast beef, then, if there be no humble bee honey today. Some oysters on spinach with capers while we wait for the roast beef, and a mermaid pie of eel, pork, and spices to push the roast beef down!"

Peaches headed for the kitchen. Falstaff turned back to Oxford.

"There's more," Oxford said.

"More?" Falstaff asked, his eyebrows rising. He took a long sip on his beer, signaling he would make no more interruptions. His feet, however, were drumming on the floor.

"Elizabeth signed an order that I receive an annual pension from the Exchequer in four quarterly installments, backdated to the beginning of the year."

"How much?"

"One thousand pounds."

The big man sat straight up. "Son of a glover! A thousand pounds! *A thousand pounds!*"

Oxford put up a hand. "To be used by me to finance plays, and to pay Lyly and the others to write replies to the pamphlets being printed by Martin Marprelate."

Falstaff was so thrilled that he began to bounce up and down in his seat, sliding off the bench into the aisle where he began dancing. For a large man, he was surprisingly nimble.

"Will you sit down?"

"Can't help it. Sorry." He forced himself back into his seat. "When the good times roll, the fat man rolls with them!" He winked at Oxford. "Plays, and money to pay your bills. What more could you ask for?" Here he suddenly stopped. "Who else knows about this?"

"Only you."

"Not even Shackspear?"

"No, He's not to be told."

"Good. If it gets out that you have money, everyone will start pestering you." He sounded like he was talking from experience.

"I'll let Nigel handle the money, so he will have to know."

"But no one else," Falstaff insisted. Before he could say more, Shackspear loomed up next to them.

"My Lord," Shackspear said excitedly. He made like he was going to slide in next to Oxford, who made it clear that Shackspear was to sit somewhere else. Shackspear tried to assume a more dignified position. "I came to see if there were any plays I could take to Henslowe."

"Do you think I wrote a play on the way back from Greenwich?"

"But Mr. Henslowe," Shackspear began again, only to be interrupted by Falstaff, who began making low growling noises.

Oxford spoke before Shackspear could ask Falstaff what he was doing. "I have decided, William, that your first name has too many syllables in it."

Shackspear's eyebrows went up.

"Too many," Falstaff said, resuming the low growling sounds.

"Too many?" Shackspear asked in a high voice. He sounded like a wounded lark in a barn trying to escape from two cats below him.

"Yes," Oxford said. "*Will-Eye-Um*. Three syllables. You haven't done enough yet to have a name with three syllables in it. I am I, not you, so I will take the 'I' from the middle of your name. You will be 'Willum' until I decide otherwise."

Falstaff was now both growling and snorting as he tried to keep himself from laughing.

"But my name is William," Shackspear said plaintively.

"Objection!" Falstaff bellowed, scaring Shackspear.

"Sustained!" Oxford immediately cried.

Shackspear was completely confused. "It's my name," he said.

"Hearsay," Falstaff announced.

Oxford agreed. "You only know your name is William, I mean Willum, because someone told you so. That is hearsay."

"Which is inadmissible," Falstaff said gravely.

Shackspear was about to ask what suit in law or equity had declared his name inadmissible but then thought better of it.

"Willum," he said. "Well, I've been called worse."

"By your friends, no doubt," Oxford said.

Shackspear showed no reaction to this. "Is there nothing I can tell Mr. Henslowe about the next play?"

"*The Famous Victories of Henry the Fifth*," Oxford announced. "By order of the Queen!"

Falstaff blew his imaginary trumpet again.

Shackspear blinked. "Good. Good. But, after that?"

Oxford rounded on him. "Art thou not a lover of English history?"

"Of course I am, my lord, but the playgoers want to see comedy. Make them laugh!" he said. He punched the air in front of him.

"You mean," Oxford asked in astonishment, "that comedy should appear in a history play?"

"No, no, I mean, write a history play for the Queen, and a comedy for William!" He blinked. "Willum, I mean."

"Hmmm," Oxford said. He turned to Falstaff. "Can a history play have comedy in it?"

"Why not?"

"I don't think so, my lord," Shackspear said, starting to look worried. "A comedy. Maybe twins again."

"No, I'm done with twins. How about friendship and love, infidelity and treachery, and the way people act when they fall in love."

The thin smile on Shackspear's face showed that he was not very impressed. "And a servant who has a dog named Crab."

"A dog named Crab? Oh, I like that, my lord. It's a shame that Tarlton is dead these past twelve months. He would have been perfect for the role. He's done a bit with a dog, he has, and had the ladies' eyes pouring tears onto the ground."

"I thought you might play the dog."

"Let me play the dog," Falstaff interrupted. "I can run sidewise, like a dog named Crab must've done, and bark most excitedly."

"Well," Shackspear said, "it sounds wonderful. "How long will it take?"

"To finish them both?" Oxford asked.

"Either one," Shackspear said hopefully.

"Months," Oxford replied. He sounded as if someone had died.

So did Shackspear. "Well, fare thee well, my lord, and you, too, Sir John. I will visit you at Oxford House to see how the play, uh, plays, are coming."

"You will do nothing of the sort. If you so much as show your bladder face in Candlewick Street again, my dog here," he said, pointing to Falstaff, "will remove your stones from your crotch!"

Shackspear started backward as Falstaff started to howl and reach over the end of the table to grab Shackspear, who jumped away.

"My lord," he wailed. "You jest too much."

"Willum," Oxford said, seriously. "If you want to play author, ye must learn to take it."

"Yes, my lord."

"Ye need to laugh more," Falstaff said solicitously, a serious look on his face. "Get rid of those dark bags under yer eyes." He turned his head and showed Shackspear a broad grin, his yellow teeth leaping out between his thick lips. "Like mine."

"Yes, yes," Shackspear said. He bowed and headed for the door.

Falstaff watched him go. "His skin is not thick enough to take every caliver you fire at him, my lord."

"Money will make him crawl, Sir John, and his skin is tough. My abuse of him will be my fee for seeing his name on the plays I write."

# ~ 20 ~
## Oxford Court – The Next Morning

To Richard Field in Blackfriars," Oxford said to Robin as the two of them came out of the library. "You have your list?

"I do, my lord."

"I want *The Arte of English Poetry* and the second edition of Ovid's *Metamorphoses*. Richard has just printed them both."

"Another Ovid?" Robin asked. He picked up Oxford's copy of the 1567 edition from where it lay peeking out from underneath the papers that littered the top of the table. Robin thumbed the pages of the book like it was a deck of cards. "This one is dog-eared, my lord, but still serviceable. Why do you want another copy?"

"Lord Burghley did not like the original, which was done by my uncle, Arthur Golding, while Arthur was my tutor at Cecil House. Burghley thought Arthur's translation was too loose and I am worried that Burghley may have convinced Richard to make changes. I told Richard I will have the Stationers Company on him if he does."

Robin turned to leave.

"Wait! One more." Oxford took the sheet of paper out of Robin's hand and scribbled "*The History of the Damnable Life and Deserved Death of Doctor John Faustus*" on it. "I want to see how much Marlowe borrowed when he wrote *Faust*. If he borrowed much, he is less of an author than London thinks he is. If he borrowed little, or twisted what is there into his immortal Helen …" Oxford stood there, looking through a window at the end of the hall. Robin waited. The two men stood immobile for a few moments before Oxford came back to life. "If he did, he is the genius people claim he is. Out with you!" he cried, pushing Robin toward the door. It opened before he could get there, admitting John Lyly, who walked past Robin without acknowledging him.

"My lord, I came as soon as I heard. As the doves coo when the sun is warm, friends flock together to hear your dulcet tones."

"You think I have money."

"I thought you would not send for me unless you had *something*," he said, starting to look worried. "But how could you have any money? You sold all your estates!"

"Not all, my old friend." Oxford put his arm on Lyly's shoulder and steered him into the library. "I need you to write a reply to Martin Marprelate. His *Epistle* has been followed by a new pamphlet called *The Protestation of Martin Marprelate*."

"I know it not, but his prior works burned my ears to read them."

"Here is his latest." Oxford handed Lyly a ragged pamphlet. "I will pay you well, but you must be silent about my involvement in this. I never gave you the pamphlet or commissioned your response."

Lyly nodded.

"In addition, you will pen a comedy that I will lay out for you. Again, it will be published as yours. I will have no connection with it. Again, you shall be well paid for your effort."

Lyly smiled, reminding Oxford of the little man who had been his secretary years earlier. Lyly had aged in the interim—his skin was beginning to look like cracked plaster in an abandoned house—but it could not mask the eagerness that was still there. "What shall it be?" Lyly asked, eyes bright.

"Endymion."

Lyly grabbed a quill out of the inkpot in front of him and scribbled down the name. Oxford began to dictate.

"Endymion confesses that he has fallen in love with the Moon goddess, Cynthia."

"The Queen?" Lyly asked, looking up. The worried look had returned.

"Of course not."

"Thank goodness. I don't want to go to jail again."

Oxford went on. "Cynthia is cool to Endymion's passion, she being a goddess and he being mortal. There is another woman who also loves Endymion. This second woman resents the fact that Endymion is in love with Cynthia. She hires a sorceress to put Endymion into a deep sleep. Cynthia comes upon Endymion but doesn't know why Endymion is asleep. A magic fountain tells her she must kiss Endymion to wake him."

Lyly's pen flew across the page. He looked up. "And?"

"She kisses him and he awakens. The play will end with everyone getting married, except for Endymion, who cannot marry Cynthia because she is a goddess and too far above his station."

"You are *sure* this is not about the Queen?"

"Do you want the money?"

"Well, with the marriages, it is at least a comedy."

"You will have a magic fountain that speaks," Oxford said. This made Lyly smile. "Write something about fairies. She loves them."

"I thought you said this was not about the Queen."

"I did. It isn't."

Lyly screwed up his face. "You had something about fairies in *The Comedy of Errors*."

"So I did:

> *We talk of goblins, owls, and elvish sprites:*
> *If we obey them not, this will ensue,*
> *They'll suck our breath, or pinch us black and blue.*

"How about this?" Lyly asked:

> *Pinch him, pinch him, black and blue,*
> *Saucy mortals must not view*
> *What the Queen of Stars is doing,*
> *Nor pry into our fairy wooing.*

"Excellent!" Oxford said.

"This is like old times. Work with me on this, your lordship."

"I have another play to write. Two, in fact, but will hand one of them to another."

"The man called Shackspear?"

Oxford started to disagree, but then shrugged. "Yes. A new light from Stratford, the one on the Avon."

"We hear his plays but when we hear him speak …"

"He speaks with his pen, not his voice."

"Ah. But where is the comedy in this play?" Lyly asked, pointing to the pages in front of him. "There must be more than weddings."

"There is a noble knight named Sir Tophas who thinks he is the paragon of virtue and manliness, though he hunts only swallows and insects. Pick up your pen and listen to what he says. He is speaking to two servants he has decided to kill:

Samias:   *Sir Tophas, spare us.*

Tophas: *You shall live. You, Samias because you are little; you, Dares, because you are no bigger; and both of you, because you are but two; for commonly I kill*

> *by the dozen, and have for every particular adversary*
> *a peculiar weapon. [He displays his weapons.]*

Samias: *Say we know the use, for our better skill in war?*

Tophas: *You shall. Here is bird-bolt for the ugly beast, the blackbird.*

Dares: *A cruel sight.*

Tophas: *Here is the musket for the untamed, or (as the vulgar sort term*
*it) the wild mallard.*

Samias: *O desperate attempt!*

Tophas: *Here is spear and shield, and both necessary:*
*the one to conquer, the other to subdue or overcome the*
*terrible trout, which, although he be under the water, yet*
*tying a string to the top of my spear and an engine of iron*
*to the end of my line, I overthrow him, and then herein I*
*put him.*

"This is very good," Lyly said, not looking up as his pen sped across the page.

"Sir Tophas will keep the audience laughing while Endymion sleeps away on the stage."

"A most curious work," Lyly remarked.

"You will be well-paid."

"Then I will well-write," Lyly said, gathering in the papers he had been writing on.

"But render the reply to Martin Marprelate first," Oxford said. "Anthony will draw pence for another broadside against the rogue. Bring your contribution tomorrow. Will you have it by then?"

"I will, my lord. And even though *Endymion* is not a comedy about Cynthia, you will put in a good word for me if she decides it is?"

"Of course. But she will know it is my gift to her for a kindness done to me. It's your opportunity to run riot with words, my little man, as only you can."

"Oh, my lord," Lyly said, his face beaming, as he headed for the hall. "I'll make her sing …" but Oxford, nodding yes and yes, propelled him out the front door.

# ~ 21 ~
## The Trunk of Plays

Robin returned that afternoon, his arms full of books wrapped in old paper. He hurried in to the library where he dumped them on the table.

"I was unable to get the *Faust* book," said Robin. "Abel Jeffes is on the continent buying new books and won't be back until next week."

"This is food enough," Oxford said, arranging the books in front of him.

"Mr. Field was glad of your business and asked me to commend him to you, which I do now," he said, doing a quick bow.

"I am sure he did." Oxford picked up one of the books and looked at the cover. "*Menaphon*," he said. "A new effort by our old friend, Robert Greene." Oxford opened the book and began turning pages. "A lengthy preface: *To the Gentleman Students of Both Universities* by Thomas Nashe." He turned the book over. "Who is Thomas Nashe?"

"I know him not, my lord. Master Fields recommended the book, not the preface."

"I've seen the book in manuscript," Oxford said. He began paging through the preface. "It appears that Mr. Nashe is eager to tell the world that he disdains those who think they can '*out-brave better pens with the swelling bombast of bragging blank verse.*' Oh, rich. '*Bragging blank verse.*' He is new from Cambridge and obviously studied under Gabriel Harvey. Wait, it gets better."

> *Yet English Seneca read by Candlelight yields many good*
> *sentences, as Blood is a begger, and so forth; and if you entreat*
> *him faire in a frostie morning, he will afford you whole*
> *Hamlets, I should say handfuls of Tragicall speeches.*

"Oh, my lord," Robin said.

"So Mr. Nashe has heard of *Hamlet*. Does he know it's mine? He won't come right out and say. The libel laws in England are very strict." He returned to Nashe's preface. "So who is Mr. Nashe aiming at?" His eyes sped over the pages. "Ah, the quarry is in sight:

> *The Sea exhaled by drops will in continuance be dry, and*
> *Seneca, at length must needes die to our Stage; which makes his*
> *famished followers to imitate the Kid in Æsop.*

"Mr. Kyd," Robin said.

"Confirmed by the following," Oxford said. "'*Sufficeth them to bodge vp a blanke verse with ifs and ands.*'" He looked at Robin. "*The Spanish Tragedy*. And Mr. Nashe should have added 'buts' to his list as well."

"'Buts?'" Robin asked.

"Mr. Kyd 'bodged up' his play with 'ifs' and 'ands' when he couldn't get a line right, but he used 'but' even more. There are more than two hundred and fifty 'buts' in *The Spanish Tragedy*, a hundred in the third act alone." He returned to the book but Shackspear appeared in the doorway before they could go any further. He also had a copy of *Menaphon* under his arm. He was obviously upset.

"My lord, the players are laughing at me," he said, holding up the book in his hand. "Burbage says someone named Tom Nashe is claiming that I 'bodge' up my verses with 'ifs and ands.'"

"He's talking about Kyd," Oxford said:

> **And** *with that sword he fiercely waged war,*
> **And** *in that war he gave me dangerous wounds,*
> **And** *by those wounds he forced me to yield,*
> **And** *by my yielding I became his slave.*

"But Burbage was happy to point out that I—I mean, you—did the same in *Titus:*

> *Go pack with him, and give the mother gold,*
> **And** *tell them both the circumstance of all;*
> **And** *how by this their child shall be advanced,*
> **And** *be received for the emperor's heir,*
> **And** *substituted in the place of mine.*

"That was Aaron talking. What can you expect from a blackamoor who is the essence of evil?"

Shackspear was not convinced. "I think Nashe is talking about me. I mean, you."

"Of course not. If you'd read further, you'd see that he goes on to rail at a writer who leaves the trade of noverint to try his hand at writing plays. Were you ever a noverint?" Shackspear shook his head. Oxford went on. "Was I?" Shackspear shook his head again. Lords never worked a trade.

"And Nashe says his target feeds on crumbs that fall from the translator's trencher. I've not translated anything. And you don't speak any foreign languages, so how could he be talking about you?"

Shackspear had to nod yes, then no. He was beginning to think he was the target of Oxford's words and not Nashe's.

"And Nashe goes on that the man he is talking about 'runs through every arte and thrives by none.' How old are you?"

"Five and twenty, my lord."

"And thus too young to have run through *any* art, much less *every* one. So he is obviously not talking about you."

Shackspear nodded.

"Burbage is having you on." Oxford turned back to the book in his hand. "As for this, Greene has underwhelmed us again. *Menaphon* indeed. A princess shipwrecked on the coast of Arcadia—oh that's very new—do we hear Sidney?—who disguises herself as a man."

"I hear it's been done many times."

"Yes, but Greene takes it a step further. The princess, disguised as a man, is wooed by her father *and* her son, while at the same time she carries on a love affair with her husband who is *also* disguised." He sighed. "Now, that *is* new."

"It sounds dizzying."

"Indeed. The character who gives his name to the book is a shepherd who follows the princess around like a puppy dog. The reader will discard the book before he reaches page ten."

This made Shackspear feel better. "But I came to find out how my lord fares in writing *The Famous Victories* …," but Oxford put up a hand, interrupting him.

"I am making progress. My brother-in-law, Lord Willoughby, is returning soon from France where he has just put Henri IV on the throne of France. I will write a march to celebrate his victories!"

"My lord!"

"Ta-ta," Oxford said, turning away.

"My lord," Shackspear said in a different tone. He turned and left.

After he was gone, Robin walked over to the table. "He's not going to go away, you know."

Oxford put *Menaphon* down. "Yes. Come with me. I have an idea. We'll to the trunk of plays." They climbed to the third floor. Robin had never been to the third floor. The room they entered was filled with old furniture. Oxford pulled a heavy trunk away from the wall and opened the lid. They sank to their knees. Oxford kneeled to paw through the papers in the trunk; Robin kneeled in reverence, eyes wide. "Here is the mother lode," he thought to himself. "Here is where genius sleeps."

Oxford grabbed a page and held it up. He scanned it and threw it to his left. He picked up another and did the same. Robin tried to read the pages as they were discarded but could see nothing. Oxford was throwing them aside as if they were shards of broken glass, but Robin was certain they were diamonds. Every so often, Oxford would read something from a page before he cast it aside. "*Timon*," he said at one point.

"*Timon*," Robin said, rolling the word around in his mouth.

"An effort distilled from anger. A man who gives everything to his friends who then abandon him when he has no more."

"Oh," Robin said. "A play about you," he almost said aloud.

"No female characters. No romance. Do not write from anger, Robin. Your effort will be as cold as Damascus steel on a winter morning." He threw *Timon* onto the other discarded pages.

Robin forced himself to keep silent. Oxford reached back into the trunk. "Ah, *The Contention between the Two Famous Houses of Yorke and Lancaster*." He held up a fistful of loose pages. "A juvenile effort," he said. *The Contention* joined *Timon* on the floor.

"Might I look through them, your lordship?"

"No."

"I would not think less of you, my lord."

"I would think less of me, and my name would glister no more in your mind. Besides, if you read these early efforts of mine, you would learn the wrong way to write plays." He slammed the lid shut. They rose to their feet. Robin thought his trip to the room had been wasted. To his surprise, Oxford handed him a sheaf of pages. "*The Famous Victories of Henry the Fifth*, a fledgling barely hatched out if its egg. The Queen wants history; you shall write it. Add feathers, Scribbler, and see if the heir of your first invention has wings."

"My lord," Robin stammered as he took the pages from Oxford.

"When you have something, bring it to me. I have a play to write."

## ~ 22 ~
## Oxford Court – Late September, 1589

Robin ran into Oxford's bedroom. "My lord," he said, running over to where Oxford lay on the floor tangled in blankets and sheets. "I heard this loud thump and …"

"Yes, yes," Oxford said, down on one knee as he struggled to pull the bedclothes off himself. "I was having such a good time," he said, eyes bright, looking up at Robin. "Proteus and Valentine arguing; servants pushing and shoving each other. Divine Silvia! Oh, divine Silvia!

> *What light is light, if Silvia be not seen?*
> *What joy is joy, if Silvia be not by?*
> *Unless it be to think that she is by*
> *And feed upon the shadow of perfection.*

"My lord," Robin said, pulling Oxford to his feet. "Leave off Silvia and Proteus. Come downstairs with me. Frangellica has a hot loaf of bread filled with the stew you didn't eat last night."

"Nay, nay, Robin. My head is full of nighttime enchantments that flee before the sun. Quick! Grab pen and ink! Help me capture them before they wisp out the window with the morning dew!"

Robin headed for the door, Oxford trailing behind in his nightshirt, exclaiming to the still sleeping house:

> *Except I be by Silvia in the night,*
> *There is no music in the nightingale;*
> *Unless I look on Silvia in the day,*
> *There is no day for me to look upon;*

They headed into the library. When they had captured all Oxford could recall, the two of them sat across the table from each other, Oxford bedraggled, still in his nightshirt, his head drooping.

"I love it," he said, his tired eyes trying to focus on Robin across from him. "I love it when I get it right. But I love *hearing* it even more. On the page, the black ink is lifeless; on the stage, it comes to life!" A sly look came over his face. "*Titus* was performed twelve times by the Admiral's Men. I saw every performance."

"You did? How? We none of us went with you."

141

"I couldn't go as the Earl of Oxford, could I? But as someone else? Nigel taught me how I could shift into madman's rags and assume a semblance that dogs disdained, or dress like a fop all clothed in French cuffs and ruffs. His favorite outfit is a matronly widow with broad hips who can push her way into the theater." Oxford wiggled his hips. "He calls her 'Ms. Frummage.' She's my ticket to the theater."

Robin was shocked. He couldn't imagine Oxford dressed in a wig and farthingale. Oxford was amused. "How can I be a playwright if I've never been a player?"

"But as a woman?"

"Boys play women all the time. You would be amazed how much you can learn watching men as a woman."

Robin was suddenly worried that Oxford would ask him to dress up as a woman and accompany Oxford him to the next play. Oxford saw his worry.

"You've never wanted to be someone else?"

"No, my lord."

"You should try it. It will make you a better playwright. As for *Titus,* I went back to see it to understand why it succeeded when I had done everything I could to make it fail. But I soon forgot why I had come as I became one with the audience as we followed the story I had written. The rapture they felt washed over me, a beautiful gift from them to me. Who cares whether Shackspear gets the praise as long as I can swim in a sea of love like that!"

This confession unnerved Robin. He knew his master was exhausted. He realized he had to get his lordship back to thinking about plays. "And how goes the play about the two gentleman who live in Verona?"

Oxford pursed his lips. "It's going well, and not well. Proteus and Valentine are best friends from birth.

> *I know him as myself; for from our infancy*
> *We have conversed and spent our hours together:*
> *He is complete in feature and in mind*
> *With all good grace to grace a gentleman.*

"Twins again," Robin said

"Not quite. Well, sort of."

"And the purpose?"

"To dazzle the Queen. She will recognize that the poetry for Silvia is meant for her. She will like that. But the play, softened by laughter from servants more skilled than those in *The Comedy of Errors*, will tell the story of what happens when two men fall in love with the same woman."

"A triangle," Robin said.

"Which I will complicate by making one of the men abandon his betrothed when he sees the woman his best friend is in love with."

"A cad."

"His name is Proteus."

"Then he is well-named."

"Yes. 'The Devil hath more shapes than Proteus.'"

"Who said that?"

"Arthur Golding."

"The man who translated Ovid?"

"Well, he had some help."

"How was that?"

"He was my tutor at Cecil House. I read his early draft and saw he would make Ovid dark and turgid, like everything else he wrote, so I started leaning in over his shoulder and making suggestions. He resisted at first but then began to see the value of what I thought he should add to his effort. Arthur frowns when someone mentions the *Metamorphoses* because he's embarrassed by how licentious it is, but inside he glows. He knows it's made him immortal."

"What about Proteus and Valentine?"

"They will be two sides of the same person."

Robin rolled his eyes. "I should have known. *The two gentlemen of Ver-One-A.*"

Oxford looked away. "At the beginning of the play, Proteus will be in love with Julia, a commoner. Proteus will tell Julia that Valentine, his best friend:

> *After honour hunts, I after love:*
> *He leaves his friends to dignify them more,*
> *I leave myself, my friends and all, for love.*
> *Thou, Julia, thou hast metamorphosed me.*

"But, when Proteus tells Valentine of his love for Julia, Valentine scoffs:

> *To be in love, where scorn is bought with groans;*
> *Coy looks with heart-sore sighs; one fading moment's mirth*
> *With twenty watchful, weary, tedious nights:*

*If haply won, perhaps a hapless gain;*
*If lost, why then a grievous labour won.*

"Valentine thinks he is immune to love. He goes off to Milan and promptly falls in love with Silvia." Here Oxford began to sing 'Oh, Silvia,' but stopped himself. "Silvia returns the love and the two of them make plans to elope."

"Proteus, meanwhile," Robin said, partly to bring Oxford back from Silvia, "is still in Verona mooning over Julia."

"Yes, but not for long. He is also ordered to go to Milan. He leaves a heartbroken Julia behind him but, as soon as he gets to Milan and sees Silvia, he falls in love with her and immediately forgets Julia."

"Does Proteus tell Silvia of his love for her?"

"Of course."

Robin looked disgusted. "And does she throw over Valentine and run to Proteus?"

"She tells Proteus to go home."

"Excellent. And does he?"

"Of course not. He wants Silvia. He devises a plan to get Valentine out of the way. He tells Silvia's father what Valentine is up to. The father banishes Valentine, thus clearing the field for Proteus."

"How awful. Proteus is unfaithful to Julia *and* to his friend."

"Yes."

"And what of Julia, still languishing in Verona?"

"That's where I'm stuck. I need to bring Julia to Milan so I can get her between Proteus and Valentine, but I don't know how to do it. Young women don't pick up and go to a distant city. She needs a reason to go, as well as permission and an escort."

"Why not dress her up as a boy?" Robin asked. "She can go to Milan on her own and offer to be Proteus's page. He won't recognize her, of course. After all, it's a play. He'll think she's still in Verona."

"And Proteus will use her to carry his love messages to Silvia!"

"And Julia will stand next to him while he woos Silvia!"

"Oh," Oxford cried, reaching for pen and paper. "Oh!! The audience will cry out to her: 'Proteus! Proteus! The page is Julia!"

Robin, a warm smile on his face, leaned on the table and watched Oxford write.

## ~ 23 ~
### *Two Gentlemen of Verona*

Oxford met Robin at the bottom of the stairs. The young page was coming from the kitchen, elderberry jam on his lower lip. He fell into stride as Oxford came off the bottom of the stairs.

"And now, my young scribe, more of *Two Gentlemen* this morning," Oxford announced, moving briskly down the hall. "Are you up for it?"

"Aye," Robin answered enthusiastically. He looked up at the heads that lined the hall as they headed for the library. "You must tell me someday, my lord, who shot these animals, and how their heads came to be mounted above us."

Oxford slowed. "The elk," he said, twisting to look up, "was brought down by my grandfather, the Fifteenth Earl. The boar over the front door was killed in France by my father, Earl John."

"In France?" Robin asked. "How came it to be hung here?"

"The boar came charging out of a thicket at my father. He leaped off his horse, took out the only sword he had, a 'dancing rapier' one only wears to court balls, and killed the boar with one thrust. The French were amazed. 'Tut,' my father told them as he cleaned off his sword and re-sheathed it. 'Any English schoolboy could have done as well. To fly the boar before the boar pursues were to incense the boar to follow.' The French were so impressed they had the boar's head mounted and sent to England as a memento of my father's visit."

"This was before you were born?"

Oxford nodded.

"But, my lord, if his stroke had been off an inch," Robin began.

"I wouldn't be here."

Robin gulped. "And the others?" he asked, looking up at the remaining heads.

"I have no idea," Oxford said, continuing toward the library. "No one brought me here while I lived at Hedingham. My mother disliked London and my father had no time for me. When he died, my grandfather was already dead. Thus, there was no one left to tell me how they came to be mounted above us."

They turned into the library. Oxford went around the table to the window that looked out on the garden.

"I was fourteen when Falstaff brought me here for the first time. The caretaker did not recognize me. Falstaff was outraged. He picked the fellow up by the ears, like he was a beagle that had just pissed the carpet, and told him to get the keys or he would add his head to the wall. Falstaff used the occasion to tell me I was far too friendly with people, particularly servants. I should cultivate disdain and a look that implied violence was nearby. If anyone protests, he said, say "I am that I am," which is as good a quote as any from the Bible.' I was surprised to hear Falstaff quote scripture, but he was always surprising me."

Oxford went silent again. "Departing inward," is how Nigel described such moments to Robin. After a minute, Oxford shook himself.

"Well, back to work on *Two Gentlemen*." He began to hunt for the papers left on the table the night before. "I gave up last night when I could not get a scene right."

"Which one is that, my lord?" Robin sat down at the table.

"Julia is bantering with her maid, Lucetta, who is a saucy wench. They toy with the names of different gentlemen Lucetta thinks Julia should be interested in but Julia is already in love with Proteus."

"Not knowing, of course, what a cad he is."

"Hush. You assume she will reject him when she learns how unfaithful he is."

"She doesn't?"

"You don't know women yet." He looked at the papers in his hand. "Julia cannot admit to her maid that she is in love with Proteus."

"Why not?"

"If she did, it wouldn't be a game. She gets angry with Lucetta, who has just brought her a letter from Proteus, and orders Lucetta out, then orders her to return, and eventually tears up the letter without reading it, which she immediately regrets. *O hateful hands, to tear such loving words!* She tries to put them together again: *Thus will I fold them one on another / Now kiss, contend, do what you will.* But the last line lacks two syllables! It has kept me up half the night!"

"'Embrace,' my lord," Robin suggested.

"Which means?"

"'To take or clasp in the arms, to press to the bosom, to hug.'"

"Oh, excellent. 'To clasp in the arms, to press to the bosom.' Perfect! But how came you by this word."

"From 'brace' for a pair of arms. The 'em' reinforces the wrapping of the arms."

"Like the 'm' in bosom."

"That was Sir John's suggestion.'"

"Yes. Well done, Scribbler."

Robin's face reddened.

"Any more words?"

"You mean, new ones?" Robin asked. He blinked. "No, my lord," and then rushed on when he saw the disappointment in Oxford's face. "Of course, I have to have a setting, something that spurs me on."

"Uh, huh."

"Like a scene." He did not think Oxford believed him. "I love words, my lord, I really do. I like fat, buttery words."

"Fat, *buttery* words?"

"Like oily, ooze, unctuous."

Oxford's eyebrows went up. "And?"

"Uh, sniggly words, like cowlick, gurgle, babble, and bump."

Oxford nodded. "Good words, good words all. I will charge you with bringing them to the table while I work."

"I will, my lord. Thank you, my lord."

Oxford added 'embrace' to the line he had been working on. "I can now proceed to Milan, where Valentine is wooing Silvia. Valentine has a servant named Speed who is, as usual, smarter than his master." He glanced at Robin. "Which is true only in plays, of course."

"Of course."

"Silvia had asked Valentine to write a letter for her to send to a 'secret nameless friend of hers.' Valentine can't figure out why she would want him to write a letter to someone he doesn't know. Speed laughs:

> *O excellent device! Was there ever heard a better,*
> *That my master, being scribe, to himself should write the letter?*

"The letters are intended for Valentine?"

"Yes."

Robin blinked. "So you are working on a play in which Julia tears up letters and tries to put them back together, and at the same time you have Valentine writing letters to himself, but he doesn't know it."

"Not even after Speed explains what is going on. Listen:

| | |
|---|---|
| Speed: | *Why, she woos you by a figure.* |
| Valentine: | *What figure?* |
| Speed: | *By a letter, I should say.* |
| Valentine: | *Why, she hath not writ to me?* |
| Speed: | *What need she, when she hath made you write to yourself? Why, do you not perceive the jest?* |
| Valentine: | *No, believe me.* |

Robin shook his head. "Valentine lacks wit, that's for sure. But Silvia woos him 'by a figure? By a letter'?"

Oxford had a look of mystery on his face.

Robin turned away. "Another puzzle. And if I don't cypher this out, I am Valentine and not Speed."

Oxford remained silent. Robin screwed up his face. Then he turned to Oxford. "No."

"Why not?" Oxford asked. "Can't I have fun?"

"The letters Julia tears up are your plays? And Valentine is you, writing to a reader he doesn't know?"

"And?"

"And?" Robin said, forcing himself to keep digging. "A letter and a figure? The only letter I know that is also a figure is 'O.'" A wry smile spread across his face. "Which stands for 'Oxford,' of course."

"Of course."

"And Silvia is the Queen, ordering you, Valentine, to write plays."

"Well done!"

"And Proteus is also you, the other half of the two gentlemen of Ver-One-A."

Oxford smiled.

"Are you going to do this with every play?"

"Yes. Every play. Footprints everywhere.

> *Someone, somewhere, someday will say:*
> *'The Earl of Oxford wrote this play.'*

Robin groaned. "Then we need to come up with something better than a figure and a letter."

---

They worked far into the evening. "A ladder made of cords?" Robin asked, looking up from the mess of papers scattered in front of him. His hands were covered in ink. He was puzzled. "Why doesn't Silvia just open the back door and let him in?"

"'Tis more dramatic to snatch her from her window. Plus, I need Valentine to hide the ladder under his coat where the Duke will discover it and banish him from Milan."

"And the Duke will know to look for the ladder in Valentine's coat because Proteus will tell him about it."

"Yes."

"Proteus is most awful, my lord."

"Yes."

"He has not only forsaken Julia, his betrothed, but arranged to have his best friend banished. The audience will not like him."

"No."

"But this is a comedy, isn't it? You don't want the audience to *hate* him, do you?"

Oxford did not reply. The two of them sat either side of the table without speaking. Finally, Robin spoke: "I think you should make him confused."

"Confused?"

"Yes. He's a young man, and young men are subject to certain humors more than women are."

"Oh? And what humors are those? Being a man, I need education here." Robin ignored Oxford's comment.

"Heat, most of all. Proteus sees Julia, and the heat rises in him. He then sees Silvia, and the heat she causes in him displaces his love for Julia, as one heat displaces another. He's confused."

"And how will I do that? Banners over the stage: 'Proteus languishes in heat!'?"

"No. Have him speak the anguish he feels over what he's done."

"By addressing the audience directly?"

"Yes."

Oxford shook his head. "When a performance begins, the audience and the players agree to pretend that the audience is not there. The audience acts like it's peeking through a hole in a wall."

"A hole in a wall?"

"Yes."

"Not very often, from what I've seen."

"No, but when it's a great play, such as *Titus* or *Tamburlaine*, the audience forget they're there. And, silent though they be, they are part of the performance, as any rehearsal in an empty room will show you. You urge me to have Proteus breach this wall by speaking directly to them?"

"Not to them directly, but indirectly by voicing his inner thoughts."

"Most unusual," Oxford said. "As if he were alone."

"Yes."

Oxford thought for a moment. "All right."

> *To leave my Julia, shall I be forsworn;*
> *To love fair Silvia, shall I be forsworn;*
> *To wrong my friend, I shall be much forsworn.*

"Good. Good," Robin said. He picked up his pen and began to take down Oxford's words.

> *I to myself am dearer than a friend,*
> *For love is still most precious in itself;*
> *And Silvia--witness Heaven, that made her fair!--*
> *Shows Julia but a swarthy Ethiope.*
> *I will forget that Julia is alive,*
> *Remembering that my love to her is dead;*
> *And Valentine I'll hold an enemy,*
> *Aiming at Silvia as a sweeter friend.*
> *I cannot now prove constant to myself,*
> *Without some treachery used to Valentine.*

Robin finished writing. "'*I to myself am dearer than a friend*' and '*Love is still most precious in itself.*' He loves only himself."

"Have I rescued him?"

"If he can be rescued."

"The servants shall show him up. They shall discuss the faults and virtues of a serving maid to offset the description of Silvia."

"No requests to look at Belgia, I hope."

"No Belgia, Robin. The stands will not come down when this play is performed. 'Tis intended for Silvia and will be performed at court. I will cascade poetry over her like she has never heard."

*O, how this spring of love resembleth*
*The uncertain glory of an April day,*
*Which now shows all the beauty of the sun,*
*And by and by a cloud takes all away!*

"Lovely," Robin said as his pen raced over the page, "but Shackspear will not want another *Comedy of Errors*, my lord."

"This he will like. There will be a dog in it."

"I have not seen the dog yet, my lord."

"I have not written the dog yet."

Nigel appeared at the door to the library. "Begging your pardon, my lord, word has come that Lord Willoughby has returned from France."

"That is good news!" Oxford exclaimed. "I shall now finish the March. Thank you, Nigel. Robin, you are to Willoughby House to find out when my sister plans the dinner for her husband's return. Tell her I will have Digby send her oysters from Colchester, the finest in all of England. Fat, salty, and green-finned beauties bred in pits made for the purpose at the mouth of the River Colne."

Nigel stepped back into the library as Robin went out the door. "Yes?"

"Sir Robert Cotton would like a word with you."

"About what?"

"He did not say."

"Tell him I am not interested in buying any manuscripts today."

"He said his purpose in coming was not commerce. He said he needed to talk to you about your former tutor, Mr. Laurence Nowell."

This surprised Oxford. "Let him in."

Nigel left and returned with a tall, elegantly dressed gentleman.

"Sir Robert," Oxford said, standing up.

"So sorry to bother you, my lord, but I have the unfortunate duty of handling the affairs of Mr. Nowell, who went off to the continent eighteen months ago and has not returned. His wife has filed papers to have him declared dead, and I am named his executor."

"I am so sorry."

Sir Robert nodded. He thought Oxford was expressing concern for the burden Nowell's disappearance had added to Sir Robert's life.

"To hear of Mr. Lowell's disappearance," Oxford added. "He was a brilliant man."

"Indeed."

"And your business with me?"

"I have been told that Mr. Nowell lent you a manuscript called *Beowulf*."

"*Lent* is not the proper word, Mr. Cotton: *gave* is more accurate. When Mr. Nowell was one of my tutors at Cecil House, he showed me a manuscript he had gotten from one of the monasteries Henry had dissolved. We spent some hours translating the Norse and, when he left, he gave it to me to add to my library."

"So you have it?"

"No, I sold it to Cyrus Foalger a year ago."

"Foalger?"

"The collector. You know him?"

"Yes."

"Well, then, you must seek it from him. But why the interest? Nowell thought I could turn the story into a play, but what could I do with a monster, and no women, or plot? You've missed nothing, Sir Robert. Foalger bought fool's gold."

"Hmm," Sir Robert said, a touch of disappointment in his voice. "Nevertheless, I must, as executor, seek out all I can find about the whereabouts of Mr. Nowell's estate."

"I would be willing to sign an affidavit."

"That would be very kind of you, my lord."

Sir Robert turned to leave. Oxford walked him to the door of the library. "Foalger is obsessed with Chaucer. Something by Chaucer might pry *Beowulf* out of his hands without having to pay him any money. That is, if he still has it."

"Thank you, most sincerely, my lord,"

# ~ 24 ~
## Lord Willoughby's

There was a spring in Oxford's step that Robin had not seen for some time. Tobias led them up Wood Street toward Cripplegate. Oxford was carrying "Lord Willoughby's Welcome Home" under his arm. Robin had his lute in a leather bag over his shoulder.

"I love it that my brother-in-law is back. He is the calmness to my storm. He is the silent listener to all my plaints and ideas. He is the sea into which my tears can fall and never fill him up."

"Marlowe," Robin said.

"Is it?"

"Sounds like it to me."

"Not the Earl of Oxford?"

Robin shook his head.

"Hmmm."

Robin knew his master's head was full of plots and poetry. He worried that Oxford, for lack of space, like the third floor storage room filled with mildewed furniture and "worthless" plays, was beginning to confuse what he wrote with what he had heard or read. Might it be the Achilles' heel to his master's perfect recall? Robin did not like to think his master might be ageing. "And who is Lord Willoughby, my lord?"

"He is husband to my sister Mary, who is such a shrew that any husband would become silent if he had to live with her long."

"Is that why he has been away?"

"No. Her tongue doth wag, and some have said that she should be whipped with the stick with which she whips others, but he loves her dearly. He has been abroad because the Queen likes him to be ambassador for her. Twice to Denmark, more recently, to France where he lead English troops that put Henri IV on the throne."

They were now through Cripplegate. A few blocks brought them to the Barbican district and a three-story brick-fronted house. "Willoughby House," Oxford said. Stairs led up to a lower porch. Tobias stationed himself to the right of the stairs while Oxford and Robin went up to the entrance where two servants in blue livery waited to usher them in. Oxford and Robin climbed another set of stairs where an older servant banged a wooden staff on the floor and announced the arrival of the Earl of Oxford.

"Edward de Vere, Earl of Oxford, Lord Great Chamberlain of England, Viscount Bolbec, and Lord of Badlesmere and Scales." He glanced at Robin out of the corner of his eye: "And servant." With a tip of his head, he signaled Robin to disappear into a nearby chamber, as Oxford proceeded down the splendid window-lined gallery that overlooked out over London and the Thames. Servants lined the inner wall, holding plates of oysters, beef purses, dried plums soaked in wine and ginger, and pigeon breasts roasted in pastry shells the shape of Lord Willoughby's coat of arms. Two more held trays filled with glasses of wine.

Oxford's sister, Mary, was nowhere to be seen. Peregrine Bertie, Lord Willoughby, stood halfway down the gallery on the other side of an opening that led down two steps to where a group of musicians was quietly playing. Willoughby was talking with Sir Francis Vere, Oxford's cousin, and Sir Thomas Cecil, Oxford's former brother-in-law. Sir Francis, dressed in sober browns and tans, was a lean, muscled man in his late twenties who had the look of a man who had spent a lifetime outdoors in military service. Sir Thomas was in his late thirties and looked as though he had spent his life in a dining room. He should have been his father's favorite, being the eldest, but Burghley preferred Thomas's younger brother, Robert. Thomas had learned to content himself with living on a vast estate and making himself into a country gentleman. He was dressed in a doublet, bombasted galligaskins, stockings and hat, all made of pale green brocade edged in an intricate lace. A white sash across his breast would have held a rapier if he had worn one. Lord Willoughby's open gown over a plain shirt made for a subdued contrast.

Oxford walked down the gallery toward them, downing a cold oyster and a beef purse as he went. He was pleased that he had talked Nigel out of dressing him in the new scarlet doublet Nigel had laid out for him. This wasn't the court, Oxford had explained; he did not need to impress anyone. A simple doublet and cape in deep blue was more than adequate for the occasion, particularly when Nigel, at the last minute, added the bright white French ruff.

"My lord," Oxford said, as he came up to Willoughby. "Sir Thomas, Sir Francis," he said, bowing to the men.

"My lord," they replied, bowing in return.

Oxford reached over and took a glass of wine from a servant. "A toast to the safe and successful return of my Lord Willoughby."

"Here, here," Thomas and Francis said, clinking glasses with Willoughby and Oxford.

"How doth thou?" Willoughby asked.

"Well, thank you. And congratulations, Sir Francis," Oxford said, "on being knighted for your bravery in the field."

Sir Francis demurred. Lord Willoughby spoke up for him. "Well deserved, and long overdue." Willoughby extended his glass to Sir Francis. The others followed. "Now Sergeant Major General of Her Majesty's forces in Holland."

"Indeed," Sir Thomas said. "It must give the two of you much satisfaction to have helped Henri to his throne." A smirk implied he thought the French needed all the help they could get.

"Yes, brave deeds, Sir Francis," said Oxford. "Acts that burnish the family name."

Sir Thomas leaned in toward Sir Francis. "The Queen well-liked your feats of arms," he said, letting everyone know that he was in on the latest gossip. "She said it reminded her of Sidney."

Oxford looked away. Willoughby nodded wanly. He hated court gossip. He once said he would never be a "reptilian," meaning someone who crawled on the floor to obtain favor, and the remark had not gone down well with Elizabeth. She may have sent him to Denmark and France as punishment for his frankness. Or, as someone else suggested, she realized the very quality that made him unwelcome at court was just what she needed in an ambassador to a foreign court.

"If my guests will allow me to see that the dinner is being properly set," Willoughby said. He turned toward the room where the musicians were playing. Sir Francis followed. "If I may assist," he said, following Willoughby out of the gallery and leaving Oxford and Sir Thomas alone.

"How doth thou, Sir Thomas?" Oxford asked. "I have not seen you since the celebration at St. Paul's."

"I'm in town for business. My father prefers I stay in the country while he grooms my half-brother, the worm, to take his place."

Oxford nodded sympathetically.

"You remember him whining to be picked up and claiming he couldn't run outside and play when we all knew he could." Sir Thomas sipped his wine. "Father decided I could not follow in his footsteps because my mother came from lesser stock. But look at me," he said. "How could he not think that I am a worthy successor?"

"We can't all be perfect, can we?"

"No." Cecil took another sip. "It's a burden."

The servant at the head of the stairs announced two new arrivals: "Henry Carey, Lord Hunsdon, and Miss Aemilia Bassano."

Oxford and Sir Thomas turned to look down the gallery. Lord Hunsdon had arrived at the top of the stairs. Hunsdon was sixty-two with a face the color and texture of old leather; the woman with him was still in her teens and glowed with the freshness of youth. Hunsdon stood with his shoulders back: his mother had been Mary Boleyn, mistress to Henry VIII before Henry fell in love with her sister, Anne. When Henry found out that Mary was pregnant, he married her off to a courtier and elevated her new husband to the peerage. Hunsdon was their first child. Everyone, including Hunsdon, thought Henry was his real father. If so, he was Elizabeth's half-brother; if not, he was her cousin. Either position granted him royal favors which, surprisingly, he had not abused. He grew up a gruff, hardheaded soldier who brought glory to Elizabeth's reign. Elizabeth had rewarded him accordingly. She appointed him Lord Chamberlain in July, 1585. In this position, he supervised the Office of the Revels. He had no interest in the arts himself, being a soldier who slept better in the field than in a bed, but a peer of his status was expected to be the patron of a company of players, and so he had formed Lord Hunsdon's Men. He had arrived for Lord Willoughby's dinner dressed in a military outfit without decoration, his grey jacket sprinkled with red buttons peeking out of their holes like foxes peering out of their dens.

In contrast, the young woman on his arm was an explosion of color. She wore a doublet of peach-colored satin covered with white cutwork and a kirtle of like color layered with Venice gold lace and lined with orange-colored sarcesnet. In her left hand she carried a bag of crimson taffeta that was embroidered with spangles and gold. A delicate, translucent silk veil did little to hide her lovely young face.

Hunsdon and the young lady walked down the gallery toward the two men. Sir Thomas was transfixed; Oxford was mesmerized. Her olive skin bore no traces of the white lead and vinegar that court ladies customarily hid behind. Her brown eyes were limpid pools, eyes no English woman had ever possessed. They reminded Oxford of Virginia Padoana, the woman he had lived with in Venice and the reason he had not seen more of Italy, but the skin of the woman approaching him was darker than Virginia's. It looked thick and sensuous to the touch. She smiled at him. He realized his loins were on fire.

"Oxford, Cecil," Hunsdon muttered, as he came up. Oxford and Sir Thomas nodded. "Miss Aemilia Bassano," Hunsdon said, introducing the young lady. The two men bowed.

"Buongiorno, signorina," Oxford said.

"Buongiorno," she replied.

"Come è possibile che un tale bel gioiello d'italia si ritrova a freddo, grigio Inghilterra?"

"Non un gioiello, signore."

"Ah, ma un diamante e dal piombo mantiene il suo valore." Oxford said, implying that she deserved a better companion than the old warrior standing next to her.

"Por favore, eo no parlo Italiano. Si prega di non parlare italiano," she said, smiling lightly.

"Eh?" Hunsdon said.

Aemilia Bassano kept her eyes on Oxford as she spoke to Hunsdon. "I asked Lord Oxford to speak English because my lord does not speak Italian."

"Just so," Hunsdon said.

"Lord Oxford flatters me by quoting from *Hero and Leander*, an unpublished poem by Christopher Marlowe. He must speak English, my lord, or you will miss the literary allusions Lord Oxford slips into what he says."

This took Oxford by surprise. He *had* been quoting from Marlowe's poem, which Marlowe had refused to show to anyone, particularly rival poets. Oxford had talked the Countess of Pembroke into getting her hands on it for a few hours so Oxford could read it quickly, yet Aemilia Bassano was so familiar with it that she was able to recognize a line from it *quoted to her in Italian*!

Her mastery of the three men was complete. Sir Thomas had lost his voice upon her approach. Hunsdon was content to bask in the glow the young woman cast over him and cared not that she might be flirting with Oxford in a language he did not understand.

"It was an excellent allusion," Aemilia Bassano added, her eyes flashing the way a fire flares up and settles back. She knew exactly what Oxford had implied: even a diamond set in lead her worth retains.

"Dinner is served," a servant announced from the end of the hall.

Willoughby returned to the gallery. "Sir William is late. We will go in." He led his guests down the few steps into the room where the musicians were playing. Oxford caught a glimpse of Robin peeking out of a small door as the party crossed the room to the steps that led up to the dining room, which was only separated from the musicians by a low railing. Lord Hunsdon and Aemilia Bassano went ahead of him; Sir Thomas followed.

As he walked up the steps, Oxford realized that the woman on Lord Hunsdon's arm must have heard *Hero and Leander* from Marlowe himself! A surge of jealousy coursed through him. He had just met her and he was acting as if she were his wife *and* that she had cheated on him! *How marvelous*, he thought to himself. He was alive again. "Whoever loved that loved not at first sight?" he mouthed to himself, and immediately grimaced. "Marlowe! Damn him!" He must not put off any longer meeting the man who had stolen Faust and the goddess walking a few feet in front of him. "Was Marlowe the better poet? Was Marlowe the better lover?" Oxford's jealousy added to the frisson he felt as the guests arrived at the dinner table.

Lord Willoughby walked to the head of the table and stood with his back to the crackling fire. He pointed to the nameplates that indicated where everyone was to sit. Oxford's was at the corner of the table to Willoughby's right. Sir Francis took the chair opposite Oxford. Aemilia Bassano sat down next to Sir Francis while Lord Hunsdon took the chair to her left. The chair next to him remained empty, as did Lady Mary's at the end of the table opposite Willoughby. Sir Thomas took the chair at the end of the table on Oxford's side and sat down, leaving the two chairs between him and Oxford empty.

Oxford's sister, Lady Mary, came bustling into the room. "Welcome all," she said. The men rose to acknowledge her. "Where are Sir William and his lady friend, Peregrine? And Gabriel Harvey?"

"Gabriel Harvey?" Oxford exclaimed.

"Yes. You two have so much fun with each other I thought he should come to the party!" Lady Mary smiled brightly. Her auburn hair was held back tightly in a bun. A simple necklace graced her open-neck dress.

"I've not laid eyes on Gabriel Harvey since Audley End," Oxford said. He was irritated.

"Oh, well, then, all the better," she said, abruptly turning and disappearing into the room behind her.

"I didn't know he was coming," Willoughby assured his brother-in-law.

Oxford shrugged.

The men sat back down. Servants began bringing in food. Hunsdon took a kickshaw off a platter held by a servant. "I say, Edward, I thought you and Harvey got along. I remember him telling the Queen at Audley End that you should 'throw away your bloodless pen' and take up arms."

"You were there?" Oxford asked, surprised.

"I've been everywhere," Hunsdon said, a leer on his face as he tilted his head toward the lovely woman seated next to him.

"That was ten years ago," Oxford said. "More recently, he's taken to describing me as a curious fellow, among other things."

"Well," Hunsdon continued, "one can't let little people get under one's skin."

Aemilia Bassano was watching a servant put more kickshaws on the trencher in front of her. "If he does come, why not ask him why Tom Nashe calls him 'huddle duddle, my lord?'"

Oxford was stunned again. Nashe's preface to Greene's *Menaphon* ridiculed Harvey for wanting to limit English poetry to hexameters. Aemelia Bassano had obviously read it. Before Oxford could say anything, the steward announced Sir William Knollys and Miss Mary Fitton. The men rose to greet them.

"Forgive me for being late, Lord Willoughby," Sir William said. "My apologies to your lordship, honorable guests." His face told everyone that the childlike woman next to him was the cause of his late arrival. "May I introduce Miss Mary Fitton," Knollys said to the room, referring to the woman next to him. Mary Fitton was no bigger than a minute. She bowed and smiled at Oxford. He suddenly remembered they had met at a play at Westminster. At the time, Falstaff had described her as nothing but hair and eyeballs. Oxford thought the description still apt: her arms and legs were sticks; her head was crowned with an explosion of hair out of which two large, bright eyes beamed at him.

Lady Mary emerged and pointed to the chairs between Oxford and Cecil. "Take a seat," she said in a high, excited voice. "No apologies necessary, Sir William. My husband, the military commander, insists we eat when the hands of a clock point to certain numbers. Oh, to be ruled by machines!" Lord Willoughby smiled wanly.

They had barely pulled their chairs out when Gabriel Harvey burst into the room, flying past the steward who was preparing to announce his entrance. "Mr. Gabriel Harvey," he said to Harvey's back.

Harvey nearly collided with Oxford. "Oh," he said. "I didn't know you were coming."

Oxford smiled and pointed to the remaining chair at the far corner of the table. Harvey nodded to everyone. "Je suis désolé d'être en retard," he said, and headed around the table. The last guest had arrived.

The servants came in and placed a plump pie in front of each guest. Hunsdon immediately picked up his knife and stabbed the one in front of him. A bird flew out, startling him as it fluttered past his head. The other guests began to attack the pies in front of them, releasing a cloud of birds up to the ceiling. Each pie contained six finches: Hunsdon's pie had been filled with silver-headed hawfinches; Oxford's with red crossbills; Aemilia Bassano's with golden-breasted serins; Sir William Knollys's with house finches; Mary Fitton's with red-faced goldfinches; Sir Thomas Cecil's with redpolls; Sir Francis Vere's with greenfinches; and Gabriel Harvey's with common linnets.

Lady Mary clapped her hands to shoo the birds. "Oh, they took so long to find. I drove the bird man on Tower Hill crazy."

"At great cost, I'm sure," mumbled Willoughby.

"Don't fret, dear," said his wife. "You and I shall each have a pie *sans* finches." A servant lowered a smaller pie in front of her husband as another servant placed one in front of Lady Mary.

A purple finch landed on Aemilia Bassano's shoulder. She turned her head to look at the bird, which appeared stunned. After all, it had just been stuffed into a pie and nearly baked to death. It looked at Aemilia Bassano with trusting curiosity.

"Which is more beautiful," Oxford asked, "the lovely finch or the lovely woman on whose shoulder it sits?"

Aemilia Bassano gave Oxford a thin smile. Was she pleased with his attempt at gallantry, or did she think the image clumsy? He couldn't tell. Her eyes returned to the finch, which suddenly flew into the rafters, eliciting more laughter from the guests.

"And what word do we use to describe these birds now over our head?" Harvey asked.

"If all were black, we'd call them a murder of crows," Sir Thomas said, caught up in the excitement.

"If doves, we'd call them a flight," Lady Mary said.

"A siege of herons, if they had long legs and necks," Lord Hunsdon added.

"Or an exaltation if they were larks," Oxford said.

"A gaggle, if geese," chimed in Mary Fitton.

"No, my dear," Sir William said, shaking his head. "In the air, they would be a skein of geese."

"Just so," Hunsdon said. "Or so says the *Book of St. Albans.*"

Mary Fitton looked not the least discomfited by Sir Williams's correction. She leaned forward to look past him at Oxford, a broad smile on her face. Oxford looked away. She was obviously trying to flirt with him. Aemilia Bassano watched with amusement.

"Well done all," Sir Thomas said, "but I would have preferred pheasants," he said, acting as if he were aiming a gun and tracking a flight of birds, "for then we could call them a nide of pheasants."

"Funny you should say that, Sir Thomas," Lady Mary said. She did not explain. Servants placed more pies in front of the guests.

Hunsdon dug into the pie in front of him. "Roast pheasant!" he exclaimed. He stabbed the pie in front of him. "And it's dead! Not warmed up and able to fly away, *but dead!*"

"Hear, hear," the others agreed.

The pheasants were quickly consumed. A larger baked pastry in the shape of a castle was brought in, evoking the first response from Sir Francis. "Bergen Op Zoom," he said, leaning forward to look at the pastry.

"Where you earned your knighthood," Willoughby said.

Sir Francis smiled as he looked over the details the cook had incorporated into the pastry. "Would that it had been as easy to capture as it will be to eat," he said. Everyone laughed.

"I approved the expenditure for this part of the meal," Willoughby said, pleased not only with how the pastry had turned out but also with the fact that his wife was in the room to hear him say so. A murmur of appreciation went around the table.

The castle made of pastry contained ducks cooked in the French style with anise and orange sauce. A servant dug them out and passed them around. They quickly disappeared along with the roasted sweet potatoes. Ipocras wine was poured into their glasses to wash down the duck. Fruit, wafers, and vin douce followed.

The desserts were simple. Some had expected sweets in the shape of swans, or cakes in the shape of polar bear heads, the latest craze from Frobisher's voyages, but Lord Willoughby must have put his foot down when it came to the end of the meal, having lost control over the finches.

"I have a gift for my lord," Oxford said. He unrolled the music for the March he had written. "It is *Lord Willoughby's Welcome Home.*" At this cue, a servant brought in the virginal and laid it on the table in front of Oxford. Robin came in with his lute in his arms. "My servant, Robin, will accompany me on the lute." Oxford began to play. Robin joined in. They sang in unison through the first stanza and then sang harmony in the stanzas that followed:

> *Stand to it, noble Pikemen, and look you round about;*
> *And shoot you right, you Bowmen, and we will keep them out;*
> *You Musquet and Calliver men, do you prove true to me,*
> *I'll be the foremost man in fight," says brave Lord Willoughby.*

There were many stanzas, the March concluding with:

> *To fight with foreign Enemies, and set our Country free,*
> *And thus I end the bloody bout of brave Lord Willoughby.*

Everyone applauded. "For you, dear brother-in-law," Oxford said, handing the music to Willoughby.

"You are too kind," Willoughby replied.

"More music," Mary Fitton said, clapping and leaning forward, ignoring Sir William beside her. "I love music!"

Oxford glanced across the table to see what Aemilia Bassano thought of his March. Her sphinx-like eyes revealed nothing.

"Another two-part melody, then," Oxford went on, "a song about a shepherd swain." He looked at Robin and the two of them began to play and sing, Oxford singing the first line, Robin singing the second:

> *Come hither, shepherd swain!*
> *Sir, what do you require?*
> *I pray thee show to me thy name;*
> *My name is Fond Desire.*
> *When wert thou born, Desire?*
> *In pride and pomp of May.*
> *By whom, sweet boy, wert thou begot?*
> *By fond conceit men say.*

Everyone applauded again. Oxford glanced at Aemilia Bassano's face.

"'Tis quaint," she said. "Obviously something dusted off for older sorts than me."

Oxford's face fell. Mary Fitton rushed to his defense. "I loved it, and I'm younger than she is," she said, referring to Aemilia Bassano.

Aemilia Bassano raised an eyebrow.

Harvey, uncomfortable with what he considered sentimentality and bad poetry, interrupted. "You know what Plato's disciple said about fond desire."

Hunsdon interrupted him. "Philosophy gives me a headache, Master Harvey," he said. Laughter greeted this remark. "Don't get me wrong. I love philosophy—just so it's written in a language I don't understand!" He put his head back and laughed. The table joined in.

"Which includes English," Harvey added, swept up in the moment.

The laughter stopped. Hunsdon glared down the table at Harvey. "So why does Tom Nashe call you 'huddle-duddle,'" he asked, reaching back to pull out the only thing he knew about Harvey.

Harvey looked stricken. He had offended the man who had the power to block what he wanted to publish and send him back to Saffron Walden where he had been born. "My lord," he began, but Oxford, of all people, waded in to smooth the conversation.

"My lord," he said, speaking to Hunsdon, "I am sure that Master Harvey meant that philosophy written in English cannot be understood, *even* by those who speak it!"

Everyone laughed again. "Oh," Hunsdon said, surprised.

Harvey nodded his head up and down and thanked God that Oxford's quickness had saved him.

"Although," Oxford continued, with a nod in Harvey's direction, "some might say the same about your poetry, Gabriel, old man."

"My lord," Harvey protested. His fear of Hunsdon had been replaced with worry that Oxford would write something that would skewer him forever as a foolish figure. "I apologize for describing your hat as 'an apish cap.'"

"*Clasped close to my pate like an oyster?*" Oxford asked. He let Harvey hang for a moment. "Forgiven long ago," he said breezily. "Your description was apt. It *did* look like an oyster. I love that little cap. I would have worn it today had I known you were coming." Harvey looked relieved once again. "But you are not forgiven for your hopping hexameters," Oxford continued, the friendliness in his voice disappearing. "It would 'rather holte and hoble than run smoothly in an English tong,' You would ruin poetry if your suggestions were adopted."

"Gentlemen," Lord Willoughby said, raising a hand. "Arguing over poetry would be even worse than arguing over philosophy."

"Here, here," Hunsdon said. The others agreed. They had no interest in watching Oxford and Harvey fight over English poetry.

"But the same cannot be said of the theater," Aemilia Bassano said. "Marlowe's *Dido*, or Shakespeare's *Titus*, his *Comedy of Errors*."

Oxford's heart jumped at her words. The woman opposite him loved poetry *and* the theater. He would woo her with poetry at first, he decided immediately, and plays thereafter.

"Me," Hunsdon said, eager to put a word in. "I'm for a jig or a tale of bawdry."

"Or a little sleep," Aemilia Bassano added, to which everyone laughed, including Hunsdon.

Lady Mary announced that the meal would be followed by an interlude of music played by the musicians in the well that adjoined the dining room. "Please come with me." Everyone rose and drifted after her to the railing that separated them from the musicians. As the music filled the room, Oxford maneuvered himself next to Aemilia Bassano. He whispered in her ear:

> *If your lips should lock with mine,*
> *Your lips are lost, your lips are mine.*

She smiled. Without looking at him, she whispered:

> *If my lips do lock with thine,*
> *On loan they'll be and never thine.*
> *For what I share shall still be mine,*
> *Though loaned to you, forever mine.*

Oxford was stunned. She had not only responded in verse but doubled his two lines to four! He leaned closer.

> *But once your lips, though always thine,*
> *Are lent to me, the rest is mine,*
> *For lips once kissed, the rest is missed,*
> *And must be lent and must be kissed.*

Her smile widened, but only on the side away from Hunsdon.

> *And so I'll lend so you can kiss,*
> *So not one spot you'll ever miss;*
> *But once you're through, all shall come back,*
> *To surfeit me and leave you rack't.*

She turned and walked back to the table to retrieve her wine glass.

"God help me," Oxford said to himself.

The music continued for a little while and then Lord Willoughby nodded to his wife. Lady Mary stepped back from the railing to address her guests. "If the ladies would be so kind as to follow me." She turned toward the opening behind her. Aemilia Bassano followed but Mary Fitton looked at Sir William with a frown. She did not want to leave. Sir William's face made it plain that she had to follow the women and leave the men alone. She tossed her napkin onto the table and, glancing at Oxford, followed the other women out of the room.

Oxford noticed that Lord Hunsdon was eyeing Robin as he followed the women out of the room.

"Lovely boy," Hunsdon said with more interest than one would have expected.

"A sight, my lord, that surely pales in comparison with your companion."

"Ah, but young boys are in season when women are unsweet," Hunsdon replied, looking slyly at Oxford. "Something you once said, Edward? And who knows how long Mistress Bassano will be sweet."

Oxford bristled. Willoughby reached over and placed his hand on Oxford's arm. "My lords," he said.

Hunsdon paid no attention. Years of dealing with treachery had fine-tuned his ear for mockery. Harvey's jibe and Oxford's explanation may have been no more than innocent dinner-table talk but Hunsdon sensed they were trying to make him look foolish, something he was aware was easy to do if the field of battle was poetry or theater. Oxford's lust for Aemilia Bassano was also beginning to rankle him.

"There was that Italian boy, what was his name," Hunsdon asked.

Oxford forced himself to be calm. "Orazio Coquo was a fine Italian musician who came back with me from Italy. He returned home after a year. The Queen, if you remember, loved his voice."

"Those of us at court," Hunsdon began, but let his voice trail off.

"Orazio was never ill-treated by me," Oxford protested, his temper rising. The gloves were off now. Hunsdon thought Orazio Coquo had been one of Oxford's lovers, and that Robin was merely the latest to serve his lordship in that capacity. "Robin has lived in my house with honor and been treated the same way. I owe no explanation to you."

"My lords," Willoughby said. "This discussion is unbecoming." Sir Francis looked away, as did Sir Thomas. "As for my brother-in-law, Lord Hunsdon, I can assure you that I would know of such behavior if your insinuations were true."

Oxford stood up, grim-faced. Hunsdon also rose, a smug smile on his face. He loved a fight. And he hadn't given up on pursuing Robin.

Oxford and Willoughby walked out into the gallery, Sir Francis and Sir Thomas following them. Knollys and Hunsdon waited for the women to return to the dining room. Mary Fitton came out first and went to Knollys, hooking his arm as she towed him toward the gallery in pursuit of Oxford. Robin came through the door next.

"Ah, my young lad," Hunsdon said, pleased to have a chance to talk to Robin alone. "What say you to playing some music at a dinner I'm planning next week?"

Robin shook his head. "I would need the permission of my master, your lordship," he said, trying to walk around Hunsdon.

Hunsdon grabbed Robin by the arm. "I'm sure you would find it most interesting if you came."

"My lord," Robin said, slowly pulling his arm out of Hunsdon's grip. "You mistake me. I am not what you think I am."

"So says the callow youth, not having had the pleasure of mine company."

"A pleasure I must regretfully decline, my lord," Robin said, finally pulling free. He headed toward the door to the gallery.

He found Oxford lingering with Lord Willoughby. Robin went past them and down the stairs to the street. Hunsdon followed with Aemilia Bassano. "My lord," she said to Willoughby as the two of them swept by Oxford, ignoring him.

Oxford followed them, at a distance. Outside, he found Robin and Tobias waiting for him. Tobias moved off downhill, Oxford and Robin striding off after him.

"Wasn't she marvelous?" Oxford exclaimed, striding off after Tobias. "Her eyes! Her long, dark hair! Did you not find her a jewel in the night?"

"I liked her not, my lord."

"What? How can ye say so? Just one glance through those dark lashes," Oxford said, placing a hand across his chest and sighing, "and I am undone."

"Then remake yourself, my lord. She is one of those women who eat men and spit them out."

Oxford smiled, a combination of smug pleasure and condescension. "You're too young to know."

"Aye, that too."

"I am with sonnets. Handfuls of them. I am for whole volumes in folio!"

"We have plays to write. You were to help me finish *Henry V*."

"And so I shall, but now I must find words to pour my soul into so that she can see on cold paper how hot my heart is."

"Oh, Lord," Robin sighed.

"Yes?" Oxford asked, distracted.

"Not you, my lord."

"She was raised at the Willoughby estate in Norfolk, where she grew up with Peregrine and his sister, Susan, now Countess of Suffolk. It is no mystery that she breathes poetry and letters! I am on fire!"

"Methinks she does not return the heat, my lord."

"But she will. She will open her arms to me when she hears poetry composed in her honor:

*She hangs upon the cheek of night*
*Like a rich jewel in an Ethiope's ear;*
*Beauty too rich for use, for earth too dear!*
*I ne'er saw true beauty till this night.*

"It is not yet night, my lord."

They went through Cripplegate.

*If I could write the beauty of your eyes,*
*And in fresh numbers number all your graces,*
*The age to come would say this Poet lies,*
*Such heavenly touches never toucht earthly faces.*

"Ah, Aemilia!" Oxford exclaimed to the sky.

"Methinks, my lord, she is not by."

"Who?"

"The woman you cry out to."

"I do?"

"Aye, as men do when they are in love."

"You call me fool."

"No, my lord. The servant cannot call the lord fool."

"And my Aemilia …"

"Is not your Aemilia …"

"Yet."

"And may never be, my lord, from what I saw tonight, and what I have seen of other men in love."

"And what is that?"

"That one moment's mirth is followed by twenty tedious nights."

"Yes," Oxford said.

"Where love brings nothing but scorn and heart-sore sighs," Robin continued.

"Indeed!" Oxford seemed invigorated by Robin's criticism. "I am a fool in love, a votary to fond desire! Tell me I waste my time on trifles when I should be writing plays and poems."

This surprised Robin.

"Took the words out of your mouth?"

"Yes, my lord."

"And I will give them to Speed and Launce, loyal servants to Valentine and Proteus, who will chide their masters, as you chide your master now. Chide me, young Robin! Call me fool."

"How, my lord?"

"By telling me how men act foolishly when they are in love!"

"Well, they wreathe their arms about themselves."

"Good. Good. Like a French malcontent."

"They sigh, like a schoolboy who's lost his books."

"Excellent."

"And look around in fear, as if they were about to be robbed."

"Yes."

"And suddenly weep like a young wench who has just buried her grandma."

"Wonderful!" Tears began to form in Oxford's eyes. "Which shall I do? Sonnets to my lady love, or lines for Speed and Launce to speak?"

"The play, my lord. The sonnets can wait."

"No, my love for her is real; the theater is for make-believe. The play can wait."

## ~ 25 ~
## Sonnets for Aemilia Bassano

Robin!" Oxford called, leaning into the hall from the library. Robin came running from the kitchen. "Hurry!" Oxford said, waving his arm. He ducked back into the library. Robin followed him into the room and slid into a chair, pen at the ready.

Oxford was on the other side, scrabbling through the papers he had left on the table during the night. The pages were torn and mutilated, no two the same size, scraps saved from the wrappings that had carried books and pork shoulders home to Oxford Court. Paper was expensive, even for the Earl of Oxford, or, more accurately, for Nigel, who was berated by Oxford for not having enough paper in the house. Consequently, every scrap was saved so that Oxford would never run out when the Muse seized him. The Muse had seized him the night before at Willoughby House and Oxford was now searching for the fruits of his all-night labor. Some slips of paper had fallen to the floor. He bent over and picked them up. Scanning them, he sorted them like a deck of cards, throwing some back onto the floor while he organized the rest.

"Ah!" he said, pulling out a scrap to look at it more closely.

*Shall I compare thee to a summer's day?*

He quickly stopped to search through the remaining papers in his left hand. Robin lifted his pen and waited. Oxford pulled out another scrap and held it up:

*Thou art more lovely and more temperate:*
*Rough windes do shake the darling buds of May,*
*And summer's lease hath all too short a date.*

Robin's pen sped across the page.

*Sometimes too hot the eye of heaven shines,*
*And often is his gold complexion dimm'd,*
*And every faire from faire some-time declines,*
*By chance or natures changing course untrim'd:*

Oxford let the first two slips of paper fall like the petals of a flower onto a cleared area of the table and began reshuffling the remaining scraps:

169

*But thy eternall summer shall not fade,*
*Nor loose possession of that faire thou ownst,*
*Nor shall death brag thou wandr'st in his shade,*
*When in eternall lines to time thou grow'st,*

He pulled out a slip hiding behind the remaining pieces in his hand and concluded:

*So long as men can breath or eyes can see,*
*So long lives this, and this gives life to thee.*

He turned to see what Robin thought of the sonnet.

Robin took his time finishing the last line. "Good," he said, without looking up.

"Good?" Oxford asked. "Only good?"

"Very good, my lord."

"*Very VERY* good, young man."

"I liked it."

"Will she?"

Robin made a face. "Comparing her to a summer's day is a nice way to compliment her."

"But?"

"But then it wanders away, I think."

"Wanders away?" Oxford grabbed the sheet of paper Robin held in his hand. He reread the poem. "How."

"Well, you impress the lady by saying nice things about her but the poem will be remembered because of you and how you wrote it, not because of her. You don't even describe her. It starts out complimenting her and ends up patting you on the back."

"Is that bad?"

"You tell her that summer is short, beauty fades, and when she's dead, your poem will live on."

"Hmm. Should I send her a different one?"

"It might be a good idea."

"I have one that begins, "Not marble, nor the gilded monuments of princes, shall outlive this powerful rhyme" and ends "So, till the judgment that yourself arise, you live in this, and dwell in lover's eyes."

"She's still dead and your poem lives on."

Oxford was starting to get irritated. "Then how about this?" he asked, picking up a page off the table. He eyed Robin. "Tell me if *this* one pleases Your Excellency:"

> *Some glory in their birth, some in their skill,*
> *Some in their wealth, some in their bodies' force,*
> *Some in their garments. though new-fangled ill,*
> *Some in their hawks and hounds, some in their horse;*
> *And every humour hath his adjunct pleasure,*
> *Wherein it finds a joy above the rest:*
> *But these particulars are not my measure;*
> *All these I better in one general best.*
> *Thy love is better than high birth to me,*
> *Richer than wealth, prouder than garments' cost,*
> *Of more delight than hawks or horses be;*
> *And having thee, of all men's pride I boast:*
> > *Wretched in this alone, that thou mayst take*
> > *All this away and me most wretched make.*

"Well," Robin began, but Oxford interrupted him. "Now, pay attention, you puppy-dog." He came around the table and handed the poem to Robin. "You know nothing of women. This poem will be the key that unlocks Aemilia Bassano's heart, so rewrite this in round hand and take it to her this day."

"Aye, my lord," Robin said, reaching for a clean sheet of paper. "I was going to say I like this one."

"You do?"

"Yes. It's you: 'birth, wealth, hawks and hounds, horses,' most particularly in "thy love is better than high birth to me.' She'll know what that means. And you end the last line with the verb 'make,' a strong verb: *'wretched in this alone, that thou mayst take all this away'* and *'me most wretched make,'* the verb slamming shut the poem like an iron gate!"

Oxford was surprised. "Yes," he said. "An iron gate. A prison cell. 'Me *m*ost wretched *m*ake.'"

Robin started to copy the poem onto the new page. "And where shall I find Mistress Bassano?" he asked.

Oxford was basking in the warm glow he always felt when he finished a poem or a scene and someone liked it. He did not hear Robin for a moment. "What? Oh, you will find her at Lord Hunsdon's in Blackfriars. I will pen the next sonnet while you are gone, which you will deliver tomorrow, and so on, until she admits me to her presence."

"Very well, my lord."

Robin found Blackfriars to be a jumble of buildings alongside a muddy stream struggling to reach the Thames. A child beggar with no legs pointed out where Lord Hunsdon lived. He said it used to be the place where Paul's Boys performed before the court banned them for being too saucy. He said he was an actor who played with the Boys. "For three years I was the jewel everyone came to see," he said, "and then an ox cart cut off me legs." He held out his hand for a coin. "I was Campaspe. John Lyly loved me."

Robin eyed the filthy urchin, who was seated on a mat of rags, his stumps pointed at the people passing by.

"He's no player," a wide woman swathed in blankets snorted as she went by in the bustle of people around them. "He was King Johan last week; this week he's Campaspe; next week he'll be Titus. Just you watch."

"Go on," the urchin called out, throwing something at her he had in his hand. "Mind your business, you!"

Robin pulled out a halfpenny. The urchin pointed to a rabbit warren of rooms and apartments he could see through a doorway. He leaned in. "And where does Lord Hunsdon live in there?" he asked, holding the coin out for the urchin to see.

"You want information like that for a ha'penny?" the urchin asked, looking away.

Robin's hand returned the coin to his pocket.

"Through the courtyard," the boy said quickly, "and up the stairs to the second floor." He held out his hand again.

Robin showed him the halfpenny again. "You weren't a player, were you?" he asked, looking closely at the boy, who was surprised by the softness he heard in Robin's voice.

"Course not," he said, snatching the coin. "What, me dress up like a girl and walk around in a dress? You theater types are easy to spot," he sneered in a voice that suggested that he detested them as much as people with two legs. "When I say I'm Campaspe, I get a lot more." He turned away, knowing that Robin would part with no more coins.

Robin went through the courtyard. He climbed the stairs to the second floor. The landing was dark. He found a door and knocked on it. A porter opened it.

"Yes?" The porter said, running his eyes over Robin. He looked like he'd been sleeping. He was irritated.

"I have something for Miss Aemilia Bassano from my Lord of Oxford."

"Have you now," the porter said. "I'll take it."

"I think not."

Robin made no move to give him the sonnet. "Wait here," the porter said. Aemilia Bassano appeared a few minutes later.

"You have something for me?"

"Yes, madam." Robin held out the poem. She took it and slipped the purple ribbon off. "It's from Lord Oxford," Robin added.

"What is your name, young sir?"

"Robin, madam.

"The bird or the man?"

"Your servant, madam."

"I thought you were Lord Oxford's servant."

"I am, madam, but he told me to deliver this to you and await your instructions. Therefore, I am your servant until you acquit me of my duty to you."

"Well-spoken, servant." She made no effort to unroll the poem. Instead, she reached over and touched his chin. She was undoubtedly attracted to him, which made Robin uncomfortable. "Your beard should be in by now, young servant, and if it do, it will do you well."

Robin pulled away. "It does me well now, madam." He pointed to the poem she held in her hand. "An you read my master's praise of you, madam, you would know he loves you with sighs of fire and words that sing, and you will quickly forget the humble servant who has delivered it."

"I will be the judge of that," she said, her eyes still on him. "I need not read your master's poetry to know he sings an old tune. He is a noble lord but I seek after fresh youth and new words that have not been sung before."

"But, madam," Robin began, but Aemilia Bassano put a finger to his lips to hush him.

"Get you to your lord. Tell him I cannot love him. Tell him to refrain from sending you to me again, though, if you come you will be well-received." She smiled seductively at him. She held out a coin. "Take this for your pains if not your love."

"Madam, I am no fee'd post. It is my master who is without recompense. Fare thee well."

"And you, young sir."

———————————

"She never read the poem?" Robin nodded. "How can that be? She must have taken it to read it in her chamber, away from prying eyes."

"I think not, my lord."

"Why so?"

"She said for me to come no more."

"A playful trick, a common one women use to set the hook before they reel in their prey."

"She is not the fisherman, my lord. You are. I think she likes not the bait you cast in front of her."

"Impossible!"

"She said she sought after fresh youth and new words that have not been sung before."

"But I wrote these words last night!"

"Women are a mystery to me, my lord."

"I cannot be so answered. She cannot withstand the beating of so strong a passion. I will redouble my efforts. She has just made the prize more valuable."

He threw himself into a chair and began writing furiously. When he finished a line, he scanned it and threw it on the floor and grabbed another piece of paper. Robin tiptoed out of the room.

# Sonnets for Aemilia Bassano

## ~ 26 ~
## Blackfriars – The Next Night

It was a cold, gusty night. Rain battered Robin like grapeshot as he ran down the street that led him to Blackfriars. The child beggar with no legs was now scrunched up against a wall.

Robin stopped. The beggar looked at him but his eyes were blank. Robin bent down, worried the boy had gone blind. "Hello?" The boy focused on him. "You have a family?" Robin asked.

The boy blinked. "Of course, I do. Can't ye see em?" He waved an arm at the empty street. "They're all around me." He turned away.

Robin realized the boy had lost more than his legs when the oxcart ran over him. "Take this," he said, dropping a few pennies into the boy's hands. "It's all I have."

A hand caught the pennies and slipped them inside the blanket the boy had wrapped around himself. "I see a man here needs not live by shifts when in the streets he meets such golden gifts."

Robin looked at him. "From whence come these lines?"

"*Comedy of Errors.* Act III, Scene 2."

"How dost thou know this play?"

"A friend carried me on his back to see it. The line spoke to me."

"So you *were* a player."

The boy reached up to wipe the rain off his face. "I was."

"But the woman going by ..."

"She and I were playing you."

"Acting all the time, of course."

"Now you see me; now you don't." He smiled slyly. "I need to live by shifts, unlike Antipholus of Syracuse. Without legs I cannot be a player, but begging is a creative art too, and I can be a player on the stage wot is the street." He held open a purse that glistened with wet coins.

"And your new profession brings you more than when you strode the stage with two good legs."

"Yer eyes are beginning to see, young sir." The boy cocked his head. "Ye want your pennies back?"

Robin suddenly felt like the boy had him on the end of a fishing line and had been playing him so gently he did not know the hook was in his mouth. The rain was beginning to run down his back.

"No," he said. "You keep them." He turned into the courtyard toward Lord Hunsdon's lodgings and mounted the stairs to the second floor.

The porter said nothing when he opened the door. Aemilia Bassano soon appeared.

"My little Robin," she said, taking his face in her two hands, elegantly gloved in white kidskin studded with jewels and tufts of fur.

Robin pulled back. "I bring you my master's love," he said, holding out the new poem Oxford had given him.

"You are your master's present," she said in a husky voice. "Sometimes the box is worth more than the gift it brings."

"Not in this case, madam."

"In carrying out your duties to your master, young servant, you neglect your duties to yourself."

"What duties would those be, madam?"

"To accept the love I offer you, for love sought is good, but unsought, even better."

"Undoubtedly true, madam, but 'tis a gift I cannot accept, being bound in duty to my lord to serve his interests and not mine."

"And in serving your master you bewray yourself, and pay a high price to boot, for you will not find finer lips in all of England," she said, pursing her lips and bringing her face closer to his.

"Spare me an inventory of your charms, madam," Robin said, turning his head away. "You have mistook me."

"Indeed." She sighed. "Had you the years of a man, you would not turn away such favors as I offer you now."

"Something I also lack, madam. Will you nothing to my lord?"

"Ah, me," she said. "Very well. Go, young Robin. Tell your master I will read his poetry and send a message whether he is to come or no. Perchance if he does, you will show him the way."

"Most gladly, madam."

"Good even, then."

"Good even."

M y lord," Robin said as he came running into the library, "Kit Marlowe has been arrested."

"Wherefore?"

"He was with Thomas Watson in Hog's Lane when Watson got into a sword fight with a man named Bradley and killed him. The beadles have taken them to Newgate Prison."

Oxford jumped up. "God's blood! 'Twould be a terrible loss if Marlowe were to swing for being too close to Tom Watson when he lost his temper. We'll have to get him out."

"I did not know you thought so highly of Mr. Marlowe."

"He has sauce in him, this Marlowe, and deserves to live another day. He opened *Dido, Queen of Carthage* with Jupiter dandling Ganymede on his knee, a scandalous way to begin a play that was supposed to be about a woman's love for a man. The court went into a frenzy trying to figure out who Marlowe was aiming at when they saw Jupiter lusting after the boy."

"And who was he aiming at?"

"They thought Raleigh was the target because he had a cabin boy on his last voyage who, someone said, had the eyes of a woman."

"And that was enough?"

"It is if you're the favorite of the Queen and hated for it."

"So who *was* Marlowe aiming at?"

"I don't think he was aiming at anyone. He was just down from Cambridge and knew nothing about the court, but those who spend their time fawning over the Queen think every character they see in a play is an attack on someone, a bad habit they picked up from my early plays. I think Marlowe opened with Ganymede on Jupiter's knee to see what would happen, the way a man might throw a fox into a henhouse to see which way the chickens ran."

"But you laughed at *Tamburlaine,* and said Marlowe was no better than Greene or Lyly."

"I laughed at *Tamburlaine* because it was a juvenile effort, but I saw greatness lurking. Do you not remember the kings harnessed to pull Tamburlaine across the stage in a chariot?"

> *Holla, ye pamper'd jades of Asia!*
> *What, can ye draw but twenty miles a-day,*
> *And have so proud a chariot at your heels,*
> *And such a coachman as great Tamburlaine?*
> *The horses that guide the golden eye of heaven*
> *And blow the morning from their nostrils*
> *Are not so honour'd in their governor*
> *As you, ye slaves, in mighty Tamburlaine.*

They were going so fast Robin thought he needed a horse to keep up with his master. Oxford seemed to be exploding with energy. Oxford kept talking as they raced on.

"The description of horses that '*guide the golden eye of heaven and blow the morning from their nostrils*' is a brillian parody of all those who have tried to wax poetic about the rising sun and failed."

"Such as," Robin said.

"Such as Thomas Lodge: *Mark how the morne in roseat colour shines/And strait with cloudes the sunnie tract is clad!*"

"More morn than dawn, my lord."

"And *Sweet Helen!*" Oxford sang out: "*Make me immortal with a kiss!*" He embraced the air in front of him as they turned into a side street.

> *Her lips suck forth my soul: see, where it flies!*
> *Come, Helen, come, give me my soul again.*
> *Here will I dwell, for heaven is in these lips.*
> *O, thou art fairer than the evening air*
> *Clad in the beauty of a thousand stars;*

"I sat in the theater watching *Faust*, grinding my teeth as Marlowe's lovely words poured over me. Sturmius had urged me to write a play about Faust, but I had put it off because I didn't think I could do justice to a mad philosopher who sells his soul to the devil. Marlowe had no such problem. I heard his words, '*O, thou art fairer than the evening air clad in the beauty of a thousand stars!*' and told myself I had to meet him. Is genius visible? But how could he be so gifted? He is the son of a cobbler and can count no ancient lineage."

"How then, my lord, can he pen words that may be some of the loveliest poetry in the English language?"

"Because he has noble blood, Robin, which was introduced into his lineage by moonlight. Someone slipped in at the window or over the garden stile while the master of the house slept."

"Oh."

"Else, anyone can write."

They had arrived at the prison, a pile of red bricks that was part of one of London's gates. Beggars slept against the walls. Wives and children sat in clumps hoping their husbands or sons would soon be let out. Oxford banged on the iron gate. A filthy older man, large, with a lumpy face, peered through the gate.

"I am the Earl of Oxford," Oxford said. "Let me in."

The man on the other side of the gate looked him up and down but did not open the gate. A clerk appeared after a moment, a younger man with long, greasy hair and the remnants of a jacket on him.

"I want to see Christopher Marlowe," Oxford said.

"Have ye got a writ or a bond?"

"No, I do not."

"Then ye can't see him."

"I will go to the Privy Council," Oxford said, raising his voice. "Mr. Marlowe is in favor with Sir Thomas Walsingham," he added.

"Then ask Sir Thomas for a writ."

Robin slipped around Oxford.

"Did ye not see *Tamburlaine?*" he asked the clerk.

The clerk sniffed. He had a runny nose. "The play?"

Robin nodded.

"Don't remember if I did."

"*Is it not passing brave to be a king, and ride in triumph through Persepolis?*"

"Ah," the clerk said. "The shepherd which conquered the world."

"Right. Him that's in there under the name of Marlowe wrote it. And if he dies, there won't be any more *Tamburlaines.*"

"Ah," the clerk said again. Then his face clouded over. "But there won't be any more *Tamburlaines* anyway. He died at the end."

"Marlowe is bringing him back. From the dead," he quickly added. "Think of the loss if we never see Tamburlaine again. Think of who will be blamed if it gets out he died because you put him in the hole."

"I don't put no one in the hole," the clerk said. "I just record who comes in and who goes out. 'Thomas Watson, gentlemen; Christopher Marlowe, yeoman.'"

Robin squeezed his hand between the bars, a shilling sticking out between his knuckles. "He'd be better off on the Master's Side, don't ye think?" The clerk looked down at Robin's hand and saw the glint of the coin. He put his hand below Robin's, who dropped the coin into the clerk's opened palm. "And we'll be back with a bond or a writ."

The clerk nodded and shambled off.

Oxford and Robin turned to retrace their steps down the alley. Oxford eyed his page, now walking alongside him. "Back from the dead?"

"Well, Walsingham's name wasn't getting us anywhere."

"And how do you know so much about Newgate?"

"Sir John oncet took me on a tour of the pubs that live off the prisons. It took us fourteen hours to visit them all."

"And I imagine he was well-greeted at every one."

"Aye. We could do with a bit of Sir John," Robin said. "It's been quiet."

"Hush, dear Robin. I need to work on *Two Gentlemen*. And Shackspear has left us alone, hasn't he?"

"Well, not exactly. He came in unannounced the other day when I was on my way to the library. I had *Famous Victories* under my arm. 'Hallo' he says, seeing the script in my hands. Before I could duck away, he pulls it out of my hands. 'Aha!' he cries and heads for the door. 'Wait!' I called after him, but he did not stop. I was going to tell you but then I heard Marlowe had been arrested"

"Nothing lost."

"You don't care?"

"No. The Queen has her history play, doesn't she? And you have your first play, Robin. Welcome to those who are *heard* but not *seen*."

"Uh, thank you." Robin said. "But what about Marlowe?"

"Find out what his bail is. Get it from Nigel and take it to Henslowe's lawyer. I need Marlowe alive and in the field against me. We shall tilt against each other, he and I, and I shall be the better for it. Off you go, now."

## ~ 28 ~
## Christopher Marlowe

The door to the Boar's Head swung open. Christopher Marlowe stood in the doorway, rain streaming off him. He stepped in and held out a card for Peaches to look at.

"Follow me," she said. She took him to the booth where Oxford was seated.

"Ah, Mr. Marlowe," Oxford said, getting up. "It is a pleasure to meet you. Please sit down." He gestured toward the empty bench across from him.

Marlowe did not sit down. He remained standing where he was, water dripping off him onto the floor. Dark circles rimmed his almond-shaped eyes. His clothing was soiled and rumpled, his hair long and greasy. His mustache drooped. His protruding lower lip gave the impression he was silently scoffing at something. A thin beard trimmed into the shape of an inverted triangle clung to the bottom of his lower lip, ending before it reached the point of his chin.

He held out the card he had shown Peaches. "I was given this card and told Will Monox had arranged for my release from Newgate."

"Just so," Oxford said, not looking at the card.

"You are Will Monox?"

"I am. I am known by many names. My given name is Edward de Vere."

Marlowe finally recognized him. "Ah. And my lord would prefer not to be known as the man who bails out murderers and playwrights."

"I arranged for the release of the playwright," Oxford said, "not the murderer. You will do well on the murder charge. As to the charge of being a playwright, the verdict on that is not in yet."

Marlowe stiffened. "I stand before no court when it comes to my art."

"Indeed you do. If you did not seek glory from your writing, you would discard a play the moment it was finished. You would stuff it in the stove that heats the dingy rooms you share with Thomas Kyd. Instead, you show your work to others and allow your plays to be performed. Let us desist with false modesty, Mr. Marlowe. We both love applause."

"I don't like owing people."

"An admirable trait, one which I have more honor'd in the breach than the observance. But you owe me nothing, Mr. Marlowe. Please. Sit down."

"I cannot stay long."

"Of course not."

Peaches appeared with a trencher of roast beef and a tankard of ale. She put them down on the table in front of Marlowe. The aroma from the roasted meat washed over him. His shoulders slumped. He had eaten nothing while he was in Newgate. He lowered himself onto the bench and picked up the knife Peaches had left on the table. He put his thumb on the meat and cut into it.

"Let me congratulate you on your *Tamburlaine* and your *Faustus*," Oxford said, as Marlowe sliced off a piece of meat.

"But not my *Dido?*"

"That too. Jupiter's love for a boy, delicately fleshed out with fine phrases: '*I love thee well, say Juno what she will.*' You have no idea how much you upset the court."

Marlowe waved the knife to show he could care less about what the court thought about him.

"And the university wits even more."

Marlowe scowled. "How so?"

"They think English poetry should ape Latin hexameters. They heard Virgil when they sat down to write poetry in English. They want to duplicate the way the Romans created stress in the first four feet of a line of poetry and then resolved it in the last two, but that doesn't work in English, does it? Gascoigne thought each line should be the same as the next 'so that the first syllable sound short and the second long.' Short-long, short-long. Boring! I went to see *Dido* and your first line leaped out at me: '*Come, gentle Ganymede, and play with me.*' An explosive first word, a flag stuck in the ground, declaring that English poetry was not going to be composed of 'short-long, short-long' hexameters."

A slight smile crossed Marlowe's face.

Oxford saw the smile. He continued. "I thought your opening line sounded a lot like '*Come live with me and be my love.*' He looked slyly at Marlowe.

Marlowe was cutting another piece of meat, his head down. "One must have fun," he said in a low voice.

"Indeed. You went on to write *Tamburlaine*, which showed that *Dido* was no accident: '*Is it not passing brave to be a king / And ride in triumph through Persepolis?*' 'Is-it-not PASSing' blew up the Harveys and the Spensers. Those of us who love poetry began to thirst for your unbridled line."

Marlowe showed no reaction to this as he bit into a piece of meat.

"But you went far beyond merely upsetting the university wits; you made Tamburlaine a shepherd who conquers all of Asia, and, in doing so, walked him out to the edge of sedition."

"Did not Henry Tudor take the crown from Richard?"

"Yes, but no one can write about that while his granddaughter sits on the throne. There were many who thought your play was about the succession, since our beloved queen has no heir and refuses to name one."

Marlowe grunted. "The play was about Tamburlaine, the man who would be king, the apparition that appeared in my room one night at Cambridge and refused to go away."

"You were possessed."

Marlowe cut himself another piece of meat and looked across the table at Oxford. "Why do you say that?"

"I have had similar experiences," Oxford confessed.

"More than once?"

Oxford nodded. "It leaves me exhausted, a shell of myself."

"So where lie *your* pages?"

"Oh, here, there."

"But not on the stage."

"Not recently."

Shackspear suddenly appeared. He was surprised to see Marlowe. "Mr. Marlowe," he said. He turned to Oxford. "My lord."

Marlowe went back to eating. "Mr. Shackspear," Marlowe growled. "He who steals my lines and twists them into something I didn't write."

This stopped Shackspear for a moment. "Well," he said, after a moment, flashing a wide grin. "Whose lines can't be polished up a bit?" He looked as if he and Marlowe were fellow artists sharing a piece of good news.

Marlowe froze. A slice of meat dangled from the end of his knife.

"Willum," Oxford said.

"Yes?"

Oxford motioned toward the door.

Shackspear looked at the knife still upraised in Marlowe's hand and recalled that Marlowe had just been arrested for the murder of a man named Bradley. "Right," he said. "Right. My lord; Mr. Marlowe." He left.

Marlowe put the slice of meat in his mouth and continued eating. Neither man said anything for a while. Marlowe finally put down his knife. "Something is amiss here," he said, wiping his mouth on his sleeve. His eyes had that sleepy look cats get when they have been well fed. Oxford realized Marlowe hadn't blinked since he'd sat down at the table.

"Anyone can write," Oxford said, shrugging.

Marlowe shook his head. "You know that's not true. Spenser said a certain lord sleeps in idle cell, a line that everyone has been trying to cipher out. I think the cell is a person, not a room."

It was Oxford's turn to say nothing.

"At the end of *Titus* I went looking for Mr. Shackspear. I wanted to speak with him. When I found him, I was surprised to see how dim the light was in his eyes. I wanted to press him about how he had written *Titus*, but there was no time to have a proper conversation with him then. I promised myself I would follow up when I had the time but I have been on the continent since then and not had the opportunity."

"And seeing him now, you still find the light somewhat dim."

"I find no light at all."

"And what would you have said to him if I had not sent him away just now?"

Marlowe studied Oxford. "Am I speaking to my Lord of Oxford, or to the author of *Titus Andronicus*?"

Oxford did not answer.

Marlowe took a swig from the tankard in front of him. "I would have asked the author of *Titus* why he wasted so much effort on a tale of hack and hew."

"*Titus* left fewer bodies on the stage than *Tamburlaine*."

"True, but *Tamburlaine* came first, and *Titus* is but a pale imitation."

"Imitation, yes, but not pale."

"It is a pale imitation," Marlowe repeated. "People love *Tamburlaine* because they can stand in the pit and imagine themselves being king of Asia. No one wants to be Titus. He lost twenty sons before the play begins and sees his daughter raped and mutilated!"

Oxford could not admit he had written *Titus* to fail, and that its success meant that he had failed in a different way.

"And *Comedy of Errors*," Marlowe continued, rolling his eyes. "The challenge in that play was how to keep the audience from leaving the theater while Antipholus of this and Antipholus of that came and went. The stage was a whorehouse and the doors were opening and closing so fast you couldn't tell who had come in and who had gone out!"

"But it worked."

"Barely. It's as thin as the paper it was written on."

Oxford was beginning to realize that Marlowe had an immense ego. Oxford wanted to tell him how *Titus* came to be written but resisted the urge. "So why don't you write a comedy and show us how to do it?" Oxford asked, a hint of sarcasm slipping into his voice.

"'Twould be too easy."

"Too easy?"

"'Tis tragedy over comedy, my lord, poetry over prose. You know that."

"Do I? So what drove you to write *Tamburlaine*?"

Marlowe smiled as they returned to a subject he liked to talk about. "It was the first fledgling to leave the nest," he said. He looked around to see if anyone was close enough to hear him. He leaned forward. "I met Thomas Watson at Cambridge. He introduced me to Sir Francis Walsingham, who thought there were Catholic plots to overthrow the Queen in every report that crossed his desk. I realized I could benefit from his fears, so I volunteered to work for him as an intelligencer. I needed money; he needed information. He agreed and sent me off to the Low Countries where I proved a most valuable servant."

"How so?"

"His spies were paid for what they produced, so they produced fiction. What I gave him was true, and from this he learned he could trust me. He asked me to do more and this kept me away from Cambridge so much that the dons were going to deny me my degree when I came back. I asked Sir Francis to help me. He had the Privy Council write a letter telling Cambridge to give me my degree."

He looked at Oxford, as if to say, "Do you think you could have pulled that off?" Oxford's budding resentment of Marlowe grew.

Marlowe went on. "The letter from the Privy Council showed me how much power I could wield if those around me thought I was working for Sir Francis. I became an actor, if you will, playing a role that made me a more important person than I really was. My peers sensed this and became afraid. The real Kit Marlowe disappeared. Or did the real Kit Marlowe surface? I don't know."

"And what does this have to do with *Tamburlaine*?" Oxford asked, tired of listening to Marlowe go on about himself.

"When I was in my room at Cambridge at night, I saw vast lands and great battles. No poem could contain what I saw so I decided to write a play. I knew audiences were tired of morality plays. They wanted men who were larger than life and who could take them away from their dreary, drudge-filled lives."

"Tamburlaine," Oxford said.

"Aye. Tamburlaine. But how was I to get Tamburlaine past Tilney? He would never let a character appear on an English stage and proclaim that the East Indians lived ten thousand years before Moses, or that there are an infinite number of universes we cannot see."

"Dangerous thoughts."

Marlowe nodded. "Yes. So I went to Sir Francis and made another bargain with him. I told him that Tamburlaine would establish me as a heretic playwright. People would open their hearts to me. I, in turn, would pass on to him what they said, which would be worth a river of gold to him. A word to Tilney and Tamburlaine was approved."

"I always wondered how it was allowed."

"Now you know."

"A dangerous game, Mr. Marlowe."

"Not if you know how to play it. There were complaints after it came out, of course, but *Tamburlaine* was such a huge success Tilney couldn't call it in. To calm them down, I gave them *Faustus* and *The Jew*."

"Which are not exactly hymns to Christianity."

"I know where the edge is. But enough about me. What is Shackspear working on now?"

"Something about two gentlemen who fall in love with the same girl."

"A tale oft told. Does anyone die in it?"

"No."

"A comedy then."

"Yes."

"How does it end?"

"I, uh, he doesn't know."

"I would tell Master Shackspear to throw away his comedies and challenge me with tragedies. Comedies are froth." He blew the head off the fresh tankard of ale Peaches had just put in front of him. "Tragedy is what we will be judged on."

"He's trying."

"Not if he's working on comedies. The audience laughs, leaves and forgets. No one forgets *Tamburlaine*."

This was too much for Oxford. "I hope our meeting does not cause you any difficulties with Sir Francis," he said, the sarcasm now audible in his voice.

"I can assure you that you are of no interest to Sir Francis," Marlowe said smugly, as if he were a government minister who had been granted access to a secret report. "He knows you are weak in body and without friends to cause any combustion in the state." Oxford bit his lip. Marlowe went on. "If he asks me about our meeting, I will say we met so I could find out whether you knew of anyone harboring thoughts against the crown."

"And what will your report be?" Oxford asked, realizing that he was extremely irritated that Marlowe had acted throughout the conversation as if he outranked Oxford.

"That I found nothing, my lord." A chuckle escaped from him. "There has been nothing to report since Lord Howard told his examiners in the Tower that you said the Bible was written by a man and not God, and that you could write a better book in six days." He leaned forward, a touch of admiration appearing in his voice for the first time. "Everyone at Cambridge hears about what you said to Howard as soon as they arrive there. Most leave religion at the door, like the provincial clothes they discard upon arrival, and quote you to those who still go to church. You are the rebel aristocrat to the Cambridge youth. They love your outrageous statements more than your plays, which are …," he paused, "old-fashioned."

"Old-fashioned," Oxford repeated.

"Yes." Marlowe said, sounding like they were discussing someone else's plays. "And now the Earl of Oxford …"

"Sits in idle cell," Oxford said, interrupting him. He suddenly realized that he did not want to hear any more from Marlowe about his life and work. "But what about you? What are you preparing for the public to worship?"

"Nothing at the moment. Translations put chinks in my purse, and my pen to sleep."

"And what will you write when you wake up your pen?"

"*Edward II*. He lost his crown when he could have kept it."

"'Tis a subject far removed from Tamburlaine."

"He is, but it is more difficult to write about weak characters who fail than strong characters who succeed. And you? What are you working on?"

"A sonnet."

"To one you love."

"Yes."

"A woman, I hope, and more real than Sidney's Stella."

"Most definitely."

"I wish you well, my lord. And, pray tell, what if any history play is next for Master Shackspear?"

"King John."

"A king far different from Titus."

"Yes."

Marlowe stood up. He was no longer interested in Oxford. "Fare thee well, my lord. If fortune smiles, we shall meet again and speak of King John."

"And Edward."

Oxford watched him go. "He'll not last long with that ego. But throw not the book away because the cover offends. How does he approach his craft? Does he write without thought? Without notes? The other playwrights are all pygmies in comparison. I need to know how he can trail lines of poetry across the page that sparkle like dew on a cold morning. I shall meet with him again."

## ~ 29 ~
## *Two Gentlemen* Finished

Nigel found Oxford in the library standing next to the table, staring at the foul pages of *Two Gentlemen*. Oxford looked up, his eyes bleary. Nigel brought himself to full attention. "Lord Wessex requests a moment of your time, my lord."

"About what?"

"He seeks your daughter Lisbeth's hand in marriage."

"At this hour of the morning?"

"I'm afraid so, my lord."

"Tell him I have no money."

"Very good, my lord." Nigel left the room. Robin came in.

"It is finished," Oxford said, dropping his quill on the table.

Robin gathered up the pages and sank into one of the chairs. He began reading. Oxford sat down in the chair in the corner just inside the door. Neither said anything. Robin looked up at Oxford after a while.

"Rather quickly ended, my lord," he said. "Valentine comes upon Proteus about to rape Silvia and rescues her. Good. But he should have killed him. Instead, he accepts Proteus' apology for trying to rape Silvia *and says he gives Silvia to him.*" He looked at Oxford in bewilderment. "Julia then faints, which is understandable, having just seen the man she loves try to rape Silvia, but Silvia says nothing"

Oxford shrugged. "They *both* can't faint."

Shackspear came bustling through the door. He did not see Oxford sitting in the corner behind the door, but he saw spy the pages on the table.

"Hello," he said. "A new play." He picked up the pages and began to read them. Robin and Oxford watched him.

"I say, there is nothing funny here except Launce and his dog."

"You like the dog?" Robin asked.

"I'd like him better if Launce had more to say than 'I think Crab, my dog, be the sourest-natured dog that lives.'"

"What would you suggest?" Robin asked, glancing over at Oxford.

"Launce is all wrapped up in his dog. He should be babbling about how everyone else cried but his dog did nothing!"

"So?"

"I would have Launce describe how his family cried when he told them he was going to Milan:

> *My mother weeping, my father wailing,*
> *My sister crying, our maid howling,*
> *Our cat wringing her hands,*
> *Yet this cruel-hearted cur shed not one tear:*
> *Why, my grandam, having no eyes, look you.*
>     *Wept herself blind at my parting.*

"Well-done!" Oxford said, startling Shackspear.

"My lord!"

Oxford came over to the table. "Write it down," he told Robin.

"You like it?" Shackspear asked.

"Particularly the grandam who, having no eyes, weeps herself blind."

"Oh," Shackspear said, not knowing how to take this.

"There's meat here for those who treat lines like these as chicken bones to suck on after the play is over and wax eloquent over hidden meanings."

"Oh," Shackspear said again. He was still lost.

"You conjugate 'weep' through every member of Launce's family, including the cat that wrings its hands despite the fact it doesn't have any, but you don't go far enough." Oxford took off one of his slippers. He threw it on the table. "Look, ye," he said: *"This shoe is my father."* He threw his second slipper onto the table: *"No, this left shoe is my father. / No, no, this left shoe is my mother."*

Shackspear stepped back. Robin also was taken aback by this. He knew his master had been up all night but this play-acting bordered on lunacy. Had he finally gone around the bend?

"A character who has spilled his banks creates an energy that flows into the theater. If you're going to take a character out to the edge, Willum, take him all the way out. The audience will become nervous. In their nervousness, they will laugh. Launce goes on:

> *This shoe is my father.*
> *No, this left shoe is my father.*
> *No, no, this left shoe is my mother.*
> *Nay, that cannot be so neither.*

> *Yes, it is so, it is so, it hath the worser sole.*
> *This shoe, with the hole in it,*
> *Is my mother, and this my father.*

Shackspear interrupted. "So Launce will cry out, his mind running hither and yon, pitching up words that have no meaning when he hears them, like this:

> *A vengeance on't!*
> *Now, this staff is my sister, for, look you,*
> *She is as white as a lily and as small as a wand:*
> *This hat is Nan, our maid.*

Oxford cut back in:

> *I am the dog; no, the dog is himself, and I am the dog--*
> *Oh! the dog is me, and I am myself; ay, so, so.*

Robin was scribbling all this down. He added, without looking up:

> *Now the dog all this while sheds not a tear nor speaks a word;*
> *But see how I lay the dust with my tears.*

The three of them stopped. Oxford looked at them. "This rivals the best music that William Byrd ever wrote."

Shackspear was pleased. "They'll be rolling in the aisles."

"The Queen will love it," Robin added. He was aglow; his master had accepted words to add to a play. Shackspear thought he had finally crawled up out of a hole and joined Oxford and Robin on the wide field where genius played. Oxford was already listening to the applause he knew would come.

"But how can this be the end?" Shackspear asked. "There are four players still on the stage. Two are women. One is lying on the floor in a faint; the other speaks not another word!"

"You forgot the ring Proteus gave Julia," Robin suggested.

"Yes. Thank you," Oxford said. "Let me see. She is page to Proteus at this point, disguised as the boy Sebastian."

"And lying on the floor," Shackspear reminded them.

"Proteus will demand the ring of her," Robin said."

Oxford began dictating:

Proteus:  *Where is that ring, boy?*

Julia:    *Here 'tis; this is it.*

Proteus:  *How! Let me see:*
          *Why, this is the ring I gave to Julia.*

Julia:     *O, cry you mercy, sir, I have mistook:*
            *This is the ring you sent to Silvia.*

Proteus: *But how camest thou by this ring? At my depart*
             *I gave this unto Julia.*

Julia:     *And Julia herself did give it me;*
             *And Julia herself hath brought it hither.*

Proteus: *Julia!*

"After which, Proteus will apologize for everything, and, chameleon-like, immediately profess his love for Julia."

"Not yet, my lord," Robin said. "Julia needs to speak to Proteus of her sacrifice:

Julia:     *O Proteus, let this habit make thee blush!*
             *Be thou ashamed that I have took upon me*
             *Such an immodest raiment, if shame live*
             *In a disguise of love:*
             *It is the lesser blot, modesty finds,*
             *Women to change their shapes*
             *Than men their minds.*

"*Than men their minds!*'" Oxford exclaimed. "How lovely! Oh, if man were constant he would be perfect. And Proteus, who is anything but constant, will say to Julia:

             *What is in Silvia's face, but I may spy*
             *More fresh in Julia's with a constant eye?*

"Oh," Robin said, his voice a mixture of disgust at Proteus and admiration for the easy grace of Oxford's poetry.

"Oh?" Oxford asked.

"Oh, how fitting that Proteus would turn back to Julia with the same speed he left her for Silvia."

"Quite so."

"Interesting," Shackspear said, "but how does this all end?"

"I don't know," Oxford said. "You two work it out."

## ~ 30 ~
## More Sonnets for Aemilia Bassano

Oxford came out of the library clutching a sheet of paper in his hand. "Robin," he called.

Robin appeared from across the hall. "My lord?"

"A new sonnet for Mistress Bassano."

"Please don't make me go back, my lord."

"Wherefore?"

"The lady likes me too much."

"You have obviously misinterpreted the signs she has given you."

"Most likely, my lord, but I would prefer not to repeat the first two visits. The lady frightens me."

Oxford laughed. "As she would, seeing such a one as you whose beard has not yet come in."

"She said as much, my lord."

"She did?" Robin nodded. "Well, tell her my beard is black and that she cannot abide the beating of so strong a passion as that which fills my heart. Go. Tell her that. And take my latest sonnet to cloy her with."

"Yes, my lord."

Shackspear came through the front door. "My lord," he cried out as he came up to them. "Henslowe and Burbage are sniping at each other over which of them will stage *Famous Victories,* but the Queen has instructed Mr. Tilney to have it shown in the presence room at Westminster. I asked Mr. Tilney to let me have a few run-throughs but he simply raised an eyebrow and told me the date and time the play would be presented before the Queen."

"How fortunate," Oxford said.

"Fortunate! It will be a disaster, my lord! The venue will be too close for a first performance." He looked earnestly at Oxford. "The players will need time to get the timing down right. Sets must be assembled. Clothing must be designed and made. The seamstresses will have us by the short hairs if they know we have a deadline set by the Queen that we can't make!"

"You need money."

Shackspear began to say no but it came out yes.

Robin and Oxford could the change flash across his face. Oxford was impressed. Shackspear *had* been concerned about the staging of the play. Maybe he wasn't completely about the money. Maybe he was beginning to see that he was part of a larger scheme, *the creation and presentation of a new art form.* Oxford remembered Shackspear dressing him down after *Titus* was performed:

> *I know the theater business, and you don't. I want money because money buys respectability. You were born with both; I was born with neither. I want the biggest house in Stratford. I want my father to have arms. I want people to call me 'Master Shackspear,' like Marlowe just did out of ignorance.*

Oxford stood there, like a sailor on a ship, sensing a change in the wind. *Could the moron from Warwickshire be metamorphosizing into a literate person?*

"My lord?" Shackspear said, interrupting Oxford's reverie. He was not used to Oxford disappearing right in front of him. Robin had smiled to himself as Shackspear grappled with what had happened.

"What? Oh. Drifted off for a moment. Get what you need from Nigel."

"It still won't be ready. Must I attend?"

"Of course. You are the author."

Shackspear looked like a husband who had just been told that his wife had run away with a man who owed him money. "At least it will be the night after *Two Gentlemen* is put on. She'll like that. Maybe that will help *Famous Victories*."

"We shall find out, won't we? And you, Master Robin, have an errand to run."

"Yes, my lord."

Robin found Mistress Bassano not at home. The porter wanted to take the sonnet but Robin managed to keep it away from him. The beggar-boy was nowhere to be seen. It was December and the city was withdrawing into itself. People were closing shutters and doubling doors as the damp cold of winter began to work its way through clothing and walls to chill London's citizens to the bone.

## ~ 31 ~
### *Two Gentlemen* before the Queen

Falstaff came barging into Oxford Court: "Your carriage awaits you, my lord," he said, sweeping his filthy hat off his head.

"What carriage?"

"*Your* carriage."

"I don't own a carriage."

"You do now."

"How can that be?"

"Because I have purchased one for you."

"With whose money?"

"With *your* money," Falstaff said, exasperated. "It's *your* carriage."

"I didn't tell you to buy me a carriage."

"How could you? I was not here."

Oxford was now the one exasperated. "I don't know what you're talking about. Where have you been?"

"Away!"

"And what did you bring back this time?"

"A carriage!"

Oxford laughed. Robin, looking back and forth between the two, realized this must be some sort of ritual.

"Actually, you haven't paid for it yet. Lord Rich loaned it to me to bring it back to London. We'll arrive to see *Two Gentlemen of Verona* in a carriage pulled by a pair of matched coach fellows."

"But Lord Rich did not loan *me* the carriage."

"No, but you can ride with Sir John Falstaff."

Oxford frowned. Out of the corner of his eye he saw Robin trying not to giggle. They had missed the loud braggart now standing in front of them, eyebrows raised, as if to ask, "Are we all ready?"

"What were you doing at Lord Rich's estate?" Oxford asked.

"He invited me out to 'bell' his hounds." He looked at Robin. "I am an excellent tuner of hounds."

Robin glanced at Oxford, who was doing his best not to look at either of them. Robin thought they were setting him up for another tall 'Falstaff' tale. "And what, pray tell," Robin finally asked, "is a tuner of hounds?"

Falstaff drew himself up. "There are very few of us these days left who can 'tune' a pack of hounds. Fortunately for you, the man who is the best at this is standing in front of you." He showed his profile.

"Why would anyone care what a pack of hounds sounds like?"

"Nay, nay, young Robin. It's not enough that a pack of hounds can follow the scent of the fox; the baying of the hounds must be matched in mouth like bells, each onto each so that the cry they send up fills the sky with music as they course across the hills."

"And how do you 'bell' them?"

"I take the entire pack into the stable yard, each on his own leash, where I serenade them. This incites them to howling, and I can identify the ones that need to be weeded out. One rough voice, one squeaker, can ruin the entire pack. I point to the squeaker and a servant drags him away, and I begin howling again, until the remaining hounds sing as one. Would you like to hear me?"

"No!" Oxford immediately said. "No, thank you, John."

Falstaff was disappointed. So was Robin.

"And the carriage?" Oxford asked.

"For a pittance, my lord, you can own this carriage and arrive at state functions in style. Hatton bought one a few weeks ago."

"You could take Mistress Bassano for a ride in it," Robin suggested, which Oxford thought was a cheeky remark for his page to make but quickly saw that Robin was angling for a ride in the carriage.

"Ah, Mistress Bassano," Falstaff said. "Lord Hunsdon won't be getting one any time soon. His opinion is, "It's horse or foot or nothing at all!"

"And then you'll suggest we use it to ride to the theater," Oxford said.

"Of course!" Falstaff exclaimed. "Over the bridge to the Rose; up the hill to the Theater."

Robin headed for the front door. "Let's take a look."

"There's a lad!" Falstaff said. The two of them went out the door. Oxford sighed and followed them. Outside, he found a pair of chestnut-colored palfreys hitched to a black-lacquered carriage. It was a cold day but the top was down. Lord Rich's coat of arms emblazoned the middle of the door.

"No, Sir John. I cannot ride through London in a carriage that has Lord Rich's arms on it."

"Not to worry, my lord." Falstaff opened the door and flipped a cloth over the sill. "Ta-da!" he said. "He who was known is now unknown."

"And what keeps it from blowing aside, like a skirt, to show underneath what is supposed to be hidden?"

"For they are weighted with lead, my lord, which, thankfully, are not used by the ladies to hold down their skirts on windy days …"

Oxford felt like he was being captured by pirates again. "All right. All right. To Westminster."

Falstaff pointed to a dirty lump of white stone that projected from the ground in front of Oxford Court.

"Oh, yes," Oxford said. "Touch the Stone." He brushed his hand over the top and climbed into the carriage. Robin followed him, a quizzical look on his face. "London Stone," Oxford said. "The center of England since the Romans founded Londinium. They measured distances from it. It brings you good luck if you touch it."

"'Twas the stone Jack Cade struck with his sword when he declared himself Mortimor," Falstaff said, as he settled himself into the carriage. "Reason enough to touch it."

The coachman brought the horses to life and the carriage headed off. The streets were filled with passersby. Grimy urchins darted under the horses' hooves and squealed like pigs to try to make the horses rear up, but the horses had been well-trained and ignored them. None of the passengers minded the biting cold because the air would have been just as bitter had they walked or ridden a horse.

The carriage finally arrived at Whitehall. A few other carriages were delivering their passengers. Falstaff dug his elbow into Oxford. "See?" he said. "A carriage attracts as much attention as a cape from Miss Peggy, or a new set of Eye-talian gloves."

They went into the presence hall. A low stage had been set up at the far end of the room. The Queen came out a few minutes later and took her seat. Everyone applauded and the play began.

"Your Majesty," one of the actors said, coming forward and bowing. "My lords and ladies, gentles," he said to the people in the hall. "The story we bring is one of loyalty and disloyalty, of faith and faithlessness, and," he added with a grin, "a dog that refuses to weep when his master is ordered away from his home. Our story begins, then, in fair Verona, where Valentine and Proteus are discussing Valentine's leave-taking for Milan and Proteus' love for Julia."

He bowed and left. Two men came out on the stage. Valentine spoke first:

> *Cease to persuade, my loving Proteus:*
> *Home-keeping youth have ever homely wits.*

Proteus the proceeded to tell Valentine he must stay for his new love for Julia. Valentine heads for Milan and Proteus walks to the edge of the stage to anguish over his struggle between following his childhood friend and staying to woo Julia:

> *He after honour hunts, I after love.*

When Proteus' father appeared and ordered him to Milan, Launce bursts into his long speech about Crab, the dog who shed nary a tear over his master's leave-taking. The audience loved it.

It was at this point that Lord Hunsdon and Aemilia Bassano arrived. Hunsdon walked forward through the seated onlookers and nodded to the Queen. Two people seated near the stage got up and headed to the rear, leaving their chairs for Hunsdon and Bassano. They sat down and turned their attention to the stage, but not before Aemilia glanced in Oxford's direction and smiled slightly.

Oxford was thrilled. His enthusiasm was brought up short, however, when he heard Speed welcoming Launce to Milan. "Padua, you idiot," he growled under his breath.

"My lord," Robin said, leaning in toward Oxford. "Speed is in Milan."

"Of course he is, but I wrote Padua."

"But you mistook the town. I changed it to Milan."

"And committed error, boy," Oxford said. "You think I didn't know where Speed is when he welcomes Launce to Padua? *It's a joke!* Launce is an idiot and Speed is playing with him. Launce doesn't realize that Speed has welcomed him to the wrong town."

"Oh," Robin said.

"I *know* what I write, young man. If I write 'City,' do not change it. If I dictate 'Temple,' do not make it 'temple.' I know what I'm doing."

Robin nodded and looked chagrined.

Proteus' soliloquy, "*to leave my Julia, shall I be forsworn; to love fair Silvia, shall I be forsworn; to wrong my friend, I shall be much forsworn,*" was almost long enough to put everyone to sleep. They awoke when

Lucetta started dressing Julia as a boy, and laughed when Julia rejected Lucetta's suggestion that she wear a codpiece. "They love cross-dressing boys," Oxford said, speaking of the audience's love of a boy playing a girl dressed as a boy.

"Yes," Robin said, relieved that Oxford was no longer upbraiding him.

The audience loved watching Proteus manipulate the Duke into banishing Valentine, and Launce and Speed going back and forth about a kitchen wench, particularly when Launce said, "Well, the best is, she hath no teeth to bite!" Christopher Hatton was in the audience and not happy to hear the line. Oxford had abused him in the first act when Speed and Launce went on about a shepherd and a sheep. There were snickers then; now there was out-and-out laughter.

The play ended quickly. "Too quickly," the Queen said to Shackspear as he knelt in front of her. She knew Oxford could hear her. "Silvia was about to be raped when you jumped us to her wedding and ended the play in less time than the rape would have taken!" The audience laughed. "Give the ladies something to say next time. No woman would stand mute in the presence of what you have just given us." She rose. "And where is the history play you've been promising?"

"*The Famous Victories of Henry the Fifth*, Your Majesty. It is ready for the feast of St John the Evangelist."

"Don't let me down," she said.

Shackspear bowed low, beads of sweat visible on his forehead. She was pleased. Nervous subjects who sweated in her presence were visible proof she could still evoke fear in her subjects.

She left the room. Aemilia Bassano drifted up behind Shackspear and placed her hand on his arm. Oxford saw what she was doing and pushed his way through the crowd to get to them.

"Silvia," he heard her saying to Shackspear. She repeated Valentine's lines:

*What light is light, if Silvia be not seen?*
*What joy is joy, if Silvia be not by?*

"Yes," Oxford said, bustling up next to them and interrupting her. "Pretty good, don't you think?"

Aemilia Bassano agreed. She was beaming. "A new poet has been born," she said to Oxford, as if she were giving him great news. She turned back to Shackspear.

*Except I be by Silvia in the night,*
*There is no music in the nightingale.*

"Yes," Oxford interrupted her again, resisting the urge to reach over and lift her hand off Shackspear's arm.

"This, my lord," she said to Oxford as she continued to gaze into Shackspear's eyes, "is the poetry I was waiting for when you and I spoke at Lord Willoughby's."

"If you would excuse us," Oxford said to Shackspear. The smile on Shackspear's face was replaced by the realization that Oxford, his face o'erhung by angry clouds, could destroy him with a word.

"Don't let us hold you up," Aemilia Bassano suggested, letting go of Shackspear's arm. Shackspear gave a cursory bow and left.

"Madame," Oxford said, "you've sent my page away three times."

"Yes. He is such a sweet boy. So loyal to his master."

"A loyalty few others could muster in the face of your beauty."

"Whereas you are a man and would, no doubt, succumb more quickly."

"I would resist, of course …"

"Why?" she asked blithely.

Oxford blinked. "Only long enough to show my respect for you."

"How nice." He was losing the wit game they were playing.

"I have poetry that far exceeds Valentine's praise of Silvia."

"Your poetry is antique, my lord; Shackspear's is new."

"Yes, yes, he does well, but he enjoys the field without competition. Let me join the lists, Madame. If you could but see the fire I have captured on the written page / you would find that your champion stands in front of you and not on yonder stage."

This turned her head. "A poet who utters verse when others speak prose?" She looked into his eyes, reevaluating him, when she suddenly saw Lord Hunsdon coming toward them. "Very well, my lord. Tonight is not convenient. Tomorrow is Christmas and we dine with the Queen. But I will be at home the next night, St. Stephen the Martyr, and my Lord of Hunsdon will be elsewhere. Knock three times and say you are Edward VII." She smirked at him.

"Thank you, Madame," Oxford said, bowing. As he turned away, he almost ran into Hunsdon. "My lord," he said as he passed him.

## ~ 32 ~
## Christmas at the Boar's Head

The Christmas feast held each year at the Boar's Head was open only to those who were part of the London theater scene. But not everyone came who could come did come, because the bill for the feast was paid by the loser of a game played at the end of the meal, and the fear of being stuck with the bill kept many away.

There were no decorations. A long trestle-table was centered in the midst of the four massive posts that held up the ceiling. A dozen or so chairs surrounded the table. The kitchen fires had been lit early and geese and venison had been hung over the open fireplace at the rear. A street-urchin crouched in a corner was basting the meat with a capon sauce made of onions, claret wine, oranges, and lemon peel. With his other hand, the boy rotated wire baskets that held partridges over the fire. Lobsters grappled with each other in a wicker basket that would be swung over a cast-iron pot in a corner of the fireplace when the call came to cook them. Steam was just beginning to rise from the pot.

Falstaff was the first to arrive. He placed himself at the end of the table closest to the door. A line of saltcellars stretched down the table. They looked like tiny birds trying to run away from him. A great mug of beer sat in front of him. He sprawled in the chair chewing on a partridge leg stolen from the spit the street-urchin was turning.

Oxford and Robin came in from the street. Robin had his lute over his shoulder.

"My lord," Falstaff called out, deftly tossing the partridge leg toward the fireplace. The street-urchin caught the leg in mid-air and dropped down behind a chair to finish the meat Falstaff had left on it.

"Sir John," Oxford said.

Thomas Digby came out of the kitchen.

"Thomas!" Oxford cried. "I had not expected to see you."

"And who else would bring oysters from Colchester? Fat, delicious Colchester oysters? I have them nestled in seaweed-filled baskets that will soon go in over the fire. When they're done, we'll douse 'em with a sauce of fresh cream and cheddar cheese."

"Have a seat, my lord," Falstaff said grandly, gesturing toward the left side of the table. Oxford walked around Falstaff and took a chair in the middle. Robin followed. Peaches brought out a tray of kickshaws and mugs of spiced beer.

"Merry Christmas, Peaches," Oxford said, bowing slightly to her before he sat down.

"And Merry Christmas to you, my lord." She curtsied without spilling any beer. She placed the mugs and kickshaws on the table.

Oxford peered into his mug. "He didn't ruin the beer this year, did he?"

"I didn't ruin it *last* year," Falstaff growled. "It's the same as it always is: five yolks of eggs in three pints of beer, a half-pound of sugar, a touch of mace, cloves, ginger, all in a pot placed over the fire. Just before it boils, I pour it into a new pot and add a dish of sweet butter."

"Yum," Robin said.

"Taste it for yerself," Falstaff said to Oxford. He leaned back, his head cocked, as if to say, "How could you doubt Fat Jack's Christmas beer?"

Oxford took a sip. "Mmm. Indeed, 'tis just as good as last year."

"Which means?" Falstaff asked, arching an eyebrow.

Oxford took another sip and pronounced it good.

Falstaff glanced at Robin for his opinion. "I like it," Robin said. Falstaff glowed. "I may not know how to write plays, but I know how to make Christmas beer."

The door burst open and four men tumbled into the inn. "Are we late?" the first called out. It was Anthony Munday. He was obviously drunk. "We've been in the Steelyard and lost track of the time." The three men behind him nodded their heads in agreement. They were William Kemp, Augustine Phillips, and John Heminges. They looked like sheep that had just been let into a pasture they did not recognize. They swayed back and forth, bumping into each other. "Please?" Kemp asked. He started to do a jig.

"No jigs!" Oxford immediately said. Kemp stopped.

"Since it's Christmas," Falstaff said, stroking his beard, "and we being Christians, we shall admit even the likes of you."

The men cheered. "God bless you," Munday said. The clump of men lurched forward.

"Right side, gentlemen," Falstaff instructed them. They headed around the corner of the table, a few of them patting Falstaff on the shoulder as they went by.

Peaches brought out more kickshaws and beer. The newest arrivals grabbed the mugs in front of them and toasted the other patrons already seated, Oxford first: "To his lordship," they sang out. Kemp quickly added: "Who has always nursed his Heliconion imps!" They all cheered.

Oxford raised his mug. "I drink to the general joy o' the whole table." The door opened and Shackspear and Thomas Nashe came in.

"My lord," Shackspear called out. He was having difficulty focusing. It was obvious the two of them had also been drinking. "Mr. Thomas Nashe and Mr. William Shackspear request the honor of being part of your company this Christmas day."

"Willum," Oxford muttered.

"Willum," Shackspear quickly corrected himself

"And how comes it," Falstaff asked, "that you stand here with Mr. Nashe, who libeled you in his introduction to *Menaphon*?"

"For because he didn't," Shackspear said. "He was speaking of Mr. Thomas Kyd." He looked at Nashe for confirmation. Nashe nodded his head up and down.

Falstaff guffawed. "And, if Mr. Nashe had staggered in with Thomas Kyd, he'd have said it was *Shackspear* he had written about!" This was greeted with great laughter. Shackspear and Nashe grinned as well, although it was unclear whether either understood what Falstaff had said. Falstaff pointed down the table. "As Master of Misrule, I order you Willum Shackspear, to the far end of the table." More laughter followed. "And Mr. Nashe to the left side of the table."

Shackspear disengaged himself from Nashe and began parading down the right side of the table. He stopped between Phillips and Heminges and put an arm around Phillips. "My Lavinia," he cooed. "A better woman than any woman ever was." He tweaked Phillips' cheek. "What is it, Lavinia? Cat got yer tongue?" Everyone laughed except Oxford. "Did you enjoy the rape?" More laughter. Shackspear turned to Heminges. "And Lucetta," he said, reaching for Heminges's crotch. "You were a gravelly-voiced maid with ideas about codpieces, I think." Heminges grinned and twisted away. Shackspear next focused on Munday. "And Anthony," he said, "how could I have written all I have without standing on your shoulders?" Munday smiled, confused by drink and not understanding what Shackspear meant.

Falstaff hoisted his mug. "To the rising star from Stratford," he said. "May there be many more plays from the rustic genius from Warwickshire!"

All save Oxford raised their mugs. "More plays!" they called out. Oxford left his on the table.

"I will make you immortal, gentlemen" Shackspear told them, looking round the table, "as I will be."

Lyly came through the door before anyone could react. The little man had found an old coat that had been expensive when new but was now torn and stained. "My lord," he said coming up to the table. "With your permission, I would like to be accepted as a guest at the Christmas dinner that, I most confidently believe, will be served in the Boar's Head Inn this Christmas day."

The other patrons cheered. Munday raised his mug. "To our Euphues," he said. "Give us a taste!"

Lyly's face glowed. He drew himself up. "Something from *Euphues*, then." They all put down their mugs as Lyly raised his chin:

> *It is virtue, yea virtue, gentlemen, that maketh gentlemen;*
> *That maketh the poor rich, the base-born noble,*
> *The subject a sovereign, the deformed beautiful,*
> *The sick whole, the weak strong, the most miserable most happy.*

The men cheered, but more to cut him off than to praise him. Like everyone else, they had had enough of Euphues. Lyly took their cheers as praise.

"Join us," Oxford said, gesturing to a chair to his left. Lyly padded around the table. Robin slid left, giving his chair to Lyly.

"I much liked *Endymion*," Oxford said, "particularly '*pinch him, pinch him, black and blue.*'"

"Thank you."

"And the songs. I may borrow them back."

"Of course," Lyly said again. "A gift once given should be returned with interest."

"Only loans earn interest, my friend; gifts come without strings."

Lyly shrugged. "A point a lawyer would make, but not a poet."

"Or a playwright," Oxford added. "And what said the Queen about *Endymion*?"

"She liked it well," Lyly said, smiling. "She thought it was about her." Oxford tried to look surprised. "She especially liked being called

'Cynthia, the Moon Goddess.' She said she was tired of being called 'Diana' all the time."

Munday raised his mug and stood up. "With your permission, gents, a song from Master Lyly. I shall sing *Cards and Kisses* from *Campaspe*." Robin picked up his lute to accompany him.

> *Cupid and my Campaspe play'd*
> *At cards for kisses, Cupid paid:*
> *He stakes his quiver, bow, and arrows,*
> *His mother's doves, and team of sparrows;*
> *Loses them too; then down he throws*
> *The coral of his lips, the rose*
> *Growing on's cheek (but none knows how);*
> *With these, the crystal of his brow,*
> *And then the dimple of his chin:*
> *All these did my Campaspe win.*
> *At last he set her both his eyes.*
> *She won, and Cupid blind did rise.*
> *O Love! has she done this for thee?*
> *What shall, alas! become of me?*

The men applauded. Munday bowed.

Falstaff shook his head. "I much prefer Mr. Lyly's *O For a Bowle of fatt Canary*." He did not rise. Robin began to play again.

> *O For a Bowle of fatt Canary,*
> *Rich Palermo, sparkling Sherry,*
> *Some Nectar else, from Juno's Dairy,*
> *O these draughts would make us merry.*

He would have continued but the door opened and Philip Henslowe and Ned Alleyn fell into the inn.

"Gentles!" Henslowe called out. "Ned and I wish you Merry Christmas!"

The men at the table pounded the table with their mugs.

"To the right, gentlemen," Falstaff instructed them. Henslowe and Alleyn went around Falstaff and pulled out chairs. The men at the table cried out "Tamburlaine! Barabas! Valentine!"

Alleyn surveyed the table. He threw his head back. He was a large man with broad shoulders and a shock of thick hair. He called down the table to Shackspear: "Tamburlaine and Barabas, yes, but Valentine? A better part next time, Master Shackspear, not someone who gets banished from the play and screwed-over by his best friend."

"Noted," Shackspear said. "I shall craft you a part the likes of which you have never seen, for which you will have to wear a farthingale."

The table roared.

"What? Ned Alleyn plays naught but men!"

Their laughter at this was interrupted by the door opening again. Robert Greene, followed by his man, Ball, came in. Greene was a big man but Ball was even bigger. He kept process servers away from Greene, the red-bearded overweight man who had stopped in front of him. Greene started to fall over. Ball steadied him. Greene pushed him away.

The guests booed.

"Wherefore?" Greene asked, glaring at them as he stood up to his full height. He was nearly as large as Falstaff.

"Alphonsus!" someone shouted. "Bejazet!" someone else called out. "Venus!" Shackspear added.

Greene reacted like the schoolyard bully who's just been called an asshole. His bleary eyes ran down the table until he spied Shackspear.

"Thief!" he called out. "You stole *Procne*!" He started around the table but Falstaff was instantly on his feet. He put an arm out and stopped Greene. With his other arm he held off Ball, who had come up to protect Greene.

Greene started to push into Falstaff when he saw Oxford looking at him disdainfully on the other side of the table. He stepped back and motioned for Ball to back off. Peaches burst into the room.

"Gentlemen!" she said. "'Tis unbecoming to fight on Christmas Day!"

"She's right," Oxford said. "Stand down, John Greene. Take a seat next to Mr. Nashe." He pointed to an empty chair. "You should thank him. His preface to *Menaphon* likely increased the sales of your book."

Greene pushed Falstaff away. "Wait outside," he growled at Ball. He walked around Falstaff and sat down.

Peaches had a tray full of mugs. "More beer, gentlemen?" She put the tray on the table and began handing out mugs.

"Mr. Greene," Henslowe called out. "Anything new for the Rose?"

"*Orlando Furioso*, Mr. Henslowe."

"Which is about what?"

"A man who falsely accuses his wife of cheating on him. His accusation sends her to her death but, of course, she does not die, and they are reunited in the end."

"Already done," Lyly announced. "1582. The Children of Paul's played it before the Queen. *Ariodante and Genevra* they called it."

"Not the *Furioso* I will write," Greene said. "No euphuisms, no mincing words," he said, "or," turning to Shackspear, "stupid jokes."

"Stupid jokes?"

"Like 'boots' in Two Gentlemen." Greene made a face. He began speaking in a falsetto voice: "'He was more than overshoes in love – 'Tis true, for you are over boots in love – Over the boots? Nay, give me not the boots – No, I will not, for it boots thee not.'"

The actors cheered. Greene was amazed. "That is funny?" They cheered some more. "How can jokes like that please *anyone*?"

"Because the public likes them!" Munday said. The rest nodded their heads up and down.

Greene was mystified. "I shall not let my art die to earn the sweaty claps of the unwashed."

"Better sweaty claps than none at all," Kemp said.

"Hear, hear," someone said.

Greene wanted to say more but Peaches and the other servants began to bring in trays of roast goose and venison. She served them up with onions simmered with raisin and mushrooms fried in clarified butter, piles of whipped carrots, and bowls of goose fat to dip manchet bread in. The street-urchin swung the basket over the boiling pot in the fireplace and the lobsters began to dance. Digby came out with bowls full of shucked oysters. He put one in front of Falstaff and slid another down the table to Robin.

"Who is missing?" Kemp asked as he scooped out a pile of carrots with his hand.

"Heywood is working on a new play," Lyly said.

"Did he say what it was?" This from Henslowe.

Lyly shook his head.

"And Marlowe?" Oxford asked.

"On the continent," Alleyn said.

"We could do with a new play from him," Henslowe said.

"And not from me?" Shackspear asked.

"Master Shackspear," Henslowe said, "*Two Gentlemen* was good fun, and *Titus* made em forget Tamburlaine for a few days, but you haven't done a Faust or a Barabas yet."

The men at the table mumbled agreement. Oxford looked down at the table.

Peaches came out with more food. "What happened?" she said. "The food's so good ye can't speak? This group? Ye need a song."

Robin piped up. "My Lord of Oxford wrote a March for Lord Willoughby," but Oxford waved him silent.

"I have a song," Kemp announced. "It's *Hold Thy Peace*, a catch-song for three voices. Who will sing it with me?"

"I will," Shackspear said.

"And I," Munday said. Robin strummed a chord. All the men reached under the table to grab their crotches. "Hold thy peace" may have meant "shut up" when originally written but men in pubs had long ago decided it referred to a private part of their bodies. Peaches groaned and headed back to the kitchen.

"Hold thy peace," Kemp began. "I prithee thee, old they peace, thou knave."

"*Hold thy peace*," Shackspear said, coming in at the wrong point.

"No, too soon," Kemp said. The song came to a halt. Kemp began again. This time Shackspear got it right. Munday came in to start the third round and soon everyone else joined in, pointing at someone else and singing, "*Hold thy peace, thou knave!*"

A round has no end and Kemp's song would have gone on forever had Henslowe not put up his hand. "Something softer," he pleaded. "And prettier."

"*Of All the Birds That Ever I See*," Oxford said, gesturing to Robin. The knives and trenchers were put down and silence fell over the table. Robin picked up his lute and began to sing:

> *Of all the birds that ever I see,*
> *The owl is the fairest in her degree,*
> *For all the day long she sits in a tree,*
> *And when the night comes away flies she.*

The men joined in the chorus:

> *Te whit te whoo, to whom drinks thou?*
> *Sir knave, to you! This song is well sung,*
>
> *I'll make you a vow, and he is a knave*

*That drinketh now!*

They all drank from their mugs. Robin continued:

*Nose, nose, nose, nose,*
*And who gave thee that jolly red nose?*
*Cinnamon and ginger,*

But Falstaff cut in, his finger alongside his nose.

*Nutmeg and cloves,*
*Gave me this jolly red nose!*

They cheered. Peaches and Digby came out with plums, preserved lemons, sweetmeats, and cinnamon water to end the meal. "D'ye know that Peaches here has a fair voice?" Digby asked. "She sings a lovely song! I heard her in the kitchen."

"Sing!" the men called out. They began pounding the table with their tankards.

Peaches looked down her nose at them. "Like 'ell I will."

"Peaches Bottomsup!" Lyly sang out. "Peaches Bottomsup!" someone else said. They all began to chant: "Peaches Bottomsup!"

"I hain't singin'," she said.

"Your last name is *Bottomsup*?" Shackspear asked in disbelief.

"And wot's it to you?" Peaches replied.

"'Bottomsup?'"

"*God's blood!*" Oxford exploded. "Why not? Isn't your name *Shackspear*?" Shackspear had forgotten Oxford was still there. "As ridiculous a combination as 'bottom' and 'up', wouldn't you agree? When I hear your name *I see a Warwickshire shithouse with a spear leaning up against it*."

Shackspear protested: "But some pronounce it '*shake*-spear.'"

"Then why don't you write it that way?"

"Would it make a difference? No matter how I spell it, people know who I am. Were I called 'Susan' I would still be 'William.'"

"'Willum,'" Oxford said.

"'Willum,'" Shackspear agreed.

Henslowe did not understand what was going on. "And if the Boar's Head was called the Pig's Head, it would still be filled with those of us who need a home away from home today," he said, showing everyone his teeth, which brought laughter from the men at the table.

"And what about John Heminges?" Lyly asked, pointing across the table at the round-faced man who had so far been silent. "You just married the widow Knell. What're you doin' here?"

"Ah," Shackspear said, looking enviously at Heminges. "Nothing like a widow. Well-grooved and hungry!"

Heminges did not like that. He glowered at Shackspear. He had a stutter that disappeared when he was onstage. Or when he was angry. He had been Mephistopheles in *Faust*. He made Lucetta famous when he (she) urged Julia to put on a codpiece in *Two Gentlemen*. The Richard Burbages and Ned Alleyns needed Heminges and the other players to feed them lines or die as they hacked their way through a play.

But the other men at the table thought Lyly had asked a good question: Why wasn't Heminges at home with his new bride? She had been widowed when her former husband was killed in a fight outside a pub in one of the provinces. Heminges had married her soon after.

"For because, because I, …, I would have missed this!"

The men cheered. "A home away from home," Munday said.

"Time to find out who pays for the meal," Falstaff announced. Digby brought out a wooden board made of five squares. Each was about a foot on each side. He placed one of the boards in the middle of the table and butted the other four against the sides of the first one to form the floor plan of a gothic church. Black lines on each piece ran from corner to corner and from the middle of each side to the middle of the other. Holes had been drilled where the lines crossed.

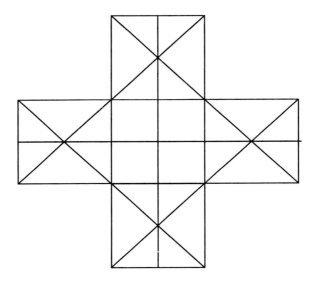

211

"Quincunxes," Robin said, looking at the board.

Everybody looked at him with a puzzled look on their faces. Oxford smiled. "He remembers the grove of trees behind Cecil House," he thought.

Digby did not like the interruption. "We'll have no word games here, Master Robin. This be a *real* game." He opened a leather bag and dumped out the playing pieces. A bronze boar and sixteen hounds tumbled out. They each had a peg in the bottom that fit into holes on the board. Digby planted the boar in the center; the men placed the hounds around the outside edges.

"Gentlemen," Digby said. "Ye know this as 'fox and geese' but in this house it's 'boar and hounds.' Since ye're all curs, ye play the hounds. The earl plays the boar. If the hounds surround the boar, ye win, but watch out! The boar can jump ye! If he gets all of you, Lord Oxford wins and the last hound he gets pays for the dinner!"

The pieces began to fly across the board, cheered on by cries and yells. Peaches kept the mugs full of beer. Oxford rarely took his hand off the boar as he chased hounds across the board, scooping them up and dumping them in a pile, but sixteen hounds were too many for him to catch and he was soon penned in.

"Hooray!" the men cheered, relieved that they would not have to pay for dinner.

Oxford stood up. "It appears, gentlemen, that I have lost."

"Again!" Munday gleefully added.

Oxford put a finger to his lips. There was a slight smile on his face, rather silly, really, brought on by the beer and the camaraderie of Christmas at the Boar's Head. "Shh," he said. They all laughed.

The door opened. A man they did not recognize stepped into the inn. He was of middling height and wore a fur hat and thick overcoat. He closed the door behind him and looked over the men seated at the table. His eyes lit on the Earl of Oxford.

"My lord," he said, coming across the room toward Oxford. He reached into a pocket in his overcoat and pulled out a thick packet of papers with a wax seal embossed on them.

"Zounds!" Falstaff called out.

"An apparitor!" Greene shouted, jumping up.

They grabbed the newcomer.

"On Christmas day?" Henslowe asked in disbelief.

"Make him eat his summons!" Greene called out. "Wax and all!"

The papers were ripped out of the man's hands and dumped on the table.

"A little sauce will help it go down," Nashe said, spooning some plum relish across the papers. Greene added a smear of goose fat and mashed the writ into the man's mouth. He fought back but Falstaff and Greene were too big for him. He gagged. Smiling bravely, he chewed the papers up and started to swallow them.

The table cheered. Greene and Falstaff relaxed their grip.

"And who is suing our lord of Oxford?" Henslowe asked.

The man was coughing and gagging. He did not know. "It was on the papers," he managed to get out, spitting out shreds of papers and dollops of relish.

"Well," Oxford said, looking at Falstaff and Greene, "what a fine job you two have done. With the suit papers in his gullet," he motioned to the man they still held between them, "how am I to find out who sued me?"

Falstaff and Greene, looking sheepish, let the man go. He reached into his pocket and pulled out another set of papers. He looked nervously from Falstaff to Greene. There were still flecks of uneaten paper on his lip.

"A second copy, my lord," he said, holding out the papers to Oxford.

Oxford took the papers and unfolded them. "Do you always carry a second copy with you?"

"Only when Mr. Greene might be about." Everyone laughed. "His man, Bell, has forced me to eat more than one summons intended for Mr. Greene."

"It appears that your profession is a hard one," Oxford said. He glanced at Robin who reached into his pocket and handed the man a coin. "For your pains," Oxford said.

The man bowed and nodded. "The food is usually not this good," he added, looking up at Falstaff and Greene. More laughter followed.

"You should have something to wash down your dinner," Oxford said, opening the papers. Robin gave the man a beer. He gulped it down

"Now who has sued me?" Oxford asked. He looked at the papers. "Christopher Hatton!" he exclaimed. "God's bodkin! What have I done to him?"

"You put him in *Two Gentlemen* as a sheep," Falstaff said, easing himself back into his chair.

Oxford scanned through the suit papers. "He says he's bought Burghley's claims against me—*'for good value'*—*Hah!*—for what Burghley says I owe him."

"How much is that?" Falstaff asked.

"£22,000."

"Ouch!" cried someone.

"Well," Henslowe said, getting up. "I haven't got that in petty cash."

"Nor I," said Munday.

The party was over. They all rose. "Money owed can kill the best party," someone lamented. "Merry Christmas" and "My lord" were heard as they headed for the door, the process server slipping out in the middle of them. Shackspear came by and looked like he was going to say something but did not. He followed the others out the door, leaving Oxford with Falstaff and Robin.

Oxford was still going over the papers. "£11,000 to the Court of Wards," he read. "£4,000 for forfeitures of covenants upon livery of title to my lands, £3,000 upon my wardship, and £4,000 for sundry other obligations."

The beer had gone flat. The geese carcasses, ribs sticking through the picked meat, reminded Falstaff of a ruined abbey he'd seen in Sheffield once. He reached into his pocket and pulled out a package wrapped in paper. He handed it to Oxford.

"What's this?" Oxford asked.

"Something you love: a bag of samphire plucked from the cliffs of Dover yesterday morn."

"The rules say no presents."

"Which is why I got you one."

Oxford tucked the package into his shirt.

"To cheer you up," Falstaff said. "And tomorrow night I shall carry you in Lord Rich's carriage to Aemilia Bassano where you shall sport and forget all these papers," he said, waving an arm at the suit papers lying on the table.

"Yes," Oxford said, but there was no energy in his voice. "Thank you, Sir John, for the samphire." He got up and started toward the door. Halfway there, he tottered a bit to the left, as if his feet wanted to go into the kitchen. He stopped and took stock of himself. Everything in order, his right foot struck out again. The left followed and this time he arrived at the door without further incident. He climbed the steps to the street and disappeared.

"He's over forty, you know," Robin said, gathering up the suit papers left on the table.

"Tut," Falstaff said. "Those without beards have no license to speak of getting old. He's got lots left in him, I tell ye."

"He's still over forty."

Falstaff sighed. "Time should never have been invented. It slices up your life into tiny pieces. If I were king, I would hang the rogue who first came up with the idea, and banish all the clocks."

"You? King?"

"The Queen has no heir, and she refuses to name one. Maybe she'll name Edward as her successor. He's got as good a chance as anyone else. And if he becomes king, he'll make me Lord Chamberlain."

Robin scoffed. "He's got as much chance of becoming king as he has of bedding Aemilia Bassano. And if he succeeds Elizabeth, he'll never make you Lord Chamberlain. Lordy, imagine what would happen if he did."

Falstaff liked the idea. He heaved himself erect. "You could be Gentlemen Usher, you know." Robin's face showed what he thought of this idea. "You'll take these to Malfis?" Falstaff asked, referring to the suit papers.

Robin nodded.

"Very responsible," Falstaff said. "Men of parts, like his lordship and miself, need the likes of you. I thank you. For him and for me."

They headed for the door.

# ~ 33 ~
## William the Conqueror

Falstaff was sitting outside Oxford Court in the coachman's seat waiting for Oxford. It was a dark, col night. The carriage had been closed up. Oxford came out and ran his hand over the top of the Stone before he climbed into the carriage.

"I'm not sure that a fancy carriage is the best way for a prospective lover to arrive at a lady's house, Sir John, particularly when the lady is living with Lord Hunsdon."

"Do not be of concern," Falstaff said. He cracked the whip and the carriage began to move. "I have left the cloths inside the cabin this time. Anyone seeing us will think Lord Rich has gone for an evening ride."

They were quickly in Blackfriars where Falstaff came to a halt outside Lord Hunsdon's lodgings. Oxford got down, his new sonnets under his arm. He told Falstaff to drive on. "I won't be needing you, Sir John. I will be spending the night." Falstaff nodded and drove off.

Robin had described the entrance to the compound where Hunsdon and Aemilia Bassano lived. The inner courtyard was not lighted but Oxford found the stairs and climbed to the second floor. He knocked on the door. No one answered. He knocked again. Another minute passed before the door was opened slightly. It was the porter who had greeted Robin.

"I am the Earl of Oxford. I have an appointment with Mistress Bassano."

"Do you," the porter replied, looking Oxford up and down. He made no move to open the door any further.

"I do," Oxford said. "If you speak with your mistress, you will hear it directly from her."

"I have just come from speaking with my mistress. She is indisposed." He grinned.

Oxford glared at him. "Go back in and remind her that I am waiting."

"I'm afraid I cannot do that, my lord." The porter leaned forward, as if he were letting Oxford in on a secret. "She said I was to tell you that William the Conqueror came before Edward VII." The porter

216

smiled and showed all his teeth. The shock on Oxford's face made the porter think Oxford hadn't understood him. "The new playwright," he explained, motioning with his head toward the rooms behind him. "Shackspear. My mistress is in love with words, you know. His words, at the moment. I'm afraid he is at his game." He winked slyly at Oxford.

The porter's words froze Oxford to the floor. The porter continued smiling at him as he slowly closed the door. Oxford finally turned, as slowly as an ancient tree falling over in a forest. He found the stairs in the dark and put an arm out against the wall to steady himself as he descended the stairs. His head was reeling. "Shackspear!" he said through gritted teeth. "*Shackspear!*"

The night was still and cold. A snowflake landed on his lip. It tasted bitter. Another landed on his cheek and quickly folded up its delicate filigree as it melted. "My love for Aemilia," Oxford muttered to himself as more snowflakes melted on his face. "As pure as snow on a raven's back, melted into nothing by Shackspear!"

He walked out to the street. He turned left and began walking away from the Thames, his legs made of lead, his heart made of stone. He felt like he was lying prone in a massive crypt and a heavy lid was being lowered over him.

He passed Cowslip Street. In the distance, he thought he saw Falstaff and the carriage waiting farther down the street. The snow had covered them in a white blanket. Oxford told himself it must be someone else. He did not want to see Falstaff. He did not want to see anyone. He wanted to be alone. He continued walking north, deeper into the dark city.

There were few lights and fewer people. The night watchmen would be out soon in their long belted coats, waving their halberds in the air and accosting whomever they saw. They always assumed anyone still out was up to no good.

"Shackspear," he kept saying to himself. "Shackspear. The monster I created is robbing me of my love as I trudge through the snow. My Aemilia doth swoon *over words I wrote!* Even now, as I am pelted by freezing snow, "he lies beside her wrapped in her warmth!" His fury was almost enough to melt the snow under his feet. He stumbled forward, his rage making him more beast then man.

He walked through Cripplegate. He had gone a mile farther when he heard hoof-beats behind him. He turned and looked back but could see nothing in the falling snow. The hoof-beats stopped. He started to walk again and the hoof-beats started up again. He looked back; they stopped. This went on for some time. Each time they got closer, and he was getting more and more tired. Finally, the carriage was alongside him. The door was open. He pulled himself up and fell into the carriage. Falstaff reached down and flicked the door shut with his whip. The carriage started up again. Oxford lay in a crumpled heap on the seat, his head buried under him.

It was after midnight when the carriage wended its way back to Bishopsgate. The gate to the city was closed. The bells of St. Bennett rang three times from deep within the city. Falstaff turned the carriage left along Hunnsditche outside the city's walls. At Aldgate, he turned left again, away from the city. When dawn began to appear a few hours later, the carriage was stopped on the crest of a hill looking out over Essex. The North Sea slept under a gray blanket in the distance. London lay behind them. Oxford peered at the lightening sky. "*Look how envious streaks lace the clouds in the east,*" he said to the cold air. "*Night's candles are burned out. There will be no sun today.*"

Falstaff coughed. "*Dawning day new comfort doth inspire,*" he said.

"You quote *Titus* to me?"

"'Twas written by a fair writer, as I recall."

"His ending was not a good one."

"Whose? Titus's? Or the author?"

"Either one."

"Titus, my lord, was a character in a play. You are not. Forget this woman who has bewitched you. If this night is any indication, her keeping will cost you more than she's worth."

Oxford pulled his head back into the carriage. He did not want to be lectured.

Falstaff snapped the whip. The carriage began to move, this time heading back toward the city. Falstaff drove it through Aldgate, which was now open. Farmers were bringing their produce in to sell it at the morning markets. He drove the carriage on through Eastcheap to Oxford Court where Robin had been up all night waiting for word of his master. He heard the carriage and came out to open the door. Oxford managed to climb down. He was freezing. His legs felt like the wobbly pillars he'd seen in the Roman Forum. "I write no more," he mumbled as Robin took him by the arm. Nigel came out with a blanket. He wrapped it around Oxford and led him into the house.

Robin came over to the carriage. "She wouldn't see him?"

"Worse. She was in bed with Shackspear."

"Oh, my God," Robin said.

"He needs sleep, but he has to be at the court this afternoon for the playing of *Famous Victories*. I'll be back to pick him up." Falstaff touched the horses with his whip and the carriage went off through the people thronging Candlewick Street."

"My play," Robin said to himself as he watched the carriage disappear, a smile trying to sneak across his face.

---

Oxford caught an hour's sleep before Nigel roused him to get ready to be picked up by Falstaff. A leather jerkin and long coat was Nigel's attempt to hide as much of Oxford as possible. His fresh appearance included a new set of heeled leather shoes that made him taller than he really was. They were soft calfskin, tan on top, black along the sides and tips. He needed every inch the new shoes gave him. His rejection by Aemilia Bassano had taken something out of him, the way the summer sun can wilt crops in the field. Robin helped him into the carriage and went with him to the palace.

The presence chamber was packed. The Queen came out and the play began. The audience liked it. They applauded when Henry V told the French ambassador that England would send cannonballs to France in exchange for the tennis balls the French had sent to him.

When the play was over, the Queen looked at Shackspear, her long fingers pulling him to her. Oxford slid along the wall to hear what she said. Shackspear came over and saw that she was furious. "If thou thinkest such thin gruel is what we had in mind when we told you to write about kings, we are greatly disappointed. In the rush to get to your next comedy, you have buried three plays in this coffin. Before we are barely seated, the play is over. More is expected." She waved a hand, dismissing him. Shackspear quickly backed away.

The Queen's eyes settled on Oxford, who walked over and bent his knee.

"Your Majesty," Oxford said. Looking up, he saw that she was seething.

"My lord, I warrant you paint your forebear, the Eleventh Earl of Oxford, with more color than history allows, but Master Camden will advise me as to that. We are not surprised. Poetic license is to be expected in drama. Your re-invention of Sir John Oldcastle and Derrick Carver as thieves and clowns is sure to inflame the Puritans and give me more trouble than I deserve, but that I can accept as the price for seeing our history brought to life. What I will not tolerate, however, is the use of a play to pressure me into making a decision in your favor."

Oxford did not understand.

She waved a hand at him, her long fingers reaching out to tell him to keep still or they would reach for his throat. Her voice lowered.

"I come to see a play about English history and you show me Prince Hal committing robbery on the highway in Kent. That's bad enough. But the audience laughs because they know the robbery you have just presented them was committed by *you* when you were scant twenty-three! Don't deny it! You robbed Lord Burghley's men on Gad's Hill. Lord Burghley, despite his humiliation, begged me to pass on it because you had just recently married his daughter. I should have ignored his plea and gotten rid of you then."

The venom with which she said this was something Oxford had never heard before. "Your Majesty, Gad's Hill is long past."

"Be silent!" she almost shouted. He could see she was breathing hard. Her voice took on the hiss of a snake. "Your cousin, Thomas Trussell, lies in the Counter, waiting to hear5

'45768 whether he will hang for a robbery *he* committed on the highway in Kent. The Trussells wring their hands and beg me to pardon him, telling me he drank too much and made a poor choice of friends. But justice must be blind, must it not, my lord? How can I save a Trussell from the scaffold when the Smiths go to the gibbet every day? This situation was complicated enough without you presenting me with a play that has Prince Hal committing the same crime Sir Thomas stands convicted of, and for which *you* should have been convicted! *You wrote this to make me pardon Sir Thomas*!"

Oxford blinked. "I did not, Your Majesty. The story about Prince Hal is extant. Hall has written about it."

"But Hall did not write about Thomas Trussell!" She banged her fist on the arm of the chair. "I will not be manipulated!!" The blood vessels in her temple were pulsing. "Doubtless, both you and your cousin are half-mongrels, your father having married a commoner in your case, which explains all."

Oxford's reaction to this remark could not have been greater had the Queen reached over and slapped him. She immediately regretted her outburst. They looked at each other, frozen in silence for a moment.

Oxford made a long, formal bow. "My mother may have been common, Your Majesty, but she came from a distinguished family.

And I, always learning from the fountain of wisdom that sits on the throne of England, now knows why your Majesty rejected me so many years ago."

He stood up. He did not ask for permission to leave. He turned and walked away, the sound of his hobnailed shoes hammering the hardwood floor as he crossed the room.

"Edward," Elizabeth called after him. He did not answer.

## ~ 34 ~
### *Pericles, Prince of Tyre*

Oxford was seated on a chair in the great hall pulling on a pair of boots. Falstaff sat across from him, sprawled across a blackened wooden chair with gnarled lions' heads carved into the end of the arms. One of Falstaff's legs, wrapped in billowing striped pants, was draped over one of the arms, turning the lion's ferocious gaze into the face of a frightened cat peering out from under a collapsed tent made of bright fabric. The fat man was working a toothpick in his mouth. Robin and Tobias were carrying bundles of books and bags full of clothing past them to the horses waiting in the street.

"Must you to Billesley again?" Falstaff asked.

"Aye. The farther from London the better." Oxford stood up and stomped his feet deeper into the boots. "I am done with plays. I am done with the court. Thomas is still in the Counter so Billesley is mine to use."

Falstaff pulled the toothpick out of his mouth. "That may not be true, my lord."

"Why is that?"

"The Queen pardoned him last night and gave him back his lands, including Billesley."

"She pardoned him?" Oxford was incredulous.

Falstaff nodded. "And it's going to cost some a pretty penny."

"Why is that?"

"Her Majesty said she was going to hang Sir Thomas to make him an example of what happens to those who rob on her highways. Bets were placed as to when he would be executed. Given how long it took her to send Mary to the block, the spread was wide, but no one bet she would pardon him. The lawyers say the bet was forfeit when she pardoned him. Everyone wants their money back."

"And I cannot use Billesley."

"That I do not know."

"Why not Hedingham?" Robin suggested. "I've never been there."

"No," Oxford said.

"And Frangellica?" Falstaff asked.

"Frangellica is returning to Italy. Nigel will stay here to manage the Court."

"Ah."

"Ah, what?"

"Ah, leaving Nigel behind means you are not closing Oxford Court." Socrates ambled by on his way to the kitchen. Falstaff shifted in his chair. "Someone has to take care of the cat."

"Piss on Socrates. There will be no more play-sheets for his arse to kiss."

Nigel went by carrying a small trunk out the front door. Falstaff watched him go. "So is this all on account of that dark-eyed woman?"

"No. It's on account of the Queen."

"She liked not the play."

"She did not. But I'm leaving because I finally learned last night what she *really* thinks of me."

"Another Harwich?"

"Worse. More like the Greeks giving dead Achilles' armor to Odysseus."

Falstaff whistled. He had not read the classics. In fact, no one knew whether he could read or not, but he had listened to more than one poet crying into his beer over the dishonor Ajax felt when the Greeks at Troy voted to give Achilles' armor to Odysseus instead of to him. Ajax, the bravest warrior in the Greek camp after Achilles, was not pleased. He announced he was going to kill all the Greeks, but Athena cast a spell over him and made him think a herd of cattle were his companions. When she lifted the spell and Ajax saw the dead cattle lying around him, he killed himself in shame.

"This will cost you the pension she gave you," Falstaff reminded him. "She tied it to the plays, you know. No plays, no pension."

"I care not. Tobias will teach me how to live off the forest."

"And Robin will cook what he finds," Falstaff said.

Robin's face showed a look of surprise as he went by carrying another satchel. He glanced from Falstaff to Oxford but kept going.

"She will come after you," Falstaff said. "She does not do well with subjects who disobey her."

"*I care not!*" Oxford shouted.

"And what about Shackspear?" Falstaff asked, still lolling in the chair.

"I have left a going-away present for him, an old play: *Pericles, Prince of Tyre.*"

Robin had never heard of *Pericles*. "Which is about …?" he asked, stopping on his way back to the library.

Falstaff smiled, showing his broken teeth, which Oxford thought looked like the walls of an abandoned castle. "It begins, lad, with a king offering his daughter in marriage to the man who can solve a riddle."

"And what is the riddle?"

Oxford supplied it:

> *I am no viper, yet I feed*
> *On mother's flesh which did me breed.*
> *I sought a husband, in which labour*
> *I found that kindness in a father:*
> *He's father, son, and husband mild;*
> *I mother, wife, and yet his child.*
> *How they may be, and yet in two,*
> *As you will live, resolve it you.*

Robin's jaw dropped. "The king is … with his own daughter?" He looked from Oxford to Falstaff and back again. "Was this ever acted on stage?"

"No," Oxford said. "Nigel will deliver it to Shackspear when he comes looking for me. Thank God I will not be here."

Falstaff chortled. "And if he gets it past Tilney and onto the stage, the Queen will personally send him back to Stratford, minus a few body parts first."

"Aye."

Robin was still standing between them, transfixed. "But why, my lord, would you write a play in which a king is …?"

"Good question," Oxford said. He did not elaborate. "Find Malfis, Robin. Ask him if Sir Thomas will lease Billesley to me. Perchance my cousin needs the revenue."

Robin headed for the door.

"And Marlowe?" Falstaff asked.

"What about Marlowe?"

"You will no longer combat with Christopher Marlowe?"

Oxford was fiddling with his gloves. "And what makes you think I have anything that might challenge Christopher Marlowe?"

"For because I paid good money to Dr. Forman to cast a horoscope for you. He told me that if you could put the Queen out of your mind, plays would flow out of you like a river."

"Simon Forman knows nothing about the theater."

"I did not ask him about the theater. I asked him about the future, and he knows that."

"Hah! Did you tell him the Queen has forbidden me from writing plays *but forced me to write plays for an idiot?* Did you tell him I've been cuckolded out of the woman I want *because she swoons over poetry she thinks was written by the idiot?* Did you tell him *the Queen called me a mongrel?* Did he say that the planets are lining up to send a flaming comet down to incinerate me in my own house?" He looked up at the ceiling, spreading his arms wide. "*I would welcome it!*"

Falstaff sighed. "Don't put down your pen, Edward. You only wound yourself when you do that."

"I'm not wounding myself; I'm saving myself. I finally know what the Queen thinks of me. I will not crawl back to her. I will not give her the plays she wants. I don't care if she takes my pension away because *the monster I have created will lose his muse and, without me, he will lose the woman he has stolen from me.*"

"Now *that's* a worthy cause," Falstaff said. "But, Edward, my boy, in the process, you do yourself injustice. Your motto has always been 'I am that I am.' I fear you have forgotten it."

This brought Oxford up short. "You taught me that in this very room."

"It was a lesson you already knew. Forget the Queen *and* this Bosoomo woman …"

"Bassano!"

"Bassano, and serve yourself first."

"I *am* serving myself first!" Oxford shouted. "*I am not going to write any more plays!*" He headed for the door.

"I suppose I shall have to return Lord Rich's carriage," Falstaff sighed.

"God's blood!" Oxford cried, as he slammed the door behind him. "*I don't give a statue's tit what happens to Lord Rich's carriage.*"

225

# 1590

## ~ 35 ~
## Billesley Hall

**M**alfis sent a messenger after Oxford to tell him that Sir Thomas had been advised to visit the Continent until Her Majesty forgave him. Thus, Billesley would be available for Oxford to use for the time being.

It was snowing when they finally arrived. To their surprise, the house was empty. "Hello?" Oxford called out as they came in. No one answered.

"Gone to other employment," Robin said, as he and Tobias carried in what they'd brought with them. Robin first built a fire in Oxford's room and made sure his lordship was abed before he went downstairs and got the stove going in the kitchen. He heated up some soup and took it up to Oxford with the stale bread they had brought with them from London.

Robin and Tobias were both up early the next morning but their master did not to appear. It was cold outside. Robin later took up breakfast for Oxford. It was a piece of stale cheat, a beaker of ale, and an eel Robin had washed in the springhouse. Oxford was not in a good mood. The breakfast did nothing to rouse his spirits.

"God's blood," he said, trying to force down the eel. "Did ye wash this at all?"

"Aye, my lord. Over and over. The salt is a little thick."

"A little?" Oxford gagged. "Richard must have brought this back from the Third Crusade." He took a swig of ale to wash away the taste. "Where is Tobias?"

"He's setting up his snares. He promises us supper."

"Can he cook?"

"I don't think so, my lord."

"God," Oxford muttered. He tried to force down another piece of eel.

Robin served dinner in the dining room at noon. Oxford was looking forward to a good meal. He took the cover off the plate and looked down at Tobias's hare. It looked like it was running sideways across the serving plate. Patches of hair still clung to its hindquarters. Oxford poked a knife into it. The animal split apart, its insides floating out into the grease it had been cooked in.

"Did you gut this thing?"

Robin swallowed. "Was I supposed to?"

Oxford looked up in amazement. "You didn't gut it? I thought you knew how to cook."

"I never said I knew how to cook, my lord. It was Falstaff who said that."

"What! Are you without voice? Without pipes?"

"I'm sorry, my lord. I heard him say it to you as we were packing to leave London and that someone would be here who would do the cooking, so I just, well, I …"

"You said nothing!"

Robin nodded. He put his head down.

"Falstaff!" Oxford shouted. He banged his fist on the table. "That whoreson sack of guts!" Then he suddenly burst out laughing. His laughter soon became uncontrollable. Tears streamed down his face. Robin watched in astonishment. Tobias peeked around the corner to see what was going on.

Oxford finally forced himself to stop. He dabbed his eyes with the cloth Robin had put on the table as a napkin. "Falstaff," he said. "*Sending me off to Warwickshire with a boy who can't cook!*" He started to laugh again. "He's probably digging into a thick roast this very minute, knowing that we would be sitting down to eat something awful, *like a hare with its hair still on it!*"

This made him burst out laughing again. "A *hare* with its *hair* on it," he said, picking up the cloth again. "If Falstaff were here, he would say: *There's a hare in your soup, my lord!* Or worse—*there's an heir in your soup!?*" He pushed the cloth into his face, trying to make himself stop laughing.

Robin backed away, thinking his master had gone mad.

Oxford finally pulled the cloth away, tears streaming down his face. "That's awful. Even when he is not here he is the cause of wit in others, *however poor it may be!*" He pounded the table again. "I'm going to *kill* him!"

He forced himself to calm down. "I apologize, Robin. You are not at fault. I took you into my service to be my secretary, not to cook for me." Robin's face showed his relief. "But don't let this happen again. If Falstaff makes any more suggestions that defy reason, *tell me immediately*. In the meantime, you will to Stratford today and find us a cook."

"Do not be hard on him, my lord. He loves you."

"Hah!" Oxford said. "*Hah!*"

"He does. He loves you more than I do."

This surprised Oxford. He looked at the young page, whose face was grief-stricken. The boy obviously felt he had failed his master. "No, Robin, Fat Jack's love for me is wasted, as is yours. No one has ever loved me for who I am. They only said they loved me because of my titles, or my money, or the words I wrote, but they never loved me."

"Falstaff does not love you for your titles or your money or your words, my lord," Robin said, a bit of defiance in his voice.

"Ah, who knows why Falstaff does anything."

"True, but he never does anything by compulsion. Were he to think you as empty as you describe yourself, he would have left you long ago."

Oxford considered this. "You may be right," he said, grudgingly. "He certainly says what he thinks. And he's no coward." He put the napkin down. "He was knighted for bravery in the border wars. I met him at Cecil House, when I was sent there at the age of twelve. He found me young and foolish and decided to devote himself to making me worse."

Robin blinked. "He would never do that."

"It had nothing to do with me. He couldn't stand Burghley—he never said why— and decided to make me so unbearable that Burghley would throw me out, which would have cost the old goat money and prestige."

"But he didn't."

"No. Instead, he took a liking to me. He started making himself available, always lolling just around a corner, and suggesting I stop acting impulsively, like stealing a fish from a passing fish vendor. I was arrogant and proud at the time and thought I could do whatever I wanted. I was the Seventeenth Earl of Oxford, wasn't I? He was trying to get me to understand there were limits." Oxford's face darkened. "I hadn't learned that when I caught one of the undercooks at Cecil House spying on me from behind a hedge."

The memory of that bright summer day flooded back into him. "It was common knowledge that Burghley used all the servants in Cecil House as spies, so I shouldn't have been surprised, but, for some reason, the sight of the undercook threw me into an instant rage."

"What happened?"

"I was in the privy garden at the time, playing at sword fighting with my tailor. When I saw the undercook spying on me, I ran over to the hedge and thrust my sword into it. I didn't know where he was. The sword struck him in the leg. He screamed in pain and fell through the hedge at my feet. A river of blood began to run out of his leg and across the bright green lawn, turning it red."

"My lord!"

Oxford appeared dazed. Robin could tell his master was reliving the sight of the cook bleeding to death at his feet. "It is amazing how much blood a body can hold," Oxford said softly.

"Did he die?"

Oxford nodded grimly. "It took twenty minutes. *Twenty long minutes.* I can still hear him crying out against the pain. He clutched his leg and tried to stop the bleeding. No one did anything to help him, including me. We stood there and watched him slowly die. His cries grew fainter and fainter until he finally fell back dead."

"My lord, how awful!"

"I was quickly hurried away. A coroner's inquest was convened the next day to decide whether I should be charged with murder. I was in shock and didn't know what to do. Burghley told me not to worry. He said he would tell the jury I had killed the cook in self-defense and the matter would be over."

"But that wasn't true, was it?"

"No, it wasn't."

"What happened?"

"The jury was assembled the next day but, before Burghley could testify, Falstaff walked past him into the room where they waited and said the cook was drunk and ran onto the end of my sword."

"But that wasn't true either."

"No, it wasn't. In fact, Falstaff wasn't even there."

"My God!"

Oxford nodded glumly. "The jury immediately accepted Falstaff's testimony and returned a verdict that the cook had killed himself."

"*Killed himself?*"

"*Felo de se. He killed himself.*"

"But there were other witnesses. The tailor, for example."

"They didn't want to hear anything else. Falstaff had given them what they wanted—a way to avoid charging me with murder and risking Lord Burghley's wrath for sending me to the gibbet."

"But Falstaff's testimony was false."

"Yes, it was."

"Did you know what he was going to say when he went into the jury room?"

"No. I was waiting outside, ready to testify, when he came out. The jurors followed him almost immediately. They streamed by me, most of them looking the other way, but some smiled at me. One congratulated me! I was completely confused. How could I be congratulated when I had just killed a man? It wasn't until later that I learned that I had been spared by an out-an-out lie! I was humiliated. I said it wasn't true, but no one wanted to listen to me. Burghley announced the decision 'a good day's work' and told me to forget the cook."

"My lord!"

Oxford nodded. "It took Falstaff only a few simple words to put truth to sleep: *The cook was drunk! He ran upon his lordship's sword!*" Oxford shook his head in amazement. "The act of killing the cook took no more than a few minutes; it took less than that to make it disappear!"

Robin's face mirrored the sadness he could see in Oxford's. "Perhaps the verdict was for the better, my lord."

"Was it? Telling the truth had been drilled into me from birth. '*Vero nihil verius*' is my family's motto. '*Nothing truer than truth.*' That day it became '*nothing truer than lies.*'"

"And Falstaff?"

"His lie and my cowardice made us partners. He took me down to the river that evening. We sat and watched the boats going by on the Thames. He told me there were times when a man's imagination must overcome facts, no matter how large they may loom. 'Sometimes

Fortune's wheel needs a nudge,' he said. 'The jurors wanted a way to get out of the box you had put them in. I gave them a way out.'"

"And saved your life in the process," Robin added.

"Yes, but at what cost? I told Falstaff I owed the undercook a death. I expected Falstaff to laugh at me but he didn't. He told me the poor man was never coming back, no matter what I did. Sending me after him would only compound the loss. We sat there, watching the sun set over Westminster. 'With the sun, young Edward, goes the death of the undercook,' he told me. He was wrong about that; with the sun went my honor. And it was *not* the end of what happened that day because not a day goes by that I don't think of the poor man and what I did to him."

"What was his name, my lord?"

"Thomas Brincknell."

"Do you know what they did with his body?"

"No."

"He must have been denied burial in sacred ground, my lord. The jury said he killed himself. A person who commits suicide can't be buried in sacred ground, right?"

"I don't know what happened to him." He did not want to talk about what happened to the undercook.

"But he *didn't* commit suicide, did he? Falstaff can trick a jury but he can't trick God, can he?"

"I don't know," Oxford said again. "I don't think so." He looked the saddest Robin had ever seen him. "And in recounting how Falstaff helped me when I was young and foolish, I realize I have been remiss in my service to you."

"How so, my lord?"

"I have failed to ask you to let me read your *Famous Victories* before Shackspear took it from you. Castiglione would chastise me, were he alive, for giving you a play to finish and then showing no further interest in it. I apologize, young Robin. Forgive me."

"My lord, it did need help. The Queen did not like it."

"'You have buried three plays in this coffin,'" Oxford said, mimicking the Queen's nasally voice. Robin giggled. "She complained it was too short but she didn't say she didn't like it. Silence is high praise from her. Congratulations, young Scribbler."

Robin was embarrassed. They fell silent. After a moment, Robin spoke first. "Did you write Prince Hal's robbery into the play, my lord, to pressure her into pardoning Sir Thomas?"

Oxford shook his head. "'I don't think so. She wanted a play about English kings. I knew *Famous Victories* was sleeping in the trunk upstairs. I gave it to you and thought no more about it. But I was aware that Sir Thomas languished in the Counter, so maybe he *was* in the back of my mind. Sometimes, when I am writing, I see someone looking up at me through the words I have written, like a watermark on the paper. It also happens occasionally when I hear something I wrote being spoken on the stage."

"Such as?"

"Such as when I gave Valentine a rope ladder. You asked me why a rope ladder. I said the ladder would let Silvia's father discover Valentine's plans and banish him. But when I heard Silvia's father speak, I realized I had been thinking about my father and how he used a wooden ladder to abduct Dorothy Fosser from her house. Perhaps the Queen was right. Maybe I *was* trying to help Sir Thomas."

"But she still didn't have the right to call you … to call you what she did," Robin said.

"No." Oxford said, scowling. "Enough. Off you go, Robin. To Stratford. Find someone who can cook for us."

"Yes, my lord."

———◆◆◆◆◆———

Robin returned later that afternoon. "The owner of an inn in Stratford sent me to Charlecote Hall where I met the man who has cooked in Sir Thomas Lucy's kitchen for some time now. His name is Ethelbert, and he should be here this evening."

Ethelbert did not appear until the following noon, however. He was almost as wide as he was tall, which was not much. But his grim face spoke of a man who did not love food. "I was a butcher's son, my lord," he announced in a gravelly voice. "I learned to cook at the feet of my mum. She still cooks for Sir Thomas, who has sent me to serve you, having heard of your grace's many accomplishments in the arts." He bowed.

"Has he," Oxford said. "Do you skin animals before you cook them, Ethelbert?"

This surprised the new cook. "Of course, my lord." He looked at Robin. His face gave away that he had been told the earl was a strange one. Oxford's question had confirmed it.

"What will you cook tonight?"

"I netted some pink trout this morning. I will bathe them in spring water with a little salt for two hours, then coat them with elderberry jam and roast them. I will toast some cheat to mop up the sauces …"

"You're hired," Oxford broke in. And with that he got up and returned to his room.

## ~ 36 ~
## Robin Is Gone

Robin and Tobias soon realized that Oxford had no interest in doing anything except loading up his arms with books each day in the library at the north end of the house and carrying them back to his room where he would settle down in front of the fire, spreading them out all around him. Robin would bring him breakfast and his master would spend the day reading.

None of the books made their way back to the library, and soon teetered in piles and lay strewn across each other like drunken students passed out after a party. Two narrow paths cut through the books, one from the doorway to the fireplace and the other from the fireplace to the bed. A pile near the door finally fell over one night, blocking Robin from getting in the next morning.

"My lord," he called from the hallway, trying to push the door open. "I would be happy to carry some books back to the library."

Oxford pushed the books away and opened the door. "But what would I do if you took one back I wanted to read?"

Robin sighed.

Oxford walked through the books to the fireplace.

"Will there be no more plays, my lord?"

"No more plays. You know that. Why do you ask?"

"Because you have *always* written plays, my lord, and poetry and songs. Now you do nothing but read."

"Yes. Words flow into me now instead of out."

"Will they flow out again someday?"

"No."

"Your decision is final."

"It is."

Robin's face fell.

"I am sorry, Robin. When we met at Greenwich you asked if you could come join me at the Folly. I said yes, but the Folly is no more. The man who extended that invitation is empty as well. Instead of playing the lute and writing plays, you find yourself a servant far from

233

London with nothing to do. You will wither away if you stay here. I shall write a letter of recommendation to Lord Strange. He will find a place for you. His company recently performed *Titus* at the Rose."

This did little to make Robin feel better, but his face showed that he agreed it was time to go. "I will take the letter, my lord," he said quietly.

"Then fetch me pen and paper."

Robin maneuvered though the piles of books to fetch a sheet of stationery from Oxford's portable writing desk. He dipped a quill into a pot of ink and presented them both to Oxford, who picked up a large book to use as a writing desk. In a moment, the letter was done. He handed it to Robin.

"If it pleases you, my lord, I will leave now. The day is young."

"As are you. I shall miss you, Robin, and the gift of words you have given me."

"Which shall dwindle if I stay."

"Dwindle?"

"Diminish, my lord. From 'dwine,' to wind down slowly."

"I shall use it."

"How, my lord? You write no more."

"Oh. Yes. I'd forgotten."

"If the muse returns, send for me. I will come."

"Yes. Thank you, Robin, for all you've done for me." Robin expected his master might put an arm around his shoulder but Oxford remained where he was, back straight, head upright.

Robin left. Oxford pushed his way through the books to the window to look toward the Avon. Robin soon appeared going down the lane, a sack over his shoulder, his footprints in the snow slowly saying good-bye. His faint image soon went behind a copse of trees and disappeared.

Oxford remained at the window. "He will do well," he told himself. He will not 'dwindle,' no matter what he does. Oxford then realized that he had never asked Robin to show him what he had written on his own. "Hadn't Falstaff said Robin was 'scribbling' all the time in a back room off the kitchen. He must have been writing something" Instead of asking what he was writing, Oxford had repaid the boy with indifference.

Oxford leaned on the desk in front of him and stared sadly out the window, but nothing moved in the checkerboard of fields and hedges that stretched down to the river. He watched a line of shadows come toward him as the sun set behind the Hall, the last rays of sunlight flashing momentarily off the ponds and streams, and then off the river itself before the darkness took all the remaining colors and left only the snow to illuminate the night.

Oxford returned to his chair and picked up a book. He opened it. His eyes ran down the page but his mind gave no meaning to what he saw. He put the book down and closed his eyes. "If I fall asleep, Robin will not wake me for dinner or drape a blanket around my shoulders." He missed the little page already. Oxford had missed few people during his life. His father, Earl John had been gone before he had a chance to learn to miss him. His mother, Margery, had abandoned him to Burghley and quickly remarried, cutting away whatever love he had felt for her. No one took their place. Falstaff was always in the background, but Oxford could never bring himself to share his innermost thoughts with a landless knight. When Oxford came of age, his grapplings with women momentarily dulled his lust but did nothing to satisfy any deeper needs he had.

The pattern, once begun, was never broken. His affair with Ann Vavasor had been full of words and passion but contained few quiet times where he could drop his guard and show her the boy he was before he became the Seventeenth Earl of Oxford. Nan, the woman he married, was a mystery he had never solved. Other women counted for less.

The sole exception was Virginia Padoana, the woman he had lived with in Venice. She had wrapped him in her arms and began to worm her way inside him when he had suddenly run away to Siena one night to see the plays there. He said he would return but she knew he wouldn't. He journeyed on to Rome, Messina, Sicily, and the Dalmatian coast before returning to Venice for a short visit on his way back to England. 'The Queen calls me home,' he told her, standing awkwardly in the entryway to her pallazo on the Campo Santa Geremia. From the sadness in her eyes and the gentle hug she gave him, they both knew the queen had nothing to do with his departure.

Aemilia Bassano had momentarily rekindled memories of Virginia but Amelia's haughtiness and pursuit of Shackspear had quashed any fantasy Oxford might have had about her. Worse, **Aemilia**'s heartless dismissal of him, not just because she was convinced that Shackspear was the author of the plays but because she was young and he was old, had brought him face-to-face with the realization that he had somehow crested into middle age. His days of wooing a woman were obviously drawing to a close.

The house was silent; the night sky was empty of wind. Tobias was, most likely, out in the fields somewhere. Ethelbert was in the basement, preparing supper. Oxford felt empty as well. In the past, he would have papered over Robin's departure with a burst of activity, frenetically writing plays or poetry, or racing about the countryside in pursuit of deer or rabbits, but he knew there would be no frenzy this time. He could only hope for a dreamless sleep and escape in all the books that lay around his feet.

## ~ 37 ~
## John Shackspear

Spring arrived late in 1590. The gray winter lingered on, bringing day after day of cold, damp weather over the mountains from the Irish Sea. Oxford remained in his room and ate little of what Ethelbert cooked for him. This continued for quite some time until Tobias came in one morning and told Oxford that Ethelbert needed money.

"Money?"

"Yes, my lord."

"Don't we have any?"

"I don't know, my lord. I don't understand money."

"Didn't Nigel give you money when we went out?"

"No, my lord."

"Then what did you do when I told you to pay someone?"

"I didn't pay them."

"You didn't?"

"I didn't have money. Nigel told me to smile and walk away when you said pay someone. No one objected. I was doing my duty, wasn't I?."

"Yes. Of course. Who has been buying the food here?"

"Robin?"

Oxford looked away. "I hate money."

"What shall we do, my lord?"

"I'll have to borrow. We'll go to Stratford tomorrow. Someone there will know of my credit."

"Then we are not returning to London, my lord?"

"No."

This made Tobias feel better. He did not like cities.

There were no horses so Oxford and Tobias had to walk the half-dozen miles to Stratford. Oxford went out ahead, invigorated by the cold air. Stratford soon appeared in the distance. Fields and outbuildings marked the edge of town. The streets were foul with offal, muck heaps, and reeking stable refuse. They came upon a tall man emptying pots into a large pail. He was wearing a worn felt coat that hung to his knees. His hair was long and greasy, his shoulders were stooped, and his beard was thin and unkempt. His black eyes were separated by a long nose that hung like a raven's beak over a narrow mouth.

"Good day to you, sir," Oxford said. The stink from the pail washed over him.

The man turned to look at him. "Eh? Oh, good day." He stood erect and reared his head back. "There are two types of men in this world, gentlemen," he said magisterially: "Men who piss, and men who piss and empty piss-pots." He tipped the pot into the pail.

"Ah, a philosopher," Oxford said.

"Nay, sir. A whittawer. The townspeople dump their night soil at the end of the street and leave their piss out for me to pick up."

"You make gloves."

"The best in Warwickshire." The man began to walk into Stratford. Oxford and Tobias walked with him.

"Pray, sir, tell us your name," Oxford asked.

"John Shackspear."

"Do you know Will Shackspear?"

"The Will Shackspear what lives in London?"

"Aye. The playwright and actor."

"He's my son," John Shackspear said, turning into a side lane." Oxford and Tobias, surprised looks on their faces, followed him. "But he hain't no theater man."

"He isn't?"

"No. He's in London getting rich, he is."

"Has he made his fortune yet?"

"Not that I know of."

"You sound disappointed."

"Of course I am. Who do ye think takes care of his brood while he enjoys himself in London? He should be here, in Stratford, taking care of his dad, he that raised him, and his wife and kids!"

They had arrived at an open lot. A wide pit took up the center. A young man was thigh-deep in the pit treading animal hides in a thick, sulfurous bath. John Shackspear walked up to the edge of the pit and poured in the piss he had collected. "So you know my son?"

"Not really."

A small boy of five or six wandered down the street toward them, his nose running. He was wearing a ragged shirt. He had no shoes on his feet.

John Shackspear turned on him. "What're ye doin' all the way down here?" he yelled. "Away, you whoreson rabbit, away!"

The boy stepped back a few feet but did not leave. He stayed just out of reach, looking at John Shackspear with a dull, vacant stare.

"Go on!" Shackspear said, waving an arm at him. Shackspear lunged at him. The boy turned his head but did not move.

"Your boy?" Oxford asked.

"William's."

"Hamnet?"

"Aye."

Oxford looked at the child. "I heard he was named after a play."

Shackspear laughed. "Is that what Will says in London? Naw. He named him after Hamnet Sadler, he did, my best friend." The child was now staring blankly into the pit. "I told you Will was smart," Shackspear went on, his admiration for the story about Hamnet's name temporarily displacing his rancor toward his son.

"The boy looks…," Oxford said, searching for the right word.

"Odd," Shackspear said. "Yes. He's a fire made with little twigs, he is. Not much there. Gets it from his mother's side, not mine."

Oxford forced himself to stop looking at the boy. "Are there any money lenders in town?"

"No," Shackspear said. He looked at Oxford more closely and lowered his voice. "How much ye need?"

"More than I think you can spare," Oxford said, beginning to move off. "I also need to send a letter to London. Where can I do that?"

"The Bear," Shackspear said. "They'll know someone who's going up soon."

"How often does that happen?"

"Every day or so."

"Thank you, Mr. Shackspear."

The child was now watching Oxford with the same dull eyes with which he had gazed at John Shackspear. "Fare thee well, young Hamnet," Oxford said to the boy.

"You too, sir," Shackspear said. "And who shall I say I've had the pleasure of talking to when next I see my son?"

"Marlowe," Oxford said, without thinking.

"Christopher Marlowe? I saw one of your plays right here in Stratford." His face darkened. "Of course, right after that Will left for London, sticking me with this," he said, "and his sisters and mother."

Oxford's face hardened. He began to walk back down the lane.

"Nice talkin' to ye, Mr. Marlowe," John Shackspear called after him.

Oxford rounded the corner. "Shackspear," he said to himself through clenched teeth.

Tobias came up alongside him. "Shackspear said he did not want to see his son's face, remember?"

"Yes. '*If I see his face and he pulls at my leg, I will not be able to leave. In staying to love him, I will be trapped again.*'"

"We just saw the son's face," Tobias said.

"You're not Shackspear," Oxford said. "He lied when he said he named his son after *Hamlet*. He lied when he said he left Stratford *because* of Hamlet. Now we hear that he left Stratford *because he saw a play by Marlowe*! It is not his son's face that keeps him away from Stratford. It is greed that keeps him away. He will do anything to get what he wants. I will not let the Queen couple me to him again. I will not be the engine by which he achieves his dreams."

# ~ 38 ~
# The Earl of Surrey

Oxford came down the stairs. "Where's supper?" he asked Tobias.

"Ethelbert has not come back from Charlecote, my lord."

"How long can his mother take to die?" Oxford was irritated. "Do we have anything to eat other than what I found in my room just now?"

Tobias shook his head.

Oxford went back upstairs. He walked over to the table under the window where Robin had left some oat cakes and dried fish. He picked up a cake: it was as hard as a paving stone. He sniffed the fish: it stank. He cranked the window open and threw them out into the darkness falling over Billesley.

"Reduced to this," he muttered to himself. "Driven to reading the thoughts of other men, plays by other playwrights, poetry by other poets."

Hunger reached into his midsection and bent him over. He grabbed the bed post at the foot of the bed to steady himself. The ferocious wooden hawk at the top leered down at him. He looked away. "I would understand the inmates in Bedlam now," he said to himself. "I will go back and find Tom. He and I will sit along the road and beg alms. 'Twould be just and compact; ending my life in drooling blather across from the Folly where so many of my dreams came to nothing."

He was dizzy. He lowered himself onto the end of the bed. A book from one of the piles slid into his leg. He kicked it into a larger pile that fell over in a series of thuds and crashes. He kicked another book, causing a second pile to topple over with a crash. "Nothing but a base football player," he muttered to himself.

"*Edward!*" a voice thundered, shattering the silence of the room.

He looked up, startled. A man was standing next to the fireplace—a man who was cradling *a head in his right arm*! His *own* head, Oxford realized. The face on the head was pale, and bloodless. A look of surprise was frozen on it. The eye sockets were empty, full of dust.

241

Blood dripped off the arm that held it. More blood obscured the coat of arms on the shirt the man was wearing.

"Sweet Jesus," Oxford said, trying to stand. "All that is good in Heaven defend me! Who are thee, O ghost?"

"I am thy father's sister's husband," the ghost said in the saddest voice Oxford had ever heard.

Oxford sank back onto the bed. "Lord Henry."

"Yes."

"How have I offended thee, my lord?"

"I left ye the sonnet and ye forged it anew; ye took the morality plays and created new worlds no one had dreamed of. But then ye laid down your pen. In this thou hast offended me."

Oxford looked like he was about to speak. The ghost held up his hand.

"I must be brief. Methinks I scent the morning air." The ghost shifted the head he was holding, which seemed to look out the window and then to look at Oxford. "List, list to what I have to say. I am doomed to walk the night and suffer pain till Lord Burghley comes to join me. When he does, I shall be there to greet him, and there take my revenge."

"Burghley? How has Lord Burghley done thee harm, my lord?"

"List, list. Like thee, I was young and foolish once. In my foolishness, I failed to mark those men who gathered like hovering kites as Great Harry sank toward death. The king saw traitors everywhere. He imagined that the men around him would block his son from succeeding him because the boy was of so few years at the time. I suggested he appoint my father, the Earl of Norfolk, as the boy's protector, but the Duke of Somerset craved the position for himself. He whispered in Henry's ear that I was plotting to put my father on the throne. Somerset had Harry send my father and me to the Tower. Six days later, I was executed. My father was to follow the next day but Harry died during the night and my father was spared."

"So it was Somerset who sent you and your father to the block."

"No. Somerset only wanted us out of the way until Harry died. Burghley urged Somerset to have us executed while we were in the Tower so that my father could not challenge Somerset after Harry's death. Somerset balked. Burghley said he would take care of the problem himself and there would be no blood on Somerset's hands.

He slipped death warrants in front of Harry and lifted Harry's hand to sign them."

"For you *and* your father?"

"Yes."

"Why did he want you dead?"

"He had come upon me in St. Paul's one day and lectured me about leading England astray with poetry that was the work of the devil. I laughed in his face. To me, he was a palace bureaucrat frightened by new ideas, but I misjudged him. He bided his time and remembered my laughter. When Harry began to see traitors everywhere, Burghley realized he had an opportunity to show Somerset how loyal a servant he could be, and a way to pay me back at the same time."

"How came you by this information, my lord? You died only a few days after you were arrested."

"I didn't know why I had been arrested at first. In the Tower, I learned that the executioner will tell a prisoner the cause of his death if he is rewarded enough. My son had already carried bags of gold to him to make sure he brought his sharp axe. I had my son double the amount to find out who had decided I should die. As I put my head onto the block, the executioner whispered 'William Cecil' in my ear! The axe fell the next instant. The look of surprise you see on my face was made permanent by my death. 'William Cecil' was the last thing I heard."

"Most monstrous!" Oxford cried. The fire flared up again. The ghost shifted away from it. He went on.

"Burghley has done well since he brought about my death. He has been knighted and made Baron Burghley. He has been named Lord High Treasurer and Secretary. I cannot bring an early death to him, so I must linger here in torment awaiting the day when he passes over. The scented gardens of Heaven can wait. When the little Welshman dies, I shall escort him to St. Peter, who shall send him down to Hell!"

Oxford shivered. "What can I do, my lord?"

"I passed Burghley on the grand staircase at Stamford late one night recently. He could see me. He knew immediately who I was. Had he died then, the surprise on his face would have exceeded the surprise you see on mine. He knows I wait for him. He guesses what I have in store for him. He spends the time he has left making sure the account he leaves behind will be favorable to him. He rewards historians, Camden most of all, with money and access to documents he selects so they will write well of him. He is manicuring history the way he manicures the lawns behind his house. I know you hate him as much as I do. I have watched you scourge him in your writings. I was waiting for your latest invention when I discovered that your revenge had gone to sleep. I have come to whet your almost blunted purpose, Edward. I will take care of Lord Burghley when he dies, but I need your help whilst he lives."

"I am no historian, my lord."

"No, but I have seen what you can do with words:

> *What fool hath added water to the sea,*
> *Or brought a faggot to bright-burning Troy?*

Or:

> *When to the Sessions of sweet silent thought,*
>
> *I summon up remembrance of things past.*

"You are alive; I am dead. I *cannot* write, but whilst ye yet live, ye mope about in a drafty manse in Warwickshire *complaining that the Queen treats you poorly*!"

"But she has."

"Ye should have yer head cut off!" He tipped the bloody head, but the sight so horrified Oxford that the ghost immediately righted it. "Do ye think she would have called you 'mongrel' if the word hadn't been whispered in her ear?"

"Burghley?"

"And who do ye think planted the idea ye wrote *Famous Victories* to force her to pardon Thomas Trussell?

"Burghley?"

"You and the Queen are naught but strings on Burghley's orpharian, but neither of ye hears the tune he is playing. Pick up your pen, Edward! Avenge my death!"

"But the Queen has taken my pen."

"And who told Elizabeth to stop ye from writing plays?

"Burghley."

"Of course, grown cleverer than he ever was when I was alive. He didn't need an axe to behead you. He had the Queen cut off yer hands! Aye, I know what ye intended with *Titus*. But then ye found Shackspear, and the Queen began to think she had been too quick to silence your voice, so Burghley, ever-so-sly Burghley—always lurking on the sidelines—suggested she let you write *but give the credit to Shakespeare?*"

"Burghley!"

"Aye, beheading you *again*."

Oxford looked defeated. "But what can I do? Anything I write will be Shackpear's. My name will be buried where my body lies."

"How long do ye think the name of the true author can be kept secret? A year? A week? Shackspear is too stupid to hold it in. He'll drink too much in a pub one night and start babbling. Or someone connected with the court will write a letter that will lie in a forgotten drawer until it's found years from now. The English love a mystery, Edward. As Shackspear becomes more famous, more questions will be asked. Thou wilt be known, my son, *thou wilt be known*."

Oxford looked unconvinced. The ghost went on.

"He forced ye to marry his daughter; he humiliated you with scandal when ye returned from Italy; he made sure the Queen never gave ye a command that would add fame to yer name; and he's blocked yer every effort to practice your art."

Oxford was filling with anger.

"It will be revenge enough for both of us if ye can show the world who he really is. Make those who read about him in the history books laugh at him in the theater. Give England the plays Burghley has denied them. In the end, yer name will be returned and we will both be revenged!"

Oxford had a grim look on his face. "I will, my lord."

"There is one more thing. Ye live in dangerous times, Edward, as I did when Harry lay dying. There will be a fight over who succeeds Elizabeth. When she begins to sink toward her grave, the Somersets of your time will come out. They will appear from corners of the realm you never heard of. Anyone hoping to be the next king of England will send you to the Tower because *you sign your name with a crown and seven checks!*" The head in the ghost's arm snorted. "Ye can't stop yerself from reminding everyone that Elizabeth promised to make ye Edward VII, and this will be yer undoing. What was my mistake? I drew up a design for a new coat of arms, that's all, but that was enough. Burghley used my drawings to convince Harry I was planning to succeed him. *You, on the other hand, give them cause to imprison you every time you sign your name!*"

He shifted his head to his left arm and held out his right hand. "My hour has come. I must go." Oxford let go of the bedpost and stepped through the books toward the ghost. He took his hand. It was warm and wet.

"What, Edward, ye've not seen ghosts afore?"

"No, uncle."

"Ye told Arundel that your stepfather visited ye at Greenwich and threatened ye with a whip."

"A fairy tale, my lord. Being witless, my audience reveled in mine, and believed everything I told them."

"Ye told them ye made love to a mare."

"A *mère*, my lord. A *woman*, not a horse."

The ghost began to laugh, but stopped immediately. "That hurt." He pressed his head against his side. "But soft. I must go. Pick up your pen, Edward. Write for both of us!"

The ghost faded from view. The fire had gone out, leaving Oxford in darkness. He collapsed onto the bed and fell immediately into the sleep of the dead.

# Thomas Digby

M y lord! My lord!" Oxford opened his eyes. Tobias was leaning over him. "Master Thomas Digby is here!"

Oxford looked at the window. The afternoon sun filled the room. "Digby? My steward! Come all the way from Hedingham Castle?"

"Yes, my lord."

Oxford looked over toward the fireplace, half-expecting to see the Earl of Surrey staring at him, but the ghost, if that's what Oxford had seen, was gone. He stood up, wobbling slightly. Tobias steadied him. Did a ghost really visit me the night before, he wondered, or was it a dream brought on because I was famished? He saw a spot on one of the books lying open on the floor. He bent down. The blot was reddish brown. He touched it: it was dry. He read the line next to the blot: *Philip, bastard son to King Richard … killed the Viscount of Limoges in revenge of his father's death.*

"Come, my lord."

"Yes," Oxford said. He left the book where it lay, open to the page with the blot. One never closed a book with a blot of ink that might be still drying. "Or of blood," Oxford said to himself, and then laughed. It was ink, he told himself, not blood, *although he wanted it to be blood.* He wasn't Lisbeth's father for nothing.

"My lord?"

"Nothing." He followed Tobias down the stairs and out the front door where they found Digby unloading two pack horses in the courtyard.

"Thomas!" Oxford called out.

"My lord."

"What brings you here?"

"I saw Nigel in London and he suggested I come out to see you. He had correspondence for you, as well as two cases of wine from Bordeaux."

"Château Coutet?"

"I know not the name, my lord." He pointed to a box lying on the ground. Oxford fell upon it. He pried off the slats, exposing a large glass bottle wrapped in straw. He held it up.

"It *is* Château Coutet! Did you bring else?"

"Oysters from Colchester."

"Oysters?"

"Belly down, wrapped in damp cloth, as tasty as the day they were pulled from the Colne."

"Marvelous!" Oxford exclaimed. He pulled open another box and found a string of sausages. "Ethelbert!" he shouted. Ethelbert immediately appeared. "We have something good to eat!" he said as he threw the sausages to him. "*Finally, something good to eat!*"

Oxford put a bottle under his arm. "Bring the oysters, Thomas." They went into the dining room where Oxford attacked the bottle with a knife. Digby poured the oysters out on top of the table. He sat down, pulled out his knife and began to pry them open.

Ethelbert came in with two glasses and put them on the table. Oxford opened the bottle and filled the glasses. Digby handed him an oyster and opened one for himself. The two men tilted back their heads and threw down the oysters, draining the wine from their glasses. "Ah!" Oxford exclaimed. He put down his glass and tossed the empty oyster shell into the wooden box. "You have brought manna from Heaven, Thomas. Catherine de Medici never tasted better fare in Florence!"

"Aye."

"Did you know, Thomas, that oysters swim up to the surface at night and open their shells to the Moon which, being so delighted to see them floating on the sea, cries tears that fall into their shells and become pearls."

Digby grunted.

"I swear," Oxford said. "I've seen them! I've been there" He pried open another shell and looked inside. "Have you ever found any pearls when you opened an oyster?"

"No, my lord."

"They're in there," Oxford said. "You have to look quickly. Sometimes they disappear as soon as the shell is opened!"

"Which would explain why I've never seen them."

"So what of Hedingham?" Oxford asked, reaching for another oyster.

"We're making progress replacing the lead and copper the Earl of Leicester took away while he had custody of the Castle, as well as repairing the buildings he let decay."

"And what news of London?"

"Nigel says Lady Mary has published her *Arcadia*."

"Ah, finally."

"You know of it?"

"Philip, her brother, began it before he died. It's a long, complicated work in prose. She was determined to finish it as a gift to him. I told her she should simplify it."

"It was too complicated?"

"A man is in love with a woman who is never allowed to leave her home. To gain access to her, the man disguises himself as a woman but, once inside, his love thinks he's *truly* a woman and treats him like a sister. Her father believes he's a *woman* and tries to seduce him. The mother figures out he's a *man* and pursues him."

Digby crossed himself. "God save us. With stories like that, the deer will be chasing the hounds and the titmice will be bedding down with the sparrows."

Oxford laughed, a hearty laugh that echoed through the empty house. He hoisted his glass and sang: *"Leave not a rabbit in his burrow."*

*"Or a buck in the bracken,"* Digby added.
*"Or a fish in the pond,"* Oxford went on.
*"Or a bird in the sky."*

The two of them sang the rest together:

*Trap 'em and shoot 'em!*
*Hook 'em and bait 'em!*
*Run 'em to ground,*
*To bake in a pasty*
*And serve all around!*

They clicked their glasses and laughed some more.

"You wrote that little ditty when you were ten, my lord."

"I cannot believe I still remember it. 'Twas my first effort at expressing the joy of mastering the chase and learning how to sit quietly with you at the edge of the pond and lure fat bass out from under the bank beneath us."

"Come back to Hedingham, my lord. See the sun in the morning, clear and bright as crystal. Sit back in the evening and feel the contentment ye only feel after a day on horseback or hard work in the barns and fields."

Oxford shook his head.

Digby was disappointed. "Well, if ye'll not come to Hedingham, then, we'll to business." Digby reached for a satchel on the floor. He pulled out a package wrapped with string and put it on the table. He cut the string with his knife and pulled out a letter. He handed it to Oxford. "From Malfis."

Oxford took the letter and read through his lawyer's advice "He has filed a demurrer to Hatton's lawsuit. He tells me to pay no mind to it." Oxford flipped the letter aside. "Not that I was going to anyway. Anything else?"

"Money from Nigel," Digby said, pulling out a leather bag, "and a letter from the Queen."

Oxford pried the seal off the envelope and pulled out the letter. "God's blood," he said. "I am commanded to meet the Duke of Saxe-Coburg at Colchester and escort him to Havering-in-the-Bowerie, where we are to wait until word is sent to bring the Duke to Hampton Palace."

"Oh, my lord. You could be stuck at Havering for weeks."

"*I'm supposed to entertain him*, she says. And she would *like* a new play."

"A command," Digby said, pouring himself more wine.

"Aye. Her 'mongrel' count shall provide amusement for the Duke."

"'Mongrel'?"

"Her dog, her spaniel, *the slave who fetches her slippers*," Oxford replied, his voice rising. He threw her letter onto the floor.

"Ye can't refuse."

Oxford reached for the wine and poured himself another glass. Silence fell over the room. His face darkened. Digby watched him warily. "All right," Oxford said at last. "I will give her a play."

"Robin said you had given up writing."

"I did. But what if I told you that someone said I should pick up my pen and write again."

"And who was that?"

"The Earl of Surrey."

"The Poet Earl? He was beheaded before you were born."

"Indeed. I know that *too well*. Thomas, do you believe in ghosts?"

"Aye," Digby said, looking around the room. He crossed himself.

"The ghost of my uncle, the Earl of Surrey, visited me last night."
Digby nodded.

"And told me to write," Oxford continued.

"So what will it be?"

"A play about a bastard."

"And what will ye call it?"

"*King John.*"

"He was not a bastard, my lord."

"No, but one of his liege men was. Holinshed writes that '*Philip, bastard son to King Richard … killed the Viscount of Limoges in revenge of his father's death.*' King Richard earned lasting fame by reaching into the mouth of a lion and tearing out its heart. His bastard son is all I need. He shall be the hero of the play, despite his smudged ancestry."

Digby shook his head. "The Third Earl of Oxford was one of them who forced John to sign Magna Carta. Elizabeth won't like that."

"The Third Earl will make no appearance in this play. Or, if he does, there will be no mention of the charter. I shall call it *The Troublesome Raigne of John King of England.* The title of the play will put her on edge. When she hears nothing about the Magna Carta, she will realize I have been playing with her."

"For which you will be punished."

"She won't be able to. She would have to admit she expected it. She will grind her teeth in silence."

"You could addle her with another king," Digby suggested.

"King John will serve, but the Bastard will be my interest in the play. The actors will fight to play him. I will make John a weak king with a weak claim to the throne. She will recognize I am talking about her."

Digby now looked concerned. Oxford went on.

"There will be a boy named Arthur who will be better descended than John. John will fear that Arthur will overthrow him when Arthur grows to manhood. John will muse how sweet life would be without Arthur, and one of his minions will murder Arthur."

"Mary," Digby said softly. The wine had lost its taste. "For the love of Jesus, my lord. She'll know you're talking about Mary, and her claim that she was better descended than Elizabeth."

"Let her wriggle. Burghley made Mary look guilty, but kill an anointed queen?" He looked dark. "Kill one and kill them all."

"You sat on the jury. Isn't England better off with Mary gone?"

"Yes. But there's a price for doing your duty when a queen goes to the block, Thomas. Elizabeth will know what I'm up to when she hears John berate Hubert for killing Arthur, who was the true heir."

"Perhaps she would be better pleased with a comedy?"

"No comedy can raise the question of who a rightful successor is."

Digby shook his head. "Ye might as well try to hold a tiger by his tooth than bring up the succession question in front of her."

Oxford smiled. "She will know I am the Bastard, and forgive the rest."

"Well, if you intend to write this play, you need to know when the Duke arrives." He got up and retrieved the letter from where Oxford had thrown it. "April 16," he read.

"God's blood!" Oxford said. "We must leave tomorrow."

## ~ 40 ~
## Oxford Court

Nigel greeted Oxford at the door. Oxford went by him, heading for the library. "Find Robin," he said.

Nigel followed at a slower pace. He stopped in the doorway. "I regret that the house is not in readiness for your arrival, your lordship. We did not know that you were returning to London."

"I need Robin."

"Young Robin left for the continent three weeks ago, my lord."

"What? He was to Lord Strange."

"Lord Strange apparently wants everyone to think he would like to have a troupe of players, but Robin learned that he had no interest in actually financing them. Robin said he would go to Italy to, as he put it, see the sights you so often described to him."

"I cannot work without Robin."

"May I suggest re-engaging Mr. Lyly?"

"No. Not the little man again. No."

Someone knocked on the door. Nigel went to see who it was. Malfis came in. He was carrying a sheaf of papers under his arm.

"No, no, *no*!" Oxford said, turning away.

"A few signatures, my lord, and I shall be out from underneath you."

"Underneath me?" Oxford turned to see if Malfis was being clever but found only a tight-lipped industrious lawyer laying out sheets of paper on the table. Nigel picked up a pen and held it out to Oxford.

"What are these?" Oxford demanded to know.

"Bonds, agreements, loans, and an affidavit to prolong Sir Christopher Hatton's entanglement in the suit he has filed against you. A writ of *Quominus* in the Exchequer will raise the question of whether Hatton can succeed against you when you owe the Queen so much money yourself. Any money Hatton might obtain from you will be money denied the Queen, and so I will add her as a defendant alongside you, which will delay the case for several years." It was obvious that the detailed explanation and the sight of the legal papers on the table gave Malfis a warm sense of accomplishment.

Oxford took the pen. "I need an amanuensis, Malfis, not more papers to sign." Malfis' index finger pointed to the first signature line. Oxford carefully wrote his full signature, seven checks and crown, ignoring the voice of his uncle to stop signing his name as Edward VII. He was in no mood to be cooperative with anyone, living or dead. Malfis' finger moved on to the next blank signature line. Oxford resisted the urge to write across his solicitor's finger and kept on signing where Malfis directed him.

"You have an amanuensis, my lord," Malfis said, once he was certain Oxford had arrived signed the last document. "Young Robin, I believe."

"Robin has gone to Italy."

"How unfortunate." Malfis slid the papers into a folder. "If I may, my lord."

"What?"

"I have a friend who is a fine lawyer from Shropshire."

"I need a secretary, Malfis, not more lawyers."

"My friend has a son, name of John, who is about fourteen now. The boy is quick-witted and well mannered. The father intends to send him down to Oxford in a year or two but would like to season him with some experience in London before he goes."

"Have you met the boy?"

"I have. He is of slight build and lacks the fair appearance that leads so many young men astray at his age. His father says he is too much into the Psalms and needs a bit of leavening."

"A follower, then."

"He will do what he is told."

"Send him round."

"My lord," Malfis said, bowing slightly. He tucked the papers under his arm and left.

---

The thin, gangly youth Malfis had described arrived at Oxford Court the next day. Falstaff opened the door for him. "Ahn-tray," the big man boomed.

The boy stepped into the hall. Falstaff looked him up and down.

"Not much meat there, boy," he announced.

"Yes, sir," the boy said. He had no idea who Falstaff was. He did not even know who Oxford was. His father had told him to present himself at Oxford Court and be respectful.

"Do ye eat?"

This question froze him. He looked at Falstaff, who obviously spent considerable time eating. He looked down the immense hall lined with the heads of animals. Was he supposed to eat? Not eat? What should he say? Falstaff leaned in to see if the boy had heard him.

"Yes sir," the boy said, as he peered sideways at Falstaff, who was breathing the odor of foul onions all over him.

"Follow me," Falstaff said. He marched off to the library. The boy followed. "Sit," Falstaff said, pointing to a chair.

"Yes sir," the boy said.

"Yes sir, yes sir. You keep this up and I'm going to name you 'Master Yes sir.'"

"Yes sir," the boy said, then instantly shut his mouth. "No sir," he quickly added. His fright was now complete.

Falstaff left the boy and went looking for Oxford. He found him coming down the stairs. "Your new secretary awaits you in the library, your lordship."

"What think you of him?"

"I'm going to miss Robin."

Oxford went into the library. Nigel followed. The boy tried to stand and banged both his knees on the underside of the table. His eyes filled with tears. "Your lordship," he managed to get out.

"What's your name?" Oxford asked.

"Arthur John Marston, your lordship, but everyone calls me John."

"Can you take dictation?"

He nodded, surprised at another question he hadn't expected.

"Get him a pen," Oxford ordered. Nigel handed the boy a pen. There were scraps of paper on the table. The boy pulled one over in front of him.

"Not that one!" Oxford slid the paper to the end of the table and replaced it with another piece. "Write down what I dictate." The boy dipped the pen in the ink pot and readied himself.

"Come live with me and be my love."

"Oh," John Marston said. "Did you write that? That's lovely."

Oxford glowered. "Write!" he commanded, pointing to the paper.

John Marston bent his pen to the paper. Oxford looked over his shoulder. "Good." Oxford walked away around the table. "Have you eaten this morning?"

The boy was surprised again. "Yes, my lord. A spelt cake, left over from last night. The cook grilled it over the kitchen fire." The boy was frantic. What did his breakfast have to do with his new employment? "And onions," he quickly added. Falstaff's foul breath still hung over him. If the large man loved onions, maybe he should say he did too.

Oxford came around the table. He leaned over and sniffed John Marston's breath. "Tell the cook to put more in."

"Yes, my lord." The boy breathed a sigh of relief.

"King John," Oxford said, pointing to the paper in front of the boy.

The boy wrote 'King John.' Oxford looked over his shoulder. "John Marston, I will speak you a scene. Do you think you can take it down?"

"Aye, my lord."

"Good. There are four players in this scene: King John, Queen Elinor, Robert Faulconbridge, and his older brother, the Bastard."

"The Bastard?" The boy looked up in dismay.

"You won't go to Hell for writing it down."

"I won't?"

"No," Oxford said. "'Tis only ink on paper."

The boy smiled wanly. "Why is he called the Bastard?"

"Because he is a bastard," Oxford said, his amusement at the boy's discomfort beginning to be displaced by irritation at all the questions. "His father was Richard Coeur-de-Lion, who snuck into the bed of the Bastard's mother and fathered him."

The boy's eyes got bigger.

"Pen to paper," Oxford ordered. John Marston put the pen down on the page. "King John has been told that the Faulconbridge brothers are at odds with each other. Robert, the youngest, says he should inherit his father's lands because his older brother is a bastard. The Bastard disagrees."

"Do we have to call him the Bastard?" the boy asked, looking up.

"It is not 'we,' John Marston; it is 'I.' And yes, he shall be called the Bastard throughout." Oxford pointed at the paper. "No more questions. You are nothing more than my pen. Do you understand?"

"Yes, my lord."

"King John asks Robert: '*What art thou?*' and Robert, the younger brother, answers: '*The son and heir to Faulconbridge.*'"

The boy began to write. Oxford continued. "King John wonders how this can be since the oldest son always inherits his father's lands: "*You came not of one mother then, it seems.*" The Bastard speaks up:

> *Most certain of one mother, mighty king;*
> *That is well known; and, as I think, one father:*
> *But for the certain knowledge of that truth*
> *I put you o'er to heaven and to my mother:*
> *Of that I doubt, as all men's children may.*

Queen Elinor is shocked by this:

> *Out on thee, rude man! Thou dost shame thy mother*
> *And wound her honour with this diffidence.*

The Bastard:
> *I, madam? no, I have no reason for it;*
> *That is my brother's plea and none of mine;*
> *The which if he can prove, he pops me out of*
> *At least five hundred pound a year:*
> *Heaven guard my mother's honour and my land!*

King John:
> *A good blunt fellow. Why, being younger born,*
> *Doth your brother lay claim to thine inheritance?*

The Bastard:
> *I know not why, except to get the land.*
> *But whether I be as true begot or no,*
> *That still I lay upon my mother's head.*

King John:
> *Why, what a madcap hath heaven lent us here!*

Oxford stopped. "Robert has been waiting his turn to speak."

Robert:
> *My gracious liege, when that my father lived,*
> *Your brother did employ my father much,*

The Bastard interrupts him:

> *Well, sir, by this you cannot get my land:*
> *Your tale must be how he employ'd my mother.*"

Falstaff guffawed.

"Get out," Oxford said. Falstaff rolled into the hallway and disappeared. Oxford went on. "Queen Elinor has taken a liking to the Bastard. She says to him:"

> *I like thee well: wilt thou forsake thy fortune,*
> *Bequeath thy land to him and follow me?*
> *I am a soldier and now bound to France.*

Bastard:     *Brother, take you my land, I'll take my chance.*
             *Madam, I'll follow you unto the death.*

Qn. Elinor:  *Nay, I would have you go before me.*

Oxford stopped. "What say you, John Marston? Will you stay?"

"Yes, sir," he said, then quickly looked around to see if Falstaff was still in the room. "Aye," he added.

"Good. Nigel will tell you where to sleep. I'll tell you when." He suddenly remembered that Frangellica had left for Italy. He turned to Nigel. "And who has replaced Frangellica?"

"No one."

"*We have no cook?*"

"Well, your lordship, Frangellica made plans to cook for the Italian ambassador but she didn't like him."

Frangellica suddenly appeared in the doorway. "Buongiorno, signore!"

Oxford bowed to her. "Buongiorno, Frangellica! Come sei stato?"

Nigel, pleased that he had well-served his master once again, motioned for the boy to follow him. John Marston, eyes wide as the sound of Italian filled his ears, followed Nigel out of the room.

## ~ 41 ~
## The Bastard

Oxford found John Marston down on his knees the next morning in front of the window in the library. The boy jumped up when he heard Oxford come into the room.

"Mr. Marston, God will think less of you if you cut off your prayers the moment you hear someone coming."

"My lord, I, I …"

"You suddenly became more worried about your lord here on Earth than the one you were praying to in Heaven."

"My lord, I mean …" The boy was flustered.

"Back on your knees," Oxford said. John Marston knelt back down. Oxford knelt beside him. "Hands clasped," Oxford said, clasping his hands together. John Marston imitated him. "Silently now, young man. God hears all."

The boy was so shocked by this that he didn't close his eyes. He remained staring at Oxford who had shut his eyes tight. Oxford cracked an eye open and looked sideways at the boy, who quickly closed his. The two of them remained kneeling for a minute. Oxford got up and brushed off his knees. "I apologize, Mr. Marston, that Oxford Court does not have a proper chapel where you can pray. However, if I were choosing a substitute, kneeling in front of this window would be an excellent choice."

"Your lordship does not mind?"

"Not at all, as long as your worship does not interfere with me."

"Yes, my lord."

"To your station, then," Oxford said, striding around the table. John Marston, his face mixed with relief and wonder, ran to his chair and sat down. He picked up his pen and waited.

Oxford was excited to be back at work, stealing facts from Holinshed and Foxe and remolding them into a story he could parade across the stage. John Marston worked hard, confirming the opinion Malfis had given of him. After a long day, the boy would stagger off to a supper and sleep while Oxford would stay up, correcting the copies and adding new lines. At times he would simply make a mark to indicated he would dictate an insertion to the boy in the morning. Other times, something he had read would prompt him to pull out earlier pages and make changes to them. One such time occurred during the second week they were working together.

"I need more here," he said, pointing to where King John had dismissed Robert's claim that his older brother, the Bastard, was illegitimate. "I realize that King John would not have accepted Robert's tale that his older brother was a bastard. A child born during marriage is legitimate:

> *Sirrah, your brother is legitimate;*
> *Your father's wife did after wedlock bear him,*
> *And if she did play false, the fault was hers;*
> *Which fault lies on the hazards of all husbands*
> *That marry wives.*

"The king would have pointed out that the older brother could have been hid away if he were indeed the fruits of adultery:

> *This calf bred from his cow from all the world;*
> *He might have hid.*

Oxford pointed to the paper in front of the boy. "Add that here," he said.

John Marston scribbled the words on the page. "Hid?" he asked.

"Think Moses."

"Ah," the boy said. "Has it happened in modern times?"

"Lord Hunsdon."

John Marston looked up. He knew who Lord Hunsdon was, but the great man's "hidden" birth was news to him. Oxford explained.

"King Henry got Hunsdon's mother pregnant and then married her off to a man who raised Hunsdon as his own."

The boy's jaw dropped. "How awful." He tried to digest this. "Are there others?"

"How can we know, if they're all hid."

This astonished the boy even more. "Hidden in plain sight."

"In plain sight." Oxford smiled, knowing that the boy would now eye every man he met and wonder if he were looking at a 'hidden calf.'

"But why add this to the play?" John Marston asked. "The Bastard was not hid."

"The Queen will know what I'm intending."

"The Queen?"

"Who else do you think I write for? The swine in the pit? Hah!"

"The Queen," John Marston repeated reverently.

"Back to work. We are now at the point where King John will suggest to Hubert that it would be meet if someone got rid of Arthur."

"Who is Arthur?"

"The rightful heir to the throne."

"And what happens?"

"Arthur dies."

John Marston threw down his pen. "I hate my name."

"Ease yourself. There are many Arthurs. Think of King Arthur."

This soothed the boy. "Will I have to write of his death?"

"No. Arthur will die offstage."

"How old will he be in the play, my lord?"

"You could play the part."

"I shall decline the honor, if asked."

"Then you won't be asked. In real life, Arthur died mysteriously. In the play, he will die while trying to escape."

"Offstage."

"Offstage. But before he dies, Hubert will be ordered to put out Arthur's eyes with hot pokers."

"Put out his eyes? With hot pokers?"

"Aye." Oxford looked down on the boy. "How like you the effect."

"Most hideous."

"Exactly. Arthur recoils in horror from Hubert:

| Arthur: | *Must you with hot irons burn out both mine eyes?* |
| Hubert: | *Young boy, I must.* |
| Arthur: | *Have you the heart? When your head did but ache,*<br>*I knit my handkerchief about your brows,*<br>*The best I had, a princess wrought it me,* |
| Hubert: | *I have sworn to do it;*<br>*And with hot irons must I burn them out.* |

261

| Arthur: | *For heaven sake, Hubert, let me not be bound!* |
| | *I will sit as quiet as a lamb;* |
| Hubert: | *Come, boy, prepare yourself.* |
| Arthur: | *O heaven, that there were but a mote in yours,* |
| | *A grain, a dust, a gnat, a wandering hair,* |
| | *Any annoyance in that precious sense!* |

Oxford paused as John Marston caught up to him. The boy looked up at Oxford. "The irons must be cold by now, my lord."

"You think?"

The boy nodded. He did not want to hear anything more about Hubert putting out Arthur's eyes. Oxford waved a hand to indicate he would say more. John Marston dipped his pen in the ink pot and readied himself.

| "Arthur says: | *Lo, by my truth, the instrument is cold* |
| | *And would not harm me.* |

John Marston bent to his writing. Oxford saw a slight rise in the corner of the young man's mouth. Oxford couldn't resist drawing John Marston back out to the edge. "Hubert replies: *I can heat it, boy.*

| Arthur: | *No, in good sooth: the fire is dead with grief.* |
| Hubert: | *But with my breath I can revive it, boy.* |
| Arthur: | *An if you do, you will but make it blush.* |
| Hubert: | *Well, see to live; I will not touch thine eye* |
| | *For all the treasure that thine uncle owes:* |
| Arthur: | *O, now you look like Hubert! all this while* |
| | *You were disguised.* |
| Hubert: | *Peace; no more. Adieu.* |
| | *Your uncle must not know but you are dead;* |
| | *I'll fill these dogged spies with false reports you are.* |
| Arthur: | *O heaven! I thank you, Hubert.* |

"You approve?" Oxford asked.

"Yes, my lord. The audience will love it."

"That they will. And their hope for little Arthur will carry them through the next few scenes. Thank you, John Marston."

John Marston blushed. "You're welcome, my lord."

262

## ~ 42 ~
## *King John* before the Queen

The applause was dying away. The Duke of Saxe-Coburg and his train applauded mightily, even those who did not understand English. For the Duke, the play was a continuation of the good time he was having in England. Oxford had taken him hunting at Sible Hedingham and out into the mud at the mouth of the Colne searching for clams, something the Duke had acquired a taste for when he was a student at Cambridge. As they stood on the edge of the muddy flats that stretched southeast toward the English Channel, Oxford had taken off his boots and showed the Duke how to find clams by digging into the mud with his toes. The Duke happily discarded his boots and followed Oxford out into the flats. His entourage was dismayed. With great reluctance, they took of their boots and waded out into the mud. The Duke announced he had not been happier in years, what with all the stuffiness of the court he had to preside over, and declared himself Oxford's liege friend for life. When he was finally introduced to the Queen, he reported how happy he was with Oxford who, unfortunately, was too far away from the Queen to see the wry smile on her face as she listened to the Duke describe how Oxford took him tramping out into the black mud at the mouth of the Colne.

"Well done, Master Shackspear," Elizabeth said, still clapping. "You have given me a history that will strengthen the resolve of my people." She looked off toward Oxford, who had folded himself into a corner of the Great Hall where the play had been staged. "Although at least one character is not in the history books, I believe." Oxford began moving closer to hear what she had to say. "And what can we expect next? Another history play?"

"A comedy, Your Majesty," Shackspear blurted out. He did not want any more English kings.

"What about a comedy *and* a history play?" the Queen asked.

Shackspear bobbed up and down. "Most assuredly," he said, a broad grin on his face. Oxford groaned.

"Well, then, a comedy and a history play." She rose. She leaned over to straighten her dress and directed her voice at Oxford, who was now close enough to hear her. "We liked not the allusion to Mary, but you have finally given me a history play."

"One of many," Oxford said.

"Yes." Someone had given her an orange before the play. She still held it in her hand. "You are a juicy orange, Edward, full of fruit, but no orange ever squeezed itself."

He bowed. "I shall consider myself well squeezed."

She decided to ignore his remark. She swept from the room. Her ladies-in-waiting swept the floor with their long dresses as they followed her out of the room. One of them glanced at him for a second. He was so surprised that he did not see Shackspear come up from behind.

"Well done, don't ye think?" Shackspear said, a self-satisfied smile on his face.

Oxford turned to him. "What happened with *Pericles*? Someone told me they saw it. Not only that, but they liked it. "

"So did Tilney, my lord, after he took out the first two acts."

Oxford bristled. "You cut one of my plays?"

"Not me, my lord: Mr. Tilney did. I thought the first act was a grabber. Even the nut-crackers could have figured out the king was sticking his own daughter!" His face glowed. "Which was why Tilney, with as big a frown as I've ever seen, tore off the first two acts and handed back the rest."

Oxford glowered. "And now you get the Queen to stick me with writing two plays instead of one."

"Yes! A comedy and a history play!" Shackspear was glowing.

Aemilia Bassano glided up. She laid her hand on Shackpear's arm.

"Welcome back, my lord," she purred, looking at Oxford. "Isn't fortune smiling on William? A comedy *and* a history play!"

"Yes. Not one but *two* commissions. With your permission." He bowed and turned away. Halfway across the room Lord Burghley angled away from the courtiers he was entertaining and intercepted Oxford.

"Edward, my boy. So good to see you. How foolish of me to think you had disappeared into Warwickshire, never to be seen again." He was beaming. "And writing plays again. Filled, as always, with characters who look suspiciously like you." Oxford began to turn away but Burghley put his hand on Oxford's arm and lowered his voice. "I have met with Lord Montague at Oatlands. He was kind enough to consider an offer to marry your daughter Lisbeth to his grandson, the Earl of Southampton."

"What need have you to talk to Lord Montague? The Earl is your ward. You control his destiny, as you did mine."

"Your grandfather was not living when I arranged for you to marry Nan. It is true that I do not need Lord Montague's permission, but it is meet that I consult him to see where he lies on the issue."

"And where does he lie?"

"In favor of the marriage."

"And what about Lisbeth? What says she?"

"She is docile and obedient. She looks to her grandfather for advice in this matter."

Oxford doubted that very much. From their fiery meeting at Cecil House, Lisbeth seemed anything but docile and obedient. She must be a handful for the old man, he thought. "And the Earl? He is, what, sixteen now?"

"He is, and the flower of his generation. Great things are expected of him."

"And if he meets those expectations, who better by his side than your oldest granddaughter?"

"Who is your oldest daughter."

Burghley's eyes were glowing. He loved matchmaking when it advanced his family interests, particularly when he had the extra pleasure of knowing his detested former son-in-law would be forced to cooperate with him. He knew Oxford would resist at first—he always did—but, in the end, he would have to agree because Southampton was an excellent match for Lisbeth. Oxford's family line stretched back hundreds of years, whereas Burghley had been a baron only less than twenty years. He so wanted to strengthen his status among the aristocratic families of England, and intended to do so by marrying his children and grandchildren off to the scions of noble families. Marrying Nan to Oxford had been his first success; marrying Lisbeth to the Third Earl of Southampton would cement his family's rise into the first ranks.

"He is a talented young man," Burghley went on. "Other poets are dedicating works to him. He is an excellent choice for Elizabeth."

"And for your family."

"As for yours."

Oxford knew he couldn't block Elizabeth from marrying Southampton. "If Lisbeth says aye, her father says aye."

Burghley smiled, letting Oxford know he was enjoying the feeling of besting his former son-in-law once again. "The Earl speaks highly of your poetry, my lord. A sonnet or two urging him to marry might find a receptive ear. Tell him he should bear children. Tell him he will see himself live on in their faces."

*And you in their children*, Oxford almost said aloud.

"Don't stand in the way of happiness," Burghley urged, sensing Oxford slipping away from him. "Help me with this."

Oxford forced himself to speak. "I will."

"Splendid." Burghley gave Oxford's arm a squeeze, bowed slightly, and moved off. Oxford could hear the old fox humming to himself as he disappeared into the crowded room.

John Marston appeared. "Is that Lord Burghley?" he asked.

"Unfortunately."

"Unfortunately?"

"I must write sonnets, John Marston."

"About what?"

"About making babies."

"Making babies?"

"About getting married and having children." He raised his right hand, index finger extended. *But were some childe of yours alive that time, / You should live twice in it, and in my rime.* Something like that. I like the challenge."

"And the plays, my lord?"

"A comedy and a history play."

"What shall they be?" The boy's face showed his eagerness.

"You pick the king."

"Henry VI."

"Why so?"

"His father, Henry V, was too noble, too incorruptible to be the subject of an interesting play."

"You think?"

"Yes. His son, Henry VI, is much more interesting. He threw all of his father's conquests away and let England be torn apart."

"You've been reading Holinshed: the three 'd's; disagreement, dissension, and disorder."

"Aye, my lord."

"Henry VI reigned a long time. I don't think I can fit him into one play."

"Then perhaps it will take two." He eyed Oxford to see how his master took this. "There are plenty of scheming men and devious women in Holinshed: Joan of Arc, Queen Margaret, Suffolk, Clifford …"

"Gloucester, Jack Cade, young Bolingbroke."

"A hell infested with devils!" John Marston burst out. The pious, quiet boy had a darker side. John Marston assumed a more sober attitude. "And the comedy?"

"Something I will shove up Burghley's nose."

"Eeeuh."

"Don't worry. They only put lords in the Tower."

They started to leave the audience room. "Why did the Queen thank that man Shackspear for *King John,*" the boy asked as they crossed the room, a puzzled look on his face. "He didn't write the play; you did."

"You *and I* wrote the play, John Marston."

"But she thanked him, not you," he said. "Or me," he mumbled to himself in a lower voice.

"Yes."

"I am confused."

"The Queen has ordered it thus. As she is the head of the Church of England, she is infallible, is she not?"

"The Puritans disagree."

"And the Catholics," Oxford reminded him.

"Yes. And the Catholics."

"And what say you about the Muslims?"

"The Muslims?"

"Or the natives who live in the forests of North America who have never even heard of Her Majesty."

The boy smiled weakly.

Oxford continued. "Think you there is only one Heaven?" The smile disappeared. Fear ran across the boy's face like a summer cloud on a warm day. "Perhaps, John Marston, we shall find a row of gods sitting on large thrones when we die. One for each religion. An attendant comes up and asks us what religion we practiced whilst we lived."

"My lord," John Marston said weakly.

Oxford looked at the boy and saw how worried he was. "Forgive me, John Marston. I am taking out my anger at the Queen, and Shackspear, on you."

"I am still confused," the boy said again. "I like certainty."

"There is little of that, I'm afraid. Take Shackspear. The Queen has decreed, for reasons you need not know, that I shall write plays and Shackspear shall get the credit."

"My lord!"

"You've seen it done. Just now, in fact. And she has ordered that no one, upon pain of death, shall reveal the secret."

John Marston looked up in fright. No one had told him he might learn secrets that would cause his death!

"What you just learned will never appear in Camden, John Marston. Not everything that happens makes it into the history books."

"Lord Hunsdon," the boy said quickly.

"Bravo!" Oxford clapped him on the shoulder. "Feeling better now?"

"Yes, my lord. Thank you, my lord."

## ~ 43 ~
## The Queen and Lady Elspeth Trentham

The Queen caught Elspeth Trentham glancing at the Earl of Oxford as she and her ladies-in-waiting were leaving the hall where they had just seen *King John*. A trusted lady-in-waiting for over ten years, and still unmarried at thirty, Lady Elspeth had been away dealing with her father's estate. Elspeth was long-legged and high-hipped. Her eyes were deep brown and almond-shaped, her nose long and regal, her hair auburn in color and long enough to reach her waist. She was wearing a dress that covered her bosom, knowing that Elizabeth did not like displays that put her at a disadvantage.

Elizabeth paused at the doorway to let her ladies-in-waiting glide past her. They were all dressed in white and looked like an eyrar of swans floating down the Thames. "Elspeth," said the Queen, as the younger woman came up to her. "He's been had by many and kept by none."

"Your Majesty," Elspeth said, trying to look surprised. "I only *glanced* at him."

The Queen knew otherwise. "Lord Burghley thought the Earl would appreciate his daughter, but he never did. He's lightning in a bottle."

"One cannot catch lightning in a bottle, Your Majesty."

"Exactly."

The Queen started to walk after the other ladies-in-waiting, who had drifted down the hallway. Elspeth walked alongside her.

"He has no wife and I have no husband," Elspeth said.

"You speak boldly."

"I was raised in a household of brothers, Your Majesty. As you have often said, if a woman remains silent, she cannot be heard."

Elizabeth smiled. "And he has no heir. If he dies without a son, 500 years of English history will die with him."

"I am not interested in being a brood mare for him, Your Majesty. If I continue to like what I see, I believe I can bring some order and direction to his life, the keel to his rudder."

"Well, he is not getting any younger."

"Neither am I. Will you let me have him?"

Elizabeth did not answer for a moment. She liked it that Elspeth had no illusions about marriage. They were alike in that regard. She also knew that Elspeth was asking for permission to marry Oxford for more than the sake of simple court etiquette. Elspeth wanted to make sure Elizabeth did not want him for herself. Or, whether she would never let anyone else have him.

Elizabeth wondered if she had finally freed herself from the passion the Earl had brought to her life when he had beguiled her with poetry, kisses, and stories about Italy. "But that was years ago," she reminded herself. "It is too late to marry now." She glanced at Elspeth as the two of them continued down the hallway. "Yes," she said aloud. "You will make him a good wife. Particularly one such as you. You may have him."

"Thank you, Your Majesty."

"Time will tell whether I should have denied the gift."

"Yes, Your Majesty."

"Well, then, if he is to be mewed up into marriage, we must contrive his capture. He is a fool with loose change when it comes to novelties, but poetry sweeps his judgment away."

Elspeth laughed. "I am no poet, Your Majesty."

"I wasn't thinking of you. We will find someone to write a poem in praise of you and have it published. He will jump in with his own poems, and you will have him."

"Where shall I find such a poet?"

"Leave that to me, my dear."

Oxford watched Elspeth conferring with the Queen. He saw Elspeth throw back her head and laugh. He heard a throaty contralto, surprising in a woman. To Oxford, her voice came from somewhere deep inside her, down near her sex, if he thought about it, which he did. In truth, he imagined that if he pulled her dress over her head, he would not see her sex as well as he could now, hearing her laughter. It was not a matter of pictures but the way frankincense evokes Araby, or how the perfume of a flower can bring back memories of a summer romance. The sound of her voice was enough to evoke all his romantic sensibilities. He was being swept away. And he loved it.

270

## ~ 44 ~
## A Poem for Lady Elspeth

Falstaff looked up as Oxford sat down across from him. "Where's your faithful assistant?"

"He thinks the Boar's Head is a den of iniquity."

"I should hope it is. Otherwise, I would have to go elsewhere."

Shackspear loomed up. "My lord," he said, bowing. He swept a new hat off his head. He looked better with it off. "Some men are able to wear hats," thought Oxford, and Shackspear is not one of them. "The comedy," Shackspear said.

"It was a history play, wasn't it?"

"Well, yes, but if you could work on the comedy, it would help put some angels in my pocket."

"You need to worry about the angels up there," Oxford said, pointing toward the ceiling, "not those that have not yet found their way into your pocket."

"With all due respect, my lord, I need the angels down here first. Otherwise, I may be seeing those up there sooner than I would like."

Falstaff bolted out of his seat and, with a sweeping gesture, grabbed Shackspear around the shoulders. He pulled Shackspear into himself, swallowing him up. "Nay, Master Shackspear. You and I are both going down, down, down," he said, his voice descending as he drove Shackspear toward the floor, "into the sulfurous pit!"

"Sir John!" Shackspear cried, trying to wriggle out from underneath him. "Forbear, Sir John." He looked desperately at Oxford. "My lord!"

Oxford leaned forward. "If I were you," he said, pausing dramatically, "I would run!"

Shackspear tore himself away from Falstaff and bolted for the door.

"I love seeing his nether parts rounding a corner," Falstaff said, sitting back down.

"Would that you could make him disappear completely!"

Peaches came up with a beer and put it down in front of Oxford.

271

"I don't beat up and dent the pots I use, my lord," she said in a scolding tone of voice, motioning toward Shackspear, now disappearing through the front door. "Ye need him."

"Aye, but I don't bang him around anymore than you do your pots, do I? We can hear you in the kitchen!"

"Oh!" She turned and headed back to the kitchen.

"She has a point, my lord. Shackspear may be a provincial hack but he has, of late, added a few things to your plays, hasn't he?"

"Nothing of note," Oxford said dismissively.

"But the Queen liked the play."

"Aye, but not because of anything *he* added. She wants two more. A comedy and a history play."

"Which'll it be?"

"Henry VI for the history play."

"And the comedy?"

"An idea that came to me while Burghley was asking me to help talk the Earl of Southampton into marrying Lisbeth."

"Ooo, that'd be a good match."

"Yes. But, as the old man bobbed and weaved in front of me, looking like a fat turkey trying to find a bush he could hide behind, I suddenly remembered how he had forced me into marrying Nan. I never bedded her, you know."

"You didn't?"

"I was having too much fun with the Queen."

"Ye couldn't have both?" Falstaff was puzzled.

"I didn't want to consummate the marriage in case the Queen decided to marry me. If she did, I could get an annulment."

"Oh. Ye mean ye wanted to be able to tell the truth."

Oxford frowned. "Yes. As difficult as that may seem to you."

Falstaff showed Oxford a toothy grin. "The truth works some times."

Oxford gave him an exasperated look.

"And what will the play be about?" Falstaff asked.

"An apology to Nan."

"Nan?"

"For accusing her of cheating on me."

Falstaff blinked. "She did, didn't she? And ye took her back, didn't ye? Something about her slipping into yer bed before ye left for Italy, and not realizing that you were doing it with yer own wife."

It was painful for Oxford to hear Falstaff describe what happened in such stark terms. The fat man's face showed that he was having trouble accepting what otherwise looked like a very tall tale.

"Yes, bedding down with your wife and not knowing it is a bit difficult to accept."

"Oh, I don't know. I've awakened in the morning and found I'd gone to bed with someone I thought was someone else. A sheep even, once."

Oxford was not interested in hearing Falstaff expound on other examples of being tricked in bed, least of all with a sheep. "I came back from Italy and was told Lisbeth wasn't my daughter. Then I was told she was because Nan had been slipped into my bed before I left! Cuckolded and then tricked! Doubly damned! People laughing at me for not keeping my wife on a tether, and then laughing harder when they heard I had accepted her outrageous claim that I had slept with her *but didn't know it!*"

 Falstaff was confused. "I know ye had doubts. But now ye believe her? What changed your mind?"

"Seeing Lisbeth at Burghley's house last year. As I listened to her, I realized I was looking at myself. Her eyes are my eyes, Jack. Her nether lip is my nether lip. She scoffs before anyone speaks, same as I do. She holds her head back in imitation of me, yet she never saw me while she was growing up. She is my daughter, Jack. Nan told the truth, and I was wrong for doubting her. I owe them both an apology."

"And all this came from watching Burghley bob up and down in front of you like a fat turkey looking for a place to hide?"

"Yes."

"So who will you be in this play?"

Oxford feigned surprise. Falstaff scowled. "Truth. Truth, my lord."

"I will be Bertram, if you must know, a young count whose father has just died. Bertram will be forced to become a ward of the king. Bertram's mother will grieve at his going: 'In delivering my son from me, I bury a second husband,' to which Bertram will answer: "I must attend his majesty's command, to whom I am now in ward, evermore in subjection.'"

"And Nan?"

"She will be a young girl named Helena, raised in the same household but far below Bertram's station. 'Oh, that I should love a bright star, and think to wed him, he is so above me.'"

"And Bertram, of course, will have nothing to do with Helena."

"No. He will leave her behind when he joins the king but she will follow him. Whether she gains him or not will be the engine of the play."

"I see a dark bed at night."

"Aye."

"And Bertram will marry in the end."

"It's a comedy."

Falstaff sighed.

"Why sighest thou, Jack? Comedies always end with a wedding."

"Yes, but will a marriage at the end make all well?"

"It will. *All's Well That Ends Well.* That's what I'll call it."

"Little mirth there. A married man is a man that's marr'd."

"Then I will have a cowardly varlet full of words make the groundlings laugh."

"Oh, an excellent device. I begin to like this man."

"You should. He will be a marvelous imitation of you."

"No stage is large enough to hold Fat Jack!"

"He will not be fat."

"Then he will not be Jack."

"But since every thought runs out of his mouth the moment they are formed …"

"I hold in more thoughts than the ocean has water."

"An easy claim to make, since we cannot tell what is withheld when so much comes forth."

They were interrupted by John Lyly, who came high-stepping into the Boar's Head. "My lord," he called out. "Mr. Tilney has promised me a pound if I can write a poem for him by noon tomorrow."

"About what?"

"Elspeth Trentame."

"*Elspeth Trentame?* You mean *Elspeth Trentham?*"

"He said 'Trentame' to me, my lord."

Oxford blinked. "In her praise?"

"Yes. He said the poem must be no longer than eight lines, and each line should start off with a letter from her name, in the order in which her name is written."

"An acrostic," Oxford said.

"I knew that," Falstaff quickly added.

"Will ye help me?" Lyly pleaded.

"Did Tilney tell you who had charged him with this task?"

"He did not."

Oxford started to think.

"You know this lady?" Falstaff asked.

Oxford waved him away. His eyes rose to study the ceiling. Falstaff and Lyly went silent. They sat back and waited like cats at a mouse hole to see what came out. Lyly soon started drumming his fingers on the table but Falstaff scowled at him and the little man put his hands behind his back. A few minutes later, Oxford began speaking, conducting with his right hand, finger pointed upwards:

> *Time made a stay when highest powers wrought*
> *Regard of love where virtue had her grace,*
> *Excellence rare of every beauty sought*
> *Notes of the heart where honor had her place;*
> *Tried by the touch of most approved truth,*
> *A worthy saint to serve a heavenly queen,*
> *More fair than she that was the fame of youth,*
> *Except but one, the like was never seen.*

"Oh," Lyly exclaimed. "So quickly! And no paper! No pen!" He ran off to the kitchen.

Falstaff chuckled. "*A worthy saint to serve a heavenly queen / More fair than all except but one, the like was never seen.*" Oh, that's good. A bow to the lady and a deeper one to the Queen."

"One must never forget she who sees everything."

"And this 'worthy saint' has caught your eye, judging from how easily this poem was given voice. Wherefore the interest?"

"She is long-legged and high-bosomed, Sir John, and I shall have her."

"And that is all?"

"That is all."

Falstaff did not believe him.

"What?" Oxford asked.

"After Billesley, my lord, you, me, and Tobias swore we would stay bachelors, no matter what. We all agreed that marriage marks the end of a man."

"I'm not marrying her. I'm only trying bed her."

Falstaff shook his head. "I see clouds on the horizon. This woman will be the end of you."

"Jack: *it's a poem.*"

Lyly interrupted them again. He had found pen and paper. "Please, my lord?" Oxford obliged, and a happy John Lyly was soon skipping out the door with his one-pound poem.

"And notice, Sir John, that *again* the author will be unknown."

## ~ 45 ~
## Miss Trentham

The Queen lingered at Hampton Court Palace before moving upriver to Windsor. Oxford lingered as well, eager to catch another glimpse of the tall, long-legged lady-in-waiting who had glanced at him after the performance of *King John*. In hopes of catching her, he forced himself to sit through a performance of *Friar Bacon & Friar Bungay*, Greene's latest attempt to make people forget Marlowe and *Faust*, which did neither. When it was over, Oxford sidled up to Elspeth. She was taller than he had remembered. Was it the shoes hidden beneath a silver dress that fell to the floor? In bare feet, she might be as tall as he was in his stockings. Horizontally, he thought to himself, she'd be no taller than any other woman he had slept with.

"My lady," Oxford said.

"My lord."

"'Tis a pity there is no dancing after the play," he said, looking into her dark brown eyes. They seemed to have no bottom. He had the distinct impression they would pull him in if he leaned any closer to her.

"I hear tell you are a fine dancer. You come well-advertised."

"With all my gifts?"

"With all your faults."

"Are there many?"

"Yes."

"Which one do you think is the worst?"

She frowned slightly. Oxford couldn't tell whether she was dandling him or pondering the question.

"Ardor when first intrigued, and then of little faith thereafter."

"Ooo," he said. "I am usually the one who wounds with words."

"So I'm told."

He tried unsuccessfully to look hurt. He wasn't used to dealing with someone so forthright. Her personality reminded him of a clear stream running over hard slate.

Then she surprised him. "My condolences on the loss of your wife, my lord," she said. No one at court had mentioned Nan's passing in the two years since she had died.

"That is very kind of you, Lady Elspeth. And let me say that I am sorry to hear of your father's passing."

She accepted his condolences. He waited for her to say more but she did not continue the conversation. He wasn't used to people saying nothing. He lived on words. They were the air he breathed. His admiration for her grew by leaps and bounds as they stood there looking at each other, saying nothing. After what seemed an eternity, she spoke.

"And how goeth your son, my lord?"

Another surprising question. "Oh, Edward. Well, my lady."

"And your daughters?"

"Also well, my lady." An eyebrow on Lady Elspeth's face rose slightly. "Actually," Oxford confessed, "I have no idea."

"And the reason therefor?"

He winced. "The lady gives no quarter."

"I only seek the truth, my lord. Is not your motto, 'vero nihil verius?' Is not family as important as truth?"

This completed his discomfiture. She had put him on his heels. He was not used to being the tennis ball in a conversation; he was usually the racket. Here was a woman who asked probing questions, with no malice in her voice. Oxford thought he might have heard a touch of kindness.

"I know little of my daughters, my lady, or how Edward is proceeding. I am not without fault in this, but circumstances have prevented me from being the father I should be."

"I do not judge, my lord. I ask because I have no children myself. I am a woman of few words; not every thought is given speech by my lips. And so my questions may sound more froward than intended."

"'Tis not a fault," he said, knowing full well she had included him with those whose every thought runs out over their lips. "'Tis a virtue."

"One I have guarded."

"And guarded well."

She began to walk down the corridor. Oxford fell into step beside her. She glanced at him. "When I came to court ten years ago, my lord, we crossed paths here at Hampton Court. You showed me a hidden garden where the caretaker grew herbs and flowers. It became my secret hideaway. I have often wanted to thank you for that."

He recalled meeting her. He had just plucked a flower when he saw a tall, gangly girl look in. He gave her the flower and recited a poem—a poem intended for Anne Vavasor. The woman girl showed no reaction and he had concluded that she did not like poetry. The woman standing by him now was so different from the one he had met in the garden. He realized he wanted to know more about her when she suddenly ended their conversation.

"I regret to say that I must depart, my lord. I have to return to Staffordshire. You and I have exchanged more words than I am accustomed to speaking in so short a time. You have inquired of much private matter, the keeping of which I would greatly appreciate."

Oxford bowed. "I am a locked casket. But will you return to Windsor in time for the Christmas festivities?"

"I will, my lord."

"And may I have more conversation with you then?"

"I will husband my words to have enough when next we speak."

"Because you have no husband to husband them for you now."

"As you have no wife."

"And what did Her Majesty say about me just now when you talked together?"

"That you are lightning in a bottle."

"I'm so glad she thinks that."

"She said you would. And the play we shall see at Christmas?"

"A comedy about a noble earl forced to marry below his station."

"Be clever, my poet lord, but do not do it with bitterness."

"There will be no bitterness. The story will be an apology."

"That will be something new, from the little I know of you."

"There is always much that is new in me, my lady."

"Except for pride, apparently."

"'Tis not a sin to boast of what is true."

She laughed. "Apparently not."

"I lived for some time at Windsor when I was young and know it well. A grotto below the castle is most excellent in moonlight."

"My lord, I am a chaste lady."

"Bring your serving lady with you. I will have a supper by candlelight waiting for us there that will bring you much delight."

They had come to a door that led further into the palace. She continued on. "Until Windsor, then, my lord."

Oxford watched the door close. How had he missed her? A jewel hidden in plain sight. Unsullied as well as unmarried! She had run her eyes over him the way a breeder runs his hands over a stallion. He would court her with poetry. "I am with sonnets," he said aloud.

Elspeth, meanwhile, was striding down an arcade that ran alongside a narrow garden. She went past Lord Henry Howard, who was leaning up against an arch.

"Your ladyship," he said, stepping out.

Elspeth went by him. Howard fell into step with her, his narrow nose and thin beard pointing down the gallery.

"He is poison, my lady," he whispered.

"Who is, my lord?"

"The lord you were gazing at."

"I am not in the habit of gazing at lords, my lord."

"He hath abused and polluted the noble women of England."

"Including the Queen?"

"Of course not." He cast a glance over his shoulder. "He also likes boys."

She scoffed. "With three daughters and a son?"

They were almost to the end of the gallery. "He suffers from the Neapolitan Malady," he said, as she opened the door.

"Who says I will let him into my bed?"

"But he will want an heir."

"Of course, he will, but who says he must be the father?"

She slipped through the door, leaving a thoroughly shocked Henry Howard behind her.

## ~ 46 ~
### *Henry VI* and a Sonnet for the Earl of Southampton

Oxford found John Marston on his knees. "Up, lad," he said, as he sat down at the table. The boy jumped up and took a position to Oxford's left. Oxford began scribbling on a piece of paper. "Henry VI engaged in many wars," he said, as he continued writing. "His reign is too long to chronicle everything, so I will pick and choose what to write about, and then I will take liberties with Holinshed to make drama out of what he sees as only history."

John Marston looked over Oxford's shoulder to see what he was writing. It appeared to be a hodgepodge of scribbles.

"Notes," Oxford said, without looking up. "Like spilling soup onto a table to find out what's in it. I'll save those worth keeping and discard the rest." He held the paper up. "We will add ideas as they come. In the meantime, I will dictate scenes that you will transcribe and throw on the floor in the corner."

The boy looked at him. "I will throw them on the floor?"

"Yes. When we think we have enough, we will sift through them and string them together. I will fill in any gaps with new work."

"Instead of plotting out the play and then writing the scenes?"

"Holinshed has provided the plot. We need only add the characters. The bad shall triumph; the good shall be ground under."

"The Queen will not be pleased with so black a drama."

"She will know Bolingbroke is coming."

"Oh."

"Where do you think we should start, young sir?"

"At the beginning, my lord."

"Which is?"

"The funeral of Henry V. With mourners black-draped in Westminster Abbey."

"Sidney's funeral."

The boy was taken aback. He had remembered the stately line of mourners that had followed Sir Philip's casket. He had hoped Oxford would think his idea a stroke of genius, but his master had seen through him immediately. Crestfallen, he hung his head.

"It is no sin to steal from others in the theater, John Marston, as long as you rework it to make it your own. You have come up with a good idea. We shall use it to open the play. And the mourners, because their new king is a boy, will begin to argue among themselves about what course the kingdom should take." He gestured for John Marston to pick up his pen. "Gloucester will say:

> *We mourn in black: why mourn we not in blood?*
> *Henry is dead and never shall revive:*
> *We with our stately presence glorify,*
> *Like captives bound to a triumphant car.*

The boy began to write. "*Like captives bound to a triumphant car?* Is this not *Tamburlaine* speaking to the kings he has yoked to his chariot, *Holla, ye pamper'd jades of Asia! / What, can ye draw but twenty miles a-day?*

"Why do you scowl? Is Marlowe not worth emulating?"

"He is, my lord. Particularly when you rework his lines, but leave in a hint of the original."

"If the listener is looking."

John Marston smiled. "If you can listen with your eyes, you can taste with your ears." He giggled.

"To work," Oxford said. "Henry's glory will not last long:

> *Glory is like a circle in the water,*
> *Which never ceaseth to enlarge itself*
> *Till by broad spreading it disperse to naught.*

"Who speaks this?"

"Joan of Arc."

"The witch."

"Was she?"

"Yes, my lord. She was Catholic."

"John Marston, *everyone* was Catholic in Henry's time."

"Oh."

"But Joan will serve us better as a witch than a martyr. I will make her despicable so that she is booed when she is dragged off to be burnt."

John Marston looked worried. "How will you do this, my lord?"

"By having her reject her own father, who has come to save her:

Joan:    *Decrepit miser! base ignoble wretch!*
              *I am descended of a gentler blood:*
              *Thou art no father nor no friend of mine.*

The boy's jaw dropped. "She says this to her own father?"

Oxford continued: "Her father protests:

Father:   *I did beget her, all the parish knows:*
              *Her mother liveth yet, can testify*
              *She was the first fruit of my bachelorship.*
              *God knows thou art a collop of my flesh.*

"She is so without grace that she would deny her own father, who is standing in front of her?"

"Listen."

Joan:    *You have suborn'd this man,*
              *Of purpose to obscure my noble birth.*

"She goes on:"

              *I am Joan of Arc, who hath been*
              *A virgin from tender infancy,*
              *Chaste and immaculate in very thought.*
              *Canst thou burn a virgin?*

The boy looked up. "Can they?"

"Of course they can. And they will. But she isn't finished scrambling to save her life. She announces that she is with child. The lords who are piling on the wood exclaim '*A holy maid with child!*' but keep piling on the wood. Then she tells them the father of her child is the Duke of Alençon, no, the Duke of Anjou."

"My lord, she is most reprehensible."

"She will exit the stage, clawing and snarling, but not before she curses them all for causing a maid's death."

"A maid who is with child?" the boy asked. Oxford nodded. "How can a maid be with child?" Oxford smiled. John Marston's eyes got bigger. "Oh, no."

Oxford was enjoying the boy's discomfiture. "Her father is standing there and she continues to reject him as she is burnt."

The boy's face took on a frightened look. "Jesus?"

"'Tis only a play," Oxford said, which did nothing to help John Marston feel better. Oxford leaned in toward the boy. "And there will be three messengers."

"Oh, no. Three wise men."

"And three ignoble lords—Winchester, York, and Somerset."

"Who will each have three attendants," the boy suggested.

Oxford nodded. The boy gripped the edge of the table. He stared straight ahead, waiting for Oxford to continue.

"And three powerful women."

"Joan of Arc," the boy said, squinting hard to remember what he had read in Holinshed, "Queen Margaret, and …"

"The Countess of Auvergne."

"I do not recall her."

"I have not invented her yet. She will combat with Talbot."

"Oh," the boy said, relieved to be on safer ground. All England worshipped Lord Talbot.

"Now that you know the course I intend to sail, I charge you with reading through Holinshed to make a list of scenes you think should be in the play. Read also my uncle's translation of *The History of Trogus Pompeius*."

"Your uncle?"

"Arthur Golding."

"He who translated Ovid's *Metamorphosis*?" Oxford nodded. "I found a copy, all dog-eared and scribbled over, lying on a chair in the day room."

"You didn't like it?"

"I was loathe to glance at it. My father made me read some of the Reverend Calvin's sermons, which Mr. Golding had translated, but no one told me he translated Ovid."

"Did you glance inside?"

John Marston nodded. "It didn't seem to be by the same man."

"It wasn't. Now you to your work and me to mine. I am to Cecil House to steal Guiccardini's *La Historia d'Italia* from the library."

"My lord," John Marston protested.

"Borrow, then. Burghley won't miss Guiccardini. He doesn't read books."

# ~ 47 ~
## Cecil House

Oxford slipped Ferrentino's *Historie* into the octavo page he held under his arm and headed for the stairs. On his way to the second floor, he met the Earl of Southampton coming down.

"Henry," Oxford exclaimed. "I have a sonnet for you."

"No doubt encouraging me to marry."

Oxford nodded. He began to declaim:

> *From fairest creatures we desire increase,*
> *That thereby beauties Rose might never die.*

Southampton put up his hand. "My lord," he said in a sad voice. "No more, please. The beauty in your lines stillborns any beauty in mine. Who can write poetry after they have read *Thou art thy mothers glasse and she in thee/Calls backe the louely Aprill of her prime*. Or this one sent to me last week:

> *Is it for fear to wet a widow's eye,*
> *That thou consum'st thy self in single life?*
> *Ah! if thou issueless shalt hap to die,*
> *The world will wail thee like a makeless wife.*

I can bear no more. Your gifts are jewels to others but hideous laughter to me, dashing my feeble efforts as a poet."

"But, my dear Henry," Oxford protested, "I sent them to you as *petits cadeaux*, mere nothings, to urge you to marry Lisbeth."

Southampton looked away. He wrapped his long fingers around the railing. The ends of the sleeves of the elegant black silk shirt he was wearing were shrouded in lace that extended almost to the tips of his fingers. "Her grandfather has also strongly urged me to do so, but I'm afraid I cannot."

"Why is that?"

Southampton's long auburn hair fell across his face. "My lord, I do not mean to offend, but I will not make the same mistake you made in marrying Nan."

"I had no choice. Lord Burghley commanded it."

"As he commands me now to marry your daughter. I have no objection to Lisbeth, my lord, but I know how much you suffered as his son-in-law. I will be at his mercy if I marry her, and so I have decided to take a firm stand on this and not agree to take her as my wife." He was clearly uncomfortable at having to be so frank.

Southampton's decision was disappointing, but Oxford realized that he was proud that the young man could express himself so honestly. "I will not add my voice to Lord Burghley's, then," Oxford said. "I will advise him to drop his request that you marry Lisbeth."

Southampton was immensely relieved. Having successfully portrayed himself as a man, the adolescent immediately reappeared. He reached for Oxford's hand. "Thank you, my lord. I regret that I will not have the honor of becoming your son-in-law …"

Oxford waved him off. "A loss for both of us, I agree. I will speak with Lord Burghley," he repeated.

"Thank you, my lord." Southampton said once more, now all smiles. "With your permission." Oxford nodded and the tall, lanky boy, more bones than flesh, bounded off down the stairs.

Oxford watched him go, then he followed him down the stairs and headed for the front door. Before he got there, Lisbeth slipped out of a hallway and intercepted him.

"You bastard!" she hissed. She struck her father on the arm. "You took my mother! Now you take the man I wanted to marry!"

"Lisbeth!"

"No!" She pushed him away, nearly knocking him over. "You said something to him. You made him change his mind! *What was it?*"

"I didn't make him change his mind. I was in favor of the marriage, and told him so."

"Liar!" She burst into tears. "*Liar!*" She turned and ran through the door at the end of the hallway, slamming it behind her.

"What have I done to deserve to be so misunderstood?" Oxford asked himself. He sighed. "What, ye expect justice?" he heard Falstaff say. Oxford looked around the empty hall. Servants knew when to disappear. They had all drifted around a corner, like sparrows folding themselves into a thicket when a storm is coming in. I could do with a little justice, Oxford thought to himself as he went out the front door.

## ~ 48 ~
## The War of the Roses

John Marston looked up. "But how did the two sides come to adopt roses as their emblems? I found nothing in Holinshed about that." Socrates leapt silently onto the far end of the table and sat down, as if he too wanted to know the answer to the boy's question.

"I will invent it. Richard and Somerset will repair to the Temple Garden with their followers where they will argue about who should control the young king. Richard berates them:

Richard:  *Since you are tongue-tied and so loath to speak,*
          *In dumb significants proclaim your thoughts:*
          *From off this brier pluck a white rose with me.*

John Marston picked up his pen and began to write.

Somerset:  *Let him that is no coward nor no flatterer,*
           *Pluck a red rose from off this thorn with me.*

Warwick:  *I love no colours, and without all colour*
          *Of base insinuating flattery*
          *I pluck this white rose with Plantagenet.*

Suffolk:  *I pluck this red rose with young Somerset.*

"And so it goes. The tension among the men builds and builds …," but Nigel interrupted him to announce that Shackspear was at the door. Shackspear pushed his way past Nigel into the room. He waved a sheaf of papers in his hand. "Sir Thomas Lucy is much offended with me for how I described him in *The Poacher of Arden Forest*."

"As well he should be."

"May we add a few lines to *Henry VI* to ease his anger? You know, make him feel better."

"We?"

"Well, Lord Strange's men think I am the author." Shakespeare smiled obsequiously. "And, to lessen the burden of writing a short scene, I took the liberty of penning a few lines that might make Sir Thomas think better of me."

"A difficult task," Oxford commented.

Shackspear took this as permission to read his notes. "Sir Thomas comes upon Talbot's body and begs Joan of Arc let him take it away:

> *Is Talbot slain, the Frenchmen's only scourge,*
> *Your kingdom's terror and black Nemesis?*
> *O, were mine eyeballs into bullets turn'd,*
> *That I in rage might shoot them at your faces!*

"*Eyeballs into bullets turn'd? Shoot them at your faces?!!*" Oxford tried not to laugh. 'Do you think his ancestor had eyeballs that looked like bullets?"

Shackspear was confused. "I don't know."

"*Yes*. I'll wager he did. Why not? If you think Sir Thomas will be pleased to hear that his ancestor's had eyeballs that could be turned into bullets, have him on. After all, it's *your* play."

This encouraged Shackspear. "And Joan of Arc will marvel at Sir Thomas' bravery in seeking to retrieve the body of such a man as Talbot:

> *I think this upstart is old Talbot's ghost,*
> *He speaks with such a proud commanding spirit.*
> *For God's sake let him have 'em; to keep them here,*
> *They would but stink, and putrefy the air.*

John Marston looked at Oxford. "Would Talbot's body stink?"

"It is the witch who is speaking." He had a mischievous look on his face. He glanced at Shackspear. "'We will take your lines." Shackspear's face lit up. "*Now, leave us*! I have the comedy to work on."

"Yes. The comedy. *Henry VI* would be good also."

"*Out!*"

Shackspear was almost giddy. "What should I do with this?" he asked, waving the papers he held in his hand.

"Throw them on the floor," Oxford said, pointing toward the pile of papers in the far corner.

Shackspear thought he was being told to throw his newly-minted scene away. He glanced at John Marston, who, with a nod of his head, let him know that the script for *Henry VI* did indeed lie on the floor. "Do ye think I can play Sir Thomas?" Shackspear asked.

"You would make a fine Sir Thomas," Oxford deadpanned.

"Thank you, my lord," Shackspear said. He bowed and left.

"God save us," John Marston muttered.

288

## ~ 49 ~
## John Marston and the Nature of Sin

D espair not, John Marston. The end is in sight." The young boy's head was sagging onto the table. *Henry VI, Part I,* had been shelved while the boy and Oxford worked day and night on *All's Well.* Oxford had become obsessed with getting the play down on paper, for, to him, a play did not exist until it was written down. He was in love with his own voice, John Marston had realized early on, and was his own best audience. John Marston's arm ached. He glanced at the window, now flooded with morning light.

"Bertram is most reprehensible, my lord."

"That he is."

"Is there no way he can be redeemed?"

"No."

"Why can he not reform himself after he is confronted with Diana? 'Tis a comedy, my lord. Don't comedies end in marriage?"

"Yes."

"But there is no marriage here." He rummaged among the papers on the table and held up a sheet. "At the end, Bertram doesn't say 'yes, my love, I will love you forever,' he says:

> *If she, my liege, can make me know this clearly,*
> *I'll love her dearly, ever, ever dearly.*

"He's still wiggling. He's not committing himself to anything. And Helena is not much better:

> *If it appear not plain and prove untrue,*
> *Deadly divorce step between me and you!*

"What a set of vows! Can't we rewrite the end? What is this play about?"

"Me," Oxford said.

"*You?*" The boy's jaw dropped. "You're the noble lord who marries a woman beneath his station? Was Nan beneath your station?"

"She was until the Queen made her father Baron Burghley."

"And Lord Burghley ordered you, his ward, to marry her?"

"He did."

"And you refused to, ah, um," the boy continued, running out of words.

"Yes."

"But in the play, Bertram sleeps with Helena without knowing it." John Marston listened to what he had just said. His eyes got big. "Did *you* do that?" Oxford nodded. The boy's astonishment was now complete. "How could you …? Of course, I have no experience in these matters …" His voice trailed off. He looked around, embarrassed. "*I'll love her dearly, ever, ever dearly,*" he muttered to himself. "Oh, I should've seen that."

Neither said anything for a moment. Then, the boy looked up at Oxford. "Did Bertram sin when he slept with Helena? After all, he *thought* he was sleeping with Diana?"

Oxford smiled. "You mean, does sin lie in the act, or does it lie in the heart? 'Tis a question that has confounded better minds than yours and mine, John Marston."

"I do not like writing a play where a man violates his marriage vows, if only in his heart."

Oxford's smile disappeared. "You didn't write the play, young man: I did. You will not go to Hell for writing down what I say."

The boy looked like he would. Oxford suddenly did not care. His droll interest in watching the boy grapple with sin disappeared as the questions he boy asked pushed him back to his own thoughts about what had really happened with Nan.

"To bed," he said curtly.

# 1591

## ~ 50 ~
## Aemilia Bassano (Again)

Elspeth Trentham did not return for the Christmas season. The administration of her father's estate had detained her. Without Mistress Trentham to distract him, Oxford buried himself in working on *Henry VI.* The pile of papers on the floor grew until Oxford decided there was enough for at least two plays. He assembled enough for the first part and went over it with John Marston. "Most diabolical, my lord," John Marston said, a satisfied look on his face, "ending Part 1 with King Henry accepting Margaret of Anjou as his new queen when the audience knows she is already the secret lover of the man Henry sent to woo her."

"A bridge to bring the audience back, John Marston."

"There are many scenes left," the boy said, pointing to the pages on the floor.

"Marlowe wrote *Tamburlaine* in two parts. We have enough for two plays and more. What say we outdo Marlowe with a third play?" John Marston eagerly agreed. "The civil war between the houses of Lancaster and York will begin in Part 2 and blood will flow in Part 3. Take Part 1 and make a clean copy in your round hand for Shackspear."

John Marston began gathering up the papers. "Lord Strange's Men are rehearsing *All's Well*," he said. "Mr. Tilney says it will be performed the third night after Christmas. *Henry VI* will follow a week later."

"And which company will perform *Henry*?"

"The Admiral's Men. Ned has already claimed the part of Richard for himself."

"He sees what's coming."

---

Oxford and John Marston were in the audience when the first part of *Henry VI* was performed before the Queen. She was pleased. "You have finally brought us what I had hoped for when I told you to write history plays," she said to Oxford. "Take this to the playhouse and bind my people together. They will newly embalm great Talbot with tears when they see him alive and well on the stage."

Her reaction to *All's Well* a week later was different. She did not like it. "Must you keep giving us you, over and over again?"

"Ever," Oxford deadpanned, which only exasperated her more.

"Nan is dead. Why must you give us Helena?"

"And Bertram? Was he not base?"

"He still is."

Oxford found he was surprised by this. Her remark had cut him. She saw his reaction. "Maybe he *has* changed," she said, her voice softening. "Maybe the Bertram I knew as a young man no longer exists. I hope so. This is getting tiring." She waved a hand as if the play hung in the air like vapors that should be dispersed. "Can't you leave off holding yourself out to the public as a motley fool? You are goring your own thoughts, and selling cheap what is most dear."

"I may look askance on truth, your Majesty, but I am a poet, and a poet can only cultivate what grows in his own garden."

"You have exhausted your garden, my lord. Seek other gardens. Your genius, fertile now, and well-tilled, needs to make new fruit we haven't tasted yet."

She looked away. The interview was over. Oxford bowed. As he left the hall, Aemilia Bassano took his arm and steered him into an alcove.

"My Lord," she said, squeezing his arm as her dark brown eyes drank him in. "I was such a fool to be taken in by *him*!" she said, tilting her head in the direction of Shackspear, who was watching them from the stage. "I was blinded by the brilliance of *your* words, my lord, and o'erlooked where they came from, a fault women commonly suffer when a chiseled face or a flashing eye is all they see." Oxford did not think Shackspear had a flashing eye or a chiseled face. Neither did she. "He has a bladder face and drooping eyes. Being a poet myself, I saw more in him than was there because, unbeknownst to me, I was being swept away by *your* words, not his."

Oxford was thrilled to hear this; he was even more thrilled to have Aemilia's arm over his. He instantly forgot how cruelly she had treated him. He imagined himself once again standing outside her apartments, a new sonnet in hand. "And how came you to such enlightenment?"

"I told him I would be Silvia one night and he would be Valentine. I asked him to woo me off to sleep with Valentine's description of life without Silvia."

*"What light is light, if Silvia be not seen?"* Oxford began.

A tremor ran through her arm. Her eyes closed for a moment, then flashed open. "He could not recite a word of it! The mask instantly fell off his face. He was not the author! But who was? Your face appeared in front of me, like thunder and lightning together."

Oxford put his hand over hers and squeezed it:

> *What joy is joy, if Silvia be not by?*
> *Unless it be to think that she is by*
> *And feed upon the shadow of perfection.*

"Oh, my lord," she said, her eyes fluttering again. "Forgive me."

"A wish easily granted. And, if it is my 'Will' you wish to enjoy, I can give you that wish as well:

> *Thou hast thy 'Will' and 'Will' to boot,*
> *And 'Will' in overplus to entertain my suit:*
> *Wilt thou, whose will is large and spacious,*
> *Allow me to made addition of it?*

A smile flooded across her face. "New poetry, freshly made? And punning on his name?" Her eyes fluttered again. "What was it you whispered to me at Lord Willoughby's? *If once your lips should lock with mine?*"

*"Your lips are lost, your lips are mine."*

She leaned into him, her lips almost brushing his cheek. "I would fain lose my lips, my lord, but not tonight. Tomorrow night. Lord Hunsdon is to the border in the morning."

*"And, when thou art away,"* Oxford said, *"the very birds are mute."*

She shuddered, then looked at him slyly. "I have a copy of *I Modi*," she said, searching his face to see how he took this. Oxford's jaw dropped. "Would you help me go through it?" she asked, a look of innocence on her face.

"Yes. Of course. The drawings you are referring to are by Julio Romano, my lady. I met him while I was in Italy."

"You did? And did you see his book while you were there?"

It was now Oxford whose eyes were fluttering. That the two of them might soon be looking at Romano's exquisite renderings of people making love made Oxford's knees weak.

"Is it possible that a man and a woman can experience love in so many different ways?" she asked, obviously hoping the answer was yes.

"Oh, indeed, my lady." Oxford said emphatically.

"There are sonnets with each one, my lord, in Italian."

"Pietro Aretino wrote them. The poet of love. He was hounded out of Italy for writing them. We shall read them together."

She slipped her arm out from his. "Tomorrow, then."

"Tomorrow."

Shackspear suddenly appeared. "Go away," Oxford said.

## ~ 51 ~
## Signore Baldini's Love Philtre

Oxford ran into Falstaff as he came out of Oxford Court. "Can't stop," he said as he hurried off down Candlewick Street. Nigel appeared in the doorway. He and Falstaff watched Oxford disappear. "Now where' is *he* going?" Falstaff asked, hands on hips.

"I have no idea, Sir John."

"Is Mistress Trentham back?"

"He did not mention Mistress Trentham. He is with sonnets, Sir John. When he is like this, he runs in and out at odd hours of the day and night and clogs my ears with sound."

"Lordy, lordy."

"I can never make sense of what he says. Do you know how many poems I have been forced to listen to?"

Falstaff nodded. "We all bear the cross of poetry."

"Indeed."

"I worry about him when he is like this."

"We all do." Nigel looked up at the sky. Darkness was falling. "He ran right by the roast duckling Frangellica had prepared for supper. He may be gone for days. One never knows. The duckling should not go to waste. If you wish, Sir John, you may sup here till he returns. Frangellica would be pleased that someone of your gustatory tastes enjoyed the meal she made for his lordship."

Falstaff's face lit up. "Always ready to help a lady," he said. He heaved himself over the door sill and headed for the dining room.

Oxford did not return. He let himself in the next morning. He found Falstaff snoring in the day room. Falstaff cracked an eye open. "Eh?"

Oxford tried to look blasé but a mischievous grin kept trying to spread across his face. Falstaff sat up and saw it. "Eh?" he said again.

"Mistress Bassano has decided that a certain provincial cow patty is not what she had imagined he was."

Falstaff sat up. "Son of a glover! She has discovered the true author."

"Yes. And she is chagrined to have thought otherwise."

Falstaff swung his legs over onto the floor. "And eager to make up for the error of her ways."

"Most ardently."

"God be praised."

"Lord Hunsdon will be away, but …"

"No 'buts.' 'Tis wonderful news that doesn't allow for any 'buts.'"

Oxford bit his lip. Falstaff scowled. "What?"

"She is a lady who, stroked with poetry, becomes the most erotic woman I have ever known."

"Oooh. I should have stayed in school. Does she make the beast with two backs?"

"I expect that and more. She has a copy of *I Modi* and wants to do every scene."

"*I Modi?*"

"The picture book that shows all the ways a man and a woman can make love."

Falstaff's eyes glistened. "You borrowed it, of course."

"She won't give it up. She said she has need of it when she has no need of men."

"Who said men seek paradise above when heaven lies between a lady's' legs."

"But a woman like this needs more than poetry and a picture book, Sir John."

Falstaff saw the concern on Oxford's face. "You haven't bedded her yet."

Oxford shook his head. "We were interrupted. Lord Hunsdon returned unexpectedly."

"Ah, so ye're worried that whoever gets into her boat must have an oar long enough to row her to shore." He eyed Oxford. "But this has never been a concern of yours, my lord."

"No, but it's been some time since I've been with a woman, Jack. I am two score and more now and can no longer strut from dusk to dawn. If she begins to find my poetry wanting, Mistress Bassano may find me lacking in other areas as well."

"Ah. So you need to strengthen yourself."

"I would hate to lose her because I cannot stay in the lists as long as she'd like."

"I wish I could help you but, having no need myself …" His voice trailed off. Oxford looked discouraged. "What about Nigel?" Falstaff suggested. "He's got a box full of jars and bottles he's always dipping into."

"Yes. But are they for help with women? I don't even know whether he likes women."

"Ask him."

Oxford found Nigel in the pantry. Oxford's inquiry made his faithful steward uncomfortable. He told Oxford there was nothing in the house that might help him. "But may I suggest Signore Baldini, my lord?"

"Signore Baldini! A brilliant idea, Nigel. Thank you."

Oxford put his head in the day room. "Baldini," he said to Falstaff, who was looked like he was going back to sleep. Oxford grabbed a wool throw off the back of a chair and headed for the door. "Tobias!" he called out as he went out the front door. Tobias quickly followed.

Oxford found Signore Baldini lining up glass bottles on a shelf at the back of his store. "Maestro Baldini," Oxford announced as he came bounding into the shop. Baldini groaned. Oxford came around the counter. "Why doth thou despair, my good friend? My good *Italian* friend?"

Baldini forced himself to smile. "How does my good Lord of Oxenford?"

"Well, well. But I do not come for perfume this time, Signoree."

"No?"

"I come for love potions."

"Ah," Baldini said, relieved that he would not be forced to give up one of his treasured perfumes. "I sell no love potions.'"

"Your brother sells love potions in Venice, does he not?"

"Yes. But he is in Venice."

"Didn't I meet you in his shop there? Weren't you helping him? Powdered rhinoceros horn, I think," Oxford said, trying to remember. "Dried bull testicles, and God knows what else."

"I didn't sell any of those to you."

"I didn't need them then."

"But I don't have them here. That was Venice; this is London. I sell only perfumes here."

Oxford didn't believe him. "Maestro Baldini," he pleaded. "You can trust me!" Baldini resisted. "My old friend?"

Baldini sighed. "If you insist."

"Mio bellisimo amici," Oxford exclaimed.

"If you will excuse me." Baldini went through the curtain into the rear of the shop. He returned in a few moments with a purple vial. He took out the stopper and held it up to Oxford's nose. "Ground penises taken from giant blue spiders found only in the Persian Gulf. They do it all night. It's guaranteed to work."

"Excellent!" Oxford said. He took the bottle and headed for the door. "My man, Tobias, will pay you."

"Of course," Baldini said. He listened to Oxford and Tobias go down the alley. A dark-eyed woman slid through the curtains. She ran a hand up Baldini's arm. "Ground penises? Giant blue spiders? Is that *your* secret?"

He laughed. "*I am Italian*," he said. He kissed her. "He only visited my country. I was born there. I do not need any help."

"I could swear I smelled poppy seeds."

Baldini shrugged. "He's an English lord, a fool. But sometimes a suggestion can be enough to produce the desired results."

She ruffled his hair. "*Il mio uomo italiano*" she said, pulling him through the curtain into the back area.

## ~ 52 ~
## The Boar's Head

The Boar's Head was empty. The afternoon sun had taken the hangers-on out to Finsbury Fields to shoot arrows and argue over whether Spanish boots had finally gone out of style. Oxford was sitting in a booth, head bent over, his pen scratching across a scrap of paper. Other scraps littered the table in front of him. He picked up the page he had been writing and leaned back to scan it. "God's blood!" he muttered. He crumbled up the page and threw it to the floor. He pulled a new sheet to him and began again.

Falstaff was lying on a bench behind Oxford. "So, armed with Signore Baldini's love potion, you return to your lover's arms."

"Aye, but a sonnet will make her love me even more."

"You'll need more than poetry to hold onto her. She is very young. She calls your poetry 'antique.' Does she not say you are old?"

"She says I am young."

"Then she is truly in love, for no one loves lies more than lovers. They see beauty where none exists, and wonder, when love is gone, what made them think otherwise while they felt love."

Oxford ignored him. His pen kept moving across the page. When he finished, he held up the sheet of paper and began to read:

> *When my love swears that she is made of truth,*
> *I do believe her though I know she lies.*

"She lies?"

"Shush."

> *But wherefore says she not she is unjust?*
> *And wherefore say not I that I am old?*
> *O! love's best habit is in seeming trust,*
> *And age in love, loves not to have years told:*
> *Therefore I lie with her, and she with me*
> *And in our faults by lies we flattered be.*

Falstaff snorted. "But, in speaking truth to her, your 'lies' will shattered be."

"She'll love it!"

"Not as much as you do."

Oxford ignored him. He pulled out a lavender colored piece of paper that smelled of ambergris. He began transcribing a fair copy of the poem onto the clean page. The graceful secretary script that Sir Thomas Smith had taught him flowed across the page. This was the part of being a poet Oxford loved most, when the vaporous ideas in his mind flowed out across the clean linen paper and took on the permanence of words chiseled in stone. He felt the gods over his shoulder nodding approval, declaring any change unnecessary. No blot must mar what he had written; no further refinement was necessary.

Shackspear suddenly appeared. Oxford put his arm over the piece of paper and looked up. "What do *you* want?"

"Henslowe won't stage the first part of *Henry VI*."

"Wherefore?"

"Because he says he hasn't got enough chinks to pay for it! There are twenty players in the opening scene, all dressed in black. Cloth is expensive, and the seamstresses will charge a pretty penny to sew it into stately robes. Henslowe said Leicester may have been rich enough to pay for Sidney's funeral but he didn't have enough money to restage it!"

"How was it put on before the Queen?"

"Tilney loaned us robes from the royal storehouse."

"Then ask Tilney to loan them again."

"He says they're not to be used for public performance."

"What about Burbage?"

"He won't talk to me since I gave *King John* to Henslowe. Richard wanted to play the Bastard and can't stand it that Ned Alleyn is tearing up London instead of him."

"Why do you always bring trouble?"

"I don't bring trouble, my lord; you do. It's your script. There are too many characters. The more players there are, the more the play costs."

Oxford realized that Shackspear was lecturing him about money, something Nigel was always doing. He was about to send Shackspear packing when he remembered the Queen ordering him to spend some of the money she gave him on staging the history plays. He screwed up his face: "How much?"

"£5."

"£5!" It sounded like a lot but, truthfully, Oxford had little idea what £5 would buy. The two of them sounded like they were bartering over a pair of gloves, or a new hat. *How could such a noble pursuit as penning a play about an English king come to this?* Silently, Falstaff began to laugh in the booth behind him, making Oxford's bench wobble back and forth. Oxford gripped the table. "Get what you need from Nigel," he said.

"No," Falstaff announced, startling them both. Shackspear jumped when Falstaff sat up. "Nigel should pay Henslowe."

"Yes," Oxford said.

"And get the costumes back once the play has run," Falstaff continued.

Shackspear was elated. He bowed immediately and turned away, worried Oxford would change his mind if he stayed any longer. He was so happy to get the money to put on the play that he did not see Christopher Marlowe pass him as he headed for the door. Oxford, in the meantime, started rereading his sonnet to Aemilia Bassano.

"My lord," Marlowe said.

Oxford, startled, looked up. "Mr. Marlowe."

Marlowe gestured toward the seat on the other side of the booth. "May I?"

Oxford nodded. He slid the lavender page into the papers on the table as Marlowe sat down cross from him. Another interruption, Oxford said to himself. He had had more than enough of Marlowe's condescending pronouncements, brilliant as they might be.

"Mr. Shackspear," Marlowe said, referring to Shackspear with a nod of his head. "Is he the dog come to fetch his master's slippers, or, should I say, his master's newest play?"

"It depends on who the dog is."

"We know who the dog is. The master gives instruction; the dog fetches." Oxford said nothing. Marlowe went on. "I want to apologize for my actions when we met last time, my lord. I erroneously concluded that you were one of those nobles who seek literary fame by surrounding themselves with poets and writers. I expected you to ask me to join your group of parasites so I could add 'glister' to your reputation."

Oxford tried not to show his reaction to this impertinence. *He needed Marlowe?* He looked away.

"You didn't, of course. Instead, you graciously overlooked my arrogance and suggested I talk to Thomas Churchyard about a place to live. Your servant Robin took me to him. Thomas welcomed me and offered me his apartments, which was very generous. Unfortunately, his rooms are in the bell tower at St. Paul's."

"Your own tower," Oxford couldn't resist saying.

"The bells kept interrupting me."

"Interrupting you."

"I started cutting the pull-ropes to get some sleep, but the monks figured out who was doing it and asked me to leave."

"And Thomas?" Oxford asked, suddenly concerned. "Was he evicted as well?"

"No. They know he's deaf. No need for him to cut the pull-ropes. He's still there. He suggested I ask Thomas Kyd if I could move in with him, which I did. Churchyard talks more than I like, but I learned a lot about you from him. And from Kyd. They showed me some of your earlier works. They told me how you had helped them when they were in need. They made me go with them to see *All's Well That Ends Well*."

"Which, I am sure, was not worth your time. Too much 'froth.'"

"No, my lord. I found much to admire, although I may be a poor judge of comedy since I am so melancholic."

Oxford's irritation was growing. "Oh, I am sure there must be something you have written that would serve to fill out a comedy."

Marlowe finally heard the sarcasm in Oxford's voice. "Yes, some things I wrote at Cambridge made me smile when I re-read them later. You've never groaned over a line when you came back to it?"

Oxford's was about to say no but waved a hand at the papers all around him. "Unfortunately, it seems to happen all the time."

Marlowe nodded. "I expect you might laugh at much that I have written."

This surprised Oxford. "You need have no such fear, Mr. Marlowe. Your art has lifted English verse into a realm of imagery and melody of speech that did not exist before you came along. '*Who ever loved that loved not at first sight?*' And '*Come live with me and be my love.*'"

It was Marlowe's turn to be surprised.

"I love the hidden jests," Oxford said, a sly look on his face.

"Jests?"

302

"Tamburlaine's splendid description of himself in Act IV:

*I'll ride in golden armour like the sun;*
*And in my helm a triple plume shall spring,*
*Spangled with diamonds, dancing in the air,*
*To note me emperor of the three-fold world;*
*Like to an almond-tree y-mounted high*
*Upon the lofty and celestial mount*
*Of ever-green Selinus.*

"Is this not the *Fairie Queen* in a higher register?" Oxford asked. "Spenser wrote:

*Upon the top of all his loftie crest,*
*A bounch of haires discolourd diversly,*
*With sprincled pearle and gold full richly drest,*
*Did shake, and seemd to daunce for iollity;*
*Like to an almond tree ymounted hye*
*On top of greene Selinis all alone,*
*Whose tender locks do tremble every one*
*At everie little breath that under heaven is blowne.*

Marlowe smiled. "'*With blossoms brave bedecked daintily* was so awful, I could not keep myself from trying to improve it. More 'polished', don't you think, to use Shackspear's phrase?"

"Neither of us could have written '*A bunch of haires discolourd diversly.*' No knight ever wore hairs on his helmet that were *discoloured diversly*. Your plume of feathers much improved the idea."

Marlowe almost looked embarrassed. Then he grew serious. "But you did the same thing to me, my lord. You twisted '*Is this the face that launched a thousand ships / And burnt the topless towers of Ilium?*' into '*Was this fair face the cause, quoth she, / Why the Grecians sacked Troy?*'" Marlowe shook his head. "I made Spenser better; you made Marlowe worse!"

"'Twas a clown speaking," Oxford said, dismissively. "How can a clown be poetical? It was just 'froth.'"

"Great poets do not mimic poor ones."

"Then why mimic Spenser?"

"He is well-known at the moment. And, if a man's verses cannot be recast so that they are recognized by others, the first poet is more dead than if he had died alone in a little room."

Oxford agreed. But Marlowe had apparently like something in *All's Well*. Oxford could not keep himself from asking Marlowe what he had found of interest in the play.

Marlowe leaned forward. "You posed a wonderful question: Did Bertram sin when he slept with Helena?"

"You, too?" Oxford looked away. He remembered John Marston's intense eyes as the young boy had asked the same question.

"If he didn't recognize her, he's committing adultery, at least in his own mind. But how could he can get in bed with his own wife and not recognize her?"

Oxford shrugged. "It can happen."

Marlowe shook his head. "No. It strains credulity to ask the audience to think he doesn't know who she is. It destroyed the all-important illusion that reality is being presented on the stage."

"So you left."

"No."

"Why not?"

"Because I wanted to see how you handled this question. How could Bertram not know he was sleeping with his own wife?"

"But he'd never slept with her before," Oxford said, unable to keep himself from defending Bertram. "She was new to him."

Marlowe was unconvinced. "I listened to Helena arrange to take Diana's place in Bertram's bed and sat forward, eager to see what you did with the question of where sin resides? In the heart? Or in what a person does? What did I get? Disappointment! He sleeps with her and the play creaks on!"

Oxford did not like to hear that his play 'creaked on,' but he couldn't tell Marlowe that *All's Well* was based on his marriage to Nan. Oxford had expected the audience would think his dilemma funny; Marlowe apparently took the play as a study of sin, and had failed. Oxford reminded himself that he had written a comedy. Why did Marlowe and John Marston think he was doing something else?

Marlowe pressed on. "It starts off so promisingly in what Helena says after Diana agrees to take her place with Bertram:

> *Let us assay our plot, which if it speed,*
> *Is wicked meaning in a lawful deed;*
> *And lawful meaning in a lawful act,*
> *Where both not sinne, and yet a sinfull fact.*

"This is good. This is very good. Is it *wicked meaning in a lawful deed*? Before the audience can grasp the nature of the problem, Diana wonders whether *she* is committing sin:

*In this disguise, I think't no sinne,*
*To cosen him that would unjustly winne.*

"But, like Helena, she dances away! I told myself patience—Bertram will resolve all. I expected him to speak volumes about sin and put the churchgoers to wiggling and squirming, but he says *nothing!*"

"Yes. I know. He's such a cad." Marlowe was imagining Bertram as an individual; Oxford was having trouble separating himself from the character he had created.

"The play is much like the case of Edmund Plowden, charged with attending Mass but acquitted when it came out at the trial that the man he thought was a priest was, in fact, a government agent!"

*"The Case is Altered."*

"Yes! Was Plowden guilty because he *thought* the agent was a priest? Did Bertram sin because he *thought* he was in bed with Diana when he was actually in bed with Helena? *All's Well* was poised to address the nature of sin and did nothing!"

Marlowe had become irritating again. "Then why don't you rewrite Bertram's lines to make Her Majesty's subjects 'wiggle and squirm'?'" Oxford was done with Marlowe. He scooped the papers on the table into a pile and stood up.

Marlowe was dismayed. "Please, my lord, do not go. I am too frank sometimes. It comes from spending too much time alone."

"Alone?"

"All my life." Peaches appeared with fresh beer. Marlowe took his. Oxford remained standing. He wondered how much they'd had. He thought it must be quite a lot.

"My father slept with a cobbler's hammer in his hand," Marlowe continued, "and used it on us if we caused him offense. My mother died when I was young. I have no memory of her. I had no brothers, only sisters, who are good for nothing but washing and cleaning." He took a sip of his beer. "At Cambridge, my poverty continued. The other students taunted me about being the son of a cobbler so I hid in my room, where I became a prisoner of my mind, my male soul breeding thoughts on my female brain."

Oxford sat back down. He had never imagined himself as a 'male soul breeding thoughts on a female brain,' despite also being alone when he was young. "And what came of this incestuous union?"

Marlowe did not understand. "My what?"

"This union between your male soul and your female brain."

"Ah. *Tamburlaine. The Jew. Faustus. Dido. Hercules.*"

"*Hercules?*"

"Yes."

"I have not heard of it."

"And never will. Or the play about Odysseus and the journey he went on after he came home and killed the suitors. Or the play about Alexander's minion."

"You tore them up."

Marlowe laughed. "I burned them. It was winter. The pages were worth more as heat for my room than a record of how much I had failed as a playwright." He took another sip of his beer. "I got rid of them," he said, a slight slur now audible at the edge of his voice. "Bad plays are like disease: they must be cut out."

"And which one of my plays would you put into the stove?"

Marlowe paused for a moment. "*Titus* was a bludgeon. *Comedy of Errors* was Plautus in English. Proteus in *Two Gentlemen* was a sharper knife, but, just when I was giving up on you, along comes Bertram and the Bastard."

Oxford was not pleased to hear his plays chopped up into one-word bits, but was surprised to hear praise in Marlowe's voice. "You would have kept *King John*?"

Marlowe nodded. "The Bastard was a fascinating character. And Queen Elinor." He waved his mug in the air, surprising Oxford even more. "What a woman!" He put his beer down and looked at Oxford. "I have never been able to write women."

"They have always been a mystery to me," Oxford agreed, with more emphasis than he had expected.

"From the waist down, they are centaurs," Marlowe said in a gravelly voice, scowling over the top of his mug. "Below the girdle lies the sulphurous pit, burning, scalding, stench ..." His voice trailed off. He looked across the table at Oxford. "But let us talk of something else. I liked how *King John* ends, the king burning from within, like his kingdom. The Bastard races to his side. The king is grateful:

> *Oh Cozen, thou art come to set mine eye:*
> *The tackle of my heart is crack'd and burnt*
> *And all the shrowds wherewith my life should sail,*
> *Are turned to one thread, one little hair.*

"Only you, a wolfish earl, could write a scene about the death of a king like that. The son of a cobbler could never mount so high." Marlowe took another pull on his beer. "But I heard nothing about Magna Carta."

"The Queen hates Magna Carta. She says it never took place."

"But one of your ancestors was there, wasn't he?"

Oxford nodded. "Robert, Third Earl of Oxford. Three hundred years ago." He meant this as a simple statement of fact. Marlowe took it as a put-down. It brought back to him the taunts from the students at Cambridge that his father lacked a title. "I must remind myself," he said, drawing himself up, "to strike my father when I see him next for having failed to provide me with famous forefathers."

Oxford was surprised by this. He leaned forward. "Mr. Marlowe, care not who your ancestors were because you will be remembered long after I am gone and my title is extinct. Your plays will live on. They have your name on them: mine do not. I will disappear while you ride a wave of fame into the future."

Marlowe blinked. He knew he was immortal; he hadn't realized that the man sitting opposite him was not. "And why is that, my lord? Why is Shackspear allowed to claim that he is the author of the plays you write?"

"I am forbidden to tell you." Marlowe's question, boosted by all the beer they had drunk, made Oxford as angry over his disenfranchisement as Marlowe had been over his lack of ancestors. "But enough of that. Let us return to poetry. Tell me how you wrote 'come live with me and be my love?' Eight words that would be poetry enough to admit you into the pantheon of poets had you written nothing else."

"By writing 'come be with me and be my love,' and throwing it on the floor, as you have done here," he said, pointing to the floor.

They both laughed.

"What makes one line poetry and another doggerel?" Oxford asked.

Marlowe shrugged. "I cannot tell until I have read it. If it's poetry, I keep it; if not, I throw it away."

"Aye."

"The muse knows," Marlowe muttered into his beer.

Oxford suddenly remembered that Falstaff was lying on the bench behind him. He braced himself, expecting to hear Falstaff's deep voice announce 'my nose knows,' but not a sound was heard. The big man must have fallen asleep. Or maybe showing restraint for once. "And now?" Oxford asked Marlowe.

"*Arden of Feversham*. Tom Kyd and I are working on it."

"A murder committed by fools. Will it be a comedy?"

"I will make it a tragedy."

"If you do, the men who carry out the murder should be named 'Shakebag' and 'Black Will.'"

Marlowe did not understand at first. Then he leaned back as a smile spread across his face. The two of them began to laugh. "'Shakebag' and 'Black Will,'" they said together. Laughter filled the inn. "Two buffoons for one," Marlowe said.

"How much more fun will it be to have *two* Shackspears on the stage, each dumber than the other."

"Shakebag and Black Will," Marlowe said, starting to laugh again.

"But how goes *Edward II*?" Oxford asked.

"Well." Marlowe said, as he drained his tankard. "But let us speak of new poetry. What say you to *My flocks feed not*." Oxford blinked. "Does your lordship not tilt at poetry?"

"Oh. Yes, I do. I didn't understand." He pursed his lips. "*My ewes breed not.*"

"*My rams speed not.*"

"*All is amiss.*"

They laughed and clinked mugs.

"*Love's denying*," Marlowe said, beginning a new round.

"*Faith's defying.*"

"*Heart's renying.*"

"'Renying?'" Oxford asked. "What is 'renying'?"

"To 'disown, to become a renegade.'"

Oxford shook his head. He thought Marlowe had invented a word to fill out a rhyme, a serious offense in a game of "carry on, if you can.'"

"The first round is inconclusive," Marlowe announced.

"Something more difficult, then," Oxford said. "*Crabbed age and youth cannot live together.*"

Falstaff snorted. Oxford had unconsciously introduced his sonnet to Aemilia Bassano into the contest. Marlowe did not hear Falstaff's reaction. He pressed on with the game. "*Youth is full of pleasance, age is full of care,*" he said.

"*Youth like summer morn, age like winter weather.*"

"*Youth like summer brave, age like winter bare.*"

"*Youth is full of sport, age's breath is short.*"

"*Youth is nimble, age is lame.*"

"*Youth is hot and old, age is weak and cold.*"

"*Youth is wild, and age is tame.*"

"*Age, I do abhor thee, youth I do adore thee,*" Oxford said, ending the poem.

Marlowe beamed. He was obviously having immense fun. "*Love, whose month was ever May, Spy'd a blossom passing fair.*"

"Enough!" Oxford said, putting up a hand. "You are hot and I am old." The beer was getting to him. He blinked to clear his eyes.

Marlowe was also having trouble focusing. His head had become a heavy ball. Each time he nodded, it went lower. He became fascinated with how heavy it felt. Oxford watched, entranced, as Marlowe's head drifted back and forth, slowly descending each time until it finally touched the top of the table. It rested there for a second, then snapped up, eyes wide open. "What heavenly odor steals over me?" Marlowe asked, looking around. He spied the lavender paper. "Ah, your poem." His head slumped back onto the table. "Aemilia Bassano," he mumbled. "Now *that's* a woman worth a poem."

"Aemilia Bassano?" Oxford asked. He lowered his head alongside Marlowe's to get his attention but the younger man had fallen asleep. Oxford's forehead gently touched the table alongside Marlowe's. The table was cool to the touch. It felt good to rest for a moment. He closed his eyes and was instantly asleep.

Peaches arrived to clear the table. "Sir John," she said. "What about these two? They're so full of words their 'eads have fallen over onto the table."

Falstaff rolled out of the booth and stood up. He brushed himself off. "Peaches, my lass, my doll."

"Don't 'doll' me." She swept the mugs and plates into her skirt. "What about them?"

"Let 'em sleep. They can do no harm with their mouths shut."

Peaches headed toward the kitchen. Falstaff surveyed the two men, as lifeless as the gargoyles over the entrance to St. Paul's. "If they with words could do as well with swords," he began, and then caught himself. A beatific smile spread across his face. "I'm a poet."

"Like 'ell," Peaches said, coming up behind him.

"Peaches, lass, let me finish. I was about to say that if they with words could do as well as others do with swords, by God, England'd be the master of the world. But 'til words pierce flesh like Damasque'd steel, I'll keep my sword, thank you very much, and stand guard."

"Very dramatic, but I don't see no sword."

"It's hidden." He put his arm around her.

"Not if ye know where it's hiding," she said, reaching into the folds of his breaches and fishing around. She pressed herself against him, rubbing what she called the porch to her front door against his thigh.

"Peaches!" Falstaff said. "Is the door open?"

"The girls are waiting."

"Mustn't let the poets see something they can't put in words." He draped his arm around her, his hip against hers, as they disappeared into the back of the Boar's Head.

# ~ 53 ~
## A Sonnet for Aemilia Bassano

She rejected it?"

John Marston nodded, his thumb and forefinger holding out the lavender page Oxford had told him to deliver to Aemilia Bassano.

"Wherefore?"

"'Crude,' was all she said, before she went back inside."

"*Crude!* It is *perfect!*"

"She did not say so, my lord."

Oxford grabbed the page. "It scans well, the rhymes work, no awkward feet. How can she say it is crude?"

"Perhaps she did not object to the poetry, my lord, but what it said about her."

Oxford remembered telling Digby that fancy words did not make a dull subject poetic. Digby had been praising a poem by George Gascoigne about hawks, a subject Digby loved dearly. Oxford rated the poem as poor poetry and dismissed Digby's enthusiasm. Oxford heard his own voice in John Marston's comment. "You mean, John Marston, that Mistress Bassano might not like reading that she was sleeping with an older man."

Marston nodded. He craned his head to look at the page Oxford still held in his hand: "First, you tell her that you '*believe her*' though you know '*she lies.*' How can you believe her if you know she lies? Truly, my lord, a sentence was never more twisted than this one. Then, you tell her that '*she thinks me young*' when maybe she doesn't. You conclude:

> *Therefore I lie with her, and she with me,*
> *And in our faults by lies we flattered be.*

"I overplayed my hand."

The boy nodded again.

"What else did she say?"

"She mentioned a younger poet, my lord."

"A younger poet?"

311

"'A fresh voice,' she said, 'who surpasses all that have gone before.'"

"Marlowe," Oxford said bitterly. He balled up the sonnet and flicked it down the table. Socrates ducked as it went whizzing by. Oxford got up and walked out of the room, as angry as John Marston had ever seen him.

The boy walked to the end of the table and picked up the crumpled poem. Socrates watched him warily. "Worth keeping," the boy said to the cat as he unfolded the paper and walked out of the room. "She didn't like it, but I do."

## ~ 54 ~
## The Geneva Bible

Falstaff came into the library and found Oxford bent over a sonnet. "My lord," he called out, interrupting Oxford's concentration. "Henslowe is playing *Harry VI* day in and day out. All London loves it. Even the Queen says that you have finally given her what she wanted."

"So?"

"Ye made my ancestor, Sir John Falstoffe, a coward! Talbot, of all people, rips the Garter off his leg:

> *I vow'd, base knight, when I did meet thee next,*
> *To tear the garter from thy craven's leg!*

"My namesake, and the honor of my family! Disgraced on the stage! I demand another be named!"

"He is not your namesake, Jack. He is from Norfolk. You are from Sheffield. The man who fought alongside Henry died childless in an empty castle. He left no descendants. He is no ancestor of yours."

"Then why call him 'Sir John Falstoffe?'"

Oxford shrugged. "John Marston thought it was a good idea."

"John Marston?" The clouds hanging over Sir John's face became darker. "Then use the name, but why make him merely a buffoon!"

"*Merely?*"

"I am nimble Jack Falstaff, to those who hang on my wit; Sir John to those in authority; and Big John to the ladies. The man I saw on the stage was none of these."

"Aye."

"But the audience thinks he is. He is to me as Shackspear is to you—*a fraud!*"

"Ah. Then I shall rename him."

"Ye better. Ye have not the magic to capture John Falstaff on stage. All ye have is words. Ye cannot capture the spirit, the vastness of what is inside."

"Which *must* be vast, seeing as how vast the outside is."

Falstaff nodded. "Make him a Lollard. You had an Oldcastle in *Famous Victories*. Use that name. It'll piss off the Puritans."

Oxford nodded. "Lord Cobham is a descendant of Oldcastle. Robert Cecil married his daughter last year."

Falstaff's face lit up. "Then it will piss off Sir Robert too! Two pricks knocked off their lofty branch with one shot! All London'll be laughing. That'll be better than free beer." Then he frowned. "Well, maybe not."

"Cobham is nothing at court and won't be able to force Tilney to make me change the name."

"But what about Sir Robert?"

"He won't lift a finger. He isn't happy about the match."

"Good." Falstaff leaned over to look at the sonnet Oxford was working on. "Another 'she lies with me and I with her'?"

"Hardly."

"So you still pursue her?"

Oxford snorted. "She has gone over to Marlowe."

"God be praised."

Oxford looked at him in surprise.

Falstaff became serious, a state not often seen in the man. "That woman is a siren, if ever there was one. She would have pulled Odysseus over the side even if he had stuffed his ears with beeswax from Mount Olympus!"

John Marston came bustling into the room. His arms were loaded with books. The boy unloaded them onto the table. His eye fell on the open Bible Oxford was in the process of underlining.

"My Lord!" the boy exclaimed. "You draw lines in God's word!"

Falstaff walked over to the corner and lowered himself into a chair.

"'Tis only a book, my young friend."

"Nay, my lord, *it is God's word!*"

"In Italian, in Greek," Oxford said, waving his hand over other Bibles on the table. "This is the Geneva Bible, which I prefer above others."

John Marston made the sign of cross. Oxford had underlined a verse in *I Samuel*. Without looking down, Oxford recited it: "*But the Lord said onto Samuel, look not on his countenance nor on the height of his stature, for God seeith not as men seeith. For man looketh on the outward appearance, but the Lord beholdeth the heart."*

"'Tis blasphemy to write in the Holy Book."

Oxford sighed. "The Holy Book is written by men, John Marston."

"By *God*," the boy insisted. He looked up at Oxford with open, searching eyes. "My lord," he began. "You know I love you and admire you, but sometimes I feel the Devil is in this house, and if I stay here longer I will be utterly corrupted, and when I die I will go straight to Hell."

"'*It is dangerous to touch pitch lest perchance one be defiled by it*,'" Oxford said quietly.

"Where is that from?"

"Ecclesiastes 13:1."

"Yes."

"Is it time to go, then?" Oxford asked. The boy nodded. Tears began to well up in his eyes. Oxford reached up and put his arm on the boy's shoulder. "Your father will be proud of you," he said. "You have been of great assistance to me, John Marston. University awaits. I thank thee for your service." The boy now looked like he would burst out crying. "Nigel will give you your pay. Tell him to give you an extra angel to buy books."

"Thank you, my lord."

"Off you go, John Marston."

The boy ran for the door. He was as much embarrassed by his emotions as he was eager to flee.

"And *now* what will I do for a secretary?" Oxford asked, but not loud enough for the retreating boy to hear. "As glad as I am to get rid of my 'mincing minister,' my 'Puritan Presence,' I have lost an arm."

"Would ye take Robin back if he were around?" Falstaff asked, draping a leg over one of the arms of the chair.

"He is in Italy." Oxford looked at Falstaff. "Is he not?"

"Could be. Maybe not."

"Well, he's no good to me in Italy."

"But what if he returns?"

"What are you not telling me?"

"Nothing."

"Don't 'nothing' me."

"I'll see what I can find out."

"You rogue."

Falstaff stood up, a shocked look on his face. "How ill-treated I am here." He brushed some imaginary crumbs off his chest and headed for the door. Oxford heard him whistling to himself as he went out the front door.

## ~ 55 ~
## Robin Returns

Falstaff steered Robin into the library. "Look what I found, your lordship." He pushed Robin into the room.

"What's the play?" Robin said, striking a jaunty pose.

Oxford leaned back in his chair. "Welcome back, young Robin. Are you game?"

"As game as *ever*," Robin said, stressing the last word. Oxford laughed. Robin walked over to the cabinet and opened it without asking. "And what has my successor done with my inks, my grinding stones, my quills?" He began to rummage in the cabinet. "I am sure he did know that a pinch of verdigris casts a gray shade on the ink, a touch his lordship much prefers." He glanced at Oxford. "If I remember rightly."

"Your predecessor knew nothing of verdigris," Oxford said. "He was a scowling Puritan who saw the Devil everywhere."

"As does Sir John," Robin said, not looking at Falstaff leaning against the doorjamb.

"Yes, but Sir John is his second cousin."

"If not his father and son."

The two of them looked at Falstaff to see how he took this. He made the sign of the cross. "The son *and* the father, dear boy."

They all laughed. Oxford turned back to Robin. "What took you so long?"

"I heard my master had a secretary."

"I heard you went to Italy."

"The plague kept me in France."

"Where he learned to soak his head in something better than Mallard grease," Falstaff said.

"French pomade." Robin bent over, showing Oxford the top of his head. Oxford remembered looking down at Robin's head the day they first met on the seawall at Greenwich Palace. It was just as shiny now as it had been then.

"And the mustache?" Oxford asked.

"If you can call it that," Falstaff said, coming over to look at Robin more closely. "He drew it with a pencil, I warrant." He grabbed the mustache and gave it a tug.

"Ow," Robin cried out, pulling away.

"Son of a glover," Falstaff said, surprised. "It *is* real!

"You're damn right it is!" Robin said, rubbing his upper lip.

"And swearing now," Falstaff said, tsk-tsking.

"France can do that to a man," Oxford said.

Robin surveyed them both. "And is this how you treat those who return to your service after a long voyage overseas?"

"France doesn't count."

"It's farther than the miles it takes to get there," Robin said, smoothing his hair. "All that glisters in England is dulled by France. The ladies are lovelier, the wines are sweeter, and the music is better. Even the mud doesn't cling to your boots as much as England's does."

Oxford glanced over at Falstaff. "Good thing he didn't get to Italy. Can you imagine the hats he'd be wearing?"

"Or the gloves? They'd be spangled with jewels and perfumed with scents that rot a fighting man's bones."

The two older men surveyed Robin, standing defiantly in front of them. "A few more pounds," Oxford commented after a moment.

"And a mustache," Falstaff added.

"And a touch of surliness. But, tell us, Robin, did the lovely ladies detain you in Paris the whole time you were 'overseas,' or did you see anything of the rest of France?"

"I did. The limpid Loire, the mighty Rhone, and the Castle of Tournon.

Oxford sat up. "Tournon?"

"A jewel hanging over the Rhone halfway to the Mediterranean."

"I know it well. I spent a fortnight there on my way back from Italy. How did you come to see it?"

"A group of ladies decided to flee the cold weather in Paris. They took me along."

"A *group* of ladies?" Falstaff asked. "They did not mind having such a fair, young man amongst them on their trip?"

Robin coughed. "I did not have my mustache yet, Sir John."

"Oh."

"You obviously earned it on the trip," Oxford added.

"Yes."

"Tell me about Tournon."

"Truth be told, the ladies were eager to escape the cold as much as the courtiers who were pursuing them in Paris. A pedantic windbag at court suggested they go to Tournon to study philosophy and literature. A drawbridge would keep out any men. Their time in Tournon would be known as the 'academy without love.'"

"And they took you with them?" Falstaff asked.

"I was not yet a man, Sir John. I didn't know what love was."

"Oh."

"We traveled down to Tournon and the ladies pulled up the drawbridge, but we had barely settled in when the Paris suitors arrived and began to storm the castle. The ladies told them to go away and had servants throw offal on them."

"That's offal!" Sir John said.

Oxford groaned. "*That's* offal!"

Falstaff protested. "Wherefore, my lord? It almost rhymes!"

Oxford waved a hand. "Please. Let me hear the boy. How long did their resistance last?"

"A week, my lord."

"Extraordinary."

"Indeed. Two of the women who had been blistered by comments made in Paris persuaded the others to hold out longer than they wanted."

"But, eventually, they gave in."

"Only because the men convinced them that they were dying from the meager food to be had in the village at the bottom of the hill."

Oxford shook his head. "And so the women gave in?"

"Yes."

"What manner of philosophy did they engage in?"

"The pedant had the men put on a play called *The Nine Worthies*."

"Oh, dry stuff."

"And how long did all this last?" Falstaff asked.

"Until the wine ran out. The ladies decided Paris was not as cold as they had remembered. They loaded everything into the carriages and returned to the city. They made the pedant ride an ass back to Paris to punish him for turning them away from love."

"Ye'll never forget how you got your mustache," Falstaff said, relishing the thought of being trapped in a carriage with a bevy of French beauties.

"Aye," Robin agreed. "But what's the play? I have had enough of women and drink."

Oxford smiled. "*Henry VI*, in all its parts," he said, gesturing toward the mess of papers in the corner of the library. "Your task shall be to arrange them in scene order so that we can decide what next to present to the Queen."

"*Next?*"

"Shackspear has already staged Part 1 before the Queen."

"The play in which Joan of Arc grovels and lies before she is taken off to be burnt? It was much discussed in Paris before I left. The way you treated Joan of Arc was greatly resented. Mr. Shackspear would be well-advised to put off traveling to France for a few years."

Oxford turned and smiled at Falstaff. "Ah, Jack, the first benefit of having that Warwickshire hack claim he wrote the plays! I can go to Paris now and not worry about an irate Frenchman putting a knife in my back."

"Oh, let's go, my lord," Robin said eagerly. "I can be an excellent guide."

Oxford shook his head. "The Queen will not allow it."

Robin was disappointed. "So Shackspear is still carrying your plays to the playhouse?"

"He is."

Socrates appeared from under the table and sauntered past Robin, rubbing his coat across the boy's leg. He continued out the door and down the hall toward the kitchen.

"Well, someone is glad to see you," Falstaff observed.

Robin smiled. "Will there be more plays after *Henry VI?*" he asked.

"What do you think?"

"I remember the trunk upstairs."

"No. The plays in the trunk will stay there. Let them rot. I have better ideas, newly egged in my brain. Their shells are cracking. A comedy about Tournon, except I will make the men vow to give up love and have the women knock down their doors. It will be full of 'fat, buttery' words. I will need you to give me new ones. Will you help me?"

"I will, my lord."

"Parts 2 and 3 of *Henry VI* are lying on the floor. The Queen wants to hear the rest of the play sooner rather than later. And I shall expect music at supper tonight."

"Most definitely, my lord. I have a new lute, a gift from a lady who said my instrument was not equal to my fingers."

"I've had the same thing said to me," Falstaff said, stroking one of his mustaches.

"Of, for the love of Michael," Oxford said. He stood up. "While you get settled in, Robin, we are to the Boar's Head." He headed for the door. Falstaff followed. "No more Master Mincing," Oxford said. He sounded pleased.

"'No more Master Yes Sir, Yes Sir.'"

"Aye."

"He never did fit in, did he?"

"The Puritans ruined him before he got here."

"And what of Mistress Bassano?" Falstaff asked, as they went out into Candlewick Street.

"Done."

"Done?"

"Finished."

"Over?"

"Over! No more! Non plus! Fini! Nienté! Terminó! *Bih-TUH!*"

"Bih-tuh?"

"'Finished' in Turkish."

"What happened?"

"She found Marlowe." The frown on Oxford's face deepened. "The first time, I lost her to myself. She thought my words were Shackspear's. That was ironic. Now she knows the words are mine, but she prefers Marlowe's. That's tragedy.

*Was it the proud full sail of his great verse,*
*Bound for the prize of all too precious you,*
*That did my ripe thoughts in my brain inhearse,*
*Making their tomb the womb wherein they grew?*
*Was it his spirit, by spirits taught to write*
*Above a mortal pitch, that struck me dead?*

A woman going by in the opposite direction lurched away from him. Madmen were common in London. Most people thought they were easily detectible, although they argued over whether you could tell a madman by the words he uttered or the way he moved. The woman had obviously concluded that Oxford was mad on both counts.

Falstaff reached out to steady Oxford and steer him around a horse and cart coming toward them. "Finished, you said."

"Yes."

They reached the Boar's Head. Falstaff stepped down and pushed open the door. "Peaches'll get ye an ale, my lord, and you can wash this woman out of your system. All women. We bachelors be. God be praised."

## ~ 56 ~
## Ankerwycke

The Thames rises in foothills far to the west of London, threading its way through Oxford, Reading, and other towns before coming out into a flat valley and flowing through London to the sea. When the river is low, it wanders back and forth like an indolent Asian courtesan reluctant to finish its journey to the sea. When it rains, the river grows larger and muscles its way through the valley, scouring new channels the boatmen can use to transport goods and people upriver. Spring had been cold and wet, and the river now widened and swirled away from the shore, forming a deep eddy that looked inviting, at least to Oxford, in the heat of the early summer afternoon sun.

"It's a god, you know," Oxford said, dragging his fingers through the water. He was leaning over the edge of the flat-bottomed barge he had hired to carry him and his baggage to Windsor, where the court would be moving to let Greenwich Palace be swept of decaying rushes and scrubbed clean. Robin sat in the center of the boat playing his lute, sending soft waves of music into the heat that hung over them. The sumpter horse on the river bank leaned into the tow rope as it dragged the barge upriver against the current.

"A god?" Robin asked, putting his lute aside. He peered over the side from under the awning he had built with sticks and a tablecloth he found in one of the trunks. "It looks like water to me."

"You've no imagination, Robin. It is a god in liquid form, fitting itself into every surface it touches, folding and unfolding as it rolls along, giving life to the fish and plants it washes through, watering the fields it passes, and giving me balm as it runs through my fingers."

Robin wasn't convinced. Oxford lay back on the cushions and pulled a shawl over his head. "I am Cleopatra descending the River Cydnus to meet Antony." He looked away, but not because Robin was having no truck with rivers as gods, or Oxford as Cleopatra. To Oxford, he was now Cleopatra and Robin was Mark Antony, and their gazes should not meet.

"Ye'd make a poor Cleopatra," Falstaff rumbled from where he had hid himself among the trunks at the rear of the barge.

"I would make a *great* Cleopatra. You have no imagination, either one of you." His tone was more mischievous than dismissive. He went back to dragging his fingers in the water. "Like Plutarch. Listen to how he describes Cleopatra's meeting with Mark Antony:

> *The barge's poop was of gold, the sails of purple, and the oars of silver, which kept stroke in rowing after the sound of the melody of flutes, hautboys, citherne, viols, and such other instruments as they played fit the barge.*

Oxford sniffed, as if the odor from a passing cow pasture had just washed over him. "That's *awful!*" He rearranged himself on the cushions, his hand on the rail: "How much better this?"

> *The barge she sat in, like a burnish'd throne,*
> *Burn'd on the water.*

"Oh, 'burn'd on the water!'" Robin muttered, warming to Oxford as Cleopatra. Oxford went on:

> *The poop was beaten gold;*
> *Purple the sails, and so perfumed that*
> *The winds were love-sick with them.*

"'The *wind* was '*love-sick*' with the *sails*?'" Falstaff asked incredulously. Robin waved an arm to silence him.

> *The oars were silver,*
> *Which to the tune of flutes kept stroke, and made*
> *The water which they beat to follow faster,*
> *As amorous of their strokes.*

"Lordy, lordy. The water now wants to be 'stroked'!"

Oxford stretched out an arm and lay back.

> *Cleopatra did lie in her pavilion,*
> *On each side her stood smiling Cupids,*
> *With divers-colour'd fans, whose wind did seem*
> *To glow the delicate cheeks which they did cool,*
> *And what they undid did.*

"'Undid did?'" Robin asked.

"Try not to understand it and you will."

Robin blinked. "What play is this from, my lord?"

"One I haven't written yet."

"*Another* play you haven't written yet?"

"Yes.

*From the barge*
*A strange invisible perfume hits the sense*
*Of the adjacent wharfs. The city cast*
*Her people out upon her; and Antony,*
*Enthroned i' the market-place, did sit alone,*
*Whistling to the air; which, but for vacancy,*
*Had gone to gaze on Cleopatra too,*
*And made a gap in nature.*

Falstaff was incredulous. "The *air* went to gaze on Cleopatra?"

"And made a gap in nature," Robin added enthusiastically, "leaving Antony alone in the marketplace!"

"You like it?" Oxford asked.

Robin nodded. "Most assuredly, my lord!"

Falstaff turned over unseen among the trunks. "I've seen him like this before, Robin. He's going to see that Trembling woman again in Windsor. This is not good. We'll have to watch him like hawks, we will."

"Oh, pshaw," Oxford said. He fell silent, the better to enjoy the echoes of what he had just written, if only on the air that occasionally touched him lightly across the brow.

"But why do you imagine yourself as Cleopatra and not Mark Antony?" Robin asked.

"Because she likes strong women," Oxford said, without further explanation. Robin knew who he meant; so did Falstaff. The Queen was always lurking in Oxford's poetry, peering around a curtain like Cleopatra batting her eyes at Antony.

The barge was now being towed through tall grass. Oxford leaned over and pushed the grass aside—watching the frogs, startled by the sudden appearance of the barge—leap away to higher ground. A field suddenly appeared. Oxford could see a crumbling building in the distance.

"Ankerwycke," he said, sitting up. "I was a student there, Robin, before my father died."

"In a priory?"

"No, in the great house behind it. The priory had been abandoned long before I came here. Sir Thomas was my tutor. He gave me little time away from my studies, but on hot days like this he would let me to run down to the river and swim across to the other side. There I could walk in the field where Earl Robert, Third Earl of Oxford, and other great barons forced King John to sign Magna Carta." The trees across the river opened up to show them a vast, empty field.

"Runnymeade," Robin said in a hushed voice. And then: "You swim?"

"You don't?"

Robin shook his head. "I would sink. 'Tis not fit for a man to swim."

Oxford laughed. "I did it all the time as a young lad. Are you afraid?"

"Of course not."

Oxford began slipping off his clothes.

"My lord," Robin protested.

"Who's to see us?" Oxford jumped into the river.

"My lord!" Robin exclaimed in a higher voice, standing up and knocking over the little awning he had made.

To Robin's surprise, Oxford stood up. "Look! It's shallow enough to stand. It feels wonderful!"

Robin remained rooted to the deck of the barge.

"Come, young sir, shed your clothes and join me."

A loud splash was heard from the rear of the barge. Falstaff had thrown himself overboard, making a giant wave that washed over Oxford. He came up and rolled onto his back. "I was dying from the heat!" he called out. "A man of my kidney—think of it—that am as butter to a hot plate!" He swam across to the sandbar on the other side of the river and pulled himself out of the water, looking like a beached whale just arrived from the southern ocean.

"What tempest, I trow," Oxford called out as he swam after him, "threw this whale, with so many tuns of oil in his belly, onto the shore?"

Falstaff ignored him. He rolled over onto his back and slid partway back into the water.

"Stay the horse, bargeman!" Oxford called out. The sleepy man on the horse pulled on the reins and the horse came to a halt. His two companions, manning long poles at the stern of the barge, staked the barge to the bottom to keep it from sliding downriver. They leaned on their poles and goggled at the earl and his knight who had so easily shed their clothes and wallowed in the water like fish.

Oxford was about to lay himself out alongside Falstaff when he saw something on the other side of the river. He pushed himself into the water and, with powerful strokes, recrossed the river to the barge where he pulled himself aboard and grabbed a shirt and breeches. He stepped ashore and walked upriver past the tow-horse and the man astride it. He headed for an old man sitting on a bench under the first course of trees. The old man was wrapped in a gray wool blanket, his head sticking out like a bulb of garlic just plucked from the ground.

"Too cold, young man, for you to be in the river," the old man said, as Oxford came up to him.

"Sir Thomas," Oxford said quietly.

The old man squinted at Oxford. His eyes looked like windows covered with white curtains. "Who calls my name?"

"Edward, Sir Thomas. Edward de Vere."

Sir Thomas studied him. "Do I know ye?"

"Do you not?"

Sir Thomas thought about this. "I knew an Edward once. I had hoped that he would be Aristotle to my Plato, but …" His voice fell.

Oxford dropped to one knee. "I am he, Sir Thomas. You taught me Greek, Latin, the hemispheres at night. Poetry. Simples composed off warm peat and the gills of fish."

Mention of the gills of fish apparently unlocked the old man's memory. "He did well at first."

"And since."

The man's face folded itself into a frown. "No. Nothing has come of the young man I knew as Edward."

"Sir Thomas," Oxford protested.

The old man put up a hand. "I grant you the poetry had moments of grandeur. *If care or skill could conquer vain desire.* Best of all were the comments to Thomas Watson's sonnets in *The Hekatompathia.* They were sublime! The author of the comments was not named, of course, which was good, good—one should let one's scholarship shine without calling attention to it—but I knew it was you. You called young Watson to account for using a figure in rhetoric I had taught you. You wrote, *which of the Greeks is called παλιλογιά or of the Latins reduplicatio,* meaning somewhat tedious or too much affected? To give an example, you went to Susenbrotus for a quote out of Virgil!"

"You remember all that?"

Sir Thomas beamed. "Few others could have been more excited to read those words. I recognized that the seeds I had planted here at Ankerwycke had borne glorious fruit. No one else was capable of tossing off a poetic term in Greek and Latin and then quote a phrase from Virgil that a German scholar had used."

Oxford let himself sit down on the bench next to Sir Thomas.

"And so, when I read your comments," Sir Thomas went on, "I closed Watson's book and smiled as I have smiled few times in my life." His breath was short and raspy. His face clouded over again. "But nothing more. Nothing." He looked at Oxford. "Ye took what God had given ye, and what I had taught ye, and instead of working to take my place, ye spent it on crude shows for the playhouse. Ye did this because it was easy. Things *always* came too easily for ye. Yer a bankside poet, Edward de Vere, because it is easy." He looked away.

Oxford wanted to tell him about the lines he had just composed about Cleopatra's barge, but the old man's ears were stopped. He remembered how excited he had been to describe to Sir Thomas the Queen's visit to Hedingham when Oxford was only eight and the joy of seeing his first play. But Sir Thomas had waved him silent. "There is more beauty in one line written by Horace than all the plays that have ever been written," he had pronounced. Oxford now realized that Sir Thomas had not changed, but Oxford had, and he felt no need to apologize for it.

Oxford stood up. Sir Thomas gazed past him. "You're blocking my view," he said, waving at Oxford to move to one side. "There is much argument there but I canna hear it when you stand in the way!"

Oxford walked back to the barge. Falstaff had somehow gotten himself on board. Robin could tell that whatever had passed between his master and the old man had not gone well. "Aweigh, ho, bargeman," Oxford called out as he climbed over the railing and sat down at the bow, pulling his damp shirt about him. The sun had slipped behind a low-hanging cloud in the western sky. The heat was fading. The horse leaned into the tow rope and the men at the stern pulled out their poles as the barge resumed its journey to Windsor, now just a few miles ahead of them.

## ~ 57 ~
## Windsor

The barge had not gone a mile when a barefoot Oxford grabbed his shoes and jumped into the water. The Thames had narrowed. "Robin," he called, wading across to the opposite bank. Robin took off his shoes and followed. On shore, Oxford put on his shoes and strode out into an open field. Robin hurried to catch up. Windsor Castle was now visible above the copse of woods that lay ahead of them in the distance.

The two said nothing as they hiked across the field. A farmhouse soon appeared. Cattle and sheep grazed in small groups in the open fields around it and looked up puzzled as Oxford and Robin went by them. "Frogmore," Oxford said, gesturing toward the farmhouse. A large tree loomed up in front of them, split it in half by lightning. Oxford stopped beneath it.

"Herne's Oak," he said, looking up.

"Who was Herne?"

"He was the keeper of Windsor Forest until he started poaching the royal deer he was supposed to protect. When he got caught, he was so ashamed of what he'd done he hung himself from this tree. People say he comes back on horseback in winter, antlered like the deer he poached, waving chains and leading a horde of demon hounds behind him. He glows in the dark, they say."

Oxford set off again. Robin ran to keep up, nervously looking back at Herne's Oak.

"When I was twenty-one," Oxford continued, "I spent a month in Windsor," Oxford added.

"Serving the Queen?"

"No. I came here to get rid of an illness that had kept me from joining my uncle on the border."

"But why here, my lord? Why not stay in London?"

"I needed rest. And I had to get away from the court."

"But you could have gone anywhere."

"I wanted to be near the old man you saw me talking to just now on the riverbank. Sir Thomas visited me here while I convalesced."

"What did he say that upset you today, my lord?"

"He said I had failed him. He said I had wasted my talent in writing plays instead of becoming a scholar like him."

"But you have no interest in being a scholar, do you?"

"No. I am a playwright. And my plays will be better than anything the Latin poets wrote, despite Sir Thomas's love of them." Then his face darkened. "Except that, if I write, I must hide behind that Warwickshire peasant, so I write, but is it me? No, it's him. Which is worse, Robin? To write under a mask and die unknown, or not write at all? Is there *any* difference?"

Robin disagreed. "I swear by Herne's ghost, my lord, that I shall make those who come after us know that *Titus* and *All's Well* were …"

"I know your love for me, little Robin, as you know mine for you. I cherish your vows to unmask Shackspear, but what can you do?"

"Yes, I may be little and of no importance, but I know who wrote the plays, my lord, and I shall make sure your name is not forgotten."

Oxford smiled. "Thank you, dear Robin."

The day had become hotter but they were soon at the outskirts of Windsor where the dirt path became a paved street and houses built of local stone on either side cooled the air. They turned into High Street, which ran past the castle and down to the Thames. At the bridge, they turned right and walked along an embankment paved with large stones. Wooden tables had been set out where the paving ended. A sandy beach ran on for a few yards before disappearing into a thicket of willows that hung over the river. A tavern made of rough stone faced the tables.

"The Garter Inn," Oxford announced, "where I stayed many years ago. There are cool winds that blow through the second floor."

They went inside and found a man in his late thirties wiping his hands on a rag. His face was pockmarked and full of dark bumps. Robin thought he looked like a pancake that had been left on the stove too long. "My lord," he said, coming over to Oxford.

"Where is mine host?"

"I regret, my lord, that my father passed away five years ago."

"I am sorry to hear that. Doubtless, you carry on his excellent service."

"I try to, my lord."

"You have received my instructions?"

"I have, my lord. Everything is as you requested."

"Good. The barge will be here shortly with my baggage. In the meantime, would you please bring us an ale? We will repair to the embankment to watch the barge come around the bend."

"Yes, my lord."

Oxford and Robin went outside and found the barge in the process of tying up. Falstaff, his hat unfolded and his belt buckle lined up with the center of his belly, waited on the edge of the boat to disembark.

"My lord and Robin," he announced, stepping nimbly onto the embankment as the innkeeper appeared with two beers. Oxford took one but Falstaff reached over and took the other, downing it in one long draft, accompanied by more sounds than were issued by any waterspout ever seen at sea. "Ah," he announced loudly when he had finished. He handed the empty tankard back to the innkeeper and wiped off his mustache. "Another one, prithee, good fellow."

"You're welcome," Oxford said. Robin frowned.

The innkeeper took Falstaff's empty mug and started for the inn. Robin touched his arm as he went by to remind him that he needed to bring three beers the next time. The innkeeper nodded and continued on.

Falstaff peered down the embankment to where the stone paving ran off into the sandy beach. He walked through the tables to the farthest one. He grabbed it with both hands and flipped it over his head. He carried it off the embankment onto the beach. Slipping his boots off as he walked, he waded out into the river and flipped the table into the water with a splash. He pressed it down. Satisfied that it would not set off for London, he turned to walk back to Oxford and Robin, who were standing on the embankment with their mouths hanging open. Falstaff stopped at the edge of the water and looked up at them.

"What are ye, a bunch of mussel-shells? Grab a bench and join me. It's been a hot day and I've bled enough fat off me today to grease every pan in the great Olney pancake race!"

Oxford laughed. "You expect us to join you *in the river?*"

"You think I'm doing this *for the dolphins?*" Falstaff climbed up onto the embankment. "Ye 'fraid of being laughed at?" He picked up a bench. "Ye too 'gentrified' to sit in the water? Too old to do the unexpected anymore?" He tucked the bench under his arm and headed back to the water. "Time to fetch the casket, Robin. His lordship is done. Finished. *Bit-tuh.* Dead, top to bottom. Don't know why I waste my time." He walked out into the water and put the bench down next to the table. The bench, though, was not as heavy as the table and had other ideas. It started to surge off. Falstaff grabbed it and forced it under him. He sat down, his back to Oxford and Robin. "Aaahhh," he said, as the water washed over his legs and lower torso. "The river is balm to the king's jewels, which are always on fire."

"From the pox, no doubt!" Oxford called after him. "If ye have anything at your age, it's an ember in a fennel stalk!"

"Edward, me boy, ye do me wrong. The ladies love what I bring them. The Golden Rod. The Staff of Plenty. Their faces light up when they see me."

"Because they hope you've come to pay your debts."

"Edward, Edward." Falstaff turned to look back at them. His face asked the question: Were they going to join him in the river, or not?

Oxford laughed. He grabbed a bench and headed for the water. Robin followed. They waded into the river and sat down across from Falstaff. The river was up to their waists and cool from the spring runoff.

The innkeeper came out with the three beers and stopped. He did not see them at first. When he did, he walked into the water without taking his boots off and handed them the mugs.

"Well done," Oxford said to the innkeeper.

"Thank you, my lord."

"There's a man," Falstaff said.

"So, Jack, what are we doing here?" Oxford asked.

"We're having our legs washed by a river god, ye know, what some call the Thames. Isn't that right, my lord?"

The innkeeper came back out. "Will there be anything else, my lord?"

"Eel pie!" Falstaff immediately said.

"I'm sorry, your worship, but we are out of eel pie."

"Pike, then."

"That, too."

"Sturgeon?" Falstaff asked, his face beginning to show worry. The innkeeper shook his head. "Perch." The innkeeper shook his head again. "Trout!" Falstaff almost shouted. The innkeeper was now the one starting to look worried. "Blast it, man!" Falstaff exploded. "This is the Thames! I'm sitting in it! You're inn is right there! Wherefore is there no fish?"

The innkeeper smiled weakly. "For because my wife does not like them," he said, glancing over his shoulder.

"Well, then, man, get rid of your wife and *get me some fish*!"

The innkeeper did not know what to say.

"Would you have beef?" Oxford asked, watching a saw-toothed strand of grass disappear under Falstaff's side of the table and reappear on the other.

"Yes, my lord," the man said. "Boiled beef."

"Boiled beef!" Falstaff immediately exclaimed, startling the man again. "But only if we can have it with Tewkesbury mustard!"

"We have Tewkesbury mustard, your worship," the innkeeper said. Falstaff smiled broadly. The innkeeper headed back to the inn.

"Not without mustard," Falstaff called after him.

This brought a smile to Oxford's face. Falstaff gave Oxford a sly look. "And what *about* Tewkesbury mustard?" Robin asked.

"John Donne was on a ship in a great storm. Everyone thought they were going to drown. Donne, on his knees, promised God that he would never eat boiled beef again if God allowed him to live."

"And was he spared?"

"He was."

"And did he eat boiled beef again?"

"He did."

"How could he do that?"

Falstaff took over the story. "He claimed his promise was not that he would never eat boiled beef again, but that he would never eat boiled beef again *without mustard*!" He put his head back and roared.

"But that's trying to trick God, isn't it?" Robin protested. You can't trick God, can you?"

Falstaff looked at Oxford. "Didn't we rid of John Marston?"

Oxford motioned for Falstaff to leave Robin alone. "If Donne's to be punished, it will have to be later."

"If at all," Falstaff mumbled.

"Otherwise, Lord Burghley would be writhing in pain now. But come, let us find a better subject to debate while seated in the Thames."

"Amen to that," Falstaff agreed.

Oxford pointed to a window on the second floor of the inn. "Up yonder is the room where I spent six weeks lying on the window sill and gazing out over the river. Sir Thomas made me drink gallons of Devil's Bit and the essence of violets."

"Did it work?"

"I got better, didn't I? And above us is Windsor Castle," he said, pointing to the walls high above the inn. "I found a grotto up there." Robin strained to see it in the fading light. "You can't see it from here," Oxford said. "In truth, you can't see the cave until you're nearly on top of it. A path leads down to it from the castle walls and ends at a small terrace hidden by an overhang."

"What adventures did you have there," Robin asked.

"None. I was alone, remember, and sick. Now, however, I will use the grotto to lure Elspeth Trentham to a dinner by candlelight."

Falstaff guffawed. "Lordy, lordy. It didn't take a grotto for ye to bed Anne Vavasor."

Oxford ignored him. "Robin, you and I will carry a small table and chairs up to the cave. I will have the innkeeper make us a meal of river trout, eel grass, and artichoke flowers you will collect from the verges of Datchet Mead. We will borrow a dozen fishing rods from the village and hang small lanterns from them to light the path." Falstaff groaned.

The innkeeper came back and waded into the river. He laid three plates of boiled beef and mustard on the table.

"More beer," Falstaff ordered.

"It's right behind me," the innkeeper said. A boy younger than Robin came down the embankment carrying a tray of mugs. Beyond him was a bevy of ladies, all fancifully dressed, walking down the embankment. Elspeth Trentham was among them. Oxford stood up. His first instinct was to run, but any hope of slipping into the trees behind him was dashed when Elspeth's sharp eyes spied him standing in the water. He decided to walk up onto the embankment and greet her.

"My lady," he said, as he came up to her, water pouring off his breeches.

"My lord," she said. "Dining in the river?" The ladies behind her giggled

"It has been a hot day, my lady."

"Does the Thames flow with beer, my lord? If it did, I am sure I would have found you with your head in it." This elicited more giggles.

Falstaff, his back to them, chortled.

"A pleasant suggestion, my lady," said Oxford, trying to make light of his predicament. "But for now I can only offer you the coolness of the river after the heat of the day. Would you care to join us?"

A flicker of her eyebrows told him what she thought of his idea. "A most generous and, at the same time, most unusual offer," Elspeth replied, "which I must, unfortunately decline. I bathe only once a month, my lord, and see no reason to combine my bath, not due for another three weeks, with my supper."

Oxford moved closer to her. "Had I known you would be here I would have sought you out before dining anywhere, much less in the Thames." He took another step closer, his boots squishing. "You have been gone many months, my lady."

"I had more business to attend to than I had planned. And I became ill, unfortunately, which prevented me from returning to court until now."

"God be praised that you have recovered, my lady."

"Thank you."

"And, having recovered from your illness, would you be so kind as to dine with me this week?"

"Here?"

"In the private grotto I described to you last time we spoke."

"Oh, yes. No, thank you. Now, unfortunately, I must leave, my lord."

She turned away from him before he could say more. The ladies who had come with her fell in behind Elspeth, leaving Oxford standing in a widening pool of water on the embankment.

Falstaff snorted. "Even the air is gone," he announced, picking up his tankard and waving it like a wand, "leaving a gap in nature, and Edward standing in the marketplace alone."

Robin giggled and looked away.

Oxford walked back to them. "No need to hide your smile, Robin. Sir John never gets my lines quite right, but I am always amazed to find out that he has heard them at all." He sighed. "But have no fear, my friends—I shall prevail with Mistress Trentham. She *will* dine with me this week."

"And why do you say that?" Robin asked

"Because she wants to marry me."

"She does?"

"Why else would she spend time with someone as old as I am, bantering with me as she does whenever I speak with her? I am unmarried, and so is she. I have no heir; she has no children. And so she fishes for a husband."

"All I heard was no," Falstaff said.

"And who has always told me that a 'no' is but one step on the way to a 'yes'?"

"But is the 'yes' ye seek her consent to marry?"

"Of course not, Sir John. To bed her is all. Did you think I wanted to marry Aemilia Bassano?"

"No, but this 'un will not give up her knot unless she thinks a priest will replace it with a tighter one."

"John. Was there ever a deer that laid down in open field and said 'shoot me?' The more she twists and turns, the better the chase!"

Falstaff grumbled. He stood up, grabbing the bench he had been sitting on before it took off downriver. "Into the inn, lads. The river god has turned cold."

## ~ 58 ~
### *Henry VI, Part 2*

*enry VI, Part 1*, ended to tumultuous applause. The Lord Admiral's Men had presented it before the Queen and the lords and ladies who had packed St. George's Hall in Windsor Castle to see it. Edward Alleyn was basking in the audience's applause for his role as the evil Richard. They knew he would take the throne as Richard III. Robert Armin received even louder applause for playing Jack Cade, the rebel leader who had hung a clerk with his inkhorn around his neck and struck London Stone with his sword. The loudest applause was heard as Shackspear joined the actors on the stage.

The Queen had watched the play from a raised platform along the north wall. She came down to mingle with her people. Oxford saw Elspeth with the Queen. He and Robin pushed their way toward them.

An older and much larger man blocked Oxford's path. "I say, old chap, what," he said, smiling broadly. He had a ruddy face and a beard that sprayed out either side of his open mouth. He looked like a ship rushing downwind in fifteen knots of wind.

"Baron Rycote," Oxford acknowledged.

"Capital play, what?"

Oxford nodded. Years earlier Oxford had nicknamed Baron Rycote 'Count What?' for the way he peppered his conversation with the phrase, pronouncing it with a rising inflection at the end. The court, eager for every witty remark tossed their way, immediately adopted the Baron's new title. The Baron, however, was a bit hard of hearing and still had no idea how much fun everyone was having behind his back.

Rycote shook his head. "Remarkable, Shackspear, what?" I spoke with him this morning and could find nothing to mark him as the playwright of *Titus* or these *Henry* plays." He waved a hand at the stage behind him. "How can that be? But my groom—he's as dumb as a post, but can the man ride horses, what? I think Shackspear is like my groom. He can't talk much, but he knows how to write plays."

Before either man could say more, Shackspear appeared. The Baron immediately accosted him. "Notably discharged," the Baron said, taking Shackspear's hand and pumping it up and down. "The decapitated heads were the *pièce de résistance,* what? How many were there?"

Shackspear looked distracted. "Four, your lordship."

"How did you make them bleed?" the Baron wanted to know. He turned to Oxford. "Even back here, we could see the blood, what? Couldn't you see the blood, my lord?" Oxford had to nod. "Marvelous," the Baron said. "The height of good theater."

Oxford decided he had had enough and began to turn away but Shackspear reached around the Baron and plucked Oxford's sleeve. "And the blood costs a lot of money, my lord. And all the extras. Stage directions, too. *"Enter Cade and all the rabblement.* We could've used half the citizens of Windsor. We need leaner plays."

Baron Rycote overheard this and was puzzled. He opened his mouth to ask what was going on when two gentlemen, successful members of the rising merchant class, pushed their way into their midst.

"Mr. Shackspear," they both said together. One leaned in toward Shackspear. "Cade dies because he is famished?" he asked, a look of incredulity on his face. *O, I am slain! famine and no other hath slain me."*

Shackspear was surprised to hear a complaint. The second man pushed past his friend. "That's just poor writing," he said. "The real problem is that Cade promises the rebels a world in which there is no money and the king feeds everyone, and where everyone wears the same livery *so they may agree like brothers*!" Shackspear glanced at Oxford, who had stopped to listen. The second man went on. "Jack Cade is the most dangerous man in the play," he said, his voice lowered, his eyes glaring at Shackspear.

"Why is that?" Shackspear asked.

"Because he wants everyone to be *equal.* That's *dangerous!* Why would you put words like these in the mouth of a man who leads a revolt against the king? Is this what the peasants in Warwickshire want?" Shackspear blinked. "I am to Tilney," the first man said. "It was an outrage for you to put this on before Her Majesty, but it will be treason to play it before the people. The unemployed and the shiftless are restless. Hearing Jack Cade promising them free beer and equal treatment will be like bringing a torch to a dry hay field." He turned away. His companion followed him.

Shackspear, thoroughly confused, looked at Oxford.

"Maybe you should read what I write before you put it on," Oxford suggested. "And I must remind myself," he said to Robin, next to him, "to check on what my faithful secretary adds in those never-ending squiggles he pens between the lines I write."

"You put those lines in Cade's mouth, not me," Robin protested. "You wrote that the pissing conduit ran with claret, and the lines about how the skin of a lamb, scrubbed clean, as parchment, can undo a man."

"Ah, yes. Do you know how many times a lambskin with a seal on it has done me in? But, truthfully, I had Jack Cade die of starvation?"

"You did, my lord. You said Cade could not die a hero's death. And when I asked you about his speeches about equality, you said, 'Doesn't the poor man want an equal share?'"

"True," Oxford said. They were now coming up to Lady Elspeth. She was standing to one side of the Queen, who was listening to a petitioner. "My lady," Oxford said, stopping to her left.

Elspeth kept her eyes focused ahead of her. "I told the Queen that I found you dining in the river," she whispered.

"Whereupon I am sure she frowned."

"She smiled."

"No. She must have frowned."

"She smiled! Why dost thou doubt me?"

Oxford moved closer and drank in Elspeth's perfume.

"I never met anyone like you," she said, still not looking at him. Her comment was frank assessment, not a compliment.

"Of course not. I am different."

"Oh," she said, exasperated.

"And our dinner in the grotto?"

Elspeth looked up at the ceiling, painted in a profusion of red and white roses. "The Queen has suggested that I should go," she said, obviously reluctant to admit what the Queen had recommended.

"Her Majesty is wise."

"She said it would be good for me."

"Her wisdom knows no bounds."

"Oh," Elspeth said again.

"My servant, Robin, will explain all to your maidservant."

He moved closer to her. He lowered his voice. "The Moon will be full. There will be lanterns to light your way, and candles to fill the air with the scent of Arabia. The table will be scoured with aromatic herbs. And the poetry? Such that you have never heard." His face was now almost brushing her cheek. "*If once your lips should lock with mine,*" he began, but she cut him off, a look of disdain on her face.

"Something new, my lord. Those words are stale." She saw the surprise on his face. "You think she didn't come swishing through the court reciting your poetry like she was handing out nose gays at a May festival? She apparently has greater talents than Lord Hunsdon gave her credit for. Her lips apparently *did* lock with thine." She sniffed. "I go off to Staffordshire and you run off after every farthingale in town."

Oxford was stunned for a moment. He wanted to tell her he was free to see whomever he pleased, but caught himself before he spoke. Lady Elspeth was obviously jealous. This made him feel better. "I am sad to hear you were distressed by my conduct while you were away, my lady."

"I was not distressed," she said. "Only disappointed."

He leaned in closer. "Something new, then:

> *Take all my loves, my love, yea, take them all;*
> *What hast thou then more than thou hadst before?*
> *No love, my love, that thou mayst true love call;*
> *All mine was thine before thou hadst this more.*

This surprised her. She had expected more lips and kisses, not words of love. She kept her gaze fixed straight ahead. "I am not one who is made weak-kneed by sweet-sounding words, my lord."

Oxford went on:

> *Lascivious grace, in whom all ill well shows,*
> *Kill me with spites; yet we must not be foes.*

The Queen began to move. The bevy of ladies around her stirred.

"I must leave now."

"But will you come?"

"I will."

"Your ladyship," Oxford said, bowing and backing away.

340

## ~ 59 ~
## The Dinner in the Grotto

L ady Elspeth and her chambermaid appeared at the postern gate at the appointed hour. Oxford bid the ladies welcome. The two women stepped through the thick stone walls of the castle onto the brow of the cliff. Trees grew below them on every outcrop large enough to hold a seed. The three of them descended through the trees on a path that wove back and forth, their way lighted by lanterns hung from fishing rods. Robin flitted alongside, just off the path, dangling a tiny fairy from a fishing rod in front of Oxford.

The path ended at the entrance to a cave. The sun was setting, silvering the Thames far below. A pale Moon hung over the eastern sky. A table awaited them. Robin, his hair shining in the light of the torches, appeared behind one of the chairs, holding his lute. A large vase in the middle of the table held a freshly-picked bouquet of flowers.

"Lady Elspeth," Oxford said, gesturing toward the table. "If you would be so kind as to join me for supper." Robin and the chambermaid drifted back up the path to give Oxford and Lady Elspeth some privacy.

"I think not," Lady Elspeth said.

This surprised Oxford. "But you agreed to dine with me here, your ladyship."

"I did so expecting I would meet Edward de Vere tonight."

"You have, my lady." He held out a hand to her. She did not take it.

"No, I have met only the theater impresario." She gestured toward the table, the candles, and the flowers. "The stage has been set."

"Impresario?"

"The one who puts on the play but who hides in the wings." She began to move toward the path. "You are in love with *being* in love, my lord, but I do not think you know *how* to love. Else, why so many lovers, blooming like flowers, and gone as quickly?"

"My lady?" Oxford was indignant. No one asked about affairs at court. They were always short. She must know that she was holding him up to a standard he was not prepared to defend.

341

"Anne Vavasor disappeared rather quickly, didn't she? And Aemilia Bassano. What of her? She lasted even less time, or does she wait in the wings for you when you tire of me?"

The smile on Oxford's face disappeared. "My lady," he began, but Elspeth was not finished.

"And the others? No, I will not be just a bedmate for a few nights, my lord, and then watch you move on to someone else."

"My lady, I swear to you that I sought nothing more than your company at dinner tonight."

"Hah! I have three brothers, remember. I know what you planned."

"Then why treat me thus, my lady? If all you wanted to do was heap abuse on me, you could have stayed in your rooms and saved yourself the trouble."

"I press you on this, my lord, because I wouldst not marry a man who is here today and gone tomorrow, whose love is like lightning, gone before one can say 'it lightens.'"

"Marry?"

"I will not frown and be perverse, and tell thee nay to make you woo me, though I know you would."

"Marry?" Oxford asked again. He looked like a man who had just heard a foreign word he did not understand.

"Yes, marry. I didn't come here tonight to let you bed me. I would have given up my virginity long ago if all it took to purchase it was a dinner under the stars. My interest is in marriage, my lord. Were my father still alive, he would have spoken to your father, and you and I would have been spared having to talk about this ourselves."

Oxford was speechless. He felt like he was in a play he had not studied and the player opposite him was reading from a script he had not seen. "It must be a comedy," he told himself. "All comedies end in marriage."

Marriage, in fact, was the furthest thing from his mind. Yet this woman who stood in front of him was bold and blunt, and he liked that. And he was weary of the unsettled life he had been leading. And she was making him realize that he was becoming tired of waking up in empty rooms at the Folly or Oxford Court or in the Savoy, and almost never in the same bed—even if he awoke with a companion beside him.

Elspeth was unnerved by his silence. "Forgive me for my bluntness, my lord, but, growing up, there was no time for foolishness, what with my brothers idling away in London and the squires in the neighborhood pursuing me like dogs in heat."

"God be praised, then, that Elizabeth called you to court," Oxford said quickly, hoping to slow her exit.

"I did not see it that way at first, my lord. Instead of clumsy country squires, I had to deal with courtiers like you."

"But you have done well," was all he could think to say.

"I have. But I didn't save my virginity to give it up to one who is well-known for slipping through the casement window as soon as the cock crows." Her words were harsher than she had intended, however, and when she saw his reaction she added hastily: "But no one has ever proposed a late-night supper in the mouth of a cave, either."

"Does that make any difference?"

"I don't know." She looked exasperated. "You are the silliest man I have ever met."

"Ah, and my heart sings that you find me so." He touched her arm.

> *If I profane with my unworthy hand*
> *This holy shrine, the gentle fine is this:*
> *My lips, two blushing pilgrims, ready stand*
> *To smooth that rough touch with a tender kiss.*

"You are hopeless," she said, pulling her arm away. "More lips; more kisses. If we have a son, he will grow up to be a clown and play fools on the stage."

"You talk of a son?"

"And what is the purpose of marriage? You lack an heir, my lord. But I fear that if I give you a son, you will drag him off to the theater and he will waste his patrimony the way you have wasted yours."

The smile left Oxford's face. He had decided enough was enough. "You, Madame, are ill-equipped to speak of marriage or the theater, or whether I have wasted my patrimony. You live in a world where coins represent success. All you have to do is open a strongbox and count them out. You may think me silly but I am dedicated to a higher purpose. I am dedicated to words. What I write will live on long after great deeds done in battle are forgotten. Eyes yet unborn shall weep to hear a player speak my lines from a stage not yet built."

Instead of being angry, a faint smile appeared on Elspeth's face. "For the first time, my lord, I hear Edward de Vere, speaking his heart. You must understand I am without education. My brothers went to university, a privilege denied to me because I am a woman. I had no neighbor to sit down with me and teach me about books or poetry, and so I am afraid I bring little more with me than my name and title, my father's wealth, and a shrewdness in business learned from dealing with men who would have cheated me if I had let them. I have no ability to know a good line of poetry when I hear it, or whether the lines written down for actors in a scene should be shouted from the rooftops or the paper used to wrap a pie on its way to the oven."

This surprised Oxford. "Forgive me, my lady. I am not used to such honesty, being a courtier who lives, as you know, in a world of lies and half-truths. Your words wash over me like water from a cold mountain spring. I can teach you how to love a poem."

"I will try, my lord. But let us put this matter of marriage behind us."

"You have decided not to marry me?"

"No, my lord. I mean, yes, no …" They both laughed. "I mean, let us agree on the terms and put our marriage behind us. I am tired of being sole."

Oxford was surprised again. He started to resist but found he did not want to. She may be kidnapping him, but something told him it was alright. "Well, then, if we agree, who will give you away?"

"The Queen said she would like to."

"I suppose she would."

"I know she was your first love," Elspeth said, her eyes searching his.

"One of many," Oxford said quickly, trying to make it sound like a fling, but she heard more emotion than he intended.

"She still pines for you. We can see it in the corner of her eyes sometimes when you are mentioned."

"Anything between us was long ago," Oxford said dismissively, trying to get the Queen out of the conversation.

"Was it? I'm not sure. She has confided in me. I know how she feels about you, but I don't know how you feel about her. I need to know. Will you carry your love for her into a marriage with me?"

Oxford tried to look like the idea was ridiculous, but Elspeth was having nothing of it. "No," he said at last. "I will not."

She could hear truth in his voice. "One more thing. It seems that you have never let *any* woman into your heart. If we marry, will you let me into yours?"

Oxford felt like he had stepped onto a ship and the first mate had begun to load him down with ropes and gear. "You are forcing me to sail in new waters, my lady, waters for which I have no charts. I feel out of my depth. Can I?" he asked aloud. She waited. "Yes," he finally said.

"Good." She reached across and shook his hand. "We have a bargain."

Oxford was dazed. Part of him was gleeful, like a little boy on a sled flying down a hillside in winter. "I *like* this woman," he told himself, and he loved adventures where he did not know the outcome, but another part of him was screaming *"What are you doing?"* He looked down at Elspeth's hand and thought of all the other contracts he had entered into with such a simple handshake. But no other contract had involved so much mystery as this one did.

Lady Elspeth returned to business. "I would prefer that someone other than the queen give me away. While her presence would bless our union, I will convince her that my Uncle Clarence, brother to my father, is a better choice."

"God bless Uncle Clarence."

Elspeth smiled. It was the first genuine smile Oxford had seen. He pounced on it. "I see a chink in your armor," he said, suddenly feeling affection for her. To himself, he imagined how difficult it must have been for her to survive, being a woman without a father or a mother. How many layers has she covered herself with in order to survive that *and* ten years at court? How similar are our histories?

"What chink is that, my lord?"

"Your smile. Smiling will do in all your defenses."

"But not tonight. Leave my defenses intact, if you will."

"To our marriage, then," he said. He bent over and gave her a kiss which, to his surprise, she returned. She pulled away.

"Will you write a play for our wedding, my lord?"

Oxford nodded. "*Love's Labour's Won.*"

"Which will be about what?"

"I don't know."

She looked at him closely. "Will it be about us?"

"I don't know."

"No, it won't," she said, looking stern.

"Then it won't be."

"The supper is cold," said Elspeth, which Oxford took as her way of saying she did not want to stay. She slipped her arm into his. "Our courting has not been what you expected, has it?"

"No."

She squeezed his arm. "Then write a play about the romantic love I have denied you."

"I'm working on it."

# ~ 60 ~
## A Marriage Contract

**M**alfis pushed open the heavy oak door and stepped into the Boar's Head. His eyes, even aided by the best spectacles money could buy in Antwerp, were unable to penetrate the thick fog of smoke and stale air that filled the tavern. He swept a perfumed handkerchief to his mouth.

Peaches saw him standing in the doorway. "Your grace," she said.

"Hardly," he replied. His eyes panned across the Inn, avoiding eye contact with Peaches, as if she might reach into his soul and steal something valuable from him if he looked at her. "I seek the Earl of Oxenford. Is he here?"

Peaches pointed toward the back of the inn. "The Earl of Ox*en*ford is there," she said with a smirk, emphasizing the extra syllable Malfis had added to Oxford's title.

Malfis understood her amusement. No one referred to the earl by his proper title any more, but Malfis had none of the disdain for language and grammar that the younger generation was so eagerly adopting. He had no doubt the theater was to blame. The Veres had been the Earls of Oxenford for 500 years, however, and they would never be called the earls of Oxford while he was in earshot. Oxford signed his name *Edward Oxenford* because Malfis had told him this was the proper way to execute legal documents. The ornamentation that surrounded Oxford's signature was of no interest to Malfis as it neither added to nor took away from the legal significance of the signature itself. Thus, the careful lawyer missed the sly allusions to royalty in the swirls and checkmarks that had so irritated the Queen.

Malfis found Oxford hunched over a table in one of the booths. Crumpled balls of paper surrounded him and littered the floor. Falstaff lay in the opposite corner of the booth, looking as if Oxford had crumpled him up and thrown him there as well.

"My lord," Malfis said, bowing slightly.

Oxford looked up. "Malfis! Have I been sued again?"

"No, my lord." Oxford thought his solicitor looked a trifle disappointed. "I came to extend my congratulations on your betrothal."

Falstaff's eyes flew open. He sat upright. His eyebrows fluttered like signal flags on an admiral's flagship. "Betrothal?" he shouted. "Betrothal?"

Oxford shrugged. "I have had conversations with a young lady about marriage."

"Marriage!" Falstaff practically shouted once more. "What need have ye of marriage, Edward?" he asked. He opened his arms wide. "Who needs a woman when you have me?"

Oxford looked at Malfis, who was waiting for Falstaff to let him return to the business he had come for, but Falstaff was not finished.

"What about yer promise never to marry?! You, me, and Tobias! We declared ourselves bachelors forever, right here at this table!"

"'Twas a promise made after much strong drink."

"'Twere signed by your own hand."

"On greasy paper that carried pigs' feet to the Boar's Head."

"And 'twas the grease that sanctified it! Not as regular as words on vellum, and no hanging seals, mind ye, but 'twas legal, a recording of the promise made by the words we spoke!" He looked up at Malfis. "I am right, am I not, counselor?" Malfis, slightly amused to hear Falstaff's description of a contract, said nothing.

"Then I am forsworn," Oxford said.

"And I am forsaken," Falstaff added. He put his massive hand on Oxford's arm "Who was it that cut Samson's hair! A woman! Who lured Ulysses' men off his ship! Women! They all feign interest in sex the day before the wedding and forget our nether parts the day after." He dropped his voice. "Ye've made it past forty, Edward: hold out a tiny bit longer. In a year or two ye'll be invisible, like me!"

"Invisible? Ye'd have to lose a ton of flesh to become invisible."

"I'm not talking about flesh. I'm talking about the day a woman walks by and doesn't see you. Not when ye'r young and she glances elsewhere to lead ye on. *When she doesn't see ye at all.*"

"It must have been terrible."

Falstaff, exasperated, twisted away. Malfis stood patiently next to the table. He had no idea what Falstaff and Oxford were talking about. Argument was beneath him. "My lord?" he said. Oxford looked up. "I have been instructed by the lady's solicitor to draw up a marriage contract, which I hold in my hand."

"Oh, this is bad," Falstaff said. He lay back in the booth.

348

"He has given me a draft in your favor for £5,000, which I will take to your banker as soon as I leave here."

"£5,000?" Oxford exclaimed.

Malfis handed a large piece of paper to Oxford, who looked at it closely. Falstaff sat back up and leaned across the table to look himself. Oxford handed it back to Malfis.

"Is this her dowry?" he asked.

"Her solicitor said it is not. Therefore, it is a gift, which will not have to be repaid if you do not marry her."

"Why would she give me £5,000?"

"I have no idea, my lord." He slipped the draft into a pocket inside his jacket. "Intentions are irrelevant when dealing with a financial draft. The terms are contained within the four corners of the document. Whatever else the maker may have had in mind is irrelevant." He patted his jacket where the draft now lay hidden. "With your permission."

"Yes, yes," Oxford said.

Malfis left.

Falstaff shook his head. "Oh, this Trembling woman is a frightening one."

"Why, Jack?"

"To her, marriage is a business investment, like buying tithes or rents."

"But she *gave* me the money. If she were treating it as an investment, wouldn't there be conditions?"

"Why did ye give £3,000 to Frobisher?"

"I was told he would come back with something of value."

"Right."

"So?"

"This Trembling woman wants to find out whether yer interested in her *or* her money. If ye take the £5,000 and run, she'll consider it well spent, having found out before the marriage that you are a cad."

"Oh."

"Send it back, Edward. It is Judas money." Oxford did not say anything. Falstaff pressed on. "And what if ye marry her and she finds out yer not what she thinks you are?"

"In what way?"

"In bed!"

"Hah! No worry there."

"Ye sure? Ye got something from Signore Baldini to help ye in the lists with that Bossoomo woman, *but ye haven't found out yet if it worked!*"

This brought Oxford up short. Falstaff was right. He hadn't slept with a woman in a long time. What if he 'failed at the hips' when Elspeth Trentham let him into her bed? He pushed the thought away. "She's enough to stir my blood, Sir John."

"Oh, she'll stir yer blood, all right, but it's performance she'll be after, and performance leaves the stage long before desire does."

Oxford did not like this suggestion, but realized Falstaff was desperately firing every gun he had to prevent Oxford from marrying Elspeth Trentham. "You forget I am without an heir. Sixteen of my ancestors have preceded me. I see them at night, floating over my bed, their faces asking me when I am going to father a son. I saw them while I composed the sonnets I wrote for the Earl of Southampton. They circled my head saying, *the sonnets are for you!* I am forty-two, Sir John. Time is running out."

"Then choose someone else to be yer brood-mare, Edward. You're playing with fire if you marry this Trembling woman."

Oxford smiled. He liked the image. "But the fire warms me, Jack."

Falstaff could see he was losing. "Ye'll pay more than ye think, even if you get the heir you want. I've told ye there are only two types of happy people in this world: *married women and single men!*"

Oxford smiled. "I will take the money *and* the woman."

"And lose me in the process," Falstaff said, folding himself into the corner of the booth. "Something wicked this way comes," he mumbled into the wall.

## ~ 61 ~
## Oxford Court – A Month Later

Nigel opened the front door. A gust of wind blew a cloud of leaves in from Candlewick Street. They swirled around his legs like intruders looking for a place to hide. Elspeth Trentham and Oxford followed the leaves into the house. "Your ladyship," Nigel said, bowing to Elspeth Trentham. "Your lordship," he added, closing the door behind them.

Oxford began taking off his gloves. "Elspeth, this is my steward, Nigel," he said by way of introduction.

"An honor," Nigel said, bowing again. "And my congratulations on your betrothal."

Elspeth nodded. She walked into the hall. The wind was strong enough to force its way through cracks around the door and lift carpets that lay scattered across the slate floor. The fireplace in the left-hand wall sent out a burst of smoke into the hall.

"You have a nest of storks on top of your chimney," Elspeth commented, directing her remark at Nigel.

"Yes. They are supposed to bring good luck, your ladyship."

"It's not good luck if they stop up the chimney. If you look outside you will see that they have already left for the winter, leaving their empty nest behind."

"Yes, my lady." Nigel bowed again. He did not look at Oxford.

"Come," Oxford said to Elspeth. "Let me show you the library." He took her into the large room on the left. The long table was covered with papers. More sheets lay scattered on the floor. As they stood in the doorway, a large pile of what looked like laundry suddenly came to life. Falstaff had been sleeping in the far corner. Without apparent effort, he was suddenly standing in front of them. He bowed deeply. "Forgive me for being asleep when you arrived, your ladyship, but, as you can see," he said, gesturing toward the window, "the sun is still up."

"Sir John Falstaff," Oxford said.

Elspeth looked him over but said nothing. She was about to leave when Socrates ambled out from under the sideboard and walked across the front of her legs, rubbing against her.

"Does this live here?"

"He does," Oxford said. "His name is Socrates."

"An odd name."

"He never answers questions. He likes you."

"Does he." This was a statement, not a question. Elspeth walked back into the hall. Oxford followed. Falstaff looked at Socrates, now ambling after them. "Traitor," he said under his breath.

Elspeth looked up at the heads that lined the walls. "A lovely collection," she said, "I suppose there is a story behind each one."

"I wouldn't know. My father never brought me here before he died so I know nothing about them except for the boar's head, which my father killed with a dancing rapier while he was in France. Pity, history. So much that happens, and so little of it remembered." Elspeth surveyed the rest of the hall. "Does your ladyship hunt?" Oxford asked.

"Of course. The stag. The fox."

"And fly at geese with hawks?"

"No. We did not have the money to hunt with hawks. Hawking is a sport for the nobility, my lord."

Oxford nodded. "I'm told the snow geese have arrived. Digby, my man at Hedingham, has been training an eyas no bigger than two fists side by side. He says she will bring down a goose three times her size."

"If she comes back."

"Digby says she will."

"Not if she's like the hawks you've written about, my lord. You have likened them to women."

"I have?"

"*If women could be fair and yet not fond,*" she began:

> *How oft from Phoebus they do flee to Pan*
> *Unsettled still like haggards wild they range,*
> *These gentle birds that fly from man to man.*"

"You do me honor, my lady. I did not think you knew any poetry of mine." He tried to quickly run through the poems he had written and what she might think of them.

352

William Byrd turned your poem into music. I heard it performed at court in 1589. You must have been away at the time." Oxford tried to recall where he was in 1589. He shivered as he remembered eating salt fish and enduring Ethelbert's uninspired cooking. "I was sulking in Warwickshire, my lady."

"You must have enjoyed writing the last couplet."

*Who would not scorn and shake them from the fist,*
*And let them fly, fair fools, which way they list?*

"An early poem, my lady." He could tell that she was not going to let him duck away that easily. "One written before I had the privilege of meeting your ladyship."

Her face told him he was losing. She looked up at a small balcony on the right-hand wall. It was so small it might have been designed as an architectural feature, but a pair of narrow doors gave promise that someone could walk out onto it. "What is that?" she asked.

"I'm not sure."

"You've never gone up to find out?"

He shrugged. "My bedroom is on the other side. Is there a room up there, Nigel?"

"I have heard that Earl John slept in the room behind the balcony when he stayed at Oxford Court."

"It's a bedroom, then?"

"Not now, my lady. We use it for storage. It is above the day room, and about the same size. If memory serves, another balcony overlooks the garden outside."

"Two balconies?" She looked at Oxford. "May I?"

"Of course." He gestured for Nigel to show her the way. The three of them climbed the stairs at the end of the hall and turned right. A hallway led to the room behind the balcony. Nigel opened the door. He held it aside to let Oxford and Elspeth walk in. They found a room filled with furniture, rolled up rugs, and trunks. Elspeth pushed her way through the confusion till she found the doors to the balcony. She opened them and stepped out onto it. She leaned out and surveyed the hall.

"Do, my lord, return to the first floor and observe your bride from her airy perch."

Oxford went back down the stairs and looked up at Elspeth. "My lady," Oxford said, getting down on one knee. "Your audience of one swears his love to you by yonder Moon," he said dramatically, waving an arm at the ceiling, "that tips with silver all the tree tops—"

"Do not swear at all," she called down, interrupting him, "or, if thou wilt, swear by the lord, our gracious savior, who is the god of my idolatry."

Oxford's face fell. They had never discussed religion. "Is she a Puritan," he wondered? "Will she use the tiny balcony each morning to preach to the household?

"What say you, my lord, as to the reason this balcony has been built on the inside of the house rather than on the outside?"

*To preach, of course*, Oxford almost said, but caught himself before he spoke. "To review the household staff?" he asked. He looked at Nigel, whose face, as always, gave away nothing.

"I think for air and light," Elspeth said brightly. "Let me see about the other balcony." She disappeared.

Robin came in through the front door. He closed it behind him and looked around. Falstaff was leaning on the wall next to the library door, a droll look on his face. Oxford was rising from where he had been kneeling at the bottom of the stairs. Nigel stood motionless on the first landing. All three were looking at the balcony, which was now empty. Sensing that he had obviously arrived in the middle of something odd, Robin drifted into an alcove in the entryway and disappeared into the shadows. At the same time, Falstaff slipped past him out the door.

Lady Elspeth reappeared on the balcony. "Splendid, my lord. The wind can blow from one to the other." She looked around. "Where do *you* sleep, my lord?"

Oxford pointed toward a second-floor doorway behind him. The landing at the top of the stairs ran over to the left-hand wall and then to the front of the house, jogging around the chimney that rose from the fireplace.

Elspeth looked across the hall at the second floor. "And what are the other rooms used for?" She looked at Nigel for an answer.

"Rooms that my lord uses to write in."

"And the one over the entryway?"

"That, my lady, is the 'Hamlet' room."

"The 'Hamlet' room?"

Nigel feared he had misspoken. He cleared his throat. "Lord Oxford repairs to the 'Hamlet' room when he feels moved to work on a play that bears the same name. No one is allowed in, including myself."

Lady Elspeth looked down at Oxford. "I remember hearing something about a Hamlet play when I came to court."

"Nothing of any regard, I am sure."

Frangellica suddenly appeared from the kitchen in the rear. She stopped to take in Oxford at the bottom of the stairs and Lady Elspeth standing on the balcony. "Signora," Oxford said to her. "Permettetemi di presentarvi la mia promessa sposa, la signora Elspeth."

"Signora," Lady Elspeth called down before Frangellica could say anything.

Frangellica was surprised to hear Lady Elspeth speak Italian. She bent her knee. "Benvenuto a casa nostra. Siamo molto onorati, la mia signora."

"Grazie mille," Lady Elspeth said.

"You speak Italian, my lady?" Oxford asked.

"I am the master of many subjects, my lord."

Someone began knocking on the front door. Robin slid out of the shadows and opened the door. Shackspear came in. "My lord," he called out, striding into the house. He doffed the cape he was wearing. "Where is Part 3? We must not disappoint the Queen. Costumes have to be made, the players must rehearse …" He spotted Elspeth Trentham looking down at him from the balcony and stopped. "My lady," he said, bowing deeply.

Elspeth turned and disappeared into the upstairs room.

"Out!" Oxford ordered Shackspear.

"But, my lord—."

"Out! You shall have your play, but not today."

Robin reopened the front door. Shackspear, backing away from Oxford and glancing up at the now-empty balcony, disappeared into Candlewick Street.

Elspeth came out onto the landing at the top of the stairs and started to descend toward Oxford. "As for how Mr. Shackspear comes to write his plays," she said cryptically, "I know naught."

Malfis suddenly appeared in the hallway, Robin having not yet closed the front door. "Your lordship; your ladyship." He bowed. "I have completed the marriage contract."

"And what date has the Queen chosen for our wedding?" Oxford asked.

"Her majesty has suggested December 27."

"Oh," Oxford sighed. "A fortnight times four! The old dowager lingers out our desires!"

Elspeth smiled. "These fortnights will quickly sweep by in the coming weeks, my lord. The second night after Christmas is a felicitous date on which to hold our solemnities. We shall ever after add our anniversary to the 12 days of Christmas and bring light to the dark days of winter."

"And the place? Did she approve of Colne's Priory, Malfis?"

"She did not, my lord." Oxford groaned again. "Whitehall, my lord. She said the most senior of her nobles should be married where kings have tread."

"How touching," Oxford said.

"'Tis fitting," Elspeth said. "And appropriate."

"Will you sign the contract, my lord? My lady?" Malfis gestured toward the day room. Elspeth came down and she and Oxford followed him into the room.

"Now that there is time before the wedding, my lord," Elspeth said, "let us to Hedingham. You can show me the keep and we can hunt game and fly at birds with your eyas."

"When shall we go?"

"The day after tomorrow," she said, taking a chair at the table where Malfis was spreading out the marriage contract. He busied himself with the inks and quills, like a hen tending to her chicks, fussing over the signatures and seals of the earl and the woman who would soon be his countess. In a few moments, he was done and out the door with the papers.

## ~ 62 ~
## Castle Hedingham

Oxford and Elspeth Trentham sat their horses in a wheat field harrowed by a biting September wind while they watched the eyas Oxford's gamekeeper had released into the sky flash her wings like semaphores to signal her joy at being so high in the air.

"I may have urged you to set her free too soon," Oxford said.

"Nay, my lord. She will return. I raised her by hand, sealing her eyes shut with thread. She's had nothing to eat for days. Hungry she rose into the sky. 'Tis the only way to train an eyas and make her obey."

Digby's boar-bristled head was uncovered to the wind. He wore a doublet of tawny fustian that was open at the neck. Sensible hose descended into scarred leather boots whose tops had been folded over to keep out the briars. His face was a series of circles—cheeks, jowls, and chins—and eyes that squinted when he laughed, but there was no smile on his face this morning as he followed the hawk high above him.

Lady Elspeth moved her mount closer to Digby's. "I imagine you were a strict mentor to my lord, Thomas, when he was young." The question made Digby uncomfortable. Oxford answered for him.

"He was, my lady, a father to me when my father was away, and sometimes even when he was home. In his absence, Thomas became a gruff taskmaster who found little to praise in me."

Digby looked up at the sky. "I protest, my lady. I was never father to him. He is a poet who rewrites everything he hears."

Elspeth smiled. "Isn't the poet compact with the lunatic and the lover, my lord?"

"I will confess to being a poet and a lover, my lady, but no lunatic."

"Then why did you let the hart go this morning when the dogs had him cornered in the bracken?" she asked, looking at him intently.

"Aye," Digby said. "A good question. We had him. Ye let him go."

"Yes, I did."

357

"But why?" Elspeth asked.

"I thought he deserved another day."

"Another day?" Digby sounded embarrassed, which Elspeth thought belied his claim that he had little to do with Oxford's upbringing.

"He would have died a noble death," Oxford explained, "and his magnificent horns would have gored many of the dogs, but I didn't want to see him rue his death as he died."

Digby snorted. "Rue his death? He was a hart. Harts have no feelings." Lady Elspeth was silent, and Digby took her silence as encouragement. "No more than a fish served at dinner or a kine slaughtered and carved up for the table. People make less fuss over a person being hung, don't they? But a hart?"

Oxford glanced over at Elspeth. She obviously agreed with Digby. Oxford sighed. "I came upon another hart once, years ago, when I was young. I had brought him to ground with a shot from distance. I was filled with joy when I saw him fall, having 'led' him exactly as Thomas had taught me. But when I found him, his life was running out of him and he was no longer food for the table but a living, breathing thing. I reached in to cradle his head, which was drooping from the magnificent rack he carried. Tears coursed down his nose, making dark the ground beneath him. We looked at each other, my tears matching his. He breathed forth such groans that their discharge almost stretched his leather coat to bursting. His eyes told me I had murdered him. Sighing, he died."

"Sighing?" Digby asked.

"His antlers hang in the Great Hall at Hedingham."

"Ah," Digby said. "I remember the hunt. Ye never told me."

"I never told *anyone*. Your reaction would have been the same then as it is today—disbelief, followed by laughter. Back then, I pushed away the image of the dying hart and said nothing. This morning, I remembered his death. I always felt that I should have tried to save him. When I came upon the hart this morning, I told myself I could save *this* one, and I did. I care not what people think any more, Thomas. I am different. I was different even then, but didn't know it."

Elspeth sat her horse watching Oxford. Digby glanced at her and decided he did not want to know any more about dying harts. His master *was* different. Always had been. Why should he be surprised? He looked up at the sky. "I may have whistled her off too soon." He brought up a small silver pipe banded by tiny roses and pomegranates.

He put it to his lips and blew a high-pitched call. The eyas dropped toward them momentarily before soaring off. They could hear the tinkling of the silver bells that hung from her jesses.

"*Look*!" Oxford exclaimed, pointing to the northwest. A chevron of snow geese were powering their way across the sky toward them.

"*Here they come*!" Digby cried. "Fat, foolish snow geese. The first sign of fall. Now, where is that eyas?"

They looked up and saw the hawk come around a cloud. The bird turned north against the wind and began to climb.

"You see, my lady? She's climbing to gain height so she can kill a goose, which is much bigger than she is." The eyas suddenly folded its wings and dove toward the weary geese. The eyas smashed into one of the stragglers. The two birds, now one, spiraled away from the other geese and plummeted toward the earth.

"*Aha*!" Digby cried triumphantly. "No haggard trained to chase birds into the river can compare with an eyas that strikes from above! *Tater*!" he called out. A black dog sleeping a few feet away jumped to his feet. Digby pointed to the sky. "*Fetch*!" he shouted in a booming voice trained to be heard across open fields. The dog took off. Digby dug his heels into his horse and sped after him.

Oxford and Elspeth followed. "Tater?" Oxford asked as they hurtled down the hill.

"Short for potato," Digby called back over his shoulder, "that vegetable Raleigh brought back from the new world. It's supposed to have aphrodeesical properties."

"You need help?" Oxford asked. Digby did not know whether Oxford was referring to retrieving the goose or help with his wife, Nell. "I don't need help with neither," he shouted. Elspeth, flying downhill with them, laughed aloud.

They found the eyas on a low-lying branch looking very pleased with herself. Digby pulled a piece of meat out of his pocket and showed it to her. He extended his arm, covered with a scarred leather glove, and the eyas stepped onto it. With his other arm, he slid a T-shaped wooden stand out from under the saddle on his horse and drove the pointed end into the ground. He transferred the eyas to the crossbar and tied her jesses to the bar. He handed her the piece of meat and stepped back. The eyas clamped the meat against the crossbar and glared furiously at him.

Tater came trotting back with the goose. "Good boy," Digby said, taking the goose. He hooked it over the saddle on his horse and pulled out a small table, two folding stools, and a charcoal brazier. The brazier was filled with split pine splints packed in lard. He had a raging fire going in seconds. Unfolding the table, he laid the snow goose in the middle, cutting down the center of the breast. He cut off a small piece and threw it to Tater. He cut the liver out and laid it on the table where he cleaned it with a few strokes of his knife. He produced a bottle of Madeira wine and a blackened pan filmed with goose fat. He added a splash of the wine to the pan and placed it on the fire. In seconds, it was smoking. Digby picked up the goose liver and laid it carefully in the pan.

Elspeth sat down on one of the stools. "So this is how you treat his lordship when you go hunting?" she asked. She was impressed.

"Only when the snow geese come in, your ladyship." He pulled out three wooden tumblers and poured some Madeira into them. He took the pan off the fire and slid the trembling goose liver onto a polished hickory trencher he had produced with his free hand. With a flourish, he placed the trencher in front of Oxford and Elspeth.

"Ah," Oxford sighed, taking in the bouquet rising from the sizzling goose liver, the wine, and the goose fat. He took out a small knife and sliced the liver into three pieces. He used the tip of his knife to carefully place one piece on the trencher in front of Elspeth. He speared a second piece and held it out for Digby, who took it with his thumb and forefinger. Oxford impaled the remaining piece on his knife and swept it into his mouth. The three of them closed their eyes and bit into the goose liver, savoring the gift the snow goose had unwittingly given them.

"Marvelous," Oxford announced. "No finer taste ever passed Cleopatra's parted lips. For this service, Thomas, I shall knight you."

Digby's eyes opened wide. "My lord," he said, downing the rest of the goose liver in one gulp. "I would forgo the honor." He turned to Elspeth. "I am a simple man, my lady. He will make me something I am not. Think of me as a tree in the forest, if you will, a walnut perhaps, brown and hard. Wood from the tree would make a sturdy chest but wouldn't it be better to leave the tree where it is? If he makes me a knight, my friends will forsake me. They will think I have put on airs. I must decline the honor," he said emphatically. His eyes pleaded with her to help him.

Oxford laughed. "So, you are a man of metaphors," he said, knowing that Digby had no idea what a metaphor was. "You liken yourself to a tree in the forest. Is this tree sobbing?" He took a bite out of the goose liver still dangling from the end of his knife.

"With all due respect, my lord, no tree ever sobbed. You twist my words, as lawyers and poets do, giving them meaning they were never meant to have. I prefer simple words—distance, weight, color—not descriptions that have more meanings in them than flowers on a bush in spring time."

Oxford forgot the goose liver on the end of his knife. "Oh, no," he said. "Words can be things of beauty, Thomas, not simply measurement of time or distance. They can transport you to magical places:

> *Was this the face that launched a thousand ships,*
> *And burnt the topless towers of Ilium?*

Digby repeated the first line, exaggerating the emphasis he had heard: "Was THIS the FACE that LAUNCHED a THOUsand SHIPS," he said. "Sounds like Old Pete thumpin' across the deck of the *Bonaventure*."

Elspeth laughed. Oxford ignored her. "Ah, but hear the third line," he said, but Digby put his hand up. He wanted nothing more to do with topless towers and whatever Ilium was. "How about this, then?" Oxford asked.

> *The labouring man, that tills the fertile soil*
> *And reaps the harvest fruit, hath not indeed*
> *The gain but paine, and if for all his toile*
> *He gets the straw, the Lord will have the seed.*

This surprised Elspeth. She had never heard this poem before, but had no doubt Oxford was the author. Here he was, she thought, expressing concern for the "labouring man," little different from his grief over killing a sobbing deer. The man she had picked to be her husband was more than just a theater impresario. He was truly different, she thought, deeper than his titles and lurid past would suggest.

Digby was grappling with simpler issues. He shook his head. "This is probably one of your poems," he said. "Only the 'lord who gets the seed would write a poem about the 'labouring man' who doesn't."

Elspeth realized that the two men had forgotten she was there. They had unwittingly lapsed into a pattern from earlier times when they would switch back and forth between mentor and student, servant and master, friend and friend, jousting with each other the way they must have done a hundred times.

"Still not good enough?" Oxford asked. "How about this?"

*A crowne of bays shall that man weare, that triumphs over me:*
*For blacke and tawnie will I weare, which mornyng colours be.*

"This I like somewhat," Digby conceded. "Blacke and tawnie be Oxford colors, so this be by a Vere, if not by you. And black and tawnie be mourning colors too, my lord, so I think you're asking one word to speak twice at oncet. And if bays mean laurel, then you're off again in ancient Greece, crowning someone who triumphs over you."

"I didn't say he triumphed over me, only that he might."

"Another reason to distrust poetry." He turned to Elspeth. "I prefer animals and birds. They're easier to understand. Take the eyas here. She's no 'haggard' that will wander off like a Winchester whore."

"Yes, a big day for your eyas."

Digby nodded. His face showed that it was time to clean up. "My lady, be aware that my master is infected with a serious illness." He said this loud enough for Oxford to hear.

"And what is that?"

"Something he calls his Muse."

"And how does this illness show itself?"

"By making him stay up at night and scratch words on paper by candlelight when he should be sleeping so he can rise early and hunt."

"And when did this illness first appear, my lord?" Elspeth asked, turning to Oxford.

"When the Queen came to visit us at Hedingham. I was eight at the time. You remember, don't you, Thomas?"

"How could I forget? Three hundred carts trailed the Queen's carriage. The visit sent your father to the money lenders."

"Yes, but the third night I saw my first play! *King Johan*!"

"I remember the visit, my lord, but not the play."

"No one remembers the play. When I went to court, I fell in love with plays. A poem is a conversation with one person. A play is a conversation with thousands of people, all at once."

His eyes were glowing. Elspeth reached over and touched his arm. "Night draws on, my lord. Let us be inside the walls of Hedingham Castle ere it falls. The darkness hides more things than will ever appear in one of your plays."

## ~ 63 ~
## That Night

Servants swept the plates and mugs off the table. "Come, my lady," Oxford said. "Let me show you Essex. The setting sun is painting the countryside with colors that are more gold than gold."

They climbed the curving staircase to the top of the keep, coming out into the evening air. Elspeth walked over to the parapet and looked down at the ground a hundred feet below. The houses that made up the village of Hedingham huddled below them less than a mile away. Beyond, fields rolled away toward the setting sun.

"These lands were called Goshen when they were given to my forbear, Aubrey, 500 years ago."

Elspeth looked out over the countryside, the soft evening breeze ruffling her hair. "You love Hedingham, don't you?"

"Yes. I look out and see where my horse fell when I was young. I cast my eye at the pond beyond the trees below us and remember Digby teaching me how to outwait the fish. What I see is mine. What I breathe is mine."

"But you want to write plays. Can you write them here, my lord, so far from the city and the playhouses you love?" He looked like he hadn't asked himself the question. "As for me, I have no wish to live here." She saw his surprise. "Forgive me, my lord, but as beautiful as Essex may be, I have had enough of country living. I do not want to look south from this tower and dream of playhouses I cannot visit and people I cannot see because they are four days away on horseback. Let us live in London."

"I would have both, if I could, but, if you wish, we will to London, though I fear that you think little of plays, my lady, including mine."

"I love plays, and think much of the man who writes them," she said, slipping her arm under his.

"My lady," Oxford said, taken aback by her arm around his waist.

"Be not concerned, Edward. There is no one up here to see us. Even the birds have flown down to roost for the night. We are alone in the night sky." He was still wearing his boots; she was bare-foot, and half-a-head shorter. He slid his arm around her. She tucked in against him. "Do I shock thee, Edward? Am I different from other women?"

"Yes."

"Never speak of them."

"No."

"Tell me if I offend. I want the man, not the fool who sprinkles glysters among the more easily dazzled ladies at court."

"You have him."

She slipped out of his grasp and turned to face him. She held up her hands, palms out. "Place your palms against mine, Edward. Close your eyes. Be thou the king you can be, not the fool hiding behind every witticism that floats to your lips. I will hear you." She closed her eyes.

Oxford closed his eyes and put his upraised palms against hers.

"Do you feel it?"

He wasn't sure, but said, "I do."

"I believe you."

He still had his eyes closed. "We kiss as holy palmers kiss," he said.

She leaned in closer, their palms still touching. "Someone said you kissed well," she whispered. She kissed him and pulled away, opening her eyes. "Oh, they spoke falsely!"

Oxford's eyes flew open. "Oh, woe is me!" he said. "If I fail at the lips, I will surely fail at the hips!"

She laughed. "That's terrible." She pulled him back into her. "But the kiss wasn't." She kissed him again, long and hard, then leaned back to see his reaction.

"A fine kiss," he said, "for one who is acclaimed the only virgin at court."

"Aye, and true it is. And more virgin than your queen ever was. But of kisses, I may claim some experience."

"But never speak of the man who kissed you."

"Who said it was only one?"

"Oh."

She took his hands in hers. "I would wager that your will has not had its way for some time now."

"A wager you would easily win, my lady."

"But my deprivation has been for a lifetime, fending off what everyone tells me is most enjoyable."

"It is, my lady."

"For you, maybe, but I intend for it to be enjoyable for me as well. Can you do that?"

"I can, my lady."

"Then, to bed, my lord."

"What, now?" Oxford was dismayed. "We are not yet wed."

"Thou art an ass for hesitating, Edward de Vere, although I love thee for your caution, which is based more on stale custom than an upright heart, but I am not buying the horse without riding him."

Oxford was shocked again. Or, did he fear failure as Falstaff had been too eager to predict? "But I may hurt thee, thou being a virgin."

She laughed. "Let us see if your ancestors gave you more than length in name. Lay me down, Edward. Use all your weapons. Thrust and foin me. If I cry out in pain and not in joy, thou shalt know it!"

Oxford, now full of trepidation, took her hand and led her down to the floor below where an enormous bed had been set up. A fireplace filled the room with warm light. Oxford pulled back the covers. Elspeth let her clothes fall around her feet and slipped under the thick comforter. Oxford pulled off his and climbed in beside her. They lay on their sides staring at each other. He reached out and touched her shoulder and was surprised to find out how smooth and warm her flesh was. The sensation that ran through him was something he had forgotten.

"You remind me of a painting of Titian's I saw in Venice."

"No more words."

"Yes."

She took his hand and placed it on her breast, a velvet, warm place that had never been touched. She moved his hand down between her legs and rolled over onto her back, pulling him over onto her. He slid into her.

Feelings he had never experienced rose through his body to suffuse him with a glow poets never captured. Words could not follow where he was going.

Afterwards, she quickly fell asleep, but he lay awake, watching her. An hour before dawn, she stirred. She turned over and looked at him.

"I did not think it would be so gentle, like mist enveloping a lowland field."

"You liked it?"

"Very much." She pulled him over to her.

"Shall I play a different tune?"

"No. More of the same."

This time they both slept. They awoke to find the sun streaming through the eastern windows. Elspeth turned on her side to look at him. "Did you sleep with Nan before you married her?"

Her question surprised him. He hesitated for a moment. "Yes."

"Did Burghley find out?"

"She told him the next day. He immediately said I had 'ruined' her and that no one would have her now, but he couldn't make his face hide a glimmer of satisfaction. I knew instantly that he had arranged for her to sleep with me to force me to marry her."

"No father would do that."

"You don't know Burghley, particularly since my entrapment would insure the Queen would elevate him to the peerage."

"So you agreed to marry Nan."

"No. I refused. He ordered me to marry her, which he had the power to do, but I wouldn't. He then claimed she was pregnant."

"Was she?"

"She said she was."

"But she wasn't."

"No."

"So you married her thinking she was."

"Yes."

"And you remembered all this when you came back from Italy."

"Yes."

She put her arm around his shoulder. "I shall not claim I am pregnant, Edward, unless I am, which, with two orgasms in so few hours, is very possible, as I am told a woman cannot conceive unless she has one." Oxford laughed. His anger at Nan and Burghley was melting away. "You have good cause to mistrust women, Edward," Elspeth said slipping out of his arms, "but I shall give you no cause to think so of me." She stood up next to the bed and began to dress.

"God bless you for that, Elspeth Trentham." He rolled onto his back, his arm behind his head. "You make me say things I've never said to anyone before." He lay in the bed, looking up at the ceiling. "My mother never held me in her arms when I was little. I never saw her express any affection for my father, or he for her. From this I learned that I must never show emotion, but this has interfered with every relationship I have ever had. But now I have you. I know you love me for who I am, not because of my titles, and you won't let me dance away from you behind a veil of poetry or witty remarks."

"Thou art becoming wise, my love."

"And will become more so with every day we spend together."

He got up and walked over to the window. He opened it and looked out:

*The grey-eyed morn smiles on the frowning night,*
*Chequering the eastern clouds with streaks of light.*

"*Now* what are you doing?" Elspeth asked, laughing.

"I am an eyas, mounting into the sky."

"And am I your goose? You've already killed me twice."

He laughed, a confident, comfortable laugh. "Digby's eyas and I both began a new life yesterday, didn't we?" She came over to him and put her arms around his waist. He turned around, his face suddenly serious. "I am filled with hundreds of tales and thousands of poems. Sometimes they come out as songs to the morning. Can you live with such a man?"

"Aye. I can, and will."

He kissed her hand. "Your days at the Savoy are numbered. I can hardly wait." He kissed the inside of her wrist.

"You didn't," she said, pulling her hand away.

"But the memory, so fresh, needs refreshing."

"Not this morning, my lord. We have much to do."

"Yes, my lady," he sighed.

They continued dressing. "Now that we will live in London," she said, "it is time you deed Hedingham to Lord Burghley."

"What?" Oxford exclaimed, a shirt halfway over his head. "Why would I do that?"

"Heneage is close to getting the writs he needs to place Hedingham in the hands of the bailiffs."

"And you want me to give it to Burghley? Impossible! The ground would open up if I signed Hedingham away."

"Not if you sign it over in trust, for your daughters."

He looked at her, his mouth hanging open.

"If you do nothing, you will lose it to Heneage."

"Is there a difference? In either case, it will be gone forever."

"Not if there is a clause in the deed that allows you to buy it back."

"And what language would let me do that?"

"That you have a male heir."

Oxford stopped. "But Burghley wouldn't agree to that."

"I think he will. He is a gambler, you know. He will not be able to resist the chance that I will not give you a son. Either way, he will come across as saving the castle for his granddaughters. He will balk at first, of course, but he won't be able to pass up an opportunity to look like a caring grandfather, even if it makes you look magnanimous at the same time."

"But once he gets his hands on it, he'll never let it go."

"The trust will be for the benefit of your daughters. They will be married off in ten years and the trust will no longer be needed. In the meantime, I will have a son and you will get Hedingham back."

It was obvious that Oxford did not think her plan would work. She added one more detail.

"Burghley knows that your creditors will take the castle if Heneage doesn't. He doesn't want that to happen." Oxford stood looking at her, one boot on, the other in his hand. "You must make the offer now."

Oxford clumped over to her. "We should not let a day go to waste, then, my love, in making sure you give me a son."

She pushed him away. "The day started at midnight, my lord. You are doing very well for today. If I were you, I would rest up for tonight."

## ~ 64 ~
## Oxford Court – *Henry VI, Part 3*

"My lord," Nigel said. Oxford opened his eyes. "What?" He pulled the comforter off his face. He had been dreaming of Elspeth and Hedingham.

"Robin awaits you in the library, my lord. He is much distressed. There is scarce time to finish the third part of *Henry VI*, which the Queen expects to see on the sixth of January."

"No. I need to work on *Love's Labour's Won*." He closed his eyes.

"You informed me last night that you had finished that play, my lord."

"I did?" Oxford opened his eyes for a moment. "Yes. I did." He pulled the comforter back over his head and started to roll over.

"Robin also said to remind you that, when last engaged in writing *Henry*, you were most taken with Queen Margaret."

Oxford opened his eyes again. "Yes."

"And Richard, if I remember rightly."

"Yes. And Richard."

Oxford was suddenly alive. He swung his legs out of bed, throwing the comforter aside. "Margaret and Richard!" Nigel slid the chamber pot out from under the bed. Oxford threw off his night shirt and, without looking, relieved himself into the pot. "Margaret and Richard! The demon and the man I will make worse than Barabas." He slipped an arm into the shirt Nigel was holding. Loose trousers quickly followed. Stepping into slippers, Oxford headed for the stairs. He found Robin in the library arranging parts of the play script in the center of the table.

"Good morrow, Scribbler."

"Good morrow, my lord."

"Where do we stand?"

"Too many battles; not enough arguments."

"So you say." He threw himself into a chair and pulled the first pile of papers to him. He began to read, scanning what Robin had written. When he finished a page, he pushed it to his right. The

369

carpenter bees were soon back, buzzing as Oxford read through the first pile. Socrates leaped onto the table and sat down on one of the pages. "Richard and his brothers storming into Parliament House, throwing Somerset's head onto the floor," he said. "Good."

"Would they have done such a thing?"

"Aye, and more."

Robin tried to sit silently while Oxford sped through the script but could not keep himself from asking a question about King Henry. "You make the king very unkinglike. Why is that?"

"He was a terrible king. The nobles will be like a school of fish hemming him in, with Richard circling like a shark. Henry thinks he can save his son from them by promising Edward, Richard's oldest brother, to make Edward his successor."

"And disrupt the royal succession? Can he do that?"

"He did, but, Queen Margaret, mother of the boy being denied the right to be king, will not like it:

> *Timorous wretch! Thou hast undone thyself, thy son and me.*
> *Would I had died a maid and never seen thee, never borne thee son,*
> *Seeing thou hast proved so unnatural a father."*

"She sounds like Joan of Arc."

"Yes. Margaret is Joan's replacement. She is evil personified. She will cause untold woe to generations of Englishmen"

"*O tiger's heart wrapt in a woman's hide!*" Robin read from a piece of paper in front of him.

"How else to describe a woman who hands a grieving father a handkerchief dipped in the blood of the man's son, whom she hath just murdered? The poor man cries out: *How couldst thou drain the life-blood of the child, / To bid the father wipe his eyes withall.*"

Robin shivered. "There is blood on the hands of everyone in this play. They all deserve punishment. It is so black that shouldn't there be a character who has done nothing to deserve misfortune? Death and suffering comes to all, even those who've done no wrong?"

Oxford sat upright in his chair. "Yes." He stood up. He began to dictate: "*Enter a son who has killed his father, dragging in the dead body.*' The son doesn't know what he's done." Robin looked up in shock. "The son thinks he will find *some store of crowns* in the man's pockets and begins to search the body. He stops:

370

*Who's this? O God! it is my father's face,*
*Whom in this conflict I unwares have kill'd.*
*Pardon me, God, I knew not what I did!*
*And pardon, father, for I knew not thee!*

Robin's pen flew across the page.

"*Enter a father who has killed his son, bringing in the body,*" Oxford continued.

"A *father* who has killed his son?"

"Aye. The father exults:

*Thou that so stoutly hast resisted me,*
*Give me thy gold, if thou hast any gold:*
*For I have bought it with a hundred blows.*

"He pulls back the cloth covering the dead man's face:

*But let me see: is this our foeman's face?*
*Ah, no, no, no, it is mine only son!*

Oxford looked at Robin. "Enough?"

"They should be on opposite sides of the stage, unaware of each other." Oxford nodded. They eyed each other, enjoying the moment when a scene cries out *this works!* But Robin had more. "What do you think, my lord, if King Henry is also on stage and witnesses this?"

Oxford clapped his hands. "Oh, excellent! He will be to one side and, unlike the father and son, able to see them while they remain unaware of each other. Where is the speech Henry recites as he sits on a molehill wishing he were someone other than a king?" Oxford rummaged through the paper on the table. "Ah!" he said, holding up a paper.

*O God! methinks it were a happy life,*
*To sit upon a hill, as I do now,*
*To carve out dials quaintly, point by point,*
*Thereby to see the minutes how they run.*

"Excellent!" Robin said as he wrote this down.

"I'll flesh this out later."

"But how does the play end?"

"With a false peace."

"A false peace? Why?"

"Richard still has to kill his way to the throne."

"More death," Robin said sadly. "I bleed as I write."

Oxford put his hand on Robin's shoulder. "Forgive me. I forget that the wounds I describe are real to you. I also am tired of the slaughter. I have no blood left in me to write *Richard III*. This will be the end of the history plays: the Queen be damned!"

Robin felt better. "Your ancestors played a greater role, my lord, than you allow in this play. Can you not write more of them?"

"I must not peek out from behind the screen called Shackspear. Edward succeeded Henry, as Henry said he would, and will execute the Twelfth Earl of Oxford and his eldest son, Aubrey, because they had supported Henry. Edward had Aubrey executed six days before his father to heighten the Twelfth Earl's agony as he waited for the executioner's axe to fall on his neck. The Earl who speaks in the play is John, who became the Thirteenth Earl of Oxford. He complains bitterly about the fate of his father and older brother:

> *Call him my king by whose injurious doom*
> *My elder brother, the Lord Aubrey Vere,*
> *Was done to death? and more than so, my father,*
> *Even in the downfall of his mellow'd years,*
> *When nature brought him to the door of death?*
> *No, Warwick, no; while life upholds this arm,*
> *This arm upholds the house of Lancaster.*

"This will remind the Queen of how loyal my ancestors have been to the House of Lancaster."

"And a small fingerprint left by the author."

"That, too."

"And, if the next play will not be about Richard, what *will* you write?"

Oxford looked wistful. "My marriage is days away. You ask about the next play; I ask about the next life. I have never really been married. Falstaff warns me I am sailing too close to Charybdis and will disappear."

"Falstaff thinks he will disappear if you marry Lady Elspeth."

"I hope not. He knows the link between us cannot be broken."

"Why don't you tell him that?"

"We are men, Robin. Men don't talk like women. Sir John knows where I stand. I don't have to tell him."

## ~ 65 ~
## A Wedding at Whitehall

The wherry spun away from Baynard's Castle. "Pull! ye fish heads!" John Taylor called out. The four men either side bent their backs to the oars. John Taylor waved a slender whip made of willow that was just long enough to reach the forward oarsmen. The tide was ebbing, slowing the boat's progress upriver.

A canopy shaded the rear quarter of the vessel. Oxford lounged underneath it, as regal as Antony on his way to meet Cleopatra. Robin hung on to the thwart, his eyes wide as he watched the men maneuver the boat. Falstaff was not aboard. Nigel had heard that Sir John had gone back to Sheffield.

"It may not be the Queen's barge," John Taylor said, "but I warrant it's good enough to carry yer lordship to his wedding."

"Indeed," Oxford said.

Robin could tell his master was pleased and apprehensive at the same time. The afternoon sun, warm for a day so late in the year, silvered the surface of the river, which rippled invitingly. A brace of swans curved away from the shore and took up station behind the vessel. John Taylor noted them. "A good omen, my lord. Queen's approval." Robin leaned over the side and waved them closer.

The wherry glided past the green fields and gardens in front of the great houses the courtiers had built on the Strand between London and Westminster.

"How goes your art, John," Oxford asked.

"A hard course, as ye know, my lord. A poet is rarely loved while he still lives." He did not ask about the poem he had given Oxford to deliver to the Queen.

Oxford introduced him to Robin. "This is John Taylor, Robin."

"The Water Poet? The man who wrote *London Bridge Is Falling Down*?"

"The same." John Taylor said. He was obviously pleased. He bowed slightly, a touch of pride in his voice. He flicked the willow staff over the heads of the oarsmen to let them know he was still watching them.

"He could not cross the bridge," Oxford explained, "and so he turned his fear into art."

"It's going to fall down some day," John Taylor said. "We all know it. What ye don't know is that it's waiting for *me* to cross it before it falls. Oncet I do, it's *blam!* and me and everyone on it goes into the Thames!" He glanced at Robin to see his reaction. Robin's wide eyes left no doubt that Robin believed what John Taylor had just told him about the bridge. Reinvigorated, John Taylor turned his head upriver. "Aye, lad, I swear it, by all that's holy in Christendom. As soon as I step foot on it, down it goes! So I hain't crossed it since I made this discovery, which is why it still stands! Little that anyone knows it." His nose rose into the air. "I'll go under it, if I have to, but I'll never go over it again!"

"But won't it collapse while you are under it?" Robin asked.

"Not if I'm fast enough, lad. It's with trembling fear that I point my boat toward one of the arches and fly under it! But I'm through in a flash, I am, much quicker than if I crossed on foot, and so the bridge has no time to catch me before I'm through!" He looked back at the bridge, which was crowded with people. "Look at them. They don't know they're going to make it to the other side *because I'm not on it.*"

John Taylor turned his attention to the oarsmen who, in his opinion, had taken his speech about the bridge to slack off. "Together now, ye shriveled worms, ye dried-up inch-pizzles!"

"Give us a line, John." Oxford asked. "Something new."

John Taylor drew himself up. "This be about chance and fate. Philosoficill, if you will:

> *By wondrous accident perchance one may*
> *Grope out a needle in a load of hay;*
> *And though a white crow be exceedingly rare,*
> *A blind man may, by fortune, catch a hare.*

"And a broken clock is right twice a day!" Robin added brightly.

John Taylor frowned. "That's not in the poem."

"Oh."

"Where'd ye hear that?"

"I don't know. Somewhere."

No poet liked to hear that someone else might be having similar thoughts. John Taylor was no different. He glared at the rowers who were watching him with wary eyes. He twitched the stick and they picked up the pace a bit to keep him from using it on them.

The boat soon came alongside Whitehall Stairs. Oxford, resplendent in black silk and plumes and clasping his great grandfather's sword to his side, stepped onto the pier. He thanked John Taylor and he and Robin climbed the steps to the Palace of Whitehall. Oxford's wedding was to take place in the chapel, with a banquet and a play to follow in the great hall. A half-dozen horn players in blue with boar's heads on their left shoulders waited at the top of the steps. They announced Oxford's arrival by playing his tucket and then continuing seamlessly into a march based on the same musical motif.

"Lord Oxford's March," Robin announced proudly. Oxford acknowledged the horn players who stepped aside to let him pass between them. He and Robin wound their way through the narrow hallways to the chapel where they found Elspeth and a group of ladies waiting for them. Elspeth was dressed in a flowing white floor-length dress and veil that trailed behind her.

"My lord," Elspeth said, curtseying to Oxford.

"My lady." Oxford bowed deeply. "Greetings on our wedding day. You look beautiful."

Elspeth's brother, Francis, appeared, along with other family members who had come in through the tiltyard entrance to the palace.

"Shall we?" Elspeth asked. Oxford nodded. He preceded his bride into the chapel, where two of his cousins, Sir Francis and Sir Horatio, waited as his groomsmen. Thereafter, the Queen entered through a side door and took her place. Elspeth and her family members then came in. Elspeth was brought up to the altar by her Uncle Clarence who gave her away. The ceremony was short, after which everyone removed to the great hall next door where they were welcomed by a new musical composition by John Farmer who had come especially from Ireland to perform it.

A long table had been set up on a low stage at the far end of the hall. Oxford and Elspeth, now Countess of Oxford, took their places in the middle. Elspeth's family took chairs to the right; Oxford's cousins took two of the chairs on the left, their wives in between them. This left three chairs empty between them and Oxford.

Oxford looked at Elspeth.

"For your daughters," she said.

"Are they to remain empty?" Oxford asked, his choler rising. "Are they to be a symbol of my failure as a father?"

Elspeth put a finger to her lips.

Oxford felt tricked and penned in. He started to rise when the door at the rear of the hall opened and his three daughters came into the hall. The servant who had taken them away from him at Cecil House took up a position next to the door. Oxford's daughters, now sixteen, seven, and five, walked through the crowd to the table. Lisbeth, the eldest, was already a stunning woman, tall and graceful, with that faint look of disdain only the very rich and titled possess. Bridget and Susan were still little girls, trying to not think of all the eyes watching them as they crossed the room. The three of them stopped behind the empty chairs. They pulled the chairs out in unison and sat down, giving a perfunctory bow in Lady Elspeth's direction. Susan, closest to Oxford, cast a quick glance at him. Bridget and Lisbeth refused to look at him and stared stonily out over the heads of the people in front of them.

Elspeth leaned over and whispered to her husband: "Lord Burghley sends his regrets but his gout prevents him from attending our wedding."

"A welcome present, but what say you about my daughters?"

"I met with Hazel privately, my lord, meaning without informing Lord Burghley. I wanted to talk to her woman to woman. I explained that I was without children myself and much grieved that your daughters had lost their mother when they needed her most. I thanked her for doing her best to fill that loss. I thought our wedding might be an occasion to reunite them with you. She had some reluctance at first, but I was able to convince her to bring them today."

Oxford was watching Hazel standing against the rear wall, a woman he decidedly did not like. "And what possible lever could you have found to bring that about."

"I gave Hazel a small sum of money to cover the expense of clothing your daughters in something appropriate to their station."

"With some left over for Hazel, I'm sure."

"I would hope so. But £50 doesn't go as far as it used to."

"£50!" Oxford exclaimed out loud.

"They are here, are they not?" Elspeth gazed out over the crowd. She leaned in closer to him. "You spared no expense in your attire or the means by which you arrived today. An eight-man boat, with pilot and crew? I hoped you like being piped ashore by trumpeters dressed in your livery, playing a new march by William Byrd?" Oxford was now thoroughly discomfited. "A gift to you on our wedding day, which will be enriched by the presence of your daughters. I think the expense was worth it."

"And how much did *The Earl of Oxford's March* cost?" he asked.

"Nothing. It was a gift from William who said he welcomed the opportunity to set your tucket to music. What did you think of it?" Oxford had to admit he liked it. She looked at him. "You might thank me, if you wanted to."

"Thank you." He looked off. "Are there any more surprises I should know about?" He had a worried look on his face.

"It is I who should be worried. I am told that we shall see a play called *Love's Labour's Won*. I shiver at the prospect because I have no idea what I shall see."

"Rest assured, my lady, there will be nothing in the presentation to embarrass you or anyone else." He glanced at the Queen, who was watching them. He reminded himself that she could read lips. He slipped his hand over his face to block her view. "You will see only foolishness without hidden meanings."

"I certainly hope so."

"And I, as the poet in the family, have composed a poem in honor of our wedding." He rose. Everyone stopped talking. "Your Majesty, lords and ladies, peers and gentry, my lady, now Countess of Oxford, my daughters," he added, nodding in their direction. "I thank you all for gracing our wedding with your presence." He glanced at his daughters. Lisbeth was still staring out over the audience but he caught Bridget glancing at him before she snapped her head back to mimic her older sister's disdain. Susan was beaming at him. Her bright eyes warmed his heart. He went on.

"I have a gift for my bride. A poem for the occasion:

> *Loves Queene, long wayting for her true-Love*
> *Slaine by a Boar, which he had chased,*
> *Left off her teares, and me embraced,*
> *She kist me sweete, and call'd me new-love.*
> *With my silver haire she toyed,*
> *In my stayed lookse she joyed.*
> *Boyes (she said) breed beauties sorrow:*
> *Olde men cheere it even and morrow.*

Oxford heard a chuckle from the audience. He forced himself not to smile.

*My face she nam'd the seate of favour,*
*All my defects her tongue defended,*
*My shape she prais'd, but most commended*
*My breath more sweete than Balme in savour.*
*Be, old man, with me delighted,*
*Love for love shall be requited.*
*With her toyes at last she won me:*
*Now her coyes hath undone me.*

The Queen applauded. "Well-done, old man!" the Queen called out. Oxford laughed, a warm smile on his face. He turned to Elspeth and saw she was also smiling. He bent over and kissed her. The other guests joined in, clapping and laughing.

Elspeth rose. "To my husband," she said, raising her glass, "who is my new-love, though he be silver-haired. And, as Her Majesty says true, he is well-done."

"Like a bit of beef!" someone called out. They all laughed.

"Aye, that and more," Elspeth said, gaining a few more laughs. She raised her glass and the audience rose to their feet to applaud the newlyweds.

Oxford produced a silver box. He took out a large emerald ring and held it up for everyone to see. "My present to my bride on our wedding day," he said, handing the ring to Elspeth.

She took the ring. "And I give my present to, Edward, now my husband." She paused. Everyone waited. "Me," she finally said.

The people in the hall burst into laughter and applause.

"And what gift could surpass that?" Oxford called out.

He and Elspeth took their seats. Oxford's oldest daughter now rose. She gazed out across the assembled guests with a composure rarely seen outside the Queen's throne room. Even Elizabeth cocked her head and waited. The stony face of a sixteen-year-old had gaveled them all into silence.

"Your Majesty; learned guests. I stand to wish Edward de Vere, Earl of Oxford, Lord Great Chamberlain of England, Baron Scales and Badlesmere, the good fortune of finally having the son and heir he has always wanted." She sat back down.

The guests fluttered behind their fans and chuckled among themselves. Oxford looked down the table at Lisbeth. He was not pleased. Elspeth put a hand on his arm before he could say anything. "Peace, my lord."

"She could have called me 'father,'" he said.

"But you must call her daughter first."

"I did so when I met them at Cecil House."

"Hazel says you addressed them as 'ladies.'"

"Was that inappropriate?"

"Had I been in the room, your words would have included me. Did they include Hazel?"

Oxford was now doubly put out. "I thought this was our wedding."

The Queen rose, sending everyone to their feet. She gestured to him. Oxford went over to her. He bowed and kissed her outstretched hand.

"My felicitations, Edward. Women are like apples on trees," she said, looking out over the wedding guests. "The ones that are closer to the ground get picked too early, when they are still unripe. The ones at the top are the best because they are hard to reach. An excellent decision, my lord."

"Your Highness," Oxford said, bowing.

The Queen dropped her voice. "It would seem, however, that your daughter, Lisbeth, is so froward that she will pick herself." She smiled. "It is no marvel to teach a woman to talk; it is far harder to teach her to hold her tongue."

"Your Majesty."

"And the play?"

"*Love's Labour's Won.*"

"Is this by you, or by that fellow Shackpear?" Oxford blinked. She laughed. "Lost your wit, my lord? By my faith, it is not often I cause you to do *that*." She laughed heartily.

Oxford smiled thinly. She was taunting him about having to put up with Shackspear. It seemed that nothing was to go right for him this day. He felt like a trained pony who had been led out into an arena and asked to perform, first by his new wife, then by his eldest daughter, and now by the Queen. Anger was rising in him. "Steady, Edward," he reminded himself. He heard Burghley, of all people, sitting in the library with him when he was a boy, teaching him to push down his feelings and put on a face that told those around him nothing about what he was thinking. Unfortunately, thinking of

Burghley only made him angrier. "Your Highness," he muttered, and walked away.

The audience applauded the play. It was shallow enough that everyone loved it, even the Queen, who gestured for Oxford to come over when it was done. "A clever mix of historical figures, *commedia dell'arte*, and your beautiful words, which always pleases us. It is an excellent play, but does not show love. Even you can't write a play that shows true love."

"Why is that, Your Majesty," Oxford heard himself asking, despite himself.

"I saw *Palamon and Arcite* in 1566 and the artist so limned the lovers that I know I will never see anything that will surpass it in my lifetime. I will be content when I die that I lived to see it played."

"How fortunate."

Elizabeth arched an eyebrow. "My having seen it, or my death?"

"Either one," Oxford said, not caring any more whether she sensed his sarcasm. "With your permission." He bowed and moved off.

# 1592

## ~ 66 ~
### Oxford and Lady Elspeth Return to Oxford Court

Welcome home," Nigel said, swinging open the front door. Oxford and Lady Elspeth, now Countess of Oxford, came into the hall. Robin followed. The Queen had lent them the use of a hunting lodge in Epping Forest for their honeymoon. Frangellica had gone along and become friends with Lady Elspeth's maid, Bona Fortuna, who was round of face and stout, ideal qualifications in a maid. She would attract no attention from male servants and cause no jealousy among the female staff.

"Have you cleaned out the second-floor room?" Elspeth asked Nigel, referring to the room with the balcony.

"I have, my lady. Please follow me."

Elspeth and Oxford followed him up the stairs. Nigel had had movers place an enormous bed in the room. Large trunks stood on end along the walls. Rugs were strewn across the floor. Bona Fortuna carried a trunk into a small room off the bedroom. Oxford thought it was a closet and asked where the woman would be sleeping.

"In there," Elspeth said. "Would you have her sleep in here?"

"No, my lady. But she will be very close to us when, well ..."

"When you sleep with me?" she asked, a mischievous look on her face. "Maybe she'll learn something." She was sorting through the drawers in one of the trunks. "It didn't bother you at Hedingham when the servants were a few steps down a stairwell, or at the hunting lodge when only a blanket over a beam separated us from her."

Nigel, uncomfortable with having to listen to such details, interceded. "Your room awaits you, my lord." He gestured across the hall. Oxford made no move to leave.

"You will visit, will you not?" Elspeth asked.

"Of course. This is rather new to me, my lady. I never lived with Nan, even when we were man and wife. I expected you and I would be sleeping together, now that we are married."

"We will, my lord. Just not all the time." She smiled, but he couldn't tell whether she was giving him a 'come-hither' look, delayed for now, or was amused that he expected they would sleep in the same bed every night. Maybe both. "May I open the window, my lord?"

"Certainly." Lady Elspeth stepped out onto the balcony that overlooked the garden that lay between the day room and Candlewick Street, the same garden Oxford had let himself into when he walked back from the celebration at St. Paul's. Oxford stepped out onto the balcony alongside Elspeth. He slid his hand over her bottom.

"You *will* visit, won't you?" she asked, ignoring his hand.

"Visit?" Oxford asked.

"When you're not in your room, or writing plays in the library."

"I will be your lodger," he said, kissing her lightly on the cheek.

"I will let you 'lodge,' then, my lord."

"I may stay so much you will have to file for a writ to evict me."

"That, I doubt, my lord." She looked down at the garden. "Pity it's so gray and dried out. In springtime I shall give it a good going-over."

"That would be nice. It's been abandoned for years. Frangellica won't even use it to grow herbs. She says there isn't enough light."

"And Falstaff. Where will he be sleeping?"

"In his own apartments, my lady, over on Cheapside."

"I was surprised to see him in the library when I came here the first time. He frightens me, with his great belly and his mustachios."

"He is a good man. I am sure the two of you will become friends."

Falstaff had come into the house while Oxford and Elspeth were on the balcony. He could see them through a window in the great hall. Because the windows were open, he could hear what they were saying.

"What's a honeymoon?" Robin asked Falstaff.

"The first month of a marriage, young pup. It lasts but the time it takes the Moon to wax and wane, and then the honey is gone."

He turned and left.

## ~ 67 ~
## *Henry VI, Part 3*

The Queen was pleased. She and the audience rose together to applaud. "Well done," she called out. Shackspear came over, preening. "Go away," she said. Shackspear, shocked, retreated through the well-wishers who had begun to crowd around. She glanced over their heads, looking here and there but not at any one in particular. They began drifting toward the doorway, her gaze dispersing them like soap bubbles floating toward a drain. She caught Oxford's eye. He made his way through the crowd.

"Finally," she said, her voice mixed with pleasure at the play and asperity at how long he had taken to give her what she wanted. Before she could say more, Robert Cecil appeared.

"Sir Robert," Elizabeth said.

"Greetings, Your Majesty." Oxford knew the false smile on Cecil's face had been crafted in front of a mirror, the way one learns to play the virginal or write a flowery signature—with much repetition and little emotion. More than one member of court with had said that Cecil may have taught himself to show his teeth but he never gave you his eyes. "I bring my father's regrets, whose gout has prevented him from attending."

"*Quel dommage.* I hadn't expected him, of course. He dislikes plays. They remind him of life, which is disorderly and without direction. He wishes he could make us follow his commands, as if he were playwright, if not God."

"Yes, Your Majesty."

Cecil's fawning irritated the Queen. "What's that you're wearing?" she asked, leaning forward to look more closely at a medallion hanging from his neck.

Cecil fingered the medallion. "This is a miniature of my sister, Nan. I wear it in remembrance of her."

"But you can't see it there, can you. Why not wear it on the top of your shoe? That way, whenever you look down, your sister will be with you."

383

Oxford burst out laughing, surprising Elizabeth and Cecil. Cecil was always looking at the top of his shoes. They looked at him.

"Still laughing at my sister, my lord?" Cecil asked.

"No, Sir Robert, No, not at all. It's just that the idea of wearing a medallion on the top of a shoe—"

"Then, at the Queen? Choose your words carefully, my lord." He turned to Elizabeth. "Ma'am," he said, and walked away.

Oxford and Elizabeth watched him go. "The elf can growl," she said. "He used to idolize you when he was a boy. What happened?"

"He thinks I am the reason he could not marry one of his father's scullery maids."

"I heard something about that."

"Lord Burghley told him the girl was promised to one of my retainers and I wouldn't give permission to void the marriage contract so the girl could marry Robert."

"Which was not true."

"Of course not. Burghley told me he lied to Robert to make sure Robert did not marry the girl, and to make sure Robert would carry his father's vendetta against me for the way I had treated Nan."

"Robert resents you, my lord, for far more than denying him his love. He resents your fair looks and straight back. He was not made for sport or love, and is jealous of all the world because of it. Interestingly, these very failings are what make him of value to me."

"Will he succeed his father as secretary?"

"He will. I have already made him a member of the Privy Council. If his father's health fails, his minion will serve me well. They are both little men, made great by me, and, therefore, loyal servants." She looked out over the lingering crowd but did not settle on anyone in particular, keeping them at bay. Oxford was surprised that she would confide such information to him. She was obviously feeling comfortable in his presence, something Oxford had not felt for a long time.

"I am going to Ditchley in May," she said.

"With Anne and Sir Henry living there unmarried?"

"How can they marry, when each is married to someone else?"

"But you will honor them if you go to Ditchley."

"Yes." She looked at him. "Really, Edward, you're beginning to sound like Burghley."

Oxford did not like the comparison. Was he turning into a Burghley? Or did his surprise have something to do with Anne? "You have forgiven Sir Henry for living with Anne?"

"Have you forgiven Anne for living with Sir Henry?"

"She means nothing to me."

Elizabeth was watching him closely. She wasn't convinced he was being honest with himself. "And your son? What about him? You know what he asked me when Anne was last here at Greenwich?"

"What?"

"Who his father was."

Oxford looked away.

She did not press him. "We shall have need of entertainment, my lord. Write me a play. And come to see it performed. The visit will give you a chance to see Anne *and* your son."

Oxford did not want to do either, but her wish, as always, was his command. "If I write, the play will be about Anne and me," he said, hoping this would make Elizabeth reconsider.

"I expect it will be."

"Much ado about nothing."

"As good a title as any." She stood up and nodded to the people in the hall. "Make it sparkle, Edward, as only you can."

## ~ 68 ~
## *Love's Labour's Won*

Shackspear came in unannounced. He was waving the script to *Love's Labour's Won*, the play Oxford wrote for his wedding. He went directly into the library where Oxford and Robin were working. Falstaff was sitting on a chair behind the door.

"This is awful!" he cried. "A masque? Fairies in costume? This is what happens when you go off on your own. Henslowe threw it on the floor. How am I to feed myself if this is all I get?"

Oxford jumped up. He ripped the script out of Shackspear's hands. "How did you get this?" He was furious.

Shackspear was surprised by Oxford's reaction. He pointed to Robin. "He gave it to me."

"Your lordship," Robin began to stutter, "I thought all the plays where to be given to Mr. Shackspear …"

"No!" Oxford shouted. "This play is personal. So are the sonnets. You are never to give them to *him*," he said, pointing to Shackspear.

"So who wants masques or sonnets?" Shackspear sneered, having recovered from Oxford's outburst. "They're old fashioned. I've made little money this past year. I only get £5 a play, you know!"

"Welcome to the theater, Willum."

"Don't call me 'Willum,'" Shackspear said, glowering at Oxford. "No one calls me 'Willum.'"

Oxford took a step toward Shackspear. "Don't you *dare* tell me what to call you. You are 'Willum' until I say otherwise. You are nothing without me. You saw how the Queen waved you away. If I say the word, your days as a London playwright are over."

Shackspear remembered the Queen dismissing him. He was instantly the fawning servant again. "Okay. Okay," he said." To Oxford's amazement, Shackspear went on as if the conversation about *Love's Labour's Won* had never taken place. "Francis Langley says we can make a lot of money if we give him a little 'seed' money. He's into jewels, land, whores—"

"Get out!" shouted Oxford.

"My lord," Shackspear protested, but Oxford yelled again, "*Get out!*"

Lady Elspeth appeared in the doorway. Oxford, head down, pushed Shackspear into her.

"My lady!" Shackspear cried.

"What is going on here?" she demanded to know.

"Say goodbye to Mr. Shackspear," Oxford said, pushing Shackspear toward the front door, which Nigel quickly opened. Out Shackspear tumbled onto Candlewick Street and disappeared.

"My apologies, my lady," Oxford said. "That man is the Devil's proxy, and would never enter this house if the Queen had not forced me into an arrangement with him."

"So I have heard. Will this be happening frequently?"

"No. He got his hands on a script that was private. I forgive you, Robin, but talk to me before you give him anything again."

"Actually, it was good theater, my lord," Elspeth said. "The scene I just walked into. You are always stealing events from life. You should add this to one of your plays."

"*Never!*" Oxford said.

"Punning again, my lord? Yet I agree, he spoke most disrespectfully to you, my lord. I admire your decisiveness. Too much closeness can bring the knife."

Bona Fortuna appeared in the library doorway. "Here is your effusion," she said, handing Elspeth a glass goblet with a handle fashioned in the shape of an egret. Elspeth took the goblet and walked back into the hall.

"Now, where were we?" Oxford asked. He was still angry.

Falstaff stood up. "Time to go," he said to no one in particular. He walked around the door and out into the hall. Nigel opened the front door. "Sir John," Nigel said, as the big man lumbered past him. "Nigel," Falstaff replied, going out the door.

## ~ 69 ~
### *Much Ado About Nothing*

T he Queen wants a play," Oxford said, as he and Robin walked back into the library. Robin sat down at the table and began grinding ink. He looked up eagerly. "What shall it be?"

"It will be all about deception. It will involve two couples moving along parallel tracks, with hidden meanings. It will be be about Anne Vavasor and me. You don't know her."

"The mother of your son," Robin said brightly. Oxford looked discomfited by this. "Everyone in the palace knows about you and her, my lord. Are you and she still—?"

"No. She has been living at Ditchley with Sir Henry Lee for some time now. She bewitched him when Sir Henry was our gaoler."

"Sir Henry? How so?"

"He had a suit of armor made with her initials carved all over it, '*AV*', '*AV*', '*AV*', '*AV*,'" Oxford said, his voice rising. Robin thought he sounded like a lark singing to the sky.

"But she bewitched *you* for a while, didn't she?" Oxford's scowl returned. "Does she still cast a spell over you?"

"Me? No, no."

"But you plan to write a play about her."

"She is a remarkable woman."

"And the mother of your son."

Oxford scowl deepened. "Isn't she?" Robin persisted. "I only ask because I've never heard you mention him. He must be thirteen or fourteen now. About my age. Is he at Ditchley with his mum?"

"My little page is full of questions today," Oxford growled. He looked exasperated. "Yes, I suppose he is."

"What's he like?"

"Now, that's quite enough for now."

"My lord, 'tis no sin to be father to a son."

389

"*Enough*! I owe the Queen a play." He made a sweeping motion, as if he were wiping something away that was hanging in the air. "What *do* you know about Miss Vavasor?"

"Nothing."

"Oh, excellent."

"Why is that, my lord?"

"Because the title of the play will be *Much Ado About Nothing*. The Muse is with me when words suddenly appear as if they are popping out of a script I haven't written yet. You are my lucky charm, Robin."

"My lord!" Robin realized this made him pleased and worried at the same time.

"Mistress Vavasor shall be Beatrice in this play; I shall be Benedict. They shall be mirror images of each other. They will push and pull at each other as Anne and I did in real life."

"But they will have to marry at the end, if it is to be a comedy."

"I'll worry about that when we get there. I need to know how Beatrice would speak to Benedict. I want something new you've heard at court, or in town. This play must be *new*!"

Robin furrowed his brow. "Well, she might say '*Benedict wears his faith but as the fashion of his hat, ever changing with the next block*.'"

"Good. Go on."

"'*I wonder that you are still talking: nobody marks you.*'"

"What would he say to that?"

"'*My dear Lady Disdain! Are you yet living?*'"

"Yet living!" Oxford muttered. "Perfect!"

"My lord, what is this all about?"

"Deception."

"Deception?"

"There will be two plots, both engineered by deception."

"*Two* plots?"

"I haven't told you about the second plot?" Robin shook his head. "One plot will be about Benedict and Beatrice; the other plot will be about a pair of star-crossed lovers tripped up on their way to the altar. I will call the two lovers Claudio and Hero. Their journey will be interrupted by a scoundrel who convinces Claudio that Hero has been sleeping with another man."

"I've heard this before."

"Yes, but not the way I will tell it. Deceit and deception are always with us. It will be everywhere in this play." He noticed that Robin did not share his enthusiasm. "The character who will deceive Claudio into believing that Hero is not a virgin will be named Don John."

"Don John of Austria?"

"Aye."

"The bastard brother of the King of Spain, who slew so many of my friends in the Netherlands?"

"The same."

"Good choice. The audience will hate him."

"I hope so. Don John will outrank Claudio but fear that Claudio will displace him in his brother's eyes: *'That young start-up hath all the glory of my overthrow: if I can cross him any way, I bless myself every way.'*"

Robin picked up his pen. "I begin to like this play. How will this scoundrel's deceit be discovered?"

"I don't know."

They both fell silent. Robin spoke first. "If all the deceit is being carried out through the use of words, my lord, maybe you should create a character who mangles English when he speaks but who, unwittingly, sets matters straight."

Oxford laughed out loud. "I love thee for this, Robin! I will add the Earl of Arundel and make everyone laugh."

"The Earl of who?"

"The Earl of Arundel," Oxford said. "A most traitorous, boil-brained, toad-spotted slug! He and Lord Howard plotted to overthrow the Queen. I found out and told Her Majesty about their plans. She sent them to the Tower. In their attempts to get out, they made up bald-faced lies about me."

"Such as?"

"Charges not worth repeating."

"Were any true, my lord?"

"No. Well, some, maybe."

"How can that be?"

"They reported what they heard, but not the circumstances, and, in reporting only the words and not the circumstances, they lied."

"By telling the Queen what they heard you say?"

Oxford nodded. "Because they didn't tell the Queen that my words were uttered over long suppers and after much wine and that my sole purpose was to set the table to laughter."

"Deceiving her the way you deceived them."

Oxford thought about this. "Yes, but my deception was to bring merriment to the table. Theirs was to impute crimes to me, which is entirely different."

"So what did Arundel say that you want to use in this play?"

Oxford's eyes lit up. "Listen:

> *First will I detect him of the most impudent, and senseless lies, that ever passed the mouth of any man;*
> *His Third lie which hath some affinity with the other two is of certain orations he made to the state of Venice;*
> *The Second vice, wherwith I mean to touch him ... is that he is a most notorious drunkard,*
> *Thirdlie, I will prove him a buggerer of a boy that is his cook;*
> *Fourthly, will I truly hit him, with his detestable practice of hiring murderers.*
> *Fifthly, to show that the world never brought forth such a villainous Monster.*

Robin was shocked. "Is any of this true?"

"Of course not. Except for the first one. I love telling impudent and senseless lies. After all," he said smugly, "I am a playwright, am I not?"

Robin acknowledged that he was. His shock over what Arundel said was replaced by his realization that Arundel couldn't count. "Did he actually speak like this?"

Oxford nodded. "I will make him a captain of the night watch. He will stumble upon the solution to Don John's treachery by capturing the men Don John has ordered to trick Claudio. He will bring them before Leonato, governor of Messina.

"Messina? Where is Messina?"

"In Sicily."

"Sicily? Why Sicily?"

Oxford waved a hand. "Because Messina is a lovely city, with a castle down at the water. Don't worry: the play will be in English. What we need now is the name of the character who will speak the way Arundel does." He paused for a moment. "Ah, I remember seeing a letter Burghley wrote to Walsingham during the Babington plot. Burghley complained about the constables he saw on his way from London to Theobalds. Burghley questioned them about what they were doing and found out that the only information they had about the conspirators was that one had a big nose! Burghley referred to the watchmen as 'dogberries.' The captain of the night watch will be named Dogberry!"

"And a 'dogberry' is something only a dog would eat!" Robin said.

"Or worse!"

They both laughed.

"Here is Dogberry speaking doggerel to Leonato when he brings Don John's men before him:

> *Marry, sir, they have committed false report;*
> *moreover, they have spoken untruths; secondarily,*
> *they are slanders; sixth and lastly, they have*
> *belied a lady; thirdly, they have verified unjust*
> *things; and, to conclude, they are lying knaves.*

"Oh, my lord, we are listening to Arundel himself."

"'Tis his signature."

"And his claims are nothing but false statements: false report; spoken untruths; slanders; untrue verifications; and more lies."

"It's a play about deception, isn't it? Beatrice and Benedict will try to deceive each other that they are not in love. Don John will try to deceive Claudio into believing Hero has cheated on him, and Hero's father will deceive all by claiming Hero died of shame, when she lives!"

"Wonderful!"

"Nothing is as it appears to be."

"Yes. And the story will be told by players," Robin went on enthusiastically, "who are themselves engaged in deception by playing Beatrice and Benedict when they are people who, after the play is over, can be seen outside the theater on the streets of London!"

"Oh, Robin, you are on to me! Yes! I *love* it!"

"And isn't 'nothing' a word for a woman's vagina?" Robin asked.

"You think?"

Robin nodded. "And 'nothing' is also zero."

"It is."

The sly look on Robin's face expanded. "And might 'zero' also stand for the letter 'O,' as in 'Oxford?'"

Oxford tried to look modest and failed. "You spy me out."

Robin was pleased with himself. "You have ruined me, my lord. I see hidden meanings everywhere now."

The two of them sat across the table from each other, like runners at the start of a race, coiled up and ready to explode.

"But deception will be not enough," Oxford said, sitting up, a more serious look on his face. "I need beautiful words to fog the ears of the audience so they will not truly understand what they have heard until later when, on a subsequent reading or performance, they realize that there was more there than they thought at first."

"I am ready," Robin said, eyes bright.

"Then I will lay out for you what I have written in my mind."

## ~ 70 ~
### *Henry VI, Part 3*, at the Rose

John Heminges walked to the front of the stage. He was dressed in robes that identified him as King Edward IV. He turned to Augustine Phillips and then Ned Alleyn on either side of him. "*Clarence and Richard, brothers both, love my lovely queen and kiss your princely nephew.*"

Phillips walked over to a crib in front of Heminges and bent down:

> *The duty that I owe unto your majesty*
> *I seal upon the lips of this sweet babe.*

Ned Alleyn, robed in red as evil Richard, followed Phillips to the crib:

> *And, that I love the tree from whence thou sprang'st,*
> *Witness the loving kiss I give the fruit.*

He looked out at the audience, a sly grin on his face:

> *And when I cry 'all hail! I mean all harm!*

The audience hissed.

Heminges returned to his throne and sat down.

> *Now am I seated as my soul delights,*
> *Having my country's peace and brothers' loves.*
> *Sound drums and trumpets! farewell sour annoy!*
> *For here, I hope, begins our lasting joy.*

The play ended and the audience burst into applause. They knew there would be no joy in England until Richard took the throne and was killed at Bosworth Field. They booed King Edward's false sense of peace. The hisses swelled as Ned Alleyn, still dressed as Richard, strode to the front of the stage and sneered at them. Henslowe, off-stage, knew he had a hit. Hundreds, maybe thousands, would come to see Richard slay his way to the throne.

Shackspear was also excited. He had played the Duke of York, his first major role. He had tried to bring York's grief to life after York learns his son has been brutally murdered by order of Queen Margaret.

Garbed as York, Shackspear had wailed the loss of his son as Margaret dipped a handkerchief in the dead boy's blood and gave it to him to wipe his tears. Shackspear cried out, "*O tiger's heart wrapt in a woman's hide!*" and heard the audience break into applause. Now that the play was over, he expected to be cheered as he stepped out onto the stage and waved the bloody handkerchief around, but no one seemed to notice him. They were all booing and hissing Ned Alleyn.

Henslowe raced through the back of the theater to get to the exit door so that he could urge the playgoers to come back and see the play again. Shackspear was right behind him. "The boy with the money box says we took in £3, 16, and 8!" Henslowe gleefully told Shackspear as they raced toward the exit. "The *Jew* brought in only 50 shillings!"

"And *Orlando Furioso*?" Shackspear asked, as Robert Greene came up to them out of the crowd surging through the door.

"16 shillings."

"Mr. Shackspear," Greene announced loudly, sticking his belly up against Shackspear's. His face was red. His eyes were bloodshot. The crowd streaming by slowed to watch Greene. They could tell from his voice that a storm was coming. Falstaff and Robin were among them. Marlowe slipped in along a wall to listen as well.

Greene wagged a fat finger in Shackpear's face. "You puppet! You upstart crow! Beautifying yourself with *my* feathers! Who gave you *my* lines! I would to God I could go to the theater one day and hear a speech that did *not* come from my pen! *You are all robbing me of my words!*"

"Good Heavens," Henslowe said. "Give a playwright too much to drink and he thinks he wrote everything."

"I am *not* too much with drink!" Greene thundered. His head tilted forward, as if it were about to fall off his shoulders.

"Robert, Robert," Henslowe said. He slipped his hand into Greene's arm and turned him toward the door. "Ye need to lie down and rest." He pushed Greene off the landing. The big man almost fell. He staggered away from the theater. He wanted to stay and fight but it was a blustery March day and the wind was pushing him from behind. He finally came to a halt in the middle of the path. The crowd surged around him, laughing. He looked confused, as if he had forgotten where he was.

"Lies!" Shackspear called after him. "I wrote every word you heard in there."

"How can we be sure?" an overweight woman called out, pushing herself to the front of the crowd. She had a hand on top of her head to hold down a large crumpled straw hat. Her belly rivaled Falstaff's. "Someone else could have written wot we just heard. Where's your proof?"

"Proof?"

"How do we know ye're not just a messenger boy," she said, sticking her jaw out.

"Messenger boy?" Shackspear asked. A frightened look appeared on his face. He glanced around and spied Marlowe. "Mr. Marlowe. Please tell this woman I am the author of the play she's just seen."

A smile flitted across Marlowe's face. He looked like a banker about to tell someone their loan application had been disapproved. "Madame," he said. "Playwrights work alone. While I cannot say who wrote the play you just saw, I can assure you I did not write it."

"Mr. Marlowe!" Shackspear exclaimed.

"Ye see?" the woman said triumphantly. "Ye see? I knew it!"

Henslowe decided it was time to intervene. "Ye knew what?"

"I knew he didn't write the play. Did *you* see him write it?" She wiggled her hips.

Henslowe rolled his eyes. "And I suppose you're the author, and I should pay you instead of him."

"Yes. I wrote it! Not him!"

"That's enough!" Henslowe announced. He gave a whistle and two burly men appeared. They swept the woman off her feet and carried her away, her legs kicking. "It's his word against mine," she cried out. "He has no proof!"

Everyone in the entryway laughed. Shackspear looked relieved. "Imagine a woman thinking she could write a play! Ha ha ha."

"Not much more than imagining a Warwickshire hack with no university education could," someone called out.

"All right, gentlemen," Henslowe said, raising his arms. "The show is over. Inside *and* outside." This brought more laughter. He started pushing them toward the door.

Ned Alleyn came out of the back of the theater. He came up to Shackspear. "You've got blood on your face," he said in a low, harsh voice. Shackspear wiped his face with his hand. "Get out!" Alleyn hissed. Shackspear blinked and went back into the theater. Alleyn turned to Henslowe. "He got so carried away playing York that he put his face in the handkerchief and smeared blood all over himself!"

"I heard the titters."

"*I had to kill him to get him off the stage when he still had twenty lines to speak!* You can't have laughter in a tragedy, Mr. Henslowe. It's like a ship skirting a waterfall; the slightest laugh and over it goes! He almost cost us the play!"

"We were short of players, Ned."

"We'll never be that short again. If you give another part to him, I will leave. I will not let him turn my tragical gifts into something the audience thinks is funny!"

Henslowe sighed. Alleyn stomped back into the theater.

Marlowe pushed himself off the wall and headed for the exit. Robin came up next to him.

"Mr. Marlowe," Robin said. "My lord seeks a minute with you at the Tabard."

"The Tabard? Ah, his lordship is married now and needs separate quarters away from his wife to see the women he now writes poetry to."

Robin was indignant. "You mistake him entirely."

"I do?"

"Entirely."

"Well, then, let's proceed. But why wasn't he here today?"

"He had other matters to attend to."

They headed east. The Tabard was on Canterbury Road, south of the Cathedral, a short walk from the Rose.

"You defend your master well," Marlowe said.

"'Tis easily done."

"Why is that?"

"Because, as he passes, the ground rises to kiss his feet."

"A pleasant conceit, but not something I would write."

"Not something you *could* write." Robin said doggedly.

"An interesting comment for one who appears to be but a page," Marlowe said, the velvet edge of his voice fading a bit. Robin did not reply. They walked along in silence for a minute. Marlowe kept rolling the phrase around in his mind. "Is it Greene's?"

"No."

"He thinks he wrote everything he hears."

"He is a drunk in the last stages of his disease."

"So you are physician as well as critic?"

"I don't need to be a physician to know that John Greene drinks too much. His drinking is only exceeded by his ego. His problem grows worse because he realizes he will not be remembered well. He told himself he was outdoing Lyly and Kyd but then you came along, and now he has to contend with Shackspear. He can't compete with either of you, so he tells himself that the lines he hears must have been written by him." Robin looked at Marlowe. "You would know all this if you didn't spend so much time on the continent, Mr. Marlowe."

"It seems I have been missing a lot."

They turned into Canterbury Street.

"I don't recall 'the ground rises to kiss his feet' in any of his lordship's plays. It must be from a new work he is writing."

"It is not."

"Well, then," Marlowe said, "How came you by these words?"

"I wrote them."

"You?" Marlowe looked at the young page striding alongside him. "So you are a poet, uh …"

"Robin."

"Robin."

"But I am no poet."

"Then what *do* you write, Robin?"

"Plays, Mr. Marlowe."

"The plays Shackspear claims *he* wrote?"

"God's love, no."

"How can we be sure?" Marlowe said, smiling mischievously. "You heard the woman back at the theater. She may be on to something. Maybe *you* are the author."

"Really, Mr. Marlowe. Do you think a boy without education could write plays about Verona, or about the War of the Roses? Do you know how many sexual puns there are in *All's Well?* I don't even know what sex is yet."

"What a pity," Marlowe said, eyeing Robin.

A passerby stopped in front of them. "Mr. Marlowe," the man said. He was in his late twenties. A brown Italian cape hung off his shoulder. He doffed his cap. "I'm a bit of a player myself, I am, and can bombast out a line as good as the next:

> *I walk abroad a-nights*
> *And kill sick people groaning under walls.*

"Excellent!" Marlowe said, interrupting him. He put a hand on the man's shoulder. "Mr. Henslowe is just now at the Rose. He is seeking new actors. Present yourself to him. He may well take you in."

"Thank you, Mr. Marlowe." The man bowed.

"But do not mention my name. He loves my plays, but not me."

The man nodded and headed off toward the Rose.

"He can act?" Robin asked, as they resumed their way.

"Of course not. I get rid of my adoring public by wishing them well and sending them off on some kind of errand, as I did just now."

"I think it 'twas acting he adored, Mr. Marlowe, not you."

Marlowe looked at him again. "There seems to be more to you than meets the eye. We shall have further conversation."

When they arrived at the Tabard, Robin ran up the steps to the porch, which was filled with afternoon drinkers watching the parade of merchants, pilgrims, and townspeople streaming by. Marlowe followed him into the Inn.

## ~ 71 ~
## The Tabard Inn

Robin took Marlowe to a booth deep in the Tabard where an older woman was seated. A sputtering candle shed little light but Marlowe was able to make out that he was looking at the woman who had just finished berating Shackspear at the Rose.

"Mr. Marlowe," the woman said, in a high-pitched voice.

"Madame," Marlowe said. He bowed and turned to leave.

"Oh, sit down," the woman ordered him in a deeper voice. "Yes, it's me." Oxford pulled off the wig. "In this guise I am *Mrs. Frummage!*"

Marlowe's jaw dropped. "Whatever for?" he asked, thoroughly confused. He tried see Oxford behind the dress and apron.

"How else can I go to my plays? Or yours, for that matter?" Marlowe had been struck dumb. "You've never dressed up as a woman?" Oxford asked. Marlowe shook his head. "It'll make you a better playwright. We have boys playing women. How about a *man* playing a woman? Or a *boy* playing a *woman* playing a *man*? Yes." He stopped to think about this. "No matter." He waved Marlowe toward the bench opposite him. Marlowe sat down. "You have been away," Oxford said. "We should have renewed our acquaintance sooner."

"I've been on the continent. I would still be there if Burghley hadn't ordered me home. He heard I was making money!" He laughed, a short bark of a laugh. Oxford couldn't remember hearing Marlowe laugh before. "I was counterfeiting Spanish coins."

"Burghley should have approved of that."

"He did. But he got worried that if I got good at making Spanish coins, I'd start counterfeiting English ones."

"Would you?"

A sly smile crossed Marlowe's face. "Of course. Just imagine!"

"I'm afraid I can't," Oxford said dryly. Money was a subject that rarely crossed his mind. "Last time we met you said you had no time for art. Has that changed?"

401

"Yes. *Arden of Faversham* is finished. 'Tis not fit for my name, of course, and will go into the books as 'by anonymous,' but it will put chinks in my pocket."

"And after *Arden?*"

"*The Massacre at Paris*. Walsingham was there when it happened. He told me what he saw and showed me reports sent back by others."

"A bloody tale. My brother-in-law, Lord Willoughby, led the English troops that put Henri on the throne. I will give you a letter of introduction to him. He likewise can tell you a great deal about what happened." Oxford grabbed a sheet of paper and began to write.

Marlowe was surprised. For Oxford to drink ale with him and talk about plays was one thing; to write an introduction to Lord Willoughby was quite another. "Thank you, my lord."

"Peregrine and I are very close. He will see you. But what about *Edward II?* Have you finished it?"

"No." Marlowe's face clouded over. "I doubt I will. I saw the first part of *Henry VI* and put down my pen. How could I write something to rival that? I heard a second part was expected, and there might be a third. I decided you were going to run the table on English kings. If you did, I would be wasting my time on *Edward*."

It was Oxford's turn to be surprised. "But your *Faust* almost made *me* put down my pen! How could I come up with anything to follow that? *Comedy of Errors? Two Gentlemen? Much Ado About Nothing?*"

"*Much Ado About Nothing?*"

"Oh, right. You haven't seen that yet. But they're *all* much ado about nothing. You yourself said so—and you were right."

"What I said is no longer true. The opening scene of *Henry VI* could have been slipped into *Tamburlaine*:

> *Hung be the heavens with black, yield day to night!*
> *Comets, importing change of times and states,*
> *Brandish your crystal tresses in the sky,*
> *And with them scourge the bad revolting stars*
> *That have consented unto Henry's death!*

"Did I offend?"

"I took it as a compliment."

"Which was my intent. But I labor in the shadow of your *Faust*, as well as your *Jew*. When I write, I find myself asking, 'What would

Marlowe do with this?' and write and rewrite again." Oxford saw that Marlowe did not believe him. "We are poets, you and I. We will be measured by the words we write and nothing else. In this regard, we are brothers."

"And enemies at the same time."

"*My enemy who makes me better is my friend*"

"Who wrote that?"

"I did."

"And this is why you got me out of Newgate?"

"Of course. If you had died in there, I would have become fat and lazy. With you alive, I live in fear that you will produce something that will so o'ertake my work that the scholars who come after us will say that only one poet lived while Elizabeth reigned, and his name was 'Christopher Marlowe.' You produce masterpieces, which I have not been able to equal yet, but I intend to best you, Mr. Marlowe. As for *Edward II*, he is yours. I am done with English kings."

"My lord, the stage will suffer. Only a wolfish earl can bring our English history to life."

"That's very kind of you, but no." Oxford picked up his mug and held it out to Marlowe. "To the death!"

"To the death!" Marlowe replied, not quite sure what he was agreeing to.

"And as brothers, I think we should call each other by our first names."

Marlowe, surprised yet again, responded sheepishly. "I prefer 'Kit.'"

"Then I will call you 'Kit.'"

"But what do I call you, my lord? 'Edward' is too formal. Did you have a nickname when you were young, or are lords not allowed them?"

"I was 'Ned' until I was twelve. When my father died, I became 'Edward.' I have never again been called 'Ned.'"

"'Ned,'" Marlowe said, a slight smile on his face. "And, as friend or enemy, Ned, how do I put fear in your heart so that you become a better poet?"

"By telling me about *Edward II*. Where do you open it?"

"With the recall of Gaveston."

"Edward's lover, if I remember aright."

Marlowe nodded.

Oxford noticed that Marlowe was looking at something behind him. He turned and saw Robin sitting on a stool eating a meat pie. Oxford turned back to Marlowe. "He will not return your affections, Kit. His beauty has attracted other admirers, but he has shown no interest in their offers. I daresay he will treat you the same."

"He already has."

"He eschews men *and* women. There are men like him, you know."

"And they are wise ones, too."

"Indeed. As to *Edward II*, I offer my help. At the moment, I am embarked on a light comedy for the Queen. We could work together on both, if you wish."

Marlowe shook his head. "And make another *Sir Thomas More*? Four playwrights had a hand in that play. Dogs with ink on their paws could have written a better one."

"No, then."

He shook his head again. "You shall have to fear me from the playhouse, Ned, not from over my shoulder."

"Well, then, Kit, to our mutual success." The two men toasted each other again.

## ~ 72 ~
## "The Heat of a Luxurious Bed"

Early morning light was streaming into the bedroom. Lady Elspeth had flung open the curtains on the balcony that looked out over the garden. "My lord, arise! Come see the seed beds I have dug. They will grow flowers that will fill the hall with color!"

Oxford toddled over to the balcony and looked down at the ground below. Elspeth wrapped her arm around his waist. "Lovely," he managed to mutter. He disengaged himself and, grabbing a robe, headed down the stairs. "Awake, young page, awake!" he called out.

Robin popped out from under the stairs and looked up, still sleepy.

"Helios has driven his Chariot beyond London and spread his rosy fingers into the alley that separates Oxford Court from St. Swithins. My bed has been flooded with glorious light and sent my lovely bride into the garden to dig holes in the ground and plant seeds to grow flowers." He took Robin by the shoulder and steered him down the hall toward the library.

"How nice," Robin said, not knowing what else to say.

"No, not nice. My warm bed was suddenly empty, the sheets flung back as if I had been tossed into a springhouse. I have lost my bedmate to a patch of dirt."

"Oh," Robin said.

"But, at the same time, good." Robin was now thoroughly confused. "Good, because if she had lingered in bed, I would've lost the scene I had been dreaming about when she threw the covers off."

Robin went to the table and picked up his pen. He pulled a clean sheet in front of him. Oxford walked over to the window and opened it further.

"Don John tells Claudio that his betrothed, Hero, has been seeing a man in her bedroom. *'Go but with me to-night,'* he says to Claudio, and *'you shall see her chamber-window entered, even the night before her wedding-day!'*"

"But let me guess," Robin said as he wrote this down. "The woman Claudio will see at Hero's window will not be Hero."

"Aye, but Claudio will *think* it is Hero, and conclude that she is not a virgin because of what he *thinks* he has seen."

"Deception," Robin said. Oxford grunted. "And he will imagine that she has enjoyed *the heat of a luxurious bed*, like the one you just left." He started, surprised at what he heard himself say.

Oxford turned from the window. He walked around the table and stopped next to Robin, who cringed. Oxford stood over him Oxford saw the boy's fear in the way he crouched, waiting to be struck. "You have been beaten, haven't you?"

"Yes, my lord."

Oxford studied the boy for a moment and then walked back to the open window. "I know lords who would have your knees cracked for such impertinence," he said, "but I will not beat you."

"Thank you, my lord."

"The last thing I heard you say, young man, was that you didn't know anything about beds, luxurious or otherwise."

"Yes, my lord."

"Has Falstaff been corrupting you?"

"No, my lord."

"Perhaps we have worked together too long."

"Oh, no, my lord. Beat me, if you think it would do me good, deny me food, do anything, but do not ostracize me."

"Ostracize you? How comes it that you know that word?"

"From reading Xenophon, my lord. I search for new words because I know so few. I have no education. I fear your displeasure at my lack thereof. There are many with university degrees who would love to take my place and write down what you dictate. I live in fear that you will fall in love with another John Marston and I will awaken to be told by Nigel it was time to go. I listen to the house every morning before I open my eyes. Do I hear footsteps I don't recognize? Do I hear the voice of a new page come to take my place? Will I be gone by day's end and sleep that night in a ditch?"

Oxford walked over to where Robin sat ramrod straight, eyes focused on the bookcase on the opposite wall. A single tear had formed in the corner of his eye. "Should I leave?" he asked in a voice that trembled.

"Shush," Oxford said. He put his hand on Robin's shoulder. "We have a play to write, young man. Your place was taken by John Marston because you decided to see the world."

Robin collapsed in his chair. Fighting back tears, he picked up his pen and, looking hard at the table in front of him, waited.

"But if you would gobble up words like pigeons pecking up peas, you need to know their proper meaning. 'Ostracize' is the word for the process by which the Athenians banished men they considered too dangerous to their liberties. You are not dangerous. You are merely impertinent. Impertinent servants, in ancient Greece as well as in present-day London, are simply dismissed. Something which will not be done *today*." Oxford walked away a few steps. He put his hands behind him. "Back to *Much Ado About Nothing*."

Robin took a deep breath. He put the tip of his pen down on the paper.

"Claudio will confront Hero with what he believes has happened. Hero will drop into a swoon."

Robin started to say something but caught himself. Oxford was still standing a short distance away with his hands behind his back. "Yes?"

"With all due respect, my lord, her undoing is too great a moment to be discarded lightly."

"And you suggest—"

"That Claudio withhold his accusation until the wedding ceremony."

Oxford frowned. "No man would stay for the ceremony if he thought his bride had cheated on him."

"In real life, yes, but this is theater. The audience will know that Claudio is going to accuse Hero. The longer he stays silent, the more the tension will build. It will be like a bomb with a burning fuse."

Oxford nodded. He liked this. "So when would you have him accuse her?"

"When the priest asks him whether he will marry her."

"You will have him reject her at the altar?"

"Yes. In fact, I think I can carry it even further."

"How, my lord?"

"The priest will ask Claudio: '*You come hither, my lord, to marry this lady?*' and Claudio will reply '*no.*'"

"That's short and to the point."

"I can't think of any way to say it more succinctly."

"I'll say."

"But the others will not understand. Hero's father will say: '*To be married to her. You come to marry her.*' The priest will turn to Hero and say: '*Lady, you come hither to be married to this count,*' to which she will say, '*I do.*' The priest will then ask Claudio and Hero if they know of any reason why they should not be married: '*If either of you know any inward impediment why you should not be conjoined, charge you, on your souls, to utter it.*'"

"And this is where Claudio will announce that Hero is a drab!" Robin said excitedly.

"No. Claudio will turn the question back on Hero: "*Know you any, Hero?*""

"Lovely," Robin said. He wrote down Claudio's question. "I can hear him hanging over her as he leers at her. 'Know you any, HEER-OH?'"

"More deception?"

"Indeed, my lord. But who is this Claudio? You claim to be Benedict, and Beatrice is Anne Vavasor, but who are these two?"

"Claudio is Sidney; Hero is Nan."

"But they are both dead."

"Not if I put them in a play. When I start a play, each character is newborn. As I write, the character grows. I find the character has a history, has likes and dislikes, mannerisms that endear the character to people or make them shun him. I see Sidney when I write Claudio. Burghley wanted Nan to marry Sidney before he discovered Sidney was penniless. I became a better candidate for his daughter's hand."

"So you two competed for the same woman." Robin said, wonderingly. He obviously thought it must have been good fun.

"What do you think the tennis match quarrel was all about?"

"Oh."

"I was long married to Nan at the time, but he never got over losing her to me. He was vain and naïve and, therefore, a good model for Claudio, who will be easily gulled in *Much Ado*."

"So how does Hero answer Claudio's question?"

"'*None, my lord*,' she will say. The priest will turn back to Claudio: '*Know you any, Count?*'"

"And Claudio will tell everyone Hero is not what everyone thinks she is."

"No, not yet. We still have Hero's father, who is standing by watching all this."

"Lord Burghley!" Robin interjected.

"Very good. He is, of course, ever interrupting, ever thinking he knows everything. He says: '*I dare make his answer, none.*'"

"What does Claudio say to this?"

"'*O, what men dare do! What men may do! What men daily do, not knowing what they do!*'"

Robin was catching all this on paper. "Shouldn't he reject Hero now and be done with it?"

"Why stop when we're having so much fun?" Oxford asked. "I will have Benedict, as confused as everyone else, stick in his two pence: '*How now! interjections? Why, then, some be of laughing, as, ah, ha, ha!*'"

"Good, good," Robin said, writing swiftly.

"And to delay the ending even more, Claudio will say: '*Stand thee by, friar*,' and turn to Hero's father: '*Will you with free and unconstrained soul give me this maid, your daughter?*' The father will answer: '*As freely, son, as God did give her me.*'"

"And then?"

"Claudio will give her back:

> There, Leonato, take her back again:
> Give not this rotten orange to your friend;
> She's but the sign and semblance of her honour.
> She knows the heat of a luxurious bed;
> Her blush is guiltiness, not modesty.

Robin's pen raced across the page. "'*The heat of a luxurious bed*,'" he said. "How sad is this? Claudio cannot marry the woman he loves, and he is rejecting her because he's been tricked!"

"I will have Benedict lighten the mood," Oxford said. "He will say: *This looks not like a nuptial.*"

"Well, it is a comedy, isn't it?'

"Unless it's deceiving on that as well!"

"Oh, my lord," Robin said. They looked at each other, grinning.

"Have you got it down?" Oxford asked.

"Yes. What happens next?"

"Hero will faint, and everyone will think she is dead."

"My lord!"

"And when Claudio finds out that she is innocent, he will cry out that he killed her with shame."

"But she is alive."

"She is."

"So how does this end, my lord?" He looked perplexed

"I will bring Hero back to marry Claudio but she will be disguised so that Claudio will not know he is marrying her until after the ceremony is over!"

"Oh, my lord! More deception!"

"Of course."

## ~ 73 ~
## Ditchley House

The Queen had visited Ditchley House on one of her earlier progresses but had not returned since its owner, Sir Henry Lee, had begun living openly there with Anne Vavasor. The clucking hens at court were doubly affronted by Sir Henry's behavior. He was married and his wife was still living, although she had removed herself to a manor house on one of Sir Henry's other estates and made no complaint about Anne, which, within the tattered remains of what stood for acceptable behavior in Elizabeth's reign, might have allowed the situation to be quietly accepted if Anne had not also been married as well. This was "double adultery," some wit had commented at court. The old biddies treated events like this as so much corn thrown into a farmyard, which they felt obliged to peck up and digest, cackling to each other about the decline of civilized life and the punishment that would surely come.

And so the Queen's decision to pay Sir Henry a visit sent the court into a tizzy, which she liked very much. She also liked Sir Henry. She had given him her scarf to wear in the 1581 tournament. The Queen's interest in forgiving Sir Henry may have been encouraged by her memory of the time she had spent in the east wing at Ditchley enjoying the view of the afternoon sun setting over of a pond in the distance. And so it was that at the conclusion of *Henry IV* she had told Sir Henry how much she liked her earlier visit, knowing full well that he would immediately ask her to come to Oxfordshire again, which he did. She said she would come in May.

It was January when she told Sir Henry how much she liked her last visit to Ditchley. Perhaps the leaden English sky had burnished her memory of the prior visit, but the prospect of viewing the afternoon sun at Ditchley helped her get through the rest of the winter. She also took quiet pleasure in watching people try to fathom why she would reward Sir Henry's outrageous behavior. But, aside from the fun of surprising and upsetting everyone, she would have done the same thing if she had not been Queen and had fallen in love with a married man. As a result, the impending visit took on the aura of an adventure into the forbidden, and not only for the Queen.

Sir Henry was both thrilled and terrified. He had months to make Ditchley sparkle, but he knew a lifetime would not be enough. He would have to find something to satisfy the Queen's love of gifts while, at the same time, expressing his gratitude for the forgiveness she would bring to Ditchley. Anne suggested a new portrait. Sir Henry commissioned Marcus Gheerhaerts the Younger to paint a larger-than-life full-length portrait of Elizabeth—making sure she would appear younger than she was—which the Dutchman, to Sir Henry's immense relief, finished on time. The painting was installed in the Great Hall the week before the Queen's scheduled visit.

The day everyone had been waiting for finally arrived. Carriages and wagons wended their way across the countryside bringing members of Her Majesty's court, visiting dignitaries, poets, painters, players, and their baggage and servants. Arriving last, the Queen cantered up the drive on a red stallion she had mounted a mile earlier to show everyone that a horseman still ruled England. Sir Henry's guests, including Oxford and Lady Elspeth, waited under the portico. Elizabeth dismounted into Sir Henry's arms, who gently lowered her to the ground. He immediately bent his knee. "Get up, Sir Henry. I would rather have you upright and able to walk than bent over and unable to be the host I expect you to be."

She walked past him into the foyer and immediately saw the portrait. She stopped in front of it. The portrait showed her standing on a map of England. Sir Henry waited expectantly.

"So much better than gloves or perfume," she finally said, gazing upward at the painting that towered over her. "Gloves last fewer than two or three wearings, perfume scarce more." The remark was intended to needle Oxford for the gloves he had brought her from Italy and the perfume he had given her more recently. "I will hang it in the great hall at Hampton Court."

More gifts and a lavish banquet followed, after which a very pleased Queen led Sir Henry, Anne Vavasor, the Earl of Oxford, Lady Elspeth, and scores of other nobles out into the warm sunshine behind the house where the rear yard sloped dramatically, creating a natural outdoor theater. The lawn at the bottom of the slope ran to a pond in the distance. Half a dozen chairs had been placed in the middle for the Queen and the most senior guests. Blankets and cushions had been laid out down the slope and across the bottom of the hill for the rest of the guests to sit on.

The Queen sat down on the middle chair and asked Anne to take a chair to her right; Elspeth was told to sit on her left. "Just like old times," she said, leaning back in her chair and patting their hands. Oxford sat next to Elspeth while Sir Henry took the chair next to Anne.

James Burbage came up to the Queen and bowed. "Your Majesty."

"Mr. Burbage. What is the play?"

"A romantic comedy set in Italy in which two couples are frustrated in their pursuit of marriage, one by outside interference, the other by internal bickering."

"You give away too much. Who are the players?"

"Lord Strange's Men."

"And where is Lord Strange?"

"In the library playing billiards with his brother."

She harrumphed. "At least they came. Lord Burghley begged off *again*. His gout grows worse the farther I go from London. And Sir Robert is detained on business." She looked around. "Perhaps he likes not the playwright. Which reminds me," she said, turning her attention back to Burbage, still standing in front of her. "I thought Shackspear was giving his plays only to Henslowe. How did you get the performance of this one?"

"I understand Mr. Alleyn said something to Mr. Shackspear after a performance of *Henry VI* that led Mr. Shackspear to believe his plays would be in better hands if they were acted by Lord Strange's Men at the Theater instead of by Mr. Henslowe's at the Rose."

"And where is Mr. Shackspear? Is he not here?"

"I'm afraid he is not."

Oxford leaned forward. "He sends his regrets, Your Majesty. He is an artist, you know, and very anxious when a new work is unveiled. He asks that you forgive him for not being here."

"More forgiveness? I forgive Sir Henry and everyone thinks I will forgive anything?" She said this loud enough to make sure everyone understood she would brook no further requests for 'forgiveness.' "Should I forgive you," she asked Oxford, "for telling me that Shackspear asks for forgiveness?"

"Perhaps he was worried you might order him to visit his wife and children, who are less than a day's ride from here in Stratford."

"And he would not want to do that?"

"He prefers London, Your Majesty."

She knew it was far more likely that Shackspear had been ordered to stay away, and probably by Oxford. She turned back to Burbage. "And who will play the clown?"

"Will Kemp waits to entertain you."

"A good choice. And the name of the character he will play?"

"Dogberry, Your Majesty."

"Dogberry," she said, trying unsuccessfully to suppress a smile. "With a name like that, how can he not be funny? Let us have the play."

Benedict and Beatrice were soon sparring in front of the Queen and Sir Henry's guests. "*I wonder that you will still be talking, Signor Benedict: nobody marks you. / What, my dear Lady Disdain! are you yet living?*" and so forth, which quickly set the audience to laughing.

The play went by quickly, but one scene jumped out at Anne Vavasor. Don Pedro, the king of Spain, told Beatrice she had lost the heart of Signor Benedict. Beatrice agreed:

> *Indeed, my lord, he lent it me awhile; and I gave*
> *him use for it, a double heart for his single one:*
> *marry, once before he won it of me with false dice,*
> *therefore your grace may well say I have lost it.*

Anne blinked. Oxford had twice gotten her pregnant. Everyone knew of the second pregnancy, which ended with the birth of their son in a room next to the Queen's bedchamber. No one knew of the first pregnancy, which ended in a miscarriage at three months. No one, that is, except Oxford. The hairs on the back of her neck stood up. Was she Beatrice? If so, Benedict must be Oxford! But Shackspear had written the play, she reminded herself. How could Shackspear know anything about her relationship with Oxford? She forced herself to calm down. The pressure of preparing Ditchley for the Queen *and* having to deal with the man she had once loved was beginning to affect her judgment. She straightened herself in her chair and concentrated on listening to the play.

Her consort, Sir Henry, saw connections of a different sort. When Don John appeared, Sir Henry sat bolt upright. "Don John!" he called out. "The Butcher of the Netherlands! If not for him, we would still have Sidney!"

The audience cried out an agreement, whether in ignorance, like Sir Henry, or out of courtesy to their host was impossible to tell. Don John had died long before Sidney had died at Zutphen. The Queen knew this. She smiled. She would not spoil Sir Henry's party by correcting him in front of his guests. She looked at him, her loyal spaniel, and smiled. He was ecstatic. She glanced at Oxford while she selected a cool drink from a servant standing behind her. She knew the mention of Sidney would irritate the Earl.

Sir Henry's remark was quickly forgotten. The audience became transfixed as Claudio was maneuvered into believing Hero had given up her chastity the night before her wedding. They squirmed when Claudio falsely accused Hero of cheating on him. Some cried out 'she's innocent!' When Claudio gave Hero back to her father, Hero fainted dead away. The audience, desperate for comfort, listened enraptured while Hero's father and the priest concocted a plan in which they would claim that Hero had died of slander and thereby trick Claudio into marrying a woman who would turn out to be Hero in disguise.

If the audience loved being told they would witness another wedding where Claudio would be tricked *again*, they loved Will Kemp as Dogberry even more. When Kemp reported to Don Pedro what he had learned from interrogating Don John's henchmen, there were many who knew they were listening to the Earl of Arundel, for the Earl's inability to keep his threes and twos in proper order had become the fable of the court.

At end of the play, Benedict told Beatrice: "Peace! I will stop your mouth with a kiss!" and the audience broke into applause as he took Beatrice into his arms. With these words, Anne knew then that Oxford had written the play. He had said the same thing to her one night when she had been rattling on about something, and the kiss had swept her away.

To her surprise, she realized she was warmed by the memory of their time together. She glanced past the Queen at Oxford, who was watching her out of the corner of his eye. A faint smile crossed his face. Anne smiled back. It was as if he had reached across and squeezed her hand. The play was a gift to her. Her smile told him she accepted it.

The sun was now dropping below the tree line. The Queen had not missed the connections between Benedict and Oxford, as well as those between Beatrice and Anne, and she very much liked Dogberry as the Earl of Arundel. She turned to Burbage, who had been standing behind her. "But no marriage, Mr. Burbage?"

"Your Majesty?"

"A comedy ends in marriage, does it not?" She turned to Oxford. "Aren't I right, my lord?"

"They have agreed to marry, Your Majesty."

"But promises do not equal ceremony, do they not?"

Oxford was surprised at this. Could she be alluding to the promises they had exchanged when they were close? But she was not bringing up memories of their past together. There was no warmth in her question. She was, in fact, irritated. She had caught the glances between Oxford and Anne and was angry that they would do it in public across her face.

The other guests spread across the hillside sensed something had gone wrong. The chattering among them died away as they realized the Queen was on the verge of one of her outbursts, which always occurred suddenly and for reasons no one could foresee beforehand.

Oxford leaned forward. "I will speak with the author, Your Majesty, and advise him to correct this deficiency. Beatrice and Benedict should get married, don't you think?"

His attempt to trick her into saying something about marriage only increased her irritation. She rose and announced that there had been too many jokes about cuckoldry and that she was retiring to her rooms, but not for that purpose, of course. This elicited some light laughter. Sir Henry announced that music and dancing would be held in the great hall. The Queen wended her way up the slope to her rooms while everyone else, following at a discreet distance, veered off to the house.

The music and dancing went on into the night. The kitchen supplied trays full of kickshaws and the wine flowed like water. It was reported that Lord Strange had won the billiards game by extending himself across the table, but had been unable to get back up to celebrate his victory. He was now sleeping soundly on top of the table while William, his brother, was lying under the table in a raft of dogs that had decided to use him as pillow and bolster for an evening nap.

Oxford gestured for Anne to follow him out onto one of the patios that overlooked the rear lawn. "Forgive me, if you can," he said, "but I could not resist the urge to put our badinage into a play. Scenes like that have been appearing in my head for years. If I didn't write them down, I would have lost them to the sickle of time. It is a billet-doux intended only for you. No one else will know you were my Beatrice."

"Then was our relationship all about 'nothing?'" asked Anne. "We spoke words of love to each other, and I have given you Edward. Were these gifts nothing?" Then she immediately caught herself. "Forgive me. I have no right to ask that of you, now that you have found a wife."

"And you have found love."

"And you have not?" She looked away. "Another unfair question. Sir Henry is not the poet you are, and he does not light up my life the way you did with your words and outrageous behavior, but I have found that there are different ways to love someone, and to be loved. I am very content."

"Then I am happy for you."

She could tell he meant it. "And should I be happy for you?"

"Yes. Elspeth loves me for many reasons; I love her in return for different reasons. The mystery is that, although few seem to overlap, we seem to grow fonder every day."

"Then I am happy for you."

"And I gain peace, for I worried you despaired that I married Elspeth instead of you."

"Not at all. You are a leaf, my lord, long gone down the stream." This surprised Oxford. He had never thought of himself as a 'leaf,' nor been told that he could be forgotten so easily. Anne read his mind. "Do not look amazed, my lord. *'Winter brings on cold weather; and we must shiver. Summer returns, with its heat. We must let be, and not seek to change those things we cannot change.'*"

"You quote me Seneca?"

"You always told me to be ready, whatever may come." She dropped her voice in an attempt to imitate him. *"We have only today; tomorrow, when it comes, will be different from what we thought it would be.* I can thank you for that. You taught me how to accept fate."

Part of him was happy she was happy; another part was disappointed to hear she was not pining for him. To his surprise, he heard himself ask after their son. "How is Edward? Is he here?"

A smile spread across her face. "He is doing well, my lord, but he is not here. Not knowing what might happen with you and the Queen, I decided he was better off if he were somewhere else today. He is in London, happily polishing armor in the Tower, a job Sir Henry has assigned him."

"He must be twelve now."

"Yes. And as tall as you are now." She did not need to add that Oxford would be proud of him. "We should go in."

"Yes."

They walked back into the house. A small orchestra was playing at one end of the hall; the Forgiveness Portrait loomed over the other end, but was apparently having no effect on the guests. A man and woman who had been drinking wine with Lord Strange in the billiards room had slipped down behind a sofa and were engaged in fumbling attempts to touch each other in ways that most, but not all, of the house guests found off-putting. A three-some hung giggling over the sofa watching the couple on the floor behind them. Those who preferred food to sex, at least when they were not one of the participants, drifted into the banqueting room. Elspeth drifted into the banqueting hall as well, where all the serious people had gravitated. Oxford looked into the room and saw there would be no fun to be had there. Taking a glass of wine from a servant, he went into the billiards room where the servants were attempting to get Lord Strange off the billiard table. "Ferdinando," Oxford said, calling the man by his given name in an attempt to rouse him.

The servants maneuvered Lord Strange to the edge of the table. He looked at Oxford, blinking his eyes in an attempt to reconnect himself with reality. "My lord," he mumbled. "How was the play?" He frowned. "Blast! I missed it, didn't I? I must try harder to see more plays. So much is expected of me." He said this with a note of tragedy. He raised his head dramatically and slipped through the servants' arms to fall into the dogs and his brother under the table.

"Leave him there," Oxford told the servants. "No one sleeps better than a drunk."

Lord Hunsdon came up. "I say, the entire Stanley family, heir to the throne if their mother dies before them, lying drunk under a billiard table."

"Fit to rule the realm," Oxford said.

"Huh? Oh, yes. I see. If Henry were alive, they'd be waking up in the pond out back!"

"Henry Tudor?" Oxford asked. "He's been dead forty years."

"Eh? Couldn't be that long." He returned his attention to the two Stanleys lying under the table. "They need a good war," he said, "something to make them appreciate life. Nothing focuses the mind better than a screaming Welshman coming at you with a knife! The smell of blood after a battle," he mused. He turned on Oxford. "Not pig's blood, like they used in *Titus*. Doesn't smell the same."

"And where is your lovely friend, Aemilia Bassano?" Oxford asked, ignoring the comment about pig's blood.

"Pregnant. I have given her a pension and married her off."

Oxford was surprised. "Are you not the father?"

Hunsdon laughed. "To steal a line from the play we just heard, '*she hath many times told me so.*' But what can you do with a pregnant woman? Not much. I had the making of a child, but she is fading, as all flowers do that are plucked too early. Let someone else deal with the issue. I am off to fresher fields."

Oxford's face showed his reaction. Hunsdon saw it.

"Don't look so shocked, old man. You did the same with Anne Vavasor." The bluff old field general smiled broadly. Oxford had not made the comparison. "Snuck up on you on that one, eh what?

Oxford did not like Hunsdon's remark. He *had* discarded Anne Vavasor when she gave birth to a son, just as Hunsdon had discarded Aemilia Bassano. Unlike Hunsdon, though, Oxford, had not provided Anne with a pension or a husband. She had found those on her own. Oxford, for the first time, saw himself as he saw Hunsdon—arrogant, powerful men using people with little thought of how their actions affected others. Oxford wondered how he could have written, "*The labouring man that tills the fertile soil / He gets the straw, the lord will have the seed*, and be indifferent to a mother and her son. *His* son, a voice reminded him. He suddenly did not like himself. Gloom descended over him. Or was it the wine? He drained his glass and angled away to get another. He had to erase the vision of Hunsdon's gleeful face staring into his, an image that damned him as pompous and thoughtless.

A table along the wall was filled with glasses filled with wine. "Soldiers on parade," Oxford said as he picked one up and drained it.

He put the glass back down and aligned it with the others. "Soldier, you're out of uniform," he said, waggling a finger at the glass. He picked up a full one and drained it. He put it down next to the first empty glass. "This won't do," he said.

"*What* won't do?" a voice said behind him.

Oxford turned and saw a tall, attractive woman in her early 50s. Her thick lustrous dark-red hair contrasted with the creamy skin of her bare shoulders. Dark brown lines had been drawn over her eyes to give her the eyebrows she no longer had. "Lettice," he said, bowing slightly. "My regrets on the passing of your husband. He was mourned by all."

"Like Hell!" the woman said in a deep voice that someone said had never been spoken in daylight. Lettice was a terror at court. 'Lettice prey,' someone had cracked once after observing Lettice disembowel a new lady-in-waiting who had made a mistake. She was the granddaughter of Mary Boleyn. She had first married the Earl of Essex and, after his death, the Earl of Leicester, both famous marriages that made her rich. She was a constant presence at elegant parties, pacing through the guests like a lioness amongst timid fawns. She terrified men, drawing them to her with her wide smile and then frightening them when they realized she was fully capable of pulling them into an adjoining room and ravaging them in ways they'd never imagined. Women feared her as well. She added to her attractiveness with necklaces made from silver coins taken off drowned Spanish sailors that she draped across her front in a web of knots and splinters taken from sunken ships. The splinters had been dipped in silver. She looked like she was stepping through a waterfall.

"No one mourned the Earl of Leicester, my lord, *not even his widow*," she said. It was obvious that she had also been sampling the wine. "You should be congratulating me on my marriage to Sir Christopher Blount."

"Which, I am told, should be a charm, being the third."

"I hope so. My first husband was *always* home but didn't love me. My second husband, 'the Earl,' as he insisted on being addressed, said he loved me but was *never* home. Why? Because he was always chasing after the Queen! She urged him on, of course, and resented me *because I was his wife!* How humiliating! I was told I was not to come to court!"

"She did the same thing to Nan."

"Oh, yes. I remember." She wobbled a bit. Realizing she was a little unsteady, she made an effort to straighten herself.

Oxford was trying to do the same, which she was not too drunk to notice. She held up her glass. "Good, eh?"

"Marvelous," Oxford said.

She looked past him at the table filled with glasses. "What were you doing just now?"

"Some are full and some are empty," Oxford announced, speaking slowly and with great deliberation. "Those that are full are out of uniform."

"Yes."

He lowered his voice. "Some can live with disorder and some cannot. Which side are you on?"

"The side of order. The full glasses need to be emptied."

"Yes." He took her glass and put it back on the table. He gave her a full one and picked one up for himself. He clinked it with hers. "To order," he said.

"To order and more wine," she sniggered, tossing back the glass. She handed it to Oxford and squinted at the table. "There are some still out of uniform."

"Yes." Oxford picked up two more glasses. They downed them both.

Lord Strange suddenly appeared. Oxford looked at him. "What said the dogs?" Oxford asked, which only confused Strange. Lettice started to laugh, confusing Strange even more. "The dogs under the billiard table," Oxford explained.

"What dogs? I don't remember any dogs."

Oxford handed him a glass of wine. "Help us drink this." Oxford waved a hand at the glasses on the table. "They are out of uniform."

Lettice giggled. "Some are full, and some are empty. Some can live with such disorder and some cannot. Which side are you on?"

Lord Strange screwed up his face. Even sober, he was not good at games. "Disorder," he said.

"No, no," Oxford and Lettice said together.

"I mean *order*!" he announced loudly.

"Bravo," Oxford said. Strange was relieved. "Drink up, my lord," Strange drained his glass and handed it back to Oxford, who gave him a new one.

People had begun gathering around. Someone explained what the game was and the others joined in. Full glasses began to disappear. The servants, under strict orders to keep the glasses full, scrambled to bring up more wine, and thus a frantic contest began between the servants and the guests in which the guests tried to drink the wine faster than the servants could bring up new bottles. The guests were on the verge of winning when the intake of alcohol began to affect them. Some began looking for chairs to sit on. Lettice announced that there were benches in the chapel that were upholstered with soft cushions. "I feel a need to commune with God," she announced, eliciting laughter. She toddled off. Those who could still stand followed her. Oxford decided to go too. Other guests, looking in from the great hall, saw the exodus and waved for others to follow.

The line of people wended its way and into the small chapel where Sir Henry's ancestors were buried. The ceiling was high but the room was not large. Stone sarcophagi crowded the room. Most had recumbent statues on top that were supposed to represent whoever was buried inside. Lettice leaned in over one of the sarcophagi. "Who have we here?" she asked, trying to read the writing on the tomb.

> *Good friend, for Jesus sake forbeare,*
> *To stir the dust encloaséd heare,*
> *The man is blessed who spares these stones,*
> *And cursed is he that moves these bones.*

"How bad is that, eh?" She put up her hand. "Hark, my friends, we shall all be dust someday, whether at the edge of a field or in a sculptured tomb like these. Think hard on what will be written after you are gone so that you are remembered well. Don't leave it to others, or you will be left with something like this." She pointed to the inscription she had just read.

"I don't see any for Sir Henry," someone said.

"That's because he hasn't died yet!" Everyone laughed.

"And when Anne dies, where will she be buried?" another asked. "She can't be buried here with him."

"Oh, don't be so quick to think that," Lettice said. "Word has it that he has left instructions for the sculptors to show him lying on top of his tomb with Anne at his feet." She leered at the people around her. "He'll need an elegy, though, won't he? Something to put on his tomb. How about if we suggest a few lines? Is anyone interested? 'Twill be a new game!"

"*Here lies old Sir Harry*," one started. "*He won the tourney and then went on a journey*," but couldn't think of a second line.

"My lord!" Lettice called to Oxford, standing along one of the walls. "What say you, my lord? Will you give it a try?"

"Yes, do," someone said. The others waited expectantly.

Oxford took a glass of wine from a man standing near him and gave him his, which was empty. Oxford looked up at the ceiling.

> *Here lies the good old knight Sir Harry,*
> *Who loved well but would not marry;*

This was greeted with murmurs of approval.

> *While he lived and had his feeling,*
> *She did lie and he was kneeling.*
> *Now he's dead and cannot feel,*
> *He doth lie and she doth kneel.*

The room burst into laughter. "Well done!" someone called out. Oxford started to bow, a big grin on his face, when he spied Elspeth and Anne Vavasor standing in the doorway. The others saw them at the same time. The chapel went silent. The guests, heads down, began moving toward the door. Elspeth and Anne stepped aside to let them leave. Lettice emptied the glass she was holding and set it down on top of one of the tombs. She followed the others out the door. Anne followed her, leaving Oxford with Elspeth, whose face showed how angry she was.

"Good thing Sir Henry is not here, my lord. He would have challenged you to a duel and the Queen would have been very upset. While you were in here doing your utmost to offend our host, Anne and I were in the garden having a very sensible conversation. You may be surprised to learn that she wishes us both well. You may also be surprised that she feels your son, Edward, needs you. And while I am trying to repair the wreckage you have left behind you, you are in here making more. It is not Anne's fault that she cannot marry the man she loves, *any more than it was your fault you could not marry the Queen!*"

This stung Oxford.

"The carriage waits in the driveway. I suggest you go outside while I go back in and give our regrets."

"We are not staying here?"

"I would feel uncomfortable if we did. I have a cousin in Neat Enstone, which is only a few miles from here. We can stay with her. She has a suite of rooms that was in ancient times used by the village parson."

"What if your cousin is not at home?"

"I took the precaution of making sure she would not be away in case we needed a place to stay."

"You expected I might do something untoward?"

"I thought it very possible, although, not being as creative as you are, I never imagined I would hear you reciting an impromptu poem that described our hostess kneeling between Sir Henry's legs. Really, Edward: you have outdone yourself."

She turned and left. Oxford found himself unable to move for a moment. The wine had gotten to him. He finally managed to walk to the carriage. His head was spinning. It had begun to rain. Tobias stood barefoot in the mud. He opened the door to the carriage and Oxford climbed in. Tobias held the door open and stood there, awaiting the Countess.

Elspeth soon appeared. Oxford slid over to let her climb in beside him. Tobias closed the door and swung himself up into the seat high up on the rear of the carriage. The coachman snapped his whip and the carriage began to move away from the house.

Elspeth put her hand on Oxford's, surprising him. "I apologized and made excuses which were accepted. Anne is very gracious. She will not tell Sir Henry what happened, nor will anyone else."

"I would not have been surprised if you had not come back," Oxford said quietly.

"You flatter yourself. We are married for better or worse." She looked out the window at the fields they were passing. Neither said anything for a moment. "Your elegy was very good, I must say, for something done on the spot."

"It was?"

"And very funny. Crude, but funny."

The carriage turned onto the main road while Oxford, still fuddled from the wine, tried to absorb Lady Elspeth's kindness.

"The manor house we are heading for has a large bed in the parson's bedroom," Elspeth said.

"Why would a parson need a large bed?"

"Foolish man. No more questions. We have been many days on the road to get here. I have missed you."

## ~ 74 ~
### *Edward II*

I t was June and the flowers were pushing up through the bare
ground when Oxford came out of the Office of Revels and saw
Christopher Marlowe going down the other side of the street.

"Greetings, Kit," Oxford called out.

"Good day … Ned," Marlowe replied. He had almost said 'your
lordship.' The two men laughed. "Visiting Mr. Tilney, are we?"

"Yes."

"Would that I could sit down with the Master of the Revels like
that. I would like to stay his hand. He shaves off too much."

"Does he? Judging from *Edward II*, he shaves very little."

"You have seen it?"

"Of course I have. Did you not look for me?"

"Of course not."

"I thought not."

They laughed again.

"And where to now, Kit?"

"To the Steelyard. I crave smoked ox tongue and only the Dutch
know how to do it right."

"And pickled herring."

"Aye."

"May I accompany you?"

"Certainly."

They turned into Thames Street.

"But you saw it twice, not oncet," Marlowe continued when they
had settled into a steady pace, side by side.

"You looked, then."

"Of course not."

"Then how do you know I came back?"

427

"Well, a glance then."

"But not a look."

"Of course not. But your second visit aroused my curiosity more than your first. Why would you return?"

"I thought I had remembered a line incorrectly."

"Did you?"

"No."

"Which line?"

"It's where Gaveston says he would *'draw the pliant king which way I please.'*

> *And in the day when he shall walk abroad,*
> *Like Sylvian Nymphes my pages shall be clad,*
> *My men like Satyres grazing on the lawnes,*
> *Shall with their Goat feet dance an antick hay.*

"And which line did you think you remembered incorrectly?"

"I thought I heard *'Like SYL-VEE-AN Nymphes my pages shall be clad,'* but on my way home, I worried Heminges might have said *'SYL-VAN Nymphes.'*"

"But the meter would have told you which was correct."

"Yes, but which word had Heminges actually spoken? Which word had 'Kit' written?"

"*'SYL-van,'*" Marlowe said. "Not *'SYL-VEE-AN.'* That word doesn't exist. Besides, it doesn't work metrically." He thought Oxford was accusing him of being a sloppy poet.

"I heard *'Syl-vi-an'* both times and thought it was intentional: three quick steps to prepare the listener for the ending of the line, *'shall-be-clad,'* which sounds like satyrs dancing across the lawns with their *'goat-feet.'* You and I have been known to invent a few words."

"Heminges has a lisp. He mangles lines. They all do, sometimes by mistake, sometimes on purpose." He sighed. "I fear Heminges is boying the part to make the audience laugh. I've heard some sniggers."

"No, he's not doing that. Burbage might, but not Heminges. It's interesting that your best art comes out when you write about a man's love of boys. Gaveston is Ganymede reborn. I half-expected you to bring Ganymede back, but he is, no doubt, being fondled in heaven and unavailable."

"Ganymede has more fans than you might think. They flocked to see him in *Dido*. Some aped his feathered hat; others mimiced the way the boy who played Ganymede minced around the stage."

"The real question, Kit, is how you got *Edward II* on the stage at all? Isn't it a play about a man's love of boys?"

"You mean, how did I get it past Tilney? 'Master No' rejected it, of course. He didn't even want to touch the pages."

"So how did you get him to approve it?"

"I went to Lord Hunsdon."

"Hunsdon?"

"He loved *Dido*. He came to every performance. He sat on the stage so he could be closer to the actor playing Ganymede. I told him that if he liked *Dido*, he'd love *Edward II*. Hunsdon went directly to Tilney. Soon thereafter, I received a message that the Office of the Revels had withdrawn its objection to the play."

Oxford shook his head. "Hunsdon cast an eye at Robin once but I thought he did it to rile me. He doesn't need boys—look at Aemilia Bassano!"

Marlowe guffawed. "He's fooled you and everyone else at court. Why do you think he wanted to be Lord Chamberlain? To be around sweet-voiced boys. He made Aemilia Bassano his mistress to squelch any questions about his 'manhood.' He never touched her."

This brought Oxford to a stop in the middle of the street. "How can you say that? She has a son by him. He has acknowledged the child as his."

"And thereby neatly blocked any claim that he was cuckolded," Marlowe said, smiling at Oxford's astonishment. "Think about it. He's three score and ten. Is he really the father of the child? Of any child? But, by acknowledging the boy as his, he puts a feather in his cap *instead of a coxcomb on his head!*"

Oxford thought back to when he was told that Nan had cuckolded him. He tried to imagine himself blithely claiming that Lisbeth was his child to stop any rumors that Nan had cheated on him, but he couldn't imagine himself being so clever. Strict rules of honor would have hemmed him in. Apparently the Hunsdons of the world had no such problems.

But if Hunsdon was not the father of Aemilia's child, who was? It suddenly dawned on Oxford that the father must be Marlowe! No wonder the man standing next to him was grinning from ear to ear.

"You," Oxford hissed. "*You're* the father! You get the use of the woman, and he gets to claim the child is his!"

Marlowe burst out laughing. "Only you could come up with that! I have *also* never touched Aemilia." Oxford did not believe him. "Truly, Ned. Have you ever seen me with a woman?"

"I don't care whether you like boys or women."

"As long as it's not Aemilia Bassano," Marlowe added.

"So, if you didn't father her child, who did?"

Marlowe shrugged. "She's had many lovers."

Oxford's head came up with a snap. "Shackspear!"

Marlowe laughed again. "Could be. But why care? It wasn't you or me. That should be the end of it."

Oxford had to agree, but the question addled him. He had wanted her so badly. Not knowing who managed to get into her bed was unfinished business. And the poems he had written! What about them? All wasted?

"So, Ned, do you think less of me now that I have confessed my love of boys?"

"It means nothing to me. Truly. In Italy, an older man who has a boy as his companion is a common sight. You could be Jupiter and dandle Ganymede as much as you want:

> *What is't, sweet wag, I should deny thy youth,*
> *Whose face reflects such pleasure to mine eyes,*
> *As I, exhaled with thy fire darting beams,*
> *Have oft driven back the horses of the night,*
> *Whenas they would have haled thee from my sight.*

"Think what those lines would bring in Venice, Kit. You could write plays there and send them back to England, avoiding Tilney *and* the Queen."

Marlowe did not agree. "I would be a fish out of water in Italy, Ned. You went there as a rich tourist; I would be a poor traveler, quickly sent to debtor's prison. What would I write about? Courtesans in gondolas? I know nothing about them."

They finally arrived at the Steelyard. A large, broad-faced man in his twenties was coming out of the inn. "Mr. Marlowe," he said, extending his hand.

Marlowe couldn't remember the man's name.

"Jonson," the man quickly said. "Ben Jonson."

"Oh, yes. Mr. Jonson. Let me introduce you to Ned Vere. Ned, Mr. Jonson is a budding playwright."

Oxford thought Marlowe incredibly cheeky to introduce him as Ned Vere. Marlowe knew it, and was enjoying the moment. He carefully avoided looking at Oxford.

"A pleasure," Jonson said. He looked at Oxford. "I've seen you somewhere, Mr. Vere. I went to the Merchant Taylor School."

"I live nearby," Oxford said. He found he liked being Ned Vere.

"And then to Cambridge for a few terms, Ned," Marlowe added, more interested in giving voice to Oxford's new name than relaying information about Jonson

Jonson's face became serious. He furrowed his thick eyebrows. "Cut short by lack of funds. But Cambridge teaches little of the world, and less of the classical arts that I crave to acquire."

"Oh?"

"Be careful, Ben. Mr. Vere also attended Cambridge."

"But only for a few months," Oxford quickly added.

"And were, no doubt, thereby spared corruption."

"Yes, thankfully."

"And what do you do for a trade, Mr. Vere? I am apprenticed to my stepfather as a bricklayer. My hands are in mortar at sunup but by afternoon they cradle a pen."

His speech was slightly slurred, making it clear that Mr. Jonson had spent the day emptying mugs of beer and not cradling a pen.

"We're for the Steelyard," Oxford said, pointing toward the door behind Jonson.

"Let me not stand in the way of progress, then," Jonson replied, stepping aside. Oxford and Marlowe walked into the Steelyard.

"*'And what do you do for a trade, Mr. Vere?'*" Oxford repeated.

"And your answer would have been?"

"I don't know."

The playwright Thomas Heywood came toward them, heading for the door. "My lord," he said to Oxford as he went by.

"Well," Oxford said, turning to Marlowe. "Ned Vere did not last very long, did he?"

Marlowe laughed. "Like a good play, it was good while it lasted." He raised his hand, as if he were blessing Oxford. "I give you permission to use the name I have bestowed upon you for whatever purpose you deem fit. Retire Mrs. Frummage. Buy yourself a large hat and baggy pants and go forth as 'Ned Vere,' common man."

Oxford thought about this. "'Twould be strange, wouldn't it, being common. What trade would I adopt?"

"Typesetter?"

"No. The sight of words on the page would be too much for me."

"Then what?"

Oxford couldn't come up with an answer. "What would I have been if I had not been born a Vere?" His mind was blank. "I am a wordsmith without words," he finally said.

"Now, *that* is a frightening prospect," Marlowe said. He put his arm around Oxford's shoulders. "You have sore need of a beer."

"Aye, but you'll have to pay for it, Kit."

"And the reason?"

"I'm a lord, and have no money."

They laughed good-naturedly as they disappeared into the darkness of the Steelyard.

## ~ 75 ~
## Rosencrantz and Guildenstern

We are to Lord Willoughby's," Oxford called up to Lady Elspeth, who was standing on the second floor balcony.

"Will you be back for supper?"

"Should I be?"

"You should."

"Then I shall return."

"And where is Falstaff? I have not seen him for some time now."

"Neither have I." Oxford looked at Robin.

"I heard he went to Seville."

"Can he do that?" Lady Elspeth asked. "Seville is in Spain. Aren't we at war with them?"

"I don't know, but if anyone can, Falstaff can. Good day, my lady. We shall see you at supper."

The two of them went out the door. Tobias met them in the street and pushed out into the throngs going by to make room for them. He was swinging the pomander out in front of him. It was early summer.

"Will Lord Hunsdon be attending?" Robin asked, as they headed toward St. Paul's. Oxford noticed he sounded worried.

"No. He has lost his young escort."

"Mistress Bassano?"

"Yes."

"Wherefore?"

"For because she is pregnant. *'She is fading,'* he said to me, *'as all flowers do that are plucked too early.'*"

Robin wrinkled his nose. "Even though he's the one that did the plucking?"

"Grieve not, Robin. She well knew the risk and enjoyed the ride. He has married her off to a court musician."

"Can he do that?"

"Who's to stop him?"

"Are you sad that she is with another man?"

"Robin. I am a married man."

"Of course."

"And well over Mistress Bassano."

"God be praised, as Falstaff would say."

"Which he *did* say. But Lord Hunsdon has done Mistress Bassano a favor. He could have abandoned her."

"But he has abandoned the child, hasn't he?" Oxford could hear the concern the little page had for the baby which was not yet old enough to feel for itself.

"Yes. But the child's new 'father' may be a better father than Lord Hunsdon would have been. Whoever he is, he will be well-rewarded, as Lord Hunsdon's 'father' was."

Robin did not understand.

"You remember Mary Boleyn?" Oxford asked.

"The *other* Boleyn girl?"

Oxford nodded. "Mary was Hunsdon's mother. Great Harry was his father."

"Henry VIII?"

"The same. Harry bedded Mary before he took a liking to Anne. When Mary became pregnant, Harry got rid of her to pursue Anne, who did not make the same mistake her sister had made."

"Which was?"

"Letting Harry into her bed before he married her."

"And so Anne became queen."

"For a few years."

"And what happened to Mary?"

"Harry married her off to a minor nobleman to act as father to the baby that was already on its way before the man met his new wife. An 'immaculate conception,' you might say."

Robin ignored the comment. "And the baby?"

"Lord Hunsdon."

"So Lord Hunsdon is Elizabeth's brother?"

"If one says Harry was his father."

"Otherwise, he's her cousin."

"Right."

"Were Hunsdon and Elizabeth close when they were children?"

"Yes. They bonded because he was of uncertain descent while she was a bastard for a while.

"How can someone be a bastard *for a while?*" Robin asked.

"A difficult concept, I agree. Elizabeth was a *sometime* bastard; Hunsdon was an *always* bastard. Elizabeth was legitimate at birth, then became illegitimate when her mother was beheaded and Parliament declared her mother's marriage to Henry illegitimate, and then made legitimate again when Henry put her back in the succession."

"What a horrible way to grow up."

Oxford agreed. "Elizabeth and Hunsdon were raised together in a court teeming with plots and conspiracies. As outsiders, they gravitated toward each other. They knew they were fledglings being raised in another's nest. The cuckoo should be part of the Tudor coat of arms."

"The cuckoo?"

"The cuckoo lays its eggs in other birds' nests, leaving its young to be raised by others."

"Oooh."

"Think of it, Robin. If King Henry had married Mary, Hunsdon would have succeeded him as king. Elizabeth would have faded into history as just another whelp thrown off by her father." Robin shivered at the possibility. "Think of what would have happened to me if my father had not married my mother? I might have been a page like you!"

Robin knew that Oxford meant no disparagement by this. His master's mind was always running in all directions, like a basset hound poking its nose in every corner, searching, searching.

"And if your parents had been noble, I could be serving you," Oxford said." They were passing a pub. A drunk lay against the side of the building. "Consider this man lying here, for example." Oxford looked down at the drunk. "What say you if I tell Tobias to scoop him up and carry him to the Savoy where you and I will dress him up in my clothes and play servant to him when he awakes?"

Robin looked down at the man lying spread-eagled in front of him. Tobias came back to find out why they had stopped.

"The challenge will be to convince him that he is the lord of a vast estate in Essex," Oxford went on, growing more excited as he talked. "We will tell him that he has been asleep for many years. We will dress him in my clothes, and tell him his long-suffering wife has been unable to wake him!"

"Who will play the wife, my lord?"

"You will."

"I, my lord?"

"Who better? You are young. In a proper dress and wig, who would know the difference?"

"*I would!*"

"Oh, Robin, do not hesitate when adventure beckons. Let's see how far we can go with this before he sounds us out. We will give him a title and parade him around as a lord from the Welsh marches just returned from years in Europe. The reptiles that infest the court will fawn over him when they think him an earl and howl in rage when they discover he is nothing but a drunk!"

Robin did not share Oxford's enthusiasm. ""My lord. We are to your brother-in-law's, are we not? Perhaps another time? A drunk can be easily found, if one is needed."

Oxford looked down at the sleeping drunk and sighed. "All right. Yes, lie there, you who would be a noble lord if I were not bound elsewhere. To my brother-in-law's, then," Oxford said. Tobias realized that whatever his master and Robin had been discussing was over. He set off toward Cripplegate. Oxford took a final look at the drunk. "How sad. Greatness for him was but a moment away. *Sic transit fortuna.*"

They were soon at Lord Willoughby's. They found him in the sunken well where the musicians had performed the last time Oxford and Robin had visited. Robin slipped up the steps and disappeared into the kitchen while Willoughby introduced Oxford to his guests: Thomas Digges and Thomas Harriot, noted mathematicians; Sir John Dee, mathematician and astronomer; and Sir Walter Raleigh, poet, ship builder and navigator. "Henry Percy is late," Willoughby said.

"Must have tripped over a thought," Raleigh commented. The others chuckled. Percy was the Ninth Earl of Northumberland and known as the "Wizard Earl" for his forays into astronomy and more occult subjects.

"And my distinguished guests from Denmark, gentlemen," Willoughby continued, gesturing to two young men walking down the steps into the room, "Frederik Rosencrantz and Knud Guildenstern."

"Greetings, young gentlemen," John Dee said. "All our best wishes to your distinguished uncle, Tycho Brahe."

"And he to you, Herr Dee," said Rosencrantz, handing Dee a package. "A gift from Professor Brahe to his learned brethren in England."

Willoughby gestured to a table surrounded by chairs. Dee sat down at one end and opened the package. He took out four copies of an ornately printed book. A copper engraving of the author poked out of each of the books. Dee held one up for all to see. It was a portrait of Brahe surrounded by an arch with the coats of arms of the royal Danish families on it. Dee put down the copper plate and picked up one of the books. Thomas Digges picked up another; Raleigh, a third; Willoughby picked up the fourth.

"His theory of the heavens made clear," Guildenstern announced proudly.

The English gentlemen paged through the books. Dee looked up. "This is most generous. There is much to learn here."

"Indeed," Raleigh said. "But does Herr Brahe still seek to explain the movements of the heavens by placing the Earth at its center?"

"He does, sir, but only for the sun and moon. The mathematical proofs of his conclusions are all here."

Dee nodded. "I think Herr Brahe is right. We must be the center. The Holy Bible tells us so. Copernicus' idea that the sun is at the center must be wrong. God could not have created man in his own image to live on a planet that was not at the center of everything."

The others murmured.

"Gentlemen: a toast," Willoughby said as a servant moved among them carrying a tray of short glasses filled with a clear liquid. "Akvavit," Willoughby said. Each guest took a glass. "A gift from our Danish friends."

"*Aqua Vitae*," Guildenstern said. "The water of life!"

"It helps for all the illnesses inside a man," Frederik added, as the glasses were filled by Lord Willoughby's serving man. A second servant came in with a tray of pickled herring.

"Then I am for akvavit," Thomas Digges said. He threw back his glass and gasped. "Oh. Oh," he said, his eyes watering. The other men laughed. "Yes, it may help all the illnesses inside a man, *but the cure may be to kill the patient!*"

"No, no," Guildenstern protested.

"Do not worry, Knud," Willoughby said. "When an Englishman is complaining, he is enjoying himself!"

Guildenstern drew himself erect. "Our uncle told us to remind Lord Willoughby that we Danes celebrate by drinking one glass after another, to the sound of trumpets, recorders, and lutes!"

Musicians appeared at the railing behind him. Willoughby gestured to them and they began playing. "We have no cannon, gentlemen, but the music may make up for it." The men began downing the akvavit.

"Awful stuff," Willoughby said *sotto voce* to Oxford. "I spent all my time at Elsinore finding places to dump it out. Flower pots; drain spouts; over the railings."

The other men, however, liked it. They asked for more. Rosencrantz and Guildenstern showed them how to drink it in one shot. While waiting their turn for a refill, the Englishmen glanced through the books the Danes had brought.

"Your son is working at the Tower Armory, by the way," Willoughby said to Oxford.

"Yes. I heard at Ditchley."

"Elspeth may have had something to do with it."

This Oxford hadn't heard. "Why would she do that?"

"Wasn't she the reason your daughters were at your wedding?"

"Yes."

"And what a lovely addition they were. Lisbeth is getting close to marrying age, Edward. You'll have to deal with that soon."

"Burghley's already tried to marry her to Southampton—he's still in wardship, you know—but Henry refused. I was all for it, but Henry told me he would never get out from under Burghley's thumb if he did so. Lisbeth thinks *I* told him not to marry her. She is furious with me."

"Women," Willoughby said.

"Aye," Oxford agreed.

The other men were continuing their assault on the akvavit. One or two may have started drinking out of courtesy but courtesy was soon overtaken by a genuine thirst for the drink. The more the men drank, the louder their voices became. Raleigh defended Copernicus while Dee said Brahe was right. The two Danes weighed in on their uncle's side, while Harriot decided to defend Ptolemy. "Why throw away the traditional explanation of the universe?" he asked in a wobbly voice, revealing that the akvavit might be having a greater effect on him than he realized.

The arguments became more intense. Oxford watched the men begin to point at the ceiling to stress an argument and then point their fingers at an adversary to drive a point home. This descended into finger-jabs. Thomas Harriot finally cried out over the din: "*Who cares?*"

Lady Mary was suddenly at the railing. Although small in stature, she had a commanding presence. "*Gentlemen! Enough!* You're arguing about the stars? Mr. Harriot is right: *Who cares?*"

The men all started talking. Guildenstern shook his fist at her. "This is too complicated for a woman to understand," he said to her, somewhat drunk himself. "*Go back in the kitchen!*"

His words shocked the Englishmen into silence. "I say, Mr. Guildenstern," Thomas Digges began, but Lady Mary needed no help to defend herself.

"*Back in the kitchen?*" she shouted. She headed for the steps, but Lord Willoughby intercepted her. "Mary, Mary," he said, turning her around and escorting her firmly back up the steps. "Please remember these distinguished gentlemen are our guests."

"*Distinguished? Distinguished? They are nothing but insects!*" she called out, trying to get around her husband. "*Tiny men arguing over stars and planets! Who Cares?*"

Willoughby finally managed to get her around the corner and out of sight.

"He needs to give her a good whipping!" Thomas Harriot said, his speech slurred. He suddenly remembered Oxford was Lady Mary's brother. "My lord," he said.

"He's right," Knud Guildenstern said, as drunk as the others and, unlike Harriot, unaware that his hostess was Oxford's sister. "In

Danemark, a woman like that would be walled into a cellar until she learned her place!"

Willoughby came back down the steps. "My apologies, gentlemen. My wife, as Lord Oxford knows, has strong opinions, which she has no reluctance to express."

"What a shrew," a thoroughly besotted Thomas Digges said, as he sank into a chair. He looked down at one of the books lying on the table. He opened it and tried to read something but couldn't make out a word. "Curious," he muttered, as his head fell onto the table.

The others realized it was time to go. "Well, Peregrine," Walter Raleigh said, getting up, "thank you for a most unusual time."

"Here, here," Thomas Harriot said. "My lord," he said to Oxford, as he headed for the door. Raleigh took one of the books and followed him. John Dee fumbled with a copy for himself. "I would like to take one of these, if I may," he said.

"Certainly," Willoughby said. He looked at Oxford.

"Thomas Digges deserves the last one, don't you think?" Oxford asked, looking down at the now-sleeping mathematician.

Willoughby agreed. "About my wife," he began.

"Peregrine: she was my sister before she was your wife. No need to say anything."

"Yes."

"Shrew that she is."

"Yes."

Oxford followed the others out the door. Robin was waiting for him on the second-floor gallery. They went down to the street where they picked up Tobias. Robin quickly noticed that Oxford had withdrawn into himself. At Cripplegate, Oxford's right hand came up, index finger extended. His head waggled as he began to conduct whatever silent music he was hearing. Robin watched. After a while, the right hand went down and the left hand, index finger extended, came up.

Robin finally felt bold enough to interrupt. "My lord," he began, but Oxford interrupted him.

"Shush," he said, now conducting with the right again as they passed the drunk still lying against the building. "Christopher Sly,"

Oxford said, pointing to the man as they went by, but not looking at him.

"Who is Christopher Sly?" Robin asked.

"He who is lying on the stones back there."

"But we don't know his name."

"That is the name I have given him in the new play I am writing. He will be asleep on the stage when the play begins. He will become more famous than he ever dreamed of, without ever knowing it."

"What play, my lord?" Robin was excited. There had been no plays for some time now, ever since Lady Elspeth had come into his lordship's life.

"Shhhh." Oxford put his index finger to his lips.

They walked along.

"*The Taming of the Shrew*, I shall call it," Oxford said after a while.

"'Twill be about your sister?"

"Aye."

"I heard her just now."

"My brother-in-law is a lion on the battlefield but retires from the field when my sister comes into view. '*In war*,' he has said to me, '*one must be brave, but in marriage, discretion is the better part of valor.*'"

"And your sister Mary will be your role model for the play?"

"Aye."

"What think you Lady Elspeth will say about it?"

"About the play? Why, she'll say nothing. It's not about her."

Oxford's left hand came up.

Robin watched him for a while. "And what is that you do when your left hand is up, my lord."

"*Hamlet*, young sir."

"Two plays at once?"

"Sometimes more." The left hand sawed the air.

"What is *Hamlet* about, my lord?"

"A young man whose father is most cruelly murdered."

"How, my lord?"

"By having poison poured into his ear while he sleeps in his garden."

"How awful."

They walked a bit further. "And your father, my lord. How did he die?"

"By having poison poured into his ear while he slept in his garden."

"No!"

"Yes," Oxford stopped. He looked at the young page. "You are the glass to my anger, Robin. I see it anew. Instead of a garden in Essex, my father will die in a garden in Denmark. Many more will die, including the two Danish visitors we just saw at my brother-in-law's."

"What?"

Oxford pointed at the sun, now sinking beyond Newgate. "We are but insects, Robin, as my sister so aptly said. We live on a speck of dust far from the center of the universe. The two Danes champion Tycho Brahe, who claims that the sun and moon revolve around the Earth."

"Should they die for that?"

"Men have died for less."

They were now in front of Oxford Court.

## ~ 76 ~
## An Heir for His Lordship

Oxford came through the front door and headed for the stairs. Lady Elspeth came out of the kitchen.

"Edward," she said. He didn't respond immediately. His left hand was still conducting. "Edward!"

Oxford stopped. "My lady."

"We sup in the dining room."

"Of course." He began to climb the stairs again.

"My lord!"

Oxford stopped again.

"I fear I shall lose you to one of your plays."

"Never! I shall return, my lady. I promise." He came back down the stairs and gave her a kiss.

"My lord! The servants!"

"I'm sure Robin knows how to kiss. Do you not, Robin?" Robin looked away, embarrassed. Oxford laughed and bounded up the stairs.

Lady Elspeth looked at Robin. "He is with a new play, isn't he?"

"Two, my lady."

"Two? I am married to a lunatic."

"An artist, my lady."

"A lunatic, if you heard what he did last week." She dropped her voice. "It was after midnight. I was asleep in my room when someone began hallooing and banging on the garden window. I thought a burglar was trying to break in. Then I saw it was mine husband! He asked if the lady of the house was home. Why would he ask? He's looking through the glass, our faces inches apart! Before I could say anything, he says: '*Is the master of the house away?*' This surprised me even more."

Robin shook his head, his eyes wide.

"'Soft, soft,' I said to myself. 'He's mad. Humor him.' I tell him the lady of the house is at home, whereupon he cries out, *I hear she is beautiful!*" Lady Elspeth turned to Robin. "Robin, I am *not* beautiful."

"My lady."

"No, no. Even to a lunatic poet. Not with this nose, these eyes set too close together. *He is imagining I am someone else!* '*Who are you?*' I ask. '*A lover in the night*', he says, '*come to take you away and ravage you!*'"

"Oh, my lady." Robin was embarrassed. "What did you do?"

"I opened the window and knocked him off the ladder." It was Robin's turn to be astonished. "I would have done the same to any man who tried to climb into my bedroom."

"But this wasn't any man, my lady; this was your husband."

"Not in the fantasy he was living. I know a test when I see one!"

"Oh, my lady. He was, no doubt, in one of his fits of passion in which his imagination outgrows his head."

"I have always been told that you don't know someone until you live with them, but I never expected that I would wake up and find my husband trying to break into my bedroom *thinking I was someone else!*"

"Oh, my lady, he didn't think you were someone else."

"Oh, yes, he did. He imagined he was rescuing *someone else!*"

Robin wanted to defend his master but Lady Elspeth would hear none of it. "What happened after you knocked him off the ladder?" Robin asked.

"He landed on his back in the garden. Looking up at me, he said: '*I always wanted to do that.*' Do what? I asked, but he did not answer. He jumped up and went into the house. I didn't see him again that night. He said nothing in the morning. Has he mentioned it to you?"

"No, my lady."

"Has he done anything like this before?"

"Not that I know of, my lady."

"Why would he want to want break into my bedroom when he can walk in through the bedroom door?"

"No doubt to imagine he was rescuing you."

"What needs he to imagine that? Am I lacking in something?"

"Oh, no, my lady. He is besotted with you. Maybe he was thinking about his father, who put a ladder up to a window one night and carried off the woman he was supposed to marry."

"His father?" Lady Elspeth asked. "And the woman let him take her?"

"Perhaps she wanted to be rescued."

"Oh, the knight in shining armor. The ladder. I suppose there was a tethered horse waiting out in Candlewick Street. Edward has been reading too much of *La Morte d'Arthur*."

"And everything else."

"Have I married a chameleon, Robin? Is there a real Edward in there somewhere?"

"Oh, yes, my lady. His head is full of poetry and plays, but Edward de Vere is indeed the right honourable the Seventeenth Earl of Oxford, and worth every moment you spend knocking him off ladders."

Lady Elspeth laughed. "Perhaps you are right. Thank you, Robin. You have given me comfort."

Robin blushed.

Bona Fortuna came out of the kitchen carrying the first plates for the supper. "All is ready, your ladyship."

Oxford appeared at the top of the stairs. "My lord" Lady Elspeth said to him, indicating supper was ready. Oxford came down the stairs and followed her into the dining room. Bona Fortuna pulled out a chair at the end of the table for Elspeth while Nigel pulled out a chair at the other end for Oxford. The table was at least twenty feet long. Bona Fortuna lifted a cover off a porcelain dish.

"Ah," Oxford said. "Osso bucco! How did you know?"

Lady Elspeth looked pleased with herself. "I heard you mumble 'Virginia' one night. My first thought was that you were dreaming about Raleigh's settlement in the New World, but then I realized no man would be dreaming about land if he uttered the name of a woman in his sleep."

"I was thinking of my investments in Virginia, truly."

"I will forgive you for such a gentle fib. However, your investments have been with Frobisher, to the northwest."

"North by northwest," Oxford said. "I am mad north by northwest."

"And in more directions than that, quite possibly."

Oxford, for once, did not respond. Nigel placed a bowl of the osso bucco in front of him. Elspeth went on.

"Something about the way you pronounced 'Virginia' made me ask Frangellica about this and she remembered Virginia Padoana."

Oxford coughed. He hadn't thought of Virginia Padoana in years. "My lady," he protested, "I have not seen Miss Padoana in decades. I've had no communication with her. I have not even *thought* about her," but Elspeth waved him silent. She didn't believe him.

"I sent a letter to Venice, asking after Miss Padoana."

"My lady!"

"I admit you might think me too inquisitive about a woman you knew 'decades ago,' but, after all, what else can a woman do when she hears her husband utter a woman's name in the middle of the night?"

"My lady, your concern does her injustice. You would have liked her. She introduced me to Titian, to Giulio Romano. I met her while attending services at San Giovanno."

She smiled at him. "You should have quit at Titian."

"Where else does one meet lovely women in Italy?" Lady Elspeth sipped some of the osso bucco. "And?" Oxford asked.

"And what?"

"What did you hear back?"

"Oh, you are interested?" He nodded, perhaps a little too much. "She has retired to a Dominican monastery in Padua."

"No!"

"Why no?"

"Virginia? In a monastery?"

"She did not lie about the osso bucco."

"So it wasn't Frangellica who gave you the recipe?"

"I never said it was."

"True. But, my compliments to Frangellica, who has outdone herself in recreating the dish. I did not realize I missed it so much."

"And Ms. Padoana? Do you miss her as well?"

"She was in another life. *In another country*!"

Lady Elspeth smiled.

Oxford ate some more of the dish in front of him. "What else did you learn from her?" he could not stop himself from asking.

"Women who share secrets, my lord, do not share them with men, even husbands. If we did, we would lose our allure."

This caused a faint smile to run across Bona Fortuna's face. But Oxford could tell there was more. "And?"

"Oh, yes. Miss Padoana wrote that you loved Carnival, and wearing masks. She sent you one."

Bona Fortuna produced a black and white harlequin mask from behind her back and took it down the table to Oxford. "Good God!" Oxford exclaimed. "The very mask I wore the night we celebrated Carnival in Venice!"

"Are you sure?"

"I wrote my initials on the inside." He motioned for Nigel to bring a candle over. He peered into the mask. His face fell.

"No initials, my lord?"

Oxford shook his head. He turned the mask over and looked at the front. "I shall give it to Shackspear," he said.

"Do not be downcast, my lord. Ms. Padoana may not have saved the actual mask, but she remembered what you wore that night and took the time to find a replacement to send to England."

"Yes. Very kind of her. She must have gotten rid of the one I left with her when she moved to the monastery." He put the mask in front of his face and lowered his voice.

> *Degree being vizarded,*
> *The unworthiest shows as fairly in the mask.*

Elspeth ignored Oxford's leap into poetry. She had learned that such digressions, sometimes in Latin or French, and once even in Greek, were common occurrences at the dinner table. "And your 'masked' appearance in Venice was not the first time you appeared in disguise, my lord, if memory serves me aright."

"Oh?"

"When I came up to London, I was told, "*Beware of the Earl of Oxford; he is not always what he seems.*""

"If he were, he'd be a dull fool," Oxford said. "And what was it that you heard about me that was the cause of that remark?"

"That you once appeared as the Turkish ambassador once."

"*Beni?*"

"Beni?" Lady Elspeth asked.

"*Moi*, in Turkish," Oxford said, an impish grin on his face. He obviously knew the story.

"*Me*, in other words, in English, the language I speak," Lady Elspeth said, with some asperity. "I do wish you would limit yourself to our native tongue when speaking with me, Edward."

Oxford had forgotten that Elspeth took his tendency to switch back and forth between languages as subtle criticism of her lack of education. He had confessed once that, when bored, he would translate speeches into another language while they were being delivered, even into Greek if he were feeling particularly feisty. "Forgive me, my lady. I will speak only English from now on."

The room went silent for a moment before she returned to what she had heard about Oxford not always being what he seemed. "The Turkish ambassador was on his way to England. Elizabeth was excited because this would mark the opening of trade relations with the orient. You and your friends decided to dress up as Turks and imitate his embassy. You sailed out of Harwich on a ship flying a Turkish flag and coasted down to Dover where you arrived as the ambassador and his retinue."

"No," Oxford said, in mock disbelief.

"Your arrival was, of course, earlier than the port commander had expected, but, voyages being as haphazard as they are, he greeted you with all diplomatic respect. You shielded your face behind clothing that covered you in every direction and deceived him. The commander ushered you ashore to the sound of cannons and trumpets and escorted you to Greenwich with great fanfare."

Oxford was beaming. He couldn't stop himself from taking over the story. "The Queen was thrilled to hear that the ambassador had arrived. She draped herself in her most costly jewels and came down to greet him. I bowed low as she extolled my virtues. That is, until I winked at her from underneath my turban and gave myself away."

"I heard she was furious."

"As angry as I've ever seen her. But I could see she was laughing inside. She had to turn her face away to hide it. She ordered me from the room. It cost a small fortune to make sure the ambassador did not find out when he arrived that he had been preceded by an imposter."

"An impossible task, given the nature of the court."

"But the Turks did not speak English and so he never found out."

"And so this is why she calls you 'my Turk'?"

"It's her way of enjoying the trick while reminding me never to repeat it. It's one of the many ways she and I talk over the heads of less agile minds."

"Yes," Elspeth said quietly. "I'm beginning to find that out."

He did not hear her. He put the mask in front of his face. "Like the mask I wore in Venice. It is good to be remembered." He looked at her through the mask. "But Virginia Padoana sent me this as a gift; are there no gifts from you tonight, my lady?"

"None that you don't have to wait for."

"I hate to wait."

"When the gift is of great value, waiting makes it of greater value."

Oxford peeked around the mask. "What gift could that be?"

"Something that needs many months."

"Months?"

"Even God needs time to make a baby."

Oxford lowered the mask. "A baby?"

"If my signs and Dr. Forman are to be believed. "

"*A baby?*"

She nodded.

"When?"

"February," Lady Elspeth said, trying not to look too pleased.

"February! I cannot wait till February!" He jumped up and ran down to where Lady Elspeth was seated. She turned her face away. He kissed the cheek she presented him. "Why didn't you tell me before?"

"I only learned this morning."

"But 'tis suppertime!"

"You were not at home when I found out."

"You could have told me when I came in the door!"

"News such as this needs proper circumstances to be disclosed."

"True. True." He looked at Robin. "Did you know?"

"Of course not," Lady Elspeth said. "Even Bona Fortuna was not told. This is business between mine husband and me."

"And wife, *and mother*!" Oxford turned to Robin. "I'm going to be a father, Robin! A son of my own!" He laid his hand on Lady Elspeth's middle.

> *This fair child come next winter's time*
> *Shall prove his worth by succeeding mine!*
> *And make me new when I am old,*
> *And warm my blood when I am cold.*

"I am with sonnets!" he exclaimed, and ran out of the room.

Lady Elspeth placed her hand on her midriff and looked at Robin. "So quickly," she said drolly. "But no words of praise for she who will bear the child?" Robin did not know what to say. "Thank God it will be a male child," Lady Elspeth said.

"You think so, my lady?"

"I pray for a son every day, Robin, but, since God helps those who help themselves, I made sure, when my time was right, that his lordship and I spent the night in the parson's bed at Neat Enstone."

"And how does spending the night at Neat Enstone ensure a son, my lady?"

A faint smile crossed Lady Elspeth's face. "A night in the parson's bed guarantees a male heir."

"Oh."

"In case you need a male heir someday, Robin. Now you know."

"Oh. Yes. Thank you, my lady."

"But why did my lord cry out, *a son of my own*? Does he have any sons that are not his?"

"No, my lady."

"He spoke it to you."

"He did? Perhaps he meant his son, Edward, by Anne Vavasor."

"No. He has never accepted Edward as his own."

"Perhaps, then, his son by Lady Anne, who died shortly after he was born?" Lady Elspeth shook her head again. "I've never heard mention of any other, my lady. 'Tis the reason he was so excited by the news."

The front door opened with a bang. Robin went to find out who it was. "Sir John!" Lady Elspeth heard Robin say. She went out into the great hall and headed for the stairs.

"My lady!" Falstaff called out to her. "Greetings! And Merry Christmas!" He left his foot in the door to hold it open. Two men were dragging a ceramic pot in from the street. The pot contained a large tree that was covered with oranges. The men bounced the pot over the threshold, loosening one of the oranges, which fell to the floor and rolled down the hall toward Lady Elspeth. Falstaff cuffed the men. "Flap-eared knaves!" he bellowed. "Cow-flops! Be thou gentle with mine tree!"

"Falstaff!" Oxford called down. "What dost thou?"

"He thinks it is Christmas," Lady Elspeth said.

"It is July, Sir John."

"Which is not too much after springtime, which quickly follows winter, which contains Christmas and your wedding, and not having heretofore brought you a wedding present, I humbly beseech my lord and lady to accept my humble gift, late as it may be."

Oxford laughed. Lady Elspeth was frowning to keep herself from laughing.

"We heard you went to Seville!" Robin said, a beaming smile on his face.

"Eh? Oh, yes. Seville. Which is why I am late with mine gift. It was a long trip, with pirates and Spaniards going at me all the way down and back!" He started shadow-fencing with invisible swordsmen.

"You mean you went all the way to Smithfield market?" Oxford asked.

"My lord. The lad thinks I went to Seville."

"And so you did."

"Which is all very interesting," Lady Elspeth said, "but why are we now graced with an orange tree that sits in our hall?"

"For because, my lady," Falstaff said, bending a knee to the floor, an effort trumpeted by loud popping sounds and stifled moans, "it is my gift to you for your garden."

Lady Elspeth placed her hand against her breast. "Why, Sir John," she said. "I am touched."

"Then my duty is discharged," Falstaff said. Nigel and Robin ran over to help him up.

"It will take more than an old man and a boy to get that tub of lard back on his feet," Oxford called down. "He's not seen his knee since he was two thumbs to a pint-pot!"

Falstaff laughed. "I wear my greatness for all to see." He grabbed his belly with his hands. "My success on the battlefield goes before me."

"If a trencher can be called a battlefield."

Lady Elspeth picked up the orange and walked up to Falstaff. She took his hand. "Sir John, I thank your giving heart, and not your belly," she said, slipping a gold coin into his hand.

Falstaff refused the coin. "'Twas not done for gold, your ladyship, though I thank thee for your kindness. 'Tis enough if I can say I am the cause of *gardening* in others!" He leaned back and started to laugh.

"Jack!" Oxford called down. "Guess what?"

"What?"

"I'm going to be a father!"

"What?"

"You already said that."

"He means I am expecting," Lady Elspeth said.

Falstaff began to sink to his knees again.

"No, Sir John, once was quite enough."

Falstaff nodded, relief showing on his face.

"I will tell people," Oxford began to declaim from the landing above them, "that I am an important man now because *I am the father of the Eighteenth Earl of Oxford!*"

"God be praised!" Falstaff said.

Shackspear suddenly appeared behind them. He angled himself around the orange tree and took in Falstaff, Robin, and Lady Elspeth before finally seeing Oxford looking down from the second-floor landing. "My lord," he said, stepping into the hall. "Mr. Tilney has called in *Much Ado About Nothing*. He said the Queen gave him strict instruction not to allow it to be played. What did you do to piss her off this time?"

"You piss off, Willum. I have no idea why Tilney called it in. They're not my plays, remember? *They're yours.*"

Shackspear stamped his foot in irritation and stormed out the door past the men wrestling with the orange tree.

Lady Elspeth looked up at Oxford. "Anne asked Sir Henry if he would speak to the Queen and call it in."

Oxford was disappointed. "'Twas my best yet. Shackspear is right to be upset."

"But you have a copy, don't you?"

"For what purpose? They're not my plays. And what use would I have of a copy? To sit up at night and grieve over my losses when the house is asleep?" His face darkened. He turned and disappeared.

Falstaff and the two men began to muscle the orange tree through the garden door. Robin went over to Lady Elspeth. He looked around to make sure no one else could hear him. "The truth will out some day, my lady and the world will learn that my master wrote the plays that carry Shackpear's name. I know it in my heart, just as you know that your baby is a boy. I have copies of everything he's written," he said, lowering his voice.

"Thank you for your good service, Robin. How came this idea to you?"

"Christopher Marlowe, my lady. He told my master to hold back the originals and give only copies to Shackspear. He said he never gives his originals to Henslowe. He said that when Henslowe wants to stage *Tamburlaine*, he has to pay Mr. Marlowe for the privilege. My lord dismissed the idea because, as he just said, he is not the author. But he had another reason for not keeping copies. He told Mr. Marlowe that copies were useless because no one sits and reads a play. 'It is an abomination that scenes invented merely to be spoken should be published to be read,' he told Mr. Marlowe. 'A play is for the theater where it comes alive. Otherwise, it is dead on the page.'"

"But you thought Mr. Marlowe had a good idea."

"I did."

"And where do you keep these copies?"

"Under the stairs, my lady, where I sleep."

"It must be crowded in there."

"I could not sleep between better sheets."

She smiled "You *are* clever with words. But I think we should keep this between us. Don't tell anyone. Not even his lordship."

"He has no reason to ask, my lady. He doesn't know I have them."

She handed him the orange. "Take this," she said. "Ask Frangellica to stick cloves in it. 'Twill perfume the plays as well as the room in which you sleep."

"Thank you, my lady."

"I notice you shaved your mustache."

"I did, my lady. It wasn't coming in much. I was embarrassed by how thin it was.

"Too early, eh? Don't worry; it will come in. Did anyone notice?"

"No."

"Men are like that. What about Falstaff?"

"I'm not sure. You have to watch his eyes to know what's going on with him. There's a lot in there if you look."

"There must be, judging from the how large the outside is."

## ~ 77 ~
### *The Taming of the Shrew*

S hrew?" Robin asked. He had found Oxford fingering the leaves on Falstaff's orange tree in the garden. They started to walk across the hall to the library. "Why work on a frippery about a noisome wife when *Hamlet* waits upstairs?"

"Because *Hamlet* is not ready. *I* am not ready."

Robin sat down at the table, a puzzled look on his face. "How can you not be ready to bring *Hamlet* to the stage? I heard it was performed years ago. Surely, you've had enough time to work on it by now."

"The *Hamlet* you heard mention about was the wail of an adolescent, quickly stuffed back into its closet."

"*Too many tragical speeches,*" Robin said.

"Too many speeches of the kind young men write, believing they know everything about life."

"But surely …"

"My being no longer young, I can finish *Hamlet*?" Robin heard irritation in Oxford's voice, but his master sounded more displeased with himself than with his page's continual questioning. "Being older, Robin, is not the same as being wise. *Hamlet* needs the distillation of experience and wisdom, something I am still acquiring. In the meantime, let us bend ourselves to *The Shrew*, something of lesser import, and thus more easily written, but which will nevertheless excite lesser minds."

Robin grumped. "I like not a play about a woman who needs to be trained like a dog."

"Or a falcon. But within your objection lies the attraction. How do I take an idea that has been the plot of hundreds of plays, banal at best and insulting at worst, and transform it into something new? How do I write a play that the burghers of England will cheer as showing the true basis of marriage—which is the transfer of wealth from one generation to another, *and* how women can feign obedience so that they rule absolutely."

"That is your intention?" Oxford nodded. "I think you've hit upon something."

"How do you think women have managed to live all these centuries? The oak is rent by the sudden storm, but the reed bends and survives. We shall show them how to bend and survive. We shall start with the drunken beggar we saw on our way to Lord Willoughby's."

This surprised Robin. He was about to ask what the beggar had to do with the play when Socrates leaped onto the end of the table. Oxford and Robin noticed. "A good sign, my lord."

"I wondered where the bugger was."

"And the drunken beggar?"

"Will be lying against a wall when the play opens."

"For what purpose, my lord?"

"Yours not to ask," Oxford said briskly. "You are my secretary. When did you become co-author?"

Robin tipped his head back and thought about the question. "Some time in the distant past, I think. A word here, a word there. Some lines spoken by Launce in *Two Gentlemen* about his dog? Julia's comment about men changing their minds?

> *It is the lesser blot, modesty finds,*
> *Women to change their shapes*
> *than men their minds.*

"And on such slender grounds, you expect to be named co-author?" Robin could tell that Oxford was trying not to smile.

"You liked it at the time."

Oxford admitted he had. "Very well. You can have co-billing alongside me, right behind Shackspear, who blindeth all as to who the true authors are."

Robin liked this. It was a promotion, of types, even if only a few words on the wind. "And the purpose of having the beggar in the play?"

"The beggar will frame the play the way yonder painting is enclosed within that wooded frame," he said, pointing to a picture on the wall. "Here's how the drunken beggar will be introduced:

Lord:              *What's here? one dead, or drunk? See, doth*
                     *He breathe?*

| | |
|---|---|
| Huntsman: | *He breathes, my lord. Were he not warm'd*<br>*With ale, this were a bed but cold to sleep so soundly.* |
| Lord: | *O monstrous beast! how like a swine he lies!*<br>*Sirs, I will practise on this drunken man.*<br>*What think you, if he were convey'd to bed,*<br>*Wrapp'd in sweet clothes, rings put upon his fingers,*<br>*A most delicious banquet by his bed,*<br>*And brave attendants near him when he wakes,*<br>*Would not the beggar then forget himself?* |

Robin's pen raced across the paper. "A 'swine' who becomes a lord. I sense Ovid nearby."

"The great poet will breathe every word in this play. The beggar's transformation will be the first of many. The transformation of the shrew will be the centerpiece. The audience will stay to see it done."

Robin waited, pen in hand. "What does the beggar say when he is aroused from his stupor in scene one?"

"He will look down at his clothes and say:

*Am not I Christopher*
*Sly, old Sly's son of Burtonheath, by birth a*
*pedlar, by education a cardmaker, by transmutation a*
*bear-herd, and now by present profession a tinker?*
*Ask Marian Hackett, the fat ale-wife of Wincot, if*
*she know me not.*

"And who is Marian Hackett, my lord?"

"The fat ale-wife of Wincot."

"Is she real?"

"Not only real but *immense*!" Oxford made like he was holding a large balloon between his arms. "Wincot is a few miles from Billesley. I went there on one of my wanderings after you went back to London. Shackspear will appreciate the reference. He will point to the fat ale-wife of Wincot as proof that he is the author of the plays."

"And what will Christopher Sly contribute to the play?"

"Nothing. He will lie on the stage thinking he is a lord. A servant will masquerade as his wife."

"His wife? If she's his wife, won't he try to get her into his bed?"

"Of course."

"But the wife will be a boy. How will that work out?"

"It won't. His 'wife' will tell him he has to watch a light entertainment before they retire."

"Which will be *The Taming of the Shrew,*" Robin said, writing down what Oxford was telling him.

"Aye."

"So *The Shrew* will be a play within a play."

"Aye."

"But Christopher Sly will be on the stage while the play unfolds,"

"Yes."

"And looking longingly at his wife."

"Yes."

"Thereby, creating, by his very presence, tension in the audience, who will wonder if he will bed his wife or no"

"Yes."

"Like a summer thunderstorm in the distance."

"You like this?"

"Yes, my lord. And the shrew?"

"The shrew will be Katharina Minola. She will be from Padua. The man who will tame her will be Petruchio. He will be from Verona."

"Verona again," Robin muttered, writing down the names.

"Is Verona unacceptable?" Oxford asked, eyebrows raised.

"No, my lord."

"Katharina is the older daughter of a rich money-lender named Baptista Minola."

"*Baptista Minola,*" Robin said, writing down the name. "These Italian names are difficult for me." He spelled out what he had written. Oxford nodded that he had gotten it right.

"The father's name is a conflation of 'Baptista Nigrone' and 'Pasquino Spinola.' The first was from Padua; the second from Venice. They were money lenders who provided me with money while I was in Italy."

Robin waited.

"Katharina is called 'Katharina the Curst' because of 'her scalding tongue.' A character says he would not marry her 'for a mine of gold.' Her younger sister, Bianca, is sweet and beautiful. She has many suitors, but cannot marry until after Katharina does. This is the situation when Petruchio arrives and proclaims his purpose for coming to Padua:

> *I come to wive it wealthily in Padua;*
> *If wealthily, then happily in Padua.*

"To 'wive', my lord? Can you make a noun into a verb?"

"Of course I can." Robin squirmed. "There are no grammar rules, Robin, only guidelines. Don't turn into Gabriel Harvey on me."

Oxford walked around the table. "Now for some of the verse I have shelved in my mind as I thought about this play." He looked at Robin. "'Shelved,' a verb formed from the noun 'shelf.'"

"Yes, my lord."

"First, the description of the paintings that Christopher Sly is told he can have brought to his room:

> *Dost thou love pictures? we will fetch thee straight*
> *Adonis painted by a running brook,*
> *And Cytherea all in sedges hid,*
> *Which seem to move and wanton with her breath,*
> *Even as the waving sedges play with wind.*
> *We'll show thee Io as she was a maid,*
> *And how she was beguiled and surprised,*
> *As lively painted as the deed was done.*
> *Or Daphne roaming through a thorny wood,*
> *Scratching her legs that one shall swear she bleeds,*
> *And at that sight shall sad Apollo weep,*
> *So workmanly the blood and tears are drawn.*

Robin's pen flew across the page. "Ovid again," Robin muttered.

"Always," Oxford said. He continued to dictate scenes and descriptions into the night. Socrates moved around the table while Oxford spoke, blessing the pages that Robin pushed in his direction by sitting, sphinxlike, upon them. Eventually, he grew tired of the game and disappeared. When Robin's head began to nod, Oxford walked over and took the pen out of the boy's hand. "Another day, young Robin," he said.

## ~ 78 ~
## The Death of Robert Greene

Falstaff's orange tree died in September. The eggplant seeds Frangellica planted in a corner of Lady Elspeth's garden fared better. Unfortunately, the dish she put together with English cheese turned out to be inedible.

Oxford and Robin had little time to work on *The Shrew* during the summer. The warm weather was taken up with joining the Queen on her visits to various estates and making a three-week trip to Staffordshire to visit Lady Elspeth's relatives. It wasn't until September that he and Robin were able to return to *The Shrew*. Oxford picked up as if he had never taken a break from the writing of it.

"Petruchio has hardened in my mind and become more blunt," Oxford said, as he and Robin took up their positions in the library. "He will dismiss everything he has heard about Katharina and claim the opposite is true:

> *Say that she rail; why then I'll tell her plain*
> *She sings as sweetly as a nightingale:*
> *Say that she frown, I'll say she looks as clear*
> *As morning roses newly wash'd with dew:*
> *Say she be mute and will not speak a word;*
> *Then I'll commend her volubility,*
> *And say she uttereth piercing eloquence:*
> *If she do bid me pack, I'll give her thanks,*
> *As though she bid me stay by her a week:*
> *If she deny to wed, I'll crave the day*
> *When I shall ask the banns and when be married.*

"This is before he meets her?"

"Aye."

"What happens when he *does* meet her?"

"This is what he will say when he sees her for the first time: *Good morrow, Kate; for that's your name, I hear.*

Katharina:  *Well have you heard, but something hard of hearing:*
          *They call me Katharina that do talk of me.*

461

Petruchio:   *You lie, in faith; for you are call'd plain Kate,*
*And bonny Kate and sometimes Kate the curst;*
*But Kate, the prettiest Kate in Christendom*
*Kate of Kate Hall, my super-dainty Kate,*
*For dainties are all Kates.*

Robin looked up. "Oh, he has renamed her! Her metamorphosis has begun! Right at the beginning! La!"

Oxford smiled. Even an audience of one could be enough at times. "Petruchio and Katharina will go back and forth at each other, but Petruchio will be more commanding than Benedict was. I need help with this, Robin. You be Kate and I'll be Petruchio. I'll speak; you respond."

"I, Kate? Why do you keep suggesting I should play women, my lord? I'm a man, though few in years."

"Yes, of course, but who else is in the room? Here's your chance, *co-author.* I'll speak; you respond." Robin, still scowling, made himself ready. Oxford drew himself up. "Petruchio will tell Kate that he has come to Padua to woo her for his wife. What would Kate say to that?"

Robin immediately responded: *"Moved! Let him that moved you hither remove you hence: I knew you were a moveable."*

"Oh, lovely! Petruchio will say: *"Why, what's a moveable?"*

Robin: *A join'd-stool.*

*"Thou hast hit it: come, sit on me."*

"My lord!" Robin said, looking up. He was blushing.

"Are they not young, Robin? Are they not courting each other? Are they not thinking of marriage? Did you not learn anything in Paris?"

Robin lowered his head. *"Asses are made to bear, and so are you."*

"Oh, excellent!" Oxford said, ignoring the possibility that Robin might be talking about him: *"Women are made to bear, and so are you."*

Robin picked up the thread: *"No such jade as you, if me you mean."*

Oxford had drifted around the table and was standing next to Robin: *"Come, come, you wasp; I' faith, you are too angry."*

Robin:   *If I be waspish, best beware my sting.*

Oxford:   *Who knows not where a wasp does wear his sting? In his tail.*

Robin:   *In his tongue.*

462

Oxford:    *Whose tongue?*

Robin:     *Yours, if you talk of tails: and so farewell.*

Oxford:    *What, with my tongue in your tail?*

"My lord!" Robin cried out. He threw his pen on the table. "You go too far!" He rose and made like he would strike Oxford.

"Perfect!" Oxford exclaimed. "Put that in. *She strikes him.*"

Robin withdrew his hand and sat back down. He wrote: *She strikes him.* Oxford continued. "*I swear I'll cuff you, if you strike again.*"

Robin:     *So may you lose your arms: If you strike me, you are no*
           *gentleman;*

Oxford:    *'Twas told me you were rough and coy and sullen,*
           *And now I find report a very liar;*
           *For thou are pleasant, gamesome, passing courteous.*

Robin:     *Go, fool.*

Oxford:    *Did ever Dian so become a grove*
           *As Kate this chamber with her princely gait?*

Robin:     *Where did you study all this goodly speech?*

Oxford:    *It is extempore, from my mother-wit.*

Robin:     *A witty mother! witless else her son.*

Oxford:    *And therefore, setting all this chat aside,*
           *Thus in plain terms: your father hath consented*
           *That you shall be my wife; your dowry 'greed on;*
           *Here comes your father: never make denial;*
           *I must and will have Katharina to my wife.*

"Well, that's direct," Robin said, hurrying to catch up. "And what says the father?"

"He is overjoyed. He can now marry off Bianca."

"What does Kate say?"

"She says she will see Petruchio hanged before she will marry him. Petruchio ignores her and tells the father:

*She hung about my neck; and kiss on kiss*
*She vied so fast, protesting oath on oath,*
*That in a twink she won me to her love.*

"Oh, my lord. Does Kate hear these words?"

"She does."

"I fail you, then. I cannot think of what Kate would say to such lies!"

"She says nothing."

"She has changed her mind?"

"Her silence suggest she has. But she is still a shrew, Robin, and Petruchio must tame her:

> *My falcon now is sharp and passing empty;*
> *And till she stoop she must not be full-gorged,*
> *For then she never looks upon her lure.*
> *Last night she slept not, nor to-night she shall not;*
> *As with the meat, some undeserved fault*
> *I'll find about the making of the bed;*
> *And here I'll fling the pillow, there the bolster,*
> *This way the coverlet, another way the sheets:*
> *And if she chance to nod I'll rail and brawl*
> *And with the clamour keep her still awake.*
> *This is a way to kill a wife with kindness;*
> *And thus I'll curb her mad and headstrong humour.*

"Is she nothing more than a wild bird to him?" Robin asked as he scribbled down Oxford's words.

"No. But she needs a husband, and he needs a wife. He commands her as a good father would a stripling son, a captain a crew that has never been to sea, a general who is given raw recruits. Like the raw recruits that become soldiers, the marriage between Petruchio and Kate will prosper."

"But she is naught but slave to him."

"Was Bucephalus only a horse to Alexander? Remember that Kate stood silent when Petruchio announced he would marry her. She will find room to be herself, as Bucephalus accepted Alexander's reins and bore his master."

Robin did not like comparing Kate to a horse, even a horse as famous as Bucephalus, but Shackspear was announced before they could continue. He stepped into the library and whisked a broad-brimmed hat off his head. An immense turkey feather, newly arrived from the colonies, wavered back and forth alongside his hip where he held the hat against his leg. "My lord," he said bowing. "I come to find out how the next play is coming."

"Why? The theaters have been closed since the authorities decided too many people were going to the Rose to see *Henry VI*."

"Aye, my lord. Thousands at a time."

"The Queen asked me to give her Talbot fresh-bleeding on the stage and, when I do, she closes the theaters."

Shackspear nodded. "Do you think she will reopen them?"

"I have no idea. But I see from the fine clothes you are wearing, you have no need of plays. Have you bought the big house in Stratford yet?"

"I have invested whatever money I have with Francis Langley. He has shown me that there are many services that can be provided to playgoers, whether the theaters are open or closed. You should let me show you how it can be done."

"Spare me," Oxford said. He noticed that Shackspear was holding a pamphlet in his hand. Shackspear held up the pamphlet. "Robert Greene's dying thoughts," he said.

"*Greene's Groatsworth of Witte, bought with a million of repentance*," Oxford said. "Yes, I have read it. '*Quia mortui non mordent.*'" Shackspear did not understand. "'Dead men don't bite.'"

"Except when they publish from the grave," Shackspear said. He was upset. "Greene has directed some of his shafts at me."

"Yes. You are '*an upstart crow, beautified with our feathers, that with his Tiger's heart wrapped in a Player's hide, supposes he is as able to bombast out a blank verse as well as the best of you.*' You are, '*in your own conceit, the only Shake-scene in the country.*'"

Shackspear beamed. "Pretty good, huh? I mean, '*Shake-scene?*' '*Shackspear?*'"

"Everyone gets it, Willum."

"Maybe I'll change my name to 'Shakescene.'"

"We're not finished with your first name yet."

This took the smile off Shackspear's face. He looked at the pamphlet again. "Greene was upset at me for my play-writing." He looked up to see Oxford's reaction to this.

"No, *Groatsworth* is directed at three playwrights: '*Base-minded men all three of you, beware of those puppets that spake from our mouths.*' He's warning them about 'puppets,' by which he means players, because players speak the words put into their mouths by playwrights. He then refers to you as a player, not a playwright."

"Oh."

"And he is quite possibly referring to you when he speaks of '*rude grooms*.'"

"'Rude grooms,' Shackspear said. "I didn't see that."

"Didn't you start your career by holding the horses of wealthy patrons who came on horseback to see a play?"

Shackspear nodded.

"And Greene must have seen you as the Duke of York in *Henry VI*."

"You think?"

"How else explain the *Tiger's heart wrapped in a Player's hide*? You went on at such length that Alleyn had to kill you to shut you up. What Greene has done is take the hide I put over Eleanor and slide it over the player with the big mouth."

"Oh," Shackpear said in a different voice.

"And don't think for a moment that Greene did not know who is writing the plays you give to Henslowe."

Shackspear nodded again. "Well," he said, "as always, it's been a pleasure." He bowed and put his hat back on his head. He adjusted the feather and walked out into the hall. They heard the front door close.

Oxford looked at Robin. "What?"

Robin shook his head. "He came in all puffed up; you plucked off all his feathers."

Oxford scowled. "Back to Petruchio."

## ~ 79 ~
## Whitehall Palace and *The Taming of the Shrew*

The Queen decreed that Shackspear's latest effort, *The Taming of the Shrew*, would be performed during the Christmas season at Whitehall. Ned Alleyn gave a dark and menacing performance as Petruchio. The audience stood at the end, cheering Alleyn as he strutted across the stage, gallantly accepting their applause. Oxford had expected the women to react differently but they stood alongside the men, applauding just as loudly. This included the Queen, who announced after the applause died away that the message of the play should be taken to heart by every woman so that they could learn how to be better wives and obey their husbands and fathers. "Few things are as difficult to accomplish as stopping a woman's mouth," she announced regally, "but Petruchio has shown us how it can be done. All hail Shackspear, whose wife, no doubt, cowers on the back stairs when she hears his boots returning home to Stratford. Hah, hah!" she laughed. "Go forth, my people, and have more talk about this."

The onlookers applauded the Queen's pronouncement. She swept from the room. As she went by Oxford, she said, without moving her lips, "*You still haven't shown us love.*"

Shackspear beamed. Well-wishers congratulated him on his latest success. "What does the fat ale-wife of Wincot look like?" one asked. "Well," Shackspear began, but Oxford was already heading for the door and did not hear Shackspear's answer. Robin trailed alongside.

"What an awful play!" Lettice Knollys proclaimed, as she came sweeping up to Oxford in a gorgeous gown of blue silk. Her red hair had been puffed out like a chrysanthemum to out-brave the Queen's thinning hair. She had apparently decided it was time to brazen her way into the performance of a play with the expectation of using her appearance as a wedge to regain access to the court. The Queen's hasty retirement may have been caused by seeing Lettice's voluminous red hair in the audience. With her long legs and waving her arms as she came up to him, Oxford was reminded of the elegant cranes he had seen tip-toeing across the salt flats near Naples. "Look at these ninnies," Lettice said, casting her eye over the women crowding around Shackspear. "Did they not hear Petruchio say Katharina was his 'household stuff?'"

> *She is my goods, my chattels; she is my house,*
> *My household stuff, my field, my barn,*
> *My horse, my ox, my ass, my any thing;*

She threw her head back in a dramatic pose. "I, a woman, despair of ever understanding my sex. How can they applaud this? And my cousin commends this to 'her people?' I feel dizzy, like I have been swept up by a wind and set down in the land of the Hottentots." She put her hand on Oxford's arm to steady herself.

Oxford looked out over the crowd. "Perhaps Katharina figured out how to manipulate Petruchio," he suggested.

"Hah!"

"No, I mean it."

"*Hah!*" she said again.

"No, then."

"Of course not. If otherwise, no message was ever so completely hidden." She spun away from him. "I need some air."

Oxford looked at Robin. "I am as surprised as she is. It was the same after *Titus*. An impulse to make fun of my sister has apparently struck a chord in men *and* women."

"Not all women," Robin said, gesturing toward Lettice Knollys. "Perhaps there may be advantages to being a hidden author, my lord, at least when it comes to this play."

"Aye. And it seems that Lettice doesn't know I wrote it or she would have said something about it, for she always speaks everything of what she has on her mind, as little as that may be. Let us go. If I tarry, I fear something bad will happen."

"It already has," Robin said.

# 1593

## ~ 80 ~
## Henry Is Christened in the Boar's Head

Robin was unable to recall later whether it was Oxford or Falstaff who had come up with the idea of bundling two-week old Henry de Vere into a silver wine pitcher—a gift from Henry Tudor to the Thirteenth Earl of Oxford for help in fending off Perkin Warbeck—and carrying the newborn baby through a winter snowstorm to the Boar's Head where he could be christened with beer.

"Gentles!" Oxford greeted everyone as he swept into the Boar's Head, the wine pitcher under his arm, a somewhat bemused baby looking out at everyone. A beaming Falstaff trailed behind. Robin, a look of worry on his face, was left with the task of closing the heavy door against the wind trying to push its way into the Inn.

The storm had forced the closure of the theaters. With nothing else to do, the players and staff, the impresarios and hangers-on, had trudged through the snow in the hope that the wintry day could be pushed aside by the ale and food they expected to find at the Boar's Head. His lordship's arrival had interrupted an argument over where a new indoor theater should be built so that plays could be put on without regard to the weather outside.

"Seneca!" Burbage called out as he stood up on the other side of the table that had been dragged in front of the inn's massive fireplace. The other men rose with him. "Our Roscius," someone else called out. "Soul of our age," said another.

Oxford was surprised. Their praise suggested they knew who had written *The Shrew* and the other plays, but, even if they did, they would never tell anyone outside the theater world.

Falstaff picked up a stool and set it down on top of the table. Oxford put the wine pitcher on top of the stool. Oxford turned the pitcher so that the bemused Henry, peering out wide-eyed from inside the blanket he'd been wrapped in, could see the men around the table.

"To Lord Bolbec!" someone said, referring to Henry by his title as heir. The men picked up their mugs and began to call out toasts. Little Henry gurgled his pleasure. His lips moved. "Look!" one of the men said. "He's trying to say something. Shut it!" The tavern went silent. They and leaned in to listen.

"*Women are made to bear*," someone whispered in a falsetto voice, eliciting a wave of laughter.

"Such wisdom, and at such an early age," Henslowe said.

"He knows his lines already," said another.

The laughter brought Peaches out of the kitchen. "Oh, God," she said, coming over to where Oxford was steadying the wine pitcher. "My lord," she protested, "he is not safe up there."

"Dark beer," Oxford said in a deep voice, as if he were taking part in an ancient ritual. "We are christening him into the fellowship of players and playwrights! Bring dark beer."

"I pray thee, my lord!" Peaches protested. She spotted Falstaff dragging a set of antlers out from behind a dark corner next to the fireplace. "No," she said again. "He's to be christened in church, my lord. Your ladyship will not take well to this."

"Shush, woman," Falstaff said, lifting the rack onto his head.

Peaches went back to the kitchen. Falstaff secured the antlers and stepped up next to the baby. Oxford placed himself on the other side holding the wine pitcher. Peaches came back with a mug she handed across the table to Oxford. Falstaff solemnly began to speak:

"*In nomine patris et filii sancti*," he said, twisting the words of the Catholic prayer to make Oxford the father and little Henry a holy son. The men applauded. Peaches knew enough Latin to understand what he was saying. She threw up her hands and went back to the kitchen.

"*In the potion add a fin of fish*," Falstaff continued, "*a cup of wine, a feather for his hat.*"

"*The twinkle in his father's eye*," Oxford said, rubbing his fingers together over the mug, "*to make the ladies love him bye and bye.*"

"*A drop of ink and parchment skin, to make him grow to be a playwright's kin*," Henslowe added.

"*A bit of iron to grow his sword*," Alleyn joined in.

"*Some fenugreek to make his half-staff full!*" Lyly cried, bringing laughter from the table and a scowl from Falstaff.

Oxford dipped his finger in the beer and stirred it. "*Round and round the mixture goes, one drop I'll place upon his nose*," he chanted as a drop fell squarely onto his son's upturned face. "'*Twill course down to his little toes, and make him what? God only knows."* Henry wrinkled his face as the drop ran over his lips.

It was at this moment that the door to the Boar's Head burst open. Lady Elspeth, snow swirling around her, stood in the doorway, looking like an angry goddess just dismounted from her chariot. "My lord!" she called out across the room. *"What hast thou done with my child!"*

The men scattered. Falstaff slipped into the shadows of the fireplace and slid the antlers off his head. Oxford held onto the wine pitcher while he and his son watched Henry's mother storm across the room toward them.

*"Thou dost humiliate me,"* she cried, pulling Henry out of the wine pitcher, *"and God as well!"* She clasped the baby to her bosom. She glanced down at her son. Some of the beer had dribbled into his mouth. His tongue was tasting it. He was smiling.

"He looks none the worse," Oxford began, but Elspeth cut him off.

"No thanks to you, my lord!" She shifted Henry away from Oxford, as if he might try to take him back. "Don't you understand that if something should carry him off while he is yet unchristened, *he goes not to Heaven, my lord, but to Limbo!"* Her words reverberated through the now-silent inn. "I go to church every day to thank God for giving us a healthy son and thou wouldst consign him to the Devil by taking him out in a snowstorm!" She looked around the room. "His christening will be in less than a fortnight. St. Paul's has been putting me off, claiming they had no time, but they know who his father is and would rather St. Swithin's had the honor." She glared at the men. She wrapped Henry in her cloak and stalked to the door where one of the men had run ahead of her to open it. She went out into the flying snow.

"Well," Henslowe said, "That puts a damper on things. Can't have a christening without a baby."

"'Twas well-done, if foreshortened" Falstaff said. "And just as good as wot he'll hear in Paul's."

"Aye," the others agreed. They all looked at Oxford to guage his reaction. He was smiling. He had apparently liked the performance and seemed to care little that his wife had interrupted it.

"When ye re-write this n some play," Burbage said, "get something larger than the wine pitcher. Something like the iron pot in

471

the fireplace there." He pointed to the cauldron bubbling in the fireplace.

"And fill it with newts and eyeballs," Alleyn said, grinning. "Something better than 'fish fins.' The pit won't like 'fish fins.'"

"They will," Falstaff protested.

"They won't," a number of others replied.

"Was he the fattest deer you ever saw?" someone else asked. They all began to laugh at the memory of Falstaff with antlers on his head.

"Be kind, my friends," Falstaff pleaded.

"We are kind; you are *kine*. As in *c-o-w*."

This brought groans. "I'd rather brave the storm than this," Burbage said, getting up, and heading for the door. The party ended.

## ~ 81 ~
## "If Thy Body Had Been As Deformed As Thy Mind"

Few of the men who had watched the baptism of Oxford's son followed Burbage out the door. The storm was still blowing, though, and most stayed. Oxford, for no reason, stayed as well. He shifted closer to the fire and basked in the sound of the others debating Thomas Nashe's latest effort. Peaches brought him a bowl of stew. Looking into the fire, Oxford realized he could not remember having ever been as content. He finally had an heir, and a wife who loved him. She would forgive him for taking their son out in a snowstorm—"My son too," he thought, "despite her claim that I had taken 'her son.'" He day-dreamed about images of spring, his favorite time of year, and watching his son become a young boy while he, the father, disgorged the plays and poetry that bubbled up inside him like the stew in the pot he was staring at.

"*My mind to me a kingdom is,*" he said to himself, "*such perfect joy therein I find.*" He drifted off. Everyone sensed he had wrapped himself in the comfort of his favorite tavern, with its fire and food and friends. They muted their voices and drifted about, never coming close enough to penetrate the invisible bubble that surrounded him. Though he could have stayed there forever, he finally tore himself away. Time to go home, Edward, he said to himself. Time to see my boy again. He heaved himself into his heavy bearskin coat, wished everyone 'Good day,' and headed out alone into the howling snowstorm.

The wind blew down the street from St. Paul's. He leaned into it. Head down, eyes focused on the slippery ground in front of him, he began to make his way toward Oxford Court.

At Pudding Lane, a loud voice called out "Hold!" Oxford looked up and was surprised to see Thomas Knyvet, Anne Vavasor's cousin, in front of him. Knyvet, a much larger man, was holding a rapier in one hand and a buckler in the other. His face was seething with rage. "If thy body had been as deformed as thy mind is," he announced loudly, as if the street were full of people eager to know what he was about, "my house had been yet unspotted and thy cowardice unknown." He started toward Oxford.

"Stay, Thomas, while I arm myself." Oxford fumbled to open his coat and pull out the rapier stuck through his belt.

"This be no Master's Prize contest, ye scurrilous dog, but vengeance for your treatment of my cousin. There be no rules. If ye be not ready, ye die; if ye be ready, ye die anyway! *Hai*!" he cried as he ran at Oxford, waving his sword in a vicious arc.

Oxford slipped in the snow and fell sideways, and Knyvet's sword missed him. Oxford managed to pull out his rapier as he fell. He thrust up at Knyvet as the larger man passed over him, striking Knyvet in the leg. Knyvet howled in pain and grabbed his leg, hopping to one side.

Oxford rolled to his feet. Knyvet turned and charged, swinging at Oxford again, but the blow glanced off Oxford's coat.

"Hold! Ye dog! We're not playing hits and passes. Stand and be killed!"

"What ails ye, Thomas?" Oxford asked, backing away. "Why now, after so many years? Anne and I are friends."

"She may have forgiven you, but I haven't!" Knyvet cried, rushing at him again. This time he held his sword upright. Oxford ducked but Knyvet hit him with the buckler and drove Oxford over onto his back. Oxford stabbed up but his rapier broke in half. "Hah!" Knyvet shouted. He stabbed down but Oxford squirmed away and the blade went through the lower part of his coat to pierce his thigh instead.

It was Oxford's turn to cry out in pain. Knyvet raised his sword to finish him off, but Oxford rolled away again.

"Avast!" a booming voice called out from somewhere in the curtain of snow. Falstaff was coming toward them, waving a broad sword. "Ye die if he does!" Falstaff called out. Knyvet sneered. He knew Falstaff was too far away to save Oxford, now lying on his back, blooding running out into the white snow. Knyvet turned to finish Oxford off when Falstaff, still yards away, flipped his sword over and threw it butt-end at Knyvet, hitting him in the head. The blow knocked Knyvet over into the snow. Oxford scrambled up against a wall while Knyvet, stunned, picked himself up.

Falstaff, quick for such a big man, retrieved his sword before Knyvet had recovered his senses. "No more fancy Eye-talian moves, Mr. Knyvet," Falstaff called out, waving his sword around like it was made of air instead of steel. Knyvet backed away, spreading his sword and buckler in a defensive position. Falstaff reached over and picked Oxford up, flipping him over his left shoulder, head down.

"Sir John!" Oxford protested.

Knyvet tried to stab Oxford but Falstaff blocked his sword. "Leave me kill him," Knyvet said.

"Nay," Falstaff said.

"Put me down!" Oxford cried. Knyvet tried to stab Oxford again but Falstaff twisted away.

"Get out of the way, fat man, or I will kill you first," Knyvet said, waving his sword back and forth.

"'Fat man?'" Falstaff said. "Is that all you can come up with? I hope you fight better than you curse." He swung his sword out to his right and caught Knyvet off-guard, knocking him onto his back. "*Alla Stoccata!*" Knyvet called out as he thrust upwards at Falstaff.

Falstaff parried the blow.

"Enough, John!" Oxford cried. "Put me down!"

"Roast Beef!" Falstaff thundered, advancing on Knyvet, who was still on his back and trying to scramble away. "Boiled Potatoes!" Falstaff called out, whirling his sword as Knyvet kept propelling himself backward through the snow, trying to get up. "Why do you flee, crab-like, my friend?" Falstaff asked, Oxford still over his shoulder. He swung at Knyvet again. "Where are your '*punto riversos,*' your '*imbrocattas.*' Didn't Signore Bonnetti teach you anything?"

"*Passata sotto!*" Knyvet replied, dropping to one knee, left hand on the ground, as he thrust up at Falstaff.

"Turnip greens!" Falstaff replied, fending off Knyvet's thrust. He whirled his sword faster, continually moving toward Knyvet, who finally turned and ran.

"Ye fight not fair!" Knyvet called over his shoulder as he put distance between himself and Falstaff.

"Of course not," Falstaff said, as he watched Knyvet disappear.

"God damn ye, John, put me down!" Oxford said. Blood was pouring over the front of Falstaff's coat. "I don't need your help, Sir John. You stopped me from vanquishing him!"

Falstaff dropped his sword and laid Oxford in the snow. "Well, as gracious a 'thank you' as I ever received."

"Why did you put me over your shoulder? Why humiliate me!"

"To get your head below your leg, Nedward. Saves blood."

"Don't call me 'Nedward.' I told you never to call me that!'"

"Your lordship, then." He pulled Oxford's coat open. "If I had left ye on the ground, ye would have bled to death before I was finished with him." He pulled Oxford's leggings apart. Blood gushed out. He pulled the belt off his coat and wrapped it around Oxford's leg, tightening it.

"Watch the jewels," Oxford muttered through gritted teeth.

"No need for them anymore," Falstaff said, standing up. "Ye went and got married." He picked up his sword and bundled Oxford over his shoulder again.

"Sir John!" Oxford cried out anew.

A trio of street urchins had been creeping toward them, drawn by the fight. Falstaff flipped a coin to the closest one. "To Oxford Court, then. Tell the lady the Earl is to Sir John's." He flipped coins to the other two. Fetch López. Bring him to my place."

"Why to your place?" Oxford asked. "Oxford Court is closer."

"Ye need a hiding place, my lord. Something is up. Knyvet would never have attacked you like this unless he thought he could get away with it. Something has changed. I can smell it."

"Your nose again."

"Aye, but a different nose."

Oxford started to ask how many noses he had but lost the thought. "'Twas Thomas who stabbed me, John," Oxford muttered as they passed by the Boar's Head.

"Aye. Thomas Knyvet," Falstaff said, trudging through the snow.

"No, Thomas Brincknell," Oxford whispered, just before he passed out.

## López and the Ghost of Thomas Brincknell

The entrance to Falstaff's apartments was off an alley that disappeared into darkness. The door was small but opened onto a large room. Falstaff kicked it open and carried Oxford inside to the uproar of a pack of dogs that leaped up to see what the big man was bringing in. Older dogs, warmed by the fire, looked up but declined to join the chaos. Marrow bones, chewed-up sticks, and other debris littered the floor.

Fox skins and huntsman poles lined the walls. Two chairs opposite the door were occupied by cats that eyed Falstaff as he carried Oxford into the room. A large table stood in the middle. Straight-backed chairs stood at military attention around it.

A fireplace took up the wall opposite the door. Shelves either side held arrows, cross-bows, stone-bows, and other weapons. An oyster table littered with shells sat in a corner. A table in the other corner held hawks' hoods and bells. A third table was covered with dice, cards, and boxes, while a fourth had a hole in its center filled with tobacco and pipes. Two or three green felt hats with their crowns punched in rested on a low bench and were filled with a dozen eggs each.

A door at the far end provided access to a garden which, from the barking and thumping that could be heard, held more dogs. A door next to the fireplace opened into a chapel that had been unused since Henry VIII had seized the building from the Whitefriars and given it to the Earl of Sussex, whose descendants had leased it to Falstaff.

The big man crossed the hall and carried Oxford into the chapel. He used his foot to pry a pew away from the wall and push it up against another one, forming a long box into which he lowered Oxford. "Thomas," Oxford mumbled. Falstaff gathered a red and black Turkish blanket from the pulpit and laid it over Oxford.

"Armado!" Falstaff called out.

The garden door opened and shut. "Master," a voice replied. The shuffling of wooden clogs could be heard crossing the hall. A legless boy, his stumps and hands shod with wooden shoes, appeared in the doorway.

"There should be some soup left on the fire. Bring it."

"Master," the boy replied, swiveling as he disappeared into the hall, closing the door to keep the dogs out.

Falstaff pulled Oxford's leg up and laid it over the back of one of the pews. He unwrapped the bloody clothing and loosened the belt tied around the leg. New blood began to flow immediately. Falstaff let the wound bleed for a few seconds and tightened the belt again. The legless boy came back in, carrying a bowl with one hand while supporting himself with the other. Falstaff dipped a cloth into the bowl and laid it against Oxford's lips, forcing some of the soup into Oxford's mouth. The boy pulled himself up over one end of the pew to see what was going on.

"Who's he?" he asked, trying to see Oxford's face, hidden by the Turkish rug.

"Nobody," Falstaff said. "No one came in today. Understand? Not a word."

The boy nodded.

"Did ye feed the dogs?"

"Yes, master."

"And the cats?"

"All."

They could hear the door to the alley open. Falstaff stood up. "Long Tom?" he called out.

"Aye." A thin man with a filthy beard appeared in the doorway. His face looked like it had been squeezed together at birth. His eyes crowded up against his nose, which, from its length, had absorbed those parts God had denied him elsewhere. His eyes twinkled and lent an attraction to his face that would not otherwise have been there. "Wot's this?" he asked, looking at Oxford and his bloody leg.

"Nobody," the boy said.

Long Tom looked from Falstaff to the boy. "Right," he said.

"And right it stays," Falstaff said. "They'll be chinks in our pockets if we keep him alive *and* no one finds out he's here. Got it?"

Long Tom nodded. A smile spread up either side of his nose. "What we have here is a mystery, then." He obviously liked mysteries.

"Aye. And if you blather about this to the people who give ye scraps and leftovers for the dogs and cats what live here, we could all be out on the street, or in the Counter, scot and lot, if not worse!"

The smile disappeared.

"Bolt the door and let no one in."

"Aye." Long Tom went back into the main room.

"He's the Earl of Oxford," the boy said quietly. Falstaff nodded. "Who would want to stick him in the leg?"

"None of yer business," Falstaff said. "Ye look after him. I'm going to find out where the doctor is."

A knocking was heard at the door. The dogs set too again. Falstaff left Oxford's side and waded through the dogs. "Announce yerself!" he called out.

"It's Robin, Sir John. I have Dr. López with me."

Falstaff opened the door. Robin and a short, dark-skinned man stood in the doorway. They were covered with snow.

"How is he?" Robin asked.

"He's delirious." Falstaff said. He reached past Robin to pull López into the room, slamming the door shut behind them. Falstaff led them into the chapel.

"Move away," López said, waving a hand at Armado. He leaned in over the pew and pulled the cloth away to examine the wound. "Nnnnn, nnnnn, nnnnn," he muttered to himself as he poked a finger in the hole in Oxford's leg. Oxford stirred, moaning. López reached into the bag he had brought with him and took out a glass jar. He opened it and stuck his index finger into the jar, bringing out a yellow viscous substance that he began spreading on Oxford's leg. "Honey," he explained, "from Mount Hybla, mixed with powdered river dust from Egypt, hot cedar oil from Lebanon, and a bit of alum and white vinegar." Oxford groaned as the mixture sank into his wound.

"Will he live?" Robin asked.

"God knows," López said, making the sign of the cross as he looked down at Oxford. "He should not be allowed to move for three days. The wound needs to form a scab. Any movement will open it up." He took out tissue paper and carefully unfolded it next to Oxford. He lifted up a spider's web and laid it on top of Oxford's leg.

"What else can we do?" Falstaff asked.

"Pray for his soul." López said, as he smoothed the edges of the spider's web over the wound. "He will not likely survive this."

"He's tougher than you think, doctor."

López shrugged. "Wrapping your belt around his leg saved his life, but we will know in a week whether you have done more than temporarily extended his life."

"Gramercy for coming so quickly," Robin said.

"*Di nada.* I owe his lordship for how he greeted me like an Englishman when I came to court. The others treated me like a Jew. A few words from him and the Queen made me court physician. Her favor made me rich. I will come back in three days." He picked up his bag and moved toward the door.

Falstaff put his hand on the doctor's arm. "Thomas Knyvet did this."

"Knyvet? Over Anne Vavasor?" López was puzzled. "That was a long time ago."

"Aye. Something else is going on. You know anything about it?" López shook his head. "Ye weren't here, if ye know what I mean." López nodded. He went out into the hall, pushing his way through the dogs.

Oxford stirred. "Thomas," he moaned.

"He plans his revenge," Robin said, buoyed by the sound of Oxford's voice.

"Nay. He thinks the undercook he killed at Cecil House when he was a boy has returned to avenge his untimely death."

"Thomas Brincknell," Robin said.

"Ye know?"

"He told me about it. And how you saved him by telling the jury that the undercook ran onto the end of his sword."

"No lie'll save him now." Falstaff said. "I will make him a merrie-go-down that will make him want to live." He snapped his fingers.

"Master," Armado said. He scuttled out the chapel door.

Robin watched him go. "I think I know him," Robin said, "but not from where."

"Blackfriars," Falstaff said, as he rearranged Oxford's blanket.

"Blackfriars? Yes. He said he'd been an actor. He quoted a line from *Comedy of Errors*. When I asked him how he came to see the play, he said a friend carried him to the play on his back." Robin looked up wonderingly at Falstaff. "You were the friend?"

"He was a good player before he lost his legs. Without his legs, he became a nobody. Among the dogs and cats, he's a somebody. The animals love him because he's down at their level. He doesn't tower over them like I do. He keeps the animals company while I'm gone and Long Tom gets the food and firewood."

"You burn wood?" Robin was surprised to hear this. Almost everyone was switching to coal.

"Coal is made by the Devil. It's black and dug out of the ground. It stinks when ye burn it. Only what God grows with sunlight goes into my fireplace."

"Oh." Robin looked around for the legless boy. "What's the boy's name?" he asked.

"Armado."

"Armado? He's Spanish?"

Falstaff shrugged. "He has no legs. What else could I call him?"

Robin giggled. "But what about the cats and dogs? And the hawk I saw in the rafters? What are they doing here?"

"For because they accept me as I am. None of them see my girth and chastise me for it. None counts my years and tell me how long ago I was young. None dismiss me because my hat is out of fashion, or look the other way when my shirt is filthy and torn. They love me no matter what." He stood up. "Armado!" he called out.

"Master."

"More stew for Robin and me at the table, if ye please."

"Yes, master."

They went out into the large room. Falstaff sat down in the chair at the end of the table and pointed to a chair next to him, Robin sat down on it. A large wooden trencher in front of Falstaff was flanked by a white stick fourteen inches long. A glass tun without feet stood next to the trencher and held the remains of a pint of beer into which someone had stuck a sprig of rosemary.

Tom came in with a pot of stew, followed Armado carrying a pitcher of beer. The dogs began yelping and trying to climb on the table but Falstaff picked up the stick and drove them away. "I've no mind to share meat with any of ye, so shut it."

The yelping died back and the dogs took up position around the table, hoping for scraps.

"Lady Elspeth will need to be told how he's doing," Robin said.

"Aye, but not tonight. It's too late. Go over tomorrow when ye get up."

Robin looked around. He didn't see any beds. "So where do ye sleep, Sir John."

Falstaff pointed to the fireplace. "Best place in the house. I kick the bones aside and lay out in front of the fire. The dogs climb onto me and act as my blankets. I sleep like the dead."

Robin smiled slightly, and tried to imagine Falstaff lying in front of the fireplace covered by dogs. "Is there no other place?"

"No beds, if that's what ye mean, but don't worry, lad. Wherever ye decide to lay out on, a dog or two will keep ye warm."

True to his word, Falstaff flipped some bones to the dogs when he was finished and used the time they fought over them to lie down in front of the fireplace. In minutes, he was fast asleep. First one dog and then another came over and flopped down next to him. Smaller ones began climbing on top until he was covered with dogs.

Robin looked around and started thinking the table might be a good place to spend the night. Long Tom and Armado had cleared it and disappeared into the back. Instead, he opted for the bench with the hats full of eggs. He put them on a shelf near the fireplace and dragged a filthy blanket over to the bench. Here he was faced with a dilemma. Should he lay the blanket on the bench to soften its hard surface, or lie on the bench and pull the blanket over him for warmth? He opted for comfort over warmth, thinking the room was not that cold. He spread out the blanket and lay down. Within moments, a terrier was sitting next to the bench at eye level, his eager face asking to join him. A somewhat larger dog took up a position next to the terrier. Robin and the dogs looked at each other. Then, the terrier vaulted on top of him. The larger dog quickly followed. The terrier flopped down over Robin's legs, the larger dog across his mid-section. Within minutes, they were fast asleep.

## ~ 83 ~
## *"Abandoned & Despised"*

Fever gripped Oxford for a week before he began to recover. López came the third day and then every day thereafter. One day he brought Simon Forman with him. They poked Oxford's wound and argued over how to treat it. Shackspear appeared another day, just as Oxford had begun to rally. He didn't say how he knew where Oxford was. He told Oxford he wanted to bring a Cambridge student by who was studying medicine and knew all the latest treatments. Shackspear raved about the student, but then let slip that he was trying to marry the young man to his oldest daughter. It was at this point that Falstaff decided it was time for him to leave. He escorted Shackspear to the door where Shackspear, irritated at being summarily disposed of, sneered, "Who needs him?" referring to Oxford. "The theaters are closed, maybe for good this time. We are to the provinces, Henslowe and Burbage too, where every play is new, *no matter how old it is.*" This got Falstaff moving and Shackspear decided he better put some distance between himself and the fat man who was now coming after him with surprising speed.

Robin rarely left Oxford's side. He would play soft melodies on his lute and sing songs about summer love. Lady Elspeth came every day. When Oxford began to rally, she brought young Henry. Oxford looked at his son and smiled. Robin saw the smile and grinned; Falstaff let out a laugh; and the dogs in the hall broke into raucous barking. Lady Elspeth kissed Oxford on the forehead and asked him to come home. He said he would. López decided the next day that the Earl would be strong enough to move within a fortnight.

One day, as he continued to recuperate, Oxford asked Falstaff why Thomas Knyvet had attacked him.

"I don't know, my lord. But I've been told that your sister, Katherine, has filed papers to strip you of your titles."

"What? Again? I was thirteen when she sued me last."

"Aye, but she lost because she didn't sue ye in the Court of Wards."

"So why now? I've done her no harm. What cause has she against me now?"

"Someone must be using her for their own purposes. Thomas Knyvet obviously thinks Katherine will be successful or he never would have attacked you."

"And who could that be? I've not offended anyone lately, have I?"

"I am making inquiries."

"And what is Katherine's complaint?"

"That your father was married to another woman when he married your mother."

Oxford was incredulous. "She would slander him in his grave?"

"It's not about your father, my lord. It's about your titles and lands. If the judges decide in her favor …"

"I will be made common and poor in the same instant!"

"Aye."

"What proof does she have?"

"I don't know, my lord. I spoke with your uncle who defended you the last time. Master Golding says a special court has been commissioned to hear your sister's claim because it involves your ancient titles."

"'Sblood, Jack! This cannot be. What does Malfis say?"

"He returns not my messages."

"Has a trial date been set?"

"No. I'm told they have to serve you with the summons first, but they don't know where you are. You're safe here, but as soon as you return to Oxford Court, they'll serve you and the trial date will be set."

Oxford looked tired. "So, what is to be done? Should I resign my titles and be done with this?"

"And where would that leave me?" Falstaff asked, indignantly. "What is Sir John Falstaff if he hath not his Earl of Oxford to serve? I am too old a dog to learn new tricks, my lord. Rest here; I will find out who is behind this." He turned to leave.

"Jack."

"Yes?"

"Twice now you've saved my life. I thank you."

"Then I say you're welcome, you're welcome."

Oxford laughed. "Three's a charm?"

Falstaff shook his head. "Fate never spoke those words."

Oxford returned to Oxford Court but took little comfort there. He wandered about the house adrift, like a ship without rigging or crew. No words of poetry came out of him. His eyes were dead. Robin stopped playing his lute and took to hiding under the stairs lest his presence irritate his master.

Oxford finally realized that Malfis was avoiding him and the messages Oxford had sent him for information on the lawsuit. He decided to go to Malfis's office and find out what his lawyer could do for him. He had not gotten far when he rounded a corner and saw Falstaff coming down the street toward him. "Jack!"

"Edward," Falstaff said, stopping in front of Oxford.

"Thou dost call me 'Edward' in a public street?'"

Falstaff did not answer right away. He put his hands on his hips and tipped his head back, surveying Oxford as if he were seeing him for the first time. "Aye, Edward. That's what I shall call ye, as all the world will, if the trial goes not in your favor."

"Jack!"

"No, no, no," Falstaff said, waving a fat finger back and forth. "I am no 'Jack' to you. I am 'Jack' to my friends, 'John' to my family, and 'Sir John' to the world, which is where I hold you to be."

"*What?*"

"Do not be dismayed, Edward. 'Tis no dishonor to quit the field when the battle is lost. But rest assured, whether the trial leaves you lord or commoner, the two of us will hoist another mug in the Boar's Head someday. In the meantime, fare thee well, Edward." He turned and started to shamble away.

"*You traitorous dog!*" Oxford called after him.

Malfis suddenly walked out of an alleyway to Oxford's right. "Good even," he said.

Oxford turned to him. "You recognize me?"

"Of course, my lord."

"That hulking beast of a human being doesn't," Oxford said, pointing to the figure of Falstaff walking away from them.

"Ah, Sir John. Yes. He has obviously abandoned you. Well, he has always been quick to jump off a sinking ship."

"A sinking ship?"

"Well, let us say 'taking on water,' my lord."

"So you've heard about Lady Katherine's suit."

"I have, my lord."

"Malfis! My sister wants to take my name away from me! She can have my estates; I will give her all the money I have, but I cannot let her take my name! You must defend me!"

"Unfortunately, my lord, I cannot."

"Why is that?"

"I am your solicitor, my lord. Only barristers can appear in court."

"Then find me a barrister."

"I have been canvassing the inns, but without success so far."

Malfis showed no pleasure at Oxford's predicament. He was simply stating the facts. Had Oxford heard a touch of joy in Malfis' voice, he would have erupted in fury. The colorless words left him drained.

"Tell me, Malfis: the outcome has already been decided, hasn't it?"

"I do not know, my lord." He looked like he was regretting that he had stopped to talk to Oxford. "But it appears that Falstaff has so concluded," nodding in the direction Falstaff had gone, "and that is not a good sign."

Oxford did not know what to say. His leg throbbed with pain. He leaned against a wall.

"I will send around as soon as I have news, my lord," Malfis said, but Oxford had already turned away. Malfis watched him go, a far older and more tired man than the lord who had sold Fisher's Folly, or even the apprehensive groom who had signed the contract to marry Elspeth Trentham.

## ~ 84 ~
## The Death of Christopher Marlowe

Oxford was coming out of the day room when Robin came running into the house. "My lord! Christopher Marlowe is slain! Stabbed in the eye."

"Where? When?"

"In a tavern in Deptford! Within the past hour!"

"Oh, Robin! *Cut is the branch that might have grown full straight, and burnéd is Apollo's laurel-bough!* Hurry! We must to Deptford!"

They ran down to the Thames and leaped into a four-man wherry. "Lads! To Deptford! Marlowe is dead!" Oxford told them. A wail went up. Robin threw them a fistful of coins at them and the boat shot out into the river.

"I killed him," Oxford said forlornly to Robin. "I met him at the Steelyard a few weeks ago. He said he had heard of Katherine's suit. He promised to help me. Now he is dead."

"Oh, no, my lord," Robin said. "He had many enemies."

Oxford shook his head. His face was grim.

The wherry was soon inside the dockyards at Deptford. Oxford and Robin headed for a cluster of buildings and inns that wrapped around the headwaters of the cove. They had no trouble identifying the inn where Marlowe had been killed: the lane in front was crowded with people and carriages. Oxford pushed his way through the people and ran into the inn through the open front door. Sir Robert Cecil was coming down the stairs. "My lord," he said.

Oxford was surprised and suspicious to see his former brother-in-law.

"You wouldst be better off not seeing him," Sir Robert said.

"Why was he killed?"

"An argument over the bill."

Oxford's face showed that he did not believe him.

"Truly. How oft do we see something insignificant have such dire results, In this case, though, it was providential."

"Why say you that, Sir Robert?"

A sardonic smile slipped across Sir Robert's face. He pointed to the stairs with the cane he was holding. "Your greatest competitor lies upstairs, forever silent. You don't appreciate that?"

"No, I do not. Everyone, including you and me, is the worst for it." He brushed past Sir Robert and headed up the stairs. A doorway at the top led into a small room where Richard Topcliffe was leaning over the body. The sight of Topcliffe, Elizabeth's favorite torturer, only increased Oxford's suspicions. Topcliffe held the dagger in his hand, having just pulled it from Marlowe's eye.

"Stabbed with his own blade," Topcliffe said, a bemused look on his face. "There were four of them. Marlowe liked not his share of the bill and pulled his knife. The man he attacked turned it back into his eye."

"Where are the others?" Oxford asked.

"In custody until we sort this out." He looked down at Marlowe's body. "It's a pity I never got to put Honest John's boots on him and find out what the Catholics are up to."

Oxford stepped past Topcliffe and knelt next to the body. Marlowe's remaining eye stared up at him. Oxford felt like he could see, in that good eye, the dead man receding at great speed into space.

Oxford stood up. "Has he any family?"

Topcliffe shook his head. "It's a potter's grave for him."

"I will take the body," Oxford said. Robin had appeared in the doorway to the room. "Get a carriage," he said to Robin, who disappeared back down the stairs. Topcliffe motioned for the men to carry the body down the stairs. They put it in a carriage Robin had found. In five minutes, Oxford and Robn were outside the local church. For £1, the vicar agreed to let Marlowe be buried in the church graveyard. A row of freshly-dug graves lay open. Marlowe's body was lowered into one. The grave diggers filled it in, leaving Oxford and Robin alone. Oxford walked over to the cemetery wall where he took piece of coal out of his pocket and wrote on the wall:

> *Reader! I am to let Thee know*
> *Marlowe's Body only lies below;*
> *For, could the Earth his Soul comprise,*
> *Earth would be Richer than the Skies!*

488

## ~ 85 ~
### *Matrimonium Clandestinum*

A bailiff dressed in a dark coat and round, fringed cap, waited for Oxford outside one of the private entrances to Whitehall Palace. "My lord," he said, touching his cap, and then, turning to Arthur Golding and Robin, touching it again to acknowledge their presence.

Whitehall was a rabbit-warren of rooms, gardens, and courts cobbled together by Henry VIII out of the former residence of Thomas Wolsey, Archbishop of York. Henry had seized it in 1529; his successors had been adding to it ever since, making it the largest palace in Europe. By 1593, it spanned King Street, a public thoroughfare that ran through its middle. The bailiff took them to a secret courtroom buried deep in the palace, a fitting place, thought Oxford, to dispense injustice.

He walked into a long, narrow room. High windows either side let in little light. A cluster of straight chairs filled the area near the door. A low railing separated them from the rest of the room. Oxford thought the chairs looked like cattle in a feed pen, waiting to find out whether they were to be let out to pasture or sent down the hall to the abattoir. A long table stretched toward the far wall, which was paneled in chestnut and covered with brightly painted coats of arms. High-backed chairs surrounded the table. A clerk sat at the end arranging papers. The chairs to his left were empty.

Eight lords were already seated at the table, four on each side. They were dressed in heavy robes and wide ruffs. All wore white caps, tight to the head and peaked. High wooden partitions behind them pressed up against the lords, who turned their heads to look at Oxford as he came in. Oxford surveyed the room, head back, trying to project as much disdain as he could.

Arthur Golding took off his hat and tried to make himself look small. He had not wanted to come. He was a great, lumbering shaggy-dog type of person uncomfortable outside his study. Oxford had pointed out that his uncle had saved him the last time his legitimacy was challenged and that Golding owed his sister, Oxford's mother, a defense.

489

A bailiff came over. He was big and beefy. "Be seated," he said, pointing to the chairs behind the railing.

"I am a party to this action," Oxford said, dismissing him.

"That will be determined by the judge," the bailiff said. Oxford pushed him aside and stepped through the bar.

Lord Ellesmere entered the room at the far end. He was accompanied by Sir Francis Bacon, whose arms were full of papers. Lord Ellesmere sat in the middle chair; Sir Francis sat down to his left. Lord Ellesmere gestured to the clerk to announce the case. The clerk unrolled a roll of parchment. "Oyer, oyer," the clerk called out. "All those having business before this honourable court draw near and give your attention." He read from the roll.

> *By order of the Privy Council, the sixth and twentieth day of June in the thirty-fifth year of the glorious reign of Elizabeth, Queen of England, etc., to the Lord Chancellor, greetings, you are hereby commanded to take whatever steps are deemed appropriate by you to assemble a jury of peers to determine whether Earl John, Sixteenth Earl of Oxford, did lawfully marry Margery Golding in Belchamp St. Paul on August 1, 1548.*

"My lord!" Oxford called out. The clerk looked up in surprise. Oxford strode to the end of the table opposite Lord Ellesmere. "This is outrageous! My mother and father, dead these many years; unable to respond to these charges; my ancestors writhing in their tombs as they hear my half-sister's crazed attempts to take my patrimony away from me! I am Edward de Vere, the Seventeenth Earl of Oxford, Lord Great Chamberlain of England, Viscount Bolbec, Baron Scales and Badlesmere—"

"Yes, yes," Lord Ellesmere said. "We know who you are. And I will overlook this gross violation of our rules in deference to your lordship's ancient title, as well as how these accusations must offend you."

"So where is she?" Oxford shouted. "Why is she not here?"

"Because, my lord, the question charged to us by the Privy Council does not arise out of any claim by your sister, although I understand why you might think that to be the case. The question of the validity of your parents' marriage has been raised in a case before the Court of Common Pleas. A John Masterson has filed suit to dispossess one Hugh Key of a lease that was granted to Mr. Key and his mother by your father, Earl John."

"What does that have to do with me or my parents' marriage?"

"Mr. Masterson says that he is the lawful leaseholder to the property in question by virtue of having purchased the lease from Sir Christopher Hatton, who, it is claimed, purchased the lease from you."

Oxford tried to think. He remembered selling a lease to Hatton. "I sold Sir Christopher the remainder interest. If Mr. Key or his mother are still living, Mr. Masterson must wait until they die."

"Mr. Key has argued as much. But he has gone further. Mr. Key has alleged that your father's marriage to your mother was invalid because your father was married to another woman when he married your mother. If so, your parent's marriage was bigamous and you are illegitimate. If so, you inherited nothing to convey to Sir Christopher. If true, Mr. Key argues, Mr. Masterson's suit must fail."

Lord Ellesmere paused. He could see the shock on Oxford's face. He went on. "Mr. Key's defense raised an issue that is beyond the jurisdiction of the Court of Common Pleas, *videlicet*, whether the marriage of the Sixteenth Earl of Oxford to your mother was valid. Therefore, the judge hearing the case in the Court of Common Pleas certified the question to the Privy Council, which, in turn, charged me with empaneling a jury to hear evidence and answer the question—did your father legally marry your mother? I will convey the jury's verdict to the Court of Common Pleas and they will continue on with the case of *Masterson v. Key*."

Lord Ellesmere was clearly enjoying himself. His use of one of Lord Burghley's favorite phrases—*videlicet*—was intended to make Oxford think the Lord Treasurer was involved in the proceeding when, in fact, he was not.

Oxford finally found his voice. "And from such an insignificant event, a defense raised in a lawsuit over a lease of property, the marriage of my parents can be ruled invalid?" Oxford blinked. "And, in the process, touch the legitimacy of my blood, and the right to my hereditary possessions?"

Lord Ellesmere nodded solemnly. "Such is the law."

"But Katherine *must* be here! She is behind this! I know she is!"

"My lord," Lord Ellesmere said, his voice becoming firmer. "In applying the law, we must deal with facts about your parents' marriage, and those facts will not come from you or your sister. Your sister was eight when your father married your mother. You were not even alive. Therefore, neither of you are qualified to provide evidence in this proceeding. Please take a seat behind the bar." He struck the bench with his gavel. "The court will come to order. Sir Francis: bring in the first witness."

Arthur pulled Oxford back into a chair in the first row but did not sit down beside him. To everyone's surprise, he addressed the judge. "Your honor," he said.

"Who are you?" Lord Ellesmere demanded.

"Arthur Golding, sister of Margery Golding, uncle to Edward de Vere. I am also brother-in-law to Earl John, may he rest in peace."

"Are you here to give evidence?"

"I was present at their wedding, your Excellency."

"Do you know whether or not the Earl entered into any prior marriages before he married your sister?"

"I do not."

"Then sit down."

"Your Excellency, in a good-faith effort to ensure that justice does not miscarry here, I would like to be heard." Lord Ellesmere's eyebrows rose. "There is the question of laches, your Excellency.

"Are you a lawyer?"

"No, your Honor."

"Then sit down!"

"But this matter was raised thirty years ago in a proceeding filed by Lady Katherine in 1563. Her claim was dismissed."

"Yes, but the dismissal did not go to the substance of her claim. It was dismissed because she had filed suit in the wrong court."

"Yes, your honor, but the law does not customarily allow a claim that has lain dormant for so long to be prosecuted, particularly when crucial witnesses have died or disappeared."

"That is true, but the question we must decide in this proceeding has arisen out of a case that is *in vivo*, so there is no staleness in the question of who is the true leaseholder in the case of *Masterson v. Key*."

Golding was forced to agree.

"But even if your contention of staleness had some merit, Mr. Golding, would you want the title to an earldom as old as the earls of Oxford to descend through a child spawned on an illegal marriage, just because justice has been asleep? That *would be* injustice." Lord Ellesmere glanced at Oxford and then pointed to the chairs behind Arthur. Arthur sat down.

Lord Ellesmere looked at Sir Francis. "Call your first witness."

"Thank you, your lordship. I call Rooke Greene."

A tall, lean man entered the room through a door in the right-hand wall. He took up a position at the near end of the table, his back to Oxford. The clerk stood at the other end of the table. The witness raised his hand. "Do you swear, under the penalties of perjury, to tell the truth, the whole truth, and nothing but the truth, so help you God?"

"I do."

"Your name." Sir Francis asked.

"Rooke Greene, esquire."

"Where do you live Mr. Greene?"

"In Little Sampford, Your Grace, County of Essex."

"Your age?"

"Three score and ten."

"Did you know John de Vere, the Sixteenth Earl of Oxford?"

"I did."

"Did the Earl marry Dorothy Neville?"

"Yes, he did. She was his first wife. She was the sister of the Earl of Westmoreland. Their wedding was feted at Castle Hedingham."

"Did Earl John and Dorothy Neville have any children?"

"Yes. Lady Katherine, who married Lord Windsor."

"Did there come a time when Earl John and Dorothy Neville stopped living together as man and wife?"

"Yes. Through some unkind dealing of the Earl, the Lady Dorothy removed herself from the Earl's presence to live elsewhere."

"How do you know this?"

"The Duke of Northumberland employed me to ask her to return to the Earl, but she refused, saying she would never live again amongst such bad company as were about the Earl at the time. His retainers were apparently unruly and had treated her poorly."

"Is Dorothy Neville living?"

"She is not, Your Grace. She died about the second year of King Edward VI's reign, near Salisbury where she had gone to live."

"Did Earl John divorce Lady Dorothy before she died?"

"Not to my knowledge."

"Did you know a woman by the name of Dorothy Fosser?"

"I did, Your Grace. She was maid to Lady Dorothy."

"Did Earl John marry Dorothy Fosser?"

"No, although he contracted to do so."

"What happened?"

"On the day before he was to marry her, he rode to Paul's Belchamp and married Margery Golding instead."

"How do you know this?"

"We all knew it. I also heard it from John Anson, who married Dorothy Fosser within the year."

"Is Dorothy Fosser still living?"

"No. She died at Felsted about the fourth year of the reign of Queen Mary."

"Did Earl John marry any other woman?"

"Yes. A woman named Joan Jockey, although I only know this by report."

"Did Earl John marry any other woman?"

"Not that I know of."

"You may stand down. Call John Anson." Greene walked passed another man who took his place. The clerk swore him in.

"Your name?" Sir Francis asked.

"John Anson."

"Your age."

"Three score."

"Your occupation?"

"Clerk to the Parson of West Turville."

"Did you know Dorothy Fosser?"

"I guess I did. I married her."

There were titters in the court. Lord Ellesmere scowled.

"Do you know whether she was ever supposed to marry the Earl of Oxford?"

"Yes. The Earl of Oxford contracted to marry her, but there followed no marriage for that after the banns were said and a license obtained, the Earl married Margery Golding instead."

"But you say there was a contract."

"Aye, but whether it was in writing or not, I know not."

"Did she pursue a cause of action against the Earl?"

"She consulted with Doctor Dale, Doctor Jones, Doctor Aubrey, Mr. Vaughan, and Proctor Biggs about the contract. They told her she should sue a commission to prove the contract, and that if it were proved, the marriage of the Earl with Margery Golding would be *matrimonium clandestinum*!" He announced this with great effect.

Anson's answer had not been what Sir Francis had expected. "Are you claiming that the Earl's marriage to Margery Golding was *matrimonium clandestinum* because of his contract with Dorothy Fosser, or *matrimonium clandestinum* because the haste of the Earl's marriage to Margery did not allow proper time for the banns to be read?"

This was too much for John Anson. The question exhausted the little legal knowledge he had. Sir Francis moved on.

"Is Dorothy Fosser, still living?"

"No, Your Grace. She died during Queen Mary's reign."

Sir Francis picked up a sheet of paper.

"Did Earl John marry a woman named Joan Jockey?"

"Yes, he did. About two years before Lady Dorothy died."

"How do you know this?"

"Joan Jockey lived in Earls Colne, where I was living at the time. Lady Dorothy was still alive and outraged that Earl John would take Joan Jockey into his house while still married to her. She wrote to Mr. Tyrell, the Earl's comptroller, to know if it were true and he wrote back that it was. We were all dismayed at the Earl's actions."

"Was the Earl still living with Joan Jockey when he entered into a contract to marry Dorothy Fosser?"

"No. The Earl had put Joan Jockey away before that."

"What do you mean, he 'put Joan Jockey away?'"

Anson, for the first time, looked uncomfortable. "Well, Lord Darcy and Lord Sheffield came to Earls Colne and, with certain others, brake open the door where Joan Jockey was and spoiled her."

"'Spoiled her?'"

"John Smith, one of Earl John's fellows, cut her face, and thereafter she was put away."

"How did this 'put her away?'" Lord Ellesmere asked.

"She was cut. Ye could not look at her, yer grace."

"Why did they cut her?"

"So that no one would want anything to do with her, including Earl John."

"Thank you, Mr. Anson. You are excused."

The witness was replaced by another man. The clerk swore him in.

"You are?" Sir Francis asked.

"Richard Enowes, of Earls Colne."

"Your age?"

"Sixty-two, sir."

"Did the Earl marry Joan Jockey?"

"He married her at Corpus Christi time at White Colne Church, which the Lady Dorothy took very grievously."

"Was Lady Dorothy still living when Earl John married Joan Jockey?"

"Yes."

"Did Earl John divorce Joan Jockey before he married Margery Golding?"

"No, Your Grace. He was still married to Joan Jockey when she was spoiled and put away."

"How do you know about the 'spoiling' of Joan Jockey?"

"I was present when it happened."

"How was she spoiled??"

"John Smith cut her nose off her face whilst the rest of us held her down."

"Do you know where Joan Jockey is today?"

"No, Your Grace."

"But she was alive and married to the Earl when the Earl married Margery Golding."

"Yes, Your Grace. As far as I know."

"Thank you. You are excused."

Sir Francis turned to Lord Ellesmere. "My lord, the evidence is clear. Earl John was married to Joan Jockey when he married Margery Golding."

Oxford slumped in his chair. Arthur started to get up but Oxford put his hand on Arthur's arm. "It's no use," he said.

Lettice Knollys, still calling herself Lady Leicester despite her marriage to Sir Christopher Blount, burst into the room. "I heard that!" she announced loudly. She swept past Oxford, using his shoulder to steady herself as she went by. In doing so, she let a small piece of paper fall into his lap.

She pushed open the bar and stormed further into the court. "You are all *worms*!" she thundered, coming up to the table. The lords seated around the table looked at her in shock. "*Worms?*" she repeated. "None of ye know not how to stand up to the *bitch*!" she announced.

"Madame!" Lord Ellesmere said, banging his gavel on the table. "You disgrace this court with your unseemly behavior. And Her Majesty with your scurrilous references."

"So ye knew who I was talking about," Lady Leicester said, causing more alarm. Lord Ellesmere motioned for the clerk to remove his reply from the record. She went on, pointing to Oxford. "His father was lawfully married to his mother!" she said. "I know how this works! Someone wants something they can't have, so they find a base lawyer who …"

Lord Ellesmere motioned for the bailiffs to remove Lady Leicester from the room. They grabbed her by the arms and began to propel her toward the door. "There are things done at night that can never be done in daylight," she shouted over her shoulder as they muscled her through the doors. Outside in the hallway, they could still hear her: "Make sure ye spell *bitch with a capital B!*"

Lord Ellesmere sat back down. He was visibly shaken. "Now, where were we?"

"I was going to sum up to the jury," Sir Francis said.

The jurors began to settle down again, shifting and rearranging themselves. They looked like hens in a roost recovering from just having seen a fox run past them. Oxford was so dispirited that he did not even look at the paper Lettice Leicester had dropped into his lap. Arthur Golding reached over and took it. He stood up.

"My lord," he called out.

"No," Lord Ellesmere said. "This farce has gone on long enough." He waved Arthur back down.

"My lord, the Earl of Oxford craves a one-day continuance."

Oxford looked up in surprise.

"No," Lord Ellesmere said again.

"My lord, you yourself have noted that this proceeding is charged with a weighty task—determining whether Edward de Vere is the Seventeenth Earl of Oxford and legal heir to his father. Should the verdict go against the Earl, it will call into question every transaction his guardians entered into while he was a minor. Lord Burghley was guardian of the Earl's person, while the Earl of Leicester was guardian of his lands. And then there are sales after he reached his majority," Lord Ellesmere's face began to show concern. Arthur continued. "Given how far-reaching the effect of such a verdict will be to the lands in the kingdom, my lord, it would cost little to pause for one day to make sure the verdict is correct."

Sir Francis had had enough. "My lord. The evidence is clear. The witnesses have sworn Earl John was married to Joan Jockey when he married Margery Golding. There is no need to wait."

"But how embarrassing it would be," Arthur said, emboldened by the fact that Lord Ellesmere had not told him to stop, "if the court ruled today and a witness appeared tomorrow who would make the jury's verdict appear ill-advised, opening everyone up to criticism that it may have been, what shall I say, premature, if not pre-determined?"

Lord Ellesmere was frowning hard. "What grounds do you have for making such a request?" He was caught between his desire to end the hearing and his worry that, if he did, he might be making a mistake.

"The Earl has been handed a note that says: 'Get a postponement for one day.'"

"Nothing more?" Arthur shook his head. "No reason given for the request?" Arthur shook his head again. "Who wrote the note?"

"It is signed 'F', your lordship."

"'F?' Who is 'F'?"

"I do not know."

Everyone in the courtroom tried to imagine who 'F' might be.

"Falstaff!" Oxford exploded, jumping up. "That bed-breaking, diseased, whoreson sack of guts!"

"My lord!" Lord Ellesmere called out. "Your dignity, my lord!"

"What dignity? You are stripping me of my dignity. And that fat knight, who has abandoned me, is the last person in the world who would have a reason for a postponement. This is just another trick!"

"It may not be Falstaff, my lord," Golding said, his eyes urging Oxford to calm down. "It may be someone else." He turned back to Lord Ellesmere. "But whoever sent the note, a day's continuance makes eminent sense. What harm can there be from such a short delay? If no witness appears tomorrow, justice will have been sharpened and you can explain to the world how far you went to make sure the verdict was fair. If a witness does appear, the court can weigh whether the testimony of the witness affects its determination."

"My lord!" Sir Francis objected. "I protest!"

"Why, Sir Francis?" Oxford asked, coming through the bar. "Something not seen yet? Something hidden? My lord," Oxford continued, addressing himself to Lord Ellesmere. "Your minion is nothing but noise." He waved a hand at Sir Francis, dismissing him. "He thinks that because what he speaks comes out of his top that it is different from what comes out of his bottom, but there are some, I wager, who would say they are the same."

Sir Francis was rendered speechless by this remark.

"My lord!" Lord Ellesmere shouted. "Your vulgarity may be sufficient proof of your illegitimacy *by itself*! But your outbursts are little more than the guttering of a candle before it goes out. You shall have one day, my lord, after which, I have no doubt, the result will be the same as that which we would have reached today had this postponement not been requested. Until then," he went on, leaning forward, his voice dripping with sarcasm, "*be thou the Seventeenth Earl of Oxford for one more day*. Court is adjourned!" He struck the table with his gavel and left the room.

"It's a trick," Oxford said to Arthur. "If it was written by Falstaff, he wrote it to prolong my agony."

"Perhaps he has a witness," Arthur suggested.

"A witness? God's blood! Forty-plus years have passed since my father married my mother! He's probably found a witness who'll say my father was married to *another* woman not yet mentioned here!"

"If that were the case, the note would have gone to Sir Francis." Oxford had no response to this. "Let's find out how Lettice came by this note," Arthur suggested.

They found Lady Leicester in the hallway. "I couldn't let you go down without a fight, Edward," she said. She clapped her hands. "I haven't had this much fun in a long time."

"'B' is for bitch?" Oxford said, smiling despite himself.

"Aren't her fingers all over this?"

"She'll make you pay."

"What else can she do? I was banned from court when I married Leicester, even though she refused to be his wife!"

"Where did you get the note?" Arthur asked.

"A boy was hanging outside the courtroom when I arrived. He said he had a note for you but was afraid to go in."

"What do we do?" Oxford asked, looking at the note for the first time. His anger was gone. He was spent.

"We come back tomorrow," Robin said. Oxford had forgotten his page was still with them. "I have a good feeling about this."

Oxford laughed. "You're such a liar."

"Yes, but I'm good at it." Robin grinned. This was so out of step with what had just happened in the courtroom that it sounded like Robin had not been there. "And, if you lose, you can write plays all the time and not have to worry about the Queen anymore."

"I can?" Oxford said. A hundred emotions flashed across his face.

"To my carriage," Lady Leicester announced. "We are all to Oxford Court."

## ~ 86 ~
## Yorick

The next day, there was no word about a witness who might testify at the trial. Everyone was downcast and despondent. Lady Elspeth decided to accompany Oxford to the trial. "I will bring Mary with me," she said, referring to the Mother of Jesus. "My prayers will save us."

Lady Elspeth had been praying more and more as the days wound down to the trial. Oxford found his wife's piety irksome. He felt it was based on desperation, and he had no doubt that no one in Heaven, if there was such a place, cared anything about him at all. After all, if Mary could help them, why had Mary not stopped the trial before it even began? As a result, he had begun to respond to his wife with sardonic, even sarcastic, remarks which, fortunately, Elspeth, wreathed in her religion, missed.

Arthur Golding and Robin also came, but neither said anything as they seated themselves in the rear of the courtroom. Oxford and Lady Elspeth sat in front, secretly fingering her rosary under the shawl she had draped around her shoulders.

The lords took their places on either side of the table. Sir Francis Bacon and the clerk came bustling in and sat down. Lord Ellesmere soon appeared. He looked at Oxford.

"Well?"

Oxford said nothing. He was numb. He looked like a prisoner waiting for the hangman to drop the platform. Lord Ellesmere shifted his gaze to Arthur Golding, who also said nothing. "Let the record reflect that the courtroom is silent, which I take to mean that there is no further evidence to be presented to the jury." He turned to Sir Francis. "You may make your summation, Sir Francis."

"Thank you, my lord." Sir Francis rose. He turned to the lords seated at the table. "My lords, your task is easy," but before he could go further, the doors at the rear of the court room burst open and an older man strode into the room. He was tall and raw-boned and dressed in home-spun woolen garments. His feet were shod in thick boots. He smelled of peat smoke and horse sweat. A long nose ran down his face the way the Apennines run down the spine of Italy. His eyes, deep-set, with fire and anger in them, surveyed the court-room without fear or condescension.

Lord Ellesmere was annoyed. "Get you hence, sir; this is a judicial proceeding."

The man paid him no attention. He walked through the gate in the railing and stopped at the end of the table. "I am Rowland Yorke," he announced to no one in particular. His voice sounded like it was coming from a room lined with stone.

Sir Francis was surprised by this. "The father of Rowland Yorke?"

"His mother has told me so," the older man said. "And, with great regret, I must admit that I am, indeed, his father."

Sir Francis turned to Lord Ellesmere, "Your Grace, Rowland Yorke, the son of the man standing in front of you, was servant to Lord Oxford on his trip to Italy many years ago. More recently, he has turned traitor while serving the Queen in the Lowlands and surrendered the Zutphen sconce to the Spanish, which rewarded him for his treachery with a pension and sanctuary. The witness is obviously here to testify in support of the Earl of Oxford; otherwise, we would have had information about him before. Therefore, his testimony is prejudiced, and I move that he be barred from testifying."

Yorke had decided that Sir Francis was not worth acknowledging. He looked at Lord Ellesmere. "My son is paying for whatever he did, having preceded me to the grave. I am here to give witness that the Sixteenth Earl of Oxford never married Joan Jockey."

"How do you know that?"

"I was servant to Earl John. I was his jester."

Lord Ellesmere snorted. "The court finds that difficult to accept."

"Judge me not by how I look today, Your Grace," Yorke said, in a tone that made it clear he was not used to being challenged. "I speak the truth. I was his jester and his fool."

Lord Ellesmere scowled back. "Then, how do you know he never married Joan Jockey?"

"Because I was there."

"He may have married her when you were *not* there."

"I would have known, had he done such when I was not there."

Sir Francis cut in. "But witnesses have said he *did* marry her."

"They lie," Yorke said simply. "Bring them here. Ye'll see."

"I think not."

"I say they have not testified truthfully," Yorke went on, his voice rising. "Bring them in." He glowered at Lord Ellesmere.

Witnesses would later say that it was at this point that Yorke bewitched Lord Ellesmere and took over the courtroom. Lord Ellesmere nodded and a bailiff opened a door. Rooke Greene came through the door. He saw Rowland Yorke and stepped back.

"Come here, Rooke Greene," Yorke said. Greene walked over to the older man, who towered over him. "Do ye know me?" Yorke asked. Greene nodded his head. "Did ye tell these gentlemen that Earl John married Joan Jockey?" Greene glanced at Lord Ellesmere. "I'm asking ye, not him. Look at me."

Rooke Greene wanted to run. "I told them what I heard. I didn't know for sure." He cast a worrisome glance toward Sir Francis.

Yorke waved Rooke Greene away. He looked at the door Greene had come out of. "Who else is in there? Come out. All of ye."

The other witnesses came out. Rowland Yorke looked them up and down. "Did ye tell these gentlemen Earl John married Joan Jockey?" They nodded. "'Twas a lie, wasn't it?"

Sir Francis reached over and touched Lord Ellesmere, who suddenly came to life. "Mr. Yorke. The witnesses were examined at length yesterday and no further examination is necessary."

Yorke ignored him. He took Richard Enowes by the ear and dragged him over to the window, knocking one of the partitions aside in the process. The clerks scattered. The lords seated at the table turned their chairs to get out of his way. "Ye see the Moon, Mr. Enowes?" Yorke jerked Enowes's' head back to make him look up through the window. "That's God's eye, Mr. Enowes. Even veiled in clouds, it's looking straight into your heart. Fear God, Richard Enowes, not the men in this room."

Yorke gave Richard Enowe's ear a yank. "I lied," Enowes said in a faint voice.

"Ye what?"

"I lied!" Richard Enowes said more loudly.

Yorke threw him aside.

"My lord!" Sir Francis called out. "This is torture, and the testimony this witness has just given must be disregarded."

Rowland Yorke headed for John Anson, but before he could get there, Anson blurted out: "Earl John did not marry Joan Jockey."

Lord Ellesmere turned to the jurors. "The objection by Sir Francis is sustained. The jurors are instructed to disregard anything these witnesses have said today that differs from what they said yesterday."

Yorke did not understand what Lord Ellesmere meant but he could sense that his efforts to correct the record were being disregarded. "Ye think what I say is nothing?" he demanded in a loud voice.

Lord Ellesmere banged his gavel on the table. "Mr. Bailiff, remove this man from the courtroom. This trial is over."

"Not if there is another witness," Yorke said defiantly.

"What do you mean—'another witness'?"

Rowland Yorke lowered his voice. "Joan Jockey," he growled.

There was a gasp in the courtroom. Richard Enowes and John Anson glanced desperately around the room.

Sir Francis exploded. "There is no Joan Jockey! No one has seen her in more than forty years! This is a desperate attempt to defraud the court by presenting a woman the Earl hopes to pass off as Joan Jockey."

Lord Ellesmere ignored Sir Francis. He was taking the measure of Rowland Yorke, who was scowling at him. Lord Ellesmere was wondering whether the tall, raw-boned man was deliberately maneuvering him into making a decision that would look bad later on. "If Joan Jockey still lives," Lord Ellesmere asked, "where is she?"

"Because the trip from Scotland wore greatly on her, Your Grace, slowing her down. I came ahead to make sure the court didn't conclude its business before she had a chance to testify."

"Scotland?" Scotland meant James, and Lord Ellesmere had no interest in bringing attention to himself by mishandling a judicial matter that might have some connection with the king of Scotland. "But she is from Essex. How came she to Scotland?" Lord Ellesmere heard himself asking.

"Because after she was cut, no man would marry her. Her mother and father were powerless to do anything, and so she disappeared into the attic of their house until they died, which was a year or two before my service to the Earl ended. When it did, I asked her to come with me to Scotland. She had returned to God, but she was Catholic. She knew she would find more comfort in Scotland than if she stayed in

Essex, so she came with me. She joined a convent of the Order of St. Clare near my home and has lived there since."

"Did Earl John know she had been cut?"

"Not before it happened. When he found out, he was greatly distressed."

"How could his retainers have cut her without orders from him?"

"They knew he was smitten with her and would have stopped them had he found out what they wanted to do. They thought that if they disfigured her, he would give her up. In this, they succeeded, but not for the reasons they expected."

"How so?"

"Earl John was horrified when he saw what they had done. The knife that cut her face cut something out of him as well. He took it as God punishing him for his sins. He returned to God, dismissed the retainers who had cut Joan Jockey, and made himself fit to marry one as noble as the Earl of Oxford's mother."

"But he had never married Joan Jockey?"

"No, my lord. As these will attest," Yorke said, pointing to Enowes and Anson cowering against the wall.

"And so where is she?" Lord Ellesmere asked, irritated at himself for having allowed Yorke to go on for so long.

"I will go look," Yorke said, but just then a figure hidden in a heavy cowl entered the courtroom. "Joan," he said, going up to her. He took her hand. "Come with me." He led her through the railing and up to the table. "Tell these gentlemen who you are."

"Joan Jockey," she said softly. Her face was hidden in the cowl, which was part of a torn and tattered gray woolen robe. A thick rope gathered the robe at the waist and showed how thin she was. She looked like a bundle of straw someone had left out in a winter field.

"A likely story," Sir Francis snorted. He turned to Lord Ellesmere. "How can we know who she is, my lord? Any woman can claim she is Joan Jockey, provided enough silver is poured into her pocket."

Joan Jockey raised her head. She drew back the cowl, letting it fall over her shoulders. The men in the room gasped. She could not have frightened them more had she come into the room through one of the windows trailing ribbons of smoke. She turned to the three men who had testified. They gaped at her as well. "I forgive you all," she said, "even you, Rooke Greene, who, wanting to be called esquire, claimed that you were not there."

Rooke Greene ran from the room. Joan Jockey turned to the men seated at the table. "They knew not what they did, my lords. They were God's instruments, sent to punish me for my vanity and foolishness. I had no business trifling with the Earl. He was far above my station. It was only when my beauty was taken from me that I could see God's beauty. Only when I was cut was I able to abandon the worship of *my* flesh, which in turn I, in my ungodliness, had made Earl John worship."

Sir John Stanhope, the member of the jury closest to Lord Ellesmere, stood up. "Enough!" he cried.

"We are not done," Lord Ellesmere told him.

"I am."

"Aye," the others agreed. They all stood up, pushing their chairs back. The men could not look at her. They waved their arms to ward her off. One made the sign of the cross. They were as eager as Rooke Greene to get away from this woman who had a hole in the middle of her face as wide as an open mouth.

"My lords!" Lord Ellesmere said. "You have not been dismissed!"

They paid him no heed, rushing from the room. The clerks and other hangers-on scurried after them.

"Gods blood!" Lord Ellesmere cried out disgustedly. He gathered up the papers in front of him and stormed out of the room.

Lady Elspeth came up to Joan Jockey. "Would you be so kind as to pray with me?" Joan Jockey nodded. The two of them dropped to their knees. Elspeth took Joan's hands in hers and the two of them began to pray.

Rowland Yorke strode back to where Oxford was sitting in shock. "My lord," he said, bending his knee.

"Yorick! My old Yorick!" Oxford cried. "I thought you long dead."

Yorke smiled. "There's still some fight in the old dog yet, eh?"

"And what a joy to see you! Thank you for the service you have just done me by coming here to stop this evil proceeding!"

"I was only doing my duty, my lord, to you *and* your father."

"Indeed. Whatever can I do to repay you?"

"Nothing. One does one's duty without thought of reward or compensation."

Oxford took his hands off Yorke's shoulders and looked him up and down. "As tall and commanding a figure as ever strode a battlefield," Oxford said, embarrassing Yorke, "or who carried a young boy up and down the stairs. Where be your jibes now, your songs?"

"Left behind, my lord. 'Twas only the noise of a young man." His eyes shifted. "Let us leave this room. These walls bleed sin." He took Joan Jockey's arm and helped her up. Lady Elspeth took her other arm, and the three of them headed for the door. Oxford, Arthur Golding, and Robin followed.

On the staircase they met Lady Leicester.

"Oh, I am too late! What happened?"

"There will be no verdict," Arthur said. "The jurors want nothing more to do with this case."

"I always thought it would turn out aright!" She reached over and gave Oxford's shoulder a squeeze.

Oxford smiled wryly, but said nothing.

Once in the street, Yorke gathered the reins to a horse a young man had been holding for him. Joan Jockey was mounting a second horse.

"My good Yorick," Oxford said. "Will you not linger so that I may ask how you have been and renew our friendship?"

"I cannot abide London, my lord, not even for one night, not even for you. Thank you for your kind offer, but I shall be on my way." He reached for Oxford's hand, folding it into his large paw. "It has been an honor to serve your house."

"Fare thee well, Yorick. I will sing of thee."

Yorke smiled. "I fear they will be songs sung to my grave, my lord. He turned his horse and began to move slowly away. Joan Jockey following apace. Beyond them, Oxford saw Falstaff sitting on a low wall.

"What is *he* doing here?" he wondered aloud. He stalked over to him.

"My lord," Falstaff said, bowing from his perch. He made no attempt to get off the wall.

"You address me as 'lord?'" Oxford asked.

"Is not that the outcome of the case?"

Rowland Yorke pulled his horse up next to Falstaff, pushing his horse between Oxford and Falstaff and leaned over. "Sir John," he said, leaning down and shaking Falstaff's hand. "I daresay I will never again have the privilege of spending days and nights on the road with you. And this thought gives me much pleasure."

Falstaff laughed. "Forgive me, Master Yorke, for not getting up but I'm waiting for my arse to arrive. It is still three miles off!" He grimaced, reaching round to rub his hind quarters.

"You need more time on a horse," Yorke said.

"I need more time in bed!"

Yorke frowned. "Sir John, I will have to spend a lot of time on my knees asking God to forgive me for all the stories and bad words I heard from you on the way here from Scotland." He dipped his head in Oxford's direction and turned his horse to leave. Joan Jockey guided her horse in behind Yorke's and the two of them rode across Charing Cross toward Watling Street and the way north back to Scotland.

"You *rode* here with him?" Oxford asked. "From Scotland?"

"Do ye think I walked?"

Oxford could not imagine Falstaff riding a horse, much less all the way to Scotland and back.

"Three horses I broke underneath me, lad," he said, looking very pleased with himself.

"So why did you treat me so poorly when last I saw you? I could've taken your death more easily than being told you were abandoning me!"

"How better to let everyone know I *had* abandoned you?" Falstaff said, a mischievous grin on his face. "What a performance, eh?" He eyed Oxford. "Fooled ye, didn't I? Even you, the 'honey-tongued writer of plays' thought his loyal servant had gone over to the enemy." He shook his head. "O, ye of little faith."

"But why couldn't you have told me? I am sore at the edges for how you treated me."

"And tell you what I was up to? No, no, no. Thou wilt not utter what thou dost not know, my lord. So I said nothing and let you believe I had abandoned you."

"My lord," Lady Elspeth said, coming up to them. "God has spoken: be thou the lord of Oxford." She said this as if it were some magical charm. Oxford expected her to sprinkle him with holy water.

"Thank you, Elspeth," he said. He was still reeling from the turn-about of his fortunes. He expected to be happy, but was surprised to realize how angry he was. Angry with everyone. Angry with Falstaff, for having abandoned him. Angry with Elspeth for burying herself in religion and walling herself off from him. He wanted to choke her *and* Falstaff. He stood in front of her, dizzy, afraid to say anything for fear it would come out wrong. To his surprise, he heard himself say, "And thank Mary, too."

Lady Elspeth smiled. "We are cold, my lord. Will you accompany us in Lady Leicester' carriage? She has offered to take us home."

Oxford looked over and saw Robin and Arthur Golding standing next to the carriage. He shook his head. "I will walk," he said. "I need to think." He walked away from them all toward the Strand.

Falstaff and Lady Elspeth watched him go. He was soon a tiny figure in the throng of people streaming down the Strand.

"I don't know how this will affect him," Lady Elspeth said, a worried look on her face.

"Aye," Falstaff agreed. He whistled for Robin. "Follow him, lad," Falstaff said, pointing toward Oxford's retreating back.

"And do what?"

"Her ladyship will feel better if she knows yer watching him. In the state he's in, he's liable to walk into the Thames and not know it until the water closes over his head."

"Sir John!" Lady Elspeth exclaimed.

"Exaggerating for effect, my lady. We poets speak like this at times. Robin'll be a second pair of eyes. Your lordship has got his life back. So have you. All of us, in fact." He was surprised to hear himself say it.

## ~ 87 ~
### *"Graze On My Lips; Feed Where Thou Wilt"*

Oxford took horse after the trial and rode north to Hedingham. He spent the next few weeks hunting and fishing with Digby, who would roust him out of bed in the morning and ride hard with him across the Essex countryside. Digby did not speak unless spoken to. Oxford had gone silent. The two of them did not need words. They ran down deer and rabbits, hunted foxes, and chased geese into the rivers. At the end of the day, they ate a simple meal either in the great hall in the castle or in the small cottage Digby shared with his wife, Nell, down the slope, after which they fell into bed exhausted.

One morning, Oxford suddenly announced that he was returning to London, and, without more, turned his horse south, leaving Digby to watch him disappear at high speed.

Lady Elspeth was walking up the hall when Oxford burst into Oxford Court. "My lord!" she cried excitedly, coming up to greet him.

"My lady," Oxford said, returning the embrace, but she could see his eyes were fixed on the door to the library. "Perhaps your lordship would like to see Henry?" she suggested.

Oxford nodded. He turned away from the library and followed Lady Elspeth up the stairs into her bedroom where he found his son, now four months old, on his back looking up at him.

"He thrives," Oxford said.

"Yes," Lady Elspeth said, looking pleased.

Oxford turned and ran back down stairs. "Robin," he called out. Robin appeared from the kitchen. "My lord," he said. He was also surprised to see Oxford. The two of them went into the library, leaving Lady Elspeth to wonder whether her doting on little Henry was contributing to her husband's coolness. "He will return," she told herself. A new play is crying out to be born. In the meantime, she would comfort herself with scripture. She sat down in a large chair near the crib and pulled the Bible into her lap. She opened to Ecclesiastes and began to read, picking up the pen every so often to make a note in the margin.

"In Venice," Oxford said in the library to Robin, "there was an artist of such skill that those with money paid immense sums for his paintings. Kings paid homage to him. He built a magnificent villa that looked out on the Island of Murano. Every evening the sea in front of his villa swarmed with gondolas carrying beautiful women. Musicians filled the air with music. This went on till midnight. He was in the last years of his life, but still possessed of all his faculties as he produced new paintings and supervised the lesser artists and craftsmen in his studio who finished the large works he had designed. Some of his paintings were large enough to cover an entire wall."

Robin sat erect, pen and ink in front of him. "And this artist was?"

"Titian," Oxford said.

"Oh. I saw one of his paintings at Hampton Court—a portrait of Boccaccio."

"What did you think of it?"

Robin made a face. "It was all brown and dull. I couldn't understand why one of the royals had bought it."

"I know that painting. I asked Titian about it. He said it wasn't his. He said other artists were constantly putting his name on paintings he never saw."

"Did you like the work you saw in his studio?"

"I liked one very much. It was of Venus and Adonis."

"I saw a Venus at Hampton Court. Someone said it was by Titian, but I didn't like it either."

"Was it Venus *and* Adonis?"

"No, only Venus. She was lying on a couch with nothing but a napkin between her legs." The face he made showed he disliked the pose more than the painting.

"She was also naked in the painting I saw in Venice but clinging to a young Adonis who was trying to escape from her."

"Escape? I thought Adonis *pursued* Venus."

"Right, which is exactly why Titian's painting caught my attention. My memory of it came back to me this week and I knew I had to return to London to capture it in a poem."

"A poem? About a painting?"

"Yes."

"And not a play?"

"It wouldn't work as a play. It will be a word painting of a love-sick queen, frantic in her attempts to bed young Adonis. Sweating lust," Oxford said, lowering his voice and leaning in toward Robin. "This is what she says to poor Adonis, who wants nothing to do with her:

*I'll be a park, and thou shalt be my deer;*
*Feed where thou wilt, on mountain or in dale:*
*Graze on my lips; and if those hills be dry,*
*Stray lower, where the pleasant fountains lie.*

Robin's ears were burning. "This is about Venus?"

"It is."

"But you said it was about a 'love-sick' queen."

"It is."

"*Our* queen?"

Oxford nodded.

Robin looked away. "My lord, this is not good."

Oxford was suddenly angry. "She abandoned me, Robin. All she had to do was lift her little finger and Lord Ellesmere and the reptiles he had assembled would have been sent off to the provinces. *Instead, she did nothing!* She wanted me gone. She wanted me common. I'm going to give the world a flushed, panting, perspiring, suffocating, aging creature, as far from the goddess of love as I can make her."

"By writing a poem about a goddess and a boy named Adonis?"

"Who do you think is Adonis?"

"Oh, no."

"This poem will paint in vivid words the time she and I spent together. It will not be pretty. The world will see her as the aggressive, imperious, demanding slut that she is."

Robin decided not to say anything about Oxford calling Elizabeth a slut. His master's anger was bubbling just beneath the surface. "Will Adonis give in to her?"

"Of course not."

"Did you?"

"Of course I did."

"What makes you think she will make the connection?"

Oxford laughed. "We once tied our horses to a tree. Hers was ripe for love, and mine tore himself free to mount hers:

> *Imperiously he leaps, he neighs, he bounds,*
> *And now his woven girths he breaks asunder;*
> *He sees his love, and nothing else he sees,*
> *For nothing else with his proud sight agrees.*
> *As they were mad, unto the wood they hie them,*
> *Out-stripping crows that strive to over-fly them.*

Robin looked faintly ill. "How does it end?"

"Adonis is killed by a boar:

> *He ran upon the boar with his sharp spear,*
> *Who did not whet his teeth at him again,*
> *But by a kiss thought to persuade him there;*
> *And nuzzling in his flank, the loving swine*
> *Sheathed unaware the tusk in his soft groin.*

"God's mercy," Robin muttered, but Oxford cut him off.

"This is not for you to decide," he said in a flattened, minatory voice Robin had not heard before. "Write down what I speak or seek employment elsewhere."

"Yes, my lord," Robin said, his head low. Something had changed. The trial had clearly affected his master.

"This is how it begins:

> *Even as the sun with purple-colour'd face*
> *Had ta'en his last leave of the weeping morn,*
> *Rose-cheek'd Adonis hied him to the chase;*
> *Hunting he loved, but love he laugh'd to scorn;*
> *Sick-thoughted Venus makes amain unto him,*
> *And like a bold-faced suitor 'gins to woo him.*

## ~ 88 ~
## Richard Field and the Printing of *Venus and Adonis*

R obin, take this to Richard Field and tell him to print it in dark ink on good vellum." Oxford held out the completed manuscript of *Venus and Adonis*.

"Yes, my lord."

"It must be perfect. No missing words; no upside down letters."

"Yes, my lord."

Tobias opened the door for Robin and found Shackspear about to knock on it.

"My lord!" Shackspear called out, planting a foot inside the door.

"Come in," Oxford said, surprising them all. Shackspear stepped inside and cast a wary glance around the room. Tobias closed the door behind him. "Willum," Oxford said, "Robin has your latest invention." He pointed to the manuscript Robin was holding.

"A new play?" Shackspear's lit up.

"A new poem."

"A new poem?" Shackspear asked in a completely different voice. "What need have I of a new poem? The theaters are closed and we are all starving. A new play to perform in the provinces would fill our pockets with money." Shackspear made a snorting noise. "Nobody pays money for a poem."

"They will for this one."

Shackspear looked from Oxford to Robin. "And why would they do that?"

"In this poem, Venus pursues Adonis."

Shackspear shrugged. "So?"

"Adonis rejects her advances."

"So?"

"Venus is the goddess of love," Oxford explained, wondering how far back he'd have to go before the dolt in front of him understood that Venus pursuing Adonis was something new.

"Ah." Shackspear looked over at Robin. "My kind of woman."

515

"A few lines will help you understand. In this scene, Venus wraps her arms around Adonis and starts kissing him furiously:

> *With blindfold fury she begins to forage;*
> *Her face doth reek and smoke, her blood doth boil,*
> *And careless lust stirs up a desperate courage,*
> *Hot, faint, and weary, with her hard embracing,*
> *Like a wild bird being tamed with too much handling,*
> *He now obeys, and now no more resisteth,*
> *While she takes all she can.*

"*While she takes all she can,*" Shackspear said, hitching up his pants.

"Go with Robin," Oxford said. "He knows what to tell Mr. Field."

Robin and Shackspear went out the door. They were soon at Richard Field's print shop. "Vautrollier & Fils," the battered sign announced to the left of the door, a sad reminder of the broken hopes of the shop's founder. Fortune had denied Monsieur Vautrollier a son and then illness had taken him off in his prime, allowing Richard Field, the young apprentice from Stratford-upon-Avon, to take over the print shop and marry the widow left behind.

Robin and Shackspear found Richard Field setting type, his fingers black with printer's ink. Field looked up, the thick lenses in his wire-rimmed glasses making him look like a fish that had just swum up out of the Thames.

"Yes?" he said.

Robin was tongue-tied. Oxford had given him no instructions beyond where to take the manuscript. Nothing had been said about whose name should go on the poem as its author. Oxford had jokingly referred to Willum's "latest invention," but was Shackspear to be given credit for having written it? Before Robin could decide what to do, Shackspear walked over to Field and stuck out his hand.

"Richard," Shackspear said.

"Ah, William," Field said. "Welcome to London. How do you find the big city? Not much like Stratford, eh?"

"No, thank God."

"I have heard of your success. I've not had time to see one of your plays but I will do so soon. How is your father, John?"

"Who knows?" Shackspear said dismissively. "I have a new poem for you to print." He motioned for Robin to hand over the manuscript. Field wiped his hands on a rag hanging from his belt before taking it. He walked over to a large table and began reading it silently.

"A poem, with a dedication to the Earl of Southampton. He'll like that, particularly the Latin epigram. 'The first *heir* of my invention?' What does that mean? Is this your first poem?"

Shackspear showed his teeth. "I am forced to admit it is."

Robin look away. Field, however, was ready to believe his countryman. "Well, then, you should put your name on it."

Shackspear hadn't thought of this. "Now, how could that have happened?" he asked, shooting a dark look at Robin.

"A defect easily remedied," Field said. "My apprentice will carve a signature block. We will use it to print your name on the poem."

"Excellent," Shackspear said.

"But where?"

Shackspear did not know. He put his finger on the dedication page. "Here," he said.

Robin leaned in to see where Shackspear had decided his signature should appear. Robin knew signatures did not go on dedication pages.

"Very well," Field said. "Your name shall go below the dedication to the Earl of Southampton."

Shackspear laughed again. "That way, if I offend anyone, I can say I am not the author!" This alarmed Field. Shackspear saw Field's reaction and stopped laughing. "No, no, Richard. I *am* the author."

Field was relieved, but the frown on his face showed that he was not a man given to joking, particularly about what he printed. "As to the spelling of your name," he said, turning back to the manuscript, "it is not something people usually pay a great deal of attention to, but we in the printing trade are trying to be consistent in how we spell words, particularly the names of people. I've seen your name spelled 'Shackper,' 'Shakspear,' 'Shakspea,' 'Shackspere,' 'Shakspere,' and 'Shakspeare.' I know you are being referred to when I hear these names, but when it comes to something that is printed, it behooves those who shepherd poets to Mt. Parnassus to make sure the author has a good name, and that it is spelled the same way throughout the published work."

"Hear, hear," Shackspear said, beaming. "I could not agree more."

"Let me point out," Field went on, "that your family name is pronounced 'shack-spear.' This is because there is no vowel after the first syllable to lengthen the 'a.'"

Shackspear did not understand. The only 'vowel' Shackspear knew was a nasty furry creature that lived in the fields around Stratford.

"By which I mean, your family name, as it is now spelled, makes a listener think of a 'shack,' which is not a good association. I suggest an 'e' after the first syllable, which, in my humble opinion, would make for a much better family name."

Shackspear still did not know what Field was talking about.

"'*Shake*-Spear,'" Field said slowly and deliberately. Robin could see Shackspear's face and turned away to keep from laughing out loud.

"Ah," Shackspear said. "*Shake*-Spear. I like it."

"'Shakespeare,' then. Closed-up. No hyphen."

The cloud on Shackspear's face returned.

Field saw Shackspear's concern. "A dash in the middle of a name is sometimes taken to mean that the name of the author is a pseudonym, and since you are the author, you don't want that."

Shackspear nodded. "No, I don't."

"*Shakespeare*," Robin said ponderously, emphasizing the second syllable. Shackspear thought the grin on Robin's face was delight at hearing Shackspear's new name.

"I shall pronounce it 'Shake-*spare*,'" Shackspear said, effecting what he thought was an upper-class accent. "After all, if we are rearranging the letters, why not brush up the pronunciation?"

"Yes," Field agreed.

Just then, Fields's wife entered the room. She had dark eyes, a sallow complexion, and a surly look on her face. She ran her eyes over Shackspear and then Robin.

"Ah, Jacqueline," Field said. "Mr. William Shake-spare, and his page." Shackspear's face glowed from hearing the sound of his new name. Robin, now page to Moron, looked on, mouth open.

Shackspear bowed. Fields's wife ignored him. "And?" she said to her husband.

"A new commission. A poem."

"A poem? You know we can't make money printing poetry." She walked to the table, opened the manuscript, and began reading some of the stanzas. "Mm," she said "Yes … Yes … There are some who might pay money to read this after all."

Field had gotten no farther than the dedication page and did not know what his wife was reading. He tried to look around her.

"*To clip Elysium and miss her joy?*" Mrs. Field exclaimed, chuckling to herself in a deep, earthy voice. "Oh, I daresay there are some who will take delight in reading that."

Her husband suddenly looked worried. "Is it bawdy?"

Mrs. Field nodded her head. "Most definitely."

"I had no idea."

"And a good thing, too," she said, "or this may have ended up elsewhere." She turned to Shackspear. "How much to print this?"

Shackspear was surprised. He had no idea he was be expected to pay the printer. He cast a furtive look at Robin who was studiously turning a knob on a press nearby and ignoring him.

"Well, madam," he began, but Mrs. Field cut him off. "Mark you," she said, "we don't finance unknown writers here, much less poets or, God forgive, playwrights. You're not one of them, are you?"

"Well," but she cut him off before he could say he was, sort of.

"The normal arrangement for unknown poets is that we give them a few copies for free, which they sell on their own."

This brought Robin into the conversation. It was one thing to laugh at Shackspear; it was quite another to let Moron give his master's work away, and to a French woman at that. "Madame," he said, "my master is not so foolish as to give away a priceless poem." He looked up at Shackspear to hint that Oxford would not like to hear that his poem had been given away for free.

Everyone in the room up to this point had taken Robin to be the silent, invisible servant, and so his decision to insert himself into the conversation took everyone by surprise. Shackspear, for his part, liked the backbone Robin had given him and tried to look aghast, signaling, he hoped, that his "page" spoke for him. Mrs. Field was about to react to Robin's comment when he walked around her and picked up the manuscript.

"*Un moment, mon petit,*" Mrs. Field said, obviously distressed that the poem was about to leave the shop. "Perhaps we can work something out."

"No, we will find a printer who appreciates great art, someone who can set in dark ink lines such as *When he beheld his shadow in the brook the fishes spread on it their golden gills*, and *Panting he lies and breatheth in her face she feedeth on the steam as on a prey and calls it heavenly moisture, air of grace.*"

Mrs. Field let out an involuntary gasp. "Enough!" she cried. "Leave the manuscript here. We will do it justice."

"But there is the matter of payment," Robin said, refusing to look at Shackspear, who was watching the page with his mouth open.

"What say you to an arrangement whereby Mr. 'Shake-spare' gets a part of the money we take in for the sale of *Venus and Adonis*?"

Robin had no idea how much someone should get for the sale of a poem. Shackspear was trying to make himself look as if he were considering the offer.

Mrs. Field took their silence as rejection. "Well, then," she said. "I think we can sell the poem for six pence a copy. I estimate that it will cost us three pence a copy to print the poem, what with the paper, ink, and time needed to make and set the type. What say you to one pence per copy? That will leave us with two, assuming that I am right. If no one buys your poem, we will be the ones to suffer. If it sells, we will both make a profit."

Shackspear and Robin looked at each other and nodded. "But you will have to let us look at your books to see how much you bring in."

Mrs. Field chuckled. She turned to Shackspear. "Your little page drives a hard bargain. He will, no doubt, become a very successful money lender." This was not intended as a compliment, and Robin knew it. He was indignant. Mrs. Field reassured him. "Do not worry, *mon choux*. It will be easy for you to see how many we print, and a quick trip through St. Paul's will tell you what we sell them for."

This mollified Robin. They all looked at each other. Mrs. Field put her hands on her hips. "We have an agreement, *mes chéris*?"

Shackspear and Robin said "Aye."

## ~ 89 ~
## The Sign of the Ship

**A**ll he said was for you to meet him at The Sign of the Ship."

"Not the Boar's Head?"

"No, The Sign of the Ship," Robin repeated. "He has news for you."

"What news?"

"He didn't say."

"Then we shall to The Sign of the Ship." Oxford got up from the table and headed into the hallway. "By the way, I can't find my Geneva Bible. Do you know where it is?"

"I believe her ladyship has it."

"What would she be doing with it? She has her own Bible."

As if she had heard mention of her name, Lady Elspeth called down from the balcony. "Are you going out, my lord?"

"Yes, my lady. I'm meeting Sir John at The Sign of the Ship."

Her face showed that Sir John's heroics in bringing Yorke and Joan Jockey to London had not changed her opinion of the fat knight. Oxford read the look on her face. "My lady, Sir John is the reason I am still Earl and you are still Countess. You should think more highly of him."

"I understand, my lord, but I find it difficult to accept his appearance and way of life."

Lady Elspeth was about to turn back into her bedroom when Oxford remembered to ask her about the Geneva Bible. "Do you know where my Geneva Bible is, my lady? It's gone missing."

"I have it, my lord. I will bring it down."

"No need," Oxford called up, but she had already disappeared. Moments later, she appeared on the landing at the far end of the hall. She had the Bible in her hands and quickly descended the stairs. She handed it to him but, as she did so, the book slipped through Oxford's fingers and fell onto the floor. Robin quickly picked it up and gave it to his master.

Oxford could see writing in the margins. "You have been writing in my Bible?" he asked, dismayed.

Her look of surprise showed that she had obviously thought she could. "My lord, I have seen you pun to page in many books, including this Bible! I was just doing the same, placing my thoughts in the margins."

"Yes, but they are *my* books."

"I apologize, my lord." She made a perfunctory curtsy. "I did not know *your* privilege was not *mine*." She turned away.

Oxford watched her climb the stairs. He did not understand her anger. "It was she who has written in my Bible, the one I have had from childhood," he thought. "My hand in the margin is a welcome sign that I have previously visited the page, like the worn sill below the door to Oxford Court, its depth silently signally how many feet have passed over it. Another hand in the margins of my books signals trespass, an intrusion, and makes me turn away."

"My lord," Robin said, not knowing what his master was thinking about. "Shall I summon Tobias?" Oxford hesitated. Before the trial, Oxford would have called out for Tobias himself. But now? "You are still the Seventeenth Earl of Oxford," Robin said.

"Am I?"

"The trial changed nothing."

"So you say. But everything seems to be changing around me. The world of the courtier is disappearing. A man's ancestry and his learning mean less and less. Is a whiffler superfluous, even for the Seventeenth Earl of Oxford?"

"How better to show the world that nothing has changed than by having your whiffler precede you through the streets, announcing to all who you are. To go alone would tell everyone that you no longer consider yourself the Seventeenth Earl of Oxford," and here Robin paused for effect, "and that your enemies have won."

Oxford looked at Robin. "Ever my loyal page," he said. "Yes. So be it."

Tobias slipped out of his room next to the front door and presented himself. He stood erect, neatly dressed in his tawny overshirt with the blue boar stitched on his right shoulder. His purple hat was firmly planted on his head. The gilded pomander swung from one hand.

"My lord," he said, in his deep voice.

Oxford waved him toward the front door. "Lead on."

Tobias glanced at Robin, who smiled slightly. Oxford knew they had been conspiring with each other. He ignored it. They went out the door and turned downhill toward the river, Tobias in the lead, with Robin just off Oxford's left.

"The trial forced me to think the unthinkable," Oxford said. "What would my life have been like had the outcome gone against me? Before the trial, I was invincible. Afterwards, well, I am changed, but I know not how, except that I came within a few words from a man's mouth of being made a common man, like you, Robin."

Robin took no umbrage at this. Oxford was descended from five hundred years of nobility; Robin did not even know who his parents were.

"That is all in the past now, my lord."

"Is it? I don't think so. It showed me that the pillars on which I have based my life can be washed away in a moment. How long did it take for Elizabeth to deny me the joy of writing plays? How many words? And take my love for Elspeth. I found her a delightful object of my affections when I first saw her at court. Now we push and pull over writing words, words again, in a book."

"She's given you a fine son."

"Yes, but have I lost him to Elspeth because I have drifted away from both of them? Is it because she is now a mother and no longer the object of my affection that *she* has changed? Has Henry displaced me in her heart? Is marriage a flower that, once the heat of the courtship is gone, withers and dies as it transforms itself into a reckoning of accounts and the raising of children?"

The Sign of the Ship came into view.

"Here we are," Robin said, relieved that their destination had saved him from more conversations about marriage, of which he knew nothing. They found Falstaff lounging in a booth.

"My lord," Falstaff said, making no effort to get up. Oxford slid onto the bench on the other side while Robin took up a position next to the booth along the wall.

"So what news?" Oxford asked.

"You were right. Your half-sister Katherine was the cause of the case against you. She thought *The Taming of the Shrew* was about her."

"About her? It was about Mary, my full sister!"

"Then why did ye call the shrew 'Katherine?'"

This brought Oxford to a stop. "I don't know."

"Maybe ye *were* thinkin' of her."

Oxford shook his head. "No, no, it was always about Mary." But he did not sound like he was sure.

Falstaff went on. "She asked Sir Robert to find a way to bring you down."

"Oh, my God. That little weasel."

"Sir Robert knew about the lawsuit between Masterson and Key and suggested the idea to Katherine that a claim that your father's marriage to your mother had been unlawful would have to be referred to the Privy Council. She expected, as did Sir Robert, as well as everyone else, that the jury would return a verdict that you were illegitimate."

"The enormity of it! My downfall brought about by a petty dispute over a lease my father sold before I was born!" His face darkened. "*The hidden hand,*" he said. "Sir Robert is a worthy son to his father."

"Some would say that the son *exceedeth* the father."

"But wait. The verdict would have voided the titles to every estate I had sold, as well as everything Leicester sold as my guardian!"

Falstaff nodded.

"Why would Sir Robert want that?"

Falstaff chuckled "He cared not a whit who might suffer as long as you were stripped of your titles and properties. But there was something in it for him too. He realized he could pick up some of the properties himself, at bargain rates, of course, and make a fortune off the bribes owners would pay him to keep their lands. He was heard joking that it would take ten years and half the solicitors in London to sort everything out."

"'Sblood, he is evil."

"Aye," Falstaff said. "But ye have to admire the beauty of it. Fill his pockets with money while reducing you to nothing. Sweet and simple."

"Forgive me for not joining in the applause. But what said Burghley about his son's scheme? Has he become so enfeebled that he would let his son strip me of my titles and the birthrights of his grandchildren?"

"Ye guess right, lad. Burghley was furious when he found out what Robert was up to. But Cecil explained that your three daughters will inherit no titles when ye die anyway, and he reminded Burghley that you now have a male heir who is not a Cecil. That was enough for Burghley to wash his hands of ye."

"Good God. And the Queen?"

Falstaff shrugged. "Ye'll have to take that up with her yerself."

"I'm still having trouble forgiving you for how you treated me in the street."

"Ah, what a performance!" Falstaff said, looking pleased with himself. He folded his thick fingers over his belly. "Not even Burbage could have done so well."

Oxford was not interested in agreeing with him. "You may have been acting, but the queen was not. Had the trial gone the other way, I would have been as forgotten as last month's plague victims." Oxford scowled. "She's going to pay for this."

Falstaff leaned forward. "You won, Edward. Let it be."

"She let me down, Jack. Sir Robert will pay as well."

"The little man?" Falstaff shook his head. "Hate is a great magnifier of what it's looking at, my lord. He's not worth it."

"Oh, yes he is."

They sat in silence for a moment. "But I am remiss in not thanking you, Jack, for finding Yorick and Joan Jockey, for riding all the way to Scotland and back ..." Falstaff was leaning back in the booth, his hands folded over his great belly again. He looked like a fat mourning dove at twilight, all puffed up and ready for sleep. "But how did you know Yorick would testify in my favor?" Oxford asked.

"I didn't."

"You didn't? You went to Scotland without knowing what he would say?"

"Pshaw. I didn't even know he was *alive* when I left."

Oxford looked at Falstaff in amazement. "Why would you do such a thing?" Falstaff shrugged. Oxford saw something cross Robin's face. "What?"

"He loves you."

Falstaff looked away, a faint smile stealing across his face.

"Not that I'm worth it," Oxford muttered.

"Now ye speak truth," Falstaff said.

No one said anything for a moment.

"I'm surprised Yorick remembered anything," Oxford said after a moment.

"He didn't."

"Then how could he testify that my father never married Joan Jockey?" Oxford suddenly looked closely at Falstaff. "Oh, no."

"I had to refill his memory," Falstaff explained. "It took me three hundred miles, more or less."

Oxford put up a hand. "No."

"He was quite a challenge! Old men forget everything except their childhood. In Yorick's case, he didn't even remember Earls Colne."

"Let me guess. You decided to remind him of his duty to come to London and testify Earl John had never married Joan Jockey."

Falstaff looked balefully at Oxford. "Ye think he testified untruthfully? Water'll run uphill before a lie will run out over his lips."

"Unless he didn't know that what he was speaking was untrue."

Falstaff shrugged. "That's possible."

"So you blathered in his ear all the way down here and convinced him my father had never married Joan Jockey."

Falstaff leaned back, a look of contentment on his face. "How'd he do?" he asked, all innocence.

Oxford was frowning. "Very well, according to your standards, which was apparently a bunch of lies!"

"Lies?" Falstaff took his hands off his stomach. "I prefer to think I was merely refreshing his memory so that he could recall that your father had never married Joan Jockey."

"Like someone helping a player remember his lines."

"More like getting a witness ready for a trial, don't ye think?"

"Still lies, Jack."

"What about Joan Jockey? Did she lie when she told the court she had never married your father? Huh?"

Oxford had no answer to this.

"But who knows what happened between your father and Joan Jockey? Maybe Joan Jockey doesn't remember. Or doesn't *want* to remember because, if she did, maybe she couldn't go on claiming she was the wronged woman who had found Jesus."

"I am dizzy," Oxford said.

"Ye want certainty, Edward, but there is none. Memories fade. An event that happened yesterday is a blur ten years down the road. Truth is not what happened in the past; it's what those alive *think* happened."

Oxford turned to Robin, who was listening to this with big eyes. "He is the devil incarnate, Robin. My father would have banished him from my presence, had my father lived to know him."

"And you would have been hung at seventeen," Robin blurted out. "And killed by Thomas Knyvet in a snowstorm. *And if you had survived that, you'd have been stripped of your titles at forty-three!*"

They were all taken aback by this, Robin included. Falstaff looked out the window at the passing boats and said nothing. Oxford sat in stony silence.

A commotion at the entrance to the tavern made them turn their heads. Shackspear was coming toward them. He had a copy of *Venus and Adonis* under his arm.

"God's blood," Oxford groaned.

"Your punishment on Earth," Falstaff said.

"My lord," Shackspear said, as he came up to them. "I am a made man. I am saluted in the street. Women beg me to come inside; men hate me."

"And he has a new name," Robin added.

Shackspear drew himself up. "William *Shake-spare*," he announced.

Falstaff guffawed. "Son of a glover."

Oxford's face darkened. "*Shake-spare?*"

"Richard Field's suggestion," he quickly added.

Falstaff started silently laughing, his belly going up and down. Shackspear pressed on. "Richard said it should be written without a hyphen, because that would make it seem like the author was soodeness, you know, not the true author."

"Which, of course, you are," Oxford said.

"What? The true author? Or soodeness?"

"God blast you," Oxford called out, striking the table in front of him with his fist. "I've had enough of 'truth'!"

Shackspear was at a loss as to what was going on, but Robin was suddenly worried that his master's name should have gone on the poem. "Was *Venus* to be printed with your name on it, my lord?"

Oxford looked like he was going to explode. "No!" he shouted, jumping up. He headed for the door. "I need air!"

A Yeoman of the Guard appeared, blocking his way. "Hold, my lord. The Queen commands your presence." Oxford saw a pair of soldiers stationed at the door to the inn. "When?" he asked.

"Now."

"What? I am not fit for her presence."

"She said 'now,' my lord."

"How do you know she meant 'now?'" Oxford asked.

"I asked her myself, my lord. She screamed *'NOW'*, and threw a book at me that looks like the one in yonder gentleman's hand." Shackspear quickly slipped his copy of *Venus and Adonis* behind his back.

Oxford drew himself up. "Well, if it is the gallows, I am ready."

"You should hope that's all it is," Falstaff said. "We shall pray for you, my lord."

"Oh, God." Oxford looked up at the captain. "You know you are in trouble when the Devil says he will pray for you." He turned to Robin. "Tell my lady I will be late for supper, Robin. Lead on, Captain. Venus waits."

# ~ 90 ~
## A Conference with Venus

The captain took Oxford deep into the palace, farther than Oxford had ever gone before. They wended their way past the courtyards and waiting rooms for other visitors, "to reach the spider's lair at the center of her nest," he told himself, for Elizabeth had obviously secreted herself in a room where no one could hear what she wanted to say to him. Oxford squared his shoulders. He reminded himself that it was she who had abandoned him and that *Venus and Adonis* was what she deserved.

The captain stopped at a plain door and knocked. A guard opened the door and stepped aside. Oxford entered the small, dark room, bare of any furniture except a straight-backed wooden chair against the opposite wall. Elizabeth sat erect in the chair, her eyes fastened on Oxford. A copy of *Venus and Adonis* lay on her lap. Four ladies-in-waiting stood to her left.

"Get out!" Elizabeth said, her voice barely audible. The guard opened the door again and the four ladies-in-waiting silently slipped past him. He followed them out and closed the door behind him, leaving Elizabeth and Oxford alone.

"How dare you?" she hissed, her voice quavering. She picked up the copy of *Venus and Adonis* and waved it at him.

"You abandoned me," Oxford said defiantly.

"I did nothing of the kind!"

"When you learned that Sir Robert was scheming to strip me of my titles, my properties, my heritage, my everything, *you did nothing!*"

"I don't control the courts."

Oxford snorted. "No lies, please! 'There are no keyholes in here with ears in them to listen to what we say,'" he said sarcastically, quoting what she had told him at Greenwich when she had ordered him to stop writing plays. "These walls," he continued, waving his arm around the room, "'will not blab or know of what we speak.'" He dropped his voice. "Speak the truth, or speak not at all."

She returned his anger. "You painted me as a '*panting, sweating, overweight, aging love goddess, with a taste for choir boys!*'" she yelled, her voice rising. She threw the book at him, just missing his head. "*Who fails to bed the boy! Me! The love goddess!* That's more insulting than all the rest! And '*To clip Elysium?*'" she laughed, almost hysterically. "'*To lack my joy?*' How dare you?"

Oxford thought her description of the poem was so good he almost smiled. He realized he was enjoying the fight, something they had engaged in many times. But was she?

"I am humiliated before all the world," she went on. A paper suddenly appeared in her hand. "My people write the Privy Council, horrified by your latest invention." She read from the paper in her hand.

> *Also within these few days, there is another book made of*
> *Venus and Adonis, wherein the queen represents the person of*
> *Venus—which queen is in great love (forsooth) with Adonis.*
> *And greatly desires to kiss him, telling him that although she is*
> *old, yet she is lusty, fresh, and moist, and full of love and life.*

She looked over the book at him. "'*Lusty, fresh, and moist?!*' *Moist?*"

"Call it in," he said.

"You know I can't. Slander runs from lip to ear, like fire across a wheat field in summer, or St. Elmo's fire through the rigging of a ship in a raging storm. It is too late. It is gone. It is part of my people's memory"

"It is never too late. Tilney can find a way to gather them in."

"At the moment, Mr. Tilney is having his thumbs lengthened by Mr. Topcliffe for having let *that* go by," she said, pointing to the copy of the poem lying on the floor. "But calling it in would only confirm what those who are loyal to me now stoutly deny."

"When the field is full of geese, they say, it is difficult to catch them all."

Elizabeth's face took on a harder look. "And you thought that my 'abandonment' of you gave you license to publish whatever you wanted to about me?"

"Does a seamen thrown into the sea have any duty to the captain who threw him overboard?"

The two fell silent. She felt old and ugly. He began to realize that his revenge may have been more effective than he had intended. He suddenly felt the need to reach out to try and wipe away all the anger that sat between them like an invisible wall.

"You remember my horse breaking away to mount yours?" he asked.

She glared at him. "I remember nothing of the sort."

"I think you do."

She looked away. "I remember you gave in."

Oxford did not know what to make of this for a second but then realized she was rankled that Adonis had spurned Venus. It was as if Oxford had not only held her up to ridicule but left behind a false account of their relationship.

"In more ways than you know."

They went silent again. Oxford then walked over and picked up the bound copy of the poem. He leafed through it. "Pages torn by many fingers, grease stains everywhere. It reeks of eyes reading and rereading passages like this:

> *And on his neck her yoking arms she throws:*
> *She sinketh down, still hanging by his neck,*
> *He on her belly falls, she on her back.*
> *Now is she in the very lists of love,*
> *Her champion mounted for the hot encounter.*

"Stop!" she cried out. "You have stripped me *naked!*"

"*You* were content to let them strip me of my ancestry!"

This silenced her for a moment. "It was not as simple as you think," she said in a quieter voice.

Oxford closed the book. "I thought you, a bastard two times over by act of Parliament, would have stepped in to stop them from making *me* a bastard. You despise me that much?"

"Yes, I know what it's like to be labeled a bastard," Elizabeth conceded. Her voice had become hard again. "Of course I wanted to help. It is ill of you to think otherwise. But there were other factors I had to grapple with. For example, what if the evidence showed that your parents' marriage was indeed unlawful? What then? If I interfered, would I become a conspirator in a plot to maintain a fraud, namely, your claim that you are the Seventeenth Earl of Oxford? I sensed Heaven frowning if I disbanded the court. Instead, I let the wheel of fortune roll without any interference from me."

Oxford looked at her in dismay. "Did I mean so little to you that you could let fate decide whether I remained the Earl of Oxford? Particularly when Sir Robert had his hand on the wheel?" His voice was once more rising in anger. "Was I nothing but an object of curiosity, a fox careening across the countryside, pursued to find out which way he turned? God, woman. I am no toy for you or Heaven to play with: I am Edward de Vere."

She sighed. "We are all illusions, Edward: you, as the Seventeenth Earl of Oxford; me, as the Queen of England. Am I truly a bastard? Many believe I am. Are you illegitimate? Some would say yes. I should have interfered and saved you from Cecil. I can see that now. Forgive me."

"Too late."

"But you have survived."

"No help from you."

"True. But you have imposed a hefty fine on me for my negligence. I will never be Cynthia again; I shall forever be Venus, thanks to you." She sounded defeated.

"Was there nothing of beauty in the poem?" he asked.

She ignored his question. "I must confess, a small part of why I did not act was the thought that you would welcome the opportunity to throw away your noble ancestry to earn fame as the true author of your plays. That door is still open," she said. "You can still take it. Falconbridge, another bastard, gave up his claim to his father's lands to accept Queen Elinore's offer to become a knight in her service. How fitting if you did the same, abandoning your claim to your father's titles to seek glory in the theater."

Oxford looked at her. Was she playing him? Did she want him gone from court? But, if she wanted that, she could order him gone.

"I want both," he said. "I am my father's son, and grandson to his father, and to every Vere back 500 years. I can feel them in my bones. You cannot resign your office as Queen of England; I cannot resign my office as the Seventeenth Earl of Oxford. I have obligations to my son, and to all his descendants."

"Here, here," Elizabeth said, clapping her hands slowly. "But what of the playwright? Where is he in all this?"

"Standing in front of you, Your Majesty. A word from you and I become visible to the world. A word from you and fame will follow me long after empires are gone and marble statues have crumbled into dust."

She looked at him balefully. "You think you will be more famous than I will be?" She cocked an eye at him. "Fortune has allowed you to remain the Seventeenth Earl of Oxford, but Fortune has not said that you can be both earl *and* playwright. If you write plays, my lord, you will not be identified as the author."

"Your Majesty, give me my life," Oxford pleaded. "Do not do this out of pique over a simple poem, mere words on paper."

"I do not do this because you have libeled me in print, although I thought of doing more to you than denying you your name on a play. No, I do this because you must remain earl. Write plays and give them to the world as William Shackspear's, if you want to, or do nothing. The choice is yours."

Oxford drew himself up. He dropped the copy of *Venus and Adonis* to the floor. He bowed. "There have been times when I thought I may have gone too far with *Venus*, but I thank you for removing any doubt in that regard. You deserve every word I wrote." He bowed again. "With your permission."

She waved a hand, dismissing him.

## ~ 91 ~
## Sir Robert Gibed at Christmas

Oxford left the meeting with Elizabeth knowing that the bond forged between them when they were lovers was no more. He felt no loss. In fact, he felt relief: he was finally free of her.

He came out into a bright, windy day, and thought he could see a hundred miles. His leg was without pain and his heels barely touched the ground as he went down the Strand and past St. Paul's into Candlewick Street. He was soon at Oxford Court where he went into the library where Robin, paper and ink in front of him looked up in surprise. Socrates, curled up in a ball at the end of the table, picked up his head.

"Aye, ye Egyptian mystery," Oxford said to the cat. "It's me." He turned to Robin. "And we have a play to write, young man."

A smile appeared on Robin's face. "And the play is?"

"Richard III."

"The king Henry Tudor deposed?"

"Shhh," Oxford said, putting an index finger to his lip. "'Deposed' is a word that's out of favor these days. It hints of a taint in the succession, a hint that never occurs when a son takes his father's place."

"But Henry killed Richard in battle, didn't he?"

"He did. And for some, 'trial by combat' justifies the result. But we can't say Richard was 'deposed' because it raises the question of whether what's good for the gander is good for the goose."

"Meaning, that if Henry could 'depose' Richard, someone else might start thinking they could 'depose' Elizabeth."

"Well done, lad."

Oxford saw the light in Robin's eyes. The boy had disappeared while Oxford was recovering from his leg injury and fighting off Sir Robert's attempt to strip him of his titles. *Venus and Adonis* had been a solo effort, written alone. He had been only vaguely aware of Robin drifting about the house while he scribbled away. In fact, Oxford realized how important Robin was because he did not draw attention to himself. The boy had seamlessly entered Oxford's service without objection from anyone. Falstaff liked him. The young page made every task into a smooth surface. It was only now, in the aftermath of so much turmoil, that Oxford had begun to realize that it was Robin's *lack* of presence that was so astonishing. Like now, finding him seated in the library, waiting for him. Oxford pushed aside thoughts of why this was so and plunged into Richard III.

"The beginning."

Robin hunched over the table.

"Richard, alone, at the front of the stage, staring out at the audience."

"What does he look like?"

"Small in stature and hunch-backed, with a limp and a withered arm."

"Ooooo."

"Listen:

> *Now is the winter of our discontent*
> *Made glorious summer by this sun of York*

"Richard is already using the royal 'our' in the first line of the play, a signal that he wants to be king, for this is how kings speak. The 'sun of York' is Richard's eldest brother, newly enthroned as King Edward. Richard's chances of being king are slim. His two older brothers, Edward and George, must die, and die without issue. These lines, spoken sarcastically by Richard, set the course of the play and feeds the audience's expectation that Richard *will* be king. They know this, of course; no suspense there. Their pleasure will be watching it done."

"He 'lours' at the audience."

"'Lours?'"

"'To frown, scowl, look angry or sullen.'"

"Oh, I love it. Thank you, Robin. The next two lines will be:

> *And all the clouds that lour'd upon our house*
> *In the deep bosom of the ocean buried.*

He will overcome his shortcomings:

> *But I, that am not shaped for sportive tricks,*
> *Nor made to court an amorous looking-glass;*
> *Deformed, unfinish'd, sent before my time*
> *Into this breathing world, scarce half made up,*

*And that so lamely and unfashionable*
*That dogs bark at me as I halt by them.*

"Oh, that's good," Robin said. "Dogs bark at him."

Oxford waited for him to catch up.

*And therefore, since I cannot prove a lover,*
*I am determined to prove a villain.*
*Plots have I laid, inductions dangerous,*
*By drunken prophecies, libels and dreams,*
*To set my brother Clarence and the king*
*In deadly hate the one against the other:*
*And if King Edward be as true and just*
*As I am subtle, false and treacherous,*
*This day should Clarence closely be mew'd up,*
*About a prophecy, which says that 'G'*
*Of Edward's heirs the murderer shall be.*

"A mystery!" Robin was excited. "But Clarence's name does not begin with 'G'."

"His first name is George."

"But isn't Richard the Duke of *Gloucester*!"

"Well done, Robin. The audience will make the connection, but King Edward and those around him will not." Robin made ready. "Clarence comes by, lamenting his name and his new imprisonment. Richard commiserates with him, and then waves him good-bye:

*Go, tread the path that thou shalt ne'er return.*
*Simple, plain Clarence! I do love thee so,*
*That I will shortly send thy soul to heaven,*
*If heaven will take the present at our hands.*

"Is this the last we see of Clarence?"

"Clarence will be knocked on the head and stuffed into a butt of Malmsey."

"On stage?"

"No. Off stage."

"Oh, but on stage would be much better, my lord. The stuffing would be well-received by the pit."

"We have higher goals here, Robin. Our task is to make Richard diabolical. To do that, I will have him approach Lady Anne, the widow of the Prince of Wales, and ask her to marry him."

"But Richard just slayed her husband, didn't he?"

"Yes." Oxford saw Robin's dismay. "Think it cannot be done?"

"'Twould be difficult, my lord, if not impossible."

"You have too high an opinion of women. Lady Anne will come out escorting the body of Henry VI to his grave. Richard will confront her. She will rail at him for causing so many deaths, including the death of her father and her husband, the Prince of Wales. Richard will not return her anger. He will tell her that he killed her husband to help her 'to a better husband.'"

"Meaning him?"

"Yes."

"Oh, my lord."

"She will resist, of course."

"I would hope so."

"She will call him a 'foul lump of deformity' and summon the Earth to 'gape open wide and eat him.'"

"Good."

"He will claim he did all the horrible deeds she accuses him of because of his love for her:

> *Your beauty was the cause of that effect;*
> *Your beauty: which did haunt me in my sleep*
> *To undertake the death of all the world,*
> *So I might live one hour in your sweet bosom.*

"She can't possibly believe him!"

"She is a woman, Robin."

"Then I am glad I am not a woman."

"She does not give in quickly, of course. No woman does. She spits on him and wishes it were poison."

"Ah! He will be so incensed by this that he will pull out his sword and threaten her with it!"

"No. Richard is nothing but milk and honey at this point in the play. He pulls out his sword, yes, but he hands it to her, telling her to kill *him*."

"And she kills him," Robin said hopefully.

"No, no, my little page. That's what the audience will expect, but Anne cannot kill him."

"Because it would end the play."

Oxford nodded. "Now you're beginning to think like a playwright." Robin was pleased. "Richard will drop to one knee and present his breast to her:

> *Nay, do not pause; for I did kill King Henry,*
> *But 'twas thy beauty that provoked me.*
> *Nay, now dispatch; 'twas I that stabb'd young Edward,*
> *But 'twas thy heavenly face that set me on.*

"She not only cannot kill him, she drops the sword. Richard tells her to pick it up, but she leaves it on the floor. 'Then tell me to kill myself,' he urges her. She says she already has.

> *Tush, that was in thy rage:*
> *Speak it again, and, even with the word,*
> *That hand, which, for thy love, did kill thy love,*
> *Shall, for thy love, kill a far truer love;*
> *To both their deaths thou shalt be accessory.*

Robin's pen sped across the page. "That hand, which, for thy love, did kill thy love shall, for thy love, kill a far truer love. Lovely. Who says you never listened to John Lyly?"

Oxford frowned. "Now, that's quite enough. You are not here to comment on my genius, or remind me of lesser lights."

"Yes, my lord."

"Where was I?"

"He asks her to marry him."

"Oh, yes. Lady Anne will waver—it's a play, isn't it?—but she will finally agree to marry him because she thinks he has become penitent."

"My lord, you do women no favor by making Lady Anne so inconstant. It beggars belief. You risk losing the audience, don't you?"

"Yes. Wonderful, isn't it? The challenge will be to make Lady Anne *so* unbelievable that the audience will think about walking out."

"I think they're already at the door."

"Not yet. For now, I must concentrate on showing how bad Richard is. This is what he will say after Lady Anne leaves the stage:

> *Was ever woman in this humour woo'd?*
> *Was ever woman in this humour won?*
> *I'll have her; but I will not keep her long.*

"He will marry her and then have her done away with?"

"Yes."

Robin looked up. "He is so evil. Who is Richard, my lord?"

"Robert Cecil."

"Oh. The withered arm. The hunchback. I should have seen it. But to paint him so black may be to gild him, my lord. There were some who liked Aaron the Moor because of how dark he was."

"Tut, Robin. Any 'gilding' will disappear at the end. Richard will fear all and trust no one. Ghosts will visit him. Richard's death will be nothing like Tamburlaine's, who bravely said his '*soul doth weep*' to see his friends' '*sweet desires depriv'd my company,*' or Aaron the Moor spitting in the face of the men burying him. Richard will be a coward at the end, running around crying '*A horse! a horse! my kingdom for a horse!*'"

"Oh, I feel better."

"I'm so glad. Now write what I speak! We must finish this!"

---

*Richard III* was presented to the Queen at Christmas. Burbage, his body humped and twisted, stalked to the front of the stage and 'loured' at the audience until the theater filled with silence. They were naught but ears now, two to a head, Oxford whispered into Robin's ear. Burbage slowly rotated his head across the pit and up through the galleries until he burst out with "*Now is the winter of our discontent*" in a voice that shook the roof and sent the rats scurrying into their hiding places beneath the stage.

Oxford saw Cecil peeking from behind a partially-opened door. He nudged Robin. "I knew he couldn't stay away."

Oxford settled back to enjoy his revenge, one eye on Burbage and the other on Cecil. "He won't like the fiends that haunt Richard the night before he dies."

# 1594

## ~ 92 ~
## A Play for Lady Mary

Lady Mary, Countess of Southampton, my lord," Nigel announced from the door of the library, "and Lady Lettice, Countess of Leicester." The women swept past him into the room. Oxford and Robin rose from the table where they had been working.

"My lord," Lady Mary said, as she came up to him. "Edward," the Countess of Leicester said. They held out their hands; Oxford dutifully kissed each hand in turn.

Lady Mary was the shorter of the two women and the larger by far. She was swathed in a broad belt made of orange cloth that reminded Oxford of the rub rail of a wide-bottomed merchant ship, which Lady Mary was beginning to resemble. Her dark hair was jammed into a wide-brimmed straw hat dyed bright yellow. A double row of large pearls hung down the front of her dress and framed a gold jewel known as a Jesus. Her taller companion wore nothing on her head. Her thick red hair fell freely over her bare shoulders and the purple and mauve silk dress she was wearing.

"And to what good fortune do I owe this visit," Oxford asked.

"I must speak with you about an important matter," Lady Mary said.

"Which is?"

"Perhaps we should closet ourselves in a more private space?" She gestured in the direction of Robin, who was standing the other side of Oxford.

"Of course." Oxford said. He gathered up the papers in front of him and bundled them into Robin's arms. "To Richard Field."

Lettice leaned over to see what Oxford had given Robin. "*The Rape of Lucrece*. Is this the 'graver labor' promised in *Venus and Adonis*?" She had a mischievous look on her face.

"I wouldn't know, would I?" Oxford said. "Shackspear wrote *Venus*, didn't he?"

"Yes, yes," Lady Mary said, frowning at Robin to send him on his way. "So we are told. But that nuddernut never wrote nanything."

"I liked *Venus and Adonis*," Lettice chimed in. "I liked it a lot. Could we glance at *The Rape* before it goes out the door?"

Lady Mary put a hand out to block Lettice from getting closer to Robin. "She is more interested in the rape than the poem," Lady Mary said, waving at Robin to accelerate his departure. "I have no time for nalacious literature, if this be like *Venus*. 'Tis all right for a late night nevening, perhaps, but I come on more important business."

"Follow me, then," Oxford said, amused at Lady Mary's natterings. The two ladies had obviously been sipping some wine before setting out on their errands that day. Oxford led them across the hall into the Day Room where they sat down in chairs arranged in the far corner. Nigel followed them in. "Would anyone care for some refreshments?" The ladies shook their heads no.

"And Lady Elspeth?" Lady Mary asked, addressing her question to Nigel.

"Her ladyship is in her private chapel, my lady, where I assume she is saying her prayers."

"As I would be doing, were I married to his lordship," she said. "To business, then. I am to marry in May."

"Congratulations. And who is the lucky man?"

"Sir Thomas Heneage."

"Sir Thomas?"

She saw the surprise on Oxford's face. "Yes, he is old and short of money but I need a husband so I can go to court. I miss the gossip and the gowns."

"A match made in Heaven," Oxford commented.

"I miss the gossip and the gowns too," Lettice complained, "but I am barred from court because I married my Robin, even though he lies six years in the ground now." The Queen learned about the marriage, which had been a well-kept secret, from Le Mothe, the French envoy, who had the distinct pleasure of telling Her Majesty what Leicester had done to pay Leicester back for his untiring efforts to block Elizabeth's marriage to the Duke d'Anjou. Elizabeth had immediately banished Lettice from court, as if it were her fault.

"You stole the only man she might have married," Lady Mary said.

Oxford did not like hearing that but showed no reaction to it. "And how did Sir Thomas come to propose?" he asked. "I didn't think he had it in him."

"He didn't."

"Then, you proposed to him." His lack of surprise showed he thought it entirely possible.

"Of course not. What do ye take me for? Men propose, not women. But what makes a man do it? They never know. Neither did he."

Sir Thomas was apparently as dense as ever, Oxford thought. "But what does this have to do with me?" he asked.

"The wedding will be at Southampton House," Lady Mary said. "I want the Queen to come. A new play will reel her in." She went through the motions of hooking a big fish and pulling it in. Lady Mary had always been an avid sportswoman. She was fond of riding across the countryside around Wanstead, even venturing as far afield as Epping Forest in earlier years, but her girth had kept her from climbing on a horse for some time now. The tenacity with which she pursued big game was replaced by the pursuit of fish. Ponds were built on her estate and she fished nearly every day of the week, punting out in small boats or sitting at the end of a pier with a rod. Lettice visited her once and started catching fish faster than Lady Mary, which put Lady Mary out of sorts. Lady Mary said nothing to her guest the first day, or the second, but when the fish kept flying out of the water on the third day, Lady Mary made arrangements for a boy to swim under the pier and attach live perch to her line so she could redeem her honor. Lettice guessed how Lady Mary had suddenly improved her luck. On a subsequent visit, she brought a salt mackerel with her and slipped the boy a coin to put the mackerel on Lady Mary's hook. When the Countess reeled in a saltwater fish, the guests and staff on the pier burst out laughing. Everyone knew what she had been up to. Lady Mary took it well—"hung on my own petard"—she muttered when she realized she had been caught, and the two women became good friends.

"But why seek a play from me? Ask George Peele, or Shackspear. I have been banned from writing plays," he said, putting on a long face as he turned to Lettice, "as you have been banned from court."

"A pig's bozzle!" Lady Mary said forcefully. "No one thinks Shacksmear wrote *Much Ado*, or *The Shrew*, or any of the other plays that have his name on them. We long ago figured out who the true author is."

"We did," Lettice agreed. "In fact, we play a game when we go to see a new one. The game is to figure out who the Earl of Oxford is thinking about when a new player appears on the stage. We lean forward and listen to every word. It's quite a feather in one's cap when one of us figures out the answer."

"Yes, yes," Lady Mary said irritably. "We knew the sheep in *Two Gentlemen* was Hatton. Richard, evil Richard …," her voice trailed off while she looked around, "was, well, you know who."

Lettice leaned forward. "Was I the inspiration for Duke Humphrey's wife in *Henry VI, Part 1*?" The glow on her face showed she thought she was.

"Part Two," Oxford could not keep himself from saying.

"Part Two, then. Queen Margaret boxes the ears of Duke Humphrey's wife for the same reason Elizabeth boxed mine—for wearing clothes that outshone hers!"

Oxford shrugged. "Oh, that's a common story. Shackspear no doubt heard it in the Steelyard."

Lettice was not persuaded. "But, if he *is* the author, how can he get away with treating making Elizabeth look so poorly?"

"If he were the author," Lady Mary added, "*the old boot would have boxed up his nuts and shipped them to the New World!*" She looked like she wouldn't mind doing the packing herself. "We know who the author is."

"Tell me I was Duke Humphrey's wife," Lettice pleaded.

"Enough!" Lady Mary said. "I need a play for my wedding. I don't care if Shacksmear puts his name on it, just so I get something outdoorsy, flowery, elegant, and filled with fancy words."

Oxford was bemused. "And the wedding is …?"

"The second of May."

"Why so soon?"

"My son, Henry, 'the Earl of Southampton,'" she said, sarcastically emphasizing her sons' title, "comes of age in October. He's putting on airs. Poets and scholars are dedicating works to him."

"Shacksmear among them."

"Aye. Him, most of all. *Venus*, with all its heavy breathing and moist places, has puffed Henry up, at least among the younger set." She suddenly realized the poem on its way to Richard Field might also be dedicated to her son. "Did Shacksmear dedicate *The Rape* to him too?" She had a worried look on her face.

"I'm afraid so," Oxford said. He looked pained, as if Shackspear was a delinquent nephew he could not control.

"All the more reason to marry in May. If I wait, I will need Henry's consent, and he won't give it. He sniffs and says Sir Thomas is beneath me. Can you do it?"

"I will speak to Shacksmear, Lady Mary, and use all my powers to persuade him to give you the play you want."

"Thank you, my lord." She stood up. "And it would give me great pleasure if you came to the wedding as well. I can assure you that it will be worth the trip, as short as that may be." She headed for the door. Lettice got up to follow her and blew Oxford a kiss.

Robin, returning from his errand, met them at the door. He stepped aside to let the women pass. He and Oxford watched them climb into Lady Leicester's carriage.

"Manuscript delivered, young man?"

"Aye, my lord." Robin was looking at the carriage as it drove off. "Did Lady Lettice just blow you a kiss, my lord?" he asked.

"Of course not. Come inside, my faithful assistant. We have a new play to write."

"And I have news, my lord. Dr. López has been arrested for trying to poison the Queen."

"Poison the Queen? Impossible!"

"He's a Portuguese, my lord, and a Jew."

"He is *not* a Portuguese, and he is *not* a Jew! He is an Englishman and a good Christian."

"There are witnesses who say the Spanish were paying him to do it."

"The Spanish? López hates the Spanish. And the Catholics too. He fled Portugal to escape the Catholics who were persecuting him for his Protestant faith. He's been the Queen's loyal servant for years! This is nonsense!"

"It was suggested to me that Lord Essex may be behind it, my lord. He's been pushing the Queen to have the good doctor executed, but she has so far refused to sign the warrant. Falstaff says something else is going on. He's trying to find out what."

"God, I hope so. He saved my life."

"Who, my lord?" Oxford did not understand. "Falstaff or López?" Robin asked. He waited for an answer, his head cocked. Oxford noted a sly look on his servant's face. "Floppy pronouns, my lord," the young boy said.

Oxford wasn't used to being examined like this. "Maybe."

"So which one, my lord?" Robin asked, still grinning.

"Both, I guess."

"Aye."

"And what is the reason you have turned pedant and are treating me as your first student?"

"*We have a play to write*," Robin said excitedly. "'Tis music to my ears, a tune I've not heard for some time."

"Ah. Well, in that case, I will forgive you for your impertinence. We should begin, shouldn't we?"

## A Double Maske

"To the trunk of plays, then," Oxford said. He vaulted up the stairs two-at-a-time, Robin close behind. They dragged the trunk over to the window. Oxford opened it. "*A Double Maske*," Oxford announced, holding up a sheaf of ragged papers. "A piece of froth," he said, "words, words, words, more than enough for the wedding of a countess." They went back down stairs to the library.

"And this is about what, my lord?" Robin sat down in his accustomed place. Socrates leaped onto the end of the table.

"It's a masque, and it's a mask. It's about the King of France and it's about the Queen of England."

"How can that be?"

"Because I will make it so."

"In 1572, Marguerite, sister to the King of France, married Henri, King of Navarre in Paris. She was Catholic; he was Protestant. The King of France and his mother, Catherine de Medici, thought the marriage would stop the killing but it didn't."

"The Massacre at Paris," Robin said. "Was Henri killed?"

"He would have been had Marguerite not forced her way into her brother's chambers and begged him to save Henri. Charles said he would if Henri turned Catholic. Henri agreed, and was spared."

"This is the same Henri who is now King of France?"

"The same."

"I have seen letters he has written you."

"He sends me special messages for the Queen."

"So you are friends?" Robin asked, his eyes wide opening wider.

"He and I became friends when I passed through Paris on my way to Italy. When I returned, he was still being held as a 'velvet' prisoner in the Louvre. The French King, and his mother, Catherine, wouldn't let him leave Paris because they feared Henri would return to his Protestant faith and raise an army to attack the Catholics."

"How awful! To be a prince and locked in a prison!"

"Yes. I decided to free him. I had met one of the ladies-in-waiting to the King's mother, Catherine, when I was in Italy. Her name was the Countess of Mirandola. I talked her into smuggling a rope into the Louvre. A few nights later, Henri came sliding down the rope into a boat I had hired. We were quickly away from the riverbank and downriver through the city walls. Horses waited for us a short distance further on. Henri set off for Navarre while I left for England."

"My lord, this is a feat worthy of our greatest knights! Why have I not heard about this?"

"Because Henri and Elizabeth asked me to keep it secret. The French would have blamed Elizabeth if they had learned of my involvement."

"What a pity!"

"Yes. Denied fame in *another* field. Just think: I could have added a rope to my coat of arms!" He laughed. "Henri escaped but Marguerite was still held prisoner in the Louvre. Her dowry had not been determined because of the Massacre. It was a great piece of unfinished business. It wasn't just beds and blankets; it was whole provinces, custom duties, and who got the taxes. Charles, the French king, finally decided to let Marguerite leave Paris to meet Henri at Nerac and finalize her dowry. Catherine de Medici went with her, accompanied by an enormous train of nobles and maids-of-honor. The Countess of Mirandola went along and wrote me every day. Elizabeth was on progress at the same time through the eastern counties of England. The English court received news every day about what was going on in France."

"Was this the 'noble progress' my lord in Gabriel Harvey praised you in a poem he read at Audley End?"

Oxford laughed. "Not just me. He had a poem for everyone. He hoped to be appointed my secretary, but he was not a poet by nature. He had to hunt for words, the way a pig roots in the ground looking for nuts. John Lyly, on the other hand, was overflowing with words. I hired Lyly during the progress and made Harvey my enemy. Lyly came back with me back to London where we began working on the *Double Maske*, which I based on the events in Navarre. The play was put on before the Queen in January, 1579. It was politely received and quickly forgotten, probably because I let myself follow what happened in Nerac, which was that Charles, the King of France, died in Paris while everyone was dancing in Nerac. The festivities ended immediately. We shall trim off the end and add a wedding."

Robin had been the leafing through the script. "There is much beautiful language here, but more is needed to carry a play."

"So what does my scribbler suggest?"

"The king tells his three companions that they will sleep no more than three hours a night, eat one meal a day, go one day a week without *any* food, and, most importantly, avoid women."

"Is that improbable?"

"Very."

"It's a play."

"Which was received 'politely' when it was first put on. The audience at Southampton House will expect more. These are modern times, my lord. The wedding guests will want something new."

"And what 'new' do you propose?

"I would keep the opening, with the King of Navarre telling his companions there will be three years of fasting."

"But one of the courtiers has not yet agreed to these conditions. His name is Berowne. He sees difficulties ahead."

> *O, these are barren tasks, too hard to keep,*
> *Not to see ladies, study, fast, not sleep!*

Robin looked up as he wrote these lines. "Let me guess. He is you."

"How can you say that? You've not heard the play."

"Do I need to? Your face gives you away. I have discovered you."

"You could have waited," Oxford said, trying to sound petulant, but he was enjoying being caught.

Robin went back to paging through the script. "You have a braggart knight named Don Armado. He must have a page."

"A little, snitty fellow."

It was Robin's turn to look surprised. "I am not a little, snitty fellow."

"Who said it was you?"

"He shall be called 'Moth,'" Robin said, writing down the name.

Oxford looked at Robin conspiratorially. "And if he be little and snitty, who do you see when you write down his name?"

"Thomas Nashe."

"Excellent!"

"There will be no doubt if we call him 'yoong Juvenal.'"

"How so?"

"Because that's what Greene called him in *Groatsworth*."

"I missed that." Oxford leaned back and looked at the ceiling. "Armado will enter in the second scene, accompanied by his servant, Moth. Armado is melancholy. '*I have promis'd to study three years with the Duke*,' he will say. Moth will respond: '*You may do it in an hour, sir.*'"

"How can that be?"

"Moth will say:

| | |
|---|---|
| | *How many is one thrice told?* |
| Armado: | *I am ill at reckoning, it fits the spirit of a Tapster.* |
| Moth: | *You are a gentleman and a gamester sir.* |
| Armado: | *I confess both, they are the varnish of a complete gentleman.* |
| Moth: | *Then I am sure you know how much the gross sum of Deus-ace amounts to.* |
| Armado: | *It doth amount to one more than two.* |
| Moth: | *Which the base vulgar call three.* |
| Armado: | *True.* |
| Moth: | *Why Sir is this such a piece of study?* |
| | *Now here's three studied, ere you'll thrice wink,* |
| | *And how easy it is to put years to the word three, and study* |
| | *Three years in two words, the dancing horse will tell* |
| | *you.* |
| Armado: | *A most fine figure.* |
| Moth: | *To prove you a cypher.* |

Robin laughed as he wrote down the words. "A braggart buffoon and his clever page. I remember the dancing horse."

"You like the clever page more, I warrant."

"Now you find *me* out, my lord."

"Armado will announce he is in love."

"I once told Marlowe that the ground rose to kiss your feet."

"I like the image."

"So did Marlowe."

"And what children has that line spawned?"

Robin became serious. "Don Armado, being a mint of words, will say:

*I do affect the very ground, which is base,*
*Where her shoe, which is baser, guided by her foot,*

*Which is basest, doth tread.*

Oxford laughed. "Well done. And Don Armado will cry out:

*Assist me, some extemporal god of rhyme,*
*For I am sure I shall turn sonnet.*
*Devise, wit; write, pen; for I am for whole volumes in folio.*

"Oh, no. You're Don Armado too?"

"Can't I be everyone?"

Robin heard a little boy, wanting every toy in the room.

The two of them sat across the table from each other, the boy the master for a moment, the master the boy. Robin broke the spell. "And then?"

"A messenger announces that the Princess of France and her ladies-in-waiting have arrived, escorted by a courtier named Boyet."

"*Boyet?*"

"Shh," Oxford putting a finger to his lips. "The Queen …"

"You mean 'the Princess,' don't you?"

"Yes, the Princess arrives in Navarre and Boyet feels he must give her one more piece of advice:

*Consider who the king your father sends,*
*To whom he sends, and what's his embassy:*
*Yourself, held precious in the world's esteem,*
*To parley with the sole inheritor*
*Of all perfections that a man may owe,*
*Matchless Navarre; the plea of no less weight*
*Than Aquitaine, a dowry for a queen.*

"To which the Princess replies:

*Good Lord Boyet, my beauty, though but mean,*
*Needs not the painted flourish of your praise:*
*I am less proud to hear you tell my worth*
*Than you much willing to be counted wise*
*In spending your wit in the praise of mine.*

Robin hurried to write all this down. "So who is Boyet?" he asked.

"Must every character I create spring from some mortal soul?"

"In your case, yes."

"Robin doth become saucier and saucier."

"And Boyet is …?"

"A courtier who will speak in rhyme. The Princess tasks him with finding out what the king and his courtiers are up to and Boyet replies that he is 'proud of the employment, willingly I go.'"

"The little minion."

"Berowne will overhear what Boyet says and describe 'the little minion' as having once stood between the Queen and the fire.'"

"Sidney."

"Some will think so, since he is well-known for having done so."

"*Boyet*," Robin said. "*The little boy.* You can't forgive him, can you?"

"How can I? But not for his tantrum at the tennis court. That I can forgive. It's his poetry I cannot forgive."

"And Berowne?"

"This is how Rosaline, one of Marguerite's ladies-in-waiting, greets Berowne:

| Berowne: | *Did not I dance with you in Brabant once?* |
|---|---|
| Rosaline | *Did not I dance with you in Brabant once?* |
| Berowne: | *I know you did.* |
| Rosaline | *How needless was it then to ask the question!* |
| Berowne: | *You must not be so quick.* |
| Rosaline | *'Tis 'long of you that spur me with such questions.* |
| Berowne: | *Your wit's too hot, it speeds too fast, 'twill tire.* |
| Rosaline | *Not till it leave the rider in the mire.* |
| Berowne: | *What time o' day?* |
| Rosaline | *The hour that fools should ask.* |

Oxford paused while Robin's pen ran across the page. It finally came to a stop. Robin looked up. "A wit contest, but little comedy."

Oxford sighed. "How about a pedant who volunteers to put on *The Nine Worthies* before the Princess?"

"Nine more actors?" Robin asked.

"Played by three," Oxford said.

"I begin to like this." Robin dipped his quill into the inkpot.

"You begin to sound like Shackspear."

Robin kept his head down and said nothing.

"The pedant shall be called Holofernes, a name taken from Rabelais' *Gargantua and Pantagruel*. Holofernes is Gargantua's tutor."

"Holofernes? Gargantua? Pantagruel? I am lost, my lord."

"You mean, uneducated."

Robin took no offense. He had never been to school. Comments like this were usually followed by a lecture in which Oxford had the unreasonable expectation—not unlike prayers sent Heavenward by churchgoers—that a few words could lift Robin out of his ignorance. Robin made himself comfortable.

"Rabelais was a great writer. I will have Holofernes put on a pageant before the ladies called *The Nine Worthies*. He will argue with another character over what type of deer the Princess has just killed.

> *The deer was, as you know, sanguis, in blood; ripe*
> *as the pomewater, who now hangeth like a jewel in*
> *the ear of caelo, the sky, the welkin, the heaven;*
> *and anon falleth like a crab on the face of terra,*
> *the soil, the land, the earth.*

"But who is Holofernes, my lord, and what is *The Nine Worthies*? And why do you want to stuff this into *A Double Maske*?"

"'*Stuff*?' Patience, my young lad. *The Nine Worthies* is a poem based on a play put on at Chester each year. It was written by a man named Richard Lloyd, who was tutor to a young nobleman."

"Chester is near the home of the Earls of Derby."

"Yes."

"Which means the young nobleman was William Stanley, your future son-in-law."

"Bravo, Robin."

"I begin to see, said the blind man. I know nothing of Richard Lloyd, but Holofernes makes me think of Gabriel Harvey."

"Does it? Holofernes will ask if he can recite an epitaph on the death of the deer, to which Sir Nathaniel will reply: *Perge, good Master Holofernes, perge; so it shall / please you to abrogate scurrility.*"

Robin grabbed his pen. "If this is what education brings, perhaps I am better off having missed it."

Oxford laughed. "Holofernes will pronounce the following:

> *The preyful princess pierced and prick'd a pretty pleasing pricket;*
> *Some say a sore; but not a sore, till now made sore with shooting.*

*The dogs did yell: put L to sore, then sorel jumps from thicket;*
*Or pricket sore, or else sorel; the people fall a-hooting.*

*If sore be sore, then L to sore makes fifty sores one sorel.*
*Of one sore I an hundred make by adding but one more L.*

"Lord, have mercy," Robin said, as his pen ran back and forth across the page. When finished, he scanned the page. "An odd rhyme. An even odder rhythm. A first line of eight or nine syllables, followed by three pairs of lines of six and three. But the pattern is quickly broken: the eighth line is not followed by a line of three but by a line of six again, and then the line of three returns! To be ended by a line of eight! And, it doesn't scan. The last line limps over the finish line, dragging a broken leg—*by adding but one more L*! The 'but' pops off the page, like a bone sticking out of a man's leg."

Oxford was enjoying Robin's attempt to understand the structure of Holofernes' epitaph.

"And the puns!" Robin said. "Awful! *Sorel* and *sore? The preyful princess pierced and prick'd a pretty pleasing pricket?* My lord, that will become the final test for every foreign speaker to show he has truly learned English! In fact, Harvey could have written this. It's *bastardized* Harvey!"

Oxford suddenly looked distressed. "Bastardized? No, no, Robin. I would never 'bastardize' Harvey's efforts. I only wish to do him justice."

"I'll say."

"It was not easy."

"And how will you end *A Double Maske?*"

"A wedding and some songs. We will get Paul's Boys to come over and sing something, particularly if I make it Lyly-like."

"Lyly-like." Robin smiled at how much his master had changed in the past few months. A comment that some lines in *Richard III* were reflections of Lyly's influence evoked a curt response from Oxford, yet here he was bringing up Lyly's name himself.

"But back to the beginning, Robin. The filling in between the high points is always the hardest part of writing a play or a poem."

## ~ 94 ~
## A Nidicock for Lady Lisbeth

Oxford was leaning back in a chair in the library when his eldest daughter burst into the room. She informed him in arch tones that Lady Alice, widowed a few months earlier when her husband, the Fifth Earl of Derby, had died from a massive dose of arsenic poisoning, *was now claiming she was pregnant!* "*How dare she!*"

"He left a present behind," Oxford drolly remarked.

"Not for me," Lisbeth stormed. "My wedding to William is now on hold. *We will have to wait till Christmas, for Christ's sake, to find out whether it's a boy!*" She glared at her father. "*Do something about this!*"

Oxford had heard about Lady Alice's claim. A son would "unearl" the dead earl's younger brother, William, who became the Sixth Earl of Derby upon his brother's death. William would now have to wait to see if Lady Alice gave birth to a son, who would succeed his father and displace William, a 34 year-old playgoer and would-be poet Lisbeth had promised to marry. Oxford shrugged. "He's a nidicock," he said flippantly. Lisbeth looked at him with wide eyes. "Truly," Oxford protested. "Sir George Carew said so. He is William's brother-in-law. He ought to know."

Lisbeth exploded. "He is *not* a nidicock!" she shouted. "George Carey is a beady-eyed, slope-headed, *pygmy marmoset!* Women run away from him when he appears. His eyes molest us more than his hands ever could."

Oxford was amused. He wasn't quite sure what a pygmy marmoset was, but he liked the description. *God*, he thought to himself: *she is so like me!* He tried not to smile. He glanced at Robin, who obviously thought Oxford should have welcomed Lisbeth instead of calling her betrothed a nidicock.

"I apologize," Oxford said. He did not have to look at Robin to see how astonished the little page was by this admission. "I was told you have rejected many fine suitors, so William is obviously a man worth fighting for. You have my permission to marry him." This stopped Lisbeth in her tracks. "And if you do, you will still be *my daughter* more than *his husband*."

This last statement surprised all three of them. Lisbeth did not know her father well enough to sense, as Robin did, that Oxford, always in love with the double-entendre, might be playing with words here. All Lisbeth heard was a father's declaration of love, which opened up a lifetime of emotions, emotions she had locked away long ago. Instead of giving them utterance, however, she immediately said something to take herself away from them.

"Easy for you to say now," she sneered, tilting her head back and presenting Oxford with the haughty look he had first seen at Cecil House. "But you couldn't find the time to tell me you were my father when I was little, like when you passed me in the hallway at Cecil House without so much as a word!"

"I did? When was that?"

"I was three. You were a giant as you came down the hall. My father! Come to pick me up and take me to my mother so that we would all be together again!" The emotion in her voice surprised her. She hurried on. "You didn't even look down."

"I don't remember," Oxford said. He was surprised at how sad he sounded. Lisbeth, full of anger and disappointment, didn't hear it.

"Of course you don't. Lady Suffolk put me in the hallway. She said you would stop and pick me up when you saw me. '*Nature will work*,' she claimed, '*and when your father sees you, I will pop out of a side room and tell him you are his daughter!*' But you didn't stop. You went by without as much as a glance."

The anger in her voice had disappeared. She was watching Oxford walk by her again, hurt all over her face. She had become a child again, alive only in her memories of the past, and her father walking away from her down the hallway.

"Lady Suffolk," Oxford said, in an almost reverential tone.

"Aye."

"Peregrine's mother."

"And a better grandmother than nature gave me."

"Did you know she convinced Great Harry to let women read the Bible?"

"No."

"She would have been the last to tell you."

Somehow, they had stumbled onto common ground. "I miss her," Lisbeth said. "I loved the time I spent at Grimsthorpe. I was only five when she died. She should've lived forever."

A heavy silence fell over the room. They had forgotten Robin. He slid a paper across the table to remind them he was still there.

"Well," Oxford said, "you have picked a fine man. If he is unearled by Lady Alice's baby, you can show everyone how much Love triumphs over Fortune by marrying him anyway."

Lisbeth laughed aloud. "Only *you* would say something like that! If a baby unearls him, he loses me as well. The baby will return him to what he was before—a second son, destined for the military or the church, but that won't be good enough for me. You think I pursued him for love? I didn't start to chase him until *after* his brother died. Lady Alice's outrageous claim will prove false eventually. If not … Well, there are others."

Oxford was taken aback. She saw his reaction. "Don't look at me like that! Someone decided to help nature along by poisoning William's older brother, didn't they? It may have been P-Pop, to put William in a position to inherit the earldom and marry me!" Oxford blinked. She might be right. Lisbeth went on. "I don't mind being a tool in grandfather's plans as long as I benefit from the scheme. I'm not my mother, thank God, moon-eyed and amazed at life as it goes by, a leaf on a stream being carried this way and that, marrying whomever her father ordered her to." She did not check to see how Oxford took this slap. "I want to have power *and* money and I will marry the man *I* want. But if P-Pop wants to have his descendants on the throne of England, and he wants me to be the vessel through which they come, I don't mind being the conduit."

"You *are* my daughter," Oxford said quietly.

"In spades. In the world I live in, success is to be had in marriages and poison. If Lady Alice is barren, I can be the mother of a king."

"You have read great Harry's Will?"

"Of course I have. The 'spine' of England. The crown was to go to Edward and his male heirs, but Edward died childless; next, it was to go to Mary and her heirs, but Mary also died childless; third, to Elizabeth and her heirs, but she has none, and is now too old to get one; which leaves Lady Margaret Clifford, the oldest living descendant of Mary Tudor, who happens to be the mother of my William. If the Countess survives Elizabeth, the Countess will become Queen. She is old, however, and has made it clear she will decline the honor. Which means William has a very good chance of becoming king. If he does, I will be his queen, and our children will inherit the throne of England."

"You *have* learned well at Cecil House."

"Far more than if I had been raised in yours. P-Pop is a fuddy old man, but you can learn a lot from him if you pay attention to what he's doing and *not* what he's saying. I am no Sylvia."

Oxford was at a loss for words.

Elspeth went on. "With this impending dignity, we would be most embarrassed if it came out that you, the father of the Queen, were writing plays." Oxford's mouth dropped open again. He could not tell whether Elspeth was speaking for William and herself, or had adopted the royal prerogative of referring to herself in the first person plural. Her arrogance was not beyond it. She gave no indication she saw his shock. Or, she saw it and did not care. "Think of it. The father of the Queen of England writing plays! That would be totally unacceptable. I think you need to find something else to do with your time."

Oxford knew Elspeth did not care about the theater, but he had never imagined that she would be standing in front of him one day wagging a finger and telling him, as the future Queen of England, that he had to stop writing plays! Before he could say anything, Lady Elspeth came into the room.

"Lisbeth!" Lady Elspeth said, coming up to her daughter-in-law and giving her a warm hug. "How lovely to see you." She turned to Oxford. "We are to the theater. A new play at the Curtain: *The Massacre at Paris.* All London is talking about it."

"It's not new."

"It's new to us," Lisbeth said. She crooked her arm through Lady Elspeth's. "I so love Marlowe. Don't you?"

"That's not fair, Lisbeth," Oxford's wife said.

"No, it isn't," Oxford grumbled.

"Can't help myself," Lisbeth said. "Can't accept plays like you do."

"But plays are good," Oxford said doggedly.

"William thinks so too. He loves them more than I do. You two will get along well."

Oxford's face softened. "Enjoy the play," he said as the two women swept out of the room.

# 95

# The Lord Chamberlain's Men

Oxford listened to his wife and daughter happily chatting with each other as they went out the front door. He sat at the table trying to understand how his daughter could be so far removed from anything he could have come up with had he tried to put her in a play. Perhaps this was why she was continually surprising him. Perhaps this was his punishment for not helping his daughters when they were young. *Or your son, Edward*, a voice reminded him, a thought which made him feel worse.

Robin cleared his throat. Oxford had forgotten he was still in the room. Oxford looked at him. "I deserve it, don't I?"

Robin walked around the table and sat down on the other side opposite Oxford. "Not being married myself, or the father of any children, I am unable to answer your question. Perhaps Lisbeth would have been different if she had been Lady Elspeth's daughter. Perhaps not. A person is rarely, in my experience, even a faint copy of their parents. A copy of an uncle, perhaps, or a distant grandmother, but rarely a parent."

Oxford smiled. "So much wisdom from one so young."

Robin leaned forward. "Everyone wants you to put down your pen, my lord. You owe it to yourself to keep on writing. And to me."

"To you?"

"Yes. I am 'Scribbler,' remember? I want nothing more than to see my plays acted on the stage. And I can't do that if you stop writing."

Oxford smiled. "Like Shackspear, who, if I put my pen down, will also be deprived. Well, at least with you I have an audience of one."

"You have an audience of millions, my lord, not including those yet unborn. The Burghleys of the world, their grandchildren, the Puritans who want to stop us from eating cakes and ale, are the thick underbrush you must push through to get to the high, open ground where everything is crystal clear and beautiful."

Oxford laughed. "And where have you gone to find such fanciful phrases? What am I growing here? Another Lyly? Please, dear God!"

"My lord," Robin said, his brow furrowed.

"Be thou thyself, Robin. I love thee for it. And thank you from rescuing me from myself. My head is an amphitheater full of characters—all me! Those 'me's' who love to grovel in self-pity gain strength when I am feeling down. They elbow their way to the front of the stage where I present a tragedy to the world—*me*! But I'm not worth watching. No one wants to hear someone else feel sorry for themselves, or watch a play about it. They want to see happiness, and people smarter than they are."

"*A Double Mask*," Robin suggested.

"Exactly."

"Master Willum Shackspear," Nigel announced. Shackspear came into the room. He was dressed in a green velvet suit and hat. He tucked the hat under his arm.

"My lord," he said, bowing to Oxford. "Robin," he added, giving a slight bow in Robin's direction. "I have good news."

Oxford stifled the impulse to ask Shackspear if he was retiring to Stratford. "Which is?"

"The theaters are closed and the Earl of Derby is dead. The Earl transferred all his property just before he died to his widow in trust for his three daughters. William, his brother, will get nothing. On top of that, the Earl's widow has announced that she is pregnant, thereby throwing the succession into question."

"This is good news?"

"The lawyers say it will take ten years for William to get the estate away from the widow. In the meantime, Derby's players are no more and there is no money for new plays. Burbage wants to found a new company *and* find a permanent home. The lease on the Theater runs out in two years."

"And what does all of this have to do with me?"

"Burbage is looking for ten players to become sharers in a new company, which will own the rights to the plays and divide up the profits. If we get enough money, we'll buy ground and put up a new theater. In the end, we will control our own destiny and make more money."

"'We'?"

Shackspear put on his best mock-humble face. "I have been asked to join."

"Who else?"

"Condell and Heminges. Kemp."

Oxford glanced at Robin. "Good men," Robin said.

"And Lord Hunsdon?"

"He has agreed to allow the company to call themselves the Lord Chamberlain's Men. The Queen suggested it. She is distressed at the declining number of companies, which is reducing the number of plays put on before her."

"But the theaters are still closed."

"She may be thinking about re-opening them, my Lord. The plague numbers are down."

"So how much are you asking for?"

Shackspear licked his lips. "Burbage says a share will cost £100."

"£100!" Oxford said. "£100," he said to Robin, wagging his head. "Pay the man."

Robin looked at him in surprise. "I don't have £100."

"I didn't think you did." Oxford looked at Shackspear. "Neither do I."

"My Lord! This is an opportunity that won't come again. There are no more Burbages or Kemps out there. Once Burbage has his sharers, no one else will get in!"

"What about Edward Alleyn?"

"He's gone over to Henslowe. He's married his daughter. Got her pregnant, I heard." Shackspear hurried on. "My lord, you will benefit from this if you help me become a sharer."

"How so?"

"Burbage wants me to join his company so he can get your plays."

"My plays?"

"I mean, my plays."

"Does he know?"

"No. He still thinks I'm the author. If I am part of the company, I can take him your plays, and you will have access to the best stable of players in England. Burbage; Kemp; Heminges; Condell. These players will stay together. They won't break up and go elsewhere, like the Queen's Men or the others. They are the players your plays deserve. They will bring life to your plays. They will stretch you."

"£50," Robin blurted out, surprising both Oxford and Shackspear. "£50 and two plays a year."

"Yes," Oxford agreed.

"My Lord," Shackspear began, but Oxford interrupted him.

"Not a farthing more. Burbage didn't invite you in for your acting abilities: he wants my plays. £50 and two plays a year."

Shackspear hesitated. "£50 and two plays a year."

"Tell him you'll go to Henslowe if he turns you down," Robin added.

"Yes," Oxford said. "Good idea."

"And who gets the profits, my lord?"

"You do. You are the author, aren't you? And I can't have filthy lucre crossing my palm, can I?"

"Yes," Shackspear said. This made him feel better. "I mean, no." He straightened himself and took his hat out from under his arm. "Thank you, my lord." He put the hat on his head and pulled the brim down at an angle. He bowed and left.

# 96

## The Execution of Dr. López

Is it today?"

"It is, my lord. Within the hour."

"Are you coming, Sir John?"

"I have a great fear of attending executions, my lord, lest some higher power, if there be one, see me there when I would otherwise have gone unnoticed. I will pass the day here, my lord, an it please your lordship."

"As you wish."

Oxford and Robin headed out the door toward Watling Street. A large crowd had already gathered. Horses soon appeared, dragging a hurdle on which López had been strapped. The horses dragged him up to the gallows where men cut López loose.

The crowd surged forward. "Burn the Jew!" someone called out. "Cut his guts out and show 'em to him!" another cried.

Constables and watchmen pushed the crowd back. Oxford was let inside the cordon. Robin slipped in with him. They went over to López, who was being stood up by the noose around his neck. The executioner slipped a long-legged stool under his feet.

"Rodrigo," Oxford called up to him.

López looked down. His eyes were bulging as he gasped for air. He danced on the stool, swaying back and forth.

"*Be it known*," López suddenly cried out in a voice loud enough to be heard across the square. The crowd went silent. "*Be it known that I have always loved the Queen as well as I love Jesus Christ!*"

This was too much for the executioner. He kicked the stool out from under López, dropping him toward the ground. The fall broke López's neck with a crack, killing him instantly.

"Nooooooo," the crowd cried out. They had come to see the executioner cut out the Jew's entrails and show them to him while he was still alive, but the executioner had killed him too soon. The executioner was also angry. He had denied himself the pleasure of cutting into the Jew and hearing him scream. In a fury, he attacked López's body, carving into his belly and throwing body parts in every direction. Blood splattered on Oxford's hands. Some hit Robin who, in revulsion, ran away.

Oxford dropped slowly to his knees. Onlookers would later report that his lordship looked like he was praying, but, in truth, he could not bear to watch López being disemboweled. Another man, Michael Lok, kneeled down next to him. Oxford owed Lok £3,000 for money invested in Frobisher's voyages. The executioner was now sawing through López's hip. "I am not here for the £3,000," Lok said. "I came for him." He gestured toward López. "He was a good man."

"Aye. A good Christian and a loyal subject."

"A loyal subject, but a Jew nevertheless."

Oxford was surprised by this. "He died a Christian."

Lok shook his head. "He said he loved Jesus as a bill of exchange, like the ones you signed in Italy. He hopes the Queen will not forfeit his property, so that his widow and children will have something to live on."

"I care not whether he was a Christian or a Jew. He was a good man."

"He was, my lord." Runners appeared with baskets to take López's butchered parts to the four corners of the city. "I am willing to enter into an exchange with you if you will do something for the Jews in London."

"And what is that?"

"Write a play about a good Jew. Not the Jew Christopher Marlowe gave us. If you do this for me, I will forgive the £3,000 you owe me."

"If I wrote such a play, no one would come to see it."

"Except that you make it so." Lok wiped his hand in the blood running from the gallows. "God's tears," he said, holding up his hand.

Oxford nodded. Tears were filling his eyes.

"If you cut us," Lok said, "do we not bleed? If you poison us, do we not die? Write a play, my lord, that shows the world how we love our children and grieve when we suffer loss."

Oxford nodded. "I will."

Lok held out his bloody hand. Oxford took it in his. Blood ran through their fingers. "In Rodrigo's name," Lok said.

"Amen," Oxford replied.

## ~ 97 ~
## The Wedding of Sir Thomas Heneage &
## The Countess of Southampton

The second floor window was open and the breeze off the Thames was ruffling the daffodils in the window box.

"'*The lovely daffodils that come before the swallow dares*,'" Oxford said, as he dealt cards to the other men seated around a small table.

"'*And take the winds of March with beauty*,'" William Stanley, Sixth Earl of Derby added, as he took his cards and began to look through them. He had a six and seven of clubs, a knave of hearts, and an ace. He tried not to smile.

"Lovely," Oxford said, referring to the poetry and not the cards he had given himself. A few shillings rested in the center of the table. Oxford shifted his cards to his left hand and picked up a meat purse. A gold toothpick rested on a tiny stand shaped like the horns of a bull. *From Crete*, the merchant had told him in Palermo, *where the Minotaur was worshiped*.

Derby tossed another coin onto the table. The two other men passed, discarding their cards and drawing new ones from the pile on the table. Oxford matched Derby and dealt two more cards to everyone else. One man immediately said "out," and dropped his cards onto the table. The other three laid their cars down on the table face up. "I win again!" Derby said excitedly as he gathered in the coins on the table.

Lisbeth came up the stairs into the room. "You not only disappear from the celebration," she said to Derby, "but take over the Countess' favorite room. Have you no shame?"

"The play was over," Derby said.

"At least you could have said goodbye to the Queen. You should have thanked her for suggesting that Tilney reopen the theaters."

They could hear the drums outside as the Queen proceeded down the pier and boarded the royal barge.

"'Twould be good to see the back of her," Oxford suggested, glancing at Derby, who had a mischievous look on his face. The other men decided it was time to leave. They went down the stairs.

"Really!" Lisbeth said. "You two!"

"Are getting along very well," Oxford said.

"Famously," William said. "The only thing we disagree on is how to rewrite the ending to the play we just saw."

"No one noticed it needed it," Lisbeth said.

"Because no one was *listening*," Derby said.

Lisbeth frowned. "'Twas only a play performed at a wedding."

"Oh?" Derby glanced at Oxford, who was shuffling the cards again.

Lisbeth walked around the table and put her hand on Derby's shoulder. Oxford reached over to gather in Derby's cards but Lisbeth saw what Oxford had dealt him. "You know he's letting you win."

"Of course I do. It's his way of welcoming me into the family."

"We're not exactly family yet," Lisbeth said, a look of irritation spreading across her face. "We still have to wait on your sister-in-law's pregnancy."

"She is not pregnant," Oxford said, laying out new cards.

"She is not?"

Oxford nodded.

"How do you know?" Derby asked.

Oxford put an index finger to his lips.

"Why didn't you tell us?" Lisbeth asked.

"I just learned myself. A whisper in my ear from someone who should have been listening to the play. Call it an early wedding present."

"Oh, Father," Lisbeth cried. She ran around and gave Oxford a hug.

She had never hugged him. He felt slightly embarrassed. "Don't give away that you know. You must carry on as if the Countess is still pregnant. Get thyself before a glass, Lisbeth, and practice the face you just showed me as you stood next to your future husband and said, with great petulance, *we still have to wait on your sister-in-law's pregnancy.*"

Lisbeth tried to look petulant. Derby laughed. "I know the face you're talking about. She won't have trouble finding it."

Oxford and Lisbeth looked at each other warmly. He could tell she was pleased to be marrying Derby for whatever reasons she may have, and without any realization as to how contradictory some of them might be. She cocked her head. "And will my lord be penning a play for our wedding?"

Oxford tried to look surprised. "I am forbidden from writing plays, aren't I?"

"Not for our wedding." She cocked an eye at her betrothed, whose face plainly showed that he also wanted Oxford to write a play for their wedding.

Oxford looked out the window at the river. "A few thoughts have come to mind."

"It must be a comedy," Lisbeth said. "Comedies always end in marriages, don't they?" Oxford acknowledged that they did. She turned to Derby. "At least two, don't you think, my dear?"

"I was thinking of three," Oxford said.

"Oh," Lisbeth said, quite pleased. "That would be very nice."

A tall man in his forties stuck his head up out of the stairwell. "My lord," he said.

Oxford turned to see who had addressed him. "My goodness. Finley."

The man called Finley came up into the room. "My lord," he said again, bowing, his head brushing the ancient beams above him.

Oxford turned to Derby and his daughter. "My lord, Lady Lisbeth, this is Finley, who I have not seen since we were students at Cambridge."

Finley bowed. "My lord; Lady Lisbeth." He stood back up, making sure his head did not hit the beams above him. He was wearing a long coat that had seen better years, and an old shirt starched and cleaned for the wedding but which still showed many errant threads at the collar.

"How long has it been?" Oxford asked.

"Many years, my Lord."

Derby rose from the table. "You two must have much to discuss."

"The dancing has begun," Lisbeth said, "and 'twas the reason I came up to get you. My lord," she said, addressing her father, "You need to honor Lady Mary, now wife to Sir Thomas, with a dance. Or so says Lady Elspeth, your wife, who suggested I find you and tell you so."

Finley stepped aside to let Lady Lisbeth and the Earl of Derby descend to the floor below. When they had disappeared down the stairs, he turned to Oxford. "Forgive me for interrupting, my lord."

"Sit down, Finley. It's good to see you. Where have you been all these years? On the continent?"

"From time to time, but mostly at Cambridge."

"You have a position there?"

"Not exactly. I have been living in the town, or in the neighboring villages, taking in students who need help in getting their degrees. It doesn't pay much, but I have to eat."

Oxford nodded.

"You remember *Palamon and Arcite?*" Finley asked. His face widened into a smile. "You helped me with it."

"Yes. *Palamon and Arcite.* The Queen mentioned it recently. She said 'the author so limned the lovers that she would never see anything like it again.'"

"That piece of frippery?"

"She was needling me. She's good at that."

"There's far better been produced since that play was put on the boards."

"Have some of them been yours? You have continued to write?"

"Yes, but I have discovered that no one wants to put on my plays."

"I am sorry to hear that."

"Don't be. It has taken me a very long time, but I am not a playwright."

"No?"

"No. But, in the process of writing many *bad* plays, I've I learned a lot about how *good* ones are written. I can take a play apart and tell you why it doesn't work."

"And what do you do with this new-found ability?"

"I have helped some playwrights with their work, but I intend to be a professor teaching the history of the theater. It's a form of art the universities have not yet recognized."

"*Yet?*"

"I see a day when Cambridge will offer a program devoted to the study of the theater."

Oxford looked away. "You know what Cambridge thinks of the theater, Finley. They think it is for bawds. They think it is the Devil's workshop. They think it corrupts the soul. I'm afraid, my friend, you may be engaged in another doomed venture."

"With all due respect, my lord, I believe I will eventually prevail. It is true that the Puritans hate the theater, as well as the dons at Cambridge who dream only in Latin, but they are not the only people who matter. I have been able to arrange for the production of plays at the colleges and shown students and faculty how the combination of plot and poetry is a new form of expression that deserves to be studied alongside literature, rhetoric, and poetry."

Oxford was still unconvinced. "Bravo, but this is a hopeless task, I fear. And I am without influence to help you, I am afraid."

"I am aware of that, my lord, but I know you will help me if the opportunity arises."

Oxford nodded. "So what brings you to London?"

"I am much taken with the plays of William Shackspear."

"Willum."

"What?"

"Nothing."

"Oh. Well, it is difficult to study plays when the acting companies refuse to print the play scripts. And what is printed is of little help because they're written from memory and contain every possible error a printer's apprentice can devise. The only way to build a program to study the theater is for me to see live performances and take notes. My mentor told me a play by Shackspear would be part of the wedding festivities today and so I came up to London to see it."

"Mentor?"

"A person whose name I am not at liberty to divulge."

"But who has encouraged you in this venture?"

"Most definitely."

"A man of the theater, then," Oxford said. He tried to figure out who it might be.

"He has been most generous."

"So what did you think of Willum's latest effort?" Oxford asked, as he got up from the table.

"A festival of language, my lord, a linguistic exuberance in which Shackspear discovers that he has no limits."

Oxford stopped. "Really?"

"With many layers. Berowne is in love with himself and seeks his reflection in the eyes of the women he meets. However, Rosaline spells catastrophe for him. She continues a series of women Shackspear can't trust."

"Like who?"

"Like Silvia in *Two Gentlemen*. In the play we just saw, Berowne says Rosaline is '*one that that will do the deed / Though Argus were her eunuch and her guard.*' The fear of cuckoldry is ever present in Shackspear's plays."

Oxford pursed his lips.

"The language is delicious. '*Light seeking light doth light of light beguile.*' That's Lylyish."

"Lylyish?"

"Yes, but far better. Because the center of the play is more than just words. It's a about love:

> *Love, first learned in a lady's eyes,*
> *Lives not alone immured in the brain,*
> *But, with the motion of all elements,*
> *Courses as swift as thought in every power,*
> *And gives to every power a double power,*
> *Above their functions and their offices.*

"And:

> *And when the Love speaks, the voice of all the gods*
> *Make heaven drowsy with the harmony.*
> *Never durst poet touch a pen to write*
> *Until his ink were tempered with Loves sighs;*
> *O! Then his lines would ravish savage ears.*

"Shear poetry, my lord. *Power* and *power* and *double power*! Music never swelled thus. And *to make heaven drowsy*!"

Oxford was, of course, pleased to hear Finley praise *The Double Maske,* even if Oxford could not admit that he was its author, but he realized that Finley's fervid imagination, something that had been very much in evidence when they were students so long ago, had not dimmed a bit. "I'm so glad you saw it performed. Have you had the pleasure of meeting Mr. Shackspear?"

"No, my lord. I was hoping he would be here, but I guess that someone as low as a playwright is not invited to the marriage of a countess and a knight, even when the playwright's work graces the occasion."

"Yes. Shall we?" The two of them descended to the hall, which was filled with dancers. The Countess of Southampton was standing at the end of one of the tables filled with glasses of wine, beer, and punch. She had a glass of wine in her hand. Sir Thomas was out on the waterside being congratulated on landing the richest widow in England as his wife.

Oxford took a circuitous route around the room, coming up next to the Countess. She welcomed him with a nod and the two of them watched the dancers execute one of the latest galliards, a *cinque pas* ending in a *lavolta*, a step which involved an intimate, close hold between the couple as the male partner lifted his female partner into the air and spun her 270 degrees.

"Obscene!" the Countess said as she watched dozens of women being lifted up and spun around in the air. "And I am so glad they are doing it at my wedding." Oxford was only mildly surprised. "We must condemn those things we love best," she confided to him in a conspiratorial voice. "Were I a few years younger and lighter, I would ask you to take a spin out there with me."

"You would be disappointed, my lady. I am a clubfoot on the dance floor, despite having been forced out of bed by Lord Burghley every morning at seven to learn how to dance."

"But not the galliard, I warrant."

"No, my lady. 'Twas not known when I was a student there."

"A pity," she said, putting down her glass and picking up another one. Oxford wondered if the sight of the women being thrust into the air was, for the Countess, the sex she would not have with Sir Thomas, who was much too old and feeble to bring her any joy on this their wedding night.

The Countess' son, Henry, now the Third Earl of Southampton, was gracefully moving through the complicated steps of the dance. "What a pity his father is not here to see how handsome a man Henry has turned out to be," Oxford mused.

"But he *is* here."

"Who?"

"His father." She took a sip of wine and looked out over the dancers.

"His father is long dead, Madame. You buried him."

"I buried the Second Earl of Southampton, my lord, but he was not Henry's father."

Oxford looked at her disdainfully. "Madame, you do yourself ill by slandering your former husband on the occasion of your second wedding."

"But the truth is the truth, is it not, my lord?" she asked, looking at him directly.

Oxford was beginning to think she may have had too much to drink, but he realized she was implying *he* was Henry's father. "Madame, you suggest an honor I must decline."

"Because you and I have never …?" she said mischievously, letting her sentence trail off.

"Yes, my lady."

"You are correct."

This puzzled Oxford even more.

"Your mistake, my lord, is assuming that I am Henry's mother."

"Of course, you are."

"I would know, wouldn't I?" The woman Oxford had thought drunk or mad now sounded completely sober. "He has your eyes and her hair, your mouth and her nose. And he gets his arrogance from both of you."

Oxford was watching Southampton dancing gracefully across the floor. She waited for his question.

"Then, if you are not his mother," he heard himself asking, "who is?"

The Countess leaned in: "She who just left in the royal barge." She gave his arm a squeeze. "*Regina Vagina!*"

*~ To Be Continued ~*

# Lineage Tables

# The Earls of Oxford

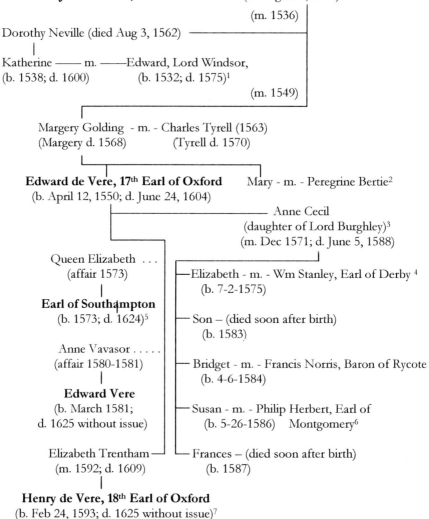

**John de Vere, 16th Earl of Oxford** (d. August 3, 1562)

(m. 1536)

Dorothy Neville (died Aug 3, 1562)

Katherine —— m. ——Edward, Lord Windsor,
(b. 1538; d. 1600)       (b. 1532; d. 1575)[1]

(m. 1549)

Margery Golding  - m. - Charles Tyrell (1563)
(Margery d. 1568)         (Tyrell d. 1570)

**Edward de Vere, 17th Earl of Oxford**      Mary - m. - Peregrine Bertie[2]
(b. April 12, 1550; d. June 24, 1604)

Anne Cecil
(daughter of Lord Burghley)[3]
(m. Dec 1571; d. June 5, 1588)

Queen Elizabeth  . . .
(affair 1573)

**Earl of Southampton**
(b. 1573; d. 1624)[5]

Anne Vavasor . . . . .
(affair 1580-1581)

**Edward Vere**
(b. March 1581;
d. 1625 without issue)

Elizabeth Trentham
(m. 1592; d. 1609)

Elizabeth - m. - Wm Stanley, Earl of Derby [4]
(b. 7-2-1575)

Son – (died soon after birth)
(b. 1583)

Bridget - m. - Francis Norris, Baron of Rycote
(b. 4-6-1584)

Susan - m. - Philip Herbert, Earl of
(b. 5-26-1586)    Montgomery[6]

Frances – (died soon after birth)
(b. 1587)

**Henry de Vere, 18th Earl of Oxford**
(b. Feb 24, 1593; d. 1625 without issue)[7]

---

[1]  Edward, Lord Windsor, died, January 24, 1574 in Venice. Oxford's half-sister, Katherine, wife of Edward, Lord Windsor, sued Oxford in 1563 to have their father's marriage to Oxford's mother declared void, which would have 'unearled' Oxford.

[2]  *See,* Peregrine Bertie

[3]  *See,* The Family of William Cecil, Lord Burghley

[4]  *See,* The Earls of Derby

[5]  *See,* The Earls of Southampton

[6]  *See,* The Earls of Pembroke

[7]  Only the earls of Oxford used "de" before their last name. All others used "Vere."

# William Cecil, Baron Burghley

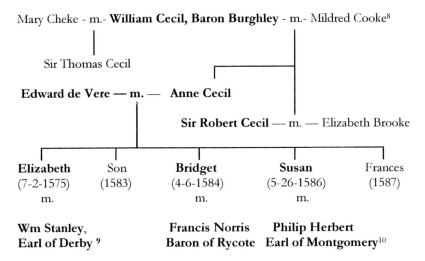

Mary Cheke - m.- **William Cecil, Baron Burghley** - m.- Mildred Cooke[8]

Sir Thomas Cecil

**Edward de Vere — m. — Anne Cecil**

**Sir Robert Cecil** — m. — Elizabeth Brooke

| **Elizabeth** | Son | **Bridget** | **Susan** | Frances |
|---|---|---|---|---|
| (7-2-1575) | (1583) | (4-6-1584) | (5-26-1586) | (1587) |
| m. | | m. | m. | |

**Wm Stanley,**
**Earl of Derby** [9]

**Francis Norris**
**Baron of Rycote**

**Philip Herbert**
**Earl of Montgomery**[10]

---

[8]  Mildred Cooke's sister Anne was the mother of Francis Bacon, later Sir Francis Bacon. Thus, Sir Francis was nephew to Lord Burghley and cousin to Robert Cecil. Sir Francis played a significant role in the trial of Essex and Southampton in 1601. Bacon's interrogation of the two men brought out answers that forced Cecil to come out from where he was hiding to confront Essex as to who had heard him (Cecil) claim that only the Infanta of Spain had the right to succeed Elizabeth on the throne of England.

[9]  *See,* The Earls of Derby

[10]  *See,* The Earls of Pembroke

# The Earls of Southampton

Thomas Wriothesley - m.-— Jane Cheney
(created 1st Earl in 1547; died 1550)

Henry Wriothesley – 2nd Earl - m. - Mary Brown[11]
(born 1545;[12] died 1581[13])　(daughter of Viscount Montague)

**Henry Wriothesley – 3rd Earl**— m. — Elizabeth Vernon (1598)[14]
(born Oct 6, 1573)[15]

---

[11] Mary Browne was thirteen when she married the 2nd Earl of Southampton. They separated in 1580 because of her alleged adulterous relationship with another man. In an attempt at reconciliation, the Countess sent her young son, the future 3rd Earl of Southampton, to her husband with a letter but the 2nd Earl rejected her offer to reconcile and kept their son away from her. The 2nd Earl died in 1581 but Mary was unable to get back her son because he went to Lord Burghley as a royal ward. In 1594, Mary Brown married Sir Thomas Heneage, who was Treasurer of the Royal Chamber. He died 15 months later in October, 1595, owing an accounting of what he had spent as Treasurer on entertainments for the Queen. The Queen demanded an accounting and the Countess submitted records that mention Wm Shakespeare as being one of the players paid by Heneage in 1594, which is the earliest known reference to William Shakespeare as a member of the Lord Chamberlain's Men. However, the play they supposedly performed before the Queen on the date specified was a play performed by the Admiral's Men; the Lord Chamberlain's Men were performing elsewhere. Since the accounting was made some time after the actual performance, there is a suspicion that the Countess, trying to avoid a massive judgment against her for money her dead husband had spent, was being creative in adding Shakespeare. Ogburn: pp. 65-66, citing Stopes. In January, 1599, almost immediately after her son's marriage to Elizabeth Vernon, she married again, to Sir Wm Harvey, with whom she had been living. Because the 2nd Earl was no longer living, Southampton had to approve the match as the senior male member of the Wriothesley family and apparently balked at her mother's choice.

[12] 5 years of age at his father's death; the Master of Royal Wards sold his wardship to Sir Wm Herbert, who sold it back to Henry's mother, Jane.

[13] The 3rd Earl of Southampton was 2 days short of 8 years old at his father's death. He became a ward of Lord Burghley and lived at Burghley House. Oxford, also a ward of Burghley, had left Burghley House ten years earlier when he came of age in 1571. Thus, the Earl of Oxford and Southampton never lived at Burghley House at the same time.

[14] Lord Burghley (*See* William Cecil, Lord Burghley), as Southampton's guardian, tried to get Southampton to marry his granddaughter, Elizabeth de Vere (Burghley Family; Oxford Family) in 1590, but Southampton refused and reportedly paid a £5,000 fine to Burghley.

[15] There is no documentation for this date except for a letter from his supposed father announcing the news of the birth of a son. There is no record of a baptism. The 2nd Earl was locked up in the Tower in 1571 for his involvement in the Ridolfi Plot; released May 1, 1573 to Sir Wm Moore; July 1573 to his father-in-law, Viscount Montague. Henry was born less than 9 months after his father's release from the Tower. The Queen may have allowed conjugal visits, but the evidence tends to indicate he was only allowed to see his wife in July.

# The Earls of Derby

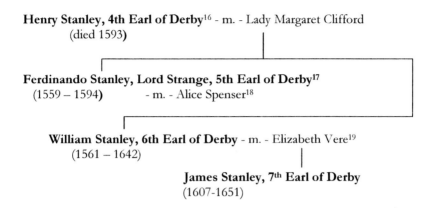

**Henry Stanley, 4th Earl of Derby**[16] - m. - Lady Margaret Clifford
    (died 1593)

**Ferdinando Stanley, Lord Strange, 5th Earl of Derby**[17]
(1559 – 1594)     - m. - Alice Spenser[18]

    **William Stanley, 6th Earl of Derby** - m. - Elizabeth Vere[19]
    (1561 – 1642)

             **James Stanley, 7th Earl of Derby**
             (1607-1651)

---

[16] Established Lord Strange's Men, which continued in existence under his two sons, and which performed many of Shakespeare's plays.

[17] Ferdinando Stanley's mother, Lady Margaret Clifford, was next in line to the throne by virtue of her descent from Mary Tudor. Ferdinando would have become heir to Elizabeth had he survived his mother *and* Queen Elizabeth. However, he predeceased both when he died on April 16, 1594. The succession would have gone to his daughters, who survived Lady Margaret, and not his brother, William, as Oxford's eldest daughter, Elizabeth, is portrayed in *The Death of Shakespeare*. Ferdinando was believed to have been poisoned by a massive dose of arsenic. He had turned in a step-brother who had tried to enlist him in a plot by the Catholics in exile to put him on the throne as a Catholic king. His act of loyalty, however, made him suspect to both Protestants and Catholics. The relatives ran to the Earl of Essex who took them into his service, which made Stanley fearful for his life. Stanley raided the main relative's house on April 2. He was dead two weeks later. He may have been poisoned by Burghley (to get him out of the way – Rowland York thought so – see Nelson p. 345), by the Catholic plotters to bring forward his brother, William, who may have been considered a better candidate, or by the relatives of the man he turned in. Burghley moved rapidly to marry Elizabeth Vere to Ferdinando's brother, William, but the wedding had to be delayed. See following footnote. Some of Lord Strange's Men formed the Lord Chamberlain's Men under Lord Hunsdon, which may have been intended to bring the players under control of the Queen. Edward Alleyn joined the Admiral's Men.

[18] When Henry Stanley died in 1593, his son Ferdinando Stanley succeeded him as 5th Earl of Derby. When Ferdinando died less than a year later, his younger brother, William, should have immediately succeeded Ferdinando as the 6th Earl of Derby. However, Alice Spenser, Ferdinando's widow, claimed she was pregnant. William was engaged to marry Elizabeth Vere. William and Elizabeth had to wait to find out whether Alice gave birth to a son, who would have become the 6th Earl of Derby and 'unearled' William. However, in December 1594, Alice gave birth to a daughter and William became the 6th Earl of Derby. He and Elizabeth Vere married in January, 1594. Some scholars believe *Midsummer Night's Dream* was written for their wedding.

[19] The eldest daughter of Edward de Vere, the 17th Earl of Oxford. Only the earls used the 'de' after their first names. Thus, Edward Vere, Oxford's illegitimate son, and the fighting Veres, Sir Francis and Sir Horatio, but Henry de Vere, who succeeded his father as the 18th Earl of Oxford.

# Peregrine Bertie
## (Lord Willoughby de Eresby – 1555-1601)

Richard Bertie (horse master) – m. 1553 - Katherine Willoughby[20] (died 1580)
(Duchess of Suffolk &
Baroness Willoughby de Eresby)
(Widow of the Duke of Suffolk)

Susan Bertie[21] — m. 1570 — Reginald Grey of Wrest,
(b. 1554)                          later restored as the fifth Earl of Kent (died 1573)

— m. 1581 — Sir John Wingfield

**Peregrine Bertie** - m.- **Mary (Vere) Oxford** (died 1624)
**Lord Willoughby de Eresby**        (m. 1577/8)
(b. 1555; d. June 25, 1601))

Robert Bertie

---

[20]  In 1577, Lady Katherine wrote to Lord Burghley that she would place Oxford's daughter Elizabeth (2 years old at the time) in front of Oxford the next time he came to see her to see if Oxford took to the child in the hope that this would reunite him with the mother, Anne, Burghley's daughter. Nelson: p. 76. Compare *The Winter's Tale*, Act II, Scenes 2 and 3, in which Leontes' baby daughter, which he thinks is not his, is placed in front of him in the belief that he will recognize her as his own. The attempt fails in the play. Whether Lady Katherine put Oxford's daughter in front of him is unknown. If so, it didn't work because Oxford continued to stay away from his wife for quite some time. Lady Katherine is well-known for many things, including talking Henry VIII into letting women read the Bible.

[21]  Susan Bertie became Countess of Suffolk upon her mother's death in 1580. Aemilia Bassano was born January 27, 1569 in Bishopsgate, London, into a family of Italian (possibly Jewish) court musicians. At age seven (1576), she went to live with the Willoughby family at Grimsthorpe Castle in Lincolnshire under the tutelage of Susan Bertie. Aemilia arrived four years before Susan's mother, Lady Katherine, died, and may have known something about the letter Lady Katherine wrote in 1577 that is referenced in footnote 1. Upon her mother's death in 1587, Aemilia became Lord Hunsdon's mistress, by whom she had a son, Henry, in 1592. Hunsdon was 45 years older than she was. *See,* the Lords Hunsdons. Bassano was then married to her cousin, Alfonso Lanier, who died in 1613. A daughter named Odillya lived only ten months. In 1611, Bassano published *Salve Deus Rex Judaeorum*, the first book of poetry published by an English woman. Bassano memorialized Susan in her book as the "daughter of the Duchess of Suffolk." Her son by Hunsdon lived to 1633.

# The Earls of Pembroke

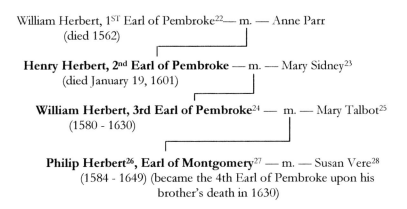

William Herbert, 1ST Earl of Pembroke[22]— m. — Anne Parr
    (died 1562)

**Henry Herbert, 2nd Earl of Pembroke** — m. — Mary Sidney[23]
    (died January 19, 1601)

**William Herbert, 3rd Earl of Pembroke**[24] — m. — Mary Talbot[25]
    (1580 - 1630)

**Philip Herbert**[26], **Earl of Montgomery**[27] — m. — Susan Vere[28]
    (1584 - 1649) (became the 4th Earl of Pembroke upon his
        brother's death in 1630)

---

[22] Established Pembroke's Men, , which continued in existence under his two sons, and which performed many of Shakespeare's plays.

[23] *See,* The Sidney Family. Mary Sidney, Countess of Pembroke, was Robert Dudley's niece and Sir Philip Sidney's sister. Mary Sidney was Henry's third wife. His first marriage to Catherine Gray was probably annulled when Queen Mary came to the throne. His second wife was Catherine Talbot, who died in 1576. When Henry died in 1601, she did not remarry, but remained at Wilton House and became a noted literary figure in Elizabethan and Jacobean England.

[24] William founded Pembroke College, Oxford, and continued his patronage of Pembroke's Men. He became Lord Chamberlain in 1615. He refused to give up the position until he could secure his brother, Philip, as his successor in 1626. William, therefore, was Lord Chamberlain in 1623 when the First Folio was printed. A relative, Henry Herbert, became Master of the Revels in June of that year. Ben Jonson, one of William's patrons, was supposed to get the office but did not. See, *The Incomparable Pair and "The Works of William Shakespeare"* by Gwynneth Bowen at http://www.sourcetext.com/sourcebook/library/bowen/12pair.htm. William and Philip are described in the dedication to the First Folio as "the incomparable pair of brethren." (Notice that the two brothers were the sons of Sir Philip Sidney's sister, Mary.)

[25] The dwarfish and deformed daughter of the Earl of Shrewsbury, by whom William had no children. He had an affair with Mary Fitton in 1600 when she was twenty years of age and impregnated her. When he refused to marry her, he was sent to the Fleet Prison. When Mary gave birth to a boy who died, he was released. He wrote a poem about the affair. See Ancilla to Chapter 24 - Lord Willoughby's. He had two children by Lady Mary Wroth, daughter of his uncle, Robert Sidney, after the death of Lady Mary's husband, Richard Wroth.

[26] Philip had a quarrel with Henry Wriothesley, 3rd Earl of Southampton, in 1610 over tennis. Compare the Earl of Oxford's famous quarrel with Sir Philip Sidney, also over tennis, in 1579.

[27] The Earl of Pembroke began paying Jonson a stipend of 100 marks per annum in 1616, increased temporarily to £200 a year in 1621. *This Star of England*, p. 1208. Philip became the 4th Earl of Pembroke upon his older brother's death in 1630.

[28] *See,* Oxford Family. Susan was the Earl of Oxford's third daughter. There is a drawing by Inigo Jones of Susan Vere dancing in one of Jonson's masques. *This Star of England*, p. 1208.

# The Lords Hunsdon

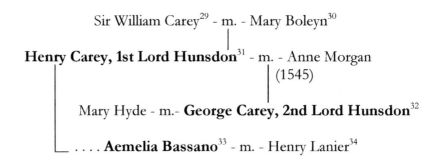

Sir William Carey[29] - m. - Mary Boleyn[30]

**Henry Carey, 1st Lord Hunsdon**[31] - m. - Anne Morgan

(1545)

Mary Hyde - m.- **George Carey, 2nd Lord Hunsdon**[32]

.... **Aemelia Bassano**[33] - m. - Henry Lanier[34]

---

[29] Gentleman of the Privy Chamber to Henry VIII. Died suddenly from the sweating sickness June 23, 1528. Henry Carey, his son, was two and became a ward of his aunt, Anne Boleyn. When Anne was beheaded in 1536, Henry was ten. His mother, Mary, died in 1543, and he was returned to his family.

[30] Sister to Anne Boleyn, who was mistress to Henry VIII before Anne. Many believed that Henry Carey's father was Henry VIII, not Sir William.

[31] Born 1526; died July 23, 1596. Appointed Lord Chamberlain in July 1585. Patron of the Lord Hunsdon's Men, and, from 1594, patron of the Lord Chamberlain's Men.

[32] Born 1547; died September 9, 1603. Became 2nd Lord Hunsdon when his father, Henry, died in 1596. However, George Carey did not become Lord Chamberlain on the death of his father. The Queen instead appointed William Brooke, 10th Lord Cobham, to be Lord Chamberlain. Cobham lived in the Blackfriars district and, despite being the patron of the Lord Chamberlain's Men, opposed the attempt in 1597 by James Burbage to have a theater built there for adult companies. This caused Burbage financial difficulty because the lease had run out on the Theatre. Burbage had bought the playing space in the Blackfriars for the Lord Chamberlain's Men to perform plays. Cobham also apparently objected to the name Sir John Oldcastle, one of his ancestors, for the character that became Falstaff. When Cobham died in March, 1597, the Queen appointed George Carey Lord Chamberlain, which post he held until his death in 1603. Cobham's daughter, Elizabeth Brooke, married Sir Robert Cecil on August 31, 1589.

[33] Mistress to Henry Carey; raised in the Willoughby family from age 7. *See*, Peregrine Bertie, footnote 2.

[34] Born in 1593. Assumed to be the son of Lord Hunsdon., by whom she became pregnant in 1592. Aemilia married Alfonso Lanier on October 18, 1592. Lanier died in 1613; Aemilia lived to 1645. In 1611, she published the first book of poetry by an English woman, *Salve Deus Rex Judaeorum*.

# The Sidney Family

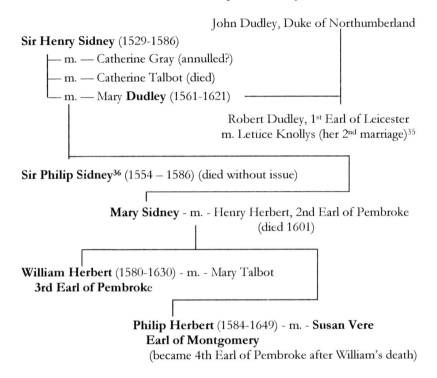

John Dudley, Duke of Northumberland

**Sir Henry Sidney** (1529-1586)
- m. — Catherine Gray (annulled?)
- m. — Catherine Talbot (died)
- m. — Mary **Dudley** (1561-1621)

Robert Dudley, 1st Earl of Leicester
m. Lettice Knollys (her 2nd marriage)[35]

**Sir Philip Sidney**[36] (1554 – 1586) (died without issue)

**Mary Sidney** - m. - Henry Herbert, 2nd Earl of Pembroke
(died 1601)

**William Herbert** (1580-1630) - m. - Mary Talbot
**3rd Earl of Pembroke**

**Philip Herbert** (1584-1649) - m. - **Susan Vere**
**Earl of Montgomery**
(became 4th Earl of Pembroke after William's death)

---

[35] Lettice Knollys was a grand-niece of Ann Boleyn. At age 17, she married Walter Devereux, 1st Earl of Essex, by whom she had Penelope Rich and Walter Devereux, 2nd Earl of Essex, as well as other children. Her first husband died in 1576. She then married Robert Dudley, 1st Earl of Leicester, in 1578. Elizabeth was outraged when she found out about the marriage and banished Lettice Knollys from court for life. It was rumored that she had been carrying on an affair with Leicester while her first husband was still alive. Some even claimed Leicester poisoned her first husband, who died of dysentery in Ireland. She had no children by Leicester. After Dudley died in 1588, she married Sir Christopher Blount, a much younger man, a year later. He was beheaded in 1601, along with her son by her first marriage, the 2nd Earl of Essex, for their participation in the Essex revolt. She lived to 1634, dying at the age of 91.

[36] Philip Sidney was knighted in 1583 when he was designated by Prince John Casimir of Poland to represent him by proxy at a ceremony inducting Casimir into the Order of the Garter. Since a representative could not be of a rank lower than a knight, Queen Elizabeth knighted Sidney so he could fulfill the honor. (This parallels William Cecil being made Baron Burghley so that his daughter's marriage to the Earl of Oxford would not be morganatic.) Sidney was wounded at the Battle of Zutphen and died October 17, 1586. His body was brought back to London in a ship with black sails. Pamphlets, poems, and sermons turned him into a national hero. He was not interred until February 16, 1588, eight days after the execution of Mary, Queen of Scots. It is unknown whether this delay was caused by lack of funds to bury him or a conscious decision on the part of Burghley, Walsingham, and the Queen to use Sidney's burial to distract a populace that might have reacted unfavorably to Mary's execution. Thousands of nobles and commoners followed Sidney's hearse to his grave and nothing was heard about Mary's death. *Hidden Allusions*, fn 19a, pp. 247-248.

# ~ Glossary ~

**acrostic**: a poem in which the first letter of each line spells a name.

**alewife**: woman who keeps an alehouse; an oily fish.

**an**: if.

**angel**: a gold coin worth 10 shillings; called so after the Archangel Michael on one side.

**apparitor**: process server.

**arras**: a tapestry, wall hanging, or curtain.

**arsenic**: poison, referred to as 'inheritance powder.'

**Bedlam**: Bethlehem Hospital, where the insane were dumped.

**bed trick**: where a man sleeps with his wife woman but thinks she's someone else.

**bergamot**: pear-shaped orange the rind of which yields an oil used in the making of perfumes.

**besmutched**: to besmirch.

**bewray**: betray; disclose.

**bill of exchange**: a written document evidencing an obligation to repay a loan.

**calliver**: a smooth-bore forerunner of the rifle.

**cheat**: whole meal bread, coarser than manchet bread.

**chirurgeon**: surgeon; doctor.

**Court of Wards** (and Liveries): established by Henry VIII to regulate feudal dues, wards, and questions of livery.

**eyas**: a sparrow hawk.

**eyrar**: a brood of swans.

**felo de se**: to commit a felony on oneself, such as suicide.

**foul papers**: the original drafts of a manuscript of playscript.

**froward**: forward; brazen.

**furniture**: baggage.

**Gad's Hill**: an area on the road from London to Canterbury.

**glister**: to glisten, to glitter.

**gremolata**: chopped herb condiment classically made of lemon zest, garlic and parsley.

**haberdine**: salt cod.

**haggard**: a mature hawk caught in the wild and trained to hunt.

*I Modi*: erotic drawings by Giulio Romano.

**Ipocras wine**: a spiced wine. When strained through a woolen cloth, the cloth resembled Hippocrates' sleeve.

**invention**: creation, but also a fictitious statement or story; a fabrication.

**groat**; an English silver coin worth four pence

**kickshaw**: appetizer, hors d'oeuvres, from quelquechose.

**limbo**: between Heaven and Hell; where babies went who died before they were baptized.

**livery**: clothing worn by servants that identified them as servants of a particular nobleman.

**manchet**: fine white bread.

**marriage *in futuro*:** a promise to marry in the future, which is not a marriage, although suit can be brought on the contract.

**marriage *per verba de praesenti*:** a marriage validated by words, even if performed in secret, if followed by consummation.

**matrimonium clandestinum:** a marriage that rests merely on the agreement of the parties, or a marriage entered into a secret way, as one solemnized by an unauthorized person, or without required formalities.

**medlar:** apple-like fruit that tasted best as it began to rot.

**mon choux:** my cabbage; my dear.

**moniment:** archaic spelling of monument; but also a record without a monument. 'Thou art a moniment without a tomb.'

**morganatic;** a marriage in which, because one of the parties is not of sufficient birth, the children cannot inherit the parent's title.

**motley:** jester, a fool; multi-colored cloth.

**ne:** neither; nor.

**Neapolitan Malady:** syphilis.

**nidicock:** a ninny; a fool.

**Orpharian:** a flat-backed stringed instrument, member of the cittern family.

**petits cadeaux:** little gifts.

**pomander:** a mixture of aromatic substances contained in a pierced metal sphere.

**quincunx:** an arrangement with four points and a fifth point in the middle

**Roscius:** a Roman slave who became a famous actor.

**samphire:** samphire, rock samphire, or sea fennel grew on rocky cliffs near the sea and was used as a condiment when pickled and in salads when fresh.

**Seneca:** a first century Roman philosopher ('readiness is all') and tragedian.

**sprezzatura:** a certain nonchalance, so as to conceal all art and make whatever one does or says appear to be without effort and almost without any thought about it.

**Tycho Brahe:** Danish astronomer who argued that the sun and moon orbited the earth.

**virginal:** keyboard instrument.

**ward:** a minor under the jurisdiction of a court; a minor whose father, a vassal-in-chief to the king, has died.

**weed:** clothes.

**whiffler:** a servant who precedes a noble to make way and announce his presence.

**whittawer:** a person who converts animal skins into white leather.

**wittol:** a man who knows he has been cuckolded by his wife and tolerates it.

Readers interested in further information about

*The Death of Shakespeare–Part One*

can visit

*www.doshakespeare.com*

to find out how to purchase

the ebook version of the book and obtain

*The Reader's Companion to the Death of Shakespeare,*

250 pages of research and comment keyed to each chapter.


*The Death of Shakespeare–Part Two*

will be forthcoming.